WITH EVERYTHING I AM

THE THREE SERIES
BOOK TWO

KRISTEN ASHLEY

ROCK CHICK
PRESS

THE THREE SERIES BOOK TWO

WITH Everything I Am

KRISTEN

NEW YORK TIMES BESTSELLING AUTHOR

ASHLEY

PROLOGUE
CONNECTION

TTHE TRAIL of blood was leading the hunters straight to him.

Normally, he would have outrun them long before now, but with his right flank wounded by the shotgun blast and with him unable to rest or transform in order to heal quickly, he was simply losing more blood, more energy, and slowing.

He tried to sense his brethren but they weren't near. They weren't due for hours.

He'd arrived early, too early.

Something had drawn him to this forest, so much as called out to him.

And, as usual, he followed his instincts.

He'd gone early and transformed so his senses would be sharper in order to seek out whatever it was.

Therefore, he'd been distracted, and if he was honest with himself, cocky. He'd smelled the hunters but he'd never expected they'd be a threat. Humans rarely were.

As he ran, he sensed it again...out there. It was close, whatever it was, and the pull of it was so strong, it made him momentarily lose focus.

This cost him. He wasn't watching where he was going. He wasn't scanning the landscape.

He skidded to a painful halt, the snow blossoming out in white wings at his sides. A sheer rock face in front of him. A dense forest of pine trees—difficult to maneuver especially injured—to his right. Hunters at his back and to his left...

He stared.

A child.

Wearing a pink hat, scarf, boots, and mittens and a navy coat, her long blonde hair falling down her shoulders.

Her green eyes were on him.

She couldn't be more than five, maybe six, alone in the snow in the forest in the dead of night.

What the fuck? he thought

She had to be lost. Her need for rescue was what he must have sensed.

But he could feel no fear from her, not even of him, and in this form everyone and everything feared him.

But obviously not her.

She was gazing at him calmly as if she took moonlit strolls regularly, and further, as if she could see him plainly in the dark.

As if she was one of his own.

Impossible, he thought.

First, she was blonde. There were no blondes of his kind. None. Not in history.

Second, he'd smell it and she smelled starkly human.

He considered transforming. However, even if the cold couldn't kill him, he didn't relish the idea of transforming into a six foot six inch naked man with a gunshot wound to his thigh in front of a child. Not to mention, the hunters, who were gaining and who he could far more easily attack as a wolf (which was not forbidden, but frowned upon even if there was no alternative as it seemed would soon be the case).

But it was forbidden to change in front of a human who didn't know about their secret culture.

Completely forbidden.

Even for him.

He heard the hunters crashing through the snow and branches, getting ever closer. He turned swiftly and growled low.

It was his vast experience there were two different kinds of human hunters.

There were those who took what they called their "sport" seriously and behaved, in their way, honorably.

These, he knew, were not those kind of hunters. Therefore, if they weren't careful (which they would not be) they could hurt *her*.

He couldn't allow that.

In fact, he'd die to stop it.

The force of this knowledge startled him but he knew it instantly and instinctively straight down to his immortal soul.

The hunters burst through the trees into the clearing where he stood and leveled their shotguns at him.

He growled again and advanced, giving them their target.

Surprisingly, so did the child and she did so rapidly.

"*No!*" she shrieked, taking the hunters' attention, and before he could move a muscle, she slid to a halt in front of him. She threw her arms wide as if to shield him with her body.

He tore his gaze from the hunters and stared at her in stunned surprise.

"*My* puppy!" she cried. "You hurt *my puppy!*"

"Get away from that animal!" one hunter bellowed, the barrel of his gun moving subtly, aiming away from the child.

"Jesus," another muttered. "What's a kid doin' out here?"

"My puppy!" she shouted again, turned, and lifted up on her toes so she could wrap her arms around his neck, pressing her face into the thick fur there. "You hurt my puppy!" she repeated on a wail as if her heart was torn apart. Then, not detaching her arms from his neck, her head rounded on the hunters again and she yelled, "Papa is going to be *so* mad."

"Kid, I said, get away from that animal," the first hunter ordered.

She ignored him. "Papa went all the way to Alaska to get my puppy for me and he got out tonight. He wouldn't come when Papa called and called and *whistled* and *called* and we were so worried, so, *so* worried, we couldn't get to sleep. We were looking for him, looking all over. Papa is just out there..." She took an arm away to point vaguely in the direction from where she came. "We were looking for him and Papa is going to be *sooo* mad that you *shot my puppy!*" She ended on a shriek, throwing her arm around his neck again, holding on tight, and pressing her face into his fur, her body beginning to shake with false sobs.

Bloody hell, but she was a cunning little human, and as a wolf, if he could laugh, he would.

Unfortunately, he could not.

Instead, he shifted his furry bulk into her and without delay she pressed closer.

"Fuckin' A," the third hunter mumbled, his eyes narrowed on the girl as he lowered his gun. "Is that Senator Arlington's daughter?"

"*Fuck!*" the second hunter hissed, lowering his own firearm. "It is."

"Kid—" the first hunter started in a soothing tone.

She pulled her face away from his neck and glared at the hunters. "Go! Go now! If you go now, I won't tell Papa it was you."

They hesitated, all their guns lowered now, their feet shuffling.

"*Go!*" she screamed, her child's voice piercing the brittle air.

"Maybe we could talk to Senator Arlington," the third one whispered his suggestion. "Explain things."

"Yeah?" the first hunter asked sarcastically, turning angry eyes at his friend. "Do *you* want to tell Senator Arlington how we were out at night and you shot his precious daughter's dog? Do you, Gary? Hunh?"

"That ain't no dog," the second hunter said, his eyes never leaving the beast. "That's a wolf."

"Don't look like no wolf I've ever seen," the third hunter noted and his voice turned greedy. "He's huge. A beauty. Got to be a hundred pounds heavier than any wolf—"

"He's a wolf, ain't no dog," the second hunter pressed.

"Jesus, Lloyd, you ever see a wild wolf stand calm next to a kid with her arms wrapped around his ruff?" the first hunter, clearly the brains of the crew, threw out.

"He's a rare breed!" the child snapped, sounding adorably impatient, making it clear their squabbling was highly annoying and she had far better things to do. Her arms tightened as she continued, "That's why Papa had to go all the way to—"

"All right, kid," the first hunter cut her off, taking a step back while throwing his arm out to indicate his friends should follow suit. "Promise you won't tell your pa you saw us?"

"Promise you'll stop hunting wolves in this region?" she shot back shrewdly, not sounding five or six but much older.

"Kid—" the first hunter started.

She interrupted him angrily. "Since you know you're not allowed."

The hunters stared at her in shock.

"They said she was weird," the third hunter, having moved back several paces, whispered in a voice that he thought only he could hear.

"I'm not weird!" the child snapped and he swung his canine eyes to her in further surprise because he, of course, could hear. Even in the form of a man he had heightened hearing, but he'd never known a human to have that kind of range.

The third hunter started then mumbled again, "Weird."

The child's body grew stiff with hurt affront.

The wolf growled.

All the hunters stared at the beast.

"Promise!" she demanded.

They were silent.

"I'll tell my papa..." she threatened.

"Okay, kid, we promise," the first hunter assured her, moving back again.

The wolf and child stood still and silent, watching the hunters retreat. A pace, two, three, four, then they turned and made their way swiftly through the wood.

"Silly men," she whispered irritably as she let him go and looked at him, her astute green eyes moving the length of him to his flank then she murmured, "Poor puppy." She patted him on the neck. "Papa will fix you, he's good at that. Let's go home."

She started walking away and he stood still, watching her, uncertain, even with his experience of all things human, inhuman, and beast, what to make of the child.

She turned back.

"It's okay, puppy," she told him. "You can trust me. I'm not weird. Promise. It's just..." she paused and quirked her head to the side. "Animals understand me. Papa says it's a special gift." She patted her thigh with her pink mitten. "Come on, we'll take good care of you." She lifted her hand to her heart, made a cross, and grinned an immensely adorable grin the sight of which he felt in his gut. "Cross my heart."

She turned again and marched away.

He followed.

Not because of her promise she'd take care of him.

Instead, because *he* needed to protect *her*.

It wasn't far, maybe a five minute trek (but annoyingly painful and lumbering for him), when they came upon a log cabin in the trees. Warm, welcoming lights flooded from its windows, a sparkling Christmas tree shown in one.

"That's home," she told him, her voice reverent. "We have another home in the city, but Momma and Papa and I like this one *way* better. We come here *every* Christmas." She turned to him and smiled a bright smile. "Come on!"

She ran the rest of the way, throwing open the door and turning again in its frame to pat her leg.

Limping less but still limping, he followed.

He entered the cabin and could see exactly why she'd prefer this place to any other.

It was small but it was homey, rustic, warm, and friendly.

He could live his life there.

She was busy rushing around the cabin and he stood in the door watching her.

"We'll get you all warm and you can rest. Momma and Papa will be home soon and he'll know what to do. Papa always knows what to do," she babbled as she bunched clean sheets on a rug before the fire with her still-mittened hands and then she turned to him and patted her leg again. "Come on, puppy. It's okay."

He cautiously limped to the sheets.

She pulled off her mitten and ran her fingers down his head. "Good puppy," she murmured.

He collapsed with a canine groan to the sheets.

"There you go," she whispered, crouching beside him to give him a rub.

Then she ran to the door, closed it, and pulled off her hat, mittens, scarf, and coat, throwing them efficiently on the couch.

She took a fluffy throw from a chair and brought it to him, tossing it on his body and arranging it carefully as he felt the healing in his flank sharpen.

No longer running, the wound would be mended within half an hour.

She sat down behind him and whispered, "I'll just lay here with you until Papa gets home." He felt her settle and press her little body down his back. "Keep you warm and safe," she mumbled, her voice turning sleepy. "Then Papa will take care of you."

Regardless of the fact that she was clearly a gifted child, like any child she was dead asleep within minutes.

And he lay beside her, letting the healing work and thinking, even though she clearly adored her father, he would be having words with a man who'd let his child—gifted or not—stay alone in a remote cabin and wander the forest in the dead of night. He didn't give a fuck that she was obviously quite capable or if she did, indeed, have a way with animals.

No *good* human parent did *that*.

He was whole again and he sensed them well before they arrived.

He carefully moved away so as not to waken her, had transformed, and was standing beside her wrapped in the throw she'd placed over him when the door opened.

His brethren glanced at him then the child then his brother Calder threw him his pants.

He pulled them on as his father walked close.

Too close to the child.

Unconsciously he straightened, pants still half unbuttoned, and moved to stand in front of her.

His father, Mac's eyes slid away from the girl and caught his.

Then he watched Mac's face gentle.

"Callum," Mac murmured softly.

"She's Senator Arlington's daughter," Callum announced, his voice low in deference to her sleep but rumbling because he was pissed way the hell off.

"I know," his father replied.

"I'm uncertain of an allegiance with a man who'd leave his daughter unprotected," Callum went on.

Callum watched something flash across Mac's face and what he saw made him brace.

"It matters not," his father said softly, and when Callum opened his mouth to speak again, Mac lifted a hand. "Senator Arlington was assassinated tonight. His wife with him."

Callum's head jerked toward the innocently sleeping child and he felt his gut clench painfully at the thought that she, especially *she*, would lose her mother and clearly beloved father on Christmas Eve.

"She was here for her safety," Mac continued and Callum's eyes cut back to him as he carried on, "*You* were here for it as well."

"I—" Callum started, surprised at this announcement and getting pretty fucking tired of surprises.

Mac got closer. "It was a test."

Callum's jaw grew tight.

He had endured a fair few of his father's tests in his very long life.

He watched Mac look back down at the girl with an infinitely gentle expression and he knew his father wasn't finished.

He wasn't wrong.

When Mac's eyes came back to Callum, he went on, "As ever, you passed." Callum watched his father smile and something oddly joyous shone in his eyes before he murmured, "And so did she."

"Would you like to tell me what you're on about?" Callum suggested.

Mac didn't hesitate. "Tonight, my son, the connection has begun."

Callum felt his body go solid before his eyes sliced down to the girl.

He looked again to his father, his voice coated in angry disbelief. "She's human."

Mac took in a breath through his nose, hesitated, opened his mouth, closed it, then opened it again to say, "She is."

"I can't be connected to a human," Callum clipped.

"The oracle has spoken," his father declared.

Callum heard his brethren pull in shocked breaths.

Mac moved even closer and his voice grew lower when he asked, "You felt it?"

Bloody hell.

He felt it.

It was bigger than him, bigger than his brethren, bigger and more important than anything.

He'd die for her.

She was, in a very important sense, his reason for being.

Hell, he'd even moved to protect her against his own father—a wolf he knew wouldn't harm a living soul unless forced to do it.

"*Fuck!*" he bit out.

"She'll be protected until the time is right," Mac assured.

Callum narrowed his gaze on him and growled, "She bloody better be."

Mac glanced to the side. "Ryon, see to it, our best men."

"But, Mac, we can't—" Ryon began and Callum watched his father's eyes narrow.

"See to it," Mac ordered.

"We're at war!" Ryon hissed. "We need every brother we have. We can't afford—"

Mac cut Ryon off by repeating, "See to it."

Callum watched his brethren shift and glance at each other.

Then their gazes moved back to him with dawning realization.

Callum had the same thought they did and he felt his body grow tight.

He looked back to Mac and asked with extreme unease, "She's my queen?"

He watched his father nod and anguish tore through him. But he didn't allow it to show, instead, he lifted his chin.

"When?" he demanded to know.

"It matters not," Mac replied.

"You're my father and you're my king, it fucking matters that you're soon to die," Callum ground out.

Mac didn't answer.

Callum leaned forward. "Why didn't you tell me?"

"I have my reasons," Mac responded.

Jesus but Mac could be mysterious and in the three hundred and fifty years of his life it never failed to piss Callum off.

"Mac—" Callum began but his father lifted his hand and placed it on Callum's shoulder.

"We're at war and this war will not end under my reign. *You* and *she*," he glanced down at the girl before his eyes moved back to his son, "will lead our people to peace."

Callum didn't know what he was feeling because there was too much to feel.

What he did know was that he didn't like any of it.

His eyes leveled on his father's and he promised, "If they bring you down, it'll be a fucking bloody peace and only on *my* fucking terms."

Mac leaned close as his fingers tightened on Callum's arm.

Then he whispered in his son's ear, "I'm counting on that."

CHAPTER ONE

CLEAR

Sonia Arlington walked through her store and switched off the many Christmas lights decorating the space.

She loved Christmas.

She couldn't help it. Her mother and father had both loved Christmas. They made it so special that the ones she remembered made the season one she always looked forward to even though her parents died during it.

She adjusted her fluffy, white scarf around her neck, pulled the white knit cap down over her ears, and transferred her dove gray suede gloves to one hand, pulling the strap of her matching stylish suede handbag more securely over her shoulder.

She took one last look at her shop, called Clear because everything she sold in it was either clear, silver, gray, or white. Everything. Furniture, clothing (though the clothes were never clear, of course), candles, jewelry, knickknacks, *everything*.

She loved her shop almost as much as Christmas.

Yuri wondered (aloud and often) why she bothered to work. He thought she was crazy, considering she had her father and mother's millions of dollars "festering" (his word) in different accounts.

Sonia couldn't imagine *not* working. What on earth would she do if she didn't work?

She knew what Yuri wanted her to do.

She loved Yuri but she still wrinkled her nose at the thought, pressed the code into the alarm panel, and quickly exited, locking the three locks to the front door.

She turned toward home.

It was four blocks away. She was wearing dove gray suede stiletto-heeled boots and it had snowed that day. Still, she walked the oft-not-shoveled sidewalks with a grace akin to a model on a catwalk.

This, her father would have said (if he'd lived to see her wearing heels and, of course, walking through the snow in them), was one of her special abilities.

She had many. All of which, her father told her, time and time (and time) again, were exceptional.

She was, her father told her, gifted.

Extremely gifted.

And for this, he explained time and time (and time) again, she should be proud.

Very proud.

But, even so, she could never tell anyone about them.

Never.

Anyone.

So she hadn't.

As she crossed the street from the first block to the second, she felt it.

And smelled it.

These, too, were part of her gifts.

She sensed things. Strange things. Eyes on her. A presence. Mostly benign but recently (and upsettingly) there were some that seemed menacing. And she smelled things. Lots of things. Things others didn't smell.

It was out there. She sensed its presence, smelled its smell. It was benign. It was even pleasant (immensely so), attractive (that was immensely so too), and it was familiar.

Very familiar.

She sifted through her memory banks but she couldn't find it.

Whatever it was, she knew it wouldn't hurt her.

In fact, she had the strange, strong desire to seek it out, to turn to it—even to *run* to it.

Even though this urge was powerful (and surprising, she'd never felt anything like *that* before), she didn't let on she sensed it. To do so would let it know she could feel it, which she could *not* do.

Her father had told her, repeatedly, she was special, exceptional, and gifted. But without him telling her that for the last thirty-one years and knowing no one around her shared her "special" talents, she'd settled into the knowledge that she wasn't special, exceptional, and gifted. Instead, she was just strange.

Even bizarre.

Definitely weird.

And that was not a nice thing to know about yourself.

The presence was moving with her, tracking her, and she ignored it as she did the many others she'd felt throughout her life (or, more precisely, since her parents' deaths) as she carried on home. Then she saw her little farmhouse on its corner and smiled to herself. The sight of her home and the peace she always felt when she saw it allowed her to be able to set the alarmingly alluring sensation firmly aside.

Gregor (*and* Yuri) had both gone nuts when she'd bought her farmhouse. Well, not *nuts*, they were too polished to go nuts, but they definitely disapproved. Firstly, because, even though a rather nice (if colorful) residential area of the city had sprung up around it, it *was* a simple farmhouse. Sonia Arlington (as they told her repeatedly), did *not* reside in something as common as a *farmhouse*.

Secondly, because when she'd bought it, it was a wreck.

Luckily, Sonia was loaded. Therefore, she'd had it fixed up.

She walked up the steps and unlocked her door. The alarm beeped when she entered and she punched in the code. She dropped her purse on the chest in the entryway, and through the dark, she went directly to the plugs that would turn on her Christmas lights. Then she plugged them in, *all* of them, and there were many...on both floors.

As she did so, the inside and outside of her farmhouse lit up and she didn't have to look at it to know it was perfect. Just as if it had been decorated for a magazine (which it had, her house was always photographed for the city's monthly magazine, every year at Christmas, twice it had even made the cover).

Sonia would have preferred to decorate herself, but even though in her early years she'd tried, she'd never had a flair for it and it always turned out wonky.

Her mother had had a flair for it. Cherise Arlington was the Master Christmas Decorator. Therefore, Sonia could not abide her own wonky efforts.

So she hired designers every year to come and decorate her house.

And it was always beautiful.

She walked straight back out the front door and down to her white picket fence to get her mail from the box that was fitted to the gatepost.

"Hey, Miz Arlington!" She heard called from her side.

She turned to see the Lanigans getting into their mini-van, their two young boys, Jed and Jake, both standing outside and waving at her.

She'd known they were there, of course. She'd heard their feet in the snow Jay Lanigan had not (and would not, because it was football season and Jay Lanigan didn't do much of anything during football season) shoveled from their drive. She'd also smelled the scent of their skin and hair. But as they were several doors down, she didn't turn to them. To do so might expose her secret and Sonia guarded against that every second of her life.

"Hey there!" she called back, feigning surprise and waving. Then she saw Joanne Lanigan round the hood of the van. "Ready for Christmas, Jo?" she called.

"If you're ready for Christmas, I'll shoot you!" Jo yelled back with a smile in her shout. "It's weeks away."

Sonia was ready in September. That was how much she loved Christmas. She planned for it all year.

"A few more things to do," Sonia lied.

"Right," Jo shouted. "We got your card today. The first one every year."

Sonia shrugged even though they couldn't see her, however she could see them, clear as day. Her night vision, another gift, was perfect. "I'm organized and don't have a full-time job, two boys, and a husband who disappears when it's football season!" Sonia replied loudly.

"Hey! I heard that!" Jay shouted from the other side of the van.

"Good!" Jo replied. "Then maybe you'll notice the neighbors see me taking out the stinking trash from September to January. Yeesh!"

Sonia chuckled to herself as she pulled her mail out of the box, turned to her neighbors, and called, "Be safe, Jay, it's supposed to snow again."

"Always!" Jay called back, not affronted by Sonia's earlier comment.

He wouldn't be. Sonia was a great neighbor.

She watched their house when they were away, including walking their completely out-of-control dogs, which was why no one but Sonia would watch their house (or dogs). She regularly babysat the boys. She threw fantastic barbeques during the summer. And she had a catered Christmas party that was so spectacular, the entire neighborhood waited with bated breath to receive their invitation and turned out for it. They did this even if they were invalid. She knew this because another of Sonia's neighbors had broken one leg and the other ankle falling off the ladder while fixing Christmas lights to his house and he'd *still* rented a wheelchair and wheeled himself to her place for her party.

Sonia waved the Lanigans away and then turned to her house.

The picket fence surrounding her property and the porch that ran two sides of the house that had a white railing were dripping with greenery, clear lights sparkling in their bows, white poinsettias affixed to the points of the drapes. Two little white sleighs filled with white poinsettias and lined with twinkling lights sat at angles pointing in at the top of the stairs. Single candles shown in every window on all sides. More greenery, lights, and poinsettias were draped around the faux widow's walk on the roof. A tall, wide, fabulous real fir tree—dressed to perfection and lit with an abundance of glimmering lights—stood in the window.

She sighed at the sight, as she did every day from the minute it was decorated. Always returning home, turning on the lights, then walking back out to get her mail so she could witness it and let the season shine down on her.

With regret, she reentered her house, took off her hat and gloves, and carefully placed them tidily in the chest by the door. She hung her scarf on the hooks at the other side of her entryway with her coat.

She walked into her house, shuffling the post (mainly catalogues) in her fingers.

The inside of her house was decorated in a way that Gregor and Yuri approved, but she'd done it only so they'd be quiet about it.

It wasn't comfortable, countrified, farmhouse splendor.

Once you stepped through the wide entryway, the whole of the downstairs was one room, the walls torn down to make it open plan. Left and right were seating areas, fireplaces on each side, their mantels festooned with Christmas cheer. The back left was a dining room with another fireplace, ditto the Christmas festooning. The kitchen was behind the right area. No festooning in the kitchen but she did have Christmas kitchen towels and pot holders and red and green plastic-ended pancake turners (which she never used as she didn't eat pancakes) sticking out of her utensil crock. The red one had a turner the shape of a bell and the green one had a turner the shape of a snowman.

The walls all around were painted in coordinating tranquil light colors of seafoam (left seating area), green (right seating area), and blue (dining room and kitchen). The kitchen was state-of-the-art. The furniture was sleek, modern, and most especially, expensive and elegant. The minimal décor was carefully chosen to augment the furniture and paint.

It looked almost like her store Clear but with subtle hints of color.

Sonia loved Clear.

She detested her décor.

But she detested Gregor and Yuri complaining even more, so she'd given in, which was once in enumerable times in her life that she'd done so since Gregor had become her guardian after her mother and father died.

She went to the kitchen and threw the mail on the counter. Without taking off her high-heeled boots, she poached a piece of fish, boiled some brown rice, and steamed some vegetables.

She ate it standing up at her counter, thinking it tasted of nothing.

Bland and well...just *bland*.

Sonia loved food. Too much. In her teens, she'd started to put on weight, Gregor had noticed and commented, often.

This was a problem, considering, even as active as she was as a child, she'd always been slightly plump. And even as careful as she was now—

and she was obsessively careful with diet *and* exercise—she was curvy and nothing she did shifted a centimeter off her bottom or her breasts, no matter what it was. And Sonia had tried everything.

Therefore, for Gregor and her own peace of mind (because Gregor could shatter it, something he did with great regularity), she was careful with her food, and once she became an adult, her drink.

She stood at her counter eating and flipping through catalogues, carefully folding down corners if she saw something she wanted to buy for Christmas for a friend, a neighbor, or one of her shop girls. Next year, of course, as her Christmas shopping was well since complete and wrapped for this year.

Once she was done eating, she tidied everything away and went to her office upstairs to check her e-mail and her Facebook page. She didn't change her status. She never did. She had few friends on Facebook because she had few friends *at all*. This was because she knew she was weird, not because people didn't like her.

Then, as it was Friday, the cleaning lady came on Fridays and the house seemed fresh and lovely (and because she always did it on Fridays), she drew herself a bath.

Fridays meant facial, manicure, and pedicure.

Every Friday.

Without fail.

Unless, of course, she had an appointment at a spa to have this done on a Saturday, which she also did, once a month.

This was because Sonia didn't have friends who she went out to drinks with (very often) and Sonia didn't date (anymore).

To get close to anyone, spend more than a small amount of time with them, meant they'd notice her gifts.

No matter how careful she could be, she'd always slip up. Friends or boyfriends had noticed in the past and it had been uncomfortable (to say the least).

So, Sonia Arlington spent most of her time alone.

Considering she was social, very social, this meant that Sonia Arlington spent most of her time *lonesome*.

As the bath was filling, she took off her clothes and put them away. She rubbed an exfoliating mask on her face and shaved her legs.

As her mostly-white, very clean bathroom filled with the fragrance of lavender coming from the salts in the bath, Sonia carefully body brushed every inch of her skin, even her back, with a handled brush. She settled in the bath and went through her extensive regime of different face masks, shampooing and deep conditioning her hair as she relaxed.

After, she alighted from the bath, toweled off briskly, and donned her robe. Then she gave herself a manicure and pedicure.

All of this was done with practiced ease and precision.

When finished, she went to her medicine cabinet and pulled out the injection.

She had an extremely rare blood disorder inherited from her father. Every night of her life (and Gregor had done it until she was eleven when he patiently taught her how to do it herself), she took the injection.

She hated them, but as her father told her—again, many a time—she could die without them.

She'd once, as a rebellion during her early teens, stopped taking them. This she hid from Gregor. He would have been livid if he'd known. He was very careful with her injections and was just as adamant as her father that she take them every day without fail.

When she didn't, it was a mistake.

Two days after she'd stopped, while she was in bed asleep, she woke having the strange, terrifying sensation she was coming out of her skin.

Seriously.

As if, at any second, her tingling skin would split and she'd boil straight out of it, her blood felt that hot. She could feel it, every last cell of blood *boiling* through her veins.

She'd crawled to the bathroom, so immense was the pain, to give herself the injection, and like now, as the needle pierced the flesh of her right buttock, she felt the injection *invade*.

There was no other way to put it. Just like the boiling of blood cells she'd felt that awful night, the injection *invaded*. Searing through her system, down to the ends of her toes, up, around, and down to her fingertips, up through her scalp, and out—even to the ends of her hair.

But this sensation only lasted minutes. Unlike that night where she'd fought it for hours before giving in.

As usual, when the burn ended, she clutched the basin, took deep breaths, and gave her system several long moments to settle. She disposed of the needle in a small sharps container and walked to her bedroom.

Gregor nor Yuri, although he'd very, very (very) much like to, had ever seen her bedroom.

This was because it was not sleek, modern, and elegant.

It *was* comfortable, countrified, farmhouse splendor.

Mismatched, homey furniture. A colorful wedding ring quilt on the bed. Scalloped shams on the pillows. Vibrantly colored braided rugs. A poofy dust ruffle and even poofier shades in the dormer windows which had even *poofier* pads on the seats.

Her bedroom was beautiful and she adored it, more than Clear, more even than Christmas.

Because it reminded her of home.

Not the elegant townhome she shared with her socialite mother and United States Senator father in DC when her father was at work. Or their gracious, rambling home in that very city.

Their real home.

The cabin in the mountains.

She glanced around her room and saw, amongst her plethora of toss pillows in the middle of the bed, her wolf. Like her Christmas lights did, every night, all year long, the sight of her wolf made her smile.

Her father had it made for her and given it to her the first Christmas she could remember.

She was two.

And she slept with it every night since she was two.

It was a stuffed animal the exact replica of *her* wolf, the one who had, very unfortunately, died the same night as her parents.

She'd known it was *her* wolf the minute she'd seen him (she *did* have a stuffed animal to prove this fact).

And she'd loved him with an inexplicable and unfathomable depth from the moment her eyes fell upon him.

Even though he'd died, he'd never left her, not once, not in all these years.

She knew this because he came to her in her dreams.

She turned her head and saw in the corner *her* Christmas tree. It was smaller and not perfectly decorated. The multi-colored lights were wonky because she put them on. The decorations didn't match because they came from her mother and father's belongings, of which she had practically nothing. This was because Gregor had sold them, given them away, or tossed them out with a thoroughness that was astonishing. Therefore, she truly had nothing but those decorations.

They were the decorations her parents bought during their marriage, were given by friends or had taken from their childhood homes. They were the decorations that hung on the tree in their beloved cabin, long since destroyed in a forest fire (yet another precious thing Sonia had lost).

Over the years, because she figured her parents would want her to, Sonia had added sweet but mismatched decorations that she'd found and fallen in love with. All of which were far from perfect but definitely perfect on her tree.

It was *this* tree she sat beside alone every Christmas morning and opened the presents friends and neighbors had given her.

This was her *real* tree.

She turned on the lights of the tree and the one by her bed. She carefully moisturized her face (so as not to destroy her manicure) and lay on the covers (so as not to destroy her pedicure) and read until her nails were dry and she was sleepy.

She then, as she did every night without fail, rubbed lotion into her feet, a different lotion on her hands, and finally, almond oil into her cuticles.

She turned out the bedside light. Her gaze went to her little Christmas tree, and again, this time with a deep contentment, Sonia sighed.

This was her absolute most favorite time of year.

Because every night, from the day after Thanksgiving until the day after New Year's, she'd sleep in a room bathed in Christmas lights.

And she'd remember a time, long ago, when she was loved.

She opened her eyes and saw her "puppy" standing by her bed.

In her dreams since the night her parents died, she'd see him standing beside her bed, staring at her with his intelligent tawny eyes. But she knew in her heart he was there to look after her, to keep her company, to keep her safe, to protect her.

Not every night (regrettably), but most nights after her parents died.

Over the years these nights came fewer then fewer, until now he only came a few times a year.

But always, one of those times was around Christmas.

"Hello, puppy," she whispered in her dream.

He sat, so huge was her puppy, and he appeared somehow regal.

She grinned at him.

He watched her.

"Is my handsome wolf coming tonight?" she asked.

Her "handsome wolf" had started coming later, years later, when she was in her late teens.

He was an entirely different kind of dream.

She hated to admit it because she loved her puppy, but she liked those dreams even *better*.

Her puppy growled.

Sonia blinked, slowly, dreamily.

When her eyes opened, her handsome wolf was there. She felt him.

The covers slid down her body, she turned, looked up, and saw him.

God, he was handsome.

And he was *huge*.

His naked body slid in bed beside her, mostly on her, and she took his warmth and his immense weight gladly.

She looked in his clear blue eyes.

"Hi," she breathed.

He smiled.

God, he had a great smile.

She wrapped her arm around him as her other hand went up, as it always did, to touch his beautiful face. Her fingertips in his thick hair, her thumb glided along his dark eyebrow then down, over this sharp cheekbone then down, along his full bottom lip.

She watched, fascinated (no matter how many times she saw it) as the tawny spikes shot out of his pupils, the normal sky-blue color of his irises was forced out, and the warm, glittering, deliciously hungry tiger's eye took over.

She lifted her head from the pillow and placed her mouth against his. "Where have you been, my handsome wolf?"

His tongue glided along her lower lip.

Sonia shivered and opened her legs so his hips could fall through.

This was, mostly, an invitation.

It was also so she could wrap him lovingly, protectively in her limbs.

She heard him growl as she felt it against her mouth.

She shivered again.

His deep voice rough with approval, he said, "Always in heat, my little one."

"Only for you," she whispered, her breath catching, her heart racing, her skin warming.

She didn't need him to touch her, kiss her, anything.

He just needed to be near and she was ready for him.

"What do you want?" his voice rumbled, his hips pressing. She could feel the promise of him and she could...not...*wait.*

"You, inside me," she answered.

"Just like that?" he teased.

"You've been gone a while," she told him and arched her back. "I missed you."

She watched close up as his face gentled before he murmured, "Baby doll."

She loved it when he referred to her as "little one" because, at five foot nine (and three quarters), she was far from little.

But she loved it even better when he called her "baby doll."

She pressed her lips against his, tightened her limbs around his body, lifted her hips into his, dug her nails into the muscles of his back, and begged, "Please, my handsome wolf, fuck—"

She didn't finish, his hips reared back, her breath caught in thrilling anticipation, and she waited for his invasion.

Sonia's eyes opened.

"Damn!" she snapped softly into the night.

Always, right before the *good* stuff happened, she'd wake up.

And always, when she woke up, she was hot and bothered.

Immensely so.

Frustratingly so.

Unless she did something about it, which she always did.

She turned to her nightstand, took out her toy, touched the button, and slid it between her legs.

Her neck arched, her body tightened, and not long later, her mind filled with visions of her handsome wolf, she made herself come.

It was nowhere near as good as her dream even as frustratingly short as her dream always was.

But it was all she was going to get.

Her "puppy" was dead and her "handsome wolf" didn't exist in the real world (alas), so her toy was all she had.

For some reason that night this upset her more than it usually did.

She put her toy away, got out of bed, and padded to her window seat to look out into the dark.

"I need a dog," she told the window.

And she did. She'd always wanted one, even as a child. Her father had actually bought her one that last Christmas and he and her mother were on their way to pick it up when they got into the accident. But after they'd been killed, Gregor, not wanting the animal in his home, had given the dog away.

A dog wouldn't think she was weird because she could see better, hear better, smell better, and sense things. A dog wouldn't care just as long as she fed it, pet it, and threw a Frisbee for it.

"That's it," she told the window, "I'm getting a—"

She stopped, her body froze, but her head jerked around to look toward the door.

Someone was in her house.

She jumped up and ran to the bedside table, yanking her phone from its cradle.

She'd pressed the nine and the one before they were on her.

This stunned her.

When she'd sensed them, they'd only just breached the door and her alarm didn't go off. She knew no one who could move that fast and that silently while at the same time disabling an alarm.

One hand at her mouth and one arm around her waist, she was swung around, her legs flying wide, and she dropped the phone.

Instinctively, her fingers formed a claw and she scratched the arm holding her waist. She felt her long strong nails (she religiously took a cocktail of vitamins every morning and this gave her shining hair and fast-growing strong nails, that, in that particular moment, she was deliriously happy for) digging in deep.

She heard his inhuman howl and was tossed away with such force she flew across the room, right through the air, and slammed into the wall.

She fell to the floor and didn't hesitate. She surged up, already on the run.

She was tagged within seconds. Her wrist caught, she was whirled sharply, the tug at her arm causing her to feel an acute intense pain up her arm and along her shoulder. She had no time to cry out, her arm was wrapped around her front, her other wrist caught and pulled forward as well. Her attacker, she noted distractedly, was huge and had enormous hands, holding both wrists tight at her front with little effort while his other hand went to cover her mouth.

His lips came to her ear.

"Play nice, queenie," he ordered.

"Jesus...fucking...God, she's a goddamn wildcat," the other swore from behind them.

Their smell hit Sonia then.

She'd smelled them before.

They'd tracked her before.

They were the menacing ones.

But they'd always kept a distance. Now, obviously, there was nothing distant about them.

This made terror slice through her.

He held her easily. His strength was hard to miss. She was kicking out with her heels, connecting with his shins, and he didn't even so much as grunt.

He could snap her neck in an instant, she knew it. How she knew it, she couldn't say. She just did.

Still, she fought his hold and only stopped when she noticed what he was doing.

Her body went solid.

He was sniffing her.

Sniffing her.

She held her breath.

"Fuck, do you fucking smell her?" he asked against her neck, his arms tightening painfully.

She felt his comrade get close but she heard him pull in breath through his nose.

Then his friend muttered, "Jesus."

"You touch yourself tonight, queenie?" her captor asked, his voice a leer.

Her body jerked with surprise.

Oh my God, she thought hysterically, *they're like me.*

"Sure she did." The other got close, bending from his enormous height to peer in her face. "She doesn't smell like that normally. I would have noticed."

For some strange reason, her captor was rubbing his temple against her neck, her jaw, her cheek. "Christ, I'm getting hard."

"What do you think?" his friend asked, getting closer, his voice dropping, becoming ugly with greed. "Will we get medals, promotions, or both, we do her before the king can claim her?"

Sonia's body locked tight as fear froze every muscle.

"Both," her captor muttered, his hand moving from her mouth, down her neck, her chest, his aim unmistakable as he continued, "Me first."

She opened her mouth to scream. Her captor's friend's hand shot toward her face and she gave an almighty heave to get loose when they heard the thundering, unbelievably terrifying howl.

Everyone froze but Sonia's eyes shot to the door.

The man from her dream stood there.

She gasped.

Then he moved, dropped down, crouched low on both legs and not even a second passed before he surged up...

And the man was gone. But, suddenly—she could not believe her eyes—*her wolf*, alive and snarling, was flying across the room.

He landed on her captor's colleague who went down with a wounded yelp.

Sonia, thinking vaguely that her fear was making her hallucinate, got one chance to look and saw a spray of blood spurting across the room before she was tossed again.

She flew through the air and fell down, the back of her head slamming against the corner of her bedside table. She felt a brief moment of pain and heard a vicious snarl at the same time she could have sworn she heard the tearing of flesh.

Then everything went black.

CHAPTER TWO

THE THRONE

RYON WALKED into the throne room of the Territorial Mansion and he felt his jaw grow tight.

Desdemona sat on the throne on the dais, her dark gleaming hair around her shoulders, her face fully made up, an honor guard of twelve flanking the back of the throne and down the steps of the dais.

She, at least, was smart enough to know if she wanted to try something it would take at least thirteen of them to bring him low.

However, she wasn't smart enough not to appear unaware of their surprise visit.

Or there was the distinct possibility she was still panting for the opportunity to see Callum and she'd hastily thrown this circus together for his benefit.

Fuck, Ryon had called her only a half an hour before and she'd managed to pull together this show.

Stupid bitch.

He barely got two steps in the room before the entire guard dropped to a knee, fell forward on a hand, and gazed at him, heads up.

Much more slowly, Desdemona gracefully alighted from the chair and she took her time moving a step to her left before she fell into the same ceremonial bow.

Ryon hadn't seen her in years and she hadn't changed. Haughty because of her high birth, conceited because of her extreme beauty, and stupid because she just plain was.

She was lucky it was Ryon moving toward her. If Callum had seen that demonstration, he'd have her head and deserve it.

He might have it anyway and deserve it more.

Desdemona, daughter of Titium and Governor of the Western Territories of the Americas, was about to learn that King Callum was not at all like the patient, generous, benevolent King McDonagh was.

Without a word, he walked up the steps of the dais, sat in the throne, and muttered, "Rise."

The guard and Desdemona took their feet.

She stepped down two steps and turned to him.

"Ryon," she greeted familiarly, and with anyone else but her— because he didn't like her *and* with what was happening in her territory —Ryon *might* have allowed it.

Instead, he sensed the eyes of the guard, he'd never liked Mona, and he *knew* the state of her territory, therefore he clipped, "You forget yourself, Governor."

He watched as her face grew pale, her mouth set hard, and her eyes flashed.

Jesus, she was stupid.

He should strike her.

He didn't. He wanted her brain functioning properly when he had a go at her.

He watched as she bowed her head and murmured, "Your grace."

He let go her silent rebellion, threw his hand out, and commented, "This is impressive. Half an hour ago, you didn't know of the king's imminent arrival."

"We're ever ready in the Western Territory, your grace," Desdemona replied.

Bullshit, she knew they were coming.

That was why they'd moved on the queen.

Could the bitch be more stupid?

"Where is he, I mean," she hesitated before finishing, "the king?"

Ryon surveyed her.

Yes, she could be more stupid. Because there was a chance she didn't even know about the queen, and even as those in her territory conspired to break the treaty, she couldn't hide her eagerness to see Cal.

She was, quite plainly, gagging for it.

In fact, there was a more than mild possibility she'd orchestrated this fiasco in order to get it.

If she *wasn't* involved in the conspiracy, this grand show was entirely for Cal.

Jesus, Cal must be a master of his own dick to inspire this kind of devotion. He'd finished the messy business with Desdemona over a hundred years ago and she *still* wasn't over him.

"He's collecting his queen," Ryon answered bluntly, exposing knowledge that had been, for thirty-one years, treated as the most crucially held state secret.

Every last guard pulled in breath and even Desdemona gasped.

All right then, perhaps she didn't know.

"The queen is in my territory?" she asked, her voice breathy and irate, not even attempting to hide her displeasure. Anyone else would find that knowledge an unreserved honor, even if they knew the queen was human.

"Yes," Ryon replied.

"I don't believe it," she whispered.

"Believe it, Mona," Ryon returned sharply. "And while you're wrapping your mind around that you better pray he gets to her before the men who were dispatched to kidnap her do."

Her body jolted and the air in the room got thick.

Finally, the bitch was smart enough to know fear and she definitely knew Cal enough to know that fear was warranted.

She leaned forward and her face was even paler, her eyes betraying her fear, but her voice was angry. "No one in my territory would *dream* of moving on the queen."

"They would and they did. We received word eleven hours ago they were taking her tonight. That's why we're here," Ryon informed her.

"That's impossible," she snapped.

Ryon's head suddenly tilted to the side and he took in a breath through his nose.

Cal was there.

As were his warriors.

He also had his queen with him.

He wouldn't have her if she hadn't been under threat.

The Mating Ceremony wasn't to commence until a year in the future. Cal was supposed to begin their regular human courtship in a few weeks at her annual Christmas party. He was to pose as the guest of a neighbor, a wolf who'd been planted in a house across from hers years ago.

This was something Ryon had talked him into doing. Cal wanted just to grab her, as was his due. Ryon, on the other hand, had been reading reports on her as well as watching her himself for thirty-one years.

Sonia Arlington needed to be courted. As a human, she'd expect it.

But being all she was, she deserved it.

It took Ryon a while to talk Cal around, most especially since his father's death Cal had been reading the reports on her as well as getting the pictures. And, because of this, not to mention the simple fact that she *was* his mate, Cal was growing impatient.

Very impatient.

But, apparently, Cal's hand had been forced and the treaty broken.

This meant war.

Desdemona's head jerked toward the door. She sensed it too.

"Impossible, Mona?" Ryon asked quietly and he watched as she slowly turned to face him, her throat moving convulsively.

Yes, Mona, you...are...fucked, Ryon thought as he rose from the throne and stepped to its right side.

The next second, Cal came through the door.

Ryon felt his jaw get tight again upon seeing Sonia, wrapped in a blanket, held unconscious in Cal's arms.

The guard and Desdemona, without delay, dropped to their knee, forward on their hand, but in the presence of their king, they bowed their heads toward the floor.

Ryon didn't drop to his knee.

He was not only a duke. He was not only Cal's cousin. He was not only born precisely one year after Cal (to the very hour, a significant happenstance in the brotherhood). But his blood had mingled with Cal's on too many battlefields for Ryon to take a knee.

He'd done it once, after the king had fallen.

Cal had forbidden him ever to do it again.

Without looking at anyone but Ryon, Cal made his way to the throne.

Ryon felt a muscle jump in his jaw at the look of fury on his cousin's face.

Cal sat on the throne, gently arranging Sonia in his lap so she was close, her forehead tucked into his neck, her hand resting on his chest, her knees cocked and tucked into his side. His arms, finally, settled protectively around her.

Ryon had seen her many times since that night her mother and father were murdered. She was a pretty child.

She was a fucking amazing woman. If she wasn't destined queen, Ryon would have taken her to his bed.

And kept her there.

Until the day she died.

Cal was a lucky bastard.

"Rise," Cal ordered, his voice an angry rumble.

Desdemona rose slowly, her eyes carefully not looking at Sonia, but also not looking at Cal.

Ryon didn't have time for Mona.

"Is she okay?" he asked his cousin, his eyes on Sonia.

"Ellington threw her across the room. She cracked her head, went unconscious. She was coming to but I sedated her for the drive to the cabin," Cal replied, his eyes never leaving Mona.

Ryon's eyes never left Sonia but his hands clenched into fists.

At this news that their soon-to-be queen had been manhandled, the air in the room again went thick. Or, Ryon could say, *thicker*.

Mona drew in breath.

Then she said something immensely stupid.

"She's human."

"*She's your queen*," Cal ground out and Mona took a step back, bowing her head while Cal went on. "Jesus, I will never fucking understand my father's decision about you," he gritted out and Mona's head bowed further as her shoulders drooped. "Tell me, Mona, how in *the fuck* could you let the treaty get broken in your territory?"

Mona lifted her head. "I had no—"

Cal cut her off. "It happened."

Mona leaned forward. "But, your grace, I had no—"

Cal interrupted her again, biting off every word. "In these tense times, it's your fucking job to monitor every goddamned wolf."

"But, Cal—" she started plaintively, and without hesitation at her familiarity with her sovereign, Ryon started forward.

"Leave it, Ry," Cal clipped and Ryon stopped and looked back.

"I'm interrogating her personally," Ryon demanded and without looking at him Cal nodded.

"Interrogating me?" Desdemona asked, a tremor of fear shifting through her voice.

"Warriors are coming, Mona," Cal told her. "Can't you hear them? For fuck's sake, do you ever pay attention?"

Mona's head tilted and Ryon listened to the sounds of the takeover of the mansion.

"The plot was hatched in these walls, Governor," Cal clipped. "By tomorrow night, we'll know who was involved."

The guard was shifting uncomfortably and Mona's mouth was opening and closing like a fish, but Cal just rose from his throne, cradling Sonia. He started to stride from the room seconds before the doors opened and twenty warrior wolves, all of whom were chosen specifically by Cal as Cal's Royal Guard, advanced through.

They parted for Cal and Sonia as if they'd practiced it hundreds of times. Cal walked through the stream of warriors and exited the room.

Ryon looked at Magnum, the leader, and jerked his head to a visibly trembling Mona.

"She's mine," he ordered.

Then he left the room much like Cal in search of his lieutenant.

CHAPTER THREE
THE CABIN

EVEN THOUGH SONIA *FELT* AWAKE, she knew she couldn't be.

She was ultra-warm and it felt like she was lying on one of those down mattress top thingies and Sonia didn't have one of those down mattress top thingies. But she was going to get one, it felt *lush*.

She also felt like she had a soft, fluffy, but snugly down comforter covering her as well as the softest sheets in the history of mankind shrouding her. Sonia owned a quilt, not a comforter, and her sheets were soft, but not *this* soft.

And lastly, she wasn't holding her stuffed wolf close to her chest and Sonia never slept without her stuffed wolf, much to the chagrin of the very few lovers she'd had in her life.

She opened her eyes to assess her dream state and found she was *definitely* dreaming.

This she knew because she saw from her vantage point of head on a fluffy down pillow (also not hers) that she was in her family's cabin, and as that cabin had been burnt to a cinder years and years ago, she had to be dreaming.

This was proved irrevocably when she heard a door open.

She tensed as she listened to booted footsteps hitting the floor. And she stared, not moving, as she watched an unbelievably tall man walk into the room.

All she saw was his back, but she also saw that his hair was dark, thick, and overlong. He was wearing one of those quilted flannel shirts, his was a brown, gray, and yellow plaid on a cream background. With this, he had on jeans and boots. She could see the tight bulky muscle of his thigh through his jeans when he crouched by the fireplace and quietly arranged some logs with gloved hands on top of an already big pile there.

"I know you're awake," his deep voice sounded and she blinked.

She knew that voice and its strange accent. Not American, not Scottish, not English, not French, a beautiful mixture of *all* of them.

Her handsome wolf.

Yes, definitely dreaming.

But this one was new.

She'd never had it in her cabin before. It was always either in her bedroom or some dream room lit by firelight, a room she'd never been in but sensed, strangely, was home.

And it had never been this vivid.

She dreamed vivid dreams her whole life. It was another gift she had that she knew others didn't. Her dreams weren't weird or disjointed. They were clear, they told stories, and she always remembered every second.

She liked this new dream.

"No, I'm not," she told his back as he laid down the last log. "I'm dreaming."

He rose, turned, and she sucked in dream breath.

God, he was handsome.

She loved every plane and angle on his face, and there were lots of them and there was lots to love. He was, put simply, beautiful.

Dark eyebrows, sky-blue eyes, strong jaw, interesting nose, full bottom lip.

He could, she noted with surprise, use a shave. He'd never been stubbly in any of her other dreams. With the thick, dark growth on his face, he looked like he hadn't shaved in days.

She'd never been one for facial hair, but on him she liked it.

She tore her eyes from his face and noticed he had on a dark gray thermal henley under the flannel.

And he had on a great black belt with a heavy buckle.

His outdoorsy outfit, not usually Sonia's thing, was *delicious*, especially on that big, muscular, broad-shouldered, slim-hipped, long-legged body.

Hell, if he was real and lived in a real cabin in the mountains and one woman caught sight of him, it would be all over. Word would get out and women would be crawling all over this place like ants on the remains of a melted fallen snow cone.

He was watching her inquiringly, so she got up on an elbow and called softly, "Why are you all the way over there, my handsome wolf?"

At her words, his brows drew together and it was a decidedly ominous look.

Sonia stared at him.

He'd never looked even *close* to ominous in any of her other dreams.

"What did you just say?" he asked, his voice strangely low and not-so-strangely (given the look) ominous.

She decided to go with it. He was always somewhat teasing and often even playful in her dreams.

"You heard me, wolf."

He pulled off his gloves and dropped them on a chair as he strode toward her.

Sonia watched him.

His grace was astonishing. He'd always been close to her bed when she dreamed of him. She'd only ever felt him join her there. She'd never seen him move.

He looked good when he moved.

Boy, she *loved* this new dream.

He stopped to tower over the bed and she dropped to her back to look up at him.

"I'm liking this dream," she informed him on a grin.

He sat beside her on the bed, his brows still drawn.

"Sonia, you aren't dreaming," he told her.

She put her hand to his forearm and tugged it toward her while saying through her grin, "Right."

He leaned forward so both of his hands were in the bed at her sides and replied gently, "Right, little one. You're awake, this isn't a dream." His blue eyes moved over her face before he asked, "Do you feel okay?"

"I feel great," she answered. Though she had to admit, even though it was weird in a dream, that her head hurt a little and she felt kind of groggy, like she'd slept a bit too long.

His hand came up and he placed it at the side of her head. It was so big it nearly covered the entire area.

His thumb smoothed over her eyebrow but his eyes never left hers.

"You called me 'wolf,'" he stated softly.

She didn't reply. She sat up, dislodging his hand, her body getting closer to his, her face getting closer to his. His body, she felt, went solid, but she ignored that too and placed her hand on the side of his face.

"I get to do the touching," she told him, as if he didn't know.

She touched his face in her dream.

Always.

She did it again, fingertips in his thick hair, thumb gliding along his brow, down across his sharp cheekbone, then over his full lower lip.

"Sonia." His mouth moved against her thumb. She lifted her gaze from his lips to his eyes, which were searching but had not gone tawny (alas). "Does this mean you feel it?"

She nodded.

Oh, she felt it all right. She always felt it in her dream.

And she hoped this dream, which was not only sharper, clearer, and more vivid than any of her other dreams, but was also lasting *a lot* longer, would not end in her reaching toward the nightstand.

He smiled.

She sucked in breath.

God, she loved, loved, *loved* his smile.

"You feel it," he murmured, his deep voice deeper, so much so it was almost a physical thing, and he looked really, really, *really* pleased about something.

It was a good look.

And the depth of his voice was an *excellent* depth.

She got closer and placed her hands on his broad shoulders, put her mouth to his, and, her eyes never leaving his own, demanded, "Are you going to kiss me, wolf, or what?"

She watched with great anticipation as the tiger's eye shot from his pupils and erased the blue of the iris.

She'd never seen the gold obliterate the blue so fast.

But she knew what *that* meant.

Then his arm sliced around her, his hips and legs shifted, and his heat and colossal weight were pinning her to the bed.

Finally!

Then something weird happened.

He didn't tease her.

He didn't let her wrap her limbs around him.

He didn't wait for her invitation.

He slanted his head and he *kissed* her.

Ho.

Lee.

Cow!

Sonia absolutely *loved* this dream!

Her mouth opened under his and that was it.

Explosion.

Not gentle.

Huge.

And consuming.

She was wrong. He didn't need just to be there for her to be ready for him.

His kiss, his unbelievably amazing kiss, sent her from aroused at his presence to burning for his invasion.

She wrapped her arms around him and kissed him back, hoping to all that was holy that he felt the same beautiful explosion.

He had to, for the minute her tongue sparred with his, his growl filled her mouth and was so intense it traveled down her throat.

That felt even better.

She arched against him and moaned right back.

His arms circled her and he rolled, taking her with him, her on top, his hands going into her hair at the sides of her head, holding it away from their faces, but there was so much of it, it tumbled down all around them.

And he kept kissing her and Sonia hoped *this* dream *and* his kiss never ended.

Ever.

His knee came up, her legs parted, one thigh falling between his, and his cocked leg landed tight against the heat of her.

Sonia's head jerked back, her mouth slowly opening in a silent moan as she felt it. The tight, hard muscle pressing powerfully against her most sensitive part.

Good goodness, she nearly came.

Just with that.

She heard another growl, it seemed far away (but was very close), and he rolled again, this time into her. She took that opportunity to kiss him again and slide herself against his hard jeans-clad thigh.

Shivers of fire shafted through her and she clutched onto his shirt like she was never letting go.

His arms tightened around her but his mouth tore from hers and he growled, "Fucking hell, baby doll."

"Don't stop," she begged, her voice sounding desperate because she *was* desperate. The dream could end at any minute. Her hand went into his hair to force his lips back to hers. "Please, don't stop or the dream will end."

She felt his body still and her insistent hand in his hair was getting her nowhere.

She opened her eyes and saw he was watching her.

"Don't stop," she pleaded.

"Sonia—"

The hand not at his head roamed, down, down, to drift over his behind. "I don't want the dream to—"

She didn't finish speaking because she heard a cell phone ringing just as she felt it vibrate against her hand.

Dreams didn't have phones ringing.

Or, they did, but only to wake you up.

She waited.

It kept ringing.

It kept vibrating.

Sunlight, his warm hard body, his tight strong arms, his heavy weight, and that damn phone vibrating against her hand all intruded.

She wasn't dreaming.

Sonia's eyes, still locked with his, widened.

Memories flooded.

The intruders the night before.

Then he was there.

Then, her puppy.

No, that couldn't be right. She was hallucinating.

But *something* had happened because he was *right there.*

How could she forget last night?

With a fearful noise escaping her throat, violently, she tore from his arms and jumped from the bed.

Stopping several feet away, she whirled to stare at him.

Her dream man.

Now up on a forearm watching her closely from a bed in her parents' cabin.

"This isn't a dream," she whispered.

But...

It *had* to be. This wasn't possible.

"Come here, baby doll," he murmured gently.

He called her "baby doll."

She closed her eyes. Then she opened them.

"This isn't a dream," she repeated, wanting him to tell her it was.

But he didn't. He moved and her arm darted up, palm out, but the rest of her body grew paralyzed with fear.

At this reaction, he stopped but her head jerked around.

This *was* her parents' cabin. She knew it.

But it was different.

The kitchen was newer, grander. It had a huge KitchenAid refrigerator and range. The countertops were nicer. The cabinets were better.

Her head jerked the other way.

There was still a big, inviting, deep-seated couch in front of a coffee table, which sat in front of a roaring fire. The couch was still flanked by comfortable club chairs. There was a large sheepskin hide tossed casually over the corner of the sofa. The rug all the furniture sat on was vast, thick, inviting you to bed down on it with a pillow, a book, and a nice comfy blanket.

But the furniture was different, newer, fluffier, sturdier, more rustic. They veritably screamed, "Take a load off and stay awhile."

Her head swung forward and she saw the enormous sleigh bed. Bigger, wider, longer, covered in a downy comforter, at the foot was a mohair throw.

Regardless of the changes, it *was* her parents' cabin.

How could this be?

Her handsome wolf.

Her cabin?

She looked back at him.

"This can't be," she whispered. "Gregor told me the cabin burned down years ago."

His face changed the second she uttered Gregor's name but Sonia was too busy registering the fact that she'd clearly gone insane to let the frightening look that crossed his face penetrate.

"It didn't burn down, little one," he said softly, recapturing her complete attention as he moved from the bed.

The instant he did she backed up two steps.

He stopped, standing at its side.

"Who are you?" she demanded.

He replied immediately, "Callum."

Callum.

Vaguely, she thought that was an interesting name. Equally distractedly, she thought it suited him.

She looked down and saw she had on the same cotton nightdress she'd donned the night before.

The memories hit her again, ugly memories, terrifying ones, and she took another step back as her head snapped up.

"They were going to hurt me," she told him.

He started walking toward her as he assured, "They won't hurt you."

She continued to retreat but he didn't stop this time.

Her hand, with its palm still facing him, had started trembling.

"They were going to hurt me," she repeated.

"They won't hurt you," he also repeated, but his voice was less gentle. In fact, it was not gentle at all. It was reassuringly firm.

His legs were longer (far longer) and he got close quickly.

She felt the logs of the cabin wall against her shoulders and stopped because she had nowhere else to go.

Then she felt his hard chest hit her hand and her hand slid up as he got even closer until he stopped, not an inch away.

She tilted her head far back and looked up at him. She felt her lips tremble and it mortified her.

She tried to stop their movement and couldn't, so through them she whispered, "Did you rescue me?"

His hands came up and she tensed but he placed them on the logs on either side of her head. He leaned down so they were face to face, so close, she could feel his breath on her skin.

"Sonia, no one will ever hurt you. Not when you're with me."

She felt a different kind of tremble slide through her body.

Because his voice wasn't firm when he said that.

His deep rich voice was rock-solid. Like those words weren't just words, they were a sacred vow.

"I don't understand what's going on," she whispered and her tense body grew tight as his head got closer but veered to the side.

Then he did something bizarre.

And, she had to admit, it was strikingly beautiful in its tenderness.

With his temple, he nuzzled her own then down her cheek, to her jaw, up again, and into her hair.

He stopped nuzzling her with his temple, but, lips to her ear, he said gently, "Get showered and dressed, baby doll. I'll finish with the wood. We'll have breakfast. Then I'll explain everything."

Sonia stood, shoulder blades against the logs of her family's long-thought-lost-but-always-beloved cabin, her used-to-be most favorite place in the world, with the heat of her dream man's body hitting her own, her fingers curled on the solid, very real muscle of his shoulder, his stubbled cheek against hers, his lips at her ear, his glorious voice calling her his "baby doll."

And she could do nothing but nod.

Sonia's senses returned somewhat to normal when Callum stepped away from her but took her hand and led her to a plethora of shopping bags that were lined against the opposite wall.

He did a sweep and nabbed the handles all in one huge fist, even though there were ten of them, some of them large. This proved her theory correct that he had every centimeter of his body under control and was stronger than an ox because she knew no man or woman (even expert shoppers) who could do that the way he did...effortlessly.

He carried the bags to the bathroom while never letting go of her hand.

He stopped her inside and dropped the bags by the wall.

Sonia stared at the bags idiotically, noting they nearly took up the remainder of space that Sonia and Callum weren't occupying.

"Everything you need will be in these bags," he announced, regaining her attention, and she watched him cock his head to the bathroom counter, "or those."

She looked to the counter to see three more bags there, but those were smaller.

She glanced back at Callum and nodded.

"When you're finished, if I'm not in the house, I'll be out back," he went on.

She nodded again.

"You'll need to make breakfast, little one. I'll be a while. The kitchen's stocked. Eggs, toast, bacon," he carried on and this last sounded like a gentle order.

She was still too deep in all the weirdness that was surrounding her to do anything but nod to that too.

With that, he left the bathroom, quietly closing the door behind him.

Incidentally, her parents' rustic bathroom had been significantly updated. It still appeared rustic but it had a claw-footed tub that could easily seat two. The tub had an elaborate spout and spray system and a shower. The basin was finished with a fabulous concrete countertop that worked really well with the log walls and wood floor. Not to mention thick-pile rugs, fluffy, soft towels, and a big mirror over the basin with a great light fixture above it.

It wasn't until *after* she'd discovered the three bags on the countertop had her favorite shampoo, conditioner, bath wash, lotion, and perfume as well her brand of razor and a variety of her cosmetics with the exact right shades and included brushes.

It wasn't until *after* she'd perused what was in the ten shopping bags and found a variety of girlie outdoor gear. Corduroys, jeans, belts, long-sleeved thermals, long-sleeved tees, henleys, sweaters, fleeces, poofy vests, and thick socks that were *all* in her exact sizes. But not her colors. She usually wore white, black, gray, or silver. There was none of that and, of course, she never wore outdoor gear and hadn't in thirty-one years.

It wasn't until *after* she'd found sexy, lacy, satiny, silky lingerie for sleeping in and even sexier lacy, satiny, silky underwear for wearing (and not a piece of it her usual classic, but utilitarian, undergarments) were also in the bags.

It wasn't until *after* she'd lotioned, spritzed perfume, gunked smoothing elixir into her hair, and put on a light coat of makeup.

It was when she was blow drying her hair with a blow dryer she found in the cabinet. She was doing it while standing in front of the mirror in a demi bra made of pale green-yellow silk topped with beige lace and matching Brazilian cut panties. Neither of which she'd even glance at in a store, but, she had to admit, they were beautiful and made her feel a little bit saucy.

It was then that her mind shuffled logically through last night and this morning and everything that had happened.

Last night, while she was innocently sleeping (for all they knew), men invaded her house.

They grabbed her, scared her nearly to death, and discussed raping her.

Then Callum came in and, obviously, saved the day.

However, afterward, he did *not* phone the police.

She did *not* wake up in a hospital bed or shaken by a uniformed officer.

Most importantly, she was *not* introduced by a proper authority to

Callum as the man who just happened to be walking past her house and heard her scream (which, she also noted, she never screamed, so how on earth had he known to come in at all!). Therefore, upon hearing her scream, he gallantly burst forth to wrest her from the clutches of evil.

This morning, when she'd woken thinking she was in a dream, he had *not* informed her firmly that she was not, indeed, dreaming. And Callum, she also noted, could be *very* firm.

Instead, he'd *not* acted like a gentleman and he'd taken advantage of her obvious confusion and vulnerability and *kissed her* and *other things as well*.

Now she found out that he knew her preferences for toiletries *and* her size.

He'd been prepared for this.

Very prepared.

She knew why and she thought it was a cruel cosmic joke that the man outside splitting logs (she could hear the axe and the logs dropping into the snow), looked like her dream man.

It was a sadistic maneuver for that *jerk* to bring her *here*.

She'd figured that out too.

Because Gregor, for some demented reason, had systematically removed every hint of her mother and father and the life she had with them. Except her stuffed wolf and the Christmas decorations, but only because she'd thrown an almighty six-year-old fit.

He'd obviously gotten rid of the cabin too and didn't have the courage to tell her he'd sold it.

After she got away from *Callum*, she was finally going to demand some answers from *Gregor*. Then she was going to tell his son *Yuri* once and for all that she was *not* going to sleep with him and definitely *not* going to marry him. Last, she was never speaking to another man *again* until the *day...she...died!*

Except, of course, Gregor, after she forgave him because, even though he was remote, she still loved him.

And, obviously, Yuri, after she forgave him too, because, even though she knew he thought differently, she'd always thought of him kind of like a brother and she loved him too.

She put on a pair of fawn-colored low-rider cords which she was *not* going to think were cute (even though they were). She added a brown leather belt with daisies stamped into the leather which was something else that she determined was *not* cute (even though it was). Then she donned a bright pink, long-sleeved henley that had a ribbon with flowers sewn down the buttoned slit at the collar which *didn't* fit her like it was made for her, *wasn't* surprisingly the perfect color for her, and *didn't* make her look really good even though she'd never have guessed it (even though it did all that).

She also tugged on a pair of thick socks that were *not* warm and snugly (even though they were).

She found there were no shoes but she didn't need shoes.

Yet.

She walked out of the bathroom and grabbed the bags (taking three trips) and carted them back into the big room.

She made the bed (angrily) as she heard Callum chop, chop, chopping outside. Sometimes, she'd hear him stop and approach the house and she'd get tense, but he did it only to stack the logs on the back porch because he never came inside.

She found coffee, poured herself a cup, and yanked open the refrigerator to find Callum had stocked it only with full-fat milk.

Of course.

He knew her clothing size but he didn't know she religiously had to drink skim in order to fit in it.

Jerk!

She made breakfast for the both of them and surprisingly she heard the back door open the minute she was done.

She heard his boots on the floor as she was busily taking the plates from warming in the oven.

He stopped at the mouth of the u-shaped kitchen.

She didn't turn. If she did, she might throw something at him.

Or cry.

Or both.

"Sonia?" he called.

"Yep," she said, flipping the oven closed with her foot and still not looking at him.

"You okay?" he asked, sounding concerned.

Jerk!

"Much better," she replied, busily loading food on their plates. "Breakfast is ready."

"I know."

That got a reaction.

She turned to look at him and was reminded of the gargantuan joke the cosmos was playing on her because he was way, way, *way* too darned handsome.

She buried that thought and asked, "How did you know?"

"Smelled it. Heard it," he replied and turned while finishing, "I'll be there after I wash up."

Since he was turning, he didn't see her mouth had dropped open.

Okay, she was cooking bacon. You could smell bacon from a mile away.

But he *heard* it?

How?

She, of course, could hear the final preparations of breakfast.

But him?

No way.

She watched him disappear into the bathroom as she felt a shiver run up her spine and decided to bury that too.

He couldn't know of her gifts so he could pretend to have ones as well. Even Gregor and Yuri didn't know. Sure, she'd often messed up around them. Still, they'd never cottoned on.

She'd found placemats and napkins, and by the time he was done in the bathroom, she was putting his plate on a mat on the bar that separated the kitchen from the living room.

He slid on the stool and looked down at his plate.

As usual, Sonia stood at the kitchen counter across from him (the last part not as usual, obviously) and ate while contemplating how she was going to get out of this mess.

Would it take a million dollars?

Two?

Three?

What would he accept to give up his game?

"What's this?" Callum asked, his voice tight in a way that sounded like he was restraining some impulse, and when she looked at him, his face was carefully blank.

"Eggs, bacon, and toast," she answered.

He looked back down at his plate.

Sonia continued eating.

"I recognize the toast," he commented with forced politeness and she looked up again to see he was holding a piece of toast between a very attractive thumb and forefinger. "Is there butter?"

"Butter is fat," Sonia replied and took a bite of her dry toast.

Callum watched her chew like it was fascinating in a watching-the-devastation-of-an-earthquake-in-slow-motion-on-TV kind of way.

"What'd you do to the bacon?" Callum inquired after she swallowed.

"I cut off the fat," she informed him. "The meat is good. Protein. The fat is bad."

His brows went up and he went on, his voice no longer polite but coated in disbelief, "You cut the *fat* off *bacon?*"

"Yep."

He looked down at his plate. "The eggs are white."

"That's because I threw away the yolks. They're filled with cholesterol."

She trained her eyes on her plate and kept eating, but she lifted her head when she heard him move.

She watched with surprise and not a small amount of annoyance as he rounded the counter, went straight to the trash bin, and dumped everything on his plate inside it.

Then she watched with even sharper surprise and an ungodly amount of annoyance when he walked to her, grabbed her plate out from under her, pulled the remnants of toast right out of her fingers, and dumped that in the bin too.

Sonia stood staring at him wordlessly as he opened the fridge, nabbed the bacon, dumped a huge lump of it into the skillet, and turned on the burner. After that, he gently moved her away from the range and grabbed the box of eggs she'd left on the counter.

As he started cracking eggs into a bowl, she spluttered, "You just... you just...just...*threw away my food.*"

"That wasn't food," he replied.

"It was breakfast," she shot back.

"It wasn't that either."

"Callum—"

He turned to her as the bacon started sizzling and advanced, quickly. She retreated, not quickly enough. Her hips hit the counter and he closed in.

His hands on the counter on either side of her, he leaned down so they were face to face. "You're too skinny. You need to eat. Not egg whites, not dry toast, and not fatless bacon."

He thought she was too skinny?

Was he blind?

Sonia couldn't move, but even so, her mouth dropped open.

He ignored her astonished look and kept talking. "No more of that shit, Sonia. Not for me and not for you either."

"Are you...?" she paused, not thinking she could say it, then she said it, "Telling me what to eat?"

"Damn right," he replied, not having *any* problem saying what *he* had to say.

He pushed away from the counter and turned back to the range.

She watched in growing horror as he cooked breakfast all in one skillet.

He didn't not only *not* cut the fat off the bacon and separate the yolks, he didn't drain the bacon grease before he dumped the eight (yes, eight!) scrambled eggs into the skillet with it. Not done, he also chucked a handful (and his hand, as Sonia had noted on several occasions, was *large*) of pre-grated cheddar cheese on the lot and sprinkled it all with garlic salt.

Further, he slathered the toast in so much butter it was the added stroke on top of the heart attack that was the egg-bacon-cheese mess.

He served this all up on the plates, got himself a fresh cup of coffee, poured a warm up in hers, dashed it with *not* a splash of milk but a *glug*, and handed both plate and mug to her.

Then he picked up his own plate, rested a hip against the counter, leveled his blue eyes on her, and ordered, "Eat."

She looked at her plate.

She had to admit, it looked really good.

And it smelled fantastic.

She looked at him.

"I can't eat this."

"Eat," he repeated.

"This is...I can't—"

"Sonia," he said her name slowly in a way that denoted strained patience. "You can eat it or I'll feed it to you."

She felt her eyes grow wide before she asked, "You're joking, right?"

He shook his head.

She looked at the plate.

He was, essentially, a kidnapper.

He was, she guessed, going to hold her for ransom if he didn't charm her (in other words, con her) out of millions of dollars.

He had been, thus far, pretty nice, even though he was a jerk.

But, she shouldn't push it.

Sonia picked up her fork and she ate.

And, while doing so, she told herself it didn't taste unbelievably great (even though it did).

CHAPTER FOUR
EXPLANATION

AFTER THEY ATE their breakfast (Sonia couldn't finish hers, which Callum allowed, but he cleaned her plate, an act she thought was borderline intimacy which caused her to feel warm and cold and scared and excited all at the same time), Callum demonstrated that he was not quite finished racking up his sins.

Firstly, he took Sonia's hand and led her to the living room.

When she said, "I'll do the dishes." He replied, "Later."

Sin number one.

Everyone knew you cleaned the kitchen right away. If you didn't, the gunk would solidify on the plates and skillets and it would take ages to soak it away. Further, Callum wasn't exactly a tidy cook; he'd made a right mess.

However, considering her varied uncertain circumstances—chief of which was the fact that she'd been kidnapped—she decided at that point not to argue about dishes.

He stopped her by one of the large club chairs, dropped her hand, but went to the fire and stoked it, throwing another log on.

He walked across the room to the other hearth situated on the wall on the other side of the bed and stoked that fire, putting a log from the huge pile at its side on the burning embers.

Then he committed sin number two.

He walked back, sat in the club chair, leaned forward, took her hand, and gave it a firm but gentle tug so she came off her feet with a small, surprised thus uncontrollable cry. He twisted her body as she fell and she landed in his lap.

She pulled up and away but his arms locked around her.

"Um..." she muttered cautiously. "What are you doing?"

"As I said, after breakfast, I'd explain," he told her, his arms growing tighter, drawing her closer. "I'm explaining," he finished.

"Um..." she muttered again, even more cautiously, trying not to get alarmed. "Can you explain sitting here while I sit on the couch?"

She thought, considering she'd just met him an hour or so ago, this was a reasonable request.

"No."

There it was. Callum being *very* firm.

Apparently he thought it wasn't reasonable.

Sonia begged to differ.

"I'd be more comfortable on the couch," she informed him.

"You'd be more comfortable in my lap if you'd relax," he replied.

Okay, maybe *she* wasn't insane.

Maybe *he* was.

Instead of relaxing, she tensed.

"I barely know you," she noted.

"We've got a week to rectify that," he returned.

She stared.

"What does that mean?" she asked.

He completely ignored her question and asked his own, "Why'd you call me 'wolf?'"

She blinked.

Then she asked, "What?"

"This morning, when you woke up, you called me 'wolf.'"

Oh good goodness.

She couldn't tell him about her dream.

Ever.

In a million years.

No one knew about her dream and she wasn't about to share it with some guy she just met, who, it was important to note, was her kidnapper!

And anyway, even *she* didn't know why she called him that in her dream.

"I didn't," she lied. "Did I?" she added for good measure.

"You did. You know you did. You remember every second of this morning."

Holy cow.

She had a great memory, not photographic but close. It was another one of her gifts.

Did he know that? And if he did, *how* did he know that?

She didn't want the answer to that either.

"I thought I was dreaming," she reminded him.

"Yes, I got that. You still called me 'wolf' and I want to know why."

"I thought this cabin had burned down," Sonia switched subjects and explained. "My parents used to own this cabin a long time ago." Not that *he*, for whatever ungodly reason, didn't know that. "I'd been told it burned down when I was seven years old. Since it's still standing, and not burned down, and I'm *in* it, which I thought was kind of impossible, though obviously not, considering it *isn't* burnt down, I thought I was in a dream. I didn't know what I was doing."

His hand, which was resting at her hip, curled around her waist. His arm, already around her waist, tightened.

Thus, he brought her closer.

Her hand at his chest pressed back.

He was stronger than her but he allowed her some space, not nearly enough, but some.

"Little one, you're holding out on me," he said quietly, his eyes serious and not happy. "I'll tell you only once. Don't do that."

She was unsure how to respond.

The fact that he knew she was holding out on him was bizarre and alarming. The fact that his eyes had grown serious and not happy was just plain alarming.

She decided to respond to the serious, not happy look in his eyes and tread very, very carefully.

But how on earth was she going to get out of this?

Oh hell, she was going to have to give him something. She hated it but she was going to have to do it.

She swallowed before she blurted, "You're very good-looking."

His head tilted to the side with a surprised jerk.

She ignored that and carried on.

"I thought," her voice cracked and she cleared her throat, "I was in a dream. I've always been…" She paused, pulled in breath then hurried on in a rush, "Once, when I was a little girl, I met this wolf." His head jerked upright and she watched with concern as his eyes grew intense. "It's okay," she assured him, misreading his look. "I was going to mention, I've always been really good with animals. He was injured but he wasn't dangerous. He let me help him."

"Sonia—" Callum started but she talked over him.

"When I met him, I brought him here, the wolf that is. And…and I *liked* this wolf. He was a beautiful wolf. I'd seen wolves before out in the woods with my father, but never one like him. He was huge and he had this dignity…" She paused again, realizing she was veering off track, and continued, "Anyway, he made an impression on me. I've never forgotten him and I think, being in what I thought was a dream, seeing you here in this cabin and the last time I was here I met that wolf, for some reason, because of him, I used that as an endearment." She sucked in breath through her nose then said, "So there, that's why I called you 'wolf.'"

And that didn't sound like a lie. In fact, she was pretty pleased with herself, and maybe that *was* why she called her dream Callum "wolf" too, who knew?

When she'd stopped congratulating herself, she focused on his face. Then she sucked in another breath.

His face was warm and gentle, and she was shocked to see, his eyes weren't blue, they were tawny.

Oh wow.

She told herself, firmly, she didn't like it when his eyes went golden (but she did).

Anyway, how did he do that?

"What?" she whispered, forgetting her travails when his eyes were like that, but his hand slid up her back to her neck, his fingers cupped her there and he forced her head to his shoulder.

"Nothing, little one," he murmured but his voice was warm and gentle too.

She took another deep breath and told herself his big warm body didn't feel great cradling hers (which it did) and his deep, warm, gentle voice rumbling in her ear didn't sound wonderful (which it also did). Then she reminded herself that she was in a frightening situation, sitting in the lap of a large, strong, albeit handsome man who was likely dangerous and *not* her dream man (even though he was, in a way).

She screwed up the courage to start talking about what *she* wanted to talk about.

"I want to go home," she told his collarbone.

"You can't, honey, not for a while," was his scary response.

"I want to go home," she repeated.

"You need to stay with me. When this is over, I don't know where we'll settle. We'll talk about it when that happens."

When *what* was over?

And...

He didn't know where they'd *settle*?

What was he on about?

She didn't care and she wasn't going to ask.

Instead, softly, she inquired, "Callum, how much for you to take me home?"

"Honey, you can't *go* home," he reiterated.

"I'll give you a million dollars."

She held her breath and waited.

He was silent.

Oh no. Had she gone too high too fast? Or would he get angry knowing she'd low-balled him? She was, he had to know since she was his mark, seriously loaded.

While these thoughts flitted through her brain she felt his body shaking under hers.

She lifted her head and saw he was smiling. The shaking of the body was him silently laughing.

"I wasn't being funny," she told him, losing patience.

"You think I've kidnapped you," he told her.

Her mouth dropped open (again).

"Sorry?" she asked after she'd closed it.

His head tipped down and he nuzzled his temple against hers in that tender way she told herself she hated (when she absolutely didn't) before saying, "Baby doll, I haven't kidnapped you."

All of a sudden she was angry because he called her "baby doll" and the fact that this man, in real life, did that was the worst cosmic joke of all.

Maybe this made her stupid, but she didn't care.

She yanked her head back.

"Okay, Callum, this is what I know," she stated. "Two guys break into my house, they grab me, discuss raping me, and suddenly, even though it's the middle of the night and I haven't made a noise, you're there to save the day. Instead of calling the police or an ambulance as I'd lost consciousness, you take me out of the city to a remote cabin in the woods. A cabin which conveniently has brand-new clothes and toiletries, all that perfectly suit me. You're all sweet, but bossy at the same time, and I know your game. You're not my rescuer. You know I'm wealthy. Name your price, give me your phone, I'll arrange the money for you, no problem. Then you take me home so I can get on with Christmas and you can go to the beach or find someone else to con."

He studied her a moment seemingly unperturbed by her understanding of the situation and the blunt way with which she informed him of that fact and replied, "All right, Sonia, now you'll listen to what's *actually* going on."

"This should be good," Sonia muttered sarcastically.

"No, it won't be good," he returned severely. "It'll probably freak you out, it's likely you won't believe a word I say, but it's also the truth."

She glared at him.

He sighed.

Then he spoke and committed sin number three.

Furthermore, he was right. What he said freaked her out. But the way he said it made her know he believed it, which made it all the worse.

"Last night, two men broke into your house. I knew they were going to do it because I had intelligence delivered to me eleven hours earlier informing me of the plot. I am, for the sake of you understanding this, the leader of a gang that has hundreds of thousands of members across the world. The men who broke into your house were soldiers from another, rival gang. *You*, little one, are important to me. *They* know this and wanted to take you from me. What they did broke a treaty that was fragile at best. Now we're at war."

Sonia was no longer glaring at him.

She was gawking.

She wanted to stop the questions from coming. She just couldn't.

"You're the leader of a gang?" she asked.

"Yes," he answered.

"That has hundreds of thousands of members?"

"Yes."

She stared at his handsome face.

He was good-looking, no doubt about it.

But he was crazy as a loon.

For some reason, she carried on.

"I'm important to you?"

"Very."

"Why?" Her voice was getting shrill. "You barely know me."

"We'll get to that later."

She blinked, shocked out of her skull then idiotically continued, "What do you mean they 'were' soldiers? What happened to them?"

"Last night, I executed them."

Sonia gasped at this news and then tensed, ready to flee.

His arms closed tight around her, negating any attempt to flee.

He was too strong, she knew it and in an instinctive effort at self-preservation, she gave up.

"You killed them," she whispered, horrified that he'd do such a thing and equally horrified that he'd tell her he did it so...very...*calmly*.

They were not good men. They were menaces. Not menaces in a getting drunk and getting in fights, being too loud at baseball games, catcalling and doing kissy faces at women when they walked by kind of way. No, they were a much, *much* worse kind. She knew this. She'd sensed it about them more than once. And they were new, the menacing presence had only been around for a short while, but she knew they'd been tracking her for weeks. And they'd invaded her home and discussed raping her.

But *executing* them?

"They touched you," Callum replied.

"I know."

"They intended to violate you."

"I know!" she shouted, and regardless of his strength, the fact that he could subdue her easily and even harm her, she started to struggle in his arms.

His hand slid into her hair and twisted.

She stilled at the onset of pain which was gentle, but if she moved, it would get worse.

His eyes were still tawny when he brought her face to his.

And his expression was fierce and ominous and very, very frightening.

"You're my mate, Sonia, my *queen*," he announced, his voice the exact same as his face, his words, quite simply, were mad. "You were destined for me before you were even conceived. I've been waiting for you for longer than you can imagine. And they touched you *before* I touched you. They committed high treason and for that alone their execution was just. But they *fucking touched you before I touched you* and for that their deaths were *not* quick."

Sonia found she was holding her breath.

Callum didn't seem to notice.

"I'll explain more as the days pass but this you know now. You're mine, Sonia Arlington. You've been mine for centuries. You have a week...one week...to get to know me and understand the ways of my culture. I wish it could be longer but because of what happened last night, my people are at war. I'm their king, they need me. I have no time to give, but regardless of that fact, I'm giving you one week. I'll use it wisely and I suggest, strongly, little one, that you do as well. This will go much better for you if you do."

"What?" she breathed in spite of herself, not understanding even *half* of what he said and not knowing which part of "what" she was asking because there was so damned much!

"What?" he repeated.

Her mind focused on one point in many. "What will go much better?"

He brought her face closer. "At the end of this week, baby doll, we're flying to Scotland. We're having the Mating Ceremony, and from that point on, you're bound to me in the eyes of my people's laws as well as yours until you die."

She'd obviously asked the wrong question.

"You're...*what?*" she shrieked. Yes, right in his face.

"I'm binding you to me."

"You're...*binding*...me...to...you," she repeated, enunciating each word with clear, open, horror.

He ignored her horror.

"Until you die."

She tried to rear back.

His hand in her hair, his arm around her body, and his strength that would make Hercules jealous made this effort moot.

So instead she whispered, "Oh my God."

He ignored that too and stated, "You may have noticed you have no shoes."

Sonia blinked yet again.

Then she nodded.

Callum continued immediately but on a different subject, "I'm going to finish outside, the storm is already here. They're forecasting snow, maybe several feet. The electricity can go out here easily and the insulation isn't the best. We need the fires. We could be snowed in by nightfall. I need to get us sorted."

With that announcement, he stood, picking her up with him. Somewhere in her fogged, distracted, ravaged, oh-my-god-what's-happening-to-me mind, she noted that no man had ever picked her up easily like that (or, at all) and held her to his chest like she weighed no more than a sack of feathers.

He turned and tucked her sideways back in the chair, her knees to her chest, the soles of her feet in the seat.

He leaned in and put a hand on either arm of the chair.

"You take some time, come to terms with what I've just said. If you have questions, we'll talk more after lunch."

She stared at his back as he walked through the cabin and out the back door.

Then she twisted her head to look out the front windows and saw that snow had started to fall.

Heavily.

She realized she'd not make it very far in a snowstorm without shoes even if she managed to escape.

And she *had* to escape.

Because she was stuck in a cabin with a murdering madman who thought she was his queen and intended to bind her to him until she died.

On this thought, to her shame, Sonia felt a single tear drop from her eye and trail down her cheek as her extreme fear overcame any courage she might have been able to muster.

That tear was joined by another.

Then another.

And then more.

CHAPTER FIVE
MISMATCH

CALLUM FINISHED SPLITTING the logs and stacking them on the back porch in which he'd fitted the storm windows that morning while Sonia slept.

He was concerned about the storm. The snowfall was forecast as heavy and this could knock out the broadband and interfere with his cellular reception. Further, if anything should happen and he was needed, he didn't want to be snowed into the cabin. He could transform and get out, but Sonia couldn't.

At any other time, he'd be thrilled to be snowed in at their cabin. Since buying it decades ago, he'd spent a goodly amount of time there. Regardless of the fact that his title came with castles in Scotland, England, and France, a mansion on the east coast of the US and his entitlement to take over any Territorial Mansion while traveling, he'd toyed with the idea of talking Sonia into settling in their cabin for a long spell after he'd won the war. At least until they started having pups. It reminded him of the years he spent in the Canadian Rockies and he liked its intimacy, the dense forest that surrounded it, sensing and smelling the plethora of wildlife all around.

She'd once told him she loved it there, which was one of the reasons why he'd bought it. The other being that *he* loved it there and it was the only place that was *theirs*, not to mention she thought she was in a dream when she was back.

He figured she wouldn't be hard to sway to his way of thinking.

This was the only thing that brightened Callum's morning.

On that thought, he walked into the house, removing his gloves and tossing them on the counter in the kitchen.

However, upon entry, his eyes went directly to Sonia.

She didn't look to him. In fact, she didn't move.

She was seated where he left her, curled up, her neck twisted to look over the back of the chair and out the window at the falling snow.

He had, for one shining moment that morning, thought she'd also felt their connection, just as all wolves do instantly, and he could gratefully dispense of this charade of courtship, claim her, mate with her, and install her at his side.

He also had, for one shining moment that morning, gloried in the fact that she was not what he'd feared when he'd read the varied reports that had been unlocked to him after his father's death, or when he'd watched her walk home last night. It was the first time he'd laid eyes on her in person since he met her that Christmas Eve years ago.

For one shining moment that morning, he'd gloried that she was instead like a wolf, lusty for life and all that it offered.

Her sultry, teasing, inviting demeanor this morning, her unbridled response to his kiss, his thigh, his touch, he thought proved that.

Her hideously healthy, unappealing breakfast and subsequent behavior had, however, eradicated it.

Callum couldn't imagine why fate had linked her to him.

She was beautiful, there was no doubting that. As he read her reports and saw the pictures of her, they stirred him. He was a man but he was especially a wolf. He'd have to be dead for her pictures not to affect him.

It was vaguely alarming, however, the colorless life she led. Hell, even her house was painted light gray. But when his brethren welcomed her with open arms, Callum hoped she'd blossom under their adulation.

Even so, he had to admit under normal circumstances, outside of noting her beauty, she'd not tempt him, and when wolves met their mates, this was not only unusual, it was unprecedented.

He'd taken more than his fair share of humans, it wasn't that.

It was that he didn't fancy blondes.

He also didn't fancy skinny women.

She was not as thin as some humans starved and exercised themselves to be, this was true, but she was definitely not as curvy as a she-wolf or the humans he'd chosen.

And he detested talk of healthy food, fat, cholesterol, and anything of the like. He wasn't attracted to women who counted every calorie, sauntered around on high heels, and wore expensive designer gear.

He also wasn't attracted to women who over-groomed, making it their ridiculous mission to have perfect hair, makeup, and nails. This did nothing for him.

Callum held in contempt the very idea of wasting precious life engaged in dieting and primping. He held even more contempt for the women who engaged in these pursuits as Sonia, he knew from the reports, not to mention her perfect nails, hair, and skin, did.

In the rare times he was not performing his duties or engaged in war, he preferred to be transformed to wolf, running outdoors. Or doing anything outdoors for that matter, preferably in a wood. Or getting drunk on real ale or whisky with his brethren. Or eating enormous home-cooked meals. Or bedding a female human or wolf, who not only knew how to play, but fucking well enjoyed it and was willing to give herself over to him so he could meet her needs, but also so he could assuage the hungry force of his own.

Not drinking martinis at elegant gathering places, shopping, or partaking of miniscule servings of haute cuisine.

And Sonia Arlington looked, acted, and it was reported that she was a woman who preferred to engage in the latter.

Nevertheless, they were connected. Even as he wondered at it, he felt it stir in his blood, in his gut, and, this morning, she'd given him a very slim hope that perhaps there was something more to Sonia Arlington.

He approached her chair and crouched by the side.

She didn't move from her contemplation of the snowfall.

"Sonia," he called softly and her head turned.

She was no longer crying but he saw the tracks the tears left through her makeup. She hadn't even wiped them away.

He felt a strange clutch in his chest at the sight. He ignored this and straightened, took her hand, and pulled her out of the chair. Holding her hand, he led her unresisting body across the room and turned her to face him.

He had little time to get her accustomed to him and teach her the ways of her new life but he knew in this moment she could use some space.

However, no one should be idle. She needed something to do.

He cocked his head to the shopping bags and his leather case.

He squeezed her hand before ordering quietly, "Unpack your things and mine. Tidy the kitchen. I'm going to take a shower."

He saw her eyes flash at his order but, accustomed to people following his commands without question, he thought nothing of it, dropped her hand, and went to his bag. Grabbing clean clothes, he strode to the bathroom.

While he was in the shower, he heard her moving around, putting away their clothes, tidying the bags, cleaning the kitchen.

Something about this annoyed him.

It was irrational but he'd prefer she was rebellious. At least that would be interesting.

In their short time together, she had displayed mild bouts of courage and fire, but she always gave in.

Too quickly.

He wiped down the mirror and stared at himself, deciding not to bother with a shave and also thinking that the week, and indeed his life with the health-conscious, pampered, obedient Sonia yawned before him.

His father had been a patient, accepting man who taught his son many lessons and tested his son many a time.

Mac had not managed, however, to teach him patience or acceptance.

Callum dumped his clothes in the laundry hamper and walked from the bathroom.

The kitchen was clean and Sonia was tucked back in her chair, a mug wrapped in her fingers held up close to her face. Her eyes were on the fire.

A she-wolf could never be still like that.

If he was here with one of his own, she'd pounce on him the minute he exited the bathroom.

Fuck, she'd be put out that he wanted to shower alone.

If not, she'd be doing something. Baking, organizing the kitchen, finding some kind of busy work, no matter what it was. Hell, even reading, or, in these circumstances, plotting.

Not staring vacantly into a fire.

His cell rang in his back pocket, and as he reached for it, he watched her turn her pretty head slowly to face him.

And, he had to admit when her green eyes hit him, she was pretty.

Very pretty.

Stunning.

He'd never tire of looking at her.

At least he had that.

He took the call and put the phone to his ear as her gaze moved back to the fire.

"Callum," he answered and walked to stand at the back of the couch in order to study her blank but elegant profile.

"Cal," Ryon said in his ear. "Thought you'd want to know, Mona had nothing to do with it."

This wasn't surprising. His ex-lover wasn't smart enough to plot against a kingdom. He'd never understand why he'd got involved with that she-wolf. She was unbelievable in bed but she was also a fucking nut.

"Two of the mansion's detail were involved. They're under guard and on their way to Scotland for trial," Ryon went on.

"Excellent," Callum muttered.

"We're still interrogating others," Ryon continued. "The two we broke swear they're working alone and didn't give us dick about how they found out about Sonia. We'll keep working them, but my gut says this isn't a clean sweep and catching those two won't nip it in the bud. It's bigger."

Callum's gut was saying that too and he hoped it was true. The rebellion had brought down his father and, years ago, his youngest brother. The treaty was too easy for them.

He wanted their blood then he wanted their capitulation.

"Keep at it," Callum ordered.

There was silence then, "How's Sonia?"

Ryon, on the other hand, made it very clear Callum's queen did not bore him.

Ryon had a great deal more patience and acceptance than Callum had. He *enjoyed* the pursuit of coy female humans. He *liked* dating, another thing Callum detested.

Callum preferred seizing. Dating, which he rarely engaged in, left him cold. Ryon took great pleasure in wearing them down, teasing and enticing them, even tormenting them before he went in for the kill.

Callum never understood it.

"She's—" Callum started but stopped speaking when he saw Sonia's entire body jerk.

Then her head twisted around to look toward the bathroom, and without delay she sprang from the chair, crashed her mug down on the coffee table, and ran to the bathroom.

"She's what?" Ryon asked in his ear but Callum was listening to Sonia's panicked, even frenzied search of the bathroom. "Cal?" Ryon called.

Callum didn't answer for Sonia ran out of the bathroom, stopped herself on a one-footed skid, and stared at him.

"My injection," she whispered.

"What?" Callum asked, staring at her pale stricken face.

She strode forward purposefully and stopped in front of him.

"You didn't bring my injection," she said.

"Cal, what's going on?" Ryon asked in his ear.

"A minute," Callum replied, took the phone from his ear and asked Sonia, "What injection?"

"My injection," she repeated. "My medication. I need it, every night." Her strange calm started evaporating and her voice rose when she demanded, "We have to go back to the city right now!"

All right, maybe she *was* staring into the fire plotting.

"We aren't going back to the city," he told her firmly.

She took the last step that separated them and grabbed his wrist, shaking it.

"You don't understand. I need it."

Callum studied her then put the phone to his ear, which was, incidentally, in the hand which was attached to the wrist she'd latched on to and she didn't let go.

"Did you hear that?" he asked Ryon.

"What's she on about?" Ryon asked back, clearly having heard it.

"You know nothing of an injection?" Callum inquired.

"Nothing," Ryon replied.

Ryon knew everything about Sonia Arlington. He'd been ordered to know and Ryon was an excellent soldier.

The best.

Callum took the phone from his ear and warned, "Sonia, it's not a good idea to play this game."

Her eyes grew wide and she shook his wrist.

"I'm not playing a game!" she shouted, her voice trembling with fear.

When Callum didn't respond, her faced blanched further. She threw his wrist from her and took a step back, digging her nails into her hair at her temples, pulling its heavy weight back, and holding it at the crown of her head.

She took a deep breath, dropped her hands, tipped her head back, and stated in a strong voice, "Callum, I'm being very serious. I've got a rare inherited blood disorder. If I don't have that injection every night, I'll get very ill. If I get very ill and die, you'll never get your kidnapping money."

Callum continued to study her without saying a word.

She was, he remembered from their brief meeting thirty-one years ago, very cunning.

She was, he knew now, no less cunning.

She took the step in his direction that she'd moved away and tipped her head back further. "If I don't get that injection, my blood will overheat. I'm not joking. It'll heat and heat and heat until it boils my organs *inside my body.*" Her hands came up to grab his biceps. "They'll fail, I'll die, but before that, I'll be in agony." Her fingers tightened on his arms.

"Callum, this is not a game. Take me home, you'll see when you *take me home!*"

God, she was good.

"We're not leaving this cabin," he decreed and she instantly made a noise of frustration mingled with fear in the back of her throat.

She stepped away again and threw her arm out to indicate the windows.

"Look at it out there!" she yelled. "We'll be snowed in within hours. We'll never get out of here. That medication isn't carried in pharmacies!"

How convenient, Callum thought.

"Of course it's not," Callum muttered.

She stepped forward and her eyes flashed before they narrowed. "It's not carried in pharmacies, Callum, because my condition is so rare, they don't have a demand for it. I get it directly from my personal physician where Gregor got it before me and my father got it before him. I need my supply from home. We can't nip out to the local drugstore and ask for a prescription to be filled!"

Callum heard Ryon calling his name from the phone still in his hand and he put it to his ear.

"Ry," he said.

"She thinks you kidnapped her?" Ryon's voice was filled with humor.

"Evidently," Callum replied with forced patience.

"That's hilarious," Ryon commented, sounding like he thought it was hilarious because he was laughing through his words.

"Ryon," Callum's single word showed his patience was waning quickly.

"Let me check it out," Ryon replied.

"She's bluffing," Callum returned.

"No harm in letting me check. If it's nothing, I'll phone you. If she's telling the truth, I'll send someone up the mountain," Ryon offered.

"Do it," Callum ordered.

"On it," Ryon answered and Callum heard the disconnect.

"I've a man checking," Callum told Sonia and he watched her eyebrows rise before she visibly relaxed.

"Thank you," she whispered with great feeling.

She was taking this too far.

"Sonia," he called, regaining her attention, which had unfocused from him in her apparent extreme relief. "I'm telling you right now, this turns out to be a game, I won't like it."

Her jaw tensed and she jerked her head so her hair shook about her shoulders.

"Call your man back," she demanded. "Tell him it's in the green box in the medicine cabinet in my bathroom. The needles in the blue box beside it. If we have to be here a week, I'll need it all." She started to turn but jerked back and raised her angry gaze to his. "*And* the sharps container."

Then she stomped, yes, *stomped* to the bathroom and slammed the door.

Callum stared at the door and instead of feeling angry at her game, he felt aroused by her spirit.

"That's more like it," he muttered then turned to add a log to the fire.

Half an hour later, after Sonia had spent some time in the bathroom arranging her toiletries, his toiletries, rearranging the towels, maniacally cleaning the mirror and basin, if his hearing was correct (and it always was), she left the bathroom.

Then she paced.

Callum, at his laptop at the kitchen bar, ignored her.

His phone rang.

She stopped pacing, whirled, and glared at him.

Callum studied her.

She looked glorious in her anger.

Yes, he liked this Sonia much better.

Not taking his eyes from her, he yanked the phone out of his pocket and put it to his ear.

"Callum."

"She's not lying," Ryon told him and Callum didn't know what to do with that information. It proved she wasn't playing a game and further provided unwelcome information that his mate had a rare blood disorder that, if untreated, could lead to an agonizing death.

Something about this rattled him in a way he never felt before in his entire life.

"Have a man bring it to the cabin," Callum ordered and he watched Sonia's shoulders fall as her head tipped back and she looked at the ceiling with closed eyes and acute relief washing over her face.

Fucking hell, if he'd called her bluff, he'd have killed her.

That rattled him further.

"I even talked to her doctor," Ryon, always thorough, said in his ear as Sonia tramped to the kitchen and started to yank things from the fridge and cupboards. "She's got a rare blood disorder. Never heard of it, it's about seventeen syllables long. Inherited it from her father." Ryon's voice lowered. "It's nasty, Cal. She could die from it."

"How did you miss this?" Callum clipped.

Ryon chuckled and Callum's hackles rose. "Mac, *and* you, I'll remind you, forbid any of the brothers spying on her when she was inside her house. Follow her to stores. Monitor her purchases and expenses. Go through her trash. But you never let us go through her house or watch her in it. She visited the doctor regularly but medical records are confidential, which, by the way, meant I had to talk fast to get the doctor to tell me anything. She has a prescription for birth control, which we knew about from a light hack into her records some time ago. She picked those up monthly from her doc along with the injections we *didn't* know about. But this disease she's had since birth. The hack Caleb just did uncovered it but we had to go back years, and even so, it was buried, almost like it was hidden. The information about her condition and the prescription for the injections was protected behind so many passwords even Caleb had trouble unlocking it."

Even though this made sense, Callum didn't like it.

Not only that they missed it, and in missing it could have killed her, but also the fact that it made him feel a strange sense of unease that the information was hidden, protected, secret. Medical records were confidential but why would this life-threatening condition be guarded so thoroughly? In case of an emergency, wouldn't that information need to be readily available?

His attention moved to Sonia, and at what he saw, he let go of the disquiet he felt. Right then, he had more important things to deal with.

"Is it snowing down there?" Callum asked.

"Flurries," Ryon answered.

"It's not flurries up here. The man you sent may need a snow mobile or an ATV, but whatever it takes, he gets that medication here by tonight. Is that understood?"

"*I* talked to the doctor, Cal. I know how important this is," Ryon returned calmly. "I sent Waring. He knows this is priority and it's for the queen. He's a good man. He'll be there with the meds."

Callum felt his body go stiff. "Does he know—?"

"Cal, don't ask that question," Ryon broke in softly. "He doesn't know what's in the parcel, just that the queen requested it."

Ryon, Callum knew, would never expose Sonia's weakness. Only the inner circle (that would be Callum, Ryon, and Callum's blood brothers, Caleb and Calder) would know of this latest development.

Callum changed the subject. "Any more on the plot?"

"We're widening the net."

"I want regular reports."

"You'll get them."

"Later," Callum muttered.

"Good luck," Ryon replied, his voice filled with humor, his overhearing the conversation between Callum and Sonia telling the tale.

Callum didn't reply. He disconnected.

Sonia was preparing lunch, which looked as if it consisted of an enormous salad and nothing else.

No, actually, Sonia looked like she was punishing the vegetables that would soon be their lunch if her frenzied use of the knife was anything to go by.

Callum shoved the phone in his back pocket, slid off the stool, and rounded the counter making his way toward her.

He got within feet when she whirled and lifted the knife, not to brandish it at him, to point it at him.

"Don't you get near me," she snapped, jerking the knife at him on the word "you." Then she turned back to the carrot she was annihilating and kept chopping. "You could have killed me."

"I'm aware of that, little one," he replied, forcing his voice to be soft.

Her shoulders tensed but she kept chopping. "I pray to *God* whoever has my meds gets here in time."

"They'll get here," he said firmly.

"I would say I'd never forgive you for this, but if this hadn't ended the way I *hope*," she whirled on the word "hope" and narrowed her gaze at him, "it will, I wouldn't be around long enough *to* forgive."

Her declaration rattled him even further but he didn't let it show.

"Stop chopping and put down the knife," Callum ordered gently and she instantly adhered to his command. Slamming the knife down on the counter and picking up the cutting board, she dumped the carrot on top of the salad leaves already in a bowl.

She did this clumsy in her anger and carrots went everywhere.

She ignored the raining carrots, slammed the cutting board back down, and reached for a cucumber.

He advanced, positioning himself behind her and caught her wrists, both of them, and wrapped her arms around her belly along with his own as he leaned down so his mouth was at her ear.

Her entire frame, from head to toe, tensed at his touch.

He ignored it and murmured, "I'm sorry I worried you, baby doll."

As a child she was, in his sharp recollection, a living doll. He'd never forgotten her, not a single feature, not a moment.

He had been pleased that morning to hear she hadn't forgotten him either and more pleased that their meeting had clearly had as profound an effect on her as it had on him. It gave him another sliver of hope that she understood their connection on some level and she might, soon, embrace it (heartily).

On that thought, he pulled her deeper into his body.

She was silent through this.

"Sonia," he called.

"I'll accept your apology the minute your *man* walks through that door."

"Fair enough," he agreed.

"Now, take your hands off me," she demanded.

"No," he replied.

She went even stiffer.

Callum ignored it again.

"My people are affectionate, Sonia. We touch. We hug. We cuddle." Amongst other, more pleasurable things he decided it sensible not to share at that moment. "You're going to need to get used to this."

"Well, I don't *have* any people therefore I'm not *used* to cuddling, touching, and hugging. *Especially* guys I've known for a few *hours*. Now, take your hands off me!" she snapped.

His response was to pull her closer.

Her response was to go even stiffer.

He decided to change the subject and said, "If you think I'm eating salad for lunch—"

"*I'm* making *you* grilled cheese sandwiches. *You* can have cheese for every meal for all I care. *I'm* having salad..." His arms got tight at this defiance but she talked right through it. "I had food enough for two meals at breakfast but I'll need something light before dinner and *you* are just going to have to force feed me if you want it any different."

Callum grinned into her hair.

Finally, he was beginning to enjoy this.

Therefore, he agreed, "All right, Sonia."

"Now, please, would you take your hands off me?"

He rubbed his temple against her hair then slid his lips around the curve of her ear.

He liked her smell. It was human but it was far from unpleasant.

As his lips rounded the curve of her ear, he felt a short tremor shudder through her rigid body before she jerked solid.

Yes, definitely beginning to enjoy this.

He moved his lips to the skin behind her ear and repeated, "All right, Sonia."

Then he let her go and watched her start to decimate the cucumber while he walked back to his laptop.

He found, twenty minutes later, she made excellent grilled cheese sandwiches.

And, he had to admit, the salad wasn't bad either.

CHAPTER SIX

KING

Sonia was standing in the kitchen boiling the kettle for a cup of her favorite herbal tea, telling herself she wasn't grateful to Callum for making certain it was stocked. But she *was* grateful. She drank that tea all the time. She didn't know what she'd do without it.

This was after an afternoon spent gazing in the fire and plotting her escape.

She did this while listening to him talk on the phone seventeen times. She'd counted. There was nothing better to do, except plot her escape, of course.

Either he was a really good actor, this was a more elaborate pretense than she imagined, or he did, indeed, have "men." At least three of them that she could count. One named Ryon, one named Caleb, and one named Calder, and all of them reported in frequently on a variety of what sounded like war-like subjects that included Callum giving a variety of leader-of-the-gang-like orders.

He also spent a good deal of time on his computer.

Luckily, the rest of the time he left her alone so she could plot her escape.

And plot she did.

She didn't have any shoes but she *did* have a bunch of socks and *he* had several pairs of boots.

Okay, so his feet were large like his hands.

But if she put enough socks on, maybe she could keep his boots on her feet long enough for her to get away.

And get away she was going to do. It had been thirty-one years since she wandered this forest with her father, but when she was a kid she wandered with him all the time and she had a good memory. Her father loved being out of doors, especially at night, and he took Sonia with him.

The animals weren't only unafraid of her, her father, too, had that particular gift. They saw wildlife in the moonlight with their night vision (her father had that too) and she remembered quite keenly that those times were magical.

She also remembered a cave not too far away that her father had shown her.

Not only shelter but she would imagine that Callum would guess she'd seek assistance, not shelter herself in a cave until the coast was clear.

She could take a blanket, wrap up some food, and she would go, hang out there until the weather cleared and then move out, find someone and report her kidnapping.

If it kept snowing, her footprints would be covered in minutes.

Further, she had better hearing, eyesight, and smell than Callum. She'd be able to sense him if he came after her.

He was, it came to her too late after all that had happened that morning, that presence she'd sensed last night, the alluring one as, obviously, the cosmos could play a pretty mean joke. She'd noticed it (and it broke her heart) the instant he walked in from finishing with the logs and it had invaded the house when she opened his bag and put away his clothes.

If he came after her, got anywhere near her, she'd know it.

Once she got her medication, she hoped it didn't quit snowing. Then she could get away from that scary, bossy (but handsome) *jerk.*

They'd had dinner and she'd made a big one. Steak, baked potatoes (with butter *and* sour cream, her hips were never going to forgive her), veggies, and rolls. She didn't want to give him reason to pin her against the counter or do anything else that set her teeth on edge and made her want to scratch his eyes out. And she told herself the meal wasn't absolutely delicious (when it was).

Now she was going to have tea, examine the cupboards to plan what to take with her, pray that his "man" could get through the thick blanket of snow that was *still* falling, and then she was going to call it a night.

Through the whistle of the kettle, she sensed it.

Someone was coming.

She didn't make a move or give any indication that she felt anything.

But she knew they were coming.

Oh my God! I hope it's park rangers, she thought.

"Wait here," Callum ordered and her head snapped up.

He slid off the stool and went swiftly to the walk-in closet. He exited carrying some of his clothes and a pair of his boots.

He walked directly to the door, turned to her, and stated, "I'll be back in five minutes. Make coffee."

Then he was gone.

She stared at the door.

What was he doing now?

Then she thought, *Five minutes.*

Did she have enough time to gather what she needed, bulk up on clothes, and get out of there? Maybe even waylay who was out there and ask for their assistance?

No.

It was too much of a risk.

She'd have to do it when he was sleeping. Five minutes wouldn't give her a good enough head start and if she didn't manage to find whoever was out there, even with her keen senses in this storm she might get lost.

She didn't need to go from the frying pan (kidnapped by a madman) to the fire (lost in a snowstorm).

She needed to stick to her plan.

She moved to the coffeepot and it was dripping away when the door opened.

Sonia turned to the door and stared.

Through its frame came Callum followed by another man, dark-haired too, also tall (not as tall as Callum, two, three inches shorter), muscular but without the same bulk. He looked younger as well.

But she stared because he was wearing Callum's clothes.

What on earth?

They entered, Callum closed the door, the man's eyes came to her face, and then he dropped immediately to a knee.

Sonia braced for action (though she had no idea what she would do) as she thought for a second he might be overcome by hypothermia or something. But she watched as his hand came out to the floor beside his knee and his head dropped down.

Then, in a strong deep voice that carried across the room, but no matter, she'd have heard it if he said it one hundred feet away and outside in this raging blizzard, he muttered reverentially, "My queen."

Sonia gawped.

He stayed bowed with head low.

"Rise," Callum murmured quietly but unmistakably regally.

What on *earth?*

The man stood and grinned at her before he turned to Callum and remarked, "She's pretty."

Sonia's startled eyes went from the man to Callum who was watching her.

"That she is," he mumbled and lifted his chin to Sonia. "Waring needs a cup of coffee, little one, something to eat. See to it."

Sonia blinked as Callum slapped the man on the back and escorted him into the room.

What was going on?

She hadn't heard a vehicle. She'd heard and smelled a person approaching the cabin.

Apparently, Callum had sensed him too!

And why was he in Callum's clothes? How did he get there on foot through a blowing blizzard *in no clothes?* And what did he mean, *"My queen?"* And what did *Callum* mean, "See to it?"

And, *what,* she felt it pertinent to repeat, *was going on?*

"Sonia." Callum's firm voice came at her and her body jolted her out of her reverie. "Coffee. Waring's been running the last ten miles."

Running?

"Yes, of course," she murmured, attempting to mask her alarm, and she had to admit, curiosity, and called to the other man, "How do you take it?"

"With two fingers of whisky," he replied, still grinning at her. He waited for Callum to set down a small satchel on the coffee table and sit before he took his seat, looked at Callum, and repeated, "Really, your grace, she's seriously pretty."

Your grace?

"I've noticed," Callum replied, humor in his tone.

In spite of herself, hearing Callum agree she was "seriously pretty" with that warm humor in his voice made a shiver dance across Sonia's skin.

She pretended that didn't happen, found the whisky, poured in two fingers, added the coffee, took it to the living room, and handed it to the man.

"Thank you for bringing my—" she started, but before she could finish Callum's hands shot out, curved around her hips, and she was flying through thin air for a moment before she landed in his lap.

This made Waring grin again.

It made Sonia twist around and glare before snapping, "Callum!"

Callum completely ignored her, his arms closing tight as he asked Waring, "You want a sandwich or do you want Sonia to grill you a steak?"

Waring patted his flat belly and said, "Had some fast food before I transformed. I'm good. The coffee and whisky will set me up. The weather's not half bad a bit down the mountain. It's just up here you're really getting it." His grin widened and he said, "And it's all downhill on the way back."

Both Callum and Waring laughed at this like it was the height of hilarity.

Sonia didn't get it.

Then again, Sonia wasn't getting *anything*. Except the fact that Callum, Sonia noted with extreme annoyance, had a great laugh.

Which was also part of the cosmos's joke, no doubt.

"So, we go on campaign, is Queen Sonia coming with us?" Waring asked, grinning at her again. "She'd be useful. Makes good coffee," he finished before he took another sip.

Queen Sonia?

Campaign?

"Likely not," Callum answered. "She's human. Only way to assure her safety."

Human?

Safety?

"Figured," Waring muttered.

Slowly, Sonia turned her head to look at Callum.

When her eyes met his, he dipped his head, rubbed his temple against hers, her body went rock solid, and he whispered in her ear, "I'll explain later."

He pulled his head back.

She glared at him and turned to Waring. "I don't think we'll be going on campaign since there are so many things Callum's going to be," she lifted her hands and made quotation marks, "explaining later that it might take until the new millennium for him to do it."

Both Callum and Waring laughed at that too.

Sonia decided not to inform them she wasn't being funny.

Then she decided, since this was way too weird for words, not to object that Callum seemed perfectly happy chatting away with Waring while she sat in his lap. Something which she was *not* perfectly happy about.

When Waring finished his coffee, Callum stood, taking Sonia with him and placing her on her feet. Waring stood after him and Callum left them to go to the laptop.

"Take this data stick to Caleb, will you?" he asked, handing the stick to Waring who took it.

"You got a backup?" he inquired and then looked at Sonia and said preposterously, "Saliva. Probably not good for data sticks."

"What?" Sonia breathed but Callum was pulling her medication from the satchel and she saw it was wrapped in brown paper and taped to oblivion.

When the satchel was empty, he tossed it to Waring.

"Good thinking," Waring said to Callum and again turned to Sonia. "That's why he's king."

"King?" Sonia whispered but Callum was beside her. His hand sliding along her shoulders, he tugged her against his side and together they walked Waring to the door just like they were an old married couple moving to wave away a party guest.

At the door, Waring turned and bowed his head to Sonia. "It was an honor to meet you, your grace." Then he lifted his head and grinned yet again.

Before Sonia could say a word, Callum squeezed her shoulder. "I'll be back in five minutes."

He and Waring walked out the door.

Sonia stared at the door and she did this for a while before she asked it, "What just happened?"

The door didn't feel like sharing its secrets.

She and a sharp knife were in the kitchen wrestling with the tape on her medication when Callum came back, again carrying the clothes.

Sonia stopped dead, package in hand, knife point inserted in a miniscule area not taped where she hoped it might find purchase, and watched as Callum walked to the closet, threw in the boots, then walked to the bathroom and came out without the clothes.

He moved into the kitchen, stopped close to her, leaned a hip against the counter, reached out, and pulled the knife from her frozen hand and set it aside. Then he took the package out of her hands.

Coming out of her stupor, Sonia asked, "Is it later?"

His eyes never leaving her, he brought the package up to his mouth, and with his even white teeth, he tore open a section of the tape. He ripped off the rest of the packaging, held both boxes in his hands, and gazed at them.

Finally, his head came up. "You need to take this now?"

"I asked if it's later," she repeated.

"And I asked if my mate needs the medication that will stop her from dying an agonizing death," Callum returned calmly. "As you can see, my question has priority."

It *was* time for her to take her medication, though she could wait. Any time in the late evening was okay.

She'd rather have a few answers.

She looked at him, saw the set of his face, and gave in.

"I could take it."

"Let's go," he said and started to the bathroom.

Did he say "let's go?"

Let's go?

Sonia stood stock still.

Callum turned back. "Sonia."

"Give me the meds. I'll—"

He cut her off by saying, "You're going to teach me how to give it to you."

She stayed stock still but her mouth dropped open.

Then she said, "No, I'm not."

To which he replied, "Yes, you are."

"No, I—"

"Sonia, come here."

"But, you—"

"Come here or I'll come get you."

Her voice grew shrill. "I can't believe you think—"

He started toward her. She started retreating.

In seconds, she was flung over his shoulder and in a few more seconds she was set on her feet in the bathroom.

She barely got her body under her control before his torso twisted and he closed and locked the door while she stared at him in irritated horror.

He twisted back and demanded, "Now, show me what to do."

She made a snatch for the boxes but he yanked them away and he was far taller and had the arm span of a giant, drat the man!

"I'm perfectly capable of doing it myself," she snapped.

"What if you're not?" he asked.

"What do you mean, what if I'm not? I've been doing it every day since I was eleven. I *am* capable of doing it," she retorted.

He bent at the waist to get closer and it took everything she had not to lean back.

"What if you're not?" he repeated. "What if there comes a time where you can't give it to yourself? You have flu and you're delirious. As your mate, I need to know how to take care of you."

Really?

Did he *seriously* think she was his mate?

She'd known him *a day*!

And it was the weirdest scariest day of *her life*!

He was...crazy...as a...*loon*!

"You aren't my mate," she snapped.

"Sonia, I am."

"You are *not*."

He straightened and looked to the ceiling before muttering, "Bloody hell."

"You can say that again," she huffed, crossing her arms on her chest.

He dipped his chin down to look at her. "Just show me how to give you the fucking injection."

"No!"

"*Show me!*" he barked right in her face.

This was one of those times that set her teeth on edge and made her want to scratch his eyes out.

Sonia did not do that.

Instead, she said, "Give me the boxes."

"Goddamn it, Sonia—" he started, but she interrupted him.

"You want me to show you? Then give me the boxes so I can gosh darn show you!" she snapped.

He scowled at her a moment before he handed her the boxes.

With *extreme* ill-grace, Sonia showed him how to load the needle and with even *more extreme* embarrassment, she turned, undid her belt and cords, and pulled her pants down to expose her upper right buttock.

"Just jab it in and press," she bit out angrily. "The faster the bet—"

She stopped talking when she felt the heat of his fingers grazing her bare skin. She jerked up and whirled.

"Callum, just jab—" she started but he set the injection aside, grasped her hips, and turned her. "Callum," she said, twisting her head to look at him then snapped, "Callum!" when his thumb hooked in her pants and pulled them a few inches farther down her hip while his other hand held her firm.

"Baby doll," he murmured as his thumb slid along her skin.

"What are you doing?" she tried to snap but it came out breathy.

His thumb stroked back, softly, even tenderly.

His eyes came to hers. "You look like a fucking pin cushion."

Her body grew tight and she looked away.

"That happens when you have to take an injection every night," she informed him. "Now if you'd just—"

His hands at her hips became arms around her belly and he pulled her into his big hard body.

"I don't like this," he said into the hair on top of her head.

He didn't like it? He should try being her.

"I don't like it either," she replied. "It's not fun. That's why it's better just to do it fast and get it over with."

For a moment, he was silent. Then he sighed.

Then, without letting her go, he reached out with one hand to nab the injection.

"Pull down your cords for me," he ordered gently.

She did as she was told, and without delay, she felt the jab.

And she felt the burn.

Her arm flew out and her fingers curled around the basin while she sucked in breath, closed her eyes, and fought the pain.

When it burned out, she found herself wrapped tight in his arms, tucked in his body with his face buried in her neck.

His warm embrace unsettled her.

Because it felt good.

She'd always battled the pain alone. It only lasted a minute or two, but it still hurt.

She'd never had anyone, not anyone, help her battle the pain. Not since her momma and papa, who held her close after giving her the injection. Gregor was not a holding close type of guy.

It also surprised her.

Callum was a pretty domineering man, though he'd also shown moments of tenderness.

But nothing like this.

Her fingers curled around his forearms, "Callum."

"It hurts." It was a statement.

"Yes."

"It looked bad."

"It's excruciating."

His arms tightened further.

"Callum, it's okay. I'm used to it."

"There's no other way?"

She shook her head.

His face shoved deeper into her neck before he whispered, "Baby doll."

Before she could say anything else, he'd done up her cords and belt then she was cradled in his arms and they were out of the bathroom, Callum striding to the living room.

He laid her on the couch and didn't hesitate in joining her, stretching out and pinning her between his big body and the back of the couch.

She looked at him and announced, "I'd like some tea."

"I'll get you some in a minute. Tell me about your thing."

"What thing?"

"Your blood thing."

She pulled in breath.

He was being way too nice. And way too concerned. And way too sweet.

And it was messing with her head.

But she thought it best to give him what he wanted. It'd be over sooner that way.

"I don't know much about it, no one does. It's that rare. I've lived with it my whole life. There's one treatment, the injection. I know that because I've talked to my doctor about alternatives, but there are none."

"Are they researching it?" Callum asked.

"No, like I said, it's rare. I'm lucky there's even a treatment."

His voice was soft when he said, "Honey, what I saw in there, that isn't luck."

There it was.

Too nice. Too concerned.

Way too sweet.

She tried to be nonchalant about it. "Trust me, Callum, if I don't take the treatment, it's that times about ten thousand," she informed him. "I tried it once, went off the meds for two days, I thought I was boiling alive."

"Jesus," he muttered on a wince.

She stared.

He was feeling this.

Deeply.

Which made Sonia feel something deeply too.

Something insane.

A strong pull toward him to soothe and comfort.

Before she could stop herself, she pressed closer and assured, "Callum, it's okay. I'm used to it." She gave him a teasing grin. "I think it was probably good I had my teenage rebellion against the injection. I learned quickly it's better than the alternative."

His eyes bored into hers and he replied, "I'm not finding this amusing."

Yes, he was feeling this.

And yes, it was deeply.

She didn't know what to do with that. It made her forget he was a madman and think he might be her dream man.

Her handsome wolf.

Which had to be why she couldn't fight that odd pull.

And this had to be why her grin faded, she pressed even closer, and her voice went soft when she said, "That's because it's not amusing. But it's two minutes of pain every day. At least there's something that helps, even if it's an awful something. It could be far worse."

His arms around her got tight and one hand drifted up her back into her hair to tuck her face in his neck.

Once he'd done this, he announced, "I'm giving you the injection every night."

Sonia's body jolted and her head jerked back. "What?"

He tipped his chin down to look at her. "You heard me."

"Okay then, why?"

"You shouldn't do that alone."

"I've been doing it alone for twenty-six years," she pointed out.

"Yes, and that stops now."

"Why?" she cried.

"You didn't see you."

"What does that mean?"

"That means you're not doing it alone," he stated implacably.

"This is ridiculous!" she snapped, trying to push away only for him to pull her back, this time even closer.

"You could barely stay standing," he told her, head still tipped down, but his eyes had gone tawny.

Well, she learned something. His eyes went gold for a lot of reasons, including anger.

Good to know.

In the face of his anger, she still retorted, "I'll repeat, I've been doing this for twenty-six years."

"And *I'll* repeat, you're not doing it alone any longer. I'm giving you the fucking injection."

Sonia glared.

Callum scowled.

His scowl, she reckoned, was a lot better than her glare.

She reckoned this because he didn't back down, she did.

"You know," she started tartly, "for a brief second there I thought you were nice, even sweet. You're not. You're a big bossy *jerk*."

His face began to soften and she saw the blue start to seep back into the gold of his irises before he started, "Sonia—"

She cut him off and shoved at his chest (to no avail) before demanding, "Can I have tea now?"

Callum sighed the sigh of a man beleaguered, which irritated her even more.

He hadn't been kidnapped. *He* hadn't been bossed around. *He* hadn't been forced to receive an injection from some woman *he* barely knew.

Why *he* sounded beleaguered *she'd* never know!

He cut into her thoughts. "I'll get you some tea then we're talking about what happened earlier when Waring was here."

She pushed up and managed to get on an elbow. "Don't do me any favors, *wolf*, I'll get my own tea, and I don't want to talk about—"

She stopped speaking because all of a sudden she wasn't on an elbow.

She was flat on her back and most of his weight was pinning her to the couch.

And, it should be noted, the tawny had beaten back the blue in his eyes and his face was so far away from soft it wasn't funny.

"Callum—"

"You call me 'wolf' when you want me near you, when you want me to hold you and when you want me to fuck you. You *don't* call me 'wolf' when you're pissed at me, is that understood?"

Sonia didn't know what came over her, she'd never felt anything like it before.

Further, it wasn't smart. It wasn't cautious. It wasn't treading carefully with a kidnapping madman.

But she also didn't care.

In the face of what appeared to be his rage, she didn't back down. No matter that he was way bigger and way, *way* stronger than she. No matter that he told her he'd executed two men last night because they'd touched her.

She was just that tired of this whole situation.

"Let me see if I've got this right," she snapped back. "You've told me what to eat. You've made me be somewhere I don't want to be. Now, you're telling me what *to say?*"

"You got it right," he ground out.

"Oh, you're right I got it right," she bit out then yelled. "You *are* a big bossy *jerk!*"

His eyes narrowed and he clipped, "I asked, is that understood?"

"I speak English, Callum, it's *understood,*" she retorted. "I also heard you say I could use that word when I wanted you near me, when I wanted you to hold me, and when I wanted you to fuck me, so don't hold your breath because you'll *never* hear me call you 'wolf' *again!*"

She was panting when she was finished, her chest rising and falling with her breaths.

His voice dipped lower just as his face dipped to hers when he warned, "I've a mind to test that threat."

Her breathing escalated, as did her pulse, but she still invited, "Have at it. Let's see if you can make today a grand slam in demonstrating *all* the ways to make your supposed mate *hate* you!"

He scowled at her.

She glared at him.

And she felt no triumph whatsoever when he broke the staring contest, did a push up, knifed away from her getting to his feet, but leaned low over her. "I'm getting you tea. You move from that couch, Sonia, this farce ends now."

Her breath stopped.

There it was.

"What farce?" she whispered.

He stayed leaned over her but threw out an arm and answered, "This one. Me giving you this ludicrous courtship. Waring called you queen and bowed to you out of deference to me and who you'll become. You defy me again, I'll take you to that bed and make you my queen right...fucking...*now*."

"Wh-what?" Sonia stammered in confusion (and a great deal of fear) as she lifted up on an elbow.

"My people don't need ceremonies and rituals, even though we have them. If I fuck you and claim you, the deed is done. You're bound to me. That's all there is for my culture that makes one bit of difference. I fuck you, you're officially my queen."

"You're...you're...*courting* me?" she whispered.

"Did you hear a word I said this morning?"

She *thought* she heard all of them.

With a swift movement, he straightened and tore his fingers through his hair, leaving his hand at his neck before looking up to the ceiling and asking, "Who would fucking believe I'd rather be on a battlefield?"

Sonia wouldn't believe it.

At that moment, Sonia didn't believe *anything*.

Except the heartbreaking fact that he was crazy as a loon.

His head tipped down and he scowled at her. "Now stay there, don't move, and I'll bring you your goddamned tea."

He stalked away and she did what she was told.

She had no earthly idea what was going on and she was getting more confused by the minute.

What she *did* know, considering the consequences, was that she wasn't going to move from the couch.

Also, she was *never* going to call him "wolf" *ever* again.

Lastly, because of that, she would always hate him, *always*.

And she would hate him because he forever took her beloved handsome wolf away.

Callum had fucked up.

He knew it and he could kick himself for it.

He'd lost his patience and his formidable temper, and further, and most regrettably, forgotten that Sonia had no idea what was going on.

He'd told her some of it but she couldn't possibly understand his mind was on a plot hatched to abduct her, debase her, and maybe even murder her. A plot which meant his people were at war, people he was responsible for and a war he *had* to win.

He'd had her a day.

Only a day.

For well over three hundred years, he knew he'd find his mate and be bound to her. He'd always hoped she wouldn't be his queen, which would mean his father's death, but, like every wolf, he anticipated with great relish finding his mate.

Now he had her not even twenty-four hours and he'd fucked it up with her.

Ryon had warned him, even so far as pleaded with him, that he needed to be gentle and tolerant with Sonia.

It wasn't simply that Callum didn't have time for this ridiculousness (which he didn't). Callum didn't date. He didn't court. He *seized*. Even if his mate wasn't under threat and his people weren't at war, he had little patience for courting and furthermore didn't like it.

And, obviously, he wasn't very good at it.

He was now king but he'd always been a prince. No one questioned him. Only a scarce few—all blood and all in his inner circle—talked back. People followed his orders and understood his position and he expected this, was entitled to it.

But Sonia didn't know that.

Any of it.

In her world, men asked women on dates. They went to dinners, movies, got to know each other through conversations.

With female humans, if he wanted them, Callum might buy them a drink then he'd find an opportunity to kiss them and that was all he had to do, *always* all he had to do. Then he'd take them to bed.

With female wolves, he never bothered with the drink.

And he'd been wrong about her.

She was fiery and spirited and whatever led her to her colorless life was lost here in this cabin.

Sonia, his mate, the woman fate had bound him to woke in his bed this morning.

Then she'd become naturally confused to be where she was, and with a stranger no less, after what had happened to her last night.

Then he'd freaked her out. She'd retreated into her shell. He'd foolishly lamented his fate but only to find she came out of that shell blazing and he had *more* fire and spirit than he knew what to do with.

His only excuse for tonight's behavior was watching her endure the torture of her injection and he wasn't even thinking about her need to take the injection in the first fucking place.

How she could do that every night of her life was a mystery.

How *he'd* endure giving her that pain, he had no clue.

All he knew was that he would find a way and she would never endure it alone again.

The thought that she had for decades tore at him.

He made her tea, poured himself a whisky, and determined that he was going to rectify the situation as he walked back to the couch. She was lying on her side, pillow under her cheek, eyes on the fire, noticeably back in her shell.

Fuck, Callum thought.

He placed the drinks on the coffee table and bent to pull her up. He maneuvered himself behind her, his back up against the corner of the couch, one leg cocked against the couch's back. Sonia's back was resting against his chest and stomach, her hips tucked in his crotch, her bottom in the seat, and he tangled his remaining leg with both of hers.

She held herself stiff. As she would.

"Grab the drinks, will you, honey?" he asked softly, and without hesitation she leaned forward, got their drinks and handed him his whisky over her shoulder without looking at him.

Yes, totally fucked it up.

He initiated damage control.

"I didn't like watching you suffer that injection," he admitted.

She hesitated only a moment before replying quietly, "Yes, I noticed that."

Callum continued, "But, this morning, I *did* like it when you called me 'wolf.'"

She remained silent but her body tensed further.

Callum carried on, "So much so, when you said it in anger, it pissed me off."

She took a sip of her tea before saying, "I noticed that too."

He slid his arm around her belly and gave her a squeeze.

He sipped his whisky.

Then he said, "You need to know what's going on and you need to know who I am which will explain why I behave the way I do."

More silence.

Callum sighed before he spoke. "I've mentioned 'my people' and 'my culture.' What I mean when I say that is, my people are different from your people. We're a secret sect of society who has been living alongside humans since recorded history."

As he spoke, her body grew even tenser and he sensed her accelerated breathing.

She thought he was a nut.

He leaned forward, taking her with him, and set his glass on the coffee table. He took away her tea and did the same. He brought them both back and wrapped both arms around her, one at her belly, one at her chest, fingers curled around her shoulder where he stroked her.

"Rest your head on my chest," he commanded, and again without delay, she did as she was told.

She was giving in.

Immediately.

Callum felt his jaw get tight as his eyes rolled heavenward.

He decided to pull out the heavy artillery.

His arms grew tighter when he told her, "Your father was a friend to my people."

Her body went rock solid before she turned in his arms and tipped her face up to look at him.

"What?" she whispered, but he saw her face was filled with wonder.

Callum could do nothing but stare.

Fuck, she was pretty but looking like that...

Unbelievable.

He lifted a hand to trail the backs of his fingers against the soft skin of her cheek, which she fortunately allowed while he answered, "Senator Arlington was a friend to our people. He was a liaison between the cultures. He was a good man. A respected man. And he was a friend of my father's."

"Really?" she breathed.

"Really, baby doll," he replied gently.

Heavy artillery was a good call apparently as she didn't pull away. Her body had relaxed into his and her face was still filled with wonder.

He shifted her thick hair away from her temple and tucked it behind her ear before he continued, "My father was king for many years. Five years ago, he was killed in battle." His eyes caught hers as she gasped and he finished, "Now, I'm king."

Her lips parted but she remained silent.

Callum went on, "The evening the future king is born, at midnight, the oracles speak. Just by speaking, they herald the future king, but mostly they talk of his bride."

"Let's go back to your father," she said quietly.

"This is an important part, little one," he told her.

She ignored him and asked, "Were you close?"

He nodded.

"Very?" she inquired.

Callum continued to nod.

The wonder slid from her features as they grew soft with uncon-cealed compassion.

"I'm sorry," she whispered. "I know how that feels."

All right.

To pretty, fiery and spirited, he could add sweet.

Sonia Arlington could be incredibly sweet.

In order not to give in to his sudden forceful urge to take her to his bed and discover just how sweet she could be, he shifted some of her hair over her shoulder. He ran his fingers through it, never taking his eyes from hers while he said, "I know you do. Senator Arlington was a fine man and my father told me he loved you very much."

Pain sliced through her eyes briefly and his arms gave her a squeeze.

She took in a soft breath and stated, "So you think I'm your bride."

He grinned and replied, "You *are* my bride. The oracles foretold you."

She nodded and went on, "And your people think I'm your queen."

He felt his grin widen to a smile as he declared, "You *are* my queen."

"And this is why I'm important to you."

"Yes. The mate of any male of my people is important, important enough to lay down his life for her. But you're *queen*. Any one of my people would lay down their life for you."

She stared at him a moment, her eyes unreadable, then she commented, "That's an awesome responsibility."

His hands moved under her arms to pull her up his chest so her face was closer to his and he teased, "And *I* know how *that* feels." He watched one side of her lips quirk up before he went on, "It's my duty to prepare you to take on that responsibility. Today has not been a good day, baby doll, but I promise you, from now on, I'll be more patient."

"This would be good," she whispered.

He grinned at her, pleased with his endeavors and even more pleased with the results, all the while wondering if it would be a tactical error to kiss her.

Then he thought, *fuck it.*

His fingers sifted into her hair and brought her face closer to his, but before his mouth could capture her own, she spoke.

"Do all your people's eyes do that?"

"The gold?" he asked in return and she nodded. "In a way," he answered. "The eyes of those of us with royal blood go gold. Others, yellow or brown."

"So only your family has that pretty color?"

Yes, Sonia Arlington was definitely sweet.

He nodded as he pulled her face closer at the same time tilting his to hers. "Yes."

Her head resisted and there was resistance in her tone when she whispered, "Callum—"

He ignored both and finally captured her lips.

She continued to resist, pushing her head against his hand and her hand against his chest.

He slanted his head, his mouth opened over hers and his tongue touched her lips.

They tasted sweet too.

He felt her mumbled, "Oh," against his tongue but used that opportunity to slide it between her lips.

His tongue touched hers, her head stopped pushing as did her hand, and she melted into him, tilting her head, her hand sliding up to curl around his neck.

The kiss was not fiery or spirited.

It was simply, brilliantly, unforgettably sweet.

And it stirred Callum in a way he'd never felt before.

Therefore, before he truly made a tactical error by exploring that feeling and pushing her too far after fucking up so royally that day, he broke his mouth from hers and tucked her cheek against his chest.

He slid his fingers through her hair and he could hear her breath was accelerated but she didn't pull away. She just lay in his arms, her cheek against his chest.

And he prayed his damage control worked.

She took in a satisfyingly fluttering breath before she asked, "Do you want your whisky?"

"Yes, little one."

She leaned forward, nabbed his whisky, and handed it to him. She leaned again and hooked her mug with her finger.

Then Sonia lay silently, cocooned by his body with her cheek against his chest, occasionally lifting her head to sip her tea while he sipped his whisky, the fire burned, and the snow fell outside.

Yes, he thought with relief, it appeared his damage control worked.

And, Callum thought, living a life like this with Sonia didn't yawn before him.

Instead, it might just be sweet.

CHAPTER SEVEN

FAMILY

"Um..." Sonia muttered.

"Quiet," Callum clipped.

Sonia tensed in Callum's arms.

It appeared her attempted escape had *not* been such a good idea.

She remained still, cradled in his arms as he marched angrily, no, *furiously* through the snow heading back toward the cabin.

She had made good her escape plan (kind of, before it was thwarted).

After their first very bad day which ended in a not-so-bad late evening, she decided to spend some time lulling him into a false sense of security before she got the hell out of there. She'd pretended, through his gentle explanations that he was king of a secret sect of society, to understand and acquiesce to his lunacy. And she found pretending wasn't hard to do because of said gentleness, his talk of her father (insane and maybe even mean, even though what he said about her papa was nice) and his father (who he obviously missed, or convinced himself he did).

Although it wasn't hard to pretend during their chat, it *was* hard when she found out he expected her to sleep with him in the big bed.

Yes.

Sleep.

With.

Him.

She demurred (as anyone would!).

He insisted (but gently).

She demurred again.

He insisted (a bit more firmly).

She gave in.

Fortunately, this was relatively easy considering he was busy with the fires. This tugged at her heartstrings as she remembered her father doing the same thing. He was always at the fires in order to keep his family warm when they were at the cabin.

In the bathroom, she'd changed into one of her lacy, sexy, silky nightgowns and slid into bed before he'd gotten a glimpse of her.

Unfortunately, after he changed in the bathroom and walked out wearing nothing but a pair of navy flannel pajama bottoms, she got a full-on view of his chest. His massive, defined, muscular chest, complete with a furring of hair that was spread in a tempting array across his chest and down his belly. Chest hair that only the hand of God could have created after which, God could only remark, "My work here is done."

Yes, Callum's chest hair was just...that...perfect.

Really, the cosmos had it out for her.

He'd slid into bed beside her and she was certain his big body would take most of the space (it didn't, she had a nice comfy section all her own).

He called a soft goodnight to which she'd replied in turn.

Then she held herself tense waiting for him to try something.

He didn't.

He lay on his back and she listened as his breathing grew steady.

It took a while but finally Sonia fell asleep.

Unfortunately, when she woke up, she found he'd turned his back to her but *she'd* turned into him and was spooning him all down his length. *Close* to his length. Her knees cocked in his, her hips snuggled in his, her arm around his waist, her torso against his back, but her forehead was pressed to his shoulder blade.

She started to pull away. Before she could succeed in this, however, his fingers curled around her wrist and kept her where she was.

"I, um...need to go to the bathroom," she told the smoothly muscled skin of his back.

He released her wrist but rolled. She scooted back to avoid his big body, but before she could scoot out of reach, his arm tagged her waist and he pulled her mostly underneath him.

Her eyes caught his and his were tawny.

Good goodness, but she liked it when his eyes went tawny (even though she told herself she didn't).

"Look forward to waking up like that every day, baby doll," he muttered, his voice hoarse with sleep.

Sonia gulped.

Callum smiled.

Her heart clutched at his smile.

His head dropped down and to the side, he rubbed his temple against hers, and then he let her go.

That day couldn't have been more different than the one before.

They did not fight.

They ate way too much and way too fatty foods.

They talked about his father, her father, and the fact they'd been long-time friends (supposedly). About his kingdom, which apparently was *world-wide* and included armies and territories which were over-seen by governors and all sorts of other stuff.

Seriously, he had a vivid imagination. It was fascinating but it was insane.

Though, deep down, the more he talked and the pride and fondness in his voice made her want to believe this world was real.

And he talked about her queendom. Essentially, she had nothing to do except the small duties of being at his side *all the time* and supporting him *in everything he wished to do.*

Even though she asked, he'd said they'd get into "the war" later.

Most of the talking happened while they were cuddling, either Sonia sitting in his lap or both of them stretched on the couch with Sonia in his arms.

Indeed, his informing her that his people were "affectionate" was an understatement. He was the touchiest person she'd ever met.

Gregor, nor Yuri, touched, hugged, or cuddled. They were often coolly affectionate but not in any physical way.

But with Callum, even when they weren't cuddling he found ways to touch her. Like while she was cooking, he'd get close, put a hand to her waist, and look over her shoulder at the food she was preparing. Or when she was playing solitaire on his computer, he walked up behind her, wrapped his arm around her chest, pulled her back to his front, and held her there for long moments before bending, rubbing his temple against hers, and letting her go.

He never said anything. He just touched.

He was, all day, as he promised, entirely different—patient and tender, sometimes teasing and sweet.

Especially when he gave her the injection. His reaction was no less severe and her reaction to his soothing embrace was no less deep.

Obviously, since he did have men (he, again, talked to them on the phone often that day and she'd even met the cheeky but deferential Waring), she decided he was a leader of a cult or something. Somehow, he'd locked on to her as his "mate," and being the leader, had convinced his people she was their queen.

They had resources. That was also obvious. Even small as it was, her family's cabin was outfitted spectacularly. His and her clothes were outdoorsy but they were of an excellent brand and very high quality. His cell phone and computer were top of the line. The kitchen was not only stocked to the gills, everything in it was the finest you could buy—from the appliances, to the utensils, pots and pans, even the food.

She didn't believe a word he said about her father but she reckoned, in his loopy mind, he did.

It was sad that this glorious man was obviously not well.

But it was scary that, as the day progressed, something was telling her she didn't care.

She understood how he recruited his followers. Because he was the kind of man you followed, even if he was insane.

There was something about him. It was more than the fact that he was incredibly good-looking (but that helped). More than the sharp intelligence in his blue eyes. More than the rich depth of his attractively accented voice. More than his manner filled with absolute confidence and exhibited through every movement of his powerful body and every word he spoke.

It was the quiet yet fierce force of his personality which was compelling and nearly impossible to resist.

As the day wore on Sonia found she *wanted* to believe in his world, to be a part of it, even (Lord forbid) the ridiculous but appealing idea of being his queen.

She was even trying to find ways to sort it in her brain. Telling herself seeing him in dreams for years meant they were supposed to be together just like he said they were. That maybe she *was* his queen. That maybe he *was* her handsome wolf.

But the logical side of her brain, which was fighting the battle of its life against Callum's captivating pull, told her there were no such things as secret sects with kings and queens and wars.

He was just a madman who kidnapped her, maybe murdered men while doing it (even bad men, but still), and he intended to make her his "mate" without her getting a word in edgewise.

Therefore, long after she heard his breathing even the second night, she made good her escape.

It scared her silly, trying to creep around silently getting prepared and out the back door, but she did it.

Even with four pairs of thick socks on, walking in his boots was clumsy and time-consuming, it was freezing and the snow was only gently falling, which meant she had to waste precious time covering her tracks.

But even though she remembered the cave being only a short, maybe twenty-minute walk away from the cabin, it took her what felt like hours to get there.

She didn't light a fire because she had no idea how, but also because she didn't want him to see it.

Instead, she carefully unbundled her medicine and food, wrapped herself in the woolly blanket she'd brought (and she was still chilled to the bone within minutes), and stayed awake until dawn touched the sky.

She fell into an exhausted sleep while considering her next step.

Then she sensed him.

Instantly awake and alert, she jumped up, but his large form was filling the mouth of the cave before she even got the blanket off her shoulders.

She stared at him.

That was impossible. When she'd sensed him, he hadn't been close.

How did he get there so fast? He couldn't sense *her* and no one could move that fast.

He had to know about the cave.

"You knew about the cave," she whispered.

"Quiet," his voice was even and calm.

She squared her shoulders, faced off with him, and told him courageously, "I don't want to go back."

"*Quiet!*" he roared, his voice *not* even *or* calm *in the slightest.*

Sonia went still.

Callum strode forward, snatched up her medicine, wrapped her in the blanket, picked her up in his arms, and strode angrily from the cave.

So much for her escape attempt. She only managed to stay away a few hours.

Seriously, she was in trouble.

And she was in even *more* trouble because she didn't know whether to be frightened out of her mind that he found her or...*elated.*

They were nearing the cabin and she knew instantly there were people inside.

So shocked at this, forgetting to hide her gift, she whispered, "Callum, there are people—"

"Quiet."

"But—"

His arms grew so tight they almost, but not quite, hurt.

She thought it prudent to be quiet, so she was.

He walked right in the porch door, through to the cabin's back door and straight into the cabin.

There were four people there. All tall. All looking a lot like Callum, three even had sky-blue eyes, but one had green. And one was a woman.

They were all staring at Callum and Sonia with knowing, amused expressions on their faces.

Callum ignored them and tossed Sonia on the bed.

Sonia bounced then settled and looked up at Callum's handsome but enraged face, not knowing what to do or if she'd live long enough to do it.

Callum's voice was back to even and calm when he stated, "So yesterday was a lie."

Knowing this voice heralded the scary roar if she said the wrong thing, Sonia decided not to speak at all.

And anyway, they had an audience.

Were they going to do this in front of an audience?

"Answer me," Callum demanded.

Apparently they were going to do this in front of an audience.

"Um..." Sonia muttered.

"*Answer me!*"

There it was, the roar.

Okay, maybe he was a murdering kidnapping madman and there was a better way to play it, she just didn't know what that was and she was so angry, she didn't care.

She threw off the blanket and got to her knees, shouting, "You kidnapped me!"

"I told you, Sonia—"

"*I know what you told me!*" she interrupted on a shriek. "That I'm your mate, your queen, yadda, yadda, yadda. Do *I* get a say in this?" she demanded.

"No, you bloody well don't!" he shouted back.

"Well, that's unacceptable!" she yelled. "It's even *insane!*"

"I take you down the mountain, I put you in your house, I take away your guard, you'll be kidnapped and killed within days," he clipped.

"Seriously," she muttered scornfully.

"Seriously," he shot back.

"I—" she started.

"Do you forget what happened three nights ago?" he demanded.

"Of course not!" she snapped.

"The threat is real," he informed her.

"Only if you didn't set it up to make me *think* it was real," she shot back.

His whole body jerked before he thundered, "Why in *fucking hell* would I do that?"

"To make me go along with your crazy plan!" she answered.

Callum growled, his head twisted to the side and he bit out, "I should have seized her, taken her to a castle, and bedded her. This would have been finished within hours, not fucking *days*, and not with this ridiculous *garbage*. But no, I listened to you."

"Don't drag *me* into this," the green-eyed man said, grinning ear to ear like their show was enormously amusing.

"Sonia, darlin'." One of the blue-eyed men was speaking to her and she moved her gaze to his. "What Callum says is true. You're his queen and you're under threat."

"You would say that," Sonia returned. "He's brainwashed you. I hate to be the one to tell you this but you're a member of his cult."

All of them, including Callum, stared at her like *she'd* lost *her* mind.

She didn't know much about brainwashing but they said brutal interventions were often the way to go when someone was addicted to something, even the charisma of another person, so she forged ahead.

Anyway, she was already screwed. She had nothing to lose.

"I don't blame you," she went on. "He can be pretty charming and charismatic. Still, he's not a well man."

The newcomers all burst out laughing.

Callum scowled at her a moment before dropping his head back and saying to the ceiling, "Bloody hell."

"Sonia," the woman called and Sonia looked at her. "Sweetheart, I'm Regan, Callum's mother."

Sonia's mouth dropped open at this news.

She *looked* like Callum, for certain. But she had to be his sister, not his mother. In fact, she looked even *younger* than he was.

"What?" Sonia breathed.

Regan came forward. "Let me show you something, sweetheart," she said softly.

She had a big, designer, leather handbag over her shoulder and from it she pulled a framed photo. When Regan got close to her, she turned the photo to face Sonia. It was a picture of her mother and father's wedding day.

Standing by her mother was a tall dignified man who looked like every man in this room, but most especially Callum. Standing by her father was the woman standing in front of her.

"Holy cow," she whispered then she looked at the woman, who, from the day her parents were married decades ago, to that very day in the cabin, appeared not to have aged a moment, and announced the obvious, "Photos can be altered."

"I'd known Cherise Mayfair Arlington for what seems forever," Regan declared. "She was a dear friend."

Oh no. This wasn't fair.

"Don't—" Sonia warned.

"She liked pink and dressed you up in it as often as she could," Regan went on and Sonia's heart slid up her throat when she heard these words.

"Don't—" Sonia repeated but that one word sounded choked.

Regan interrupted her, "Lassiter liked blue and he detested pink—"

Sonia cut her off. "This isn't even *nice*."

It wasn't nice, them using her parents against her.

Though what Regan said was true. Her father was always trying to talk her mother out of dressing her in pink and he was always buying clothes for her that were blue. It was a silly little argument that they bickered about good-naturedly the entire, albeit heartbreakingly short life she'd led with them in it.

No one could know that from doing research on her.

Sonia had even forgotten it.

"You haven't aged a day from that picture," Sonia accused.

Regan took in a breath and replied, "Our people age slowly."

She could say that again.

Regan moved slightly closer and pressed emotionally deeper. "Every Sunday, Lassiter made you pancakes in the shapes of stars."

Sonia's heart clutched.

Now, really. How did she know that?

No one could know that.

Except her father and mother and both of them were dead.

Sonia scuttled back on the bed, whispering, "Stop it."

Regan's voice grew sad and fond when she said, "Cherise told me your favorite book was *The Giving Tree*."

"Stop."

"She said she read it to you night after night."

"Stop."

"It was the only book you wanted to hear."

Sonia felt the edge of the bed and halted, staring at the woman.

Her eyes had gone tawny.

And it hit her, belatedly, that that wasn't natural, eyes that changed like that. No one's eyes did that. It was one thing for the hue to change, say, if you were wearing a certain color. But for the color to change *completely*? To that attractive but inexplicable shade which was not from nature or any nature that Sonia knew?

And it wasn't natural for dream men to come alive.

That didn't happen. To anyone.

Ever.

Her gaze slid through the ensemble—all inordinately tall, all dark, all gorgeous, all with clear intelligent eyes. Just like Waring last night.

Just like Callum.

Holy cow.

These people weren't like her people.

These people were of a different culture. They belonged to a secret sect of society who lived alongside humans.

Her gaze moved to Callum, who was watching her closely, the anger gone from his face replaced with something profoundly gentle.

"I know this is hard for you to take in, but Callum and you have been linked through eternity, even before you both existed, even before you were cells in a womb," Regan continued softly. "You're destined for each other, connected to each other. It's the way of our people. You're lifemates and, Sonia, that's a beautiful thing. Your mother and father were good friends to our people. They accepted us. They would have been so happy you were to be among us. So very happy. I promise you that, sweetheart."

As Regan spoke, Sonia never took her eyes from Callum.

"I dreamed of you," she whispered and watched as his body grew visibly taut. "Since I was a teenager, I dreamed of you."

The others started moving away but neither she nor Callum moved a muscle.

Finally, he said softly, "You know me."

"In my dreams, you've been coming to me for twenty years."

"You know me," he repeated.

Sonia nodded a jerky frightened nod. "When I woke up the other day, I thought it was another dream."

Vaguely she heard the back door close.

"Do you understand you're mine?" he asked.

It was then that she did.

It sang through her soul. It made her feel whole again after being fragmented since a Christmas Eve thirty-one years ago.

No, it made her feel truly whole like she'd never felt in her life.

And at the same exact time, it scared her senseless.

She swallowed.

Then she nodded again.

"You understand you're my queen?"

"I'm scared," she admitted freely. She had no idea why but she *was* scared. Of him, of the fact that his crazy stories were real, she was under threat, she belonged to him, his people were at war, and she was their queen.

How did one even go about being a queen?

"I'll take care of you," he replied gently.

She gazed at him long moments before nodding again.

His body relaxed.

Then, his eyes golden and shimmering, he said quietly, "Come to your wolf, baby doll."

On trembling limbs which were moving of their own accord, she scooted off the bed, rounded it, and slowly walked to him.

When she was in reaching distance, he snatched her roughly in his arms and held her close. She trembled in his embrace, terrified at the overwhelming uncertainty of her future.

He sensed it and promised again, "I'll take care of you."

She nodded, her cheek sliding against his chest.

He rubbed his temple against the top of her head then held her tight until the tremors slid away.

Finally, he asked, "Are you okay?"

She nodded again, not making her lie audible.

He tipped her face to his with a fist under her chin.

"I have to do something. I'll be back in a short while. My family will take care of you while I'm gone."

Sonia nodded again.

He bent his neck and placed his temple against hers.

"We'll have a beautiful life, you and me. I'll see to it."

"Okay," she whispered.

He squeezed her tight then he let her go.

Then he was gone.

She stared into the space he'd just occupied, her mind blank.

From afar, she heard his deep voice say, "Let's run," and she heard the answering, amused, "Fuck, yeah."

And she thought, because he was different maybe she could even tell him *she* was different. *He* above all would understand. *He* would never make her feel weird.

Her mind filled with memories of hundreds of dreams of her handsome wolf.

Her "lifemate."

Her destiny.

And those dreams...

Her dreams...

In some magical way, those dreams foretold her future of a beautiful strong man who would hold her and tease her and accept her and make her feel loved.

She closed her eyes as gladness washed over her.

Then she realized in an unwelcome intrusion on her unbound joy that she had to use the bathroom.

She was finished and had a hand on the handle of the bathroom door when she heard the murmuring voices, voices that were talking outside.

She stilled at what she heard and listened.

"...Callum nuts?" an incredulous man asked.

"Caleb," Regan replied.

"No, seriously, Regan, is he nuts?" Caleb repeated.

"You can never know who you'll be attracted to."

"A monk would be attracted to Sonia, she's fucking *seriously* pretty," Caleb returned, and understanding these words (and hoping she did not), Sonia's body went solid. "Not to mention, she's pretty freaking funny," Caleb finished.

"You know your brother's tastes don't tend to stray down Sonia's way."

"Even so, it's nuts. Did you see her?"

"I saw her."

"Ryon said Callum seemed impatient for the claiming, wanted to *get it over with* so he could get on with taking down the rebellion," Caleb went on and Sonia's briefly buoyant heart lurched before Caleb mumbled, "Fuck me."

"Caleb—"

"It was me, I wouldn't be shitty I was forced to spend a week with that woman in a remote cabin explaining the ways of our culture to her. It was me and *I* was alone with her in a remote cabin, I'd draw it out so long it'd take a year."

"Well, it *isn't* you," Regan retorted firmly.

"No, it isn't and a damned shame it isn't." He paused and went on sharply, "Not for me, Regan, for her. Woman like that? She deserves a man who wants *her*, not the mate the oracles foretold would be his queen."

Oh dear lord, Sonia thought as her lurching heart turned to stone.

"Perhaps he'll grow an attraction to her," Regan suggested.

"Oh, he'll do his duty to his people, Mac made sure of that," Caleb clipped. "The oracles said it was Sonia, Callum will mate with Sonia. The end. Every one of us expects to find the other half to our soul. Not Cal. Duty first, heart second." There was a pause and then the kicker as a finish, "Maybe, if he's lucky, as a human, she'll understand his need to fuck around on her with his kind."

Sonia sucked in breath.

"Caleb!" Regan snapped. "You don't know he'll do that. She's his mate and—"

"It's Callum we're talking about, isn't it?" Caleb returned sarcastically.

Sonia rested her forehead on the bathroom door.

"I'm not talking about this anymore," Regan replied. "I'm going to go and get to know my soon-to-be daughter-in-law."

"I'm gonna run," Caleb returned irately.

"You do that, you need it," Regan retorted.

Sonia turned her back to the door and slid down it until her bottom hit the floor. She rested her temple on her knee as she wound her arms around her calves.

Evidently, the cosmos wasn't done with her.

So it gave her the handsome charismatic king of a secret sect of eye-color-changing, slow-aging people as her destined mate.

But it also made it so that king didn't want her.

And, apparently, he was a philanderer (even his brother said so!).

Somewhere in her heart at every moment she missed her mother and father.

It was only times like these when that slightly dulled ache grew and blossomed and twisted and reminded her how truly alone she was in the world.

Not that she often found, and lost, her dream man in the span of minutes.

But Sonia Arlington had lost a lot in her life.

This was just the last in long line of it.

And, unfortunately, she'd never gotten used to it.

***

Sonia was in the kitchen with Regan watching Callum arrange greenery and lights on the mantels of the fireplaces.

The Christmas decorations were Ryon's idea.

After Sonia experienced her latest life trauma, she composed herself (she hoped), came out of the bathroom, and she and Regan made breakfast for what Regan called "The Boys." "The Boys," Regan informed Sonia, were Calder and Caleb, Callum's younger brothers, and Ryon, his cousin.

Regan was really nice, talky and chatty in a motherly way that was a little bit weird (okay, it was a lot weird) considering she looked like their sister.

Still, she took great pains letting Sonia know she was welcoming her into the bosom of her brood with open arms.

As they made huge fluffy pancakes for the men, she told Sonia stories about her momma and papa, which was the only nice thing that had happened in this mess, Regan knowing and having stories about Sonia's parents. It was something Sonia hadn't had for years and she appreciated greatly. Although Gregor was supposed to be their very best friend, he disliked talking about them, and eventually Sonia stopped bringing them up.

When Sonia told Regan this, Regan's mouth got tight in a way that made Sonia curious.

"What?" she asked Callum's mother.

Regan slid the bacon around in the skillet with a fork and muttered, "It's just..." She looked at Sonia with a carefully closed face and finished, "I've known Gregor too, for a long time. He didn't get along with my husband."

"Oh," was all Sonia said because it was obvious Regan didn't want to talk about it. As she wouldn't, considering Gregor didn't get along with her dead husband.

This was also not a surprise. Gregor didn't get along with hardly anybody.

Callum, Ryon, and Calder came back and Sonia heard it before Regan did.

She also heard who she would later know was Calder mutter before they walked into the house, "This is brilliant. Fuck her tonight, you can bring her down the mountain, and we can stop dicking around with this shit."

Sonia's heart twisted.

There you go. More proof she was just a kingly duty for Callum.

"Jesus, Calder," Ryon (she would recognize later) muttered back, his voice sounding annoyed.

She didn't let on she heard, but strangely Regan gave Calder a look when he sauntered in with the pack. A severe motherly look that made Calder ask, "What?"

To which Regan answered, "You know what."

When Callum entered, he came directly to Sonia and curled an arm around her, bringing her body front to front with his.

"How you doing, honey?" he asked the top of her hair.

"Okay," she lied to his chest and hoped it sounded like the truth.

It obviously didn't because he pulled back and looked at her with searching eyes.

She didn't know what to do to hide her thoughts from those intelligent eyes, so she used the only escape route available to her as she couldn't run to a car and drive to the ends of the earth. She wrapped her arms around him and buried her face in massive chest.

This was the right thing to do. His body relaxed but his arms tightened around her and he gave her a squeeze.

She found out during breakfast that Callum and his father before him had been protecting her since her parents died. Ryon was what they called "the lead" of Sonia's "detail."

This meant they knew practically everything about her (except her injection). They knew about Gregor, Yuri, her schooling, her friends (such as they were), her shop, her house, everything.

This explained those benign presences Sonia felt since her parents died and she felt a strange sense of relief that she finally knew what they were. However, she told herself she didn't feel a not-so-strange sense of warmth that Callum and his father had taken great pains to protect her since her parents died (but she did feel it).

Therefore, after breakfast, Ryon walked up to where Sonia was standing at the counter, scooting her pancake remains around on her plate. There were a lot of them, Regan made delicious pancakes, but Sonia wasn't hungry.

He slid an arm around her shoulders, tucked her into his side, and teased, "As an apology for stalking you for thirty years, I told Regan you clearly had a thing for Christmas." She looked up at him and he grinned down at her at which time she noticed he was nearly as good-looking as Callum. "Regan likes to shop, as those clothes you're wearing lay testament to." Sonia glanced at Regan in surprise and gratitude at learning Regan had supplied her wardrobe. She looked back to Ryon when he finished, "She ran out and got some decorations so you could have little bit of Christmas while you're stuck up here. They're out in the car."

This was such a nice thing to do, Sonia's mood lifted instantly and she had no idea just how much her expression brightened.

She also had no idea how much it transformed her "seriously pretty" face.

She further had no idea that Callum could see her plainly from where he was leaning at the end of the counter.

And no idea the intensity of the response Callum felt at seeing her expression.

She also didn't know that she'd never, not once, looked at Callum with her expression shining and unguarded. She didn't even cotton on when Ryon's body went solid and he stared at her like he'd never seen a female before.

"Really?" she breathed. "You did that for me?"

He jolted at her words, a slow gorgeous smile spread on his face, and he replied, "Really."

"Thank you," she whispered.

"Anything for my queen," he mumbled, his green eyes going soft.

Not knowing what to do, but having been told by Callum that his people were affectionate, she gave him a little hurried and uncomfortable hug around his middle.

To this, Ryon dropped his head and rubbed his temple along her hair.

That temple thing, she thought, must be some sort of Callum's People Gesture.

However, a split second after Ryon did it, Callum's voice cracked through the room with, "Ry, fucking hell. Seriously?"

Ryon pulled away and looked at Callum who was scowling at them.

"She's difficult to resist," Ryon replied strangely but with an open, roguish grin.

"Try harder," Callum returned, his voice flinty, clearly not finding whatever they were talking about amusing.

Ryon gave her a squeeze and let her go. Then the men went out to their SUV to get the Christmas decorations and Caleb came back.

Caleb still seemed in a surly mood but he gave Sonia a welcome to the family hug before tucking into his own pancakes.

They didn't bring a tree and all the trimmings. But they did bring boughs for the mantels, Christmas lights, pretty playful ornaments and knickknacks of Santa Clauses, reindeers, and snowmen to put in the greenery. There were also matching fun candlestick holders for the coffee table with festive, wonderful-smelling green and red candles. And last, a big, plump, snowman cookie jar that Regan told Sonia they were going to fill by baking Christmas cookies.

The women got down to baking while the men drank coffee (Calder and Ryon) or dealt with the boughs and lights (Callum and Caleb).

It didn't take long, but when it was all arranged, while Regan was rolling out dough and Sonia was cutting out gingerbread men, it transformed the space to almost magical.

And baking Christmas cookies like she did with her momma in that same kitchen so many years ago, with Christmas decorations in the house, jovial male voices and Regan's musical one mingling around her, suddenly cut deeply through Sonia.

Therefore, Sonia froze mid-gingerbread man when Callum plugged in the lights to the mantel in the living room and she didn't know she sucked in breath.

Regan heard it and her head turned to Sonia. "Sonia? Sweetheart?"

Sonia stared at the greenery on the mantel twinkling with lights and dangling with lively lovely ornaments and she remembered her mother's decorated mantels in that very room.

"Sonia?" Regan called again but Sonia didn't move.

It was too much. All of it.

Too much to take.

"Callum, something's wrong with—" Regan started but Sonia was already drawn away from the dough, the cookie cutter pulled from her hand, and she was being turned toward Callum's big body.

"Little one, look at me," he demanded.

Automatically, she tipped her head back to look at him.

He took one look at her face and asked, "Jesus, honey, what's the matter?"

She didn't delay in replying. "The last time I was here, my momma's decorations were on that mantel."

She barely finished talking before she was yanked into his embrace, and when his warm body surrounded her, she lost it.

She burst into loud wracking sobs. It was embarrassing and it was weak, but it was also understandable.

Her life was terrible.

It had once been perfect when her mother and father were alive. Idyllic. Wonderful. She had been protected. She had been loved. She had been told she should be proud of who she was and the gifted things she could do. And she had lived her young life knowing her momma and papa were proud of her and those gifts.

Since then, all she'd had was Gregor, who wasn't exactly loving, if he was always gruffly kind. And Yuri, who was also gruffly kind but decided not to be her brother-type-figure but instead wanted since she turned twenty-one (and he made no bones about it) to be her lover-and-husband-type-figure.

And without anyone knowing what she could do, much less being proud, she felt she was weird.

Because of that she had to hide her gifts and therefore had no true friends who knew her down to her every secret.

She was the mate to a man who didn't want her.

She was the queen to a people she didn't know.

She'd been attacked, kidnapped, and traumatized.

And now...

What?

What was she supposed to do?

She tipped her head back and wailed to Callum, "Now what do I do?"

He didn't answer likely because he wasn't in her head and didn't know what she was on about.

Instead, he picked her up cradled in his arms and carried her to a chair, arranging her body in his lap, her face in his neck, then his arms tight around her.

"*Well?*" she demanded loudly into his neck.

"You cry it out, baby doll," he answered. "Then, together, we'll get on with it."

Easy for him to say.

He was king. He could do whatever he wanted to do.

She was queen, which meant she just followed him around while he did whatever he wanted to do. Even though he didn't want her, he would, if what Caleb alluded was true, find someone he *did* want.

Deciding to forget they were in the room (though she didn't actually forget they were in the room), she declared, "Your family's going to think I'm a loon."

"Since they're all pretty nuts," Callum replied calmly, "you'll fit in."

She jerked her head back, glared at him, and demanded to know, "What are your people going to think of me?"

His big hand came to the side of her face and his thumb rubbed away the streaming tears.

Then his eyes went to hers and he replied, "They're going to love you."

How? she thought. *He* was never going to love her.

She decided to use the tactic that worked at hiding her thoughts earlier and buried her face in his neck.

Then she did as he suggested and cried it out.

While she did this, she heard Regan working silently in the kitchen and the men went out the back to let her have her moment.

When she smelled gingerbread men baking, she took a shaky breath, got herself under control, and told Callum's neck, "I'm all right now."

His hand sifted into her hair and twisted, using it to pull her head back gently, and his blue eyes scanned her face.

Then he said something in a quiet but firm voice that made her world tilt crazily.

"You've got a lot to get used to, baby doll, but I asked my family to come up here to show you that you've got family now to help you get used to it. The people in this cabin will fight and die for you. And they would never want to see you struggle, no matter what you're struggling with. Know that in your soul and never forget it."

She blinked at him (what else could she do!) and blurted, "I think your culture is very intense."

His lips tipped up in a grin and he replied in a now teasing tone, "You're learning."

It was time to move on and away from Callum, who, when he was sweet (and intense *and* teasing) she could forget he was with her out of kingly duty.

"I want a gingerbread man cookie," she announced.

His grin turned into a smile, she hated it that she loved his smile, and while she was thinking that, he replied, "Me too."

***

Sonia wandered the room in her sexy, lacy, satiny nightgown, quickly turning off lamps and blowing out the fragrant candles.

Callum was in the bathroom changing for bed. His family had left just a little while ago.

Or, she should say, he kicked his family out just a little while ago.

While she was hugging Regan good-bye, she heard Callum, who had walked with the men down the path to the SUV, speaking to his cousin.

"I see you do that again, Ry, it won't make me happy."

Ryon's voice was good-humored when he replied, "Relax, Cal."

"I'll relax knowing I'm never again going to stand in my kitchen watching my cousin mark my mate," Callum returned.

The good humor left his tone when Ryon retorted, "I said relax."

"She's your queen," Callum clipped.

"She's also Sonia," Ryon bit back. "Don't fucking forget that, brother."

Callum had no retort. Then again, she was just his queen to him.

Sonia didn't let on she was hearing anything and anyway, she didn't know what marking meant. She reckoned it was the temple thing but she could swear Regan heard them too. Though she couldn't, the men were muttering under their breath and definitely not close. She could swear this because Regan's mouth got a motherly tightness which she tried to hide when she smiled her final good-bye.

Callum and Sonia barely got back through the front door before he dragged her to the bathroom to give her the injection.

So *that* was why he threw his family out. Not because he was desperate to be alone with his mate after she'd accepted him.

Well, she figured he wouldn't want his destined-by-the-oracles queen dying of a rare blood disorder. What would his people think?

She got under the covers and told herself she didn't feel delicious anticipation that Callum was soon to be coming out bare-chested (when she did feel it).

He came into the room moments later and she watched in what she told herself wasn't avid fascination (when it was) as he went directly to the mantel to unplug the Christmas lights.

"Don't!" she blurted and he turned to her in question. "I like to sleep with them on. Can you sleep with them on?" she finished.

"I've slept in rain and snow and mud," he told her. "I can sleep with Christmas lights on."

Why on earth was he sleeping in rain and snow and mud?

She wanted to know but she didn't ask.

She didn't ask because he came directly to bed, and unlike the two nights before where he kept his distance, he curled right into her. Spooning her body with his arm around her waist, his face went into her neck.

Her body grew stiff.

Good goodness, he wanted to have sex. Mate with her so in the eyes of his people she'd be his queen and then he could stop "dicking around" up here with her.

Holy cow.

"Relax, honey," he said into her neck, pulling her closer.

She did not *think* so.

"I'm really tired," she told him.

"Then sleep," he said back.

Did he think he could have sex with her while she was sleeping?

Oh good goodness!

"Actually," she said quickly, "I thought maybe we could talk."

This seemed to be perfectly all right with him because he pulled his face out of her neck, rested his head on the pillow, and cuddled her closer.

"What do you want to talk about?" he asked.

Oh no. Now what had she done?

"Um…" she started.

He chuckled into the back of her hair and then said softly, "Baby doll, you've had another tough day. Thwarted escape, coming to terms with your destiny, meeting the in-laws, emotional breakdowns. I'm not going to come on to you after a day like that."

Well, that was a relief. It was even nice.

And, actually, sweet.

Luckily, he spoke, pulling her thoughts away from him being sweet. "Why do you want the Christmas lights on?"

"I like sleeping with them on," she told him.

"Yes, I guessed that. You had them on in your bedroom at your house too. I'm asking why."

She shrugged, willing to talk but she'd never be willing to let him in, and replied, "I just like Christmas."

He was silent a moment and then he sighed.

"We'll let that go for now."

At last, something to be thankful for. Callum, at least, was going to let her keep her own thoughts to herself.

For now.

"I'll try something else," he said.

She expressed her thanks to the cosmos too soon.

Callum went on, "You want to tell me why your entire house is clinical and pristine and not anywhere someone would want to spend time but your bedroom is the opposite?"

"My house is lovely," she retorted.

"It is," he agreed. "In a clinical, pristine, not anywhere someone would want to spend time kind of way."

Her body got stiff again. "Callum."

"But you're bedroom," he broke in. "*That's* a place you want to stay awhile."

She felt her pulse quicken on the thought that Callum thought her bedroom was somewhere he wanted to stay awhile.

However, he probably wanted to do it in someone else's company.

She decided to let him in just a little bit in order to get this over with.

"Gregor can be..." she tried to find the word, "daunting and he has a lot of opinions that he doesn't mind sharing."

"What's that got to do with your house?"

"He didn't like me buying that house so, to shut him up, I decorated it in a way he'd like," she answered. "But my bedroom is *mine*. It's my private space, a space where I can be who I'm meant to be."

His arm curled tighter around her belly and she felt his face in her hair.

"You can be who you're meant to be everywhere, honey. Just do it. Who gives a fuck about Gregor's opinion?"

"I do. He raised me. I owe him," she replied.

Callum's face came out of her hair and he said firmly, "You don't owe that man dick."

"I know you don't like him," she whispered, finding it bizarre in the extreme he knew so much about her and that their lives had been intermingled for so long and in different ways, none of which she knew about. "Your mom told me your dad didn't get along with him. But, for all this time, he was all I had. And he wasn't great at it, but I knew he tried hard and he took care of me. You might not like him, Callum, but he means something to me, he took care of me, and he did the best he could."

There was silence then she felt his face burrow back into her hair and he thankfully let it go.

"Your bedroom reminds me of this cabin when I first bought it," he told her.

"I'm not surprised." She was still whispering. "I always thought of this place as home. I guess, with my bedroom, I was trying to recreate a little bit of home."

He pulled her ever deeper into his body but lifted his head to nuzzle her with his temple.

When he stopped, he muttered in her ear, "You're home now." Then he kissed her neck softly which made a happy shiver run from her neck, down her spine.

She was far from home, she knew.

She'd never be home again, she knew that too.

But, as ever, this was as good as it was going to get.

On that thought, she relaxed into him. He read her mood, stopped talking, and shortly after, with the Christmas lights twinkling, she fell asleep in Callum's arms.

CHAPTER EIGHT
WOLF

Sonia heard a strange noise like claws clicking on wood floors and her eyes opened.

She was in the cabin, the green, red, and white Christmas lights twinkling from the mantel in front of her casting a cheerful glow to the dark room.

Her puppy was wandering across the room. He stopped and shook his massive body as if shaking off wet or cold. Then he started to lean back on his powerfully muscled haunches as if preparing to sit.

Or leap.

But he didn't when she whispered, "Puppy."

His body stopped its movement, he came alert, and his massive head swung to face her.

This *was* a dream, she knew.

Her father told her that wounded or sick animals often disappeared in order to die with dignity.

Her puppy had been filled with dignity.

And she'd known, the moment he looked in her eyes that night, if he didn't have to, he'd never leave her.

But he'd been bleeding.

So when Gregor gently shook her awake that Christmas morning after her parents died and she found her puppy gone, she knew he'd stolen away in order to die.

Even if he hadn't, that was over thirty years ago. He'd been a full grown wolf then. He couldn't have survived thirty years.

Therefore, this was definitely a dream.

Sleepily, her arm fell toward him and she whispered, "Come here, handsome."

More than half asleep, her eyelids slowly lowered but she felt the thick soft fur of his muzzle glide almost lovingly along her fingertips. It was cold and damp, as if he'd just come in from a run in the snow.

"My puppy," she sighed drowsily and moved her fingers over his muzzle to his head in a loving caress.

Eyes still closed, she finished her stroke before she tucked her hand under her cheek.

"I wish you'd bring me my handsome wolf. I miss him," she murmured as slumber started to invade.

She *did* wish that. Her dream Callum loved her. *Her.* He didn't simply feel a duty to his queen. And if she couldn't have him in the real world, she'd take what she could get in her dreams.

She felt the bed depress on either side of her just as she smelled an attractive, musky scent the likes of which she'd never smelled. She fought the permeating sleep and her eyes fluttered open.

Callum was there, not King Callum, her handsome wolf. He was leaned over, hands in the bed on either side of her. She knew this Callum was hers because his beautiful face in the twinkling lights showed a mixture of tenderness and desire, a look he'd given her many times before.

"There you are," she whispered, her hand drifting to his sinewy forearm, finding his skin cold under her light touch.

"Sonia," he murmured.

Still closer to asleep than awake, she shifted the covers off her body and invited, "Let's get you warm."

Her eyes drifted closed again as he hesitated then she felt him move into the bed. She fell to her back as he put a knee to her opposite side, shifted over her body, and settled mostly along her length, flicking the covers back over them when he was done.

She turned into him, wrapping her arms around him, and hooking her thigh over his hip.

"You're so cold," she muttered, snuggling into his body which was so cool it felt almost moist.

"Sonia."

She nuzzled closer, seduced at the same time calmed by that beautiful aroma, and she muttered a drowsy, "Mm?"

His arms slid around her as he said, "Baby doll, I'm not your dream."

Sonia didn't answer because that was silly.

This *was* her dream. Even if it was in the cabin, it started with her puppy visiting her, always.

She burrowed deeper into his big body.

"Honey," he called as she drifted back to sleep. "I want to make sure you know we're not in one of your dreams."

"Yes we are," she told him. Sleep overcoming her, she finished on a whispered sigh, "My puppy always brings you to me."

She was nearly asleep so she didn't register his body tightening.

One of her hands drifted up his back to rest between his shoulder blades. The other glided down to rest on his tight behind.

"I'm glad I'm still going to have my dreams," she muttered as she pulled his hard hips to hers just as she fitted her soft ones to his.

She was skating on the edge of dreamland when she felt his body shaking and his deep voice filled with amusement murmuring, "I'm glad too."

She slipped over the edge into sleep.

———

Sonia woke up in Callum's arms, hers around him, her thigh hooked on his hip.

Taking in her position, the soft bed, the cocoon of warmth they made, his hard frame, her entire body melted.

"Morning, little one."

Her head slowly tipped back and she looked into his sky-blue eyes.

He was very awake, and for some reason, smiling at her.

"Morning," she mumbled, immediately lost in the clear blue of his smiling eyes.

Her gaze drifted down and she got lost in the beauty of his smiling lips framed by his dark, thick stubble.

Those lips moved. "This isn't a dream, baby doll."

The residue of sleep vaporized, reality intruded, and her eyes snapped back to his.

"I know that," she lied.

"You didn't last night," he replied.

Sonia stared. Then the events of the night before came to her.

Holy cow!

"Um..." she began, her thoughts awhirl, but she stopped speaking when he rolled into her, mostly on top of her, his thigh now between hers, and her thoughts focused on one thing. "Callum—" she started to protest.

He cut her off, saying casually but with a smile in his voice, "I'm curious about these dreams."

Her eyes went wide before she could control her reaction and the smile in his voice hit his lips.

"You see, twice you thought you were in one, and twice, when you thought you were, you came on to me," he informed her.

Oh good goodness.

She decided instantly that she didn't want to dream of him anymore. Never again. It was too confusing and it was going to get her into trouble.

She tried to slide away.

He rolled over her so he was now *totally* on top of her but he put his forearms into the bed beside her to take off some of his considerable weight.

Even so, he was close, his body covering hers. She could feel the hair on his chest grazing her nightgown.

Her breath started getting heavy as the realization dawned that maybe her dreams weren't going to get her into trouble.

They might already have.

To her mortification, he went on as if he was musing, "The first time you came on strong." His face came close but veered to her side. He didn't rub his temple along hers. Instead, he brushed her earlobe with his nose. "And I liked it a lot," he murmured in her ear.

"Callum—" she began.

He interrupted her again, his head lifting, the tawny spikes slowly invading the blue of his eyes. "The second time, you were sleepy and sweet." His mouth descended, and against her lips, he declared, "I liked that too." Sonia watched close up as his eyes turned fully golden. "A lot," he finished.

"Callum—"

"So, tell me, baby doll, what do we do in your dreams?"

It was then she realized that, yes, she was seriously *deeply* in trouble.

"Callum—"

"Do we do this?" he asked, his lips leaving hers to slide across her cheek to her ear, down her jaw. She felt the shiver slither lazily along her skin as his lips came back to hers and brushed them softly.

"I think—" she started, her lips moving under his.

He cut her off again. "And do we do this?"

He came off his forearms and his big, warm hands glided down her sides and in, over the small of her back and then down over her bottom as he gave her more of his weight, something which her body adored and therefore it automatically melted under his.

Oh my lord, she thought and bit her lip

Then she tried again. "Callum, can I—?"

"And do we do this?" he repeated before his head slanted and his lips took hers in a sweet light kiss.

She tried to move her head away, but since it was resting on a pillow she had no room to move.

His mouth broke from hers briefly to mutter, "And this?"

"Cal—"

Tactical error. Opening her mouth was a very bad idea. For this time he didn't give her a sweet light kiss.

This time, his tongue invaded her mouth and he gave her a deep searing kiss.

Regardless of what her body was coaxing her to do, Sonia managed to resist but without room for her head to move, her hands went to his shoulders and pushed.

Callum, on the other hand, managed to insist. He ignored her hands and gave her more of his weight, cupping her bottom and pulling her hips deeper to his.

She felt his hardness against her and the urge instantly came over her.

Primal, animal, an urge she felt sometimes in her dreams. An urge that she had often felt budding with other lovers, and they liked it, which meant they were always difficult to get rid of.

This one, though, didn't bud, causing her to behave slightly shameless.

It bloomed, causing her to behave highly wanton.

It was so strong, even though she tried to fight it, even though she vaguely feared it, with Callum covering her, his hardness pressed against her, his talented tongue invading her mouth, she was no match.

With a whimper, she capitulated. Her hands stopped pushing at his shoulders and her arms curled around his neck, pulling him even closer.

Then her tongue tangled with his.

His head slanted further, he growled into her mouth, and she felt it blister a path straight between her legs.

Her control annihilated and she gave in to the urge.

She fully opened her legs in invitation and his hips fell through. She kissed him back as her hips lifted, pressing insistently against his hardness.

In return, he ground his hips against hers and another sharper whimper escaped her throat as her nails grazed down his back.

His mouth tore from hers but it didn't leave her skin. It went down, over her jaw, down her neck, as his hand came up, sliding along her nightgown, up her side, her ribcage, covering her breast.

Sonia arched into it, searching, demanding.

His thumb slid over her nipple and her neck bowed, the whimper turning to a deep, hungry moan.

Callum came back, buried his face in her neck, his husky voice sounding at the skin below her ear.

"You like that?" he asked, his thumb repeating the gesture and Sonia repeated the moan. "You like it," he muttered and his thumb was joined with a finger, giving her nipple a rough glorious squeeze.

"Callum," she breathed, fire racing from nipple to between her legs, her head twisting round, her mouth searching for his.

He didn't disappoint. He gave her his mouth.

She gave him her kiss.

Planting a foot in the bed, she rolled him (and he let her). Settling her body on his big one, she embarked on a frenzied discovery. The taste of his whiskered jaw, his neck, the feel of his chest under her hands. She couldn't get enough in fast enough to suit and the more she had, the hungrier she became.

He allowed this then his hand twisted in her hair with a rough demanding pull that caused a delicious pain. He forced her mouth to his and gave her *his* kiss. Deeper, wetter, longer and Sonia couldn't stop herself from rubbing her most sensitive part the length of his rigid shaft.

"Jesus, baby doll," he groaned against her mouth, his hands coming to her hips, grasping her nightgown. She lifted up, wanting it to be gone, needing to feel his chest against her bared breasts.

He didn't hesitate. He yanked it off and tossed it away. His heated tawny eyes fell to her body straddling his, his hands drifting across her ribcage and up, but she dropped her chest and pressed it to his. His rough hair teased her nipples and it felt so great, her hips reflexively ground into his.

His hands found her breasts, thumbs grazing her nipples, fingers joining for a heady roll. Then he pushed her back and up, one hand tormenting her nipple, the other cupping her breast and maneuvering her to his mouth where his lips closed over her nipple and pulled.

His mouth on her felt so good, her back arched to demand more, but her head dropped down to watch him suckling as her arm flew out to the headboard to hold on.

Her body shuddered at the beauty of the sight and the sensations.

He switched breasts and she made a harsh noise as she ground deeper into his body. His hand left her breast and plunged into her panties, finding her, and it was so fantastic, she bucked against his fingers.

The minute she did, she was flying through the air, landing on her back, Callum pressed to her. His hand went back in her panties, his fingers twitching, vibrating at the exact perfect spot.

God, she'd never felt anything like that.

And it felt *good.*

Her arms circled him, her nails grazed his back, her hips undulated against his fingers, all the while her eyes were locked to his.

Her hand moved around, across his belly, down into his pajamas and she found him.

And he was huge, thick, long, and beautiful.

She had to have him.

Now.

"Wolf," she breathed her demand. "I want you inside me."

His eyes flashed and he slid a finger inside.

She gasped and ground down on his hand.

"In heat," he murmured, his voice guttural and supremely satisfied.

"Wolf…" A sliver of pleading pierced her tone as his words in her dream were uttered in real life.

His finger slid out of her but only to flick insistently against her sweet spot.

"You need to be ready for me."

She knew she did. She'd felt him. He was not your average man in *any* sense.

"I'm ready," she whispered.

"Little one—"

Her hand stroked then it fisted around him and she pulled him to her.

"Callum," she insisted, "I'm ready."

"Baby doll—"

Her hand tightened, he groaned, she stroked and tugged, and he groaned again.

Her mouth went to his and she demanded, "Fuck me, wolf."

Callum needed no further coaxing.

He moved and her panties were gone in a flash, whipped down her legs. His pajamas were pulled down his own.

Then he rolled into her, she wrapped her limbs around his massive body and felt the promise of him.

"Wolf…" Sonia breathed.

His hips reared back, her body tensed in delicious anticipation, and then he thrust inside, impaling her, seating himself to the root, filling her so full, so deep, she could swear he touched her womb.

He stopped and dropped his forehead to hers, his breathing labored.

In a tone filled with marvel, he murmured, "You took all of me."

She did and every inch of him was wonderful.

"I'm made for you," she whispered back and watched up close as his golden eyes glittered.

Then his mouth captured hers and he kissed her wet and hot while he fucked her, deep, rough, fast, and hard and she loved every stroke, every jolt. Her body, feeling right, feeling whole, gloried in it.

He rolled them until he was on his back, Sonia straddling him, and she took over, riding him with abandon, back arched, hips wild.

Lost in what they were doing, lost in him, full of him.

He curled up. An arm going around her waist, taking her out of her rhythm and focusing her on the beauty that was him, his face hard with almost savage desire before she lost sight of him as he twisted his torso to the nightstand. She ground her hips into his and watched as he opened the drawer and pulled out a long, slim, blue, beaten-leather case. He flicked it open with his thumb and drew out a length of delicate gold chain.

He tossed the case away and his eyes came to hers.

"Sonia," his voice was rough, "are you mine?"

Lost in the moment, immediately she replied, "I'm yours."

He made swift work of wrapping the gold chain around her waist and fastening it. She saw a small charm she couldn't make out dangling from it as it settled above her hips.

His hands spanned those hips and his mouth went to hers.

But his eyes were open and the gold was so intense, it seemed to be glowing and alive.

Then he said something that settled in her brain, her heart, and sliced a heated path down to their connected bodies.

"Baby doll, you're about to be claimed."

Before she could utter a noise, he moved her. Pulling her off him, he tossed her to the side on her belly. He shifted to his knees between her legs and violently yanked up her hips so she was on her knees but her head and torso were still in the bed.

His big hands wrapped around her hips, he impaled her on his shaft, again and again. It was wild, beautiful. Her head snapped back, her hair flying over her shoulders as she came up on her hands and reared her hips back with greedy need into his thrusting ones.

He leaned over her and fisted his fingers in her hair, muttering huskily, "That's it."

He was right. That was *it*. In fact, *it* was everything.

The whole world.

She felt it coming.

And it was so huge, she feared it.

So she fought it.

"Callum—" she whispered, sudden panic in her voice.

He pulled her upright using her hair but released it and his arms went around her, one hand slid to her breast and the one slid between her legs as he continued to plunge in and out of her.

"Give in to it," he coaxed in her ear, his breathing heavy.

She continued fighting it. It was too big, huge. It would destroy her.

But it was creeping in, invading, taking over. She wasn't going to be able to hold it back.

"I can't," she breathed.

"Submit." It was a command now. He meant to be obeyed. Every movement he made demanded it.

"Callum," she whispered, frantically fighting, and losing. "It's coming."

Then it came.

Her head reared back and her body bucked as it overwhelmed her, driving through her as he drove inside her, shattering her.

He twisted her head so his mouth was on hers, taking more, draining her.

In his arms, impaled on his shaft, with his mouth on hers, everything that was him claiming everything that was her, Sonia cried out sharply against his mouth. The noise pierced the air as she shuddered uncontrollably through the longest, hardest, most luxuriously consuming climax she'd ever had in her life.

At the same time Callum's arms circled her, possessing, protecting. One at her belly, one at her chest, he pressed her down as he drove up into her one last time and the guttural roar of his orgasm mingled with her piercing cry.

After, his breath thick in her ear, her own coming in slowing pants, he didn't move. Callum held her connected to him like he never wanted to let her go.

Then his hand drifted down, his fingers trailing the gold chain at her hips, he tweaked the charm that hung there, while doing so flicking his fingers against the sensitive skin at her hipbone.

Then his hips moved, pulling out briefly and surging back in one last time, a movement that cut through her delightfully, making her moan.

Finally, he announced, his voice husky but firm in her ear, "You're claimed."

She felt claimed, completely claimed, so claimed she felt *owned*.

Sonia shivered in his arms.

Those arms grew tight and he buried his face in her neck.

Before Sonia could catch a thought, he lifted her off him and set her gently on her knees in the bed but kept her held close.

Then he did something unusual. Something strange and poignant and beautiful. Something that messed with her mind and tore at her heart.

His arm around her waist moved, his hand drifting around, back, and down to cup her between her legs from behind.

Then he rubbed his palm against her.

Her hips bucked and she whimpered.

He sniffed.

She froze.

"God, baby doll," he groaned in her ear. "I wish you could smell us," he went on, his hand gliding reverently through their combined wetness seeping between her legs. "Perfect," he kept going. "Magnificent."

She *could* smell them.

And he was absolutely right.

He dipped low, his hand sliding up to her belly then down, over the inside of one thigh then the other, coating her.

She trembled against him.

This must be something else his people did.

It was shocking, it was intense, but it was also sexy and oddly sweet.

His hand left her and his arm wrapped around her again as his mouth went back to her ear.

"That's us I bathed you with, little one. *Us,*" he growled, the intensity of his tone proving the moment was profound. "And we're...fucking...*beautiful.*"

"Callum—" she started but didn't finish.

He fell to the bed, taking her with him and arranging her body fully on top of his.

He slid his fingers into her hair and tucked her face in his neck. Leaving his hand in her hair, his other hand cupped her behind.

"You weren't blonde, honey, after that, I'd think you were one of my own," he commented, his voice clearly content.

"What?" she whispered against the skin of his neck, not processing his words. After what happened, not processing anything but the fact that she was absolutely, seriously, totally in *trouble.*

"There are no blondes in my culture," he explained. "And my people are passionate, far more than most humans, and they like to play." His fingers dug into her bottom. "You, obviously, like to play." His hand slid up from her bottom to wrap around her waist and gave her a squeeze. "This pleases me," he muttered this last sounding pleased.

Very pleased.

Even smug.

Sonia didn't know what just happened or even *how* it happened or even *why* she let it go that far.

"Callum—"

He cut her off. "Is that how it was in your dreams?"

"Um...no, not quite," she answered automatically, lifting her head to look at him, trying to ignore the fact that he looked content *and* pleased *and* smug *and* it was a great look that did serious things to her innards, and she started again, "Callum—"

He lifted his head and brushed her lips with his as he gave her another squeeze with his arms.

"So what was it like in your dreams?" he asked, grinning at her.

She was so panicked, so desperate to get the conversation on track, though she didn't know what that track was yet. She hoped to do some serious back pedaling even if she couldn't imagine how she'd manage that considering she was naked in his arms and she'd just begged him to fuck her, she answered immediately, "Well, there was no gold chain and no sex and—"

His brows shot up and he interrupted her again with, "No sex?"

"No, we just talk for a while and get started with, um…things and then I always wake up," she replied hurriedly. "Listen—"

He broke in. "Things?"

"You know, start having sex and then I wake up," she told him then went on, "Callum, I'd like to talk—"

But he wasn't listening, he was chuckling then he tucked her face into his neck again and tightened his arms.

"What's funny?" she asked his neck.

"Poor baby," he murmured, his tone low but playful. "Twenty years I've been teasing you." He rolled into her, his head came up to look at her, his hands started to glide along her skin, and his voice was husky when he finished, "I've got a lot to make up for."

"Callum—"

She stopped speaking when he grinned again and it was so wicked, so satisfied, so unbelievably arrogant and knowing, she could do nothing but stare.

"You called me 'wolf,'" he stated.

Her body went tight.

Callum kept talking, or more accurately, teasing, "Nice to know I can cut through one of your grudges with a few kisses."

At his words, she forgot everything instantly and snapped, "It was more than a few kisses and anyway, I was not myself."

"If that wasn't you, honey, then I'll do everything I have to do to keep the Sonia I just fucked. The Sonia who came for me so hard I thought her shrieks were going to blow out the fucking windows."

She'd been wrong two days ago.

He wasn't a big bossy jerk.

He was an arrogant bastard.

She tried to push away, shoving at his shoulders, saying, "Of all the arrogant—"

She was writhing beneath him when he cut her off, burying his face in her neck, "That's it, baby doll, fight me. This should be fun."

She growled low in her throat.

He chuckled low in his.

She bucked and pushed away.

He caught her hips and hauled her under him, rolling his own hips until she was forced to spread her legs.

She stilled, her eyes locked on his, and she cried, "Get off me!"

"No, honey." He grinned at her, all haughty, arrogant king. "I'm going to get *in* you."

She gave his shoulders a mighty heave and his cell rang on the nightstand.

Both their heads twisted to it and both their eyes narrowed on it but for entirely different reasons.

"Fucking hell," he muttered, reaching a long arm out to nab it.

"Get off me," she demanded again as he looked at its display.

"Settle for a minute, little one," he ordered distractedly.

"Get...off...*me!*" she snapped and his eyes sliced to hers.

"Settle," he commanded, his voice a sharp, regal crack.

She settled because, apparently, King Not to Be Denied Due to Royal Birth Callum was lying between her legs.

He put his phone to his ear and said, "Callum."

Since she was close, she could hear the entire conversation.

"Cal, brother, you need to come down the mountain."

It was Calder.

"For fuck's sake, why?" Callum clipped.

"You remember what we talked about yesterday?" Calder inquired.

"Yes," Callum answered tersely.

"Well, we flipped that brother. He's talking. Talking *a lot*. This territory is infested. It's far more dicked up than we imagined. Mona's...hell, I don't know what Mona's been doing, but whatever the fuck it is, it's not her job. Someone has to deal with her and we need to start making moves or this shit is going to start traveling," Calder answered.

"How bad is it?" Callum asked.

"The scale doesn't go up to this bad," Calder replied and Sonia watched Callum close his eyes even as she saw his face set hard before he opened them when Calder kept speaking. "Pack up your mate and bring her ass down the mountain. I'm sure you'll find time to do her here. We got more important shit to see to."

Callum's eyes came to her but she stared at his shoulder angrily at the same time pretending she wasn't hearing a thing.

"The deed's done," Callum announced and it took everything Sonia had not to react to his words.

Good goodness.

Now she was a "deed" to be "done."

Well, he'd done it all right.

"Hallelujah," Calder hooted. "I knew it wouldn't take you long," he noted with deep respect before finishing, "Now, let's get to work."

"We'll be down by early afternoon," Callum returned.

"We'll have everything ready," Calder replied. "Later."

Sonia watched as Callum disconnected and his eyes went to her.

"I'm sorry, honey, we've got to cut this short and get back to the real world," he told her, and she had to give it to him, he sounded disappointed.

But she couldn't help but think how convenient all this was.

Callum (and his brothers) making it clear (several times) that his time in the cabin with her was something he considered a frustrating annoyance. In fact he himself referred to it as a "farce."

Callum and his brother's talk about whatever-it-was yesterday.

This morning, Callum wasted no time in seducing her, claiming her, and then his brother called to say it was imperative he get back down the mountain.

Royal duty sorted, time to wage war.

"Sonia?" he called and she focused on his handsome face. "We don't have a lot of time. We need to shower and go."

"Right," she whispered, her gaze drifting away while she felt something important curl up in the region of her heart.

"Baby doll," he murmured and she looked back to him. "We'll come back. As soon as we can. All right?"

Sonia wouldn't hold her breath.

"All right," she replied.

He leaned down, brushed his mouth against hers, and then knifed up, taking her with him.

She started to reach for her nightgown but with his hand in hers, he tugged her around the bed (yes, naked!) heading toward the bathroom.

"Callum," she called, trying to yank away her hand. "You shower first, I'll start packing."

"We leave the clothes and food up here. I've people that see to the cabin. And we're showering together," he announced and her heart skidded to a halt as he pulled her in the bathroom, let her go, and twisted immediately to the shower to turn on the taps.

"Um..." she began but gulped back whatever her next words were going to be when his hands came to her hips and he hauled her to his body.

"I know this is a lot and I know it's fast," he stated abruptly. "But soon, you'll be used to me, my body, the fact that I want you naked in my bed every night and naked in my shower every morning and naked anytime you don't *have* to wear clothes. So it's best that you start getting used to it now."

She gawked at him.

How much worse could it get?

As suddenly as he grabbed her, he let her go and stepped into the shower, clearly having no time to waste.

She stared at him, clearly having no say in the matter.

With nothing for it because, she was learning quickly, when King Callum wanted something, King Callum got it, her hands went to the chain still hanging at her hips and she started twirling it around to find the clasp.

"What the fuck are you doing?" Callum bit out from the shower and her head jerked up.

"I'm taking this off before I shower," she told him, her voice small in the face of his sudden anger.

He stepped right back out of the shower (getting water everywhere, incidentally), picked her up, put her in the shower, and joined her, not hesitating in reaching for the shampoo.

"That's a claiming chain, Sonia," he informed her. "Once it's put on, you never take it off."

She blinked up at him as the water fell on her and asked stupidly, "What?"

He turned his attention from squirting shampoo in his big palm to her.

"It's a claiming chain. You humans have wedding rings, my people have claiming chains."

Her mouth dropped open.

She closed it.

His words repeated in her head and her mouth dropped open again.

Then she whispered, "You're saying you *married* me this morning?"

He barely looked at her as he pivoted her out from under the spray and put himself in her place.

"Bound you to me, yes. For life. Same thing," he replied distractedly, mind on other things, *not* just informing her of the usually joyous fact that that morning they'd essentially been wed.

She stood frozen and stared as he massaged the shampoo in his hair.

And she stood this way for a while.

He'd rinsed, and when he saw her standing there, his eyes narrowed.

Then he said, using a voice filled with strained patience, "Get a move on, honey. There's things to do."

She jolted out of her shocked stupor and automatically reached for her shampoo.

There were things to do.

Those things didn't include Sonia having a moment to process the fact that in three days her life had been turned on its head.

She used to have a quiet life, working in a shop she loved, living in a farmhouse amongst neighbors who were good people. It wasn't a great life. It was a lonely life. But there were moments of contentment and even happiness.

Now she was queen to an unknown people. She was the destined mate to a man she barely knew but she *did* know he didn't want her. And she'd just essentially gotten married to him.

As that thing that curled up in her heart tightened and prepared to die, Sonia commenced showering, naked, with her husband, a man she'd met three days before and she wasn't even certain she liked.

And she hurried through it.

Because *he* had things to do.

CHAPTER NINE
DUTY

CALLUM PULLED his SUV into the sweeping drive of The Territorial Mansion.

As he did he realized during the two and a half hour drive his mind was so focused on what was happening amongst his people, and what he had to do about it, both imminently and in the near future, he'd not said a word to Sonia.

He glanced toward her in the passenger seat and noted her eyes were studying the mansion with curiosity.

Fuck, she was pretty, sitting beside him, wearing an ice-blue thermal, a pale pink quilted vest with a collar that framed the elegant line of her neck, a woolly pastel green scarf wrapped around that neck and dangling down the front, and slightly faded jeans that rode low on her hips and cupped her ass brilliantly. He'd given her the tan leather low-heeled boots his mother bought her that he'd kept outside in the truck and she'd chosen a belt that matched.

At the cabin, while he called Ryon and Caleb to brief them on what he wanted them to do prior to his arrival, he'd allowed her time to put on a light coat of makeup and dry her thick blonde hair so it fell in sleek gleaming waves down her shoulders and back.

Examining her loveliness, the casual flair with which she wore her clothes, remembering their morning, knowing his chain hung about her hips, still hearing her heated cries and feeling her pulsating around his cock with her uninhibited orgasm, Callum felt elated.

Today, his people were going to meet their queen.

And she was fucking perfect.

"We're here," he told her, slowing as they approached the wide-stepped entry to the mansion.

"Where's…" she hesitated, still staring at the building, "here?"

"Territorial Mansion of the Western Territories of the Americas," he replied absentmindedly, his thoughts moving from the pleasant ones of Sonia to the unpleasant ones of what he would soon be forced to do, not knowing his words would sound preposterous to her as to him, they did not.

He knifed out of the car and to his vague displeasure saw she'd alighted without his assistance by the time he rounded the back to her side.

He looked up to the building and saw two of his warriors standing guard.

They appeared to be standing outside chatting as the mansion, even though it had extensive walled gardens and its function was governmental, was ensconced within the city and open for passersby to see. Humans thought it housed a large wealthy family with a goodly number of friends, though the United States government knew differently. But humans had no idea its purpose and therefore soldiers guarding the doors would seem unusual. When amongst humans, wolves did their utmost to appear "normal," and because of that, the men, who were guards, looked like they were having a casual chat.

Callum guided Sonia away from her opened door and closed it. Then he took her hand and led her up the stairs.

His two soldiers bowed their heads briefly to their king and queen, their eyes inquisitive on Sonia, grins on their faces.

Sonia automatically smiled back and nodded, not regally, sociably, as if she was walking down the street, caught a passerby's eye, and gave them a warm neighborly smile.

At her gesture, his warriors' grins turned to wide smiles.

Callum's hand tightened in hers.

Yes, Callum thought, his people were going to love her.

They entered the large entryway that led to a long, wide hall.

Ryon and Caleb were walking toward them. Caleb was carrying a thin manila folder.

"All's ready," Caleb called.

"I'll want to read the briefing report before I go in," Callum replied.

Caleb nodded and he and Ryon turned and walked back a short distance toward a closed door. They opened it, stepped through, and Callum and Sonia followed.

It was Mona's office, complete with baronial desk, gleaming wood floors on which large, thick, expensive Persian rugs lay, priceless antique furniture and heavy ornate curtains at the tall wide windows.

He saw Sonia looking around, her eyes wide taking in the opulence. Seeing what his mate saw, Callum distractedly noted with some scorn that Mona's penchant toward lavishness was evident in the government building she'd overseen creating. These were not the usual surroundings of a wolf, nothing like it.

He stopped them close to Mona's desk, leaned a hip against it, brought Sonia in close, dropped her hand, and held his own out for the file, which Caleb gave him.

His mother had stood by his father's side in everything. This was the queen's purpose, a physical show of support to the king as well as the demonstration of the solidarity of all wolves.

Regan had been with Mac during strategy sessions and on campaigns. Though she didn't fight, she also didn't complain when her accommodation was just a tent or two beds pushed together in a barrack with blankets strung around them for privacy. Also she had been at his side during summits, diplomatic assemblies, and war tribunals.

As queen, Regan performed her duties silently. Her presence was all that was required. Her understanding of events would be important during the private times she shared with Mac. She could hardly offer him what he needed if she didn't know what was happening.

There were times of separation, but they were brief and they were rare.

Sonia, Callum had decided, would do the same.

Without a word, he opened the file and began reading the report.

He felt Sonia move away and heard her say softly, "Hi, Ryon."

He glanced up and saw Sonia lift up on her toes and press her cheek to Ryon's then she leaned back and tipped her head to smile up at him.

"Hey there, Sonia," Ryon smiled down at her in turn. "How are you handling this? It's all a bit weird, isn't it?"

"Um..." she mumbled, the smile never leaving her face and the way she said her next words pointedly reflected they were an understatement, "A bit."

Ryon chuckled.

Sonia's smile brightened.

Callum's jaw tightened.

Ryon had a way with female humans, Callum knew that.

He just didn't appreciate—at all—Ryon using it with Callum's very recently and definitely spectacularly claimed bride.

But it was something his cousin didn't hesitate doing, either yesterday or now. It was also something Sonia responded to, and further, it was something Callum didn't fucking like.

Before he could say anything, Sonia turned to Caleb and said, "Hi, Caleb."

She leaned into Callum's brother and gave him a cheek touch and a smile as well but it was nowhere near as fond as the one she gave Ryon.

Still, Callum noted that even Caleb was grinning down at her with a rapt expression on his face, as if bewitched.

"Hey there, sis." Caleb made a reply that caused Sonia's body to twitch.

"I've never really been a 'sis,'" she whispered wistfully.

"You are now."

Then *Caleb* received a bright smile from Callum's bride.

Callum felt his temper rising, and because of this, when he said, "Sonia," her name lashed through the room sharp and annoyed.

She started and turned to him, her eyes confused, her face growing pale.

"Come here," Callum ordered and she hesitated briefly but moved to his side.

Both Ryon and Caleb looked at him. Ryon with annoyance. Caleb, Callum was surprised to see, with barely concealed anger.

He ignored their expressions, looked down at Sonia, and instructed, "The queen belongs at the king's side."

"I was three feet away," she replied quietly, her face growing even paler.

"The queen belongs at the king's side," he repeated, watched her swallow and felt the air around them growing thick, this coming from his family.

His gaze sliced through his brethren, nonverbally making his displeasure known, and he looked back down at the papers.

He read the three page report and the words erased Sonia, Ryon, and Caleb from his mind.

He flipped the folder shut and looked at Ryon.

"Bloody hell, Mona's an idiot," he remarked.

"Always was," Ryon returned.

"Mac fucked up, installing her as Governor of this Territory," Callum noted with frustration, handing the file back to Caleb.

Mac had left him with a rebellion, which, in a year with studied brutality, he'd quashed, forcing their signature on a treaty they vowed never to sign, and four short years later, they broke.

Other than that, and the occasional insurrection which was normal amongst intense, temperamental, and often quarrelling wolves, Mac's realm was peaceful and ordered.

There was no mess.

Except Mona.

"He thought it was a diplomatic move," Ryon replied, his eyes sliding to Sonia. "Titium was displeased with what went on." Ryon looked back at Callum. "And he'd make a formidable enemy."

Callum knew this.

During their brief fling ages ago, something which Callum engaged in regularly, a fact he thought Mona understood as every she-wolf did, she'd become infatuated with him. Because of her obsession, scraping her off had been unpleasant and eventually diplomatically sensitive.

Titium, Governor of Europe and a highly respected warrior, had spoiled his daughter. What she wanted, Titium gave her. Unfortunately, Mona was ambitious as well as obsessive. In order for her to leave his son alone, Mac had installed her as Governor of the then sparsely populated Western Territories of America.

They'd all been surprised when she'd been passably skilled at handling her province over the years, even as it emerged and populated.

They'd also all been surprised when the years passed and she never found her lifemate, something which his father knew would turn her attention away from Callum.

However, apparently, since Mac's death, she'd lost focus on her responsibilities.

This, too, Callum understood and it irritated him.

Callum was now king and the spoiled ambitious Mona would want his attention even more than before. And she'd want it so desperately, it wouldn't matter what form that attention would take.

She'd want it enough to fuck up and draw him to her territories. Something which, unless there was an insurrection, Callum, and Mac before him, rarely had to do as his other Governors ruled their provinces efficiently. In fact, it was something the Governors took pains in *not* doing because Callum's attention, unless it was for an official ceremony or a social visit, wasn't something they'd seek.

It was likely the she-wolf probably didn't even know she was doing it.

Callum took Sonia's hand and moved toward the door, muttering, "Let's do this."

"Hang on," Ryon called and Callum stopped, pulling Sonia to his side.

"Have you briefed her on protocol?" Ryon asked, getting close.

"Sorry?" Callum replied, his thoughts anywhere but on protocol, which was something, as king, he didn't have to concern himself with. Only those around him did.

Ryon gave him an aggravated scowl but turned gentled eyes to Sonia.

"Sonia, you're about to walk into a throne room in the official capacity as our queen," he explained softly. "Everyone in that room will bow to you and Callum. If you were alone, you'd walk to the throne, seat yourself, and tell them to rise. As you're with Callum, you don't say anything. Don't speak at all until Callum tells you that you can. He'll lead you to the throne and give the order. In a minute, as this happens, people will talk, but you won't. Your duty is to observe in silence, don't say a word. But pay attention, love, to everything that's going on. You'll understand why later. Okay?"

Callum found he was annoyed with himself that he hadn't thought to instruct her on the way down the mountain.

He found himself further annoyed that Sonia was gazing up at Ryon with open gratitude.

She nodded to Ryon. Callum gave her hand a tug, and without looking at her, he led a silent Sonia through the mansion and up the wide staircase to the throne room.

The doors were opened as they approached and he heard Sonia take in a surprised breath before he guided her through.

The room was filled with his warriors and the mansion's detail. Every one of them, including Mona, who was standing at the foot of the dais, dropped into the deep, heads lowered, ceremonial bow.

He strode through the room, hand in hand with Sonia whose step had faltered. Looking down at her, he saw her staring in fearful awe at the fifty large wolves who were bowed low.

He lifted her hand and tucked it under his arm, drawing her closer to him in an effort to offer her comfort.

She looked up at him, her eyes still startled, and he nodded down at her but didn't wait for her response and led her up the stairs to the throne sitting there.

Without delay, as his father had done before him and every king, prince, duke, governor or noble in history did with their mate, he sat on the throne and pulled her into his lap.

Instantly, she made a surprised noise and tried to jerk away.

His arms tightened around her, he gave her a warning shake, and her alarmed gaze flashed to his. Whatever she saw there made her stare, then her eyes went blank and her body settled into his.

"Rise," he commanded, the assemblage took their feet and all eyes turned to the throne.

He knew what they saw.

If he'd not claimed her, she'd be standing at the right side of his throne.

But, claimed and bound, now their queen, she was in his lap.

He felt another thrill of elation, understanding the overwhelming importance of the occasion as did everyone in the room.

Everyone except, he didn't think to note, Sonia.

Watching their eyes scan Sonia, he allowed himself a moment to glory in it, knowing what they saw. Even if it had nothing to do with him and everything to do with fate, he was still exceedingly proud of it.

Then he commenced business.

Not looking at Mona, he searched the room and focused on Mona's Lieutenant Governor.

"Saint," he called and the tall warrior walked toward the dais.

Callum knew Saint well. Saint had fought alongside Callum. He was a strong crafty warrior and a good friend. Thirty-one years ago, Mac had installed Saint at Mona's side to make certain she didn't discover Sonia's existence and to keep an eye on Mona.

He'd done both.

As was standard practice, Saint had also been interrogated, but not surprisingly he had no connection to the plot or, until recently, any idea the rebellion had chosen the Western Territories to assemble.

He had no idea because Mona didn't.

However, it had been Saint who'd cottoned on something was happening. He'd uncovered the plot against Sonia and revealed it to Callum.

Over the years, Saint had been reporting with growing frequency that working with Mona was becoming more and more of a chore.

Callum, unfortunately, knew everything about Mona was a chore and hadn't thought much of it.

This was his mistake.

He was about to rectify it.

When Saint stopped at the foot of the dais, Callum spoke. "By the end of the day, I'll want a shortlist of names of those you feel would best replace Desdemona as Governor of this Territory." Callum heard Mona's angry gasp and felt Sonia go still in his arms, but he continued, "If you're interested, put your name at the top of that list."

"Yes, your grace," Saint replied, relief in his eyes and a small smile tugging at his lips.

Callum's gaze went to Mona. "Desdemona, I'm removing you as Governor, effective immediately."

She leaned forward and started, "But, your grace—"

"Under your nose, a rebellion amassed in your Territory," he announced, cutting her off. "You're well aware that one of the most important parts of your duty is to be my eyes and ears in this region and to inform me if there's news of an insurrection. Nevertheless, you've flagrantly ignored missives from Scotland as to how to oversee your people to make certain that didn't happen. This meant they knew your region was weak and targeted it. There were even two amongst your personal guard who were involved. Further, because of your personal failings, for thirty-one years you put my father *and* me in a disadvantageous position because we couldn't trust you and your guard to protect my queen. Now we have a situation where, if you were doing your job, *you* would have sorted it and it would not have required my attention or I would have been aware of it long before now. But it's far worse. It's a situation where known rebels have accumulated in your region, they've conspired to break the treaty, and all of this has placed my queen at risk."

"King Callum—" Mona began.

Callum interrupted her tersely, "Mona, you best not speak. We both know your rule of this province has been a joke since it started."

Her beautiful face twisted, and, unwisely, she ignored his command and stated, "Your father never complained."

"That wasn't my father's way," Callum returned.

"*My* father—" she began, her tone turning threatening.

"*Your* father has no choice but to accept this decision," Callum retorted. "You're released," he declared with finality. He watched her body jolt and her temper flair but continued, "For placing my queen in jeopardy, you should be punished. But with respect to your father, instead, I'm giving you a year to find your mate and settle. After that year, if you don't, you'll be sequestered."

Her face paled before it flushed and she breathed, "*Sequestered?*"

"Is that not what we do when one of our females refuses to seek her mate?" Callum inquired.

"But that's for…it's for…" she paused and snapped, "for females who are mad!"

"Prove your sanity," Callum invited and saw her face change in a way he, in his impatience and anger with her, and his father in his kindness and diplomacy, had heretofore missed.

Desdemona, daughter of Titium, wasn't stupid, spoiled, and ambitious.

She wasn't nuts.

She was fucking crazy.

"I've no need to find my mate—" she started to declare.

"Desdemona—" Callum tried to break in.

She continued mutinously, "Because he's sitting right in front of me!"

The air grew dense with shock and the sounds of shuffling feet. Sonia's already tight body turned to marble against his frame and he heard her soft intake of breath.

Ryon approached to put an end to Mona's insolence but Callum lifted a hand to stop him.

The deeper she dug her grave, the deeper Callum could bury her in it, and he wanted her buried so deep he never had to see her face again.

"You declare this in front of your queen?" Callum asked with deceptive calm.

"Years ago, I felt the connection," she threw out. "And, no matter what you say, Cal, you did too. I know it."

Sonia's body moved, those movements were slight but filled with disquiet.

He gave his mate a comforting squeeze before he said derisively, "Hardly, Desdemona."

"What we had was good!" she cried desperately, leaning farther forward.

"What we had was sex," Callum returned dismissively and Sonia jerked in his arms, which didn't squeeze comfortingly this time, they tightened.

"I'm consort to a king!" Mona declared madly, moving up the steps.

Ryon shot forward, hooked an arm firmly around her waist, and stopped her.

Callum's voice lowered, but even so, he knew every wolf in the room could hear.

"You were nothing but a fuck, Mona. A good one, but I'd had better before," he moved slightly, his eyes never leaving Mona as he rubbed his temple against Sonia's hair, making his message clear before he murmured, "And definitely better since."

He heard Sonia's breathing escalate as he saw her chest start to rise and fall with agitation, but she kept her seat which satisfied him. This was an intense situation amongst a passionate people, something she wasn't used to but she was handling herself, as he had guessed she would, brilliantly.

Mona didn't handle herself nearly as well.

Fighting against Ryon's hold, she snapped, "But she's blonde. You *hate* blondes."

"I've changed my mind," Callum returned coolly.

To that, Mona's arms went ramrod straight, her face grew red, and she shrieked, "She is *not* our queen. She's fucking *human*."

Irreverence to his queen spoken aloud during an official assembly in a throne room.

Callum held back his smile.

Mona was so deep, even Titium couldn't dig her out.

"Get her out of here, Ry," he ordered.

"Released to find her mate?" Ryon asked, his lips twitching.

"Fuck no. Sequester her," Callum answered.

"*No!*" Mona shrieked while she struggled.

"Okeydoke," Ryon muttered and a few wolves chuckled.

Sonia, he noted vaguely, had clenched her fists.

As Ryon handed Mona off to two warriors who led her struggling body out of the room, Caleb climbed the dais and stood at his right side. Then his deep voice rang out in the vast room.

"Are there those in this company who have issue with our human queen?"

No one spoke.

Caleb went on, "Are there those whose allegiance lies with Desdemona?"

More silence.

Caleb's voice then announced loudly, "Then behold our new queen!"

Everyone looked at Sonia. Sonia blushed.

"You're laying it on a bit thick, aren't you, brother?" Callum muttered.

There were several chuckles, a few full-blown laughs, and a room full of smiles.

"I thought the situation warranted it," Caleb replied with a bold grin as he leaned against the side of his brother's throne.

Callum threw him a look then turned his head, his mouth seeking Sonia's ear, and he asked softly, "Would you like to meet your warriors, baby doll?"

She twisted her neck and her green eyes searched his. She pulled in breath through her nose and finally nodded.

He stood up, lifting her to her feet. He slid his arm around her shoulders and tucked her into his side.

To his men in the room, he stated, his voice proclaiming proudly, "It's time for you to meet Sonia."

"Jesus, it's brilliant finally to have something to do," Calder announced, sitting back in his chair and grinning broadly.

Callum studied his brother from his seat behind a desk cluttered with the remains of the meal they'd eaten there while going through intelligence reports and notes on interrogations. For hours, throughout all of this, except for when Caleb had escorted her to the bathroom, Sonia had sat silently in his lap, even when they ate.

Calder, Callum knew, if he had not been of royal blood, would undoubtedly be the leader of an insurrection. All wolves had an abundance of energy, a zest for life, strength in their opinions, and none of them shied away from a fight.

Calder was all that and a great deal more.

Calder, more impatient and volatile even than Callum, was a brilliant warrior, if a flawed strategist, who appeared to be at his most relaxed in the middle of a bloody battle.

His brother, Callum decided, needed to find his fucking mate.

And his brother, Callum decided, once this was finished, would go on a quest to seek her. He'd hand down the order himself.

"Though," Calder went on, his eyes flashing to Sonia before he grinned. "It's disappointing that we're not going to have the Mating Ceremony. You'd love that, Sonia," he told her. "Our people like a good party and a Mating is the fucking best."

"Maybe after this is over, Callum will give Sonia a ceremony," Ryon suggested, his eyes soft on Callum's mate.

Callum's eyes were anything but soft on his cousin.

Jesus, if he didn't know better, he'd think Ryon had a thing for her.

"A Royal Mating is even better," Caleb threw in, also grinning at Sonia. "A fucking blast."

Sonia grinned back at Caleb and Callum's arms gave her a squeeze to capture her attention.

This worked, her face swung to his.

"Would you like that, little one?" he asked gently.

She regarded him a moment before she shrugged.

"We'll talk about it later," he told her and she nodded. Callum looked at Saint. "Are our quarters prepared?"

Sonia's body jerked in his arms but Callum's attention was on Saint who was answering. "Yes, actually. They have been since you arrived. Mona ordered it."

"At least she did something," Caleb muttered and Saint laughed.

"Callum," Ryon called and Callum's gaze swung to his cousin and saw his eyes were *still* on Callum's bride. "Since this is going to go down here, and you'll likely be here awhile, why don't you stay at Sonia's?"

At Ryon's words, Sonia instantly relaxed in Callum's arms and he caught her throwing Ryon another very grateful smile.

"Fuck, Ryon, what are you on about? The king always stays at the mansion," Calder put in.

"Yes, and a female of our kind would know and be prepared for that," Ryon replied patiently. "A human in the process of being initiated to our culture, which is probably a bit overwhelming, Calder, might like the comforts of home while she gets oriented."

Sonia pressed her lips together and sighed, clearly agreeing with his cousin.

Callum would never have considered this. Then again, Callum had very little experience with female humans except, of course, fucking them.

"Would you like to go home, Sonia?" he asked, her head tipped back instantly and she nodded, this time happily, with her eyes bright on *him*, to which he smiled and murmured, "Then we'll take you home."

Which was where they were going now.

It was high time for her injection and after their play this morning he was impatient to have her again.

Further, the idea of having her in her sweet welcoming bedroom lit by Christmas lights was an idea he liked greatly. He just hoped the cleaners he'd commanded to be sent to her house had successfully scoured away all traces of the bloody mess he'd made of her two attackers.

He stood, taking Sonia with him, and setting her on her feet. "Calder, you're off tonight," he told his brother and Calder nodded. He then looked at Saint. "We'll meet tomorrow to discuss the turnover." Saint lifted his chin and Callum then looked at Ryon and Caleb. "You know what to do." They both nonverbally indicated they understood his order.

Then he took Sonia's hand and led her from the room.

His SUV was at the bottom of the steps where he'd left it and he helped Sonia into her seat before taking his own, starting the truck, and pointing them toward her farmhouse.

He'd driven several miles before the silence in the cab caught his attention and it finally occurred to him that Sonia had another full, turbulent, likely mystifying day.

"You okay?" he asked.

She was silent.

"Baby doll?" he prompted, not taking his eyes from the road.

She remained silent.

He glanced at her to see her arms were crossed on her chest, the bag filled with her medication in her lap, and she was glaring through the windscreen.

"Sonia?"

"Oh, am I allowed to speak now?" she queried sarcastically.

"What?"

"Nothing," she snapped. "Just take me home."

Fucking hell. She was pissed about something.

"Sonia, tell me what's bothering you," he ordered gently.

"Nothing. I'm perfectly fine and I'll be *more* fine when I'm finally *home*."

Callum decided that was probably not true because it appeared they would be arguing when they arrived at her home. He wasn't going to engage in one in the truck. Further, he had to take that time to control his temper that she obviously didn't realize today, regardless of how delightfully it started, the rest had been unpleasant for him to say the least. Furthermore, the coming days, or weeks, and (although he hoped to God not) possibly months would be busy and taxing.

Therefore she'd failed in her responsibility to provide him what he'd *thought* he'd explained to her during their second day at the cabin was her duty to provide. An outlet. A release. Be that in the form of a casual conversation in an SUV about his day, holding her cuddled on her sweet bed in her sweet room and talking with her about his concerns about his people, or fucking her so hard that when she came she cried out his name.

The latter of which was how he definitely decided he'd like to process his day.

And that was exactly how he was going to do it.

He turned into the short drive at the side of her house, parking behind the door of her garage, and he shut off the engine.

She didn't wait for him to help her from the SUV (another issue he had with her that he decided, astutely, to bring up later). She dropped down from the truck and stormed up to her dark house.

She stood at her front door, arms crossed, her bag with her meds dangling from her fingers, as he took his time (to calm his temper further, an effort which failed) sauntering to her house.

"I don't have the key," she told him when he arrived at her side using a voice that made this clear it was an accusation.

He had her key.

Saint had given it to him the day he'd arrived. It was on the ring with his truck keys, his SUV being something else Saint had provided for him.

He used the key to let them in while she glared at his key ring like she was willing it to combust in his fingers.

When they entered, her alarm started beeping. She turned to it and punched in the code then stomped into the house.

Callum took off his coat while slowly Christmas lights, inside and out, started twinkling from everywhere.

Callum glanced around.

Ryon wasn't wrong. Sonia seriously had a thing about Christmas.

He listened to her tramping around upstairs as he went to her clean pristine kitchen and opened the fridge, praying she had beer.

She didn't.

She didn't even have a bottle of chilled white wine.

He was searching the cupboards for spirits when she stormed in, having divested herself of her vest and scarf, and her eyes narrowed on her mail neatly piled on the counter.

"I see someone's been taking care of my house," she announced ungraciously and walked to the mail, snatching it from the counter. Not looking at him, she shuffled through it while she demanded to know, "Did you arrange that?"

"Yes," he replied, turning back to open another cabinet in which he saw, thankfully, she had a number of bottles of liquor, and one of them, to his great fortune, contained a very good whisky.

"I shudder to think of the state of my store considering I disappeared into thin air during Christmas season." She aimed a glare in his direction as he discovered where she kept her glasses. "My girls are probably freaked!"

"Only if they have the uncanny ability of clairvoyance," Callum replied calmly. "Regan arranged for one of our people, a woman who has a goodly amount of retail experience considering her mate owns Harrinton's department stores, to tell them you had an urgent situation that called you away but arranged for her to manage the store in your absence."

This knowledge gave her a start, as it would considering there was a

Harrinton's in every exclusive mall in the country. They were highly lucrative ventures and were known as the elite shopping experience.

He ignored her reaction and the fact that she didn't express her gratitude as she had to Ryon *three times* when *he'd* displayed *his* thoughtfulness, and turned to pour his whisky.

She threw her mail on the counter and stomped from the room.

He listened to her crashing around upstairs as he turned his hips to the counter, sipped his whisky, and practiced controlled breathing.

This didn't help.

Some time later, he put his empty glass on the counter, switched off the light, and followed her up the stairs.

He found her in her bedroom wearing a silvery-gray knit nightgown with a thin edge of white lace at the bodice and hem. The nightgown hugged her curves and came down to her knees. Her face was cleaned of makeup and she was throwing back the covers on the bed.

"Sonia, it's time for your injection," he told her.

"Yes, it was. That's why I gave it to myself," she retorted, climbing on the bed, and seating herself with her shoulders against the headboard.

At this news Callum's body went still as his anger escalated exponentially.

"I'm sorry?" he asked quietly.

She nabbed a tube from her nightstand. Not looking at him, she squirted lotion into her hand, bent forward, and started to massage it into her foot.

"I gave it to myself," she repeated.

The only thing from the cabin she'd packed was her medication. She didn't need anything else, his people would see to the dirty laundry and food. And, as they'd be returning, hopefully soon, it would be good that she had clothes and toiletries there. In fact, he'd order her to stock what she needed so they could return there at his whim.

He came into the room and stopped at the foot of her bed.

"I thought I explained I'd be giving you your injections."

She shifted her attention to her other foot but not to him. "You did."

"Sonia, look at me," he demanded.

She slammed the tube of lotion down on her nightstand and then turned to face him. Or, more accurately, glare at him.

"I'll not tolerate another defiance like that again," he stated.

Her head tilted to the side. "You won't? Well then..." she leaned forward and snapped, "*good*. Because you won't be defied because you won't be *around*."

He felt his muscles grow taut as his control on his temper started slipping.

"Perhaps you'd like to explain that," he invited in a way that said, very clearly, she wouldn't.

Recklessly, she did it anyway.

"After today, I've decided I don't want to be your queen. After today, I've decided I don't want *anything* to do with *you*. Not," she stated boldly, "your people, who all seem very nice, except that crazy woman who was, sadly, though you didn't seem to notice it, not well at all. But *you*. I don't want anything to do with *you*."

"Little one," he advised softly as he moved to the side of the bed, "I'd stop talking now."

"You would? Well, of course you would, since all day you've been saying *a lot* but not much of it *good*. However, since I haven't been allowed to talk nearly *all day*, I've got a lot of words left in my stockpile."

He stopped beside the bed and watched her nab a tub, open it, and start to rub moisturizer in her face.

And he watched her do this as he sought patience.

Finally, he explained, "As Ryon told you, you weren't allowed to speak in the throne room. You *didn't* speak of your own accord the rest of the day. I thought you were quiet because you were letting things sink in."

She slapped the tub down and looked up to him. "I wasn't. I had no idea what was going on! No one told me anything. Including the fact I could speak, which, I will note, you didn't even notice I didn't!"

"Sonia—"

"However," she broke in, "the fact that I *can't* for any length of time is...is...*medieval*! And that you made me sit in your lap during that... that...whatever-it-was, was..." She paused and cried, "I don't even know what it was!"

"What it was, was the way of my people," he told her.

"What it was, was *your* way because *you* are king," she shot back, grabbing another tube. "Which brings us back to my earlier point that I'm done with this queen business. Done. You can go now," she finished, dismissing him.

Dismissing *him*.

Callum lost what hold he had on his patience at the same time he lost his temper.

She'd opened the tube and started to squirt something in her palm when Callum tore it from her hand and tossed it on her nightstand. It skidded through all of the other tubes, bottles, and tubs sitting there, leaking lotion the entire way, and she glared at the mess.

He leaned down, grabbed her ankles, and hauled her down the bed.

"What are you—?"

He then entered the bed and settled his weight on top of her.

"Get off me," she demanded, shoving at his shoulders and writhing underneath him.

"Sonia, look at me."

"Get off!"

"*Look at me, goddamn it!*" he roared, she stilled and glared at him. "You want instruction, I'll give it to you but you fucking look at me when I'm speaking to you and you better fucking pay attention."

"You have my attention, King Callum," she retorted sarcastically and he sucked in breath at her tone.

Then he spoke. "Do not disrespect me even in private," he said evenly, calmly, her eyes narrowed but she snapped her mouth shut. "Good thinking," he approved tersely and went on, "I, obviously, should have explained this more clearly earlier but I didn't. Now I am. The queen's duty is to support her king. You stand by my side or sit in my lap, however I want it, and you listen, you learn, and then, after I perform *my* duties, which can often be not so much fucking fun, you're available for me."

"Available for you?" she asked angrily.

"Available for me," he repeated.

"And what does that mean?"

"It means whatever the fuck I want it to mean."

She stared at him, he watched realization dawn, then she rolled her eyes to the headboard and muttered, "I was right...medieval."

"Sonia—"

Her eyes rolled back to his and she stated tartly, "Get off me, Callum. You didn't give me a choice but I choose no. This is the twenty-first century and *my* culture doesn't tell women to be silent nor do men make women sit in their laps during official proceedings."

"My culture does," he returned. "And I *did* give you the choice and you jumped at it, I'll remind you, pretty fucking gleefully. While you sat connected to me, I asked you if you were mine. You didn't fucking hesitate saying yes. Then, the minute you reared into my cock when you were on your knees with my chain around your waist, you embraced my culture, and there's no going back now."

Her eyes grew wide in horror before she snapped, "That's crazy!"

"That may be, but you did it. After twenty years of dreaming of me and not having me you were obviously gagging for it and the minute you got your chance you fucking jumped at it. Or more to the point, opened your legs for it, rode it, and fucking *ground into it*, moaning the whole goddamned time."

Her head jerked and her voice lowered, sounding hurt, but Callum was too angry to notice. "Please tell me you didn't just say that."

"I did because *you* did," he returned. "And I know you'll do it again."

Her wide eyes widened further and her body froze beneath his.

"Callum—"

He dipped his face closer to hers and his tone was deadly when he asked, "You want to know why I know that, little one?"

"Callum—"

"Because you're not going anywhere. I'm fucking well not going anywhere. Right now, you're going to perform your queenly duties by letting me use that sweet little body of yours to deal with my day and you're going to love every...*fucking*...minute of it."

She opened her mouth to speak.

Or yell.

But Callum got there first.

Sliding a hand in her hair and fisting it, he held her head steady and kissed her, rough and hard, his tongue invading and seizing.

She fought him the entire time.

Making furious noises in her throat, she bucked under him, pushed at him, and when that didn't work, she scratched him.

He felt her nails ripping through his shirt, piercing his skin. He tore his mouth away from hers at the pain and she took advantage. Rolling him slightly away from her, she slid out from under him and nearly got to her feet when he tagged her at the waist and tossed her back to the bed.

She grunted with frustrated rage and renewed her attack and Callum found, to his utter delight, she was a vicious and cunning little fighter who'd not only rival, but best any she-wolf of his experience.

So as not to harm her using his full strength with which he could break her in two, he wasn't able to subdue her. Their rough play continued and he enjoyed every fucking second of it.

Their breathing escalated and he noticed her struggles diminish. Her pushing had turned to touching. She'd started biting him and in doing so, used her tongue liberally. And he could feel her gliding her nose along his neck, taking in the scent of him, an odd thing for a human to do but it aroused him greatly.

She didn't even notice when she stopped fighting him and started struggling to get his clothes off his body.

But Callum noticed.

He decided in that instant to allow her defiance. Hell, he'd even incite it if this was to be his reward.

They were naked and she was as she was that morning, all over him with her hands, mouth, and tongue, touching, tasting, licking, rubbing herself against him as if she couldn't get enough fast enough. Callum couldn't believe his good fortune that destiny chose a greedy little human in heat to be his queen.

She was fucking perfect.

But it was time he had his fill.

He rolled her to her back and used his hands, mouth, and tongue on her, all over her, and she was greedy for that too. Arching against him, her hands coaxing and demanding, her nails scraping or diving into his hair to hold him to her.

When Callum's mouth was at her belly, Sonia spread her legs and Callum accepted her sweet invitation. He settled between them, ran his hands up the backs of her thighs, cocking them and then throwing her calves over his shoulders.

Finally, she was right there.

The scent of her was unbelievable. He'd wanted to taste her since he'd smelled it that first night when he'd rescued her from her kidnappers.

He lowered his mouth to her and she was just as sweet as her scent promised.

The minute his mouth touched her, she went completely still a moment before he heard the low sexy whimper escape the back of her throat. Then she jerked her hips up, clearly always greedy his Sonia, demanding more.

He smiled against her and gave it to her.

As he worked her with his mouth, her movements became more agitated and her whimpers came faster through her panting until he pulled away.

When he did, she cried desperately, "No!"

He moved over her and rolled them so he was on his back.

"You stopped," she accused, squirming on top of him.

He grinned at her and lifted his head to bury his face in her neck.

He ran his tongue up its length to her ear and his body absorbed her shiver before he said there, "I'm not done eating you, baby doll. But you took all of me this morning. I'm curious to know what you can do with your mouth."

He heard her breath catch as her face twisted to his and he saw, to his delight, she liked that idea.

"Do you know what I want?" he asked, she nodded and he murmured, "Then give it to me."

She didn't hesitate a moment. She moved, positioning herself over his head and his hands slid up her outer thighs, his fingers curling into her hips as she bent her body down the length of his.

The minute she wrapped her fingers around him, he lapped at her.

When her tongue touched the tip of his hard cock, he pulled her hips down and gave her more. She learned swiftly that the more she pleased him, the more she was rewarded.

And she pleased him a good deal.

She was rocking her hips against his mouth, her fist around the base of his cock, her movements nearly frenzied, her moans vibrating against his shaft as her sweet little mouth took him deep and he knew she was ready.

He slid away from her and turned on her. He had her ass in his hands and her back to the headboard before she had the chance to wrap her arms and legs around him.

When she did, he pressed the tip of his cock to her wet tight entrance, but stopped.

Her head tipped back and her lips parted in anticipation.

But he didn't give it to her, as much as he wanted it himself.

They'd played, he'd won, and now he wanted the spoils of victory.

"What do you want?" he demanded.

Her eyes opened halfway but she didn't answer.

He placed his lips on hers. "Baby doll," he murmured. "Tell me what you want."

"I want you to fuck me," she whispered, pressing her hips into his and he pulled back.

Her mouth formed a disappointed "O" and her eyes closed.

He grinned against her lips.

Yes, she was absolutely fucking perfect.

But he wasn't quite done.

"Call me wolf," he ordered and her eyes opened again, this time not halfway.

"Callum—"

He circled his hips and she bit her bottom lip before she strained to find him.

"Call me wolf," he repeated gruffly, the feel of her, wet and open, waiting for him, was driving him mad.

"Callum—"

"Do it, little one."

"Wolf," she whispered.

"Say it all."

She pressed her body closer, her face went into his neck, and under his ear she begged softly, "Please, my wolf, I need you to fuck me."

Sonia calling him wolf, begging him to fuck her, seemed to shatter his soul.

It also shattered his control.

He gave her what she asked for, fast and rough, then faster and rougher, and the harder he took her, the higher she went until he knew it was overwhelming her.

Her neck bent sharply, her eyes sought his, and he saw the panic just as her body tightened all around him.

He lifted his hand to cradle the back of her head.

His control of his own orgasm was slipping but he assured her in a hoarse voice, "It's all right, baby doll, I've got you."

Her dazed eyes focused on him a scant second before she gave him her trust and let go.

Her head reared back, slamming his hand against the wall just as it cushioned her head from the blow. Her body bucked. Her sex convulsed, sucking him deeper inside her hot wetness. And, finally, he heard her release yelped in loud, sharp, almost feral cries.

The sound of her climax was his undoing. He surged into her one last time and joined her in a brilliant explosion with his own claiming animal roar.

When he came back from the beautiful place Sonia took him, the most beautiful of his life (and considering he was three hundred and eighty-three years old, that was fucking saying something), he felt her breath evening out against his neck.

She still held his body tight in her limbs, his cock still snug inside her, and she had pressed her face into his neck. All of this he thought was, as Sonia could very much be, sweet.

And the realization hit him suddenly like a crushing weight that he wanted her limbs around him, her breath to stir his skin, and their beautiful connection to last for eternity.

Which heralded the unwelcome knowledge he'd lived with for thirty-one years. Knowledge he'd worked time and again with Mac to come to terms with. Knowledge that, when he met Sonia as a little girl, felt their connection, and discovered she was his, he'd raged against. Knowledge that he'd buried deep until that moment.

It was the knowledge that she was a mortal human and he was an immortal werewolf and they didn't have eternity.

Instead he'd enjoy his mate for decades, not millennia.

Then he'd watch her grow old.

Then he'd watch her die.

And destiny had chosen to make her perfect, which Callum thought was a fucking cruel tease.

His arms tightened around her and he dropped from his knees to his back, taking her with him, careful to keep their connection.

When he had her settled on top, she nuzzled closer. His fingers found his chain and trailed along it and he pulled in a breath, taking in the gorgeous scent of her hair, the beautiful scent of them mingled between her legs, and the scent of...

His body froze and his head at the same time as Sonia's twisted to look at the man standing in the door.

The scent of fucking *vampire*.

CHAPTER TEN
VAMPIRES

"Who would have thought, Sonny, that when you fuck you sound like an animal?" Yuri noted blandly, standing in the door, gaze locked on Sonia.

Belying his tone, his eyes were blazing.

Then Callum watched those eyes narrow on the claiming chain Callum's hand had arrested toying with when Yuri appeared in the door and Callum bit back a wolfish howl of elation.

Before he reached out to throw the blanket folded at the end of her bed over their bodies, Callum had thoughts he was certain, if Sonia knew them, she would greatly dislike (and likely have no problem sharing that opinion).

Yuri, who so very much wanted to get his cold vampire hands on her, had walked in on them naked, still connected, her claiming chain glinting in the lights of the room, the cries of their orgasms practically still ringing in the air.

And Callum fucking loved it.

He loved that Yuri had seen everything he saw and heard everything he heard and was right now *smelling* everything he *smelled.*

Thus he couldn't stop himself from aiming at Yuri a very fucking satisfied smile to which Yuri aimed back a very incensed scowl.

"What...what are you...?" Sonia stammered, and hearing the horror in her tone, Callum smothered his chuckle and his arms tightened around her under the blanket. "*Doing here?*" she screeched.

"Father wants to speak to you," Yuri answered.

"*Now?*" she shrieked.

Yuri leaned in the doorway and stated, "When we arrived, we noticed you were busy. Therefore we waited until you weren't. So, yes, now, if you'd be so kind."

Callum was surprised he hadn't sensed them or smelled them.

Then again, he was entirely wrapped up in his pretty little mate so perhaps it wasn't that surprising.

And he thought that this just got better and better.

They'd been there awhile.

Fucking brilliant.

Callum felt Sonia's body jolt, taking him from his thoughts, but Yuri casually pushed away from the door and disappeared from sight.

Callum looked from the door to Sonia and found she was still staring across the room.

"Honey," he called, giving her a squeeze.

"Tell me I'm dreaming now," she whispered, her voice still filled with horror, as was her face. Her eyes were dazed and unfocused, and at the look of her, Callum had to bite back another chuckle. "No, this isn't a dream," she stated, her head slowly turning to face him to breathe her finale. "This is a *nightmare.*"

"Sonia—"

"They heard us," she whispered.

They did. They not only heard their orgasms, they probably heard a great deal more. Even if Gregor and Yuri weren't vampires, who had exceptional hearing, in fact all their senses were exceptional, they still would hear them. Fuck, the neighbors probably heard them.

"Sonia—"

"We're loud," Sonia went on.

"Yes, baby doll, but—"

"We were having sex," she breathed this fact as if he hadn't participated fully in the event, her eyes widening, and Callum was losing his fight with his amusement and felt his body start shaking.

"Sonia—"

"He said…" she cut him off, her dazed eyes clearing and beginning to flash. "He said…he *actually said* that I sounded like an *animal*."

"Son—"

She disengaged from him and rolled angrily away.

Callum rolled to his side, got up on an elbow, and watched as, clumsy in her fury, Sonia struggled with her nightgown.

The material was caught helplessly around her arms and her head was hidden by it but she still ranted on.

"I can't *believe* what just happened. What he just *said*. My brother!" She tugged the nightgown down with effort and then glared at Callum. "Well, *essentially* my brother saw me naked and…and…" she leaned toward him and hissed, "*fastened* to you."

"Fastened to me?" Callum repeated, the thread of humor in his tone impossible to miss and Sonia didn't miss it.

Her eyes narrowed and she snapped, "Nothing about this is funny!"

Callum thought everything about this was the height of hilarity, especially her reaction.

He didn't share that.

Instead, he said, "Baby doll, calm down."

She leaned back and her eyebrows went up. "Calm down?"

Callum exited the bed and pulled her rigid body into his arms.

"Yes, calm down. It happened. It's over. Let's get dressed and go down and see what we're dealing with."

"Oh, we'll do that, all right. We certainly will," she told him, pulling free from his arms and then jumping around on one foot trying to tug up her underwear.

Callum grabbed his clothes and pulled them on as she yanked up her panties and smoothed her nightgown down. Then she ran her fingers through her hair while walking to her chest of drawers. She pulled something out of a box on the top and twisted a holder in her hair, fixing a ponytail.

Callum had on his jeans, was shrugging on his shirt, and seeing her makeup free, in a nightgown and ponytail, her lips bruised from his kisses, her face flushed with sex, he thought she'd never looked more adorable, never prettier, beyond beautiful.

Perfect.

Without buttoning his shirt, he strode to her and yanked her in his arms. His head descended and his mouth claimed hers in a kiss so thorough, the bruising of her lips wouldn't disappear for days.

When he lifted his head, their hearts were both beating faster and Sonia looked like she was emerging from a delicious dream, a fact which made him want to kiss her again.

Unfortunately, he couldn't.

"All right, baby doll," he called softly and he saw that, with effort, her eyes focused on his and he grinned, which made her eyes focus on his mouth, which made him want to laugh but he kept speaking. "Remember I told you that you have family now and they wouldn't want you to struggle, no matter what you're struggling with?"

She blinked and then she nodded.

He dipped his face close to hers, looked her in the eye, and said quietly, "You're about to see what I mean."

Her eyes grew wide but he ignored her look, took her hand, and guided her down the stairs.

Gregor was lounging on one of Sonia's clean-lined pristine couches by her Christmas tree.

Yuri was fuming while leaning on the mantel above the fireplace.

They both came to attention and watched as Callum led Sonia down the stairs and into the room.

Callum's gaze went to Gregor and he demanded, "I'll want to know the meaning of this."

Gregor slowly closed his eyes, visibly seeking patience, and when he opened them, he said in his cool refined voice, "Remember who you're speaking to."

"I know exactly who I'm fucking speaking to," Callum returned.

"I kept her safe for you for thirty-one years," Gregor rejoined, Callum heard Sonia gasp and felt her hand tighten spasmodically in his.

He curled her hand up, drawing her nearer, and tucked it under his arm.

"You kept her safe for Lassiter for thirty-one years," Callum returned. "You vowed it, you did it. Your work is done."

"He's already claimed her," Yuri announced hostilely. "I saw the chain."

Gregor looked to his son and murmured a warning, "Yuri."

Due to Gregor's position amongst the vampires and Callum's royal standing, Callum had known Gregor all his life. However, recently, linked by the Arlingtons, primarily Sonia, Callum had grown to know Gregor and Yuri very well.

Gregor was tall, black-haired, and lean. His son was blond, like his mother, and had more bulk to his long frame.

Gregor was also quite like Mac, without the warmth. Patient and thoughtful about his actions.

Yuri was quite like Callum, as much as Callum hated to admit it. Impatient, quick to anger and when he wanted something, he fucking well got it and he'd consider the consequences later.

Except, for Yuri, he wanted Sonia.

And he would never have her.

Not only because she had been Callum's before she existed and most especially now, but also because the vampire culture didn't allow vampires to mate with mortals.

Yuri didn't heed his father's warning and his gaze narrowed on Callum. "Four days. You had her four days and you've already claimed her. Tell me, Cal, did you whisper your people's secrets in her ear as you were thrusting inside her or did you simply boggle her mind with your legendary dick and she still doesn't even fucking know?"

Callum heard Sonia's indignant intake of breath, his triumphant elation evaporated, and his temper rose.

"Do you *want* me to challenge you?" he asked Yuri and Yuri pushed away from the mantel stating he did indeed. Callum's skin prickled, he so wanted to transform to take on the challenge. But he didn't reckon Sonia, no matter how angry she was earlier and now, would like to watch her beloved "puppy" ripping her "brother" apart with his teeth.

Not to mention, he hadn't yet told her that he *was* her puppy and that her puppy was a werewolf.

"Control your son," Callum clipped to Gregor, not taking his eyes from Yuri.

Gregor sighed and noted, "You aren't helping, Yuri."

"No," Sonia stated flatly, her eyes on Yuri and they were cold. "He isn't."

"Sonny—" Gregor started but Sonia cut him off.

"Callum took me to the cabin, Gregor."

It surprised Callum to see Gregor flinch, but he recovered quickly, stood, faced her, and said again, "Sonny—"

"You told me it had burned down."

"My dear."

"You tore them away from me, not piece by piece but fast and painful, like ripping off a Band-Aid," she snapped. "Is that what you thought? If you took it away quickly, it'd hurt less?" She didn't give Gregor the chance to answer, she went on, "Well, I'd already lost them quickly once so it fucking well didn't!"

"Sonny, give me one moment to explain," Gregor said.

Sonia obviously didn't feel in a magnanimous mood for she proclaimed, "Callum gave them back to me. He took me to the cabin and he introduced me to Regan. She even has *pictures.* Do you know who doesn't have pictures of my mother and father? *Me!*"

"Lassiter and Cherise made me promise I'd erase your old life so you could live your new one," Gregor returned quietly. "I didn't like it but there were a great number of things Lassiter and I didn't agree on. But he was your father. That's what they wanted. I vowed to do as they asked and I did it."

Callum stared at the vampire.

The different immortal beings on earth all had uneasy relationships with each other. The relationship between vampire and werewolf was the most uneasy. However, Callum had always respected the vampire vow.

Any vow a vampire took he or she would never break it. They'd die to keep it and vampires enjoyed their immortality and most held it sacred. Unlike werewolves, who often skirmished and felt losses, sometimes numerous, amongst their own, vampires had only warred once in all of history. They didn't reproduce as easily as werewolves (who were quite prolific) and they had a variety of edicts that governed them which were pure lunacy but had been put in place to protect their species. Lastly, they couldn't procreate with humans, which werewolves could and did, frequently, which was one reason why Yuri would never be allowed Sonia as his mortal mate. Vampire law forbid it.

Werewolves by their nature were lusty, and unless there was an insurrection or rebellion against the monarchy, the laws were few and wolves were free to make their own lives amongst their brethren, humans or inhumans, as they liked. If Callum or his father before him or his before him attempted to enforce abundant strictures on wolves, his brethren would rebel and their culture would descend into chaos. Free to live their lives, however, werewolves were naturally warm, sociable, and practically consumed life, likely because, with their intermittent fighting, it could be shortened.

Vampires were colder, far more controlled, and practically every move they made was governed.

The differences between the cultures were even evident in their clothes. Both Yuri and Gregor were wearing superbly tailored suits. Callum hadn't even bothered to button the torn flannel shirt he wore over his jeans. He couldn't even remember the last time he *wore* a suit and didn't currently own one.

Because they were opposites, the two peoples did not get on well with each other and studiously avoided contact.

Callum had only met one vampire that he respected. His name was Lucien and Callum liked him because Lucien's intensity reminded Callum of a wolf.

Not to mention, Lucien was an epic warrior.

Sonia broke into his thoughts with an astute one of her own.

Too astute.

"You talk like they knew they were going to die," she accused and every male in the room, vampire and wolf, went still.

Callum watched with further surprise as Gregor's face slightly softened at the same time he quickly covered.

"Parents, my dear, when they become parents tend to plan for such things. Death is an ugly fact of life and when someone loves another, they'll want the one they love to be cared for if they're not around. So, Sonny, they prepared for that time, they gave strict instructions, and when I agreed to be your guardian should that unfortunate event occur, I vowed I'd follow them. And I did."

It was a good cover because it was the truth, with only the fact not shared that Lassiter and Cherise Arlington prepared carefully for their deaths because what they were doing in their lives put them in mortal danger.

Callum gazed down at Sonia to see that Gregor's words had affected her. Her eyes were bright with unshed tears and it cut him to the quick seeing them. He dropped her hand but curled an arm around her shoulders, tucking her front into his side.

She rested her cheek against his pectoral and wrapped her arms around his middle. Her soft body molded to his and she took in a shuddering breath.

That cut him to the quick as well and his arm around her shoulders grew tighter.

Sonia wasn't quite done, however.

"Why would they want you to erase them?" she asked Gregor, her voice no longer flat and accusatory, it was soft and sad.

"I've no idea, my dear," Gregor answered. "Lassiter, nor Cherise, shared the reasons behind their wishes. They just shared their wishes."

She paused a moment before she continued her quiet interrogation.

"Earlier, you said you'd been keeping me safe for Callum," she stated and inquired, "Did you know about all of this?"

The air grew heavy, this mostly coming from Callum and Yuri, but Gregor kept his cool.

"Yes," he answered simply.

Sonia's voice was barely audible when she asked, "Did my parents?"

Gregor came closer, his eyes flicking to Callum as if to assess the threat, as he would do considering he was approaching a wolf's mate.

Callum lifted his chin and Gregor crept closer.

Quietly, he replied, "Yes, Sonny, they knew about your destiny. They wanted it for you. Very much so. They were..." he hesitated and said the next word as if it cost him to do so, "*honored* that you were to be his queen."

Sonia pulled in a soft breath and her body grew tight for a second before she seemed to come to some conclusion, closed her eyes briefly, and when she opened them, she relaxed further into Callum.

"Why didn't anyone tell me?" she asked, her voice still hushed, but there was an accusatory note threading through it.

"Many reasons, my dear," Gregor replied, coming even closer. "Because you're human. Because there was the possibility you weren't safe. Because you needed to mature to a time when you could take all this in, understand it, not fear it, and accept your destiny."

Sonia gazed at Gregor a moment, letting this sink in.

Then she looked up at Callum and noted, "Your family knew too."

"We did," Callum told her truthfully.

She looked at Gregor then Yuri then back to Callum and tried to pull away but Callum held her firm.

She gave in to his hold and remarked, "If I was eventually to live amongst you, it would have made it a lot easier for me now if your family had taken me in. I would have understood your culture. I would have grown up in it."

She was right.

And she was far too shrewd.

Callum took in breath but it was Yuri who answered.

"You'd hardly have benefited from growing up with Callum and his family," he clipped and when he went on, his tone was bitter. "Trust me, things would be different about now if you grew up thinking of Callum as a brother."

Sonia, far too sweet for her own good, reacted to the bitterness, her face grew soft with understanding and sorrow, and she whispered, "Yuri."

"And Sonny," Gregor added, "your parents wanted you to grow up amongst your own. Humans. It was also their wish."

This was an outright lie, considering they were vampires.

However, for thirty-one years, Gregor and Yuri had taken great pains to live the charade of a human life.

For Sonia.

And to protect her destiny, not only as Callum's mate, but also for the reason *why* fate chose her to be at his side during this time.

She tore her soft gaze from Yuri and looked to Gregor. She pulled in a deep breath and then released a heavy sigh.

Callum decided Sonia had had enough. It was time for this to be over and therefore he announced, "Sonia's had a stressful few days. Share why you're here so we can get on with our night."

Gregor looked to Callum and replied, "Actually, I'm here to speak with you."

"So speak," Callum ordered.

Gregor took a step back, glanced over his shoulder at his son, then back to Callum and invited, "Let's walk."

Callum's eyes also went to Yuri, who was standing with arms crossed on his chest, but his face was carefully blank.

Gregor had something he wanted to share privately, not for Sonia to hear.

He looked back to Gregor. "I'll not leave Sonia. It's unsafe."

"Yuri will stay with her," Gregor replied immediately.

Callum looked at Yuri to see he was now smiling.

"I don't think so," he told Gregor. "We'll go into the kitchen."

"We'll walk," Gregor replied firmly.

"We won't," Callum returned even more firmly.

"Worried?" Yuri taunted and Callum tensed.

"Why can't you just talk here?" Sonia cut in.

"I need to have a private word with your mate," Gregor answered and it was Sonia's turn to go tense.

"More secrets?" she queried irately.

"Business, Sonia," Gregor retorted, his tone surprising Callum by turning positively fatherly and surprising Callum further when Sonia's expression turned visibly daughterly. Gregor continued, "Between his family and mine. It's late. I'm tired. I want to get this done and it won't take long," he turned to Callum. "Let's walk."

Callum didn't move a muscle.

"Callum," Gregor said on a weary sigh. "No matter Yuri's behavior tonight, Sonia's safe with him. He'd never do anything to cause a rift between our families."

"That's surprising, considering some of the things that have come out of his mouth tonight," Callum replied.

"Take a moment and stand in his shoes," Gregor retorted sharply, uncharacteristically losing patience.

Callum didn't want to do as Gregor suggested but he couldn't stop the visions from invading. The very thought of wanting Sonia and walking in on her naked and connected to a vampire made his blood start to heat.

"We'll walk," he muttered but his eyes went to Yuri. "Sonia's going directly to bed."

"I thought she and I could share a nightcap," Yuri returned acidly.

"She's going to bed," Callum repeated, and not waiting for further response, he turned and guided her up the stairs.

She was unresisting and she was silent.

Until they hit the room.

"Callum—"

"Get in bed, honey, I'll be back before you know it."

She stood by the bed and crossed her arms on her chest, declaring, "I don't like this."

Callum didn't either but he clearly had no choice.

There was something pressing on Gregor's mind and Callum's instinct was to find out what it was so he could deal with it, as well as everything else, and move on.

He buttoned the buttons on his shirt saying, "The longer we discuss this, the longer it will take for me to get this done."

Sonia didn't seem to be worried how long it would take, for she retorted, "I don't know what part about 'this' I don't like most. The fact that you and Gregor are taking a walk to talk about something you don't want me to overhear. The fact that you stated I was going to bed when maybe I don't want to go to bed. Or the fact that you led me out of the room without letting me say goodnight to the men who raised me."

Callum studied his mate. He didn't know her very well but he was beginning to recognize something about her. And that was, only Sonia could find *three* things about the vague concept of "this" to be pissed about.

"We're not arguing now," he stated decisively.

"Then we'll argue later," she returned.

With that, she climbed into bed, turned out the bedside lamp, and settled in, commanding, "Leave the Christmas lights on when you go."

Callum sighed. Then he tugged on his socks and boots. He walked down the stairs, stopped, and looked at Yuri.

"She had a break-in the night I took her," he informed the vampire and saw Yuri's eyes flash before turning hard. "Kidnap attempt," Callum went on. "The intruders were rough with her."

Yuri's voice was as hard as his eyes when he replied, "I hope you dealt with them."

"I did," Callum confirmed and he saw another flash, this one grimly satisfied, for he knew what Callum did to the two wolves who touched Sonia.

And Callum found himself grimly satisfied learning from that brief exchange that Gregor was correct. No matter Yuri's foul behavior that evening, he'd never let anything harm Sonia.

He jerked his head at Gregor, grabbed his coat, and they walked.

Gregor was silent for a block and a half and Callum was losing patience when Gregor finally spoke.

"Something's changed," he proclaimed.

"And that would be?" Callum prompted when Gregor went no further.

"Lucien has found his lifemate," Gregor shared and that news was definitely worth a proclamation.

Nearly every immortal race had lifemates.

Vampires didn't believe in them. As they wouldn't.

After they warred centuries ago, they wrote the copious laws they lived under. Amongst them they outlawed mating with mortals (and anyone else for that matter), and at that time forced all vampires to denounce their mortal or non-vampire mates. They'd even hunted, tortured, and executed vampires and mortals who refused. From that point, they'd only been allowed to mate with vampires which significantly lowered the chances of finding that one single soul in billions who you were destined to spend eternity with.

Therefore, they'd turned their backs on the idea of lifemates.

Callum grinned to himself that it was Lucien who'd declared a lifemate. That vampire had balls.

"Is it Katrina?" Callum asked, hoping it was not.

Lucien was bound to another vampire who went by the name of Katrina. Callum had also met her, she was stunning to look at but she reminded him of Mona.

"No, he was granted severance from Katrina," Gregor answered, Callum nodded, and Gregor continued. "And then he had necessity..." Gregor paused, "to dispatch her."

Callum felt his lips get tight.

Vampires officially bound themselves to other vampires but they had an out, called severance, which was like a mortal's divorce.

Unlike the vampire vow, which clearly didn't include their vows to their mates, Callum found the concept of vampire severance repulsive. Werewolves had nothing like it. A wolf would never sever from his or her mate.

Never.

However, if his mate was Katrina, Callum would consider it.

Nevertheless, "dispatching" her was beyond the pale, even for a vampire.

This idea was even more repugnant to Callum. The only thing he knew, knowing Lucien, was that if the deed was done, there was a valid reason behind it.

"Who is she?" Callum asked.

"A mortal," Gregor answered and Callum stopped short.

He turned and stared at the vampire. "You're fucking joking."

Gregor had stopped too and regarded Callum. "I'm not."

"Bloody hell," Callum muttered, finding himself concerned for Lucien.

Vampires liked their laws, had lived under them for half a millennium, and not mating with mortals was top on their list.

Lucien and his mate could be hunted, tortured, and executed.

"Are they—?" he started but Gregor shook his head.

"Things became..." Gregor hesitated, "*uncomfortable* for a while. However, several members of The Council, including, obviously, myself, saw the wisdom of rescinding that particular edict. We were successful in convincing the others as well."

Callum continued to study Gregor, keeping his face perfectly blank and his turbulent thoughts to himself.

It had begun. The Prophesies, or what he knew of them, were coming true.

Even the parts Callum had hoped would not.

Bloody hell.

"So the foundation of vampire culture has shifted," Callum noted.

"It has indeed. Not only Lucien but *all* vampires are free to take mortal mates if they so choose."

Callum's jaw grew tight and he started walking again. Gregor fell in step by his side.

They rounded the block and kept walking together silently.

After some time, Gregor spoke again, and when he did so, he did it quietly.

"This means Yuri is free to take a mortal mate."

Callum halted and turned instantly to the vampire, fighting the blinding fury that immediately started roiling inside him.

"Don't say another word," he warned.

"Callum, hear me out."

"Absolutely fucking not."

"Callum, hear me out," Gregor repeated, but Callum started walking again and Gregor again fell in step by his side.

"She's my daughter," Gregor stated.

Callum stopped once more and turned to the vampire. "She's your ward."

"She *was* my ward, thirty-one years ago. That's a long time, Callum, nurturing a mortal, watching her grow up, putting Band-Aids on her skinned knees, arguing with her about eating peas, and hoping you bought her the birthday present she wanted most of all." Callum ground his teeth together, unaffected by the depths of Gregor's heretofore unknown fondness for Sonia as Gregor finished, "Since then, she became my daughter."

"And you're saying you want me to renounce my queen, walk away from my fucking *mate*, so you can keep your daughter?" Callum bit out.

"I'm saying I don't want her to die," Gregor returned coolly. "Ever."

Callum sucked in breath. He knew where this was going.

And he had no idea Gregor felt this deeply for Sonia but he didn't disbelieve it. Gregor was not a warm male, not openly. But Sonia was a warm woman and it would be hard not to feel deeply for her, especially if you had thirty-one years of putting Band-Aids on her skinned knees and buying her birthday presents.

Gregor continued, "Yuri adores her. He has since the moment he laid eyes on her. He'll take care of her. He'll give her anything she desires—"

"You need to stop talking," Callum warned.

Gregor ignored his warning and announced what Callum already knew, "He'll give her immortal life."

Callum sucked in breath.

Vampires fed on human blood, they had since time began. As their species developed, it also developed the capacity to protect its prey. Therefore, at the exact same time vampires fed, they released healing properties into their human meals through their saliva. These properties were extraordinarily strong, they helped the bite heal and the blood to regenerate swiftly.

And, if released into the bloodstream of a human regularly and for any length of time, it could do more. Regress aging, fight disease, greatly hasten the healing of broken bones, or, say, halt the effects of a deadly blood disease.

And, if released into the bloodstream of a human regularly and indefinitely, it could keep them young, vital, and alive forever.

"I know your people don't understand this concept but this is my lifemate you're talking about," Callum growled.

Gregor's tone was actually gentle when he replied, "Lifemate? Hardly, Callum. Her life, maybe. But yours?"

Callum's skin started prickling again, even so far as stinging, and he felt his blood start to heat as the transformation started.

He hadn't transformed without willing himself to do so since he was a young wolf who hadn't yet learned control.

It took effort but he held it back and started walking again swiftly, his long legs eating the distance to round the block which would take him back toward Sonia's house.

Gregor kept up with him, pace for pace.

"Think of her, Callum," Gregor urged calmly. "What she'll go through, aging while you do not age, knowing that—"

Callum cut him off. "This conversation is over."

"Callum, you must think of Sonia."

Callum yet again halted, turned on the vampire, and took a step closer, clearly aggressive and on the offense, bending slightly so he was nose to nose with Sonia's guardian.

"I said, this conversation is *over*."

Gregor held his cool and Callum's scowl for long moments before he replied, "Fine, Callum, the conversation is over."

"Don't raise this subject again, not with me, not with Sonia," Callum commanded.

Gregor pulled in breath through his nose then sighed and agreed, "I won't raise it again, with either of you."

"Yuri either," Callum went on.

"I'll speak with Yuri," Gregor promised.

"I want your vow on that," Callum demanded.

He watched Gregor's eyes flash then the vampire nodded.

"You have my vow."

Callum felt his body relax.

But he wasn't finished. "If you and Yuri want to be a part of Sonia's life, no matter how short it may be, you'll not behave like you did tonight. Especially Yuri."

"As you can see, my news was important," Gregor returned.

"Call next time," Callum gritted out.

Gregor's jaw tensed but he nodded.

"Yuri speaks to her like that again, or to me when she's within hearing distance, I'll tear him apart, burn the pieces, and scatter the ashes to the winds."

This threat was not idle, Gregor knew it and he knew Callum could carry it out.

Yuri might be a vampire with extraordinary abilities, including strength.

But Callum was king of the werewolves and his family didn't rule because they were good at diplomacy. They ruled because they were the strongest, swiftest, most cunning, and by far the most ferocious warriors of all werewolves.

In Callum's teeth, Yuri would be shreds.

A muscle in Gregor's jaw flexed.

Then he defended, "This evening was difficult for Yuri."

"That might be so, but the past four days have been traumatic for Sonia and the man she thinks of as her brother behaving like that didn't fucking help."

Gregor held Callum's scowl for a moment before he conceded, "Your point is made. As I said, I'll speak with Yuri."

"Good," Callum bit out.

Finished with their fucking stroll and definitely finished with their conversation, he turned and walked the rest of the distance to Sonia's house. He didn't speak the entire time nor did he do so when he entered her house and took off his coat.

He was striding to the stairs, not having deigned even to glance at Yuri, when he ordered, "You let yourselves in, you'll lock up on your way out and you'll never use your keys again unless you know Sonia and I aren't in this fucking house."

"Callum," Gregor called.

Callum stifled a growl, stopped, turned to Sonia's guardian, and regarded him in silence.

"We'll expect to see Sonia during the holidays," Gregor said quietly.

"We'll see," Callum replied roughly, put them out of his mind, and took the stairs two at a time.

Sonia was asleep on her side when he'd disrobed and joined her in bed.

He fitted his body to the curve of hers, and with his arm around her waist, he hauled her deeper into his still agitated frame.

He had a great deal on his mind but the only things catching his attention were the exact things he wished not to think about at all.

He had a vast number of friends who had found their mates. Claiming stories were shared freely and outrageously amongst wolves, both male and female, even bragged about. Fuck, it was such a common practice he even knew his parents' claiming story.

Keen to find his connection, Mac had gone on a quest to seek his mate. It had lasted years, but Mac, with his usual patience, never grew frustrated.

He'd sensed Regan well before he was even in her vicinity. He'd tracked her and found her sitting on the steps in front of her parents' cottage in France, eating an apple, and apparently, as reported to Callum by Mac, waiting for him.

Mac had seized her immediately, dragged her into the wood surrounding her parents' cottage, and claimed her on the forest floor, clasping the chain he'd carried in his pocket for centuries around her waist before he'd done it.

Until the deed was done, Mac didn't even know her name.

And that was the wolves' way. Wolves didn't fuck around.

The male seized the female, claimed her, and their lives began.

Although wolves didn't shy away from talking about sex and mated wolves didn't balk at unseemly (to other cultures) public displays of affection, Callum was grateful not to know the particulars of his mother's claiming as he did some of his friends.

What he did know was that was it. Regan was then Mac's and their lives together started there. Callum wasn't a romantic and never imagined their relationship was perfect in the centuries they had together. But it was solid, it was strong, it was affectionate and tender, and last, it was loving.

What Callum had with Sonia might not have started like other wolves but with the way he felt the moment her hand drifted toward him last night while he was wolf then stroked his muzzle with drowsy affection. The way he felt when she threw the covers aside and offered to make him warm. The way he felt when she pressed herself to him and fell asleep. The way he felt when her eyes opened that morning and she stared at him with that sleepy look of love. The way he felt when she was connected to him and agreed she was his. The way he felt when the claiming was done and he smelled the beauty that was them. And, lastly, the way he felt through (practically) every moment in between, he knew it had ended that way.

Human or not, what he would have with Sonia was solid, strong, affectionate, tender, loving, as well as spirited, fiery, and unbelievably sweet. Sonia felt the pull of their connection. He knew it and she herself had declared she was his.

But now Regan was without her mate, and although his mother kept up a bright, cheerful façade, her eyes always betrayed her loss, sometimes her sorrow, sometimes even her confusion, as if she didn't know what to make of a life without Mac in it.

That was to be Callum's future. There was no way of escaping it.

And this thought didn't make him anguished.

It enraged him.

So much, he felt the change, again against his will, coming over him, heating his blood, and tightening his skin.

Any other time, he'd give in to it, become the wolf and run.

But he couldn't, not in bed beside Sonia, nor could he go outside and roam the city streets.

So he did the only thing he could do.

He fought back the change as he released his conscious human will to his innate wolfish instincts.

And his instincts told him his mate was finally at his side. She was there for him, to take care of him, ease his way, soothe his frustrations, and tame the beast within.

His hand slid over her hip, back over her bottom, between her legs, and he found her. Without easing into it or waking her, he manipulated her until he heard her breath become heavy in her sleep, her hips moving unconsciously against his hand.

And then she woke, already wet, her breath escalating sharply as she realized what Callum was doing, but she didn't begin to fight.

Callum's sweet Sonia began to moan.

Yes, asleep, awake, Sonia was fucking *his*.

His other hand pressed under her and between her legs. Taking over, he used the hand that had been working her to yank off her underwear and then it went back to start fucking her with two fingers.

Stroking deep, feeling her growing wetness coat his fingers as they drove again and again into the silk that was Sonia, his heart rate rose as his blood still boiled under his prickling skin, and his breath grew thick when he heard her moans turn to pants. She bent a knee deep to offer him better access and she wiggled out of her nightgown as her hips started jerking, demanding, slamming down on his fingers.

Christ, she was fucking glorious.

His cock hard and throbbing, he could wait no longer. He growled into the back of her hair, stopped fucking her with his fingers, and flattened his hand against her pubic bone. Using his other hand to shift her hips, he roughly pulled her up with the hand between her legs until she was on her knees and he positioned himself between them.

Then he entered her with a violent driving thrust, seating himself to the hilt.

He fucking loved it that she could take all of him. Even she-wolves couldn't take all of him.

And he loved that she was made for him. Loved not only that she understood it, but also that it was Sonia who explained it to him.

He loved it that *she* loved to play, just as much as Callum, and just as rough and hard and hungry.

Like at that very instant, Sonia was on her knees with her sex offered to him shamelessly, her thighs quivering in joyful anticipation, and he gave her what she wanted. He pulled back, surged forward, and seated himself to the root yet again.

And again.

And again.

And he did it with a ferocity he would only use with a wolf, never a human. Fucking Sonia so hard her moans were sharp and curt, jolted to silence by his thrusts.

She came up on her hands, and when she assumed the position of a wolf, his need quickened, his strokes deepened, and she took him, all of his cock, all of his power, feeding the force of his hunger.

He reached his long arm out and grasped her thick hair, using it and his hand at her waist to grind her into him as he drove into her, harder, harder. It hit his consciousness she wasn't only taking the pounding force of his thrusts, she was rearing her hips back to meet him.

He felt her sex quiver around his shaft and her breath start to rasp and he knew it was upon her.

He twisted his fist in her hair.

"Say it," he demanded.

She reared back into his cock, her rasping breath turning to scratchy cries.

"Sonia, fucking say it." His own orgasm was coming. He felt it building in his groin and he finally understood the panic she displayed the two times he had her because the force behind his oncoming climax seemed like something that would tear her apart.

Not of his will, his hand twisted again in her hair, forcing her neck to arch as she moaned deep in her throat, his own voice gravelly when he changed his command, "I want to hear you fucking *scream* it."

"Wolf," she whispered, then her sex convulsed around his cock with her orgasm and she did as he commanded, her words shrieked so loud, it wasn't a possibility the neighbors heard, it was a certainty, *"My wolf!"*

At her words, he buried himself inside her silken wetness and exploded with a guttural snarl, feeling an intensity he'd never experienced. It was akin to the change to wolf, it was like exploding out of his skin.

And the power of it was startling and magnificent.

When he recovered, he released her hair but held her hips and continued to thrust gently inside her. She'd collapsed on her front, her head in the pillows, her hair fanning everywhere, her breathing still labored. She continued to offer her sweet ass to him as he tenderly plunged inside her, her hips angled up and pressing, encouraging, a loving invitation, a tender capitulation, a beautiful reminder that she belonged to him.

He glided a hand from her hip, over her bottom and up to his chain, which had slid high up her back, catching under her breasts. He tugged it down where it caught lightly on her hips so he could remind his mate of its presence, something he never wanted her to forget. Then, still thrusting, slower and slower, he trailed his fingers along the chain at the small of her back.

Her body shivered under his as the walls of her sex trembled delicately around his shaft.

Callum forced his hips into hers, taking her off her knees, pinning her to the bed on her belly, his cock still inside her, her legs spreading pleasingly wide to accommodate him.

The change wasn't upon him anymore. His blood not boiling, his skin heated only from fucking his gloriously sweet, pretty, perfect little mate.

As was the reason for her existence, she'd sated him.

And, he was realizing with fierce satisfaction, she did it beautifully every fucking time.

Content, he placed his forearms into the bed at her sides to settle some of his weight off her body. He used his chin to shift her hair away from her face, and at her ear, pressing deep inside her one last time, he muttered, "My glorious queen, I told you we'd have a beautiful life, you and I."

And, with his still hard cock buried deep inside his queen, Callum, king of the wolves, fell asleep while the Christmas lights from Sonia's tree cast a glow on their connected bodies.

CHAPTER ELEVEN
SCALES

Still mostly asleep, Sonia's hazy consciousness registered the covers slowly sliding down her body.

She was on her belly. Even motionless she could feel the delicious ache in every single muscle and a luscious throbbing between her legs that was a vague ache but a greater feeling of gratification. The ache was the ghost of Callum pounding inside her; the gratification was the reminder of being headily stuffed full.

Her eyes fluttered open then closed as she felt the fleeting touch on the skin of her upper buttocks where the needles were jabbed for her injections.

This fleeting touch became a different kind as if lips were trailing there.

She sighed at the beauty of it and momentarily melted back to sleep.

Then she felt strong fingers grasp her hips and she was gently rolled, arms came around her, and she was lifted.

She nuzzled into Callum's warm, hard, weirdly fully-clothed body, tucking her face in his neck, and seeking slumber as he settled into the bed, his back to the headboard, his knees cocked, Sonia snug in his lap.

"Sonia?" he called and her eyelids fluttered again.

"So sleepy," she whispered, cuddling closer, one of her arms bent and pressed between them, the other hand resting on his massive chest.

"I know, baby doll," he murmured, his arms growing tight for an instant then she felt his temple glide lovingly against her hair.

"I like it when you do that," she told him, pressing her nose to his neck for a moment, then settling and sighing, exhaustion and the heavy ache of her body calling her back to sleep.

"When I mark you?" She heard him ask through her waning consciousness.

"Mm," she replied, falling briefly into a doze as his arm around her calves shifted to become fingers trailing from her knee down her inner thigh.

"Sonia, honey," Callum called and her eyes fluttered again.

"Wolf, I'm sleepy," she protested weakly and to make her point, burrowed deeper into his hard frame.

At her words, his trailing fingers became a gentle grip on the flesh of her inner thigh for a moment before they started trailing again.

"You said that, little one," he replied softly. "I wanted you to know that the men are here. You need your rest and I need to get to work so I called them here." His fingers were still trailing from knee to mid-inner-thigh and back again as he finished, "I came up to tell you because I didn't want you to be alarmed if you woke and heard voices."

"Okay," she replied, her thoughts still drowsy, her attention reverting to his fingers' movements.

He kissed the top of her head and muttered in a final way, "You sleep as long as you like."

Sonia wasn't listening.

Her body decided his fingers weren't going deep enough, and on a downward trail, her hips unconsciously, lazily, rose to lengthen their route.

Those fingers stilled.

Involuntarily, a disappointed noise escaped the back of Sonia's throat.

His hand dropped instantly and his big palm rested warmly at the juncture between her legs.

It registered on her somnolent brain that that felt nice.

His voice had grown husky when he asked, "Do you want a little play, baby doll?"

Before her mind fully woke, her body used her mouth to answer quietly, "Yes, Callum."

"My sweet greedy queen," he muttered, his voice rough and satisfied as his palm moved away but his fingers moved in. Finding her instantly, they twitched and vibrated until she shoved her face in his neck, wrapped her arms around his shoulders, and ground into his fingers.

She was panting gently against his skin when his fingers plunged inside her, stroking tender but deep.

"God, I love the feel of you," he whispered adoringly, the tone of his words Sonia missed as she focused on the beautiful tension gathering around his fingers. "Are you going to come for me, little one?"

"Yes," she breathed, pressing to meet his strokes.

His fingers drove deep and stilled as his thumb hit the core of her, pressing and twitching, and the tension built swiftly then exploded magnificently.

After, she instantly relaxed into his body as the calm of her postorgasm and Callum's warm frame enveloped her, making her feel safe.

"So wet," he muttered, his fingers still toying with her tenderly as she drifted slowly to sleep in his arms. "The times are few, Sonia, when I regret my calling as king. But right now, with you in my arms like this, so fucking sweet, so fucking wet, I'd give anything to be able to stay here with you and eat you clean instead of having to walk down those stairs."

"Mm," was all Sonia could say, having no idea that Callum had not ever shared with a living being any regrets about his royal duty. He'd further never been tempted by anything enough actually to consider, even for an instant, avoiding that duty.

The next second, the throbbing still there, with renewed and intensely more delicious vigor that lulled her body, Sonia fell asleep with Callum's fingers still playing between her legs.

Sonia woke, her eyes opening to see her pillows, and thoughts of yesterday, last night, and *this morning* crashed painfully into her head.

Her body under the covers that were tucked snug around her went rigid.

"Oh my God," she breathed to the pillow.

She felt the ache in her muscles, the insistent throb between her legs, and every inch of her skin grew hot with shame when she remembered last night (both times, but *especially* the second time) and this morning (good goodness!).

She closed her eyes tight and turned her flaming face into the pillows as Callum's words of last night echoed in her ears.

My glorious queen, I told you we'd have a beautiful life, you and I.

And she had lain under him, listening to those words, her legs spread brazenly wide to receive him, her body glorying in his weight pressing her into the bed, *him* still seated deep inside her, filling her full as she drifted into an exhausted sleep of deep abandoned contentment.

And she'd not wanted to lose him, his weight, his warmth, his shaft filling her full, making her feel whole.

My glorious queen, I told you we'd have a beautiful life, you and I.

Memories, sharp and stabbing, filled her head.

Yesterday morning, Callum claiming her and then practically forgetting about her for hours.

Yesterday afternoon, Callum telling that poor, sick, clearly demented woman she was "just a fuck" while Sonia, his mate, his supposed *wife*, sat in his lap facing his ex-lover.

He'd even rubbed his temple against Sonia's hair, making it clear to the woman, who was obviously hung up on him (and *not* in a healthy way), not to mention *everyone in that room*, that Sonia was better in bed than she was—this deepening Desdemona's humiliation to uncharted levels, not to mention Sonia's.

Then he and his people laughed and joked at Desdemona's panicked struggles and Callum's sentence for her to be "sequestered," even Ryon, who Sonia thought was a considerate man. Whatever sequestered was, but clearly, whatever it was wasn't good.

And Sonia's place, her role, as silent succor to Callum. There for nothing more than him to use her "sweet little body" when he needed to work out his day.

It wasn't medieval

It was...

It was...

She didn't even know what it was!

And the things he'd said to her last night, about gagging for it, gagging for *him*.

And Yuri.

And Gregor!

And what they'd heard and Yuri had *seen*.

And the things she'd learned from *them*.

And that morning, oh God, that morning, sitting in his lap and letting him toy with her like she was his plaything.

No, she didn't *let* him, she'd practically *asked* him.

She *did* ask him!

A beautiful life? He called that a beautiful life?

More memories flooded her mind, these at war with the first.

Yesterday morning, Callum, sexy and sweet, just like her dream Callum, teasing her in bed before he'd seduced her, and for that matter after, if only for a short time.

Yesterday afternoon, Ryon, Caleb, and Calder chatting to her like they'd known her for ages. Like she was a member of their family already. Like she wasn't weird or strange. Like she fit in.

And both times Callum tucked her hand, which was held safe in his, under his arm. Drawing her nearer. Offering his strength when she was frightened in the throne room and upset while facing Gregor and Yuri.

And, looking back at it, last night on the drive home and when they arrived at her house, Callum's hilariously strained patience at dealing with her when she was in a snit (before he became an arrogant bastard who said hideous things, that was).

And the way he held her after she'd climaxed, her back to the headboard, his hand cradling her head, something about the way he did it making her feel precious.

And the way he'd dealt with her after Yuri interrupted them, that time with amused patience in the face of her fury.

And, before they went down to face Gregor and Yuri, that kiss. That thorough beautiful kiss. A kiss that made her feel beautiful, desired, even the impossible, *loved*.

And, having a difficult conversation while facing the only family she had left (outside of Callum's now, that was), she'd relaxed in his embrace. Callum showing her physically what it meant to support her during her times of struggle by holding her close, holding her strong. Showing her in ways she didn't understand and couldn't put her finger on that he stood between her and pain. Perhaps not able to halt it completely, but he would be there to cushion the blow.

And at that very moment, tucked snug and warm in her covers, Callum did that. He did something tender in a way that made her feel he was keeping her safe.

My glorious queen, I told you we'd have a beautiful life, you and I.

Now that *could* be a beautiful life.

But that wasn't all there was to it.

More thoughts pushed the others out and invaded her mind.

Last night, waking up with his hand between her legs, the urge already on her, stronger than ever before, changing her, taking her out of herself so she wasn't any Sonia she'd ever known but someone else entirely. She was the creature he'd created. The creature he'd claimed. The creature, on some level, her mind was telling her she actually was meant to be.

And the way he took her. The way she responded to it, wanted it, lunged to meet it, her hips pushing into his, his fingers sinking into her flesh and fisting in her hair. He demanded more and more and more and she gloried in giving it to him as she took it from him, *needing* it like it was breath.

No, like there was something vital missing. Like there was some crucial part of who she was that had been lost. She felt drawn to Callum, linked to him, in fact, just as she'd thought after he claimed her, she felt *owned* by him, and in so being, only Callum could give her whatever she'd lost.

And this morning, half asleep, her instincts taking over and her brazen (again!) behavior, falling asleep with his hand still teasing her between her legs.

And the way they'd fallen asleep last night and how that didn't feel shameful or scandalous (at the time, now she was horrified), but instead it felt...

It felt *right.*

My glorious queen, I told you we'd have a beautiful life, you and I.

A beautiful life? Was all of that a beautiful life?

Did all the good that was Callum, all that was tender and affectionate and warm and teasing outweigh the things that were bad? Did it outweigh the things that caused her to feel humiliation that her life as his queen meant he felt entitled to fall asleep between her spread-eagled legs still buried inside her even though he didn't want her but only the use of her body? Did it outweigh her knowledge that something he dredged from deep inside her made her feel replete, content, whole after he'd taken her so hard, so roughly, making her scream in her climax, and then he'd pinned her to the bed under him, still full of him and feeling, insanely, that it was *right?*

Was that a beautiful life?

It was a beautiful life to him. She knew it with the way he said it, the words still echoing in her head. He'd muttered them, quiet, sated, but the way he said it was the way you'd say the sky was blue, that grass was green, the earth was round.

Like they were just plain *true.*

Then again, for him, they would be.

King Callum had a sure thing at his side at all times until the day she died. He might not want *her*, but he was a man and men, it was Sonia's experience, didn't quibble. They'd take it as they could get it, whenever they could get it and in whatever form that took (most of the time).

And, worst of all, her *parents* wanted this for her. They were *honored* she'd be his queen.

They knew his culture. They were friends with his people. They had to understand Sonia's sentence and they wanted her to be their queen, planned for it, even when she was a child.

Which meant, even though she was certain Callum would never allow otherwise, she had no choice. She was, indeed, sentenced to be his queen, trapped in this life...forever.

She wished, however, that she was with Desdemona on her way to be sequestered, whatever that meant.

Instead, she was lying in her bed aching in a way that didn't feel at all bad (even though she told herself it did). She could still feel the delicious specter of Callum seated to the hilt between her legs.

And she was praying that she could spend her years focusing on the good and being able to tolerate the bad without going completely mad.

But she wasn't certain she could do it.

However, she had no choice but to try.

Fighting back the tears that threatened and the mortification that consumed her, Sonia dragged herself from under the covers. As she did she noticed belatedly that Callum, unlike any lover before him (all of whom thought her attachment to the stuffed wolf as an adult was a little bit strange), had tucked her wolf in her arms.

Strike one for the good.

Still, the scale was tilted to the bad side as if the good side had a thimble full of cotton and the bad side held a gosh darn *brick* (or two).

By the time she'd showered, made herself up, and dressed, she had a pounding headache caused by stress, embarrassment, and the constant futile churning of thoughts in her head trying to find some way to escape.

The headache persisted even though the hot shower eased the ache in her muscles, though not entirely. And it didn't do the first thing to alleviate the gently pulsating reminder of the feel of Callum between her legs.

She heard (and ignored) the voices all through getting ready and continued to ignore them as she made her way down the stairs, into the kitchen, and straight to the coffeepot. She poured herself a mug with a splash of skim milk and went to her vitamins, taking the cocktail of supplements with the addition of two capsules of ibuprofen.

Then, because she was their queen and queens should probably not be rude, she walked around the staircase that separated and hid most of the kitchen from the dining room. She knew, from the voices she counted, that Callum, Caleb, Saint, and a voice she didn't know sat at her dining room table.

The minute she appeared in the opening between dining room and kitchen, Callum, seated at the head of the table, turned his head to look at her.

When his clear blue eyes hit her and her mind again registered his intense masculine beauty, her belly wobbled (but she told herself it wasn't in a good way, when it was) and she felt the blood rush to her cheeks as memories of the night before (and that morning) invaded.

Ignoring the wobble and the second wobble she felt when, the moment after his eyes hit her, she watched them grow soft in a *very* sexy way, she leaned against the doorjamb.

She tore her gaze from Callum and glanced about the room, saying, "Morning, guys."

Everyone greeted her with warm smiles.

She heard the legs of Callum's chair against the pile of her rug as he pushed it back and twisted it toward her and her attention went back to him.

"Come here, baby doll," he said in a rumbling tender voice that was so intimate, so knowing, she felt the pulsing between her legs escalate.

Good goodness.

Now he only had to speak to her and her body betrayed her.

If she didn't get herself together, she was never going to find a way out.

She took in breath to calm her system and walked to him. The minute she got close, he leaned forward and hooked her about the hips with his arm, drawing her nearer while being careful of her full coffee mug. He settled her, as ever, in his lap.

This time she wasn't seated there because it was her duty or that was the way he liked it. This time it was a clear affectionate cuddle.

Sonia tried to ignore her audience as she looked into his soft sexy eyes.

"Did you sleep well?" he asked.

She did. She slept the sleep of exhausted abandoned contentment both after he took her last night and after he made her climax this morning.

With her thinking hindered by her headache, she decided it best just to be truthful.

For now.

"Yes," she whispered and his eyes grew even softer and way, way, *way* sexier as the tawny slowly began to seep out of his pupils, erasing the blue, and that made her belly wobble too (and her nipples get hard besides).

Even though she fought it, she didn't win.

His head dipped down, he slid his temple along hers, which was, when he wasn't doing it to be ugly to some poor madwoman, another thing in that thimble on the good side of her scale.

At her ear he said, "Me too."

Her body, betraying her again, caused her to feel some sort of triumph at the knowledge that he liked the way they slept last night and she shivered with delight in his arms.

Those arms tightened, and as if giving her a reward for her response, he ran his lips along the curve of her ear.

She shivered again.

She felt him smile against her ear.

"Callum," she mumbled.

His lips still at her ear, he whispered low, "Right now, I want to carry you upstairs, take those fucking clothes off your sweet little body, and fuck you on your hands and knees like last night." Her heart stuttered to a halt, her body took over her brain completely, her legs shifted unconsciously as the pulse between them quickened, and he flicked her ear with his nose before he finished, still whispering, "*Just* like last night."

She turned her head slightly and tilted it down so her cheek was pressed to the now far thicker whiskers of his and her lips were at the hinge of his strong jaw before she breathed, "Callum."

"Unfortunately, my little one, it'll have to wait for later," he told her and she found she was breathing heavily, her chest rising and falling with it.

"Okay," she mumbled, and though she wanted it to sound noncommittal, even to her own ears it sounded disappointed.

She heard his arrogant satisfied chuckle in her ear before he gave her another squeeze with his arms and lifted his head away.

His spell broken, Sonia realized there were other people in the room. Her face flushed with renewed embarrassment hoping that they didn't overhear Callum's whispers and her body tensed.

Callum felt it. He had to feel it and that must have been why he quickly changed the subject and asked her, "What are you doing today?"

His question surprised her.

She didn't know. She didn't know there would be a choice.

Before he lost his generous mood, she blurted, "I'd like to go to my store."

"Perfect," he grinned, the gold retreating, the blue taking over his irises, and her mouth dropped open at his response and his grin. "Regan's been dying to go to your store. She's on her way here now. You can take her with you."

Sonia liked the idea of showing Regan her store. She was proud of Clear. It was, in the only way she'd ever get, like showing her momma her store because Regan had known her momma for ages and they'd been close friends.

"I'd like that," she said softly and Callum's eyes also went soft, this time not in a sexy way, in a tender way.

"She's also going to take you to the grocery store," Caleb announced from across the table and Sonia's head swung to face him. "You don't have any beer in your house."

Sonia glanced at the clock she could see over her sink in the kitchen and back at Caleb.

"It's 10:30 in the morning," she informed him.

"Your point?" Caleb shot back hilariously before he grinned.

Sonia grinned back.

"Queen Sonia, this is Magnum, he's Sergeant of Callum's Royal Guard," Saint introduced the man sitting at the table that Sonia didn't know. Though she had briefly met him (but didn't remember his name) in the round robin introductions yesterday after they'd dealt with Desdemona.

"Magnum," she smiled at him.

"Queen Sonia," he replied.

She threw her hand out and said to Magnum, "Considering all this queen stuff is new and I don't want to get a big head, you know, being suddenly royal and all, it's probably best to lose the 'queen' part and just call me Sonia." Her eyes glided to Saint to include him in her statement.

She felt Callum's body relax under hers and hadn't noticed it was tense. He leaned forward and grabbed his coffee mug from the table, taking her with him and bringing her attention to him. As he leaned back, his neck twisted, he looked at her and winked.

King Callum *winked* at her.

Holy cow.

Her body went statue still.

He took a sip of coffee, replaced the mug, sat back, and his hand at her hip gave her a squeeze before he called, "Baby doll?"

"What?" she whispered, still frozen, mind blank, reacting to the wink and the fact that that one wink took the cotton out of the thimble and filled it with cement.

"You okay?" Callum asked.

She blinked. Then she swallowed.

"I just have a headache," she replied.

One look at his face told her that was the wrong answer. His brows shot together and his hand at her hip gripped her harder.

"Do you get those often?" he inquired.

"What?"

"Headaches?" he asked, his voice not soft, not tender, not teasing, but sounding impatient.

"Um..." She was uncertain of the state of affairs, or more to the point, uncertain how his mood had flipped so quickly. For goodness sakes, it was just a headache. "Not really. I mean, occasionally. When I'm under stress."

"Did you take something for it?" he queried. She nodded and his hand relaxed as did his body. "Is that what I heard you taking this morning?"

She nodded again, saying cautiously, "That and my vitamins."

"It sounded like you were opening a pharmacy in there. How many vitamins do you take?"

She did a quick mental calculation and told him, "Six."

He stared at her.

"In the morning," she went on when he didn't speak. "I take a couple more at lunch."

He burst out laughing.

She blinked again at his second change of mood in the last thirty seconds then she decided to look on the bright side. At least he didn't look angry anymore.

His hand traveled up her back to cup her neck and maneuver her head toward his.

Mouth again at her ear, he stated quietly, "We'll work out that stress later, baby doll."

And, fighting the shiver his words caused, she could do nothing but nod yet again.

His other hand slid up the outside of her thigh, over her hip, and under her silk knit, wide ribbed, black turtleneck, then down, digging into the waistband of her winter white wool slacks.

This time, she hadn't forgotten their audience and she stiffened in his arms.

"Callum, what are you—?" She stopped when his long finger hooked on something under the material of her slacks and he pulled out her claiming chain. Freeing it completely, he settled it around her hips outside her slacks as she finished breathily, "Doing."

Her mind took that moment to remind her how the chain felt dangling from her body while he drove into her last night, the delicate links a tantalizing torment against her sensitive skin. And more, after they had climaxed, when she had lowered her arms and Callum was still behind her, gently thrusting inside her, the chain had slid up her waist, her ribcage, to rest on the underside of her overly aroused breasts. The charm tweaking so close to her nipple, at the time—every inch of her body so responsive—she'd had to bite her lip not to cry out in pleasure.

That reminder, so sharp it was almost as if took her back to the actual moment, made the urge start to surface, wanton impulses flooded her brain. Things she wanted to do to Callum. Things she wanted him to do to her.

"I like to see it," Callum muttered, his voice bringing her hooded eyes to his. His gaze lifted from the chain to her face and his body grew tight under hers then he whispered, "Fucking hell, baby doll."

She took in a fluttering breath and tried to calm her thoughts, focusing on his hand still moving at her chain. He was fiddling with it and her head tipped down to look.

Then her mind erased as she saw the charm for first time (as she hadn't had a lot of time yesterday and she hadn't been paying much attention to anything but to her fevered thoughts this morning).

In heavy gold, beautifully rendered, it was the head of a snarling wolf with two eyes made of yellow diamonds.

"It's a wolf," she breathed and she was so taken by the charm, entranced by it, she missed the air in the room getting tense.

She forgot the bricks on the bad side of the scale.

She forgot everything.

Except the fact that Callum had put that charm on her claiming chain.

Her head snapped up and he'd moved so close, he had to rear his own back to miss being clipped on the chin.

"I love wolves!" she cried, unable to hide the delight in her voice and still not sensing the air, which had now lightened considerably. In fact, she was so touched by this gesture (obviously someone told him that she loved wolves), that she didn't even notice the soft chuckles coming from the table.

Callum's face was back to that affectionate softness when he replied, "I know you do, honey."

"No, I really, *really* love wolves," she blurted.

The chuckles grew louder but she still didn't process it as Callum was now smiling a white gorgeous smile and his voice held his own mirth when he said, "Yes, honey, I know."

Her head again tipped down and she remarked with wonder in her tone, "He's a beauty."

"I'm glad you think so."

She whipped her head back and uttered with feeling, "Thank you."

His face dipped and he rested his forehead to hers. "You thanked me last night, baby doll, twice. But the second time was so good, you earned another charm."

Her breath caught, her breasts swelled, but she had little time for these reactions.

His mouth took hers in a thorough beautiful kiss much like the one he gave her last night, but this one was different. It was also hungry. Further, it was in front of an audience.

"Should we leave the room?" Caleb asked in a teasing voice.

Callum pulled away and glared at his brother.

Sonia, blushing, back to embarrassed, ducked her head under his chin, tucked her face in his neck, and chanced a glance at the group from under her lashes.

They were all grinning at her and Callum.

But it was Saint who noticed her pinkened cheeks and said to her gently, "I remember those first days after I claimed my mate, Sonia. You don't have anything to be embarrassed about." He looked around the table and said, "We all have either felt it or want to."

Considering Sonia's face was burning so hot, before it melted to oblivion, she decided the best thing to do was to change the subject and do it *immediately*, "You have a mate?"

"I do," Saint replied.

"I'd like to meet her," Sonia told him.

"I'm certain she'd like that too," Saint smiled.

Callum's arms came around her and she decided to take a sip of her coffee instead of giving him her attention, as giving him her attention was making her do stupid things.

Not having her facing him didn't deter Callum in the slightest.

His mouth came to her ear and he whispered, again low, "Something else we're going to do later, baby doll. You're going to tell me what was on your mind a minute ago when you looked like you look about a split second before you come."

Sonia bit her lip, slid her eyes to the side, caught the seriously sexy look on his face (or, it might have been a sexy serious look, she couldn't quite tell), and decided her best way forward was just to nod.

This was the right thing to do. He slid his temple against hers again.

She relaxed in his arms.

The doorbell rang.

"That'll be Regan," Caleb announced.

"I'll get it," Magnum offered and rose from his chair to go to the door.

"Sonia," Callum called.

Sonia kept sipping her coffee with her eyes following Magnum as she mumbled, "Mm?"

"Ryon tells me you throw a Christmas party every year."

That statement brought her head around and she looked in Callum's eyes, wondering what was on his mind.

"Yes," she answered tentatively.

"I've decided, since this situation is likely to keep us here for a while, regardless if we take care of it, we'll stay for the holidays. You should go ahead with the party."

Sonia's heart leapt and another thimble full of cement (maybe two, or even three) joined the first.

"Really?" she asked.

"Really," he replied, his eyes studying the expression on her face with a look in them she could swear was almost doting. "You like Christmas so I want you to have your Christmas just as you like it."

"Hello, all," Regan called as she came in, but Sonia only had eyes for Callum and only had thoughts on the fact that her heart had skipped a happy beat.

Not of her volition, her hand came up and rested against the side of his head.

Then she used her thumb to smooth his dark brow after which she moved it down and she used it to stroke his bottom lip.

Then she said softly, again with feeling, "Thank you."

So deep in her gratitude, she noted only in a dazed way that Callum's face was suddenly hungry, his eyes were fully tawny, and she heard him growl. It came deep from the back of his throat and seemed to vibrate through her body, sending the ever-present pulsating between her legs soaring.

"Oh my, the newly claimed," Regan observed, and both Callum and Sonia, with effort, turned to focus on Callum's mother. "It's a shame this business is happening now, you two need a few weeks alone in a castle."

Sonia stared at her but Caleb spoke in a mutter. "I just hope he can keep his mind on the matter at hand and off his dick."

"Caleb!" Regan snapped at the same time Callum bit out the same word.

"Give me a break, Regan," Caleb returned. "You haven't been here the past ten minutes. Seriously, the newly claimed, fucking hell."

Sonia, firmly out of the moment and back to embarrassed, squirmed in Callum's lap. Callum felt it and he didn't like it.

Therefore, he aimed a dark look at his brother.

"Caleb, I'll not tolerate that shit again," he warned in a dangerous voice.

"Whatever," Caleb mumbled, obviously used to Callum's dangerous voice.

"All right, moving on," Regan announced in a way that said she had *lots* of experience stepping between her battling sons. "Sonia, sweetheart, we're going to the grocery store. Callum called this morning and said practically everything in your refrigerator is white. I don't know what that means but I *do* know it doesn't sound good. Our people *eat*," she finished on a smile.

"Sonia's taking you to Clear now, Regan," Callum informed his mother. "You can go to the grocery store later."

"Brilliant!" Regan cried instantly as her eyes lighted and she clapped happily.

When she did so, Sonia noticed she was carrying a small, glossy, charcoal gray shopping bag.

Wow, it was barely 11 o'clock and Regan had already been shopping. Callum's mom was clearly *the* shopping master.

Taking her mind off the bag, her husband, and moving it to the day before her, Sonia slid out of Callum's lap, taking another sip of coffee before saying, "I just need to run up to my office and get the invitations for my Christmas party. They're ready to post. There's a mailbox on the way to Clear."

Those invitations had been ready to post, stamped, and addressed since the day after Thanksgiving.

Callum was letting her have her Christmas party, something she looked forward to all year.

And, Sonia hoped, maybe, just maybe, if things kept going like this, the good would eventually outweigh the bad.

"Excellent, sweetheart," Regan smiled warmly at her and Sonia smiled warmly back.

Another, definitely larger, thimble of cement on the good things side of the scale was Regan. Until then, Sonia hadn't fully realized what she was missing growing up with Gregor and Yuri and no motherly-type figure.

It was lucky she realized it when she actually *had* a motherly-type figure.

She smiled to herself, suddenly strangely contented. So much so her headache had disappeared. She walked into the kitchen and put her mug in the dishwasher then ran up the stairs to her office. Piling the invitations down the length of her arm, she ran back down.

Callum was in the living room, his head bent to his mother, when Sonia arrived.

Regan took one look at her and stated, "I'll go get a bag, easier to carry those."

"They're in—" Sonia started to tell Regan where to find a bag but Regan waved her hand, rushed forward, divesting Sonia of the invitations and bustling off.

"I'll find them," she muttered and Sonia watched her go.

"Baby doll," Callum called and she turned to him. He got close and grabbed her hand, mumbling, "One thing."

His head was bent to her hand and she looked down too. He was carrying a jeweler's box in plush charcoal gray velvet. He flipped it open and she saw the sparkle inside just a moment before he pulled out the two rings nestled together there and tossed the box unceremoniously on a table close to them.

Then, without further ado, he slid a set of wedding rings on her left ring finger.

Sonia held her breath and stared as he slid on the thin wedding band of gold imbedded with twinkling yellow diamonds and its accompanying yellow diamond solitaire. The solitaire was huge, so gigantic it could be seen from space, and it was set at the sides with more glimmering diamonds.

Regardless of the diamond's size, it wasn't ostentatious but extraordinary. Sonia had never seen anything like its exquisite extortionate beauty.

Callum dropped her hand in an absent way that didn't coincide with the fact he just slid a wedding ring on her finger and this jarred Sonia out of her rapt study of the rings.

Then his hand moved to the chain that was resting outside her slacks. His finger hooked it yet again and he gave it a gentle tug.

"This is important," he declared in a kingly voice and she felt her body start to grow tight at his tone as he went on, "But your people don't understand the significance so that," he jerked his head to her hand, "will declare to *your* people that you're mine."

This wasn't a romantic gesture, a gesture of love.

This was another kind of claiming, one that physically proclaimed the fact that Sonia was Callum's, his possession. He *owned* her and the fierce kingly look on his face cemented that fact.

The thimbles on the good side of the scale started trembling as Regan walked in carrying a bag filled with the invitations.

"Oh look!" she cried. "You're wearing your chain outside your slacks. What a lovely idea."

Regan approached and, woodenly, Sonia turned to her as Regan stopped close and beamed.

"I looked at hundreds of chains before I chose that one for you," Regan commented, and at her words, Sonia felt like rocks were pummeling her body. "I liked the charm," Regan went on. "Such a fierce wolf."

Callum hadn't chosen the chain or the charm for her.

Like her wedding rings, his mother had.

Kings, apparently, didn't bother shopping for their mates, even if it was for things as significant as claiming chains and wedding rings.

And, as another brick crashed down on the bad side of her scales, the thimbles that were added that morning slid off the good side in the tumult.

However, unfortunately, Sonia didn't know the way of the wolves.

She didn't know that it was millennia-old tradition that a wolf's mother chose the chain to be bestowed on his mate and therefore, in a nod to Sonia's humanity but still adhering to their traditions, Regan had also chosen her wedding rings as a matter of course.

Sonia didn't even know they *were* wolves.

So she reacted to what she did know.

She hid the fact that her stomach had tightened and her heart had hardened as Callum brushed her lips with his absentmindedly and obviously dismissed her from his thoughts as he walked back to the dining room table. This indicating to Sonia that his show at the dining room table that morning was exactly that.

A show.

Not the sweet tender behavior of newly claimed mates.

But a performance for his people sitting around that table so they would think all was well in the world of the king and his queen.

It was then her strange brief contentment fled and Sonia made the fierce determination that she'd never, *never* be deceived like she was that morning.

Never.

So when they were in bed and she felt that urge, primal and sharp, she knew, whatever it was and from wherever it came, she was obviously not strong enough to fight it.

But her heart was her own.

Her body might betray her but she vowed she'd never lose her heart.

She mentally threw away her scales as no more measuring was needed.

This was her "beautiful life?"

So be it.

She would be his queen, his "sweet little body" to use and dismiss.

And she would be his people's queen because that was her destiny, and not only had her parents wanted it for her, not only had her dreams been guiding her to it for twenty years, but Gregor had kept her safe in order that she could live that destiny.

But Sonia would hold her heart safe.

She hid these reactions and her thoughts under a falsely bright smile as Regan tucked her arm through Sonia's and led her to the door.

CHAPTER TWELVE

NEWLYWEDS

Sonia and Regan walked through the doors of Clear.

The minute the bell jangled, Mabel, one of Sonia's two shop assistants who was standing behind the counter with a tall, dark-haired, gorgeous, obviously Callum's people woman, shouted, "Sonny!"

Kerry, Sonia's other shop assistant, who was helping some customers, looked around and gave Sonia a big happy smile.

Sonia adored Mabel and Kerry. They were good workers, never called in sick, came in even when they were hungover, hid it like pros, and never complained. They were fantastic with customers and they were both exuberant, full of personality, and made working there fun.

Their reactions to her return were balm to the soul, something Sonia needed desperately.

It was like coming home.

Sonia's gaze moved to the tall woman behind the counter who studied Sonia curiously for a brief moment then bowed her head low in deference to her queen. She couldn't exactly drop to a knee in a shop amongst humans, but her message was clear.

And Sonia wondered if she'd ever get used to that the way Callum was. When they walked in the throne room and everyone sank to a knee, he'd not even glanced at them.

Then again, he'd had a lifetime of feeling entitled that people would be on their knees before him.

Including Sonia.

Sonia shrugged off these thoughts and walked toward the counter with Regan at her side, not knowing what to do about the tall woman so, when her head came up, Sonia inclined her own.

Then she greeted her shop assistants with, "Hey, girls."

"We were so worried," Mabel exclaimed as she rushed around the counter toward Sonia. "Diana said everything was cool but you never take off from work." As Mabel came toward her, Sonia had started to unwind her scarf from around her neck. Mabel suddenly skidded to a halt, her eyes wide on Sonia's scarf, and she screeched, "*Ohmigod!* Look at that ring!" She gasped then let out a strangled cry before she went on, "*Ohmigod! Ohmigod!* Did you get *married?*"

Sonia tensed and Kerry's head swung toward Sonia again. Kerry excused herself and headed their way, but Mabel had grasped hold of Sonia's hand and she yanked it to within an inch of her eyes.

"*Look at that rock!*" she shrieked. "It's *huge!*"

"Ohmigod!" Kerry cried, getting close. "This is *insane!* I can't *believe* this! Did you really get married?"

There it was, as Sonia had noted, her girls were exuberant.

Before Sonia could utter a word, Regan, on Sonia's right side, announced in a proud voice, "Sonia and my son eloped over a long weekend."

"*Ohmigod!*" Mabel and Kerry screamed in unison. They turned to face each other and then started jumping up and down, taking Sonia's hand with them as they did so, jerking Sonia's body repeatedly through her arm.

"Girls, my hand," Sonia said quietly, thinking sadly (and trying to hide it) that for all other humans, this news was reason to shriek and jump up and down.

For Sonia, it was not.

She pinned a bright smile on her face when the girls let go of her hand and looked at Sonia with their faces wreathed with glee.

"You sly fox!" Kerry exclaimed. "I didn't even know you were dating anyone."

Good goodness.

How was she going to explain this?

"Well—" Sonia began.

Mabel's ebullient curiosity saved the day as she interrupted Sonia's frantic thoughts to find a cover story with, "Is he hot?"

Was Callum hot?

Only one answer to that, and as hateful as that answer was, it was a big fat *yes*.

"Well—" Sonia started again but Kerry cut her off this time.

"Of course he's hot. Sonia's hot. Hot likes hot."

"Yeah," Mabel grinned at Sonia. "Stupid question."

"Apparently he's loaded too." Kerry grinned as well. "Heck, you sell that ring, you could feed an entire starving African nation."

This, Sonia thought with uncharacteristic bitterness, was food for thought.

"When are we going to meet him?" Mabel asked and Sonia stilled.

She could barely come to terms with fitting into Callum's life. She'd never considered that he'd have a place in hers.

And she wasn't certain she liked that idea.

"He's very busy," she demurred but Kerry talked over her.

Shoving Mabel playfully on the shoulder she declared, "Of course we'll meet him, crazy. He'll be at her Christmas party."

Oh heck.

Sonia hadn't thought of that.

"Brilliant!" Mabel shrieked.

Sonia fought the urge to close her eyes in despair and instead attempted to beam at her girls. This fortunately worked as they beamed back.

Luckily, Sonia thought, Mabel and Kerry were the kind of people who took their employer's all of a sudden "elopement" in stride. Knowing them, they probably thought it was incredibly romantic.

However, it was highly likely that others, say the guests at her annual Christmas party, would not. They would think it was curious, even weird.

Sonia sighed. So she was weird. She could live with that and had her whole life. It was the least of her worries.

Kerry took Sonia from these disturbing thoughts and turned to Regan.

"So you're mystery, hot, loaded, new hubby's mom. Dig it! I'm Kerry." She offered her hand which Regan shook.

Not to be outdone, Mabel leaned in to shake Regan's hand after Kerry while saying, "And I'm Mabel and you can tell your son I get the first congratulations kiss."

Kerry turned to Mabel and protested, "Why do you get the first kiss?"

"Because I've been in the shop longer," Mabel shot back.

"By...*a day*," Kerry returned and this was true, they'd both been with her since it opened and they started one day after the other.

"I'm sure Callum will be delighted to receive both your congratulatory kisses," Regan stated, smiling with great humor at Sonia.

Sonia was sure he'd like it too. Kerry and Mabel were both uncommonly pretty. Heck, considering what had been inferred by Caleb, Calder, *and* Yuri, Callum might see the two of them and go on the make.

"Callum. That's an *excellent* name," Kerry commented, again tearing Sonia from her thoughts.

"And, seriously, I want what you're drinking because if you're Sonia's hubby's mother, and you look like Sonia's sister, then it's got to be *good*," Mabel noted.

"First-rate skin care regime," Regan blithely replied. "I'll write down the products I use."

"Excellent!" Kerry cried.

"I'm Regan," she introduced herself. "And I'd love a tour of the store."

"I've gotta get back to my customers," Kerry said, grinning as she walked away. "I'll be back."

"I'll show you the store, come on," Mabel offered and then hooked her arm through Regan's and led her away as Regan threw a smile over her shoulder at Sonia.

The tall dark-haired lady came forward and got close.

"My queen," she said softly.

Sonia looked in her startling, clear gray eyes, something she could do as she was wearing heels and the woman was in flats. If Sonia had not been in heels, she'd be looking up.

"Please," Sonia replied quietly, "I'm Sonia."

The woman's gaze warmed and she nodded.

"And you are?" Sonia prompted.

"Diana," she replied.

"Well, thank you, Diana, for being here while I've, erm...been away. I appreciate it."

"Anything for my queen," Diana stated, but when Sonia opened her mouth to speak, Diana quickly went on, "Though, your girls are such fun, it hasn't felt like doing a duty for my king. It's been a blast. More fun than I've had in ages."

Sonia's smile was not forced but genuine when she said, "They're a bit nuts but you're right, they're a lot of fun."

A customer approached the counter ready to check out and Diana turned to her as the customer said on a smile, "Obviously this is a special occasion, I can wait for you to ring me up."

"It *is* a special occasion," Mabel shouted from across the store where she was standing with Regan and Regan was examining a delicate glass decanter. "And after the tour, I'm running out to get champagne!"

"Yippee! Champagne!" Kerry cried from her spot and the customers she was with started giggling.

"Champagne for everyone, on me," Regan declared, to which both Kerry and Mabel yelled, "Yippee!"

"Definitely fun," Diana commented on a chuckle and looked at Sonia. "I'll ring this up. Your mail is stacked on your desk. I've dealt with everything that was urgent. Same with phone messages. Anything that hasn't been seen to, I've written down for you. I was going to take them to Ki..." she stopped then went on, "um, Callum today." She smiled again and finished, "You've saved me a trip."

Sonia caught Diana's hand and gave it a squeeze. "Even if it's been fun, seriously, thank you."

Diana squeezed her hand back and said, "Delighted."

Then Diana went around the counter to wait on Sonia's customer as Sonia went to her tiny office in the back.

Within half an hour it became clear that Diana knew what she was doing. The books were done every evening. The orders had been placed that would keep them stocked for Christmas. And there was very little mail to be dealt with and most of it was junk mail that Sonia threw away. She returned the three phone messages she had and found she was completely caught up.

There came a knock on the door, Sonia called her welcome, and Diana poked her gleaming dark-hair-mixed-with-a-burnished-red head around the door.

"Regan and Mabel are off down the street to get champagne. They should be back in a second," Diana told her.

"Come in a minute and take a load off," Sonia invited and Diana gave her a grateful look.

"Things are quiet," Diana remarked as she entered and sat down. "That is, until we have to ring up Regan's purchases. She's buying half the store. Says she's doing her Christmas shopping in one fell swoop. We'll have to reorder."

This was good news. A good Christmas for Clear meant a good Christmas for Mabel and Kerry. Her girls didn't know it, but every December Sonia split every penny of the profits in half and gave them to the girls as their Christmas bonus, augmenting it from her own personal money if they had a bad year.

This year, evidently, she wouldn't have to augment.

"I get the sense my mother-in-law likes to shop," Sonia remarked on a fond smile.

"Why do you think Harrinton's is so lucrative? Regan is our best customer," Diana joked and they both laughed.

But Sonia couldn't help but think about how Regan liked to shop. And about the thousands of dollars' worth of diamonds Callum so casually slid on her finger. And the expensive way the cabin had been refitted. Also Callum's SUV, which was an SUV but it was also a *luxury* SUV. Not to mention the opulence of the Territorial Mansion.

It hadn't occurred to her before, considering she'd never seen Callum in anything but jeans and flannel shirts, but he truly *must* be loaded.

Then again, she reminded herself, he was a king and kings tended to be that way.

"So?" Diana said expectantly and Sonia came out of her thoughts with a start and looked at Diana's beautiful eager face.

"So?" Sonia parroted, confused.

Diana leaned forward and encouraged, "Tell me all about it. Every *detail*."

Sonia's head jerked, still with confusion, and she asked, "Every detail of what?"

"The claiming!" Diana cried and Sonia jumped.

"What?" Sonia whispered.

"Mine was wild. Oh my, you wouldn't *believe*," she shared, apropos of nothing, leaning ever forward. "I was just going about my business and then I felt him. And, all of a sudden, I couldn't wait. I didn't know for what but I was just excited, ready. Then Harrinton was there. He'd been running. *Running for miles*," she sat back, fanned her face then grinned a saucy grin, "which meant he was sweaty. It was the *best*."

Holy cow.

Was she...?

"He threw me to the ground right there and claimed me."

She was.

"Thank God no one was around," Diana went on, and Sonia gasped, but Diana didn't notice or was so excited to tell her tale, she didn't care and she continued, "He barely got the words out and the chain around my waist before he turned me to my knees and was on me." She sighed and finished dreamily, "It was beautiful."

Horrified at her blunt subject matter, but not able to stop it in spite of herself, Sonia asked, "What...words?"

Diana focused on Sonia. "Didn't King Callum say them?"

"Um..." Sonia mumbled.

"Oh, I forgot, you're human," Diana said. "'Are you mine?' Those are the words. It's like your 'Will you take this man...,' if you say 'yes,' it's the same as 'I do.'" She smiled. "But you know that last part, surely."

Sonia didn't.

Well, she kind of did.

But she still didn't.

Diana continued, "And then the fun stuff starts, unlike you humans, who have to wait for the party to be over. We just go for it right away. We have the party later."

Sonia stared at her trying to hide the fact she was appalled. Did they really just run a woman down and claim her?

"I still remember every second," Diana said wistfully. "It was the most beautiful day of my life."

Apparently, they did and the women liked it.

Then it hit her that Callum hadn't done that. He'd gone against the customs of his culture and he'd tried courting her first. He wasn't very good at it and he obviously didn't like to do it, but he'd tried it.

Even as king, who clearly, by his behavior, felt at liberty to do pretty much anything he wanted to do, he'd tried to give her a courtship.

It was only a week he'd given her, but if his people found their mates, threw them to the ground, and claimed them, then a week to Callum would have felt like a year of dating.

Luckily (for him), he'd only had to wait a few days.

Still, Sonia didn't know what to make of that.

Diana broke into her thoughts. "Now, tell me about yours."

"Sorry?" Sonia asked in a shocked voice. She couldn't really mean she wanted Sonia to describe her claiming.

"Tell me all about your claiming. Everything," Diana encouraged.

She *did* want Sonia to describe her claiming.

"Um..." Sonia hedged, "it's probably like your people's average, everyday, erm...claiming."

Diana burst out laughing like Sonia was an award-winning comedian on a sold-out tour.

When Diana gained control of herself, she wiped her eyes and coaxed, "No, seriously. We're talking about King Callum here. Everyone is going to want to know about *your* claiming."

Sonia hesitated before she asked, "Is it usual for the king's story to be known like this?"

Diana nodded. "Everyone knows Mac and Regan's story. But yours...I figure yours will be a winner considering it's Callum we're talking about."

"What does that mean?" Sonia queried.

But she knew.

Oh did she know.

Diana opened her mouth to speak but there came a knock on the door and Kerry stuck her head through.

"Regan bought enough champagne for customers too. We're ready to pop the cork and we need the lady of honor. Come on, Sonny!"

When her head disappeared, Diana caught her eye, smiled, and stood.

With no choice, Sonia stood too. As she did, she schooled her features, buried her sorrow and prepared to pretend this was a happy occasion full of smiles, shrieks of glee, and bottles of champagne.

Upon arrival, Sonia found that Regan had not bought *a* bottle of champagne. She'd purchased *twelve* of them, all chilled, and a package of plastic champagne glasses.

They were all standing in front of the counter and Mabel was preparing to pop the cork on one when the bell over the door went. Out of habit every eye (but Regan's) went to the door.

"Ho...my...*gawd*," Kerry breathed.

Kerry did this because Callum was walking in, followed by Ryon, a double threat of ultra-tall, dark, handsome man. Callum's eyes were on Sonia and his mouth was engaged in aiming a sexy intimate grin in her direction.

Sonia felt her belly twist at the same time the pulse between her legs quickened.

With everyone frozen at the counter staring at him, Callum walked through with his natural masculine grace. He came directly to Sonia and slid an arm around her shoulders, curling her front to his.

"Hey, baby doll," he murmured when she tipped her head back and his eyes hit hers.

In harmony, Sonia heard Mabel *and* Kerry emit lustful sighs.

"What's happening here?" Ryon asked.

Sonia began to look around Callum but his other hand came to her neck and he recaptured her attention with his thumb at her jaw, tilting her face back to his.

Then he bent his head and touched her lips.

The pulse strengthened between her legs as her belly dipped, but her brain reminded her that this was all show.

Just a show.

"We're having champagne to celebrate Callum and Sonia's weekend elopement," Regan replied and Sonia watched Callum's eyebrows go up.

"We eloped?" he asked in a low voice only she could hear.

"Apparently," Sonia whispered back.

He grinned.

Sonia stared at his mouth.

He started chuckling.

She mentally shook herself and pulled against his arm.

Callum allowed this but only so far as turning away from her front and tucking her into his side.

"Then Ryon and I are just in time," Callum announced to the group.

Kerry and Mabel were staring at him with wide eyes.

Then Mabel breathed, "You're not hot. You're *dreamy*."

Everyone chuckled except Sonia, Mabel, and Kerry. Mabel and Kerry because they were still entranced with all that was Callum. Sonia because she didn't think anything was humorous.

"Do you play basketball?" Kerry blurted.

"No," Callum answered.

"You're flipping tall," Kerry blurted again.

"Yes," Callum agreed with a thread of amusement in his deep voice.

Sonia had to do something about this. This could go on all day.

So she said, "Kerry, Mabel, quit drooling and meet my husband. Callum, these are my girls, Kerry and Mabel." She indicated each in turn. "Girls, this is my new husband, Callum." She gestured to Callum.

Callum's fingers curled around her shoulder flexed almost convulsively and definitely fiercely each time Sonia said the word "husband." Sonia thought that was a bit overkill considering no one but Sonia could feel his fingers on her shoulder.

"Ladies," Callum greeted.

Mabel tore her eyes from Callum and looked at Sonia.

"I can see why you hid him, Sonny," she observed. "I would hide him too. Good call, keeping him to yourself until you got the ball and chain on *that* leg."

There was more laughter even though no one but Sonia knew the proverbial ball and chain was worn by the wife this time. Then they heard a champagne cork pop.

Everyone looked to Ryon who'd done the deed.

"Let's stop talking and celebrate," he declared on a boom.

"Yee ha!" Kerry shouted.

Plastic glasses were passed around, even to the five customers browsing the shop. When everyone (including the customers) had a glass and were gathered close, they all turned to Callum and Sonia.

"To the newlyweds!" Mabel cried, lifting her glass.

Everyone but Callum and Sonia followed suit and shouted in gleeful harmony, *"To the newlyweds!"*

Sonia wished she could disappear.

Instead, she smiled.

Callum, on the other hand, much better at playing his part in this travesty, took her chin in his fingers, gently tipped her head back, and he kissed her.

It was soft and sweet but it was also long.

Long enough for laughter and catcalls to ring out and long enough for it to build from soft and sweet to something else. Something that required Callum to drop his fingers from her chin, slant his head, and drag her into his arms.

She was regretfully in a daze when his mouth broke from hers and his head moved, his temple sliding against her hair.

His lips at her ear, he murmured, "To the newlyweds."

Then his arms gave her an affectionate squeeze.

The hoots, laughter, and giggles surrounding her penetrated her daze and Sonia closed her eyes against the pain in her heart.

And, in Callum's ear, she whispered, "To the newlyweds."

Sonia sat on her bed and massaged lotion into her feet, absently listening to the voices of Callum and his men downstairs.

She was running through her day in her mind in an effort to control the panic, and if she was honest (which she was not), the expectation of what the night might bring.

While the champagne celebration went on at Clear, Callum had explained that he'd arrived because he, too, was curious about her shop.

But also, he explained, because he disliked being parted from her.

She'd been gone less than an hour and he claimed he disliked being parted from her.

Really.

He said this after he'd firmly detached them from the group in a way that appeared he wished for them to have a moment to their newlywed selves. They were far enough away so no one could overhear which meant, to Sonia's way of thinking, without an audience, he said it with no purpose at all.

But he said it like he meant it.

Maybe, she thought, he was trying to convince himself.

Or maybe her.

Or maybe both of them.

She'd struggled with how to respond and decided to give him a hug.

This worked. His arms closed around her and he gave her another affectionate squeeze. She made a point to remember that for future reference.

He and Ryon stayed for a while then Ryon gave Callum a look, Callum sighed with resignation, touched his mouth to Sonia's, and they left.

Shortly after, to Sonia's surprise, Waring arrived at Clear on the errand of loading up Regan's four bags of purchases, even though Sonia lived four blocks away (and Regan and she had walked) and nothing in the bags was that heavy.

Instead of packing up the bags and whisking them away for his dowager queen, he'd had a glass of champagne, managed cheekily to chat up *both* the enchanted Mabel and Kerry (who were staring at him with an amazement that was almost, but not quite, how they gazed at Callum) *then* he loaded up Regan's bags and took them away.

That was when Sonia realized that she'd suddenly acquired a number of new names on her Christmas gift list and asked Regan if they could go to the mall. Regan's eyes lit, she instantly pulled her cell out of her big leather designer bag, hit some buttons, and said into the phone, "Caleb, Sonia and I need a ride to the mall."

Why Caleb needed this information, Sonia didn't know.

It became clear ten minutes later when a shiny SUV pulled up outside Clear. Another man who was obviously one of Callum's people collected them (to Mabel and Kerry's delight as he, too, was enormously good-looking). His name was Nikolas. He seemed a bit (but not much) older than Waring, but he was far more serious and thus didn't spend any time drinking champagne or chatting up Mabel *or* Kerry, much to their obvious dismay.

He took them to the mall where, with Regan's guidance, Sonia bought Caleb, Calder, and Ryon Christmas presents and where she and Regan had a late lunch. This included a lovely, getting-to-know-you-better conversation that, luckily, didn't include Regan asking about Sonia's claiming. But, unfortunately, didn't include Sonia having enough courage to ask Regan about Diana's open curiosity about the same. Then he took them to the grocery store where Regan bought Sonia and Callum a mountain of very unhealthy food. Finally, he took them back to Sonia's house.

When Sonia alighted from the SUV and walked to the back of the vehicle to grab some bags, she heard Regan call her name.

She looked at her mother-in-law who was gazing at Sonia, perplexed.

"Sweetheart, what are you doing?" Regan asked.

Sonia, having the handles of two grocery bags in her hand, looked at Regan then at Nikolas then at Regan again.

"What do you mean?" she asked in return, for it was readily apparent what she was doing.

Before she knew it, Nikolas had silently rid her of her bags and Regan came forward, tucking her arm through Sonia's, and guiding Sonia toward the house.

Regan's head got close and she whispered, "Sweetie, you're queen. In company, queens don't carry bags."

At Sonia's horrified expression, Regan smiled an understanding smile and tugged her closer with a pull on her arm.

"It's been so very long, I forgot how strange it all was after I'd been claimed. Mac had only been a prince then, but still, the life he claimed me into was very different to the simple life I'd lived," Regan remarked and patted Sonia's arm with her other hand. "But, I promise, you'll get used to it like I did."

Sonia wasn't sure she would, and as the late afternoon wore into the evening, she was certain of it.

This was because, when they arrived in the house, she found that Saint, Magnum, Caleb, Ryon, and Callum had been joined by Julianna, Saint's mate. Julianna was a lovely woman with a bright smile and a quiet but friendly manner. She was smaller than most of Callum's people, but still slightly taller than Sonia.

After Sonia met Julianna, while Nikolas carried in all their purchases, Callum claimed her, situating her in his lap, and taking a moment to ask about her day.

While he did this, and she answered his quiet questions, Julianna put the groceries away in Sonia's kitchen.

Listening to Julianna move around in her kitchen, Sonia noticed Regan settle herself with a book on one of the couches in the living room while Nikolas built a fire.

And something about all of this didn't sit quite right with Sonia.

"Um..." she started and turned her eyes to Callum, "maybe I should help Julianna."

Callum's brows went up then his smile grew wide.

Then he said something that caused her temper to rise and her palms to itch.

"Baby doll, when no one's around, your job is to take care of me." She stared at him (as this was the point where her temper started rising and her palms started itching) and he continued, "But when someone's around, their job is to take care of *us.*"

Seriously?

He might be king but...

Seriously?

He continued, "Saint called Julianna here to do that. It's her duty. She'd be offended if you went in and helped."

Sonia decided to keep on the subject *she* wanted to discuss.

"My job is to take care of you?"

He grinned. "I thought I explained that."

He had.

He had just not done it thoroughly.

"How, precisely and in all the varied forms, am I required to do that?"

His grin turned positively wolfish.

"I'm guessing you understand the most important part."

"Indeed," she rejoined with irritation and he chuckled before continuing.

"The other parts include you cooking for me, caring for our home, our clothes, if there's no one around to do it. Understanding my schedule and providing for it. Making certain I have what I need or want available to me so when—"

"So," she broke in, "in other words, I'm to be your little wife?"

His best answer to that question was "no."

Instead, being Callum, his eyes, for some reason beginning to change to golden, he replied, "Yes."

"Did your people skip past the twentieth century?" Sonia inquired with sarcasm.

The gold obliterated the blue not, she sensed, due to anger, but, she instinctively knew, with something else. Something that made that ever-present throb between her legs deepen and his face dipped close. "Baby doll, I'd really like to give you the opportunity to work out your anger right now, but regrettably I've got things to do."

She stared then glared then asked, "What does that mean?"

She asked it, but she really didn't want to know.

However, he told her.

His face dipped even closer, veering to the left at the last minute, he said in her ear, "That means, you want rough play and I want to give it to you. But I'll have to give it to you later."

She wanted rough play? What on earth was he talking about?

She didn't have the chance to ask, not that she wanted the answer to *that* question either.

Giving her a "we're done talking about this" squeeze, Callum dismissed her, turned his attention to the copious papers and files on her dining room table and the laptop pointed in his direction.

Regardless of his inattention to her, he still kept Sonia pinned to his lap.

And he did this for a good long while.

He did this while they ate dinner. A dinner which Julianna cooked in Sonia's kitchen and served in Sonia's dining room on Sonia's plates, using Sonia's cutlery and glasses, and cleaned up after, again in Sonia's kitchen.

And he did this while the men talked, not only about the rebellion, the intelligence they were currently in the process of gathering, and the strategy they were forming to quell it, but about all things kingdom. What was happening in other regions. Saint's takeover and eventual cleanup of the Western Territories. Invitations to official ceremonies and which ones Callum would take (none of them) and who would go in his stead (mostly Regan, but also, surprisingly, once the rebellion was crushed, Ryon).

It was, she hated to admit, fascinating; this whole secret world that was obviously thriving but completely unknown amongst her world.

What was more fascinating was Callum's intense interest in all of it. Sonia had the sense that he didn't rule with a heavy hand, but he certainly liked to have his finger on the pulse of absolutely everything. He was interested in what his people were doing, making sure that they were living peaceful prosperous lives, and he took his role as their leader very seriously.

Callum interrupted the proceedings only once, to guide Sonia upstairs with his hand firm in hers in order to take her to the bathroom to administer her injection. And this he did with now practiced ease, quickly, but as usual, she emerged from the burn snug in the circle of his arms, and if Sonia still had her scales, this would definitely be on the good side.

Regan left with a hearty good-bye and warm smile to Sonia.

Julianna, who had—when she was not serving them, to Sonia's disgust—sat completely quiet in *Saint's* lap, left with Saint on a quiet farewell and a shy smile at Sonia.

The night wore on, Sonia sitting in Callum's lap, Callum seeming not to know she was there but doing things intermittently and unconsciously that made that damnable throb ache. Like fiddling with the charm on her claiming chain or occasionally drawing lazy circles with the tips of his long fingers at her hip.

Finally, when another man arrived (his name was Bodim), carrying large, scrolled up pieces of papers, which, she saw when he spread them out on her table, were maps of the Western Territories with lots of markings on them, Callum's attention turned back to her.

Mouth again at her ear and voice lowered, he ordered, "Go to bed, little one."

His ordering her to go to bed, she thought, was bad.

Escape, she knew, was good.

She instantly made a move to slip off his lap but his hand tightened, stalling her progress.

His voice a barely audible murmur, he went on to command, "Don't wear anything to bed. I want you naked when I join you."

She pressed her lips together, ignored the pulse that shot from the juncture of her legs straight to her nipples, and met the sexy serious look in his eyes (or seriously sexy look, she still didn't know which).

Without a word, Sonia slid from his lap and called her goodnights, then she went upstairs and did exactly what *she* wanted to do.

This was investigating her catalogues and trawling the Internet to find Regan's gift. She couldn't buy Regan a gift with Regan actually there, but she needed to buy Regan a gift. It was, indeed, Christmas and Regan was her mother-in-law.

She got distracted while online shopping for Regan and swerved down the road of shopping for Callum. She told herself this was because it was her queenly duty to buy her king Christmas gifts. But it really wasn't. He looked good in clothes and she found she enjoyed buying them for him. So much so, she searched for evidence of his size (and found his clothes hung in her closet, his toiletries put tidily away in her bathroom, and noted Julianna had been busy) and in the end maybe went a bit overboard.

She eventually finished buying presents for all the new entries on her Christmas list, even Julianna and Diana, both of whom she found she liked tremendously, though she couldn't quite say why. She wrapped the ones she purchased for Callum's family that day and headed to bed.

She put on her nightgown and left on her panties, defying Callum's order to be naked. Firstly, because she didn't like sleeping naked, though she didn't mind it last night (then again, she'd slept the sleep of abandoned contentment). Secondly, because she may be his queen and her duties may be extensive, but he gosh darn couldn't tell her what to wear, especially not to bed. No, strike that, he couldn't tell her what to wear *anytime.*

She finished lotioning and oiling her face, feet, hands, and cuticles. And, with the hum of deep male voices plotting in her dining room (something Sonia vaguely recognized that was tremendously weird, but she had had a lot of weird recently and now it didn't even penetrate), Sonia switched off her light.

She cuddled her stuffed wolf and stared at her tree.

And she came to the realization, as the hum of voices and the twinkling of the lights lulled away her panic (and expectation), that she'd drifted through her thirty-seven years of life in a fog.

Losing her parents so young, knowing in an integral way she was more than a little bit strange, and if people knew the things she could do, they might even fear her, Sonia had never thought to dream.

Considering she had to hide her gifts from everyone, she never fantasized about who her husband would be, what their life would be like, how many children she'd have, because how would she go about living that kind of lie?

Therefore, she never considered living with another person and deciding who would do the cooking and who would take out the trash. She never thought about how she and her partner would argue and how they would make up. Where they'd go on vacation. If she'd get impatient with him watching too many sports on TV and if he'd get impatient because it took her too long to get ready. She never pictured a time when, together, they brought out the boxes of Christmas decorations and littered the house with them. Year by year adding precious memories, purchasing new ornaments to put on their tree and sharing moments that would be cherished.

She'd bought her white picket fence farmhouse knowing she'd be the only one living in it and shrouding her disappointment that she was fated to live her life alone.

But now, she thought sleepily, having dreamed of Callum so long (an indication of her destiny before she even knew it was her destiny), she realized she *did* have fantasies of what her life would be like. They were as unobtainable as her dream Callum was (she thought then and she still did). But the feelings she had with Callum in those dreams, *that* was what she would have wanted to nurture in her real life, if it had been possible.

Not this.

Never this.

She took in a breath and let it out in one long sad sigh, closed her eyes, clutched her wolf close and fell asleep.

She awoke with Callum's mouth between her legs over her panties, the urge already upon her, overwhelming her, wresting away her control.

She fought it with her mind, but even as she did, her hips pressed up to meet his mouth as she emitted a low whimper and the throb between her legs started to devour her.

Callum's mouth lifted away but his finger replaced it, drifting light as a feather against the fabric of her panties, causing a sensual torment.

"I thought I told you to go to bed naked," Callum's deep voice vibrated between her legs and she whimpered again. Her hands going to his hair to press him back. Her hips pushing against the light touch of his finger. Her nipples, already hard, straining against the fabric of her nightgown, causing such pleasure, it was torture.

"You defy me?" he asked, still denying her his mouth.

"Callum," she whispered.

"Answer me," he commanded and she pressed up again, seeking his mouth, keeping her silence, the Sonia she knew trying to beat back the Sonia that he created.

And failing.

He shifted her underwear aside and two fingers penetrated her, not gently, brutally, and she moaned at the beauty of it, needing it, wanting it, having throbbed for it all day.

"Answer me, Sonia," he demanded.

"I..." she whimpered and for a brief moment the Sonia she'd been her whole life surfaced, breaking through the urge. "You can't tell me what to wear."

His fingers slid out then they thrust back in and she moaned, the urge rushed back, stronger than before, and she lifted her hips to meet them.

"My queen likes to play rough," he growled, sounding pleased.

"No, I—" she began but his fingers pulled out and hooked at the gusset of her panties. With a vicious wrench, the fabric tore in several places and the panties were gone.

She gasped, but his big hands slid along her inner thighs, gripping her behind her knees, lifting them to fully bent and spreading her legs wide, boldly exposing her.

Sonia felt vulnerable for a moment before his mouth came down on her and all feelings evaporated except the exquisite pulse accelerating between her legs.

He wasn't gentle with his mouth either. He was hungry, insatiable, feeding on her with his lips, his tongue, even his teeth, causing Sonia to lose any hold she had left on her true self as her body forced her to give into the urge.

She was panting, rocking her hips against his mouth, spreading her legs ever wider to give him access. Greedy for him, for what he could make her feel, reaching out and embracing the creature he could make her be. The creature, something buried inside her told her, she was *meant* to be.

She slid close to the edge, no longer scared of the enormity of it, ready to let it take her, *needing* for it to consume her so she could exist in her skin the way she was intended to. The way she only did in these times with Callum. She cried out, and the instant she did, his mouth disappeared and she was yanked from the edge.

"Callum!" she exclaimed her protest but he wasn't leaving her.

He was over her, his weight settling into her, and she gloried in it. Feeling the promise of him a scant second before he reared his hips back and impaled her, fucking her like she loved it, slamming into her violently, filling her full, again and again and again.

His mouth captured hers and he gave her a devouring kiss, his tongue invading as his shaft drove mercilessly inside her.

She wrapped her limbs around him and lifted her hips to meet his. Welcoming him. Taking him all the way in and loving the feel of him filling her full so much, she moaned recklessly against his tongue.

He pulled out and flipped her to her belly, yanking her up to her knees.

"Yes," she gasped.

This was it. This was right. This was who she was. This was who *they* were, Sonia and Callum.

Perfect.

Positioning himself between her legs, Callum leaned forward and gripped her hair, using it to yank her up to her hands.

She felt it then, the sensation that this was *exactly* Sonia. The Sonia she was supposed to be, in front of Callum on her hands and knees.

She held her breath and felt her thighs quiver in sweet anticipation, arching her back, tilting her behind, offering her sex to him brazenly.

He accepted her invitation and seated himself to the root as he yanked her hair back, arching her neck. But he needn't have done it for she threw her head back at the splendor of him.

Then he did it again.

And again.

And again.

She reared into his hips, greeting every plunge, feeling finally whole, finally right when she took him all.

The tension built and built until her blood was boiling. Until she felt she was going to come out of her skin. Until she cried out to her wolf and exploded in sheer bliss. Through her climax she felt him impale her one last time and heard, as if from far away, the depth of his answering groan.

Just as last night, after, he rocked inside her, his shaft stroking her sex gently as his fingers drifted over the skin of her bottom, the small of her back, hooking her chain and tugging until it caught on her hips. This action of Callum's, last night and just then, she felt was profound. The reminder of the chain that signified she was finally his, just as she was always destined to be.

He twisted it so the links slid around her waist, the lightest of sensations making her shiver against him.

Then, his strokes coming slower and slower, finally he started to pull away.

"No," she whispered, pressing her hips back.

He stilled, thankfully still hard and staying inside. She'd never known a man to stay rock hard that long afterwards.

"Baby doll?" he called.

She answered his call, using her mouth and her hips, still pressing into him, explaining her need. "I don't want to lose you."

He glided out and then back in one last time while murmuring, "My little one."

Then his hips forced her off her knees and her legs, of their own accord, opened wide so he could settle between them, his body both surrounding her and filling her deep.

He moved the hair away from her face before he rested some of his weight into his forearms in the bed at her sides, the rest of it settled into her.

She loved how big he was, his body, his shaft, how it surrounded her, filled her, became her whole world. It melted away her ever-present loneliness, making her feel, with Callum encasing her in his frame, filling her so deep, she'd never be lonesome again.

She tipped her bottom up into his groin, non-verbal indication of the intensity of her thoughts.

He pressed in deeper, giving her more of what she was seeking, filling her even fuller.

"You like this," he said softly in her ear.

It wasn't a question, it was a statement. There was an element of surprise, but the low rumble of his voice revealed the depth of his approval.

Sonia didn't answer.

He pushed in further and she sighed contentedly.

She felt his smile against her ear.

"I like it too," he whispered. "It's everything we are." He slid out a bare inch then settled back in. "The connection, our connection, so fucking strong."

There was a depth in his voice that slithered lazily through her system and then settled there in a way that felt like forever.

He went on, "And it's everything I am to you." His arms moved in tighter at her sides. "Your protector." He ran his lips around the curve of her ear and she trembled underneath him before he murmured, "Lift your ass for me, little one, I want to go deep." Without hesitation, Sonia did as she was told and Callum did what he wanted, muttering, "And I'm also your possessor."

She shivered in delight at this last and his arms tightened all the more.

Her arms were cocked and under her body, pinned to the bed, but she reached out a hand, laced her fingers in his, and tilted her head until her nose was resting against their hands.

She tipped her hips up again and mumbled, "For me, wolf, I just like to be full of you. It makes me feel whole. It, finally, makes me feel right."

She missed his answering growl because it was then Queen Sonia slid into an abandoned sleep. Surrounded, connected, protected, possessed, contented, and beautifully full of her king.

Sonia's sleeping body was shifted, the nightgown pulled up. Her arms, unresisting, rising to make this task easy, and the nightgown was swept away.

Then she was curled, pulled close, a strong arm circling her waist, molding her body down the side of Callum's hard one.

She rested her cheek against his pectoral and snaked an arm around his flat stomach.

She started to shift into sleep as he murmured, "The days, I can forget, baby doll. But the nights..." His voice dropped to a hoarse growl, filled with intense feeling. "The nights will be torture knowing I won't have this for eternity."

Even if she was conscious enough to process his words, she wouldn't have understood them.

However, she wasn't conscious enough for he'd barely uttered his last word before she was asleep.

Soft and fleeting, the touch of fingers trailing the pinpricks on her upper buttocks drifted. The same when the fingers became lips, something about them Sonia couldn't hold on to but it felt as if the touch yearned to be healing.

Then Sonia was being lifted.

She was cradled in the warm cocoon of Callum sitting, back to the headboard, fully clothed, in her bed.

Still half asleep in his arms, she nuzzled closer, burying her face in his neck.

His fingers invaded between her legs, toying, playing.

"The men are here."

"Mm," she replied, pressing into his hand, seeking even in her sleep.

"Sonia?" he called.

"Play with me before you go," she urged.

His arm about her tightened, his neck twisted and she felt his lips at her temple, and then Callum did as she asked.

When she was finished, he lifted her again, settled her in bed, and tucked her stuffed wolf in her arms.

Mostly asleep, she drifted further into sated oblivion.

Her eyes fluttered but remained closed when his lips glided along the curve of her ear, at the same time his hand went between her legs from behind and his fingers entered her again.

She lifted her bottom in reflexive invitation.

His fingers slid out, gliding lazily through the folds of her wetness, his mouth still at her ear, his voice husky when he stated admiringly, "Always in heat, my greedy little queen."

Then his hand disappeared, her hips settled, and Sonia clutched her wolf closer as Callum tucked her tight in the bedclothes and she drifted off to sleep.

And this was to be the rhythm of Sonia's life for a while.

Nights (and often during the days besides) being forced by the irresistible urge to "play" as she learned Callum called it. Sometimes rough, sometimes sweet, but always ending up devoured by it. And, often in the nights, desperate to keep him close, to feel whole, sliding off her knees, Callum still inside, and falling asleep with his weight surrounding her, him filling her.

Mornings were spent cocooned in his arms as Callum gave her more of what her body craved and left her tucked safe in her bed in a way her mind wished it could truly be.

All of this leaving her feeling pampered, desired, protected, and adored.

But Sonia spent her days steadfastly guarding her heart against a king who apparently wanted his queen to believe she was much desired, much adored, definitely pampered, and even cherished.

Which meant that Sonia had to guard her heart with a growing ferocity that, the longer she did it, the more the bitterness built.

CHAPTER THIRTEEN

PARTY

"Callum, this is Jay and Jo, my neighbors from down the street, and their boys Jed and Jake," Sonia introduced Callum to the family who'd just arrived at her Christmas Party. "Guys, I'd like you to meet my new husband, Callum."

Callum heard Jo gasp and saw Jay's eyes grow wide in shock and this was about the same reaction as everyone had when they met him.

His fingers, resting at Sonia's hip, tensed reflexively.

Even though it was a human word that meant little to him as it meant little to many humans, he fucking loved it when Sonia called him "husband."

And tonight she'd been doing that a great deal.

The family recovered from their surprise and the man thrust his hand out to shake Callum's.

"We're the 'J' family," he announced. Then, strangely, to Callum's way of thinking (but many things humans did Callum thought were strange), removed himself from the family legacy his wife clearly created by declaring with practiced embarrassment, "It was Jo's idea."

Callum's eyes went to Jo. "It's a good idea. My mother had the same. My brothers' names are Calder, Caleb, and Calvin."

Sonia's body stiffened beside him, which he completely ignored. She did this often for reasons sometimes unknown, sometimes she'd tell him. He had decided in the three weeks he'd known her that if it was important, she'd tell him, which she didn't have the least problem doing. The other times weren't worth concerning himself with.

"You're the 'Cal' family," Jo declared brightly, giving her husband an annoyed nudge with her elbow.

"We are," Callum stated proudly.

"Jed, Jake, your presents are under the tree," Sonia said, her eyes fond on the two young lads. "Go and—"

She didn't finish. The boys raced to the tree, both of them ending their dash dropping to their knees on a skid.

"They love your presents best every year," Jo confided and Callum turned back to see she'd leaned toward Sonia. "It's giving me a complex," she added jokingly.

That night Callum learned many people loved Sonia's presents best every year. Indeed that night Callum learned Sonia gave *everyone* presents they loved best every year. He'd never seen anything like her casual generosity.

Another in a myriad of ways he'd found in the three weeks he'd had his queen that she was absolutely fucking perfect.

"Um, it wasn't *my* skateboards I saw them racing each other on, fruitlessly I might add, through the snow on the sidewalks on Christmas day last year," Sonia replied on a smile.

"So!" Jay boomed, butting into the women's conversation and glancing between the two of them. "This is unexpected, though we've seen a lot of activity at your house lately," Jay informed them, eyes speculative, declaring openly his neighborly prying, something else humans did that mystified Callum. Wolves let other wolves be. If they wanted to share, which they usually did, they'd share. Uninvited inquisitiveness might get your throat torn out by another wolf's teeth, a strong deterrent. "Married!" Jay continued. "That's a big surprise. How did you two meet?"

Sonia tensed and opened her mouth to reply, but as usual that night, Callum got there before her.

"We didn't meet. I saw her and thought she was the prettiest woman I'd ever laid eyes on. I grabbed her, carried her up to my cabin in the mountains, and spent three days talking her into marrying me. She agreed, we did the deed, and came back down the mountain."

Callum liked this story.

He liked it because of the hilarious reactions of the humans.

"You...*what?*" Jay asked while Jo blinked at him, repeatedly and rapidly.

"He's joking!" Sonia exclaimed, going directly into damage control, as usual that night after he told this tale, leaning into him and patting his stomach.

Now her pats were much harder than they were at the beginning of the evening but they were still puny, as female human pats tended to be. Or likely male ones, for that matter, though Callum had never been patted by a male, nor would he ever be.

"We've known each other forever," she went on. "It almost feels like we knew each other since before we were born. I met him when I was seventeen. It's been an off and on, long-distance relationship. I never knew it would come to this, but when he surprisingly asked me, I said yes right away. We decided not to waste any more time so we eloped."

Callum liked Sonia's story better.

What he liked best of all was that they were both mostly true.

Suddenly, Jo's eyes bugged out, she leaned forward and grasped Sonia's hand.

Callum stiffened.

This party was not in the least like a party a wolf would throw. For one thing, no one had shown up smashed. For another thing, even though it started an hour ago, still no one was smashed.

That said, he was enjoying himself immensely, mainly due to being with Sonia, who was taking great pleasure in entertaining her friends and being with the people who clearly cared about her.

However, he was having more than a little difficulty with humans, female and male, touching his mate. The wolf's protective instinct of their mate was naturally strong. Callum's protective instinct for his queen was stronger. Callum's protective instinct for Sonia was immeasurable. You didn't approach a wolf's mate without permission, certainly not if you were a stranger to that wolf, and you definitely didn't touch her.

Even so, tonight amongst Sonia's people, he couldn't give in to the instinct. If he had, her beautifully clinical living room would be littered with unconscious bodies.

"My God!" Jo cried. "Your ring is *gorgeous!*"

"Oh Lord," Jay told the ceiling as his eyes had rolled there. "Here we go."

Jo examined Sonia's ring closer, not taking her eyes from it but still managed to bicker. "Well it *is*, Jay." She yanked Sonia's hand toward her husband, "Look at it."

Jay didn't look at Sonia's ring.

He turned aggrieved eyes to Callum, seeking male camaraderie. "She's always on me to buy her a bigger ring."

He didn't find his camaraderie as Callum replied abruptly, "So do it."

It was Jay's turn to blink, Sonia's turn to stiffen, but Jo burst out laughing.

"I like him," she said to Sonia, releasing Sonia's hand and jerking her head at Callum. "If I didn't like all that was *him*," she boldly gestured to Callum from top to toe, "then I'd like his accent. If I didn't like *that* then I'd *still* like him."

Sonia relaxed and smiled at Jo, as did Callum, deciding that he also liked Jo.

"If you want to make nice with the men in the neighborhood," Jay advised with forced joviality, "you might want to take a little care."

"It's highly unlikely Sonia and I will be settling here," Callum announced.

Sonia went rock solid at his side and Jed and Jake, who were rushing up to them with their unwrapped presents in their hands, skidded to a halt, and the cheerful expressions on their faces melted.

"Sonny's moving?" Jed, or Jake, Callum didn't know which was which, whispered.

"We haven't decided yet," Sonia said swiftly with a radiant smile at the boy and quickly changed subjects. "So, what do you think? Do you like them?"

The boys, as children do, human or wolf, immediately remembered their presents. Their faces lit and Jake (or Jed), shouted, "They're *awesome*!"

Then both boys ran forward and gave her awkward yet genuine hugs which forced Callum to release her.

This he didn't mind. Children were no threat.

Further, he liked watching Sonia's relaxed innate affection for the boys. Something which he hoped, very soon, he'd be witnessing between her and their own children.

"I'm hungry," Jay announced and then made another try at friendly discourse with Callum. "Sonia always puts on the best spread."

This, to Callum's way of thinking, wasn't true. Although there was a good deal of food and every bite-sized item he had tasted was appetizing, there wasn't enough meat, there wasn't enough cheese, and there wasn't a single thing that required a knife and fork. Most people took a small, white, china plate and a napkin and that saw them through.

The minute Callum had seen the caterers laying out the fare, he'd been alarmed. Although no one but the other wolves in attendance had his reaction.

Wolves did *not* do finger food.

"You'll undoubtedly not be disappointed this year," Callum told Jay with truthfulness.

"Go in, help yourselves." Sonia invited, giving Jed (or Jake) a playful cuff on the head and Jake (or Jed) a teasing shove on the shoulder as they walked toward the dining room table.

Then she seemed to be moving away from him, which Callum didn't like, so he hooked an arm around her waist and curled her front to front. Her eyes lifted to his and he knew she was pissed.

He grinned.

Callum even liked it when she was angry. He was pleased his queen had spirit and fire. Immensely pleased.

Her gaze narrowed on his grin, and when her eyes came back to his she irately commanded, "Would you *stop* telling that story?"

"No," he calmly replied.

She growled low in her throat.

Callum chuckled low in his.

Then she suddenly asked, "Who's Calvin?"

He felt the pain slash through his gut, his arm tightened convulsively around her, and his grin died.

"My brother," he replied tersely.

At his instantaneous reaction, sweet Sonia's eyes were no longer narrowed, but searching.

Then, her voice much softer, she inquired, "Brother?"

"Died. In battle. Years ago." His words were short and curt and he didn't try to gentle them because this effort would be impossible.

Her body jerked lightly in his arm then it, too, went soft and settled against his.

"I'm sorry," she whispered.

He was, too, more than he could say.

Callum didn't reply.

"I shouldn't have asked but I was surprised. You'd never mentioned him," she told him.

"He was the youngest of us, we didn't protect him. It's not a subject we discuss."

He felt her heave a fluttering little sigh and she lifted a hand and curled her fingers around his neck, murmuring, "Callum."

He wished he'd had her years ago when Calvin fell. That sweet sigh, the touch at his neck, the feel of her yielding body pressed to his, the murmur of his name would have gone far in soothing the grief. He knew this because it was something it did now.

He gave her waist a squeeze and informed her, "It was years ago."

"It's still fresh," she said softly.

"It'll always be fresh," Callum replied, his voice no longer clipped but quiet. "He was my brother."

She slowly closed her eyes.

Then she wrapped her arms around him, pressed her cheek to his chest, and held him close.

He closed his eyes and marked the crown of her head with his temple, pulling her even closer.

His sweet, sweet Sonia.

He opened his eyes and saw they had a mixed human and wolf audience, all of whom were watching either avidly (the wolves) or covertly (the humans), and the fact made him exceedingly pleased.

One of her shop girls, he was thinking Kerry (or Mabel, he was too focused on Sonia calling him husband for the first time to pay much attention when they were introduced) approached.

"Um…" she began tentatively. "Sonny? The caterer wants to talk to you. Something about salmon in puff pastry? She sounded like it was urgent." The girl's mischievous eyes went to Callum, and Sonia turned in his arms to face the newcomer as she remarked, "Though, urgent and puff pastry to me don't go together."

He couldn't agree more with her statement and Callum decided he liked this girl. You could see it in the light of her eyes, the fullness of her smile, the depth of her laughter, and the loving way she gazed at Sonia—she fed on life, like a wolf.

Sonia detached from Callum and mumbled, "Thanks, Kerry. I better go see what that's about." She walked away with a distracted smile in his and Kerry's direction, muttering, "I didn't even *order* salmon in puff pastry."

Kerry's eyes tipped up to him and she grinned.

Then her grin grew hard and she said, "I know you're a big guy and you could probably break me in two." This, Callum thought, though she couldn't know, was exactly true. "But make her happy, will you? I don't know why, though considering your story she was probably waiting for you to stop dicking around," she informed him baldly (and courageously). "But she's been alone a long time. She deserves to be happy. In fact, I don't know if I know anyone who deserves it more."

She gave him a look that clearly said *she* would not be happy if he didn't do as she asked, even though she knew her displeasure would be lost on him.

Yes, Callum decided, he liked her a great deal.

She tilted her head to the side, the seriousness going out of her eyes, the hardness going away from her mouth, and announced, "One thing I can say for you, you convinced Sonny to have beer. Always wine and champagne and *cocktails*. A girl needs a beer. Which I'm getting right now. You need one?"

Callum shook his head but grinned at her.

Then, with another bright smile, she wandered off while Callum thought that he didn't like her a great deal. He seriously fucking liked her.

He noticed Sonia rounding the dining room table and decided for perhaps the fiftieth time that night he liked what she was wearing. A skintight winter white turtleneck that had opalescent beading around the shoulders and down the chest which gave the impression of sparkling snow. She'd paired this with a matching slim skirt that came to her knees and cupped her ass so perfectly, it had to be made for her. She was wearing outrageously sexy, high, stiletto-heeled, gray snakeskin boots. She had her hair loose in a sleek fall past her shoulders and down her back but a pretty wide velvet ribbon was threaded through it, holding the thick locks away from her face.

She looked like a sophisticated snow angel.

His claiming chain hung outside her skirt (she always wore it visible, at his command) and her wedding rings sparkled on her finger. Both of which, even the rings, being his, Callum felt a fierce pride that she, Sonia, his mate, his queen, dressed in that fucking sexy outfit, was displaying for all her friends and his family to see.

The minute he saw her emerge down the stairs earlier that evening, he'd decided to try to find some way to fuck her with that skirt on.

If that failed, he was definitely fucking her while she was wearing those boots.

He knew every man in this room would envy him that opportunity.

And he fucking loved that.

She stopped at the outer end of the table and was talking with one of the women who came to cater her party. The woman was gesticulating wildly and Sonia was looking at the table in charming bafflement as Caleb slid up beside him.

"Stop flirting with Sonia's shop girls, brother," Caleb muttered jokingly, and Callum watched, his eyes instantly narrowing and his body immediately alert, as Sonia's shoulders shrugged slightly up.

It was a fleeting, sparse movement, but it was there, and further, her head had slanted with a nearly imperceptible jerk, moving her ear to point toward where Callum and Caleb were standing.

"Cal?" Caleb called.

"Quiet," Callum ordered, his enjoyment of the evening eroding.

Sonia had these kinds of reactions and often. Callum started noticing it the day after their first full day and night in this house.

A human might not notice but Callum definitely did.

Callum and Caleb were standing across the expanse of the wide living room, well away from the dining room table. Even without the distance, there was soft Christmas music playing, numerous people in the room creating a loud buzz of conversation, and Caleb had muttered his joke under his breath.

But Callum would bet his immortal life she could fucking hear it.

And now, with her ear pointed toward them, she was listening.

It wasn't just her heightened sense of hearing, it was more.

For instance, when they played, it didn't happen often, but she'd run her nose along the skin of his neck or the whiskers on his jaw. Once he'd even heard and felt her taking in the scent of his hair.

Female humans didn't do that, not any that he'd met.

She-wolves, however, like wolves, did it all the time, during play or just affectionately with their mate. Your mate or partner's scent was a massive aphrodisiac, but it was also another way your senses recognized a loved one. It was one of the reasons their mingled essence between her legs was so important. It was part of the claiming ritual for the male to coat the female with it, spreading their intermingled scent, a physical representation of their connection, to mark his territory after the claiming.

Further, he'd also noticed on more than one occasion Sonia tilting her head or making a face when she'd smelled something pleasant or unpleasant. Something Callum also smelled but not something any human would sense.

She had exceptional eyesight as well, something he noticed when she was sitting beside him while he was driving and she drew in a sharp barely audible breath when a car skidded on a patch of ice in front of them. The car, however, was far ahead. A wolf could see it, but a human? Not in his experience.

And there was the way that she liked to play. She certainly responded to him when he was gentle with her, but she came alive when he was rough. He'd never, not once in his experience, knew a human to get off the way Sonia did with Callum. He was careful to make certain all his partners enjoyed his play, but the depth of her craving, the intensity of her participation and her climaxes were unreal for a human, if not a wolf.

He'd put that down to their connection, but now he was questioning it.

Because she *was* still human.

Lastly, the way they fell asleep most nights, from the first night after the claiming.

It was common practice for wolves, especially wolf mates, to sleep while their bodies were connected. The male on top, the female on top, spooned, or the way Sonia liked to be connected to Callum, with Callum over her and Sonia on her belly.

It was just the wolves' way.

The first time he'd done it, he'd been so lost in the experience they'd shared, he hadn't thought of it. It was natural to him as wolf but he would never have done it with a human. Not only because his other human partners were not his mate, but because they wouldn't find it comfortable and might even find it painful.

Later that night when he awoke still connected to her, his weight bearing her little body into the bed, he'd cursed himself. He'd drawn away and pulled her close. Since that first time, he always woke shortly after, and without the cursing, rolled to his back and pulled her to his side.

The next day after the first time, from their talk in the morning, and especially that night, he was surprised and delighted to find she liked it. They didn't sleep that way every night, but if he ended their play fucking her on her hands and knees, they *always* did and it was *always* Sonia that lured Callum to her.

One night, she'd even demanded it. Hands flying back to grasp his hips, her sex convulsing tight to trap his cock, she'd slid her knees down and drew him with her between her spreading legs.

It had been the most arousing thing a female had ever done and he'd instantly had an overwhelming urge to take her again. So he did, up on his hands, his hips pistoning into her, her belly to the bed, her legs spread wide, her ass tipped up just enough so she could take all of him, and her moans and cries muffled by the pillow.

It had been, as it always was with Sonia, fucking magnificent.

What it hadn't been was anything near to anything he'd ever had with a female human.

And none of it made any sense.

Callum, being proudly wolf and being royal, did not spend a great deal of time with humans. He didn't avoid them, but his duties, the consistent skirmishes, and simply because he preferred the company of his brethren, meant he'd spent the vast majority of his life with wolves. Even though, if he caught the scent or liked the look of a female human he wouldn't hesitate in taking her, until Sonia, he preferred she-wolves and they made up the bulk of his bed partners.

Perhaps this was something human he just didn't know.

And what Callum didn't know, he didn't like.

Especially when it came to Sonia.

"Callum?" Caleb called, catching his attention as Callum kept his eyes on Sonia and he saw her force herself to relax.

She was hiding it. His instincts screamed it.

So perhaps it wasn't just something he didn't know. Perhaps it was something else entirely.

"Five minutes ago, you were wrapped in your queen's arms," Ryon noted, smiling as he approached the brothers. "Now you're scowling. What's up?"

Callum looked at his cousin.

Ryon.

His cousin, on the other hand, preferred female humans to she-wolves, though he didn't shy away from wolves. He also enjoyed spending time in the human world.

If it was something Callum didn't know, Ryon might be able to tell him.

He started to open his mouth but thought better of it when a memory pierced his consciousness and his eyes slashed across the room to the vampire.

Gregor was standing by the Christmas tree talking with one of Sonia's neighbors who Callum had met and who Callum had not bothered to remember their name.

Two and a half weeks ago, Yuri had interrupted their post-play cuddle, and when Callum finally sensed him, his head jerked to the door at the same time as Sonia's. He hadn't been paying attention for obvious reasons, but looking back, she'd appeared deeply surprised that Yuri was there.

Not only because it was surprising, and tremendously rude, that Yuri would interrupt them, but also because she'd not sensed him until the last second, which was something, just as it was for Callum, that was unusual for her to miss.

And later Gregor had wanted a private word with Callum that Sonia couldn't overhear and didn't take him to another room.

He took him for a walk and didn't speak for a block and a half.

Gregor didn't speak because he needed the distance so Sonia couldn't hear.

Callum sliced his eyes to Ryon and said, "I need to walk."

Ryon's head jerked and his gaze narrowed.

"Walk?" Caleb asked and Callum looked to his brother. "What are you on about? We're at Sonny's party. You can't leave. This is important to her."

It annoyed him that Caleb called Sonia "Sonny" when he wasn't calling her "sis." It annoyed him more that Ryon did it (without the "sis"). The only one who'd taken to doing this that didn't annoy him was Regan.

There was no reason why this annoyed him, outside of the fact it was a familiarity that was greeted with radiant warmth from his mate and she returned it, having fallen into the habit of affectionately (and adorably) calling Caleb "bro" and Ryon "cuz."

This annoyed him more because she didn't use any endearments with Callum, even though he used them frequently with her. The only endearment she'd ever uttered was "wolf" and that was only when he was fucking her or playing with her.

He scowled at his brother and ordered, "Tell Sonia I'll be back in a while."

Caleb opened his mouth but Callum jerked his head to Ryon and walked directly to the entry, grabbed his coat, and strode out the door.

Ryon was at his side within moments.

Callum didn't speak for a block and a half.

"Cal, what the fuck?" Ryon asked with irritation.

"The vampires are hiding something," Callum answered.

"What?"

"About Sonia, they're hiding something."

"That's mad, Cal, they can't—"

Callum stopped abruptly, turned to his cousin, and asked, "Do you remember Miranda?"

Miranda was a she-wolf who had, regrettably, lost her mate. It had been centuries ago, Callum and Ryon were barely battle ready, much less battle worn, and Ryon, who shared features with Miranda's mate, had been her grief-stricken rebound. He'd not been virgin but she'd still initiated him to many aspects of play and she'd done it thoroughly. She missed her mate and taught Ryon everything her mate had done to her. Ryon had been a grateful student and a willing replacement.

It was the first time either of them knew that the instinct to stay connected after play and into sleep was wolfish.

"What does she—?" Ryon started.

Callum cut him off. "Remember how she liked you to sleep with her?"

Ryon's expression altered, it became roguish. He grinned and replied, "I remember a lot of things about Miranda. I still visit her from time to time."

Losing patience, Callum resisted the urge to growl and yanked the conversation back on track. "Sleep, Ry, not play. Do you remember how she liked to sleep with you? On her belly, you over her, connected?"

Ryon kept grinning as well as missing the point. "She still likes that. One of my favorite parts about her, the reason I always go back."

"Sonia likes it too," Callum informed him tersely and Ryon's grin died. "She likes it a good fucking deal."

"You didn't..." Ryon started. "You fucking didn't..." he growled then spat, "Cal, she's fucking *tiny*."

"I know that," Callum clipped. "I won't go into how I initiated her to it but she *likes* it. Have you ever done that with a human?"

"In a sense but I've never *slept* like that," Ryon bit back. "I'd fucking crush her."

"Have you ever had a human play as rough as a wolf?" Callum pushed.

Ryon's head jerked slightly in surprise at the question and he answered, "No."

"Not even close?" Callum pressed.

"Not even close."

"You ever play with a human as rough as you would with a wolf?" Callum persisted.

Ryon's face grew dark with anger. "Please tell me—"

Callum got close. "She *wants* it that way, Ryon. She fucking *loves* it. You ever know a human, in your vast experience, who likes it like that?"

"That's impossible, she couldn't even take it."

"She takes it, Ry," Callum retorted. "She takes *all* of it." Ryon's eyebrows shot up at this shocking revelation. "And if I don't give it to her, she begs me for it."

"Jesus," Ryon breathed, staring at Callum. "How lucky can you fucking get?"

Callum didn't have time to share all the ways he was lucky to have Sonia, only some of them having to do with how she liked to play.

"That isn't my point."

"What's your point?" Ryon asked.

"That's not it, there's more," Callum informed him. "She's got heightened senses. Not as heightened as a vampire or a wolf when he's transformed, but as far as I can gather, it's close to what a wolf has in human form."

Ryon couldn't hide his response, he reared back whispering, "You're fucking joking."

"I'm not and she's hiding it and the vampires know about it. You ever experience anything like that with a human?"

"Never."

"Sense it? Get the barest fucking inkling of it?" Callum clipped.

"No, Cal, not ever."

Callum looked away, hissing, *"Fuck!"*

He didn't like what he was thinking but he couldn't help thinking it primarily because it was the only thing that made sense.

Callum had decided to give Sonia her Christmas before he launched his offensive to quell the rebellion.

He did this for two reasons.

One, he and his men had made a significant effort to hide the extent of their intelligence, something Calder had taken over gathering (and doing a great job at it, as normal) from the rebel leaders. The rebellion thought they were still gathering information and planning their offensive. They had no idea Callum's attack was coming. They had no idea Callum knew as much as he knew and therefore had planned as thoroughly as he'd planned. They had no idea that Callum knew that they were still amassing and planning *their* attack for after the New Year. Fuck, even Nikolas, one of their chiefs, Callum had asked to escort his queen and his mother to the mall (under the constant, hidden, guard of four other wolves who followed their every move, that was) in order to hide his knowledge at the depth of their infiltration. Callum spending time enjoying his Christmas with his new mate would make them think he lost focus or wasn't taking them seriously, and it would, he hoped, lull them into a sense of security.

And two, Sonia loved Christmas and Callum wanted Sonia to have her Christmas.

It was now the night before Christmas Eve. They were moving on the rebellion on Boxing Day.

There was a lot on his mind, including the fact that the rebels fought dirty and losses on both sides would likely be high.

He didn't need this shit now.

His eyes came back to Ryon's. "The minute this shit is over with the rebellion, I want you, personally, with no one knowing about it, to investigate Sonia's disease. I want to know what it is. I want to know the incidence. I want to know what it does to her body. And I want to know *exactly* what's in that fucking injection, how it works, and how long she's been taking it. If you have to torture her fucking doctor, do it, but get me what I want."

"You don't think Sonny—" Ryon started and it took everything Callum had to beat back the urge to strike at Ryon even *thinking* what he was going to say, much less saying it.

"Not a chance," Callum gritted out. "Every night I tell her it's time to take her injection and every night I watch her eyes go blank. Sonia's eyes are never blank, but to hide her distress at her nightly agony, they go...fucking...*blank*. And every night I give her that injection and every night it's like she's dying in my arms and not in a quiet pass behind the veil kind of way but in a tortured agonizing kind of way. I've never seen anything like it in my life. It's hideous. She wouldn't do that to herself if she didn't have to, no one would."

"Then what are you thinking?" Ryon asked.

"She wouldn't do it to herself," Callum explained, "but a fucking vampire would do it to her."

Ryon's face went hard for he knew it was true.

Vampires could be ruthless.

"I don't know what their game is or even if they're playing it. But, if The Prophesies go down the way they've been foretold, then—" Callum stated.

Ryon cut him off. "I'll investigate. Don't jump to any conclusions before we know."

Callum was a lucky wolf in many ways, not just having Sonia, but also a wise father, a loving mother, fiercely loyal brothers, and Ryon, far more even-tempered and level-headed than Callum, as his advisor and friend.

Ryon got closer. "Lassiter wanted his daughter raised by them instead of us and you know why. Mac agreed and made the allegiance. And Cal, you know, Mac was no fool."

Callum looked away, lifted his hand to his neck, and gave it a squeeze.

His father was anything but a fool.

Then it hit him.

Callum dropped his arm and looked at his cousin. "Do you remember the conversation I had with Gregor that I told you about?"

"The info about Lucien?" Ryon asked.

Callum's mouth went hard at the memory and bit out, "And the rest."

Ryon nodded. "I remember."

"Gregor doesn't want to lose her, thinks of her as a daughter, or at least he wanted me to believe that and he was pretty fucking convincing.

Perhaps this injection isn't for a deadly blood disease. Perhaps it isn't for some nefarious reason, doing…whatever, to Sonia, my queen, a treachery against the alliance. Perhaps it's vampiric. Perhaps they've concocted something that will lengthen her life."

"Vampire saliva is pretty powerful but it doesn't heighten senses," Ryon commented.

"And humans don't react to vampire saliva the way Sonia reacts to that injection. They aren't injecting her with that, it's something else. Wolves don't need medicines and I can't say I've a lot of experience with witnessing humans taking treatments, but I can't imagine their medicines regularly cause those kinds of reactions." Callum's gaze turned intense on his cousin. "When I say it's bad, Ryon, I mean it's *bad*."

Ryon's eyes flashed briefly before his thoughts turned and they gentled. "Poor Sonny."

This was said with feeling, too much of it. More than would be offered to Ryon's queen, even a member of his family. Callum again wondered at it at the same time he didn't like it.

However, he'd have a word with his cousin later, after all of his problems were sorted.

"The minute we deal with this fucking situation in Mona's territory, I'm taking Sonia to Scotland," he announced.

"Of course."

"I want any time she spends with Gregor or Yuri or any vampire monitored," Callum ordered.

"It's done."

Then Callum said what he had to say so he could let it go and not leap out of his skin, into the wolf, and tear Gregor *and* Yuri asunder the minute he walked back into Sonia's house. This would cause an immortal incident which could tip the scales of The Prophesies far sooner than expected.

"I find out they've been doing that to her then deceiving her to doing it to herself for thirty-one years, I swear, Ry—"

Ryon cut him off yet again, stating fiercely, "You'll have my teeth at your back."

They held each other's gazes for several long moments, Callum trying to decide if Ryon's loyal declaration was for his benefit or Sonia's.

Then Callum let it go and nodded.

"Fuck, I wish I could run," he muttered curtly, turning back toward Sonia's house. "It's too long I've spent in this goddamned city."

"You'll be home soon," Ryon replied, walking beside him. "And when you go, you'll be taking back your queen."

At least *that* was something to look forward to, so much so, Callum looked to his cousin and smiled.

Ryon returned his smile and stopped walking. Callum stopped with him.

"Speaking of your queen..." Ryon started and trailed off.

Callum automatically braced.

Ryon studied him a moment before asking, "Is everything okay with you two?"

Callum relaxed and grinned before stating, "Perfect."

And they were perfect. Not just their play, which happened as frequently as he could manage, and Sonia always greeted it with eagerness, but everything that was them was perfect.

They'd settled in a rhythm of life that pleased Callum very much.

He allowed her to go to Clear for two or three hours a day, but kept her close any other time. Mostly in his lap, liking her near, liking her scent. The sound of her steady breathing. The sight of her elegant profile if he just twisted his neck to look at it. Her sweet ass snug in his lap, his chain within reach so he could toy with the charm she loved so much and he could have the physical reminder of their bond in his fingers.

She didn't mind this, had settled into it nicely, in fact. As her reward, he often allowed her to do things around the house or go shopping with his mother or, if they were at the mansion, to wander freely so she could talk to and get to know her wolves. This last he'd noted, as Sonia was very sociable and sweet, she'd charmed the lot of them, as Callum knew she would do.

She would often stiffen and inform him of what displeased her (or not, depending), but she was Sonia. That was her way.

They did not fight as they had in the beginning. She had clearly accepted her destiny, in fact, she'd embraced it.

Ryon's eyebrows went up, taking Callum out of his thoughts when he inquired, "You're certain?"

Callum turned fully to Ryon and demanded, "What are you driving at?"

Ryon blew out a sigh and noted, "Regardless of her heightened abilities, she's still human."

"Yes, Ry, she's still human," Callum remarked with strained patience.

"And female humans are not like she-wolves."

"No, they aren't." Although Sonia, Callum thought, in many ways very much was.

"Cal," Ryon went on patiently. "Ours is a whole other world for her. A different culture, all of it but *mostly* the way a male is with his mate, what he expects of her. I've been watching Sonia, she's settled quickly, too quickly. It's strange for a human and it makes me uncomfortable."

Callum felt his gut get tight. "What makes *me* uncomfortable is *you* watching her."

Ryon's body went visibly solid and his voice was threaded with angry affront when he whispered, "You insult me, my king."

Callum studied his cousin then he reminded him, "She's my mate."

"Understood," Ryon replied. "More than probably you know."

"What does that mean?"

"That means we've grown up together, closer than brothers, and I've wanted this for you for over three hundred years," Ryon clipped. "And I don't want you to fuck it up."

Suddenly angry at Ryon's unwelcome and unfathomable implication, Callum leaned in and declared, "I'm not fucking it up."

Ryon pulled in an annoyed breath and explained, "Cal, she-wolves don't hide their emotions. You know where you stand. They're pissed, they come at you. They feel playful, they jump you. They need affection, they nuzzle you. They want something, they ask for it and you get it for them. Female humans are *not* like that. They communicate in a kind of...a kind of..." he hesitated before snapping out the word, "*code* that only *they* understand. Half the time, you'll never have any fucking clue what's going on in their heads. Female humans' minds are like the answer to the meaning of life, impossible to decipher."

"Sonia has no problems sharing what's on her mind," Callum informed his cousin, wondering, not for the first time, especially if all he said was true, why Ryon bothered with humans.

"You might think that, but with a female human you'll never know for sure," Ryon retorted.

"That's ridiculous," Callum scoffed because it bloody well was.

"That's human," Ryon returned. "I know you haven't enlightened her about the wolf within, which I understand and you know I agree she should be in the bosom of our people when that knowledge is shared. But, have you been instructing her?"

"In what?"

"In everything," Ryon replied. "Jesus, Cal, it's like moving to a new country but without the physical location changing. Everything is different. Our traditions, our personality traits, our behavior." He threw his arm out in the direction of Sonia's farmhouse. "That party, for instance. That is *not* a wolf party, and as delightful as her outfit is, that is *not* how wolves dress."

He came closer to Callum and dropped his voice lower.

"Everything we are, she needs to understand. She may be experiencing things that are confusing her, even alarming her, and she'd never let on. She'd just let them build and build until it either explodes or turns to resentment, against you, our people, her new life. Even the smallest thing, Callum, she might not understand. Female humans need communication, *a lot of it*. It's fucking annoying, but trust me, you're better off giving it to her than suffering the consequences."

Callum stared at his cousin, disliking (intensely) what he was hearing, but also smart enough to know Ryon knew what he was talking about. He'd spent a lot of time in female human company whereas Callum took what he wanted and moved on. He'd never played their games, but he knew they had them.

And furthermore, this conversation, and Ryon's coaching, went a long way to dispel his disquiet at Ryon's attention to his mate.

"Fucking hell," Callum finally muttered then yielded, "I'll talk to her."

"Smart," Ryon nodded.

Callum sighed at adding yet *another* issue to the list he would have to sort.

Then they walked together back to Sonia's house.

After they'd taken off their coats, Ryon made his way instantly to Caleb while Callum went to Sonia. She was standing amongst a group of her friends, listening and smiling, and he approached her from behind.

He knew she knew he was there because he saw, nearly imperceptibly but it was there, her body grow tight before he was even close. Understanding it now, he'd likely notice these actions far more and he began cataloguing them.

He used his smile aimed at her friends to hide his unrest, came up to her from behind, and slid an arm around her waist, placing his mouth at her ear.

"It's time for your injection, baby doll," he muttered in a voice for only Sonia to hear.

He was pleased he couldn't see her eyes, even though he felt her body tense. Seeing her eyes go blank, night after night, was like dying a little death.

She turned to him, her gaze at his shoulder, and nodded, murmuring her apologies as he led her away, up the stairs, to the bathroom.

She waited obediently as he loaded the syringe.

When it was ready, she turned her back to him, one of his arms slid around her belly as he instructed gently, "Lift your skirt for me, little one."

She shimmied it up her hips, as she did so, exposing a pair of sexy white lace panties he'd ordered her to go with his mother and buy (about a second after he'd gathered her unattractive undergarments and thrown them in the trash). She was also wearing lace-topped, thigh high stockings.

Regardless of his chore, he still felt his groin tighten at the sight.

Swiftly, so as not to prolong her apprehension, he administered the injection.

Facing the mirror, the minute the toxin entered her body, both of her hands flew out to clutch the basin and her head lowered. She sucked in a tortured breath and her pretty face twisted with suffering. Callum dropped the syringe into the sink, yanked her skirt down, and wrapped his arms around her, trying to tear his eyes from the mirror that exposed her pain, and failing.

His body absorbed the tortured shudders rending their way through hers until she unconsciously dragged in calming breaths as the pain slowly burned itself out.

When it was over, she lifted her head until it rested on his shoulder, her cheek against his. His chin was lowered to her and her hands glided along his forearms until her arms were crossed and her fingers curled around his wrists.

"I even feel it in my hair," she whispered, the ghost of pain veining her voice, and Callum's scalp stung unpleasantly at hearing the comprehensiveness of his mate's pain.

He buried his face in her neck.

"Baby doll," he murmured there as there was nothing more that he could do.

And he fucking *hated* the feeling of powerlessness that was thrust on him night after night.

Her fingers tightened on his wrists and she said softly, "It's over, Callum."

It wasn't over. It would happen again the next night and the night after that.

If it was indeed a disease, it would happen until he stood beside her burning pyre.

He didn't respond, just tensed his arms, drawing her closer.

"We have guests." she reminded him.

He took in breath through his nose, her scent, already surrounding him, intensifying, and his body relaxed at the smell and her uttering the fact that *they* had guests.

She did not say "I" but "we."

Callum liked that.

He nodded and lifted his head, his eyes catching hers in the mirror where *she*, who'd endured it, gave *him*, who'd only witnessed it, a reassuring smile.

Then he stood holding her while she reapplied her lipstick and unnecessarily rearranged her thick beautiful hair.

He led her downstairs and stood at her side as she entertained, having lost his enjoyment of the evening, and as it continued finding himself losing his patience as his need for her grew.

She, however, continued to enjoy it and that was the only reason Callum could endure.

It was late. The caterers had swept away their wares, leaving the house tidy, but Sonia still wandered it. Finding a discarded napkin here, the remains of wrapping paper there, and throwing them away while Callum shut down the house for the night.

When he guided her up the stairs, he led her to the bathroom, deciding that he'd give them a better memory of a space that had become, for him, as it had to be for her, dreaded.

At first she was confused and hesitant but that melted, as Sonia always did, when he gently placed her hands on the basin, ordered her to keep them there, and yanked up her skirt. He pulled down her panties and she stepped out of them before he commanded she open her legs. He saw, reflected in the mirror, her face grow hungry, and his need for her deepened before she did as she was told, and at once, as her reward, he slid his hand between her legs from behind, giving her what she craved.

Callum watched her in the mirror thinking distractedly, because he so liked what he saw, that he'd have to have a room paneled in mirrors at his castle in Scotland. The vision of her growing excitement erasing the earlier painful one as he brought her to orgasm with his fingers. Then, while she was still moaning her uninhibited release, he watched as he entered her and fucked her, her skirt bunched at her hips, her sweet ass willingly tilting up to take all of him. And he kept watching as he brought her to orgasm again moments before he had his own.

Then, keeping Sonia impaled on his cock, he gazed in the mirror, her hooded eyes, he noted, doing the same, as he slowly disrobed her, baring her beautiful little body still intimately connected to his. Once she was naked against him, he took his time running his hands along the skin of her midriff, her belly, her sides, and up to her breasts as he, and Sonia, watched the trail of his hands, and as he, alone, felt her sex shudder around his cock in response to their travels.

And he held her, his forearms crossed, his hands cupping her breasts, his thumbs idly stroking her nipples, his shaft still hard and buried to the root, as he memorized the look of them together. The smell of their mingled essence. The beautiful feel and sight of all that was her.

She twisted her neck, and with her lips against his skin, he watched in the mirror as she whispered there, "How do you stay so hard so long?"

"Sensory incentive," he replied softly (and truthfully).

She emitted a fluttering sigh.

He smiled.

Then he lifted her off his shaft, turned her, seated her on the basin, and lazily pulled off her boots and slid off her stockings.

He carried her to bed, his sweet little Sonia, took off his clothes, joined her, and pulled her close, on their sides, his face in her hair, her ass snug in his crotch, his body pressed to the length of hers.

His voice was gentle when he asked, "Did you have a good night, my little one?"

"Yes," she whispered sleepily, hesitated, then inquired, "Did you?"

"Yes," he answered and his arms gave her a squeeze. "I liked the way it ended the best."

"Figures," she mumbled seconds before she fell asleep.

He should have felt contentment, but these were his worst times. In the dark, Sonia near, her body relaxed in his arms. These were the times he knew he'd miss most when she was gone.

He didn't seethe against her aging, the onset of wrinkles, her gorgeous hair turning gray.

He seethed against the knowledge that one day, she'd be gone.

As with every night since the claiming, King Callum fell asleep with his queen, forced to come to uneasy terms with this vile knowledge of his future.

CHAPTER FOURTEEN
CHRISTMAS

Sonia's body was trapped between the back of the far more comfortable couch in her upstairs television room and the length of Callum's frame. Her head was resting on his chest. Her arm was draped around his stomach. Her gaze was on the television.

In this position, late Christmas Eve, King Callum watched the movie *White Christmas* for the first time.

The detritus of their feeding frenzy was on the table in front of them, something, to his surprise, which was Sonia's idea.

One of the things she had made no bones about since they met was her dislike of the wolf diet. But that morning when he'd asked how she traditionally spent her Christmas Eve and Christmas day, she'd told him in a tentative, almost, to his surprise (and foreboding) *shy* way, that both days were the *only* days of the calendar year where she ate what she wanted, how much she wanted, and didn't worry about it.

Callum hid the displeasure he felt at these words, a displeasure he felt for three reasons.

First, she'd been shy in relating this information to him. Why Sonia would be shy, considering they were lifemates, she'd been claimed, she spent most of her days in his lap and all of her nights full of his cock, he couldn't imagine.

Second, because her shyness made him realize that he'd never bothered to ask her anything about herself, her likes, dislikes, what she enjoyed doing, what she did not. So, he supposed, it wasn't unusual that she *would* be shy because she was being asked to share about herself, which was new to her. At least doing it with him was.

She needed to fit into his life, this was true. But she was also an important part of his. He'd had a lot on his mind, but regardless if it was inadvertent, the extent of his callousness shook him. Further, he wondered, as Ryon suggested, if under the surface of Sonia's acceptance of her fate, something else lurked.

Last, because she so rigidly controlled her eating, which was one of his most disliked human traits and one he would be fully breaking her of after the holidays.

Wolves didn't count calories and they were not obsessively tidy as Sonia also was. Contradictory to humans, even though a wolf's life could last eternity, they didn't squander them on trivial things. They *lived* them to their fullest, every day enjoying what life had to offer and never sweating the small stuff.

While in bed that morning, her eyes riveted to his chest, her fingers absentmindedly sifting through the dark hair there, she'd explained (while he hid his displeasure, and, later, unrest) that Christmas Eve, she relaxed, read a book, watched movies, and ate whatever she wanted. Christmas morning, she opened her presents, which she kept for some reason she didn't share under her upstairs tree. Then she went to Gregor's in the afternoon and had a late afternoon dinner with him and Yuri before she came home.

This news was, Callum thought, somehow gloomy. Although she related it in a way that seemed straightforward, it didn't change the fact that most of her beloved holiday she spent alone, and none of it, to his way of thinking, sounded very much fun.

This was also not the way of the wolf, not ever, but *definitely* not on Christmas.

And Callum determined, watching her eyes follow her fingers, even if his queen was used to her lonely Christmases, she'd have them that way no longer.

From that day on, they would be vastly different.

And Callum set about making that so.

When she was finished talking, he'd turned to her and made love to her. He'd done it slowly, taking his time, building the hunger, and when her moans slid back to whimpers, he sated it. After, still wrapped in her limbs, their bodies connected, he took the time he rarely took (because he rarely had it) to coddle her. His hands drifting idly on her skin. His nose taking in the scent of her. His lips trailing her neck, her ear, her face, and as he did so, her limbs tightened around him protectively, lovingly, and he growled his approval against her skin.

After they got out of bed, she made breakfast for them and they showered. When she was dressing and doing whatever else it was she did while preparing for her day, he placed calls, making arrangements and seeking information.

When she came down the stairs dressed in a long sleeve T-shirt and jeans, he sent her back up to dress warmer.

Without a peep, she did as she was told.

Then he took her to a sporting goods store and bought what they needed.

After that, he took her sledding.

She'd been shocked through this, to the point she didn't speak.

But once they hit the crowded, public sledding hill and she was amongst the children and parents with their own sleighs, she'd thrown herself into it with abandon.

Callum stood at the top of the hill watching her challenge the kids, who always took her up on it, and then race them down the hill, always letting them win. He'd saunter down and drag the sled back up for her, Sonia climbing by his side, his arm around her shoulders, hers light around his waist as she exchanged loud animated replays amongst her new friends. And then she'd find her next mark and challenge another child and down she'd go again, giggling all the way.

Honest to God, if he didn't know differently, watching her unabashed glee, he'd swear she was wolf.

After she'd exhausted herself, he'd taken her to the snack shop and they sat outside, Sonia in his lap. As they sat, the children giggled at them and men and women surreptitiously glanced their way (some with curiosity, most, he noted, both male and female, with envy) while they drank hot cocoa.

Then he took her home, challenged her to a board game that they played sitting on the floor in her living room by a fire he'd built. They played while they ate a late lunch and he beat her, soundly, to which she pouted, magnificently, so he gave her another chance and played her again and beat her again. But he purposefully didn't do it so decisively the second time.

Sonia eschewed dinner, preparing a feast of unhealthy snack foods which he approved of thoroughly. While she did that, Callum checked the garage to ascertain if Regan had seen to his requests, and as ever, considering shopping was involved, his mother had accomplished her mission admirably. They carted the food upstairs and nibbled on it voraciously at first, trailing off as Sonia first put in *Elf*, another film he had not seen as he didn't often waste time sitting around watching human movies, then *Scrooged* which he had seen, but only parts of it.

And finally, as the night grew late, Sonia slid in the movie she explained she watched last every year on Christmas Eve, *White Christmas*.

Elf, Callum found, was roaringly funny. *Scrooged* was also funny and clever. But he liked *White Christmas* best. It was humorous, it was sweet, it had a depth of emotion, not to mention the man called Bing could fucking sing and the lodge they were in through most of the movie reminded him of home.

Close to the end of the film, he felt her body tense and saw her hand snake from around him to fist as she brought it to her mouth. He lifted his head to see she was silently crying, having trouble holding back her sobs at a scene she'd watched dozens of times before, but obviously it never failed to move her.

He found that moment, Sonia tucked into him on Christmas Eve silently weeping against his chest, somehow touching and right then he determined it was another new tradition and he'd have it every year. Without a word, he lifted a hand to cradle her face, his thumb trailing through her tears as he watched the general's soldiers declaring their unceasing loyalty and he thought the end of *White Christmas* was the fucking best.

He used the remote to switch off the television when it was finished and Sonia immediately moved to exit the couch.

His arm tightened, keeping her where she was.

"Honey, where are you going?"

Her head tipped back to look at him.

"Well..." she started then for some reason looked beyond his ear to the arm of the couch his head was resting on. "After *White Christmas*, I clean up the mess and go to bed."

Callum turned his head, his eyes hit the clock on the DVD player, and he saw it was quarter to midnight.

Nearly Christmas.

And he decided on another new tradition.

His other arm circled her and he pulled her up his chest so they were eye to eye.

"Why do you watch *White Christmas* last every year?"

She took a fluttering breath, something she did often, something he liked because always it denoted she was feeling something deep and he liked the fact that his queen felt deeply.

Then she answered, "Because I watched it with my parents every year. They loved it." She swallowed, seeming both nervous and uncertain, and she gazed into his eyes as if trying to read him, which was odd. She was a female human who, according to Ryon, communicated in code. He was wolf and therefore, with his mate at least, an open book. She must have found what she was seeking for she went on, "If I watch it, it means, before I go to bed on Christmas Eve, I'm remembering them. They're fresh in my mind, which is the only way I can ever really have them."

Having lost Mac and Calvin, understanding her sense of bereavement and hoping to soothe her grief as she had done his, his hand went to her neck, his fingers slid in her hair, and he pulled her face down to touch her lips to his.

She relaxed in his arms and he decided, with no small sense of triumph that he'd succeeded in his endeavor.

He slid her back down his body with his arm about her and tucked her cheek to his chest with his other hand.

Then he asked, "Would you like to know how my people spend Christmas?"

She didn't answer at first, just pulled in a soft surprised breath and he cursed himself again for his insensitivity because Ryon was right. She needed information about the culture she'd be living amongst for the rest of her days and she didn't need to get it by being suddenly confronted with it in all of its, to her, peculiarity.

When she didn't answer, he prompted, "Baby doll?"

She nodded her head against his chest.

His fingers tensed in her hair then relaxed and slid through it, and again, and again, petting her while he spoke.

"We start on first December with the parties. Everyone throws one. It's like a war to have the best party so people will want to come to yours. There's one to attend every day, sometimes you'll attend two, or even three. They aren't like yours. They're a little louder, a little wilder, and my people don't only have them at night, they like celebrating anytime. They have them during the day as well. Enormous luncheons with so much food, you need a nap afterward. Full-on breakfasts, which always lead eventually to trips to the pub, and then, even later, stumbling home highly inebriated while singing Christmas songs."

He heard a surprised giggle escape her throat, sounding strangled and he realized he'd never, not once in over three weeks, made her laugh.

Not once.

Fucking hell, but he'd been buried so deep with everything else, with his mate he'd been a thoughtless bastard.

She tipped her head back and her eyes were alight when she asked, "*You* stumble home drunk singing *Christmas songs*?"

He grinned down at her, enchanted more than usual at his queen when her eyes were lit like that, and admitted, "It's been known to happen."

She pressed her lips together but he felt her body shake with laughter.

"My people like to sing," he informed her easily. "They like it best when they're shitfaced."

She burst out laughing and dropped her forehead to his chest.

There were many things he'd experienced with Sonia in the last three weeks that Callum fucking loved.

But nothing was better than feeling Sonia's body rocking with laughter, the sound of it rumbling into his chest, while she was in his arms.

She eventually gulped back her giggles, lifted her head, and encouraged, "Go on."

His hand dropped to her neck and his thumb caressed the underside of her jaw as he continued, "Christmas Eve is spent, with strict adherence to tradition, at one member of the extended family's house. You arrive for breakfast and stay through to long past darkness falling."

"Do you have a lot of extended family?" she asked.

He didn't wish to scare her with the real numbers, so he answered, "A fair few, more than attended your party last night."

Her eyes grew huge and she breathed, "That's a long time to have a bunch of people around, especially if you have to feed them."

"At the end of the evening, before anyone goes home, it's also tradition for the women to fight over who'll get to host it the next year." He grinned at her. "Sometimes it gets vicious."

She smiled back, not knowing that what he said was literal.

She-wolves could transform and they did it often, mostly to run with their mates. There were those few with that bent (in other words, their fated lifemate and their taste in play partners ran to their own gender) who were warriors, and good ones.

However, most other times, she-wolves stayed in human form.

Unless they were fighting drunkenly, thus much less in control of the transformation, over who would host Christmas Eve.

Blood was shed more often than not.

Callum decided not to share that with Sonia.

Instead, he said, "During the day, the women cook, chat, and play cards at the kitchen table."

She rolled her eyes and mumbled, "Of course they do."

He lifted his head and touched his mouth to hers until he saw her eyes roll back then he sat back and continued, "The males have a rugby tournament or some sort of sport outdoors." He grinned and informed her, "The more brutal, the better."

"Not surprising," she noted without rancor. "Intense, as with everything else, even on Christmas Eve."

His thumb slid over her lower lip because he wanted it to, not to stop her from talking, but she did so and he started again. "We all get together for an evening feast, usually getting drunk again then we have group games that pretty much descend into pandemonium. The women fight it out as to who will host the next year and then everyone goes home."

"Except for the all-day cooking and vicious battle that ends the night, it sounds kind of fun," she quipped, her lips tipped up at the ends.

"It is," he replied truthfully. "Family is all-important. That's why finding your mate is fundamental to our existence." His voice dipped lower and his arm grew tighter. "It heralds the time when we can start our own."

Her expression changed swiftly. Starting with shock then shifting to gentleness mixed with yearning, straight to alarmed, and ending in what he was surprised to see was openly false curiosity.

"What do you do for Christmas?" she asked, changing the subject almost desperately, and he wanted to understand what had been going on in that head of hers but he thought it prudent to let it go.

The mood, he sensed, was still light. He wanted that for himself, but getting the impression he'd given her a good day, mostly he wanted it for Sonia.

"You share the morning with your mate and your children, if you have them. You open your presents, you have breakfast." He grinned wolfishly. "You make love while the children are playing." She bit her lip and he went on, "Then the direct family gets together in the afternoons and we stay together into the evening, feasting, drinking, playing games. Nothing formal, everything relaxed. We have fireworks and a glass of warm mulled wine at midnight then, if you aren't already home, you go home."

Her expression shifted back to gentle and he knew it was sincere as her body had molded to his.

"That sounds *very* fun," she said softly before she made a comical disgusted face, "except mulled wine."

"We'll get you champagne," he murmured, thinking of next Christmas and Sonia standing in his arms but amongst his brethren, wrapped tight in the furs he'd give her, drinking champagne with her face tipped to the stars and the multi-colored bursts of fireworks lighting her skin and hair.

Definitely something to look forward to.

"I'd prefer champagne," she murmured back, gazing at him curiously but matching his tone as if attentive to his mood.

His eyes slid to the clock and he noted the time.

He brought her ever closer as his hand slid into her hair, tenderly fisting and twisting, he brought her lips to his.

There he muttered, "Merry Christmas, baby doll."

And he gave her a kiss that communicated the promise that her lonely Christmases past were a memory and that her every Christmas of the future would start just...like...*this.*

Her eyes were dazed when his mouth broke from hers, her breathing unsteady, and she glanced adorably unfocused toward the clock, taking in a deep breath.

When her eyes refocused, she sighed and looked back at him.

He waited, uncharacteristically patiently, as her green eyes searched his face then looked deep into his, again like she was trying to read him and she doubted what she saw.

Finally, she whispered, "Merry Christmas, Callum."

He was disappointed she didn't call him "wolf" or any other sweet nothing she could dream up.

Even so, his disappointment didn't last long since it was time for bed and the next new tradition Callum was going to introduce.

It was one Sonia liked a great deal.

And at the end of *that,* she not only called him "my wolf."

She yelped it.

Callum woke when he felt Sonia move out of his arms.

His eyes opened as his ears heard her tortured whimper.

His body froze when he saw her.

"Jesus, honey, what the fuck?" he clipped, his hand reaching out to her body, which was still under the covers but up on all fours, her head bent low, her breathing erratic.

She reared violently away from him the instant the tips of his fingers glanced her skin, but even so, he felt the tremendous heat. It felt like she was roasting.

"Sonia," his voice was sharper with his concern, "what the *fuck?*"

She didn't lift her head when she panted her extreme understatement, "Cal, something's wrong."

She moved then emitted an almost animal whine and froze.

He slid as close to her as he dared and her breaths became gasps. She sounded like she was fighting for air.

"I'm calling an ambulance," he announced.

"No!" she cried then gasped, "The syringe, did you fill the syringe?"

"Yes."

"Full, Cal. Did you use it all?"

"Of course I fucking did."

Her head twisted slowly and she looked at him, her eyes hazy but her voice was terrified when she whispered, "This is what it felt like when I didn't take the injection. This is the burn. This is me boiling out of my skin," she gasped then whimpered, terror stark in her tone like she didn't know whether to scream or wail. "Cal, this has never happened while I've been taking the medication. Something's wrong."

Dread settled in his gut with the weight of an anvil and he declared again, "I'm calling an ambulance."

"They won't know how to treat me!" she cried. "The ER people won't have even heard of this," she moaned. "I've always been scared this would happen." Then she released that animalistic whine again and Callum felt it score through his system.

"Your doctor," he said suddenly.

She lifted her head and asked vaguely, "What?"

"Baby doll, your doctor will know what to do. Do you have his number?"

"In my phone, in my—"

She didn't finish for Callum was out of bed and bounding down the stairs, literally. He planted a palm into the railing and leaped over the side coming to rest agilely on his feet on the landing. He did the same again from there and landed at the foot of the stairs.

He found her phone in her bag, the number in the phone, and he rang it while he took the stairs, three at a time, going back up.

While Sonia, who'd thrown off the covers, looked to be fighting the battle of her life in the bed, Callum went through the rigmarole of phoning the on-call doctor, who was not, regrettably, Sonia's physician. This man took too long (in other words, more than ten seconds) to promise to contact Sonia's doctor and share that they would be in touch urgently. The only positive thing that came from this was the fact that the on-call doctor seemed familiar with the lethal importance of Sonia's illness and didn't sound like he was fucking around.

Unable to touch her even to soothe her, Callum went to the bathroom and threw a towel in the tub, drenching it with cold water. Not bothering to ring it out, he carried it to the bedroom and carefully threw it over her back.

"Yes," she whimpered her relief, falling down to child's pose under the large wet towel, her arms stretched out in front of her.

Her phone rang and Callum snatched it from the receiver.

"Dr. Mortenson?" he clipped into the mouthpiece.

"You're Sonia Arlington's husband?" a man replied.

"Yes," Callum ground out. "Is this Dr. Mortenson?"

"Yes, son. My colleague said she's having a turn?"

A turn? He called this a fucking *turn*?

"She's boiling to the touch and says she's coming out of her skin."

"Did she teach you how to administer an injection?"

"Yes," Callum bit off curtly.

"Then give her an injection."

"I did that five hours ago."

"Do it again," he replied calmly. "I'll stay on the line."

Callum wasted no time. When he returned to their bedroom, she'd thrown off the towel and was on all fours again, keening low as she battled the pain.

"It's okay, baby doll, just hold tight for me," he cooed and sunk the needle into the flesh of her buttock as swiftly as he could.

She cried out, arching her back, her neck, her hair flying over her shoulders. Then she shifted, rounding her back, her head falling between her arms, her moan going low, distinct, guttural, and absolutely terrifying to hear.

He snatched the phone to his ear. Frustrated beyond anything he'd ever experienced at his impotence in the face of his mate's agony, Callum clipped, "She's worse."

"I'm counting down, son, stay with me, one minute, thirty-five seconds," and then he counted down in Callum's ear, every five seconds, as Sonia dropped to the bed and started writhing.

"Doctor—" Callum's voice was vibrating with fury.

"You can probably touch her now," the doctor said quietly then went on, "Forty-five seconds..."

Callum dropped the phone and cautiously approached his mate, who had stopped twisting. Reaching out slowly, he touched her skin, which was clammy with sweat but no longer scalding to the touch.

He slid his fingers across her skin to touch her with his full hand and she didn't cry out so he carefully gathered her into his arms and sat with her in the bed, his back to the headboard, Sonia cradled against him.

"I'm okay," she whispered into his neck, and at once his hand snaked out and snatched the phone.

"I'll want to know why this happened," Callum said into the phone.

"She's better now?" Dr. Mortenson queried in response.

"I said, I'll want to know why this happened," Callum repeated.

Dr. Mortenson sighed. "Bodies are magnificent and terrible things, son. It could be Sonia's built up a tolerance to the drug; she's been using it for years. But there are changes in life and in your body all the time. She may be releasing more, or less, hormones. She may have suffered a shock that caused a physical response in her system which triggered a change in the efficacy of the drug. Even if she's living under significantly higher amounts of stress and anxiety or depression, say the loss of a loved one, the body has physical manifestations to all of those and all of them will interact with the medication. I'll want to do blood work and she'll need two daily injections, morning and evening, until I'm happy with what I see."

Fucking hell, now he had to give her *two* of those bloody injections?

And worse, Sonia had to *take* them?

"When can she come in for the tests?" he demanded to know.

"Anytime you want. Go to St. Vincent's Hospital, give them my name. I'll send the orders. They'll draw the blood. Is she peaceful now?"

Callum looked down at Sonia who had wrapped her arm around his body, her other hand was cocked between them resting on his chest, her cheek on her hand. Her eyes, though, were on him. They were troubled, but not fevered and delirious.

"She's peaceful."

"Smart girl, teaching you to give her injection. Well done, son. We'll meet soon, I hope. Merry Christmas."

Then the bastard hung up on him.

Callum used all of his control not to throw the phone across the room. Instead he touched the button for off and tossed it on the nightstand.

He slid his fingers through Sonia's hair, took in a deep breath to regain his composure, and asked, "You okay, my little one?"

"Um...outside of being scared out of my mind?" she queried dryly. "Yes."

He had no response to that so didn't make one.

"What did Dr. Mortenson say?" she inquired.

"He wants tests," Callum replied, deciding to share the happy news that she needed two injections per day later.

She nodded.

"He also said it was smart that you taught me how to give an injection," he teased with mock arrogance, wishing to lift the mood and soothe away the troubled look in his queen's eyes. Giving her a wary squeeze of his arms, he went on, "It's lucky you were so keen to do that, baby doll."

"Shut up, Cal," she muttered in mock annoyance, not able to hide her relief.

But he froze.

She'd called him Cal and she'd done it more than once.

Something about that made him want to howl with victory as if he'd won an epic battle.

Instead, he gave her another careful squeeze.

Her head tilted down and she snuggled closer.

Then she shared, "All my life, that's been my greatest fear. All my life, I feared that would happen. When I didn't take the injection as a teen, I had to crawl to the bathroom. It seemed to take forever, it probably did. I had to stop and breathe, over and over, to get control of my limbs again. It hurt so much."

Callum so disliked her words he wished she'd stop talking, but he kept this wish to himself.

"I'd always been so scared." Her voice hitched as if she was fighting tears and he wanted to tip her face to his and comfort her, but he let her go, sensing she needed to get this out, but sensing more it was something he was going to want to hear.

He wasn't wrong.

"You want to know what I feared the most?" she whispered brokenly.

"What, baby doll?" he asked quietly.

"That it would happen when I was alone," she turned, lifted up, and tucked her face into his neck while her other arm curled around him and she pressed to him tight. "I'm so happy I wasn't alone." She tilted her head back until her lips were at his jaw and she whispered, "You knew what to do. Thank you, my handsome wolf, for taking care of me."

He felt like howling his victory at that moment too.

Again, he didn't.

Instead, he tipped his head down and he kissed her, softly and tenderly, tasting the tears on her lips.

He broke the kiss but didn't break the connection of their lips when he muttered, "Always, my little one."

She closed her eyes tight and nodded.

He picked her up and walked to her guest bedroom, throwing back the covers, placing her in bed, joining her there, turning her to his body, and pulling the covers over them.

"Um..." she muttered. "What are you doing?"

"The bed's drenched, the towel—"

"Oh," she mumbled before he finished.

"Sleep, baby doll, and when you wake up, it'll be Christmas."

She nodded, her head sliding on his chest.

He waited until her breath evened out, which took some time and he wasn't surprised. She'd been through an ordeal. Waking from sleep in the throes of it, she wouldn't be eager to go back regardless of the fact that she drifted off quickly every night since the claiming.

For Callum, who only needed five hours of sleep a night normally, he sacrificed a few to lay alert for another episode.

And as he did so, he allowed his mind to process the fact that she called him "Cal."

And he replayed, again and again, her voice whispering, "my handsome wolf."

And when he finally allowed himself to join Sonia in sleep, regardless of their recent drama, he did it with a smile.

Callum's fingers brushed Sonia's hair away from her neck.

He leaned to her ear and said, "Wake up, honey. It's Christmas."

Her eyes fluttered but stayed closed. He watched her sniff and they opened.

She came up on an arm, her fingers clutching the covers to her breasts, and stared at the coffee mug in his hand.

She looked at him sitting beside her on the bed and breathed, her voice husky with sleep and surprise, "You made coffee?

He grinned at her and replied, "I was a bachelor for many years, Sonia. I know how to make coffee," and he handed her the mug.

Her eyes grew wide but she sat up in bed, tucking the covers around to conceal her body, and took it.

He put his hands in the bed on either side of her hips and lowered his face so it was close to hers. "Now, my queen, say 'Merry Christmas' to your king."

She blinked then whispered, "Merry Christmas."

He touched his lips to hers and whispered back, "Merry Christmas."

He pulled away, leaned down, and picked up the lavishly wrapped box he'd brought into the room.

Her eyes didn't go wide this time. They nearly popped out of her head.

"What's that?" Sonia uttered on a choked cry.

He set it in her lap and reached for his own mug which he'd placed on the nightstand, saying, "Telling you, I think, would break about fifteen Christmas commandments."

She watched him sip from his mug like she'd never seen him before.

When she seemed unwilling to move, he prompted, "Open it."

She hesitated a moment, as if she'd never had a present bestowed on her and had no idea what to do, before she set aside her mug and opened the box.

She pulled out a wisp of dove gray satin, shook it out along the bed, and stared at it.

It was a full-length nightgown with thin straps that criss-crossed at the back and a full skirt that settled on the bed luxuriously.

"It's...it's—" she stammered.

Callum cut her off, informing her, "Every Christmas morning, when we were pups, Mac and Regan left pillowcases stuffed full at the end of our beds." Her mesmerized gaze slowly swung to him as he kept talking. "We were allowed to tear into them immediately. In them was candy, toys, all sorts, but always a new pair of pajamas that we had to put on before going downstairs to unwrap the presents under the tree." He gently pulled the soft fabric from her fingers and ordered, "Lift your arms, baby doll."

Almost dreamily, she lifted her arms and he slid the nightgown over her head then put his hands under her arms and lifted her free of the bed, placing her on her feet in front of him. The nightgown glided down her body to swirl elegantly to her ankles.

A perfect fit.

His mother could definitely shop.

He allowed his hands to slide across the cool material that covered her warm soft body then he bent down and picked up another box wrapped in the same extravagant manner, bigger than the first.

He gave it to her murmuring, "Now this."

She gazed at him looking baffled a moment before she took the box, placed it on the bed, and tore off the wrapping. She pulled it open and gasped. Her fingers fisted in the material in the box and she lifted the winter white cashmere robe to her face. She was holding it in both hands against her nose and mouth so, when she turned to him, all he could see was the amazement shining in her green eyes.

He couldn't stop his chuckle as he pulled her into his arms, looked down at her, and teased, "Honey, are you going to eat it or wear it?"

She pulled the robe from her mouth and muttered worshipfully, "Wear it. Definitely wear it."

Still chuckling at the tone of her voice, he touched his forehead to hers and released her so she could don her robe.

Clutching the lapels across her chest, she raised bright eyes to his, "I...this is so...I-I don't know what to say, Callum."

He felt disappointment nag at him when she used his full name. She'd called him Cal last night.

He beat the feeling back, hoping, in time, it would come again.

He curled a hand at her neck, using his thumb to stroke the underside of her jaw, and prompted, "Do you like them?"

She nodded enthusiastically.

He grinned and finished, "That's all you need to say."

She moved forward the step that separated them and slid her arms around him, her cheek at his chest, her arms going tight.

His hand at her jaw shifted into her hair and held her face against him.

"Now this is definitely better than a nod," he told her, his voice gruff.

She emitted a short happy giggle, keeping his body tight in her arms, and tipped back her head to look at him. "I'm being very rude. I should say thank you."

"I don't know. This doesn't *feel* rude," he teased and she giggled quietly again.

"Can I give you your gifts now?" she asked and his eyebrows went up.

"Do you think that's all you're going to get?"

She blinked again, adorably, and then breathed, "There's more?"

Callum used her hair to tip her head back, bent his own, and against her lips he murmured, "Yes, baby doll, there's more."

Then he gave her a Good Morning Merry Christmas kiss.

She was blinking again when he lifted his lips from hers.

He was chuckling again when he let her go, reached beyond her to nab her coffee cup and handed it to her. Then he grabbed her hand and guided her into their bedroom.

Callum had been up awhile. Long enough not only to make coffee, but also to deal with the mess the soggy towel made of their bed and collect the presents his mother had stashed in the garage yesterday while they were sledding and place them under the tree.

When they arrived in the room, Sonia stared at the tree like a thirty-seven-year-old girl who just learned there *was* a Santa Claus.

Sonia's shining eyes came to his and she smiled. "I'm guessing this means you like Christmas too?"

He slid an arm around her shoulders and grinned down at her. "All my people enjoy any occasion that gives them an excuse to celebrate. But this," he gestured to the tree, "is because *you* like Christmas so much."

Her expression changed and she was gazing at him like she did last night, like she was trying to read him, understand him, assess the validity of his words.

And, just as she did last night, she must have liked what she saw for she melted into him.

"Let's have Christmas," she suggested in a soft voice with soft eyes looking up at him.

"Let's have Christmas," he agreed on a murmur, bending his head to touch his mouth to hers.

He went to the bed, threw all her pillows on the floor by the tree, and they sat on them, Sonia declaring excitedly that this year she got to "play Santa Claus."

"You can do it next year," she assured him as she started organizing packages with what appeared to be unbridled joy.

Watching her, Callum decided that next year, and *every* year, since she obviously had so much fun doing it, Sonia would play Santa Claus.

Callum found, to his delighted surprise, that she was far more generous with him than any of her friends and neighbors. Callum also found that she liked clothes a great deal more than he suspected seeing as she hadn't worn the same outfit twice in the three weeks they'd been together. He had new cords, shirts, belts, jeans, sweaters, and even a new stylish brown leather jacket with a thick insulating layer which would be perfect when they got back to Scotland.

Clearly, these gifts were what were in the copious deliveries that she rushed to the door to confiscate from whichever of his wolves had accepted it before she ran upstairs with the packages but came back down empty-handed.

His mother had followed the same bent, buying Sonia a variety of new clothing except, unlike her normal gear, all of this was more durable and meant to be layered for easier use going in and outside in cold temperatures. Regan also bought her bath salts, lotions, and things to wear in her hair.

Sitting amongst the discarded paper, ribbon, bows, and boxes with piles of stash by both of them, Callum looked around and muttered, "We're going to need another year to use all this stuff."

Sonia, sitting with her ass to her calves, leaned forward and beamed, "I know! Isn't it *great*?"

What was great, Callum thought, looking in his queen's shining, happy eyes, was that they were done unwrapping and now they could move on to an even *more* enjoyable part of the morning.

Therefore, he reached for her and pulled her off her calves, into his arms, and buried his face in her neck.

His lips trailing up to her ear, he heard her say, "You're not quite done."

He lifted his head and looked at her only to see she suddenly appeared apprehensive.

"What is it?" he asked cautiously, not happy that the shining light had died in her eyes and anxiety had replaced it.

"You have one more present," she whispered like she didn't want to say the words.

She took a deep breath, pulled out of his arms, stood up, and started digging in the branches of the tree. She found what she was looking for and gracefully dropped to her knees. She held out a small wrapped box topped with a large bow that engulfed it.

He took it and unwrapped it while she spoke uncertainly, "I didn't know, you know, if I should, but I thought..." She hesitated. "Well, then I thought I should. But now, I'm thinking..." She paused again as he pulled the jeweler's box out of the wrapping, allowing the paper to fall unheeded to the floor, and flipped the box open with his thumb "You don't have to wear it!" she finished on a strangled cry.

In the box was a wide, simple, gold, human man's wedding band.

Staring at the often neglected symbol of another culture's connection between male and female, Callum felt something shift in him so huge it was as if the entire room moved. His chest tightened as did his gut, but his mind blanked of everything but that fucking ring.

His eyes moved to Sonia.

"You don't have to wear it," she repeated on a whisper.

He used his forefinger to lift the ring from its satin bed, dropped the box, but pointed his finger at Sonia.

"Put it on me," he ordered, his voice so thick it was almost harsh.

She studied him uneasily for a moment before scooting forward on her knees, taking the ring from his forefinger, and grasping his left hand. Then she slid the ring on his ring finger.

He stared at the gold gleaming against his skin.

"It fits," she said softly and his eyes moved to hers "Um..." she mumbled, "Merry Christmas."

Before his brain told his body to do it, Callum surged up, his arms going around her, taking her with him as he propelled them to the floor, twisting so he landed on his back and Sonia on him.

Then he wrapped his hand in her hair and crushed her mouth down on his in a bruising possessive kiss as he rolled his weight onto hers, pillows cushioning them, wrapping paper crinkling all around.

Then he took his *wife* on the floor amongst discarded Christmas paper and boxes and he did *that* in a bruising possessive way that she could not misread or misunderstand.

Even so, when it was over, their breathing had steadied, her limbs were wrapped around him and he was still seated inside her but up with his forearm in the pillow he'd tucked under her head. He was running the tips of his fingers across the features of her face when she asked tentatively, "I take it you like the ring."

His eyes captured hers and he growled, "Yes, I fucking like it."

The doubt clouding her eyes disappeared, a hint of a smile touched her mouth, and she whispered, "I'm glad you like it."

He was bending his head to kiss her again, her head was tilting to let him, when the doorbell rang.

Callum stopped his descent.

Sonia blinked up at him. "Who could that be?"

He knew who it was.

"Our family," he replied and when her eyes grew wide he explained simply, "It's Christmas."

The doorbell rang again, and when it did, Callum regretted his decision to give her the exact opposite of her lonesome Christmases past.

That was until he felt her hand at the side of his head, her thumb sweeping along his cheekbone, and he heard her soft voice say, "No, it's the best Christmas I've had in years."

Callum gazed at the tender gratitude gleaming in his mate's eyes only a second before he slanted his head and did what he'd intended to do moments before.

The doorbell rang three more times before the door was opened.

"Fucking hell, Cal, is that a *wedding band*?" Calder practically shouted at him from across the dining room table.

His family, and hers, had arrived bearing shopping bags stuffed full of even more presents. Everyone got a cup of coffee while Callum started a fire in the fireplace in the living room, Ryon started one in the dining room, and Sonia turned on Christmas music. Then they had Christmas around Sonia's downstairs tree before Sonia and Callum went upstairs and dressed in all new clothes. After that, Regan and Sonia made breakfast. It was Sonia's recipe. Crepes filled with cream cheese sweetened and flavored with almonds and citrus, drenched in a sweet slightly alcoholic citrus syrup, and sprinkled with roasted almonds.

His *wife*, he was pleased to note, when she had a mind to do it, could cook. It was fucking glorious.

Calder's exclamation came after breakfast while everyone was still seated at the table.

Sonia was walking back into the room with full mugs of coffee for the both of them and she stopped dead at Calder's words as everyone at the table, which was littered with their breakfast dishes, turned to look at Callum's left hand.

"Yes," Callum replied calmly, pushed his chair back and reached forward, snagging Sonia with an arm around her hips and pulling her to him at the same time he divested her of his mug of coffee.

"Our males don't wear wedding bands," Caleb declared, his eyes looking at the ring as if it was a rotting sinew wound around his finger.

"One of them does," Callum returned firmly, carefully seating Sonia's stiff body in his lap under the studiously remote gaze of Gregor and the openly annoyed gaze of Yuri, as well as everyone else.

"For God's sake, why?" Calder demanded to know.

"Because, this morning, for Christmas, Sonia gave it to me," Callum answered.

"It's not our way," Caleb announced dismissively.

"Maybe not, but it's *our* way," Callum stated forcefully, making his point by drawing Sonia nearer and beginning to lose his patience as Sonia's body didn't lose its rigidity. "My mate is human. This is their symbol. It means something to Sonia therefore it means something to me."

"But, what happens when—" Caleb started but Callum cut his brother off, knowing what he was going to say. Their males didn't ever wear rings because they'd lose them if they needed to transform or the rings might do harm during the change to wolf.

"Caleb, let it go," Callum ordered.

"But—" Caleb began again.

"Let it *go*," Callum bit out.

Caleb snapped his mouth shut.

"You don't have to wear it," Sonia said quietly and Callum's head twisted to look at her.

"Did you buy it to sit in a box?" Callum asked.

"Well..." she started hesitantly. "No."

"You bought it because you wanted me to wear it," he stated and she pulled in breath then nodded. "So I'm going to fucking wear it." His gaze sliced through his brothers and he warned, "Not another word."

Caleb and Calder both looked away.

Regan and Ryon both stared at Callum and Sonia and they were grinning broadly.

Gregor's lips were twitching.

Yuri looked like he'd just drunk a mouthful of sour milk.

It was Yuri's look that dissipated Callum's temper, and once he relaxed, Sonia relaxed against him.

"What's going to be funny is," Regan began, still smiling but now at Caleb and Calder, "when you two find your lifemates and you two find out what's important and what's not. Then *we* get to give you a hard time by reminding you of your behavior right about now."

"Regan," Callum cautioned, "the subject is closed."

"I just want to declare the right to say 'I told you so' at a later date," Regan shot back and Sonia emitted a soft stifled laugh.

Callum decided that since the festive mood had been put on hold for a while, he might as well go with it and get what he had to do over with.

He looked at Ryon and informed him, "Sonia had a turn last night."

Sonia got stiff in his arms again and murmured, "Callum."

But Ryon was no longer smiling as he queried, "A turn?"

He said these two words at the same time Gregor said them and Yuri's body grew visibly tight.

"That's what her doctor called it," Callum told them. "A turn."

"Really, it isn't necessary to alarm them. It wasn't that bad," Sonia put in, and at that, Callum's head twisted to look at her again.

"It wasn't *that bad?*" Callum asked in a dangerous voice.

"Well..." she drew out the word as her eyes grew wider upon looking at his face.

Then, astutely, she shut her mouth.

"What happened?" Gregor queried on a barely-there snap.

"Her blood heated and she was in extreme pain. She couldn't even endure touch," Callum informed the vampire and Gregor's eyes went to Sonia.

In an openly paternal voice denoting barely controlled patience, he said, "As I've explained time and again, my dear, you must *not* miss an injection."

"I didn't," Sonia replied, Gregor's eyes narrowed, and Callum watched him closely.

"That's impossible," Gregor noted. "The doctor assured me that, as long as you take the injection, you'll feel no physical manifestation of the disease."

"It's not impossible because it happened last night," Callum put in and Gregor's mouth got hard.

"I'll be having a word with Dr. Mortenson then. This won't do," Gregor snapped. Definitely snapped, his patience was strained beyond his capacity to control it and his anger was palpable.

Both of which, coming from Gregor, were surprising responses.

He either cared about Sonia, Callum thought, and cared a great deal, or he was angry that whatever he was injecting her with wasn't working or side effects had developed that would make Sonia, and Callum, question the treatment.

"The doctor has ordered blood work which Sonia and I are going to the hospital to see to shortly," Callum announced and then he turned to Ryon. "From this point on, anyone who's assigned to Sonia will have advanced medical training. We won't tell them why, but they'll need to be able to administer an injection." His eyes moved around the table and he went on, "And everyone at this table will learn how to do it." He looked at Sonia. "And you'll carry your medication with you at all times, and if you need it, you'll tell whoever is with you where to find it and that they should give it to you." She opened her mouth to speak but Callum looked to Ryon and finished, "And I want a supply available everywhere we might possibly go."

"Callum, really," Sonia called his attention to her. "Isn't that going a little overboard?"

"I just witnessed it," he retorted. "*You* experienced it and you can ask me that?"

"But—" she started.

"You'll not endure that again," he proclaimed, thinking, as he was king and when he proclaimed something people tended to listen (always), that was the end of it.

This was Sonia so he thought wrong.

"But—" she repeated.

"Little one—" he began.

"Seriously, Callum, it's not—"

"Sonia," Callum stated firmly, "we're not discussing it."

She glared at him mutinously and she did this for a while.

Then her glare softened and she gazed at him again like she was trying to believe he was real.

And finally, her eyes changed slowly, and he wasn't certain because he didn't fucking well understand it, but it looked in their depths like the light of hope shined.

Finally, she emitted one of her fluttering sighs and relaxed against him.

"All right, wolf," she whispered quietly, her eyes never leaving his.

At her sweet endearment, he wanted to kiss her.

Hell, he wanted to swipe the remains of breakfast off the table and fuck her until she said it again and again.

As he couldn't do that for obvious reasons, instead, he told her, "You can be a pain in the ass sometimes, baby doll."

She pressed her lips together but she still couldn't hide her smile.

When he looked at the table he noticed immediately that all the wolves were also smiling.

However, both the vampires looked worried and they didn't hide it.

Callum rose from his seat, lifting Sonia to her feet as he did so.

With his arm around her shoulders he announced, "We'll be back shortly and resume Christmas."

Then he and his queen put on their boots and coats and Callum drove his pretty little *wife* to the hospital to have her blood drawn.

Sonia, in his arms in their bedroom, tipped her head back to look up at him.

"What did you want to talk about?" she asked.

It was early evening. They'd returned from the hospital. Sonia had helped Regan prepare the enormous Christmas banquet which was all wolf. It consisted of a prime roast of beef cooked rare, sliced potatoes baked in milk, cream, garlic, and layered with cheese, thick meaty gravy, Yorkshire pudding, and green beans tossed in butter and bits of crisp bacon. It was finished with Regan's special trifle, which had more custard, more cream, less jam, and more cake than any trifle Callum had eaten.

After that, Sonia gave both Gregor and Yuri warm hugs and they left. Then Sonia rounded up Jay, Jed, and Jake from down the road. Ryon went to the house across the street where they'd planted Trenten, the warrior who'd looked after Sonia for years. They joined Callum and his brethren who had to alter their play significantly so as not to harm the humans in a game of American football in a local park. While this was happening, Sonia, Regan, Trenten's mate, Helena, and Jo were part-time cheerleaders, but mostly they sat on the sidelines under woolen blankets, sipped hot cocoa from a thermos Regan prepared, and chatted.

They'd said good-bye to their neighbors, came home, and made sandwiches from the roast beef. Callum gave Sonia her injection and Ryon started to give Callum pointed looks, which meant it was time to go.

They had a distance to travel, and at first light, they had war to wage.

Callum had whispered to Sonia he wanted a private word and led her to their room.

"I hate to say it, baby doll, but Christmas is over," he informed her and the regret could be heard in his voice.

She leaned into him and grinned. "No it isn't. We have hours left. We can stay awake until past midnight again and watch movies. I have tons of Christmas movies. We can watch *It's a Wonderful Life*. Or we can watch *A Christmas Story*, that's a funny one. Or we can—"

He cut her off with a squeeze of his arms. "We can't, honey. The men and I are leaving."

Her grin died slowly and she blinked in confusion before whispering, "Leaving? But why? It's Christmas."

He drew her closer and dipped his face to hers. "We had a great day, little one, but my warriors spent today assembling and preparing for tomorrow's battle." She pulled in breath but he kept talking, "I must go meet them."

"Battle?" she breathed.

"Tomorrow, we quell the rebellion," Callum told her and she stared at him a second before she closed her eyes tight.

When she opened them again, they were bleak and that look cut him to the bone.

"Why didn't you tell me?" she asked.

"Because I didn't want to spoil your Christmas," Callum answered.

She watched him again, her face gentling at his words, and then she took in a shallow breath and let it out on another fluttering sigh.

Then she suggested, "Maybe you should explain what 'battle' means."

"I don't have time," he replied, and when she opened her mouth he gave her another squeeze and continued, "And you don't want to know."

"But I don't...you can't...I mean, how can you battle when...I mean, will my people see it?"

He shook his head. "Your people's government knows it's coming, when and where. As usual, they've prepared."

Her mouth dropped open in horrified wonder.

His head dropped and he marked her hair with his temple. "It'll be over soon, baby doll," he assured her, lips at her ear, hoping at the same time that he was right.

He gave her another squeeze, her arms grew tight, and she jerked her head away.

"You don't...you know, as king, you don't fight." She paused and stared at him, fear obliterating the desolation in her eyes. "Do you?"

He gentled his voice further when he explained truthfully, "Unlike your generals, in our battles, I would not be a good commander if I didn't only fight at my warriors' sides, but lead them into battle."

Her body jolted, the fear now stark on her face, and she cried, "But you can't do that! You might get hurt!"

Her strong reaction pleased him just as much as it hurt him, which was to say, for both, immensely.

"Sonia, I must."

"Have you tried talking to them?" she asked desperately.

He had. Mac had. His grandfather had.

For millennia they'd attempted a diplomatic solution. The rebellion remained staunch in their beliefs.

"We've tried that," he told her.

"But—"

"Sonia, I have to go."

Her hold grew tighter.

"Baby doll, I have to go."

She stared at him as tears gathered in her eyes.

The first time witnessing his mate's utter despair at the thought of him entering battle, unable to stop himself, Callum bent his neck and kissed her, thoroughly and long enough to taste her tears yet again.

He enjoyed everything that was her, but if he never tasted her tears for the length of her short life, he'd be able to live his long one much more contentedly.

When he lifted his head she lifted a hand, slid her fingers into his hair, and then watched as her thumb slid along his eyebrow, his cheekbone then his lower lip.

"At least tell me you're a good...um, warrior," she whispered and he grinned.

"The best," he told her truthfully. "That's why I'm king."

At his words, she gave him a sad smile then got up on her toes to place her lips against his.

"Come back to me safe, my handsome wolf," she murmured there.

He wanted to kiss her then, but he couldn't. If he did, with her so sweet in his arms, he wouldn't have been able to stop.

Instead, he touched his forehead to hers, gave her another squeeze, let her go, and walked out of the room without looking back.

Outside by his SUV, he embraced his mother, took off the wedding band Sonia had given him, and handed it to her.

"Keep that safe," he growled so low even Sonia, standing at the window upstairs, tears falling from her eyes and watching him, didn't hear. "I'll want it back the instant I come home."

Regan nodded.

He swung in his SUV, and for the first time in his life before a battle, his mind wasn't on the coming fight.

It was on his queen.

Little did he know her mind was on him as well.

And she cried long after he was gone. Long into the lonely night, in her lonely bed, in her lonely room, in her lonely house that even the company of the twinkling lights on her tree and her stuffed wolf couldn't abate.

Callum's queen cried not because he was going to battle (entirely).

She cried remembering the last two days they shared. Days that cracked through the bitterness that had built around her heart. Bitterness he had broken through with his tenderness and generosity and had given her hope that her dream had finally come true.

Bitterness that slammed back with a vengeance when that dream died the minute he took off the ring he seemed so proud to wear but, as observed from an outsider who had no idea why he did so, obviously was not.

Indeed, as observed from an outsider, it appeared he didn't care about the ring or what it meant at all.

If he did, he'd understand, like her claiming chain, that he was never to take it off, and if he was truly proud to wear it, he never would.

"Sign it," Callum growled, standing over Nikolas, the only chief of the rebellion left alive. He was on his knees, naked, wounded and bloodied, before his king.

Callum was also bloodied, both from his own healing wounds and from the blood of his victims, but he had taken the time, and given it to his warriors, to don clothes.

He had not allowed that courtesy amongst the scores of defeated wolves who were all now kneeled in front of him.

He might have done, if they had not slain his brother Calvin.

And he might have done, if they had not slain his father.

And he might have done, if the battle he'd waged on three fronts in the mountains, and on simultaneous fronts in four other territories, had not taken eight days to win.

And he might have done if he'd had more sleep in those eight days, which he had not as he'd only had an hour here or there and exhaustion had settled into his bones.

And he might have done if he'd not been so fucking hungry, not having the time to eat as he didn't have the time to sleep.

And he might have done if the loss of wolves on both sides had not been so great simply due to their stubborn refusal to admit defeat because their surprise attack had indeed been a surprise, a resounding one. The enemy had been caught unaware, had never recovered, and they should have admitted defeat days ago. In fact, within fucking *hours*.

And, lastly, he might have done if he hadn't been so long separated from his queen.

But, because of all of that, and because he was King Callum, far more impatient and intemperate than his father, especially weary, hungry, and angry, their humiliation ran alongside their defeat.

Nikolas stared up at him obstinately.

"*Sign it!*" Callum barked.

Nikolas's face twisted with fury but his voice was a pained whisper when he said, "She's a pretty piece."

Callum's body grew taut but he sought patience.

"Sign the terms of surrender and accept punishment as leader of your followers. Don't sign it and we don't stop until we've brought low every last one of you," Callum warned.

"A pretty piece," Nikolas repeated quietly. "She'll make a beautiful slave."

At once, Callum's arm swung out and the back of his fist caught Nikolas with a brutal blow to his jaw, sending him sprawling on his back.

"For fuck's sake, *sign it!*" he roared, bending over the wolf.

Nikolas scrambled back to his knees and shouted fanatically, "They all will! When we align with the other immortals who believe as we do, who believe in the divine order of things, *all* the humans will be what they were always meant to be. *Our slaves!*"

Callum drew in a sharp breath through his nose.

Then he turned his back to Nikolas and walked three paces away.

Swiftly, he turned again, crouched low, and in a blur of motion, sprung up through the air and landed as wolf on the defeated leader.

He ripped Nikolas's throat out with his teeth.

First.

Then he tore the warrior's head off.

Springing back to man, he caught the towel thrown at him by one of his wolves, wiped the blood from his jaws, and sauntered to the clothes that he'd long since learned to leap out of while becoming wolf. He grabbed his pants and pulled them up.

As he did so, he turned to Ryon. "Go through every last one until one of them signs it," he gritted as he picked up his shirt and shrugged it on. "They don't sign it then send the order to the commanders on the fronts of the other territories. Give every rebel wolf the opportunity to sign the surrender." His eyes locked on his cousin. "If they don't, slay them."

"It's done," Ryon replied, eyes lit with fury even through his fatigue.

When Callum was dressed, he turned to walk away.

"Where are you going?" Ryon called.

Callum kept walking and didn't look back when he answered, "To my queen. We're going home."

CHAPTER FIFTEEN

CASTLE

Sonia woke under the heavy hides, feeling the soft sheets and the traitorously pleasant ache that sat heavy in every muscle in her body.

Then her eyes opened.

She stared at Callum's empty pillows and the memories of the last nine days crashed brutally into her brain.

Even while Callum was away battling the rebellion, Sonia spent that time adhering to his orders as given to her through Regan.

She was to train Kerry and Mabel in managing Clear as Diana couldn't stay forever, nor, apparently, could Sonia. Under his edict she also began the process of hiring a new shop assistant who her girls would eventually choose and who would work alongside them. This was because Sonia, as soon as the rebellion was quashed, Regan told her, would be moving to Callum's castle in Scotland.

She could not argue this "fact" with Regan as Regan had as little power as Sonia did.

Furthermore, Sonia couldn't argue with Regan because Sonia spent those eight days with a very concerned mother. Her mother-in-law had lost a husband and son to this rebellion (Sonia learned) and she greatly feared for her family *and* her people.

Diana, Julianna, Helena, and half a dozen other mates, mothers, or sisters of warriors away at the fight spent time at her home, the latter of whom Sonia had not met until then. But, when Regan told her they lived close, she invited them to her home (comfort in numbers, Sonia thought). They all congregated with Sonia at her house, and as they would be, were also openly troubled.

Sonia tried to be calm and as upbeat as appropriate to soothe the worries of women (especially Regan) who she grew to care about in a short period of time. It was hard not to care about women whose faces were taut with anxiety and whose lives would be a misery if their warriors fell.

So Sonia kept the coffee going (in the mornings) and the wine flowing and food available (in the evenings) and did the best she could in a tense situation that seemed to last an age and not eight days.

Therefore, as Sonia was busy seeing to her female subjects while the males were at war, Sonia would have to argue with Callum when he got home about the fact that she intended to *stay* home and not move to his castle.

While Callum battled a faceless (to Sonia) enemy, Sonia waged her own battle.

A battle within.

She battled against her feelings of fear that he would be hurt (or worse).

She also battled to control her feelings of rage that he had again, for whatever demented Callum reason, fought to win a place in her heart and succeeded brilliantly, only to prove he didn't belong there.

This was proved time and again after he took off her ring, handed it to his mother and left without a single glance at her house. A place where *he* built the best Christmas she'd had in decades only to end it by nonchalantly blowing down his own house of cards.

He proved it in making it known he was taking her away from her home, her friends, her business by doing nothing more than ordering it so and not even having the courtesy to order it to her face. He proved it by making her say good-bye to her friends and neighbors by, again, ordering it done. He proved it by making Regan take her shopping for the numerous clothes (how she needed *more*, Sonia would never know) that Regan told her would be required in her new home. He proved it by doing all of this without asking Sonia what *she* wanted, where she wanted to live, who she wanted to surround her, and what she wanted to wear.

Lastly, he proved it by his behavior the moment he arrived back safely from the fight and the hours after he swept her away.

Callum, her dream Callum, her handsome wolf, was a figment of her imagination.

No matter how he behaved sometimes, there was only King Callum, and she vowed in her head that she would always, *always* remember that.

The worst part started when Regan received a phone call in the kitchen and came rushing into the living room where Sonia was sitting with Julianna and Helena.

"It's over! Victory is ours!" Regan shouted with delight. Julianna and Helena cried out their joy and Regan looked at Sonia. "Callum, Calder, Caleb, and Ryon are fine." She looked at Helena. "Trenten is too." She looked at Julianna. "Your brother is also with us and I'm sure Saint already knows his two brothers are safe." Then she hugged herself and laughed out loud before Julianna, Helena, and Sonia surged up to hug her and each other, so great was their relief. Though Sonia's, obviously, was mixed with other things as well.

Suddenly Regan grabbed Sonia's face in both her hands and cried, "Oh sweetheart! I forgot! It's time to get you prepared!"

Before explaining a word of this statement to Sonia, Regan started dashing around the house while Helena and Julianna, still wreathed in relieved smiles, gave her hugs and fond farewells, but, Sonia noted, no explanations.

Regan was banging around upstairs when Sonia finally joined her in her bedroom. The six suitcases and one large cosmetics bag they'd purchased three days earlier were all open and littering her bed, her window seat, and even the floor.

"The boys will be here soon. You go find the things that you want to take with you. Don't worry if you miss something. Julianna can send it if you remember something you'd like to have." Then she paused, whirled on Sonia, and exclaimed, "Oh no! The boxes are in the garage. I'll need to go get them. You! Pack your clothes. I'll run and do that."

"Regan, what on earth?" Sonia started, but she was talking to no one. In the blink of an eye Regan was gone.

She followed her mother-in-law and found her in the kitchen for some reason struggling with large flat-folded cardboard boxes and tape.

Regan glanced her way before babbling, "We should have done this before but I didn't want...just in case..." She hesitated. "Well, obviously, if something happened, you'd be staying here, so I didn't..." She paused again and went on, "Anyway, Callum ordered me to do it, and if we don't get it done by the time he arrives, he won't be best pleased."

Even though Sonia had no idea what Regan was talking about, she figured that last part was the sorry truth.

Regan continued, "And Caleb said Callum wants to leave for home the minute he gets to the city so we must be ready."

"Regan, I don't know what you're talking about," Sonia told her, and Regan stopped and looked at her as if perplexed.

"You're moving to Scotland with Callum," she replied. "I thought I explained that to you."

"Yes, but—"

"There's no time to waste, Sonny." Regan threw down a box. "You do this. Build the boxes. There's that bubble wrap stuff and tissue paper for packing in the garage. Anything you want from here, pack it up in the boxes. I'll see to your clothes."

"Regan—" Sonia started again but Regan's phone rang.

She lifted a hand palm up for Sonia to stop speaking and she answered her phone. While listening, the palm went down but she twirled her hand adamantly toward the boxes.

On a sigh (even though Sonia was going *nowhere*), she started to build the boxes as Regan listened, mumbling, "Mm-hmm. Mm-hmm. Right." Regan disconnected and announced, "We have less time than I expected. The boys will be here in an hour and a half. Let's get cracking."

Before Sonia could utter a word, Regan flew up the stairs.

Sonia stood amongst the boxes and decided, for Regan, she'd do as she was asked. She could easily unpack them later when she told Callum she wasn't moving to Scotland.

An hour and a half later, Sonia stood staring out her window in shock as her six full suitcases, one full cosmetic case, *Callum's* three suitcases, and five boxes full of her family's Christmas decorations, her stuffed wolf, her photo albums, and a few odds and ends were whisked away by one of Callum's men.

That'll make unpacking tonight a bit more difficult, she thought as she bit her lip and worry began to nag her.

Any hope she had of staying put was dashed fifteen minutes later when Callum arrived.

The door opened and Sonia, sitting and enjoying a mug of herbal tea with Regan in the living room, got to her feet, turned to her mate, and opened her mouth.

She froze and stared.

Callum's body, hair, and clothes were clean, although his clothing was wrinkled.

However, the beard that had grown in the weeks she'd been with him was now immensely thick and untrimmed. Further, his hair seemed to have grown tremendously in that short time and it went from overlong to just plain *long,* falling past the collar of his shirt.

Further, his face appeared so exhausted he looked almost haggard, something she would never have guessed as he always seemed alert and energized.

And his eyes were hungry and not in a good way. The lines beside them deeper, and they were positively seething, not with anger, but with *wrath.* A rage so deep, so strong, it emanated from him and filled the room with its terrifying intensity instantly.

He looked wild, even savage, and Sonia was frozen to the spot when Callum didn't look at his mother, who had risen at Sonia's side. He came directly at Sonia and she had the desire to flee, to run away from him as fast as she could. However, her terror was so absolute it felt her feet had grown roots into the floor.

She didn't move a muscle when he used one arm to hook her brutally at the waist and yank her body so that it crashed into his. Then he used his other hand to twist viciously in her hair causing so much pain it didn't feel sensuously pleasant, it only felt like pain. His mouth slammed down on hers and he kissed her in a way he'd never kissed her before. In a way that Sonia didn't even know you *could* kiss.

It was violent and merciless and seizing and even cruel.

Therefore, when his head came up and he glanced dismissively at his mother, Sonia didn't say a word.

"We'll see you at home," he growled, his voice rough with all that was in his eyes, all that was carved in his features and every line of his enraged frame.

Then he took Sonia's hand and dragged her out to his SUV.

Yes, *dragged*.

She even tripped twice trying to keep up with his ground-eating strides and he didn't even glance at her.

She was buckled in and he was speeding casually through the streets before she realized he hadn't muttered a word to her.

He hadn't even said hello.

She was too terrified of him to suggest it or say it to him.

Definitely too terrified to tell him she wasn't going to Scotland.

He took her to an airfield, tossed the keys of the SUV to a waiting Saint, and dragged her up the steps into an aircraft.

When she got inside she saw to her shock it was a personal jet. There was a set of four wide comfortable seats upholstered in rich tan leather facing each other over a gleaming wood topped table, four more seats in the back, two on each side of a door. There was a bar and refrigerator on the wall opposite the jet's door, the bar also made of highly shined wood where glasses and bottles were in snug secured shelves. There was a television screen on the wall behind the cockpit. And there was a long, wide, deep-seated couch running the opposite side to the seating area and bar.

Callum turned to her and commanded tersely, "Strap in."

Looking into his forbidding hostile eyes, without a peep, Sonia did as she was told. She chose a seat at the back by the window and buckled in.

He stuck his head into the cockpit and said one word, "Go."

Then he strapped himself in beside Sonia.

She tried to get her heart to stop beating so crazily. She tried to find one thread of courage. She tried to catch a single thought.

She failed at all of these things in the face of this new fearsome Callum.

When they leveled off in the air, again without saying a word to her, he unbuckled her, picked her up, and carried her to the couch.

Sonia tensed as Callum all but tossed her on it then came down on top of her.

With most of his body pinning her between him and the back of the couch, he tucked her face in his neck, and within moments, the tightness left his body, his enormous weight settled into her, and he fell fast asleep.

She was shocked at this, shocked silent and still for long minutes.

Then the shock wore off and she realized she was not comfortable nor was she tired, primarily because she was scared out of her mind. But anytime she tried to shift out from under him, his arm tightened reflexively, pulling her further underneath him.

So Sonia gave up and lay mostly under him, trying to get comfortable, sometimes dozing (as he slept for nine hours straight without moving a muscle), but most of the time deciding that she couldn't live this life.

No matter how good they were, she couldn't live for the times when Callum remembered she existed and at least attempted to be the mate he didn't want to be but it was his duty to be as king. She couldn't rail against the times when he forgot to do that and was just king.

She couldn't bear this for a lifetime.

She knew she couldn't leave, but she also couldn't live like this.

She'd been right all those weeks ago. Living like this would drive her mad.

Before she came to a single conclusion and thus before she made that first plan, Callum woke.

It was moments before the captain announced over the intercom that they would shortly be landing and they needed to take their seats and fasten their seatbelts.

Callum used the restroom at the back as did she, finding it wasn't a restroom but a full-on bathroom, four times the space as in a regular airplane's. It even had a shower.

When she came out, his arm extended to her, he pulled her into his lap and kissed her, this time slowly, lingeringly, reminding her how good it could be and how much she missed it.

Her heart lurched as her belly tightened but her mind fought against the sweetness of it even as her body rebelled and relaxed into his.

Then he nuzzled her neck, flicking her ear with his nose, and he whispered, "Buckle in, baby doll. We're almost home."

She did as she was told, the frightening Callum still fresh in her mind even though his voice was no longer harsh, his eyes were no longer hungry or enraged, and his warm tone indicated an extreme sense of relief.

When they alighted from the plane, one tall dark-haired man was standing beside a hunter-green Range Rover that Callum, holding her hand, guided her to immediately.

The man was looking at Sonia curiously but he did not drop to a knee.

He bowed his head deeply to her and to Callum before he lifted his head and to Sonia, he murmured reverently, his Scottish burr evident even though he spoke two words, "My queen." When she nodded and gave him a tremulous smile, he grinned at Callum and said, "She's pretty, your grace."

"Yes, she is, Drogan," Callum answered as the man threw Callum a set of keys which Callum caught.

"Good to have you back," Drogan called as Callum practically pushed Sonia into the left side passenger seat.

"It's fucking good to be back," Callum answered, slamming Sonia's door without bothering to introduce her to Drogan.

"Hail victory, my king," Drogan went on, his voice was soft, but it was also filled with pride and relief.

"Hail victory," Callum repeated, his voice was threaded with a vein of steel.

Callum drove them through the darkening afternoon of a wooded countryside just as swiftly as he drove them to the airfield hours before.

She wanted to ask him to slow down.

She was too numb to speak.

He didn't bother.

However, finally he said, "There she is."

Sonia turned her head from her silent, angry, fearful contemplation of the countryside whizzing by on her left to look straight ahead.

On a small rise sat a castle.

In the waning light she saw it. Not exactly large and also not like any castle she'd ever seen in the times Gregor had taken her to France and Germany.

This one was like out of a fairytale.

It had eight (she counted them) turrets upon which long streaming pennants flew. It seemed to have no straight sides, no sharp angles. It was all rounded with sweeping edges. It didn't ramble across the rise but was compact and tall, at least three stories, except the turrets, which were much higher.

She barely got a good look at it before Callum swung around the circular drive, which had a small round fountain dancing in the middle, stopped the Rover, and parked.

She also barely got a good look at the two statues (she could swear they were *wolves*) guarding the banisters on either side of the six (or seven, or even eight) foot wide set of steps. These led to the studded, wooden, arched double doors that seemed fifteen feet tall and had enormous, scrolled, iron hinges.

She also barely got a look at anything in the welcomingly lit interior as he dragged her up a winding stone staircase lit by sconces and cut by thin tapestries hanging on the rounded walls.

One flight, two, three, four, and on the landing of the fifth he walked them straight into the only room that led straight off the landing. A bedroom that she didn't see at all.

Because she was concentrating on the fact that Callum was almost tearing her clothes from her body.

"Callum—" she began.

"Quiet," he ordered in his kingly voice.

"Cal—"

He kissed her.

She struggled. Not against him but against the urge which was fighting to emerge during his deep, heady, hungry kiss. She struggled because she was never going to sleep with him.

Not ever again.

But concentrating on her inner battle, she lost track of him taking off every last stitch of her clothing.

So when she was naked and he had his hands on her bottom, lifted her, and threw her on the bed, but caught her ankles and yanked her forward at the same time he pulled her legs apart, she was losing the fight in her head.

And when Callum, still fully clothed, dropped to his knees beside the bed, that was when Sonia was lost and the urge took over because he bent forward and suddenly his mouth was between her legs.

The soles of her feet planted themselves at the edge of the bed. With a brazenly deep moan of pleasure starting at the core of her, tearing its way up her throat and through her lips, her hips surged up to meet the voracious consuming demands of his mouth. He cupped her bottom in his big hands and took from her like a man who'd been wandering a desert for days without water and had just dropped to his knees at the pool in an oasis.

In what seemed like seconds, Sonia came against his mouth. Her orgasm was so intense she barely noticed him flipping her to her belly then tugging her hips up. Her knees going into the edge of the bed, he entered her savagely.

The urge devoured her, causing her to reach her arms straight out in front of her and her fingers to fist in the hides there as he took her, rough and fast and hard. Then harder, then harder, and she met his every thrust with mindless abandon and reared back in desperation to deepen the contact. Her first orgasm seemed never to stop as the next one came and then the next before he seated himself to the root one last time, filling her full, and growled his release.

But he wasn't done.

He took her again, Callum on top, Sonia wrapping her limbs around him and letting him ride her, again hard, again fast, again rough, until they both climaxed.

And he took her again, Callum behind her, his hands on her inner thighs holding her suspended and steady for his thrusts as she grasped the headboard of the bed, her head back on his shoulder, her whimpers piercing the air.

And he took her again, Sonia on top and riding his shaft, as Callum, sitting up, coaxed her to go faster with one hand on her hip and the other hand cupping her breast and feeding it to his mouth where he tormented her nipple.

And lastly, he took her again, but neither of them climaxed as they were spent, lying on their sides, spooning, his shaft sliding tenderly, almost lazily, in and out of her, and his arms were wrapped around her tight.

"Sleep, baby doll," he whispered after he seated himself to the hilt and remained there.

Exhausted, all she could do was as he commanded.

Now, she lay in his bed in his castle in Scotland, her body exhausted and aching, but content by his play. Content in the knowledge that he again fell asleep inside her and she again fell asleep full of him. All of which she told herself she would never be and would never again do.

Humiliation crept into her muscles alongside the ache, and the bitterness that guarded her heart turned to hatred.

The tears of that bitter hatred started stinging the backs of her eyes when she heard a knock on the door.

She froze and stared, silent, hoping whoever it was (for it wasn't Callum, she would smell him, and anyway, he would never bother to knock) would go away.

They didn't.

The head of a tall, very pretty woman peeked around the door. She had dark hair burnished with coppery highlights and a huge smile on her face.

"You're awake!" she said brightly, her words also softened by a Scottish burr, and she threw open the door, balancing a tray in one hand and closing the door behind her with a hefty kick of her foot.

Sonia sat up, holding the hides to her bared breasts. The woman, wearing jeans, boots, and a pretty, bright orange, woolly sweater with a fluffy scarf in orange, red and purple stripes wrapped around her neck, walked into the room. She put the tray on the bedside table and dropped immediately to a knee, head lowered.

Sonia stared at her, stunned.

Then she remembered what she was supposed to do.

"Please rise," she invited, and with abundant energy that startled Sonia so much she jumped, the woman surged to her feet.

"My queen!" she exclaimed. "I've been waiting *ages*! Everyone has! Ages and ages and *ages*! And look at you! You're even prettier than I expected!"

"Um..." Sonia muttered, taken aback by her exuberance, and, of course, the small fact she was naked in bed and confronted with a stranger. "Thank you."

The woman burst out laughing while she turned and rushed to Sonia's six suitcases (and one cosmetics case) that somehow were all lined up with Callum's cases in the room.

"She's thanking me because she's pretty," the woman said to no one. "Hilarious!" she cried.

She then started opening suitcases in apparent abandon. She was digging through Sonia's possessions while Sonia stared in shock, uncertain what to do and unable to do *anything* seeing as she was naked and the woman had four inches and at least fifty pounds on her.

"I'm Maraleena. I'm Drogan's mate," she announced while opening another suitcase and still digging. "Drogan is Steward of the King's Estates." She snatched something out of a suitcase and whirled, brandishing Sonia's stretchy, black, cotton nightie with the deep hem of black lace and matching lace covering the cotton at the bosoms. "Ah ha!" she cried and rushed to Sonia. "You can put that on. Then you need to eat. Everything. King Callum said he wanted me to bring down a clean plate."

Of course he did, Sonia thought but didn't speak aloud as she took the nightgown Maraleena dropped on the bed beside her so the other woman could start pulling covers off food on the tray.

"You're human, I forgot," she said apropos of what Sonia thought was nothing but going back to her earlier subject. "Steward of the Estates means Drogan takes care of all things castle. You know, the plumbing and heating and the cars and the gardens and the forest and stuff like that. He also helps Callum with other stuff too, official stuff. Ho hum. Bo...ring!" she decreed, lifted the tray and Sonia had just pulled the nightgown down over her hips when Maraleena planted the tray on Sonia's lap then she looked at Sonia and said, "I'm housekeeper, or I was. That means I take care of all things castle that are, you know, housekeeping things. Keeping it clean, doing the laundry, ironing, getting the food in. Though, I'm a terrible cook. Poor Drogan, he loves his food. His life is a misery with me." She grinned a grin that belied her words and then carried on, "We've a she-wolf who sees to that, or saw to it, her name is Callista."

Sonia's astonished eyes went from her tray to Maraleena. And her tray, incidentally, consisted of two eggs over easy on what looked like two *fried* pieces of bread and sat next to a pile of baked beans, a pile of sautéed mushrooms, two rashers of bacon, two huge sausages, and two patties of some kind of meat that was black. This was accompanied by a toast caddy of four half-diamonds of perfectly toasted toast and three small bowls, one of butter, one of strawberry jam, and one of orange marmalade. This was finished off with a cafetière of coffee, a mug, a small jug filled with milk, a sugar bowl, and tiny salt and pepper shakers.

"She-wolf?" Sonia breathed, forgetting her food, and she watched as Maraleena went stock still and her face paled.

Then she blinked.

Then she stammered, "Oh, it's just something we...it's just. Well..." she spluttered, her eyes lit and she proclaimed, "King Callum is known as The Wolf!"

It was Sonia's turn to blink at her, stunned silent by this news.

Callum was known as The Wolf?

The Wolf?

The Wolf?

Why had he not mentioned this to her?

Not once.

Not while she was calling him that, calling it out during her orgasms (as hideous as that memory was at the moment), cuddling her stuffed wolf, fiddling with the wolf charm his mother bought her or *any time in between.*

"King McDonagh was known as wolf too. Because of that we're all known as wolves." Maraleena beamed down at Sonia looking for some reason strangely pleased with herself and her announcement. "So, you know, if anyone mentions that, say, calls us wolves or she-wolves or... whatever, you know why."

Sonia was only partially listening.

She was more hooked on the fact that she didn't know Callum's father's full name was McDonagh.

She thought it was Mac.

Callum hadn't told her that either.

And McDonagh was a strange name (not that some of Callum's people didn't have strange names).

Was it a last name? Was it Callum's last name? Did Callum *have* a last name?

He'd never told her that either and she'd never (stupid, *stupid* her) thought to ask.

Not, of course, that she cared (anymore). It was just that his last name was probably *her* last name and she should know her own last name!

Maraleena, oblivious to Sonia's rampaging thoughts, moved back to the suitcases. "King Callum and Drogan are down in his study going over things and beginning plans for the celebration and The Mating." She lifted an armful of Sonia's clothes out of an opened suitcase and turned to Sonia animatedly. "*Two* parties to ring in the New Year!" she shouted happily. "One of them the end of those terrible rebels and the other a Royal Mating! How exciting!"

Sonia thought she should reply or perhaps ask Maraleena what she was doing with Sonia's clothes, but the former became moot when Maraleena babbled and the latter became obvious when Maraleena started to put them away.

Therefore, Sonia decided to eat and let Maraleena chatter.

"I figure King Callum will go big on both, The Mating definitely." She threw a smile over her shoulder at Sonia as Sonia forked up some mushrooms and Maraleena dumped her clothes on top of a bureau and started sorting and kept talking.

Sonia took her prattle as an opportunity to look around and finally see her new bedroom.

The minute she did she stopped eating and stared about the room in wide-eyed wonder.

It was like no other room she'd seen.

The walls were not flat but rounded, however the room wasn't a circle but seemed to go in waves.

And it was huge.

There were two, five-doored, dark wood wardrobes that went from floor to high ceiling and they also followed the wavy curves of the walls. There was a thin dresser but it was tall. There was a wider one with seven drawers and a longer one that had four drawers up and four abreast but was shorter (the one Maraleena was at presently). The walls not covered in furniture were covered in intricate tapestries that looked old but were definitely well-kept and hung from curving polished brass rails at the top edge of the wall.

There were many windows, all of them diamond paned and the glass was so old it was wavy as well, giving the gray, green, and white landscape beyond it an almost dreamy quality.

There was an oblong alcove set in one wall which was big enough to seat two and had a fluffy pad covered in hunter-green twill and humongous cushiony pillows scattered around in different shades of brown and green.

There was a circular fireplace that, she noted in shock, *was in the middle of the room.* It had what looked like a stone hood over it which served as a chimney. On one side of the fire was a half-circle comfy couch in a reddish-brown and on the other side were two cozy chairs with ottomans separated by a stout round table. The couch and chairs were also piled with big pillows, woolen throws, or soft animal hides.

The bed Sonia was in was bigger than any bed she'd ever seen, not only wider, but longer. It had four curtained posts and was covered in heavy, soft, dark hides stitched together. There were copious pillows across the head, the mattress was covered in soft, clay-colored, flannel sheets and Sonia was separated from the underside of the hides by a sheet of the same.

The floors were littered with rugs, all of different sizes, most of them large and thick and elaborately woven in browns, rusts, and greens.

Any part of the room not taken up by furniture, tapestries, or rugs was made up of a mellow golden-red-brown stone.

It was the most inviting, comfortable-looking, beautiful room she'd ever seen.

She immediately felt like crying.

For it was *this* room she sensed in some of her dreams. She knew it from the many times she'd see that golden-red-brown at the edges of her consciousness that wasn't involved with her handsome wolf or saw the dancing of the firelight on his skin.

To bury these thoughts and halt the tears she could not shed in front of Maraleena, Sonia looked down at her plate and forced some egg into her mouth.

Then she glared at her crockery on her tray for it, too, was beautiful in a sturdy handsome way with the bottom of the plate and the outside of the bowls, mugs, and jugs being a rich earthen brown, but the inside was a gorgeous muted turquoise.

Of course, only Callum could have *crockery* that she instantly loved and therefore forced herself to instantly hate.

"...executed them all," Maraleena was saying as Sonia pushed down the top of the cafetière, her words catching Sonia's attention.

"Sorry?" Sonia asked.

Maraleena was zipping up an empty suitcase and setting it aside as she looked at Sonia.

"They should have executed them all," Maraleena repeated.

"Who?"

"The rebels!" Maraleena exclaimed, not ceasing in her endeavors and heading toward another suitcase then repeatedly pulling out Sonia's jeans and cords and piling them, folded double, on the couch. "A stroke of brilliance, we all think, King Callum handing down the order to slay them one by one until they signed the terms of surrender."

Sonia sucked in breath and the oxygen burned her frozen lungs.

Slay them one by one? Sonia repeated in her brain.

"Nothing less than they deserved," Maraleena muttered, again oblivious to Sonia's reaction. "Lots of us feel they shouldn't have stopped. This has been going on years. *Years!* And what they want, what they're fighting for! And killing our males for. It's revolting. Now, finally, it's over."

Sonia decided to get her system working by pouring coffee into it which always helped, and therefore, with studious precision in an attempt to stop her hand from shaking, she prepared her mug.

Callum had ordered the executions of men.

One by one.

Until they did what he wanted.

It was barbaric.

He was barbaric.

And he was her mate, her husband, now he was her *king*!

"Anyway, it's a happy New Year with this business over and you seated in the lap of your king," Maraleena declared while hanging Sonia's pants on hangers. She threw another smile at Sonia as if she hadn't just been crowing at the deaths of multitudes of men. "Everyone's really excited."

"I'm glad," Sonia replied, but her voice sounded choked so she sipped her coffee.

It was delicious. But it didn't help.

"You know," Sonia started, wishing (desperately) to change the subject in an effort not to go stark raving mad. "I can do that."

Maraleena froze while shoving the hangers with her pants on them in the wardrobe.

Slowly, she turned and bowed her head low.

Then, deferentially, she murmured, "Yes, my queen."

But before her head bowed, Sonia saw a look on her face that was near to tragic.

"What?" Sonia asked before she remembered Callum telling her that Julianna would be offended if Sonia tried to help. So, quickly, she said, "Maraleena, I'm so sorry. I'm human and new to this royal business." Maraleena's head came up but her face had lost its cheerfulness as Sonia carried on, "I'm used to doing things for myself."

"I suspected, as King Callum's mate, you'd want to take care of him," Maraleena replied in a dead voice.

Hardly, Sonia thought but did not say out loud.

"It's not that, it's just—" Sonia stopped speaking when the hint of a light of hope lit in Maraleena's eyes.

Sonia made a decision, put the tray aside, and got out of bed. She walked to Maraleena, grabbed the surprised woman's hand, and led her to the couch. Seating them both side by side, she faced the tall woman.

Then she explained, "Callum has been kind of busy. He hasn't had time to tell me about the ways of your people and my people are very different. So, if you would, could *you* tell me what's happening here because I need to understand it so I can..." Sonia trailed off, not knowing what to say then found her words. "Be a good queen."

It sounded lame, but the hope built in Maraleena's eyes, and obviously not a woman who needed a lot of coaxing to talk, she did so.

"Well, you see, as King Callum's mate you can decide to take the running of the castle, you know, the cooking and cleaning and stuff. Queen Regan did it for King Mac." When she stopped, Sonia smiled and nodded encouragingly for her to go on and the hope dimmed as she began to get nervous, but she sallied forth. "But, you see, this is my duty to my king but it's also..." She hesitated. "My *job*. King Callum pays me to do it and Drogan and I just bought a bigger cottage because our pups are growing and we need the money, so if you—"

"You can keep your job," Sonia cut in swiftly and the light flared bright in Maraleena's eyes before she pulled a surprised Sonia in her arms and hugged her.

"Really?" she cried then went on before Sonia could reply. "Oh, I'm so happy! I'd been so worried since I heard he claimed you." She pulled back and looked at Sonia. "Drogan said we shouldn't get that cottage because we never knew when the king would find his mate and if she'd want the running of the castle." She beamed. "But I told him not to worry. I had a feeling all would be well, and now you're here and you're so tiny and pretty and *nice*. And, I know it may sound crazy, but I love my job, I love this castle, and it's an honor for anyone to be of service to our king." She pulled Sonia in her arms and gave her another fierce hug with a whispered, "Thank you."

Sonia hugged her back thinking she would like Maraleena, which was something good in a world that looked pretty dreary, and replied, "You're welcome."

Maraleena let her go and jumped up, quickly resuming work. "You better finish your breakfast. It'll get cold and King Callum said you had to finish every bite."

There it was. A reminder of her dreary world.

Sonia resumed her place in bed with her tray and she stared at the black patties.

"What's this?" she asked, forking one up and showing it to Maraleena.

"Black sausage," Maraleena answered after glancing at it and before zipping up another bag and setting it aside.

Something about her answer, though it probably wasn't her answer, it was probably hysteria, caused Sonia to start giggling but she spoke through her laughter, "I can see that, Maraleena. It's definitely *black* and it *looks* like a kind of sausage, but what *is* it?"

Maraleena grinned at her again and said, "Black sausage, blood sausage, you know, sausage made out of blood."

Sonia paled.

Maraleena laughed.

"It's really good. Try it," Maraleena coaxed.

Sonia gulped.

"Honestly, try it," Maraleena prompted. "I only get the best in. You'll love it. King Callum does."

Of course Callum would love sausage made out of blood. He'd probably drink blood if he could.

Wanting to be a good queen and nice to Maraleena, wincing the whole time, Sonia nibbled at the patty.

It was delicious.

So she decided she hated it.

"Isn't it lovely?" Maraleena asked with a smile in her voice, watching Sonia closely.

"Yes. Lovely," Sonia agreed, made a comical face, Maraleena burst out laughing again and got back to work.

As she did so, Sonia forced down too much food that she didn't want even though she hadn't eaten in ages. Alternately, when she could get a word in edgewise, she chatted with Maraleena as the woman finished with two more suitcases.

It was while Sonia was gulping down the last bit of toast with a sip of coffee that Callum arrived.

Sonia looked at him and her heart leaped into her throat.

He was wearing the chocolate brown corduroy shirt she bought him for Christmas over jeans that fit him well, and a pair of brown boots.

Since yesterday he'd had his hair trimmed but he'd also shaved off the beard.

Completely.

No stubble, nothing.

He was *exactly* the vision of her dream Callum. The vision she'd never seen in real life (except he was clothed).

She was so struck by the picture of him he was sitting on the bed grinning at her before she realized it.

Then he was leaning in, evading her coffee mug which she was holding aloft *and* her tray, to brush her lips with his.

He pulled only an inch away before he murmured, "Morning, my little one."

"Morning," she replied, but her voice sounded husky and low.

She cleared her throat.

His grin turned into a smile.

She wanted to conk him in the head with her coffee mug.

"Brilliant." They both heard muttered from Maraleena and they both turned their heads to look at her.

She was clutching one of Sonia's sweaters and watching them openly.

"You're so cute and sweet together," Maraleena noted, a big happy grin on her face. "Brilliant. I love it." Her eyes moved to focus on Callum. "Hi there, your grace, welcome home."

"Hello, Mara," Callum returned, shifting so he was sitting in bed beside Sonia. *Close* beside her, his legs straight out in front of him, his back to the headboard, and he seized her mug of coffee from her fingers and took a sip.

Sonia clenched her teeth together at the unwanted (she was telling herself) intimacy.

Maraleena continued folding sweaters like she was in a couple's bedroom every day seeing to her chores while they lounged in bed.

"Well done with routing the rebels," Maraleena threw out casually on another sunny smile in their direction.

"Thanks," Callum replied on a half laugh.

"It's celebration time," Maraleena noted gleefully.

"It is that," Callum murmured on another sip of coffee, but his arm was pushing through the pillows at Sonia's waist where it settled. His hand at her hip, finding the wolf charm through her nightgown, and as ever, he started fiddling with it.

Sonia tried not to look like she was seething while allowing herself, if only in her mind, to *seethe*.

"Can't wait," Maraleena muttered as she placed Sonia's sweaters on a shelf in the wardrobe.

"Mara?" Callum called as he set the mug on the tray and then divested Sonia of it.

Maraleena turned to the bed with her brows raised.

"You want to do me a favor?" Callum asked, holding the tray out to her.

Maraleena's eyes grew so bright they practically singed the room with their glow.

Then, for some reason, she burst out laughing, though Sonia was thinking that Maraleena did that on a regular basis. She rushed forward, nabbed the tray, and was out of the room before Sonia could make a peep.

The minute the door closed, Callum turned his body into hers, pulling her down into the bed so her head was on the pillows.

Then he kissed her, soft and sweet but also wet and lingeringly.

It was a great kiss.

Sonia's body responded, but luckily her brain did not.

Nevertheless, she was breathing heavier when he lifted his lips from hers.

"Callum," she whispered.

"You're here," he whispered back, his eyes full-on tawny, roaming her face, his fingers sifting through the hair at the side of her head. "In my arms, in my bed, in my home."

She had to stop him. She couldn't listen to this, couldn't witness it again and want it just as much as she knew he'd never give it to her.

"Callum, I feel strange." His head cocked to the side at her words and the warm look on his face vanished as his brows shot together. "Not that," she said swiftly, she couldn't bear his false loving concern, not again. "Just, I think jetlag or something. All that food. Everything went so fast yesterday. I feel weird. I think I need a shower and more coffee—"

She stopped speaking because his face relaxed and he touched his mouth to hers.

"Take a shower, baby doll," he allowed (would she *ever* get used to him telling her what she could and couldn't do and when she could and couldn't do it?). "I've got a few things to do but I'll come back and take you on a tour of your new home." His head bent and he nuzzled her neck a moment before he marked her hair with his temple and lifted his head again. "You'll take it easy a few days, get acclimatized. Is that good?"

Was he asking like he cared about her answer or was it a rhetorical question?

She answered the only way she could. "That's good."

He grinned at her.

She loved his grin just as much as she told herself she hated it.

He pushed away from her and exited the bed.

She looked at the big room and called out to him, "Callum?"

He glanced down at her, brows raised.

"Um, where's the bathroom?"

She really hoped it wasn't on another floor or something. That would be awful, climbing down those winding stone steps should she need the facilities in the middle of the night.

He smiled, planted a fist in the bed on either side of her, touched his lips (again!) to hers, pushed away, and then walked across the room and opened a door that was *in* a tapestry. The tapestry was affixed to the door in a way that it looked a seamless part of the bigger tapestry all around it. The doorknob, too, was hidden in the tapestry's design.

It was very neat and super clever.

She didn't share this with Callum.

She just threw back the hides (really? who slept under hides?), got out of bed, and headed to the bathroom.

Callum stalled her progress by hooking an arm around her stomach and she twisted her neck and looked up at him.

"I'm anxious to show you your new home, honey," he murmured, before kissing her forehead and finishing by ordering gently, but definitely kingly, "You have an hour."

Then he was gone.

She was glad for the reminder that he was king.

And the reminder that, even if she was queen and not of his people, she was still nothing but a subject.

The bathroom was (almost) as nice as the bedroom. The walls and floors were still that stone but there was a big brass towel warmer, a huge circular tub in a very pretty shade of rust, and a shower cubical tiled in rich-colored tiles. The ceramic basin was rust-colored and set in more of that mellow golden-red-brown stone. There was a set of shelves inset in a wall with stacks of fluffy neatly folded towels. The shelves also bore pretty stoneware boxes and trays that Sonia would love to fill with her girlie bits and bobs. There was a huge round mirror over the basin surrounded on the top half with brass lights. And last, twin, narrow, thin handsome cabinets on the walls on either side of the recessed basin.

Seriously, so far, Sonia could see why everyone was so happy in this castle.

She tried to hate it, she just couldn't.

She lugged her cosmetics case into the bathroom, found her stuff, took a quick shower, and did the best she could do with her hair and makeup when she didn't know where anything was.

Luckily, there was a blow dryer (as hers didn't have the right plug) and fortunately, when she was ready, she didn't look a fright as one wouldn't want to look when one was possibly meeting their new subjects as their new queen.

She decided not to wait for Callum (he hadn't ordered her to stay in the room) and she started wandering on her own.

The bedroom was the best of all but it was also the best room Sonia had ever seen in her life. But the rest was still really, *really* good.

It was all decorated in warm, rich, manly shades. The furniture was handsome and comfortable looking. There were lots of pillows and snug throws and hides tossed everywhere, all of it inviting as well as beautiful. There were tons of circular fireplaces in other rooms, not to mention wavy walls, and diamond-paned windows.

It was magical.

Sonia wanted to hate that too but she couldn't.

In her new life she'd have Regan and probably Maraleena and of course Ryon and Caleb and maybe Calder, though he hadn't been around as much and sometimes he could be surly so she didn't know what to make of him yet.

And she'd have the castle.

That just wasn't enough.

But, she decided, it was all there was going to be.

For, she decided, she'd tell Callum she'd do her duties as his queen but she wouldn't be his mate.

Last night was the last night they'd have.

Forever.

She was standing in what she guessed was a living room, though all of them kind of looked like that. Or at least as far as she got, except she found a library and what appeared to be a knitting room as there were huge skeins of wool in big wide-woven baskets by the comfy chairs. She was staring out the window at the landscape (mostly tall, rolling, snow covered woods, as far as she could see) when Callum found her.

She tensed, expecting him to be angry that she'd started the tour on her own. But he just strode right up to her, shifting to stand at her back. He wrapped his arms around her, pulled her to his front, and dipped his head to kiss her neck.

She told herself she shivered because she was cold (though that wasn't the reason).

And she decided now was as good a time as any.

Sonia opened her mouth to speak, but Callum beat her to it.

"Have you liked what you've seen, little one?"

"Yes, you have a lovely home," she told him and then went on, "Callum—"

He interrupted by correcting her, "*We* have a lovely home."

"Yes. Right. Cal—"

He cut her off yet again, informing her, "We're planning a victory celebration first. I owe it to my men. All the warriors who fought will be arriving over the next few weeks and my guard returning home." He gave her a squeeze and his voice dipped low. "Then, two weeks later, we'll have The Royal Mating." He rested his chin on her shoulder and asked, "Are you okay with that?"

As she didn't know what a Mating was, even though she heard a lot of talk about it, she couldn't exactly say.

As she didn't feel like there was anything to celebrate, though, the answer was "no."

"Callum—" she began again.

"There you are." She heard a man say and both she and Callum (though Callum didn't let her go) turned to the door to see Drogan entering while smiling.

He started to drop to a knee but Sonia blurted out, "No!" and his head jerked up as Callum's body went solid.

Oh good goodness.

She'd done something wrong.

Drogan looked questioningly at Callum.

"Keep your feet," Callum told him, his voice purely kingly and sounding annoyed.

Sonia needed to cover.

"I did something wrong," she stated, to which neither man replied so she ventured forth. "It's just that, in your...I mean *our* home, it should be casual. People should feel comfortable and not...you know..." she trailed off and twisted her head to look at Callum before asking, "Shouldn't it?"

Callum looked as annoyed as he'd sounded (and as kingly).

He didn't speak.

Sonia's heart started beating madly.

"I'm sorry," she whispered. "I'm just not used to people bowing to me and it makes me uncomfortable."

There was a long moment of silence before Callum sighed.

He let her go and looked at Drogan. "Your queen doesn't want you to take a knee in the castle, inform Mara and Callista."

"Of course, your grace," Drogan said, but his mouth was twitching and he thankfully changed the subject by informing Callum, "There's an urgent call from Duke Ryon."

Callum nodded, curled a hand around her neck, and brought her close for a kiss on the top of her head before he started to the door.

"Sonia needs coffee. Can you show her to the kitchens so Mara can get her some? Have Mara bring her to me in my study when she's done."

He didn't wait for a reply as he disappeared out the door.

Drogan came forward and held his crooked arm out, inviting, "Let's get you some coffee."

She took in a breath, let it out, and slid her arm through his.

He escorted her out the door as she announced, "So far, I'm not good at being queen."

"Oh, I don't know," he replied and she looked up at him to see he was grinning. "His grace seemed very pleased this morning with the reports we heard that, during the battles, you'd taken our women into your home, kept them company, and tried to keep their spirits up even as your own mate was fighting."

Sonia told herself that the warm feeling that bloomed in her belly was not the feeling of pride at his words (when it was).

"Okay then, I think it's all the royal stuff I'm not good at. The rules and the protocol," she went on.

"Don't worry. I'll get Mara to explain it to you. She'd love that," Drogan told her.

If Maraleena was the talker she seemed at their first meeting then Sonia was pretty certain she'd love it too, so would Sonia.

"That's a great idea." She smiled up at Drogan.

They'd gone down two flights of stairs and were in a hallway when Drogan stopped her and stated, "You should know, Cal doesn't like all that official stuff either. I only call him 'your grace' in company. I've been in his service and the service of his father for so long I never bow anything but my head to him and neither does Mara or Callista."

She stared up at him in astonishment, not believing a word he said, and also shocked because he, too, looked old enough to be Callum's brother, *not* to have served his *father*.

"But he was just so...so...*annoyed* in there," she protested.

"You're his mate and my queen. It's my duty to kneel before you, and I'm sorry, Sonia, I know it's different amongst your kind, but it's *Cal's* right to tell me that I don't have to do so."

Now how had she forgotten *that*?

"Of course," she murmured.

"You'll learn in time," he said kindly, patting her hand, and then went on to say mysteriously, "Or he will." When her brows shot up, he chuckled and finished, "Let's get you coffee."

He took her to the friendly warm (both in looks and in temperature) kitchens (three rooms!) where she met Callista, who was less chatty, not as tall, but definitely as friendly as Maraleena. Drogan left after depositing her with the women. They gave her a tour of the kitchens, Sonia had a cup of coffee, and then all too soon Maraleena led her back to Callum.

His study was also a beautiful room with inviting furniture but included a big heavily carved desk with two huge chairs facing it. There wasn't a circular fireplace in the middle but a cavernous one behind his chair at the desk in front of which stood a tall, intricately wrought iron grate.

Callum was seated in that chair. He was on the phone, but the minute she walked into the room, his eyes came to her and his arm went out to the side.

He wanted her in his lap.

She had to admit she'd been getting used to the lap business and in the end, liking it.

She didn't like it anymore.

"See you later," Maraleena whispered and then walked out, leaving Sonia alone with her mate.

With nothing for it, she approached him and sat silently in his lap as he talked on the phone, obviously to Ryon. She knew this because he kept saying "Ry," not because she was a sleuth that deciphered it from clues in his side of the conversation.

When he finally rang off, she instantly wished his attention was on the phone again for it came directly to her.

Both of his arms wrapped around her and he pulled her closer to him.

"Have you been taking your injections twice a day?" he asked, surprising her with his subject.

"Yes, Regan told me you told her that Dr. Mortenson said I should."

"Did you take them only when she was there?"

She nodded and tried not to clench her teeth at his domineering.

Seriously, he acted like she'd never taken an injection before he stormed into her life.

"Have you taken one today?" he queried.

Her body jerked and she stared at him.

"No, I didn't think. My clock is off. I don't even know if it's due," she told him stupidly, for it had to be due. It had been hours since the last one.

"We'll go up and do it in a minute," he stated, luckily without anger, then went on to ask, "Did Dr. Mortenson get the test results back?"

She shook her head. "Not that I know of. He didn't call. It can take a while sometimes."

Callum looked away and muttered, "I'll call him."

Sonia took in a deep breath and then opened her mouth to speak.

He turned back to her and again beat her to it.

"Don't do that again, Sonia."

She snapped her mouth shut.

Then, even though she knew to what he was referring, she asked sharply, "What?"

"It was explained to you that my people defer to *me* when we're together. They will defer to you when you aren't with me, but I give the commands when we're together," he told her patiently. "You don't need to keep silent anywhere but during official business, but you don't make a command like you did today with Drogan when I'm at your side."

Sonia forgot the subject *she* wanted to talk about and decided his subject was an *excellent* one to be on.

"And I explained to you that I thought that was medieval."

A muscle jerked in his jaw, indicating, perhaps, he was no longer patient when he replied, "Yes, you did. And I believe I told you at that time that it was the way of my people."

She straightened in his lap. "Yes, and *I* believe that it was also once the way of *my* people to treat diseases by using leeches, but they found another way that works a *whole lot better* so now they're doing *that*."

The gold started to penetrate the blue in his eyes when he stated in a low vibrating tone, "Baby doll, a warning, you want rough play, for once, I have the time to give it to you."

She'd learned what *that* meant and there was not going to be any of *that*.

"I don't want rough play. I don't want *any* play," she announced and the gold shot forth, obliterating the blue as his hand trailed up her spine.

"Now, that sounded like a challenge."

Oh no! Now what had she done?

She had to think fast.

She managed it just as his fingers slid in her hair and put pressure there to bring her mouth to his. "It wasn't a challenge, Callum," she whispered. "Last night was…" She fought for a word and found it. "*Vigorous.*" His tawny eyes instantly lit with humor upon hearing her word (and they also lit with something else entirely) and he grinned before she finished, "I ache a little bit."

At once, the humor swept from his features. His hand in her hair kept putting on the pressure but only to tuck her forehead into his neck.

"Poor baby," he murmured. "Jetlagged and misused by her king." His hand slid to her neck and started massaging and she told herself it didn't feel good (when it did). "I'm sorry, honey," he went on softly. "After a battle, one like that…" She tensed at his words and he sighed. "Being away from you was not good."

She wished she could believe him.

She really, *really* did.

He bent his neck to kiss her forehead and then said, "We'll give you your medicine, I'll show you your new home, and then I want you to take it easy for the rest of the day. Yes?"

Again she wondered if it was a genuine question or a rhetorical one.

She learned it was rhetorical for he lifted her off his lap and took her to their bedroom. He located her medication and gave her the injection and she found, as much as she hated to admit it, that she'd missed emerging from the burn in the strong safety of his arms.

He spent some time showing her her new home and it was obvious as he did it, in the pride that was evident in his words and his features, that he loved this castle. Then again, there was a lot to love, not only in how it looked and how much there was of it, but how it *felt*.

They went to the library where he ordered her to find a book, which she did, then he took her back to his study.

He deposited her on the big fluffy couch which was under a diamond-paned window, just as the snow started to fall outside.

He threw a warm woolen throw over her body and tucked it tight around her hips and legs and arranged a pillow behind her head. After he settled her, he picked up the phone and ordered Maraleena to bring them lunch.

He went to his desk and made calls, went through mail, and eventually started writing notes. She set her book aside and stared out at the snow wondering how she managed to find herself trapped in a fairytale castle with a fairytale king when all of it was real but none of it was true (except, of course, the castle).

Callum ate lunch at his desk.

Sonia defied his unspoken command to clean her plate and picked at her food because she was nowhere near finished processing her enormous breakfast.

Callum didn't have the chance to confront her for she curled up on the fluffy couch under her woolen throw with her hands under her cheek and fell asleep.

So she was asleep and missed it when her king glanced her way and his face grew soft.

And she missed it when he walked to her on the couch and sat in the crook of her lap.

And she missed it when he slid her hair off her neck but tucked the throw tight around her shoulder so she wouldn't get a chill.

And she missed his soft kiss at her temple before he dropped his forehead there.

And she missed him whispering in her ear in a voice threaded with an emotion that even Sonia couldn't have misunderstood, "Fuck, baby doll, I missed you so fucking much."

CHAPTER SIXTEEN

EXPOSED

Sonia sat on the sofa in Callum's study, stared out the window at the gray sky, the landscape covered in white snow, and tried to find at least a shred of courage to say what she had to say to Callum.

She'd been with Callum at the castle for three days.

Three days!

Had she told him she did not want to be his mate but was willing to be his queen as she vowed to herself she would?

No.

Had she stopped him from making love to her as she vowed to herself she would?

No.

Had she become enchanted by his castle, the people in it, the village at the base of the rise and the people in that?

Yes!

After her first quiet day of Callum-ordered rest, she woke up in his bed, in his arms, the urge nearly upon her because his hands were roaming and his lips were trailing across her shoulder.

"Callum—"

His mouth went to her ear and his arm wrapped tight around her, pulling her into his big warm body.

"Morning, baby doll."

Good goodness.

If her world was real, she would *live* for the morning when he said those words to her in his deep rumbling voice.

"Morning," she replied, trying to blot the thought from her mind.

"How are you feeling this morning?"

As her body betrayed her and snuggled closer to him, her mind latched on a way out of her first thing in the morning predicament.

"Still a little bit achy," she told him (and it wasn't a *total* lie).

"Poor baby," he whispered in her ear, and even though he sounded vaguely arrogant, she couldn't stop the tremble his being close and whispering in her ear caused. "I'll get Mara to draw you a hot bath." He bent and kissed her neck. "Have a lie in, little one."

Then he was gone, out of bed, into the shower, out of the shower, into his clothes, and with a final trip to the bed to lean down and kiss her temple, he was out of the room.

Well, she'd dodged *that* bullet and she was pretty proud of herself because the whole time he was in the shower she kept thinking of his tall, muscled, naked body with water sliding down it and she'd had the nearly overwhelming impulse to join him there.

She lay in bed practicing her words for when she would confront him.

However, she lay in bed too long for a knock came at the door.

She pulled in breath.

Then she sighed.

Maraleena (she'd learned the woman's scent).

She called a good morning, Maraleena stuck her head around the door, and smiled huge. "Hi there, Queen Sonia, you sleep okay?"

Then she was bustling in, pulling back the curtains, fussing with the throws on the couch before she headed toward the bathroom while Sonia replied, "Yes, Maraleena, I slept great."

And she had.

She'd slept like a baby in Callum's strong arms in his big bed with his heavy warm hides covering them.

"Cal says I should draw you a hot bath and Drogan says I can call him Cal in front of you," she called half this statement from the bathroom before Sonia heard the taps turn on.

"Well, Queen Sonia says you can call her Sonia," Sonia called back, throwing the covers off, her legs over the side of the bed, and finished, "Or you can call me Sonny, that's what all my friends call me."

Maraleena appeared in the doorway to the bathroom but stopped and stood still, her eyes fastened on Sonia.

"I've known you a day," Maraleena breathed, and taking one look at her shocked expression, Sonia decided she must have done something wrong.

Again.

She started walking swiftly toward Maraleena at the same time she started talking fast, "I'm sorry. I did the wrong thing again. If you have to call me Queen Sonia then do it. That's okay. I'll get used to it."

She stopped in front of Maraleena who stared down at her a moment.

Then she burst out laughing and snatched Sonia in her arms, giving her a strong hug, before, just as abruptly, she let her go.

"I just can't believe how nice you are!" she declared, walking briskly to the bed. "I was on the phone *all night* telling everyone our new queen is teeny and pretty and *nice*. And that she and our king were all sweet and cute together." Maraleena started to make the bed as Sonia tried to decide how she felt about Maraleena gossiping about her.

Since what Maraleena said wasn't bad and clearly Maraleena had double (or triple) the words any normal female had to use daily or she'd explode, she decided she didn't mind.

"If it was me, I'd probably be all queen of the castle," she went on, pulling the sheets to. She threw a smile Sonia's way. "Though I'm glad you're not."

Sonia smiled back at her and replied, "I'm glad you're glad."

She shooed Sonia into the bathroom with her hand. "Shoo. Get. Cal says you've got some aches to work out of your muscles." Her grin turned naughty. "I remember *that*. After my claiming..." She giggled. "Oo, I was aching for *weeks*. Drogan was insatiable. And rough! It was brilliant! And, I might add, two times last night, it still *is*! It's a wonder I can even *walk* today!"

Sonia stared at her, wishing she had the wherewithal not to gape in horrified astonishment.

But she did *not*.

Maraleena caught her look, her smile died, and she straightened.

"What?" she asked.

Sonia's body jerked out of its shocked stupor and she slid her hands along her belly, crossing her arms at the black fabric of her nightgown there.

"Nothing, I'm just...humans don't..." she stammered but stopped when Maraleena suddenly slapped herself on the forehead with the palm of her hand.

"Stupid!" she cried. "I forgot. You're human." She threw her arm out to Sonia. "You said Cal hadn't had a chance to explain things and Drogan told me you wanted me to teach you about protocol and such. I'm an idiot."

"You aren't an idiot, Maraleena," Sonia said softly, walked to her new friend, and asked, "I met a lady, one of yours, and she was kind of blunt too. Do all your people talk about...um, sex like that?"

Maraleena's grin came back full force. "Uh. *Yeah*." Her eyes gleamed, she leaned forward and whispered, "*Definitely*." Then she went back to making the bed. "I've never spent a lot of time with humans but I know you don't." She finished on a mumbled, "Weird, that."

Sonia smiled at the thought that someone would think the human's way was weird.

Then again, to her people, it obviously was.

"Anyway," Maraleena went on. "You have your bath. Cal says you should dress warm. I'll bring up breakfast in a bit."

"Can I have breakfast in the kitchen with you and Callista?" Sonia asked and Maraleena burst out laughing.

Through her laughter she said, "Sonny! You're *queen*! You can do anything you want!"

Sonia really wished that was true.

Alas, it was *not*.

She took a nice, long, hot bath in the big circular tub fragranced with bath salts Callum had given her for Christmas. She put on light makeup and blow dried her hair, absently acclimatizing herself to where to locate all of her things in her new surroundings as she did so.

But when she went to the wardrobe to decide on her outfit for the day she saw, with all her bags unpacked and all of her things put away, Regan had not packed a stitch of *Sonia's* clothes.

She'd only packed the clothes *Callum* bought her.

Sonia searched through hangers, piles of sweaters, and drawers for something from home, something that was *hers*.

Nothing.

That was likely an order of King Callum too!

Fuming, Sonia "dressed warm," as Callum commanded her to do, in a pair of cords so dark brown they were nearly black. To this she added a wide dark brown belt, low-heeled boots over thick socks, and a bright-salmon boat-necked sweater. The sweater was not one of Sonia's colors, but in the shop Regan had told her it was *simply her* and she *had* to buy it, so Sonia did.

She grabbed a long, thin, but woolly, hot-pink-colored knit scarf with fluffy dangling strands at the ends, wrapped it round and round her neck, and let it hang down her front, and then she stormed to the kitchen.

It was hard to keep fuming with Callista and Maraleena both so unceasingly cheerful and both so excited to share with Sonia the ways of their people.

And over a breakfast of porridge sweetened with what Callista called "golden syrup" (and it was delicious *and* it wasn't huge and artery clogging), Sonia learned a lot.

For instance, she learned that when a man claimed his mate, he and his mate would hole up for weeks (even months) after the claiming, not to be seen or heard from until they emerged for the Mating Ceremony.

And she learned that once they emerged, they told everyone about everything as in *everything* about their claiming, down to the most intimate detail. Indeed, they'd do this often over the years trying to best each other's claiming stories. And it wasn't just the males who did it for both Maraleena *and* Callista shared theirs, in shocking detail (Sonia demurred, using being human as her excuse, which luckily worked).

And she learned that the Mating Ceremony and ritual was like the humans' wedding reception except they didn't have any wedding dresses, tuxedos, champagne toasts, posed pictures, or pre-arranged dancing. They went straight to what sounded like drunken debauchery with a big buffet of food that, as Callista assured her on a wink, "In the old days, dear, we don't do that anymore," led to the male actually *mating* with the female in front of *everyone*.

Now, apparently (and fortunately), at the end, the couple just stood (or swayed, depending how drunk they were) in front of everyone and restated the words, male: "Are you mine?" female: "Yes." Then they went home with everyone shouting advice and encouragement and had sex again.

That was it!

"It's a shame those rebel rascals had to spoil things for you and Cal. Ruined your whole claiming with their antics," Callista muttered irately then added as an afterthought, "Oh, and the fact that he's king."

"What does that mean?" Sonia asked as she poured more coffee into all three of their mugs.

Callista gazed closely at Sonia, giving Sonia the (correct) impression that she hadn't quite decided about her yet, and replied, "Just that he's like his father. Mac never rested on his laurels and Cal certainly doesn't. Everyone knows no one could seize his rule. He's the mightiest warrior in the kingdom. But there's a great deal more to it and he takes it all seriously."

"Like what?" Sonia asked, curious in spite of herself.

"Like a great deal, too much for now," Callista answered but she did it on a genuine smile. "Now, dear, you need to get to your king."

Sonia stifled her sigh, dashed milk (not skim, but also not full fat, thank God) into her coffee and started to head to Callum's study but stopped when Maraleena called out to her.

Sonia watched as Maraleena pulled down another sweep-lined earth-brown mug with turquoise interior and poured in coffee and milk.

She handed it to Sonia who took it in her free hand.

"For Cal," she muttered and grinned. "He'll like that you're looking after him even though you chose for us to do the, um...bulk of it."

Sonia nodded and smiled her gratitude to Maraleena but on the way to his study she had a mind to throw his coffee mug out the window. She liked the mug too much, so she didn't.

He was sitting behind his big desk when she appeared in the door and his handsome dark head came up instantly.

Somehow from yesterday to today his desk had become covered in strewn and stacked papers and files, mounds of post, and an open laptop.

She gazed at the mess on his desk and couldn't stop herself from asking in all jest, "Are you planning another war?"

He burst out laughing and her body jerked then stilled at the rich sound.

She'd made him grin. She'd made him smile. She'd made him chuckle. She'd heard him laugh, even at her. But she'd never *purposefully* made him laugh and doing it made her feel like she'd planted her flag at the top of world's most treacherous mountain.

"No," he replied after he got control of his humor. "This is what it normally looks like."

"You need an assistant," she informed him, walking forward trying to get control of herself and sound curt, and not doing a very good job of it (because she wasn't a curt-sounding person).

"I have four: Ryon, Calder, Caleb and Drogan. None of them are good with paperwork," Callum told her on a grin.

Sonia figured that was the truth. None of those men seemed the paperwork kind.

She stopped on the opposite side of the desk and reached over it, trying to find a safe place to lay his mug. She scooted some papers aside to expose the blotter and put the mug down because he hardly could have a system going that she would mess up in that clutter.

"You brought me coffee," he stated and his voice was soft and warm.

She looked at him not wanting him to get any ideas. "Maraleena thought you might like a cup."

"I do," he replied. "Would you like to know what I'd like more?"

No, she wouldn't.

"Callum—" she began but he interrupted her.

"What I'd like is to know why you're standing over there?"

She straightened her shoulders, deciding the time had finally come, and declared, "Because we need to talk."

"You can talk in my lap."

"I'd rather talk from over here."

His voice was firm but still soft and warm when he ordered, "Sonia, come here."

That voice did weird things to her system. Weird things such as setting the urge upon her. Weird things such as making her want to sit in his lap and put her mouth on him. Anywhere. *Everywhere.*

Yes, just his *voice.*

She fought the urge back.

"No, Callum, I—" She stopped speaking because he stood up.

Then she stared at him as he rounded his desk.

She began retreating too late.

He grabbed one of her wrists, pulled the coffee cup out of her other hand, set it on some papers on his desk, and as she tried to twist her wrist free, he yanked her to him. Then she was in his arms. He walked back around the desk and sat down with her in his lap. He calmly leaned forward, nabbed her cup, and handed it to her then nabbed his.

Finally, his attention came to her and he invited, "Now, baby doll, what's on your mind?"

Nothing.

Nothing was on her mind except for the fact that she was again in his lap where she'd told him she didn't want to be.

"Sonia?"

She blinked at him, wanting to cry and scream at the same time (not to mention scratch his eyes out).

He waited.

She didn't speak. There were too many words to say and she couldn't put even two of them together.

"I see this is one of those times," he muttered mysteriously, not sounding irritated or angry about whatever one of those times was, but amused. "All right, little one, this is what we're going to do today," he told her softly. "We're going to go upstairs, I'm going to give you your injection, then we're going to go into town."

She wasn't keeping up. Her mind was churning but her body was registering the fact that she liked the safe comfort of him so close.

"To town?" she asked.

"To town," he answered. "Then we're going to come home and you're going to take it easy the rest of the day," he finished. "Agreed?"

He took a sip of his coffee, which would have given her time to agree or, say, perchance, disagree. But before she could speak, he slid her carefully off his lap, grabbed her hand, and led her out of the room and up the winding staircase.

As he did, he spoke. "I talked with Dr. Mortenson while you were napping yesterday and he said your blood tests all came back normal. He's still concerned. He says there's a specialist consultant in Aberdeen he wants you to see. I made an appointment this morning for Friday."

Sonia's mind cleared at this astonishing news and she asked, "There's a specialist in Scotland?"

"According to Dr. Mortenson there is."

"I didn't know there was such a thing," she told him.

"Well there is, baby doll. And you're lucky he's a short flight away," Callum replied, led her into the bathroom, gave her the injection, held her until the burning fire died away, and held her long after.

"Callum," she whispered when he didn't seem to want to let her go, her hands gliding along his forearms which were crossed at her belly.

In these moments, now twice a day, she could believe in him, really *believe*.

His head came up and his now tawny eyes caught hers in the mirror.

"I hope to fuck this new doctor knows another way."

His voice was rough with frustration and she could almost believe that too.

Lost in the moment, she promised, "You'll get used to it."

His laugh was as harsh as his voice before he said, "I don't think that's going to happen, baby doll."

Then he zipped her pants, buckled her belt, and took her to town.

"Town" was not a town.

It was an enchanting village. The cottages and buildings were all made of the same warm golden-red-brown as Callum's castle. There was only one cobbled street, which was lined with shops on both sides, and on small alleyways that led off the street and up the rise behind the village there were picturesque cottages and houses.

The melted snow had given the cobbled streets a glistening shine and the sidewalks were all brushed clear of snow.

Regardless of the gray day that threatened more snow, the village seemed vibrant and fascinating.

There was a bakery with jam donuts, cookies, and pastries displayed in its window, a peek inside showing different loaves of bread and rolls on wire racks behind a heated counter filled with warm savories. There was a fruit and vegetable shop with brightly-colored produce in bushels in suspended baskets outside. There was a florist with vivid blooms in steel buckets out front. There was a butcher, a drug store, a shop that looked like it sold nothing but fishing gear. Another store that looked like it sold nothing but yarn. A women's clothing store with a window that displayed more active outdoorsy gear (but the bags and sweaters looked *lush*). A gift shop, which, when Sonia stole a glance inside while they strolled past, looked like it was filled with fun bits and bobs, none of which you needed, but all of which you could convince yourself you did. And there was a café that was heaving with people eating or ordering teas and cakes.

And, lastly, even though it was a small village, it had no fewer than five pubs. Five!

Sonia would have liked the opportunity to peruse, but this opportunity didn't present itself.

Mainly because the other thing about the village was that it was busy with loads of people shopping or chatting on the sidewalks.

And all of them were Callum's people, with clear eyes, long bodies, dark hair, and beautiful faces.

And all of them, when they saw Sonia and Callum, looked surprised then delighted then they'd smile and start to drop to their knee.

And to all of them, Callum would say something like, "Keep your feet, Merriden, your queen doesn't stand on ceremony." Or, "Stand, Rhiannon, Queen Sonia isn't big on formalities."

Then they'd bow their head, grin a friendly grin at Sonia, and chat with Sonia and Callum before letting them get on their way.

There were four things that surprised Sonia about this.

The first was that Callum knew all their names. Every last one.

The second was that he apparently wasn't big on formalities either. She knew this because he chatted amiably with the villagers, his arm around Sonia's shoulders, as if they were normal people, not a king and his new queen.

The third was that everyone was so welcoming, open, full of life and smiles, and quick to laugh.

The last was that Callum acted to save her the discomfort of people bowing to her in the streets. People she had to live with and she wanted them to like her, not bow to her. She didn't want to think that was a kindness he'd shown to her, having learned she didn't like it the day before and thus stopping it from happening again. But she couldn't help but think that it was.

They slowly made their way down one side of the street, stopping and chatting along the way as everyone else gazed at them frankly and speculatively. Then they slowly made their way down the other side of the street doing the same.

At the end of their journey, Callum led them into a pub called The Claw. It, too, had diamond-paned windows, but the glass was multi-colored in ambers, reds, and greens and it had a furry paw with sharp claws painted on its suspended shingle.

The inside was inviting and warm after the cold of outside. There was a circular fireplace in the middle with a brass hood over it and a fire lit within. There were brass taps at the gleaming bar and a variety of cushioned seating. And there was another clawed paw etched in the mirror behind the bar.

Callum guided her directly to the bar, and when they stopped, he asked her, "Do you like cider?"

She gazed up at him, and figuring he wanted to warm her up with hot apple cider, though she would prefer hot cocoa but would request herbal tea, she asked, "Apple cider?"

He smiled and answered, "In a way, though not the way you're used to." Then he proclaimed, "You'll try a cider."

He turned to the bartender (who was named Ralph, by the way) and ordered their drinks and also two fish pies, though he didn't ask Sonia if she wanted fish pie, or anything to eat for that matter. He handed her a half pint glass of something cold and golden, told Ralph to, "Put it on Canis's account," and led them to a comfortable curved couch by the fire.

He shrugged off the brown leather jacket she'd given him for Christmas. But he kept on the brown, burgundy, and navy striped scarf wrapped around his throat over his thick, navy wool, cable-knit sweater (both of which Sonia had given him too). Sonia took his lead and divested herself of her own dusky-blue woolen pea coat. Then Callum sat them close together.

Sonia tasted a sip of her cider and found it was brilliant, cool but refreshing.

She didn't want to (she told herself) but she couldn't help it. She liked the village. She liked the villagers. She liked being outside in the snowy cold. And she liked the cider.

"This is brilliant," she told him as his arm slid around her and pulled her close.

"I'm glad you like it, honey."

"I like the village too," she added.

He made no response, just smiled down at her.

She didn't want to (she told herself) but she couldn't help it. She was just too curious to stop it.

"Have you lived here your whole life?"

He pulled her an inch closer and lifted his leg to rest the sole of his boot against the edge of the fireplace.

"A good part of it, yes. We spent some time in France, with my mother's people. During a time of peace, when my father didn't need me close, I lived in Canada for a while. And my father appointed me liaison to the British government for a brief period and I lived in London then."

Well, that explained his accent.

"But you like it here?" she queried.

"I like it here."

"The best?" she went on, Callum laughed and his hand gave her waist a squeeze.

"The best. Though I found it difficult leaving the Canadian Rockies. I'd been happy there," he informed her.

This knowledge settled somewhere in Sonia (and, if she was honest, it was in the region of her heart) for she'd always been happiest in the American Rockies. And, she hated to admit it, but she really liked it right there.

Belatedly, she decided to find a different, less personal subject. One that couldn't give Callum an opening through that guard around her heart.

Therefore, she inquired, "Liaison to the British government?"

He nodded and took a sip of his beer. "All governments know of our people."

She looked to the fire, sipped at her cider, and murmured, "I'm surprised about that."

His hand gave her waist another squeeze and he asked, "Why?"

She looked back at him and replied, "Because you're so secret. I had no clue."

"No one has a clue," he responded. "Unless we want them to." His face got closer and his voice got lower when he finished, "Like you."

She pressed her lips together in an effort not to respond to how much she liked his face that close and his voice that low and looked again at the fire.

His big body relaxed further into hers. "Our people intermingle with your people all the time."

"Do a lot of your people have human mates?" she queried.

"It's rare," he answered. "But it happens."

Sonia looked about the pub and saw all eyes on them and all the eyes were clear and light. All the heads were dark. And all the bodies were big and long.

She turned back to Callum and whispered, "This whole village is your people."

He looked down at her and smiled. "You noticed that?"

She nodded.

He pulled her even closer. "This is one of the reasons we need a liaison to the British government and why we have liaisons to every government. There are small countries like this around the world."

"Countries?"

"Yes, little one," he replied. "Villages, towns, even some small cities. This is our land, our country, the village and miles of wood that surround it. It isn't owned by the British government. It's owned and ruled by us. Didn't you wonder why you didn't go through Customs and Immigration when we arrived?"

She hadn't thought of it, her mind was on other things.

"No," she told him. "I'd never flown in a private jet before. I didn't think about it."

"Well," he said, "that's why. Not because you arrived in a private jet, but because we landed on an airstrip, a private airstrip, *our* private airstrip that no one uses. The roads leading to this village are not on any map. Essentially, to your people, this place doesn't exist."

Sonia didn't respond, she just stared at him.

Callum continued, "That doesn't mean that humans don't find their way here on occasion and they aren't welcome when they do. They just wouldn't be able to find their way back unless they had excellent memories and little fear of very bad roads." He gave her a quick grin before he took a sip of his beer and then went on, "There are those of us who prefer living amongst their own, being who we are and how we are and not having to keep anything secret. There are those who find their calling in the human world and their profession takes them there. There are those who just like living in the human world, amongst more people, having more opportunities. There are others who move back and forth, depending on their mood. And there are others who live here but also like to spend time in the human world." Then he finished, "Ryon's like that."

"What are you like?" she asked quietly, more curious than was prudent as to his answer.

"I like being with my people and I rarely stray into the human world," he answered honestly.

"Don't you like humans?" she blurted on a whisper before she could stop the words and then wished she could kick herself because she didn't care (though, she did).

"I do," he grinned again, his voice went soft, his eyes grew warm and his face got closer. "One in particular."

She pulled in breath and reminded herself that he could be like this, sweet and tender one minute and the next...

Well, the next he would *not*.

"So why don't you spend time with humans?" she pushed.

He sighed and pulled away, saying, "I just don't understand them."

Her eyes grew wide. "What's not to understand?"

He gazed at her a second before he threw back his head and roared with laughter.

"What's funny?" she demanded when his laughter calmed.

"You, baby doll," he was still chuckling when he responded. "How much of my culture makes sense to you?"

She had to admit, he had a point.

She didn't inform him of that fact. She looked to the fire and sipped her cider, which caused him to chuckle.

"I'll make you a deal," he said on another squeeze of her waist, capturing her attention.

She looked at him again and raised her eyebrows.

"I'll help you understand my people and you help me understand yours."

Before she could answer, she heard a noise outside. A noise that sounded like someone carrying bags slipped and fell to the sidewalk giving a startled cry of pain. She automatically tensed at the noise, as if she was going to rush outside to help, her eyes flashing to the door.

Then she realized it was a noise that Callum wouldn't hear and she couldn't help because she wasn't supposed to hear it either.

As she had many times in her life, Sonia forced herself to relax and took another sip of her drink.

"Sonia," he called and she hesitantly turned to look at him.

"Yes?" she answered, trying to look innocent and thinking maybe she failed for he was studying her closely.

He opened his mouth to speak but Ralph was there with two big plates on top of which sat smaller, oblong dishes of browned, fluffy mash potato-topped fish pies that were so hot they were steaming and looked delicious.

"Two fish pies, your grace?" Ralph asked.

Callum didn't look happy to be disturbed but he nodded, moved them to a table, and they ate their pies (filled with salmon, cream, carrots, herbs, onions, and cheese, they were to-die-for and likely a million calories each).

Their conversation died because Callum seemed deep in thought and Sonia didn't have anything to say.

After that, he took her back to the castle.

But not before taking her to the bakery and buying her a huge Viennese cookie, half of it dipped in a thick layer of chocolate. This he ordered her to eat in the Rover, and when she refused, he pulled the car to the side of the road, turned to her, and raised his brows ominously.

She ate the cookie and she hated herself for being so weak.

She hated him more.

But the cookie, she had to admit, was delicious.

Callum made Sonia take it easy the rest of the afternoon but he made her do it while lounging on the couch in his study while he sat at the desk and worked. Clicking through his laptop or talking on the phone, but mostly he seemed to spend his time writing notes in longhand.

They ate dinner, he took her to their room for her injection and after they lay on the couch in the room he called "the lounge." It was a couch *upholstered* in hides (and she told herself it wasn't soft and snugly, but it was). He threw a woolen rug over them (making them snugly too) and they watched *Cool Hand Luke*, which, according to Callum, was Calder's favorite movie, a fact Sonia didn't find surprising.

The phone rang (or, dozens of them rang all through the house) as they were winding their way upstairs to bed. Sonia was also winding herself up trying to figure out how she was going to stop him from making love to her, or more precisely, herself from wanting him to.

"You go on up, baby doll, I'll be there in a second," he murmured distractedly and peeled off into a room.

She was asleep by the time he joined her in bed.

And the urge was over her by the time he woke her with a hand between her legs and fingers rolling her nipple.

There was no chance to fight it, she was too far gone.

She arched her back and pressed her hips into his hand.

"You're still tender, honey, I'll—" he started but she rolled to him, dislodging his hands, and kissed him.

Then she did other things to him with her mouth.

Then he did things to her.

Finally he took her, not hard and rough, but slow and sweet, and she didn't cry to her wolf when she climaxed. She whispered it in his ear on a contented sigh.

In the end, she fell asleep in his arms.

She woke up in them too, just as far gone as the night before, but Callum wasn't in the mood to be slow and sweet. He was in a different mood. And, with the urge over her, Sonia liked his mood.

She liked it so much she begged for it.

After, she lay on her belly, her eyes closed, her mind trying to regulate her breathing.

She felt him lying beside her, her head was turned away from him but she knew he was up on an elbow and his fingers were trailing lightly along the naked skin of her back. His hand finally glided down over her bottom and he reached low as it slid down the back her thigh and he gently cocked her leg.

Then, just as he had done after her claiming, he coated her thighs with their combined wetness.

She felt his chest at her back and his fingers digging in her hip when he growled in her ear, "That's the most beautiful thing in the world."

Sonia didn't respond verbally but she shivered deliciously because, somewhere deep down, even though she told herself she didn't, she agreed.

His fingers gave her hip another, far gentler, squeeze.

"Dress warm before coming to me," he ordered before exiting the bed, throwing the hides over her, and walking to the bathroom.

Before he left the room, he tucked her stuffed wolf in her arms and kissed her temple.

Sonia stared at the pillows, clutching her wolf, and told herself not to cry.

She also told herself, that day, she was going to find a way to end this.

Before Maraleena could arrive, she threw back the hides, went to the bathroom, and took a shower.

However, Sonia didn't find a way to end it.

Instead, she had breakfast with Maraleena and Callista in the kitchen again and they spent that time teaching her queenly etiquette and protocol and doing it hilariously. Callista acted out the silent part of the queen while Maraleena acted out the domineering part of the king and all three of them giggled until their sides hurt.

When she arrived at the door to Callum's study, he was already striding across the room. Sonia barely got her mouth open before he took her up the stairs for her injection and then he said they were off to explore the wood.

Before she could say another word, they were off to explore the wood.

That was the worst because it was the best.

Tramping through the snow and the trees, the brisk air in her lungs, the cold on her face, the warmth in her active muscles, she could smell the wildlife, hear it and sense it all around her.

And she loved it.

It reminded her of being out with her father all those times when she was a child. She hadn't done it since he'd died and she forgot just how much she loved it.

No, how much it felt right, like she was where she belonged, like she'd come home.

And being there with the sweet tender Callum. Feeling that with him, while Callum held her hand as they trudged through snow. Stopping her every once in a while to place his hand under her jaw, tilt her head to his, and brush his lips to hers (and sometimes it was far more than a brush). Coming to a rise which exposed a new vista and both of them halting, standing close, and just experiencing the view. With all that, she allowed herself to pretend. Just that once, she allowed herself to be where she always loved to be with the man she wanted for so long to be hers.

So, when they returned, without demur, she ate lunch seated in his lap, and after lunch, she made out with him in his desk chair that was turned to face the roaring fire. She didn't make a peep when he picked her up, walked her to the couch, and set her down.

Arranging the woolly throw over her, he murmured in a tone filled with regret, "I've work to do, little one." He framed her face with his hands and touched his mouth to hers. "We'll finish in a bit." Shafts of tawny sliced through the blue of his eyes before he whispered, "There're a few things I want you to do to me in that chair."

Sonia felt the throb pulse between her legs and she also heard the soft moan that caught in her throat.

The gold took over the blue when he growled with approval, "In heat."

Then he kissed her, harder, longer, and wetter before he let her go and went back to his desk.

Once Sonia emerged from her pretend world of enchanted castles and fairytale kings you met in your dreams, she realized that she'd been in Scotland for three days.

She didn't intend to go to Scotland at all but she'd been there three days, met people she liked, and fell in love with the village and the woods.

She didn't intend to have sex with Callum again but they'd had sex six times, not passable sex, not good sex, but (as usual) *fantastic* sex.

But she *did* intend to get a few things straight, which was the only thing she *didn't* do.

And she had to find the courage to do it, and soon. Or she was going to be doing things to Callum in his chair, things her mind was making up on its own, things that were making that throb beat between her legs and her breasts swell. Things that, the very thought of them, when Callum wasn't even looking at her or speaking to her, were deeply affecting her.

And she was, she decided, in serious, *serious* trouble.

So deep was Sonia in her thoughts, when she heard the front door open, miles away (well, not exactly, just two floors of winding stairs and a long hall, but still), she didn't even think to stop from looking toward the door.

She thought about it when Callum said her name.

Her body tensed but she looked toward him.

He was studying her closely again, eyes narrowed, brows drawn.

His ominous look.

Finally, he asked, "Did you hear that?"

Oh good goodness.

She'd forgotten to hide her gift. Her father told her never, *never* to forget.

She tried to cover. "Hear what?"

Callum answered instantly, "Regan and Ryon arriving."

She stared at him.

She knew it was Regan and Ryon too, she could hear their voices and they were getting closer.

How did he—?

He interrupted her thoughts, "Answer me, Sonia, did you hear that?"

She didn't have time to think about *him* hearing the arrival of his family. She still had to cover.

"Ryon and Regan are here?" she asked, tossing the throw aside and standing.

"You didn't hear it?" he returned as he, too, stood and started toward her.

She considered running.

Instead, she lied, "No." Then she cocked her head and went on lying, "Oh. I hear them now."

Anyone would, they were coming up the stairs.

Callum stopped in front of her and looked down at her. "If you didn't hear them, why did you turn your head the minute the front door opened?"

"You can hear the front door open from all the way up here?" she asked immediately, shocked and extremely interested in this news at the same time still hiding her secret.

"I can," he replied tersely, stepping closer, making her tilt her head back to look at him, and feeling the heat from his body, then he finished with, "And so can you."

Her eyes flew wide, her mouth opened to deny it, and Regan came through the door.

"Cal! Sonny! It's so good to be home!" she cried, rushing in, her face wreathed with smiles.

Ryon was following her, his eyes were on both Sonia and Callum and they were wary like he felt the tense air.

Callum turned to face his mother.

"I hate that plane ride. It's so *long* and you're so *pent up*. There's nowhere to *roam*," Regan declared while placing her hand on Callum's biceps, giving his cheek a kiss, and then giving Sonia a hug.

After Regan moved away, Sonia tried to step away from her mate.

His arm slid around her shoulders.

Sonia stopped moving.

Callum tucked her into his side.

"But I'm home now!" Regan announced gleefully before turning to Sonia. "And I want to know how you're getting on, Sonny, but the very first thing I'm going to do is change my clothes and take a walk. Then I'm going to ask Drogan to light a fire in the knitting room and you're going to tell me *everything*. Oh, I do hope Callum took you to the village. They have the best bakery in the world and I'm French so that's saying something!" She grinned, looked between them, and teased, "Then, I suppose, I'll let Cal have you back for dinner."

"I'm glad you're home, Regan," Sonia smiled at her mother-in-law then turned her smile to Ryon. "And you too, Ryon. Glad to see you safe."

"It's good to *be* safe, Sonny," Ryon smiled back.

"Oh!" Regan cried suddenly. Sonia jumped and looked to see her mother-in-law was digging in her purse. "Things were...well, we didn't get much time and I was just so happy everyone was okay and then I was worried about getting Sonny ready." She pulled her wallet out of her purse and zipped it open. "So, I forgot, but..." Her arm extended toward Callum and she announced, "Here!"

The wedding band Sonia gave to Callum was gleaming between her thumb and forefinger.

Sonia stared at it and felt every muscle in her body grow so rigid, she feared if she moved she'd break into a million pieces.

She watched as, casually, Callum reached out and took the band from his mother, murmuring his thanks. And, just as casually, he reached across Sonia's rigid body and slid it on the finger that was curled around her shoulder.

They said that people had their limits, their breaking points.

That was Sonia's.

Something came over her. Something she'd never felt in her life. Something she didn't understand, for a moment.

Then she realized it was fury. It was a fury so mammoth, she could think of nothing else but it.

She looked up at Callum not noticing the air in the room had gone dense as all of its inhabitants sensed her rage.

"I need a word," she declared before yanking out of his arm and practically running to their bedroom.

In the seconds before Callum followed her in and shut the door, Sonia realized that the time had *come*.

She was going to do this.

Now.

She lifted her hand out, palm up, and demanded, "Give me my ring."

Callum was watching her carefully, arms crossed on his chest, as he asked, "Sorry?"

She wriggled her fingers. "My ring. Give it to me."

He wasn't watching her carefully anymore. He realized what she was talking about and his jaw clenched.

Then he asked, "Why?"

"It doesn't mean anything to you. And, when I bought it, I wasn't certain it meant anything to me." She watched the muscle leap warningly in his jaw at these words but she was too enraged to care. "But then it did. It meant something. And it isn't right, if it means something to the giver, for the receiver to wear it if it means nothing to them."

He was silent for a moment before he spoke.

Then he said in a tone that was as much of a threat as the muscle jerking in his jaw, "Can I ask why in *the fuck* you think it means nothing to me?"

Sonia ignored his tone too.

She dropped her hand and snapped, "It doesn't matter *how* I know, I just *know*. Now give me *my ring!*"

She watched his body grow taut before he stated, "You've got about two seconds, baby doll, to tell me what the fuck you're on about."

Something broke inside her and the pain was excruciating.

Because of that she leaned forward and hissed, "Don't call me baby doll."

And the second the words were out of her mouth, she saw it, clear as if she was an inch away.

His eyes instantly turned golden.

And he started toward her.

Sonia was alert enough to retreat.

"Two seconds are up," he growled as he stalked her.

She was still throwing caution to the wind in the frightening face of his mirrored fury. She might have been alert enough to retreat but she was definitely not going to back down.

"I didn't know your kind existed," she threw at him. "But you knew about humans. You knew what wedding rings were."

"And?" he clipped.

She stopped retreating, braced, and shouted, "So I had an excuse when I started to take off my claiming chain! I didn't know what it was!" She jabbed her finger at him as he stilled his progress and stared at her. "But *you* knew what a wedding ring was and you *took it off just the same!*"

His head jerked slightly, his face cleared of his fury, and he murmured, "Honey."

"Don't call me that either," Sonia snapped. "This charade is over. You don't like blondes? Great. Fine. Whatever. Consider your duty served, Callum. In public, if your people want me, I'll be their queen. My parents wanted that. It's my destiny. Even *I* feel it, though I don't want to. But in private, it's over. I'm done. If you aren't okay with that, that's good too. I'll just go home."

Sonia thought that was pretty good. However, when she focused on Callum and not what she was saying, she saw he was grinning.

Yes, *grinning*.

He was *such* an arrogant bastard!

Then he asked calmly, "What makes you say I don't like blondes?"

Sonia gaped at him.

Was he mad?

"That crazy woman said it before you sequestered her!" Sonia cried.

He started toward her again, not stalking in the same way, but definitely still stalking.

"Baby doll," he said with humor threading his tone, "She's crazy."

Sonia started retreating again in exactly the same way as before.

"Do you like blondes?" she queried with a bite in her tone.

"No," he replied honestly. Her shoulders hit tapestry and she was forced to halt at the same time she gasped at his effrontery before he finished, "Or, I should say, not until recently."

He got close and she tried, quickly, to move to the side to escape him. This failed.

With no effort at all, his arm shot out, hooked around her waist, and he pulled her in front of him. He took a step forward and she was back against the tapestries, pinned there by his tall frame.

Sonia decided she'd fight her way out of it. Not physically, she wasn't stupid, or at least not *that* stupid.

Verbally.

"You sequestered her," Sonia accused.

"I did," he replied, gazing down at her patiently, one arm around her, the other hand coming up to curl around her neck.

Sonia tried to yank her neck away.

This failed too.

She quit trying and went on, "That was cruel."

His eyebrows shot up. "Sequestering Mona?"

"No," she shot back. "*Everything* you did to Mona."

"Sonia, you don't know what you're talking about." She opened her mouth to speak but his hand at her neck moved to her jaw and his thumb pressed against her lips. "But if you'd calm down a second, I'll explain."

She jerked her face from his hand and then snapped, "I don't want an explanation. You're right, I don't know what sequestered means. But I know you humiliated her in front of a room full of men. Then you forced her to go somewhere she didn't want to go and she barely got a word in edgewise. There *is* no explanation for that."

Callum watched her speak with curiosity then he muttered, "Bloody hell, Ryon was right. Baby doll, have you been holding on to this for a whole fucking *month*?"

"Has it only been a month?" Sonia retorted sarcastically. "It's felt like *years*."

He studied her a moment still with that strange curiosity then he remarked musingly, "I thought this would be annoying but it isn't. You're pretty all the time, little one, but you're spectacular when you're pissed off."

Sonia growled and shoved at the massive wall of his chest.

He rocked back a few inches but recovered quickly and returned to his previous position.

"All right, Sonia, you obviously need to talk, we'll talk," he offered but it looked like he was fighting a smile. "Tell me what's on your mind. *All* of it."

She stared at him in astonishment.

He was enjoying this!

Her vision covered with a film of red.

She'd never been so incensed and she didn't care that he could snap her like a twig. She shoved him again, harder this time, but he just rocked back and then came forward yet again.

So she went back to her earlier strategy.

"I don't want to talk!" she yelled in his face, "There's nothing you can say about how you treated Mona. About me being here without you even asking me if I wanted to move, wanted to leave my business, my friends, my *home*. There's nothing you can say about coming back from...wherever, whisking me away, *just like that*, without even saying *hello*! There's nothing you can say about me not having any of *my* clothes here, about you taking over everything, every move I make, every-thing I wear, everything I *eat*. There's nothing you can say to explain all...things...*you*!"

He was still fighting a smile when he commented, "There's a lot there, baby doll."

"*Stop calling me baby doll!*" she shrieked.

She barely got out the word "doll" when he bent, put a shoulder to her belly, and hefted her up. She kicked out her legs and beat at his back with her fists, but he didn't notice or didn't care. He strode nonchalantly to the bed and tossed her on it.

Sonia instantly rolled, got up on all fours, and started crawling but his hands seized her ankles and he pulled her knees out from under her, dragging her across the bed, and rolling her to her back.

She growled and went at him.

In no time at all, he was on top of her and had her wrists pinned over her head.

"We'll play later, Sonia," he informed her, his face suddenly serious but it was studiously so, as if he was being serious for her benefit but still found the situation amusing. "Now we're going to talk."

Sonia gaped at him, mouth open and everything.

He thought she wanted to play?

He *was* mad.

"We'll start with Desdemona," he announced and she bucked under him but his hands tightened on her wrists and he gave her a warning shake before he demanded, "Pay attention."

She stilled and glared at him.

"There's a lot of history with Mona I won't get into," he started to explain.

"I gathered that," Sonia snapped acidly.

He watched her, still obviously trying to fight back his humor. "You've got nothing to be jealous of, little one."

"*I'm not jealous!*" she screeched.

He shook his head, ignored her screech, and continued, "Being sequestered is not a bad thing. Your people do it as well when someone is not right and they need help. Mona, as you could tell, is not right."

"She just has a thing for you," Sonia retorted.

"Yes, she does, but it's more than that," he returned smoothly. "She's in a far better place than she deserves to be. For what she did, or, more to the point *didn't* do, she should have been punished. Instead she's amongst people who will try to help her sort out her head."

Sonia's eyes narrowed on him and she asked scornfully, "She should have been punished just because she's got the hots for you?"

His painstakingly serious expression changed to genuinely serious.

In fact, deadly serious. So deadly, one look at it made Sonia hold her breath.

"No, Sonia," he stated slowly. "She should have been punished for what her inattention to her responsibilities caused. She should have been punished because what she *didn't* do meant hundreds of warriors died. *Hundreds* on both sides. She should have been punished because what she didn't do means I've spent the last three days writing letters to mates and mothers explaining that their lovers and sons died brave. Died honorably. Even though every word is *fucking futile* because *nothing* I say will ease their anguish."

At his words, and the depth of feeling with which he spoke them, the fight left Sonia. She felt her body relaxing under his as she felt her heart slide into her throat and tears start to prick the backs of her eyes.

He'd been writing a lot. She saw him doing it.

Callum had been handwriting letters to grieving mates and mothers.

She couldn't imagine writing hundreds of letters like that. She wouldn't know what to say. The task was so atrocious she couldn't ever imagine having the strength to bear it.

But Callum did. He did it at the same time he grinned at her or took her to the village or walked with her through the snow, never once letting on that this heavy weight was bearing on his broad shoulders.

For the first time since she met him the burden of his responsibility as king to his people struck her and it felt like she'd been seared by lightning.

It came out of her mouth before she could stop it. It came out softly, gently, even lovingly as the tears welled in her eyes and slid out the sides.

"My handsome wolf."

The instant she whispered those three words, his hands released her wrists and his forehead dropped to hers.

Freed, her arms wrapped around him tight.

He rolled to his side, taking her with him and curling his arms around her to hold her close.

She realized then she was another one of his burdens. A mate he didn't exactly want but he had all the same and it was his duty to do right by her.

And he was attempting to do his duty, not only to his people, but to her. His moments of kingliness were a part of him, ingrained. It was who he was.

The rest of it, his tenderness and humor, was him doing the best he could with a difficult situation.

Her destiny had brought her to him to be his queen, *his people's* queen, and she had a duty as well, to him, to his people. It was an awesome responsibility, but it was also an honor no one but *no one* of her kind would have.

But Sonia had been chosen and she'd been acting like a selfish idiot, thinking of her lost dream instead of doing her duty *to him.*

No man, not even someone as strong and charismatic as Callum, should face such a burden alone. It was her duty, her *destiny*, to stand by his side and provide what she could to help him see it through.

Still weeping silently, she tipped her head back to look at him.

"Callum—"

He looked down at her and started talking at the same time, "Your place is beside me, Sonia, wherever I go. I'll take you to visit your friends as often as we can but you belong at my side. After what happened with the rebellion, I needed to be home and I needed you with me."

"Callum—" she repeated.

He kept going. "You can't wear your fancy clothes and high-heeled shoes here. It's cold and it snows, *a lot*. It's my duty to take care of you and I did, by getting you what you needed to live your life at my side." Then he muttered with irritation, "Christ, you're the only woman I know who doesn't like new clothes."

She wanted to kick herself at throwing his generosity in his face, but instead attempted yet again to interject, "Callum—"

He kept right on talking just as, visibly, his irritation grew. "Your life is too short to worry about calories, fuck, it's too damned short to worry about *anything*. You have a beautiful body and it'll be even more beautiful when there's more of it. But you have to learn, little one, to *enjoy* your life and not waste it on ridiculous things like counting calories and making certain you've taken every last vitamin."

"Callum—" she tried again but he was on a roll.

"And when I arrived to collect you and didn't say hello it was because I'd been fighting for eight days straight. No food, no rest. And I'd left the front after having given an order, an order I knew was carried out in my absence, a vile order I had no choice but to give for they would *not* admit defeat."

Her body grew taut against his again because she knew he was talking about the executions and she fully realized the weight of his burden wasn't immense.

It was colossal.

She tried to break in. "Callum, please—"

She failed in her endeavor and he carried on, "This has been going on for too fucking long. My father dealt with it, his father before him, we've tried everything. I had no choice but to break them. I don't fucking like not having a choice and I don't fucking enjoy being forced into a corner that requires me to make a decision that means the end of the lives of men who are probably good men but they followed the wrong path. If I didn't break them, even more warriors would die, more letters would be written, this would never *fucking end.*"

She decided to wait it out. She'd created this, now she had to bear the consequences.

However, apparently, he was done, for he asked, "Do you understand?"

Sonia did understand.

Boy, did she understand.

She lifted her hand to the side of his face, her fingers going into his hair, but her thumb swept along his cheekbone and she replied softly, "I understand."

He studied her face and must have approved of what he saw for the intensity moved out of his, his big body relaxed into hers, and his fingers started stroking her back.

"So we're good?" he queried, his deep voice as soft as hers.

No, they weren't good.

But they were as good as they were going to get. And, as always, Sonia had to accept that.

Feeling his warm strong body against hers, gazing into his handsome face, allowing the stroking of his fingers to relax her, she thought perhaps she was wrong.

Perhaps, if she simply gave up her dream, she *could* do this, and she vowed at that moment she would.

Therefore, she nodded.

"All right, little one," he was still speaking softly but, for some reason, his arms were getting tighter, "we have one more thing to talk about."

Committed to her new vow, Sonia nodded again.

Then he stated, "You heard Regan and Ryon arrive."

Forgetting her vow completely, Sonia automatically jerked in his arms to try to get away.

Those arms tightened further.

Panicked, she stared at him and denied, "I didn't."

"You did," he returned firmly. "You heard the person fall outside yesterday as well." Her panic rising, Sonia kept pushing against his arms, but he held her fast. "You hear a lot you don't let on to hearing, you smell a lot too." At the extent of his knowledge, she started to struggle, but he didn't let her gain an inch. "You see a lot too. More than any human does."

"I don't," she lied.

"Sonia," he warned.

She shook her head.

His brows drew together and he asked in a far less soft tone, "Why are you hiding it?"

She stared at him and then something pierced her panic.

He'd heard Regan and Ryon as well and the person falling outside yesterday and he'd heard Waring arriving at the cabin weeks before. And he smelled them between her legs, just as she did. Thinking about it, she'd noticed it often in a distracted way that he could sense the same things she could.

And her attackers that night, they'd sniffed her. They could smell her and she'd forgotten or blocked it out of her mind, but she'd thought, at the time, they were just like her.

It was because they were Callum's kind.

So much was going on she never thought about it, but Callum consistently exhibited the same abilities, the same gifts of sight, hearing and smell that she did.

And he never hid it. Not once.

"You have heightened senses," she breathed in wonder.

He continued to watch her with knitted brows. "All my people do."

"They do?"

"Yes, Sonia, they do," he replied and his arms gave her a squeeze. "All my people do. What I want now is for you to admit that you do too."

She didn't know what to make of this. She'd never met anyone who had her gifts, except her father. She had always been the strange one, worried about what people would think, how they'd react if they knew.

But Callum was just like her.

She stared then she swallowed.

Then she thought about her destiny and how it brought her to this man who shared her gifts.

And she took a huge chance, hoping her father wouldn't disapprove, and quietly, she shared.

"Father told me never to tell anyone," she whispered and watched his brows unknit and lift.

"Why the fuck not?" he asked irately.

She shook her head and answered, "Humans don't have my gifts. He said I should be proud of them but I had to hide them from everyone. *Everyone*. I could never tell a living soul. And I didn't. Even Gregor and Yuri don't know."

His mouth got tight at that but he didn't speak.

"If they knew, Callum, they'd think I was a freak," she went on to explain. "They might even fear me." She pressed closer and her voice dropped back to a whisper. "They might even *harm* me. My senses are that good. They could think I was a mutant. They could want to study me."

As her lifelong, perhaps hysterical fears were verbalized, Callum gave her a shake. "Baby doll, no one is going to hurt you."

"Not *now*," she agreed. "I have you to protect me. But before, who knows?" she cried. "It's not just that, it's more," she added. Now that she'd let it go, after so, so long, she couldn't stop the information flowing. "Animals don't fear me. And I'm not just talking dogs and cats, I'm talking all animals. Birds and the wild animals Papa and I would see when we were out in the woods. And even more, I can feel eyes on me, smell people from far away, but I know if they're good or they're bad. I'd been sensing your people watching me for years and I knew I had nothing to fear. I also knew those men who attacked me that night before they came into my house. I knew them because I'd been *sensing* them for weeks."

It was Callum's turn to try to cut in. "Sonia—"

But it was Sonia's turn to be on a roll.

"And I dreamed of you. I dreamed of you for ages and you were real. I dreamed of you and I *in this room* and I didn't know you or this castle existed. No one does that! I'm a freak!"

His arms grew so tight, for a second it cut off her breath and she stopped ranting and stared at him.

"Baby doll, calm down. You aren't a freak. Me and every one of my own have the same abilities."

Her eyes grew wide at this revelation and she breathed, "Did you dream about me?"

His gaze grew soft and he rolled to his back, rolling her on top of him at the same time. Then his hand came up and his fingers tucked her hair behind her ear.

"No, unfortunately, I never dreamed of you," he whispered. "That, honey, is a gift all your own." She drew in breath to speak but he kept talking. "But your father was right, it's a gift. All of it and you shouldn't hide it. You *should* be proud." His thumb swept her lower lip and she trembled against him, hearing those words again, words her father said time and again but this time from Callum, spoken in his fierce whisper, his eyes never leaving hers. "You don't have to hide it here, not amongst my people, who are now *your* people. Baby doll, with me, you don't have to hide anything. You can be all you."

A relief so extreme, a relief that she never thought she'd know, hit Sonia, and it was so immense, her body sagged with it. Melting against his, she dropped her cheek to his chest, clutched his shirt in her fists, and burst into sobs.

"I never thought...it's been so...so ha-hard..." she stammered as his fingers sifted soothingly through her hair. She was focusing on his hand's movements, trying to come to terms with everything (an impossible task) when something occurred to her, Sonia's head jerked up, the tears ceased, and she asked, "Do you think I'm one of you?"

Callum shook his head. "No, baby doll. We don't have any blondes among us." His hand came to her face, he swiped at her tears, and said softly, "But you know you aren't. If you take a minute, you can smell the difference."

She took in a breath and she knew what he was saying. She'd never given herself the time to make the connection before, but his people's scents were different than hers. They were deeper, muskier, almost wild and animal but not in the least unpleasant.

In fact, she liked their smell better than humans.

"I like your smell," she blurted, meaning his people's smell (though she liked his too, immensely), but it didn't come out that way.

He grinned before he rolled into her saying huskily, "I like yours too."

The tawny was spiking through his irises and Sonia knew all too well what that meant.

And she suddenly felt vulnerable.

Exposed.

She'd never been with him knowing him the way she did then, understanding both their duties, their abilities, their connection on a level that hadn't, until that moment, penetrated.

"Callum—" she whispered but he was mostly on top of her and his face disappeared in her neck.

Then his tongue slid up its length before he said, "Regan wants you and she'll be back from her walk soon, we have to be fast."

"Callum—" Sonia whispered again but his mouth moved over her jaw, took hers in a hungry kiss, and she was instantly lost.

They were fast, or, she should say, *Callum* was fast.

With practiced ease, he'd drawn the urge over her, but even if they needed to be fast, he felt in the mood to play.

Therefore, she was fully clothed, as was he, but Sonia was on her knees in front of him. His arms were around her, one hand in her unzipped jeans, the other up her sweater having yanked down her bra. His fingers were torturing her in beautiful ways in both places.

Her head was resting against his chest, and as she ground down into his fingers, she tipped it back to gaze unfocused at his strong square jaw.

"I want you inside me," she begged.

"Tonight," he growled.

"Please," she breathed.

He gave her what she asked for but not what she really wanted and two of his fingers entered her, stroking deep.

Taking what she could get, she rode them wildly.

"That's it, baby doll," he groaned hoarsely into her ear. "Fuck yourself and come for me."

Instantly upon hearing his words, she did as she was told. Her cries piercing the air as the orgasm overwhelmed her and her body trembled in his arms.

When she was done, he was cupping her breast and her sex and his mouth was at her neck.

"You okay, little one?"

Her body wasn't okay. It was *more* than okay, happy and content.

Her mind wasn't okay either, but it was better than it had been since Callum stormed into her life and turned it on its head.

She understood him and his duty and she knew her place.

It was okay as it was ever going to be.

She decided to nod.

"Good," he murmured, his hands moved gently away, and he righted her clothing, but his arms wrapped around her and he held her where she was. "One more thing, baby doll." He was still murmuring but there was steel veining through his tone and she held her breath for what was to come next. "Never again ask me to give back my ring. No matter how pissed you are, never do that again." His arms tightened around her and he growled, "I can't wear it into battle for reasons you'll eventually understand. I gave it to Regan for safekeeping. From now on, if I need to, I'll give it to you. But it means something to me. I can't fucking imagine why you'd say it doesn't, but get that out of your head right now. Am I understood?"

Her breath caught in her lungs, the steel in his tone piercing that guard around her heart, even though she wasn't entirely certain she understood or believed what he was saying, Sonia could do nothing but nod.

Satisfied with her response, he kissed her neck, gave her a squeeze, and then pulled them out of the bed, walked them out of the room, and took her to his mother, leaving her in the cozy warm knitting room with its blazing fire and her mother-in-law smiling happily at them as he kissed her thoroughly and left.

Likely to write more letters.

She stared after him long after he'd gone.

Then Sonia Arlington sighed, finally accepting her fate, and she turned with a smile to Regan.

CHAPTER SEVENTEEN
BETRAYAL

WALKING down the hall toward the kitchen, Callum heard the three women's voices filled with laughter just as he smelled the three distinct scents.

Two wolves.

One Sonia.

As he turned the corner to enter the room, Sonia, no longer hiding her gifts, was already looking toward the door expectantly, a small smile on her face.

Callum smiled back.

She was sitting at a stool at the counter, a mug of coffee cupped in both hands. She had her long hair pulled back from her face with a wide, pale pink band and she was wearing the cashmere robe he bought her for Christmas as well a pair of thick, pale pink socks. Her face was free of makeup and he thought she'd never looked lovelier, not simply because she was, but because, since their blowout fight that afternoon a week and a half before, she'd changed.

As he walked into the room, Callum nodded to Mara and Callista but he went directly to his mate, getting close, and when he did she tipped her head back to look at him.

"Hey," she said softly, her eyes warm on him and that single word made his cock jerk.

He threaded his fingers in her thick soft hair and bent his mouth to hers.

"Hey," he replied against her lips before he kissed her lightly.

When he lifted his head, her cheeks were pink but her eyes showed her disappointment.

Satisfied with her reaction, Callum grinned.

Her gaze dropped down to his grin and she emitted a delicate fluttering sigh.

Loving that sound, Callum's hand twisted reflexively but gently in her hair.

"Do you want coffee?" she asked.

No. He didn't want coffee.

He wanted to order Mara and Callista out of the room and he wanted to lift Sonia up on the kitchen counter and do things to his queen that, just from the memories, would make certain that pink stayed in her cheeks any time she was having coffee with her new friends in this room.

"Yes," he answered.

His fingers glided through her hair as she put her mug down, got up, her body brushing his, but she didn't go to the coffeepot immediately. She stopped, went up on the tips of her toes, kissed the underside of his jaw, and *then* she went to the coffeepot.

"Big day tomorrow," Mara commented as Callum leaned a hip against the counter and watched Sonia make him a mug of coffee.

"Mm," Callum replied, his mind on his mate.

"I can't wait," Callista remarked. "My house is full. Every room, every couch. Even some in sleeping bags on the floors. The whole town is buzzing with excitement."

"I know!" Mara exclaimed. "The place is heaving. Last night, Drogan and I took the pups up to our roof just so we could look all around at the campfires dotting the hills in the dark." She clasped her hands together and breathed, "It was so beautiful, it was like a dream."

Sonia returned and handed Callum his coffee after which she slid an arm around his waist and rested her weight into his side. When she did, he pulled her closer with his arm around her shoulders.

Sonia looked to the women and stated, "It's seriously crazy. Every day for days, more and more fires. I can't believe so many people are out in this snow and cold *in tents*."

Callista grinned at her. "Our people don't mind the cold."

"They'd have to not," Sonia replied. "It was below freezing last night. Even in the castle, Callum kept the fire going all night in our room to fight back the chill."

"I'll bet he did," Mara muttered with comically wide eyes to Callista and Callum watched Sonia's cheeks go pink again, for Mara was right. Callum kept the fire going in the fireplace but he kept Sonia warm under the hides in other ways.

Callista noticed Sonia's blush and she teased, "Mara, you forget our dainty queen is a respectable human. They don't talk over coffee about all the best ways to fight back a chill."

"Maybe not, but I'm going to have words with Drogan. It's been *ages* since he's been able to go *all night* fighting back the chill."

Callista and Mara burst into hysterical laughter and Callum glanced down to see Sonia, not in the least offended, smiling at them.

She must have felt his eyes for she tipped her head back to look at him and announced cheerfully, "Mara and Callie think I'm a prude."

"You *are* a prude, Sonny!" Mara shrieked and then her gaze moved to Callum. "Still, after all this time, *no one* knows her claiming story! It should be illegal."

"I agree." Callista nodded mock soberly. "Illegal."

Sonia calmly grabbed her coffee cup, brought it to her mouth, and mumbled into it, "Lucky for me, my husband's king."

That was when Callum burst out laughing, curling his *wife* into his front. She dropped her mug and tipped her head back to grin at him.

"Find me when you're done here, wife," he ordered quietly, his hand tensing on her shoulder on the word "wife."

Her eyes flashed briefly and she nodded. He touched his mouth to hers, and with another nod to Mara and Callista, he left the room and went to his study.

Sitting at his desk, trying to focus his mind on the hundreds of matters that should be taking his attention, chiefly the victory celebration that was taking place tomorrow, he found his task impossible.

His eyes slid to the window and he saw for once the sun shining bright upon the snow.

He turned his chair to face the view and his gaze became as distracted as his mind as he looked at the over-bright vista but didn't see it.

The last week and a half had been a revelation.

Ryon was correct. Female humans needed communication and giving it to Sonia had made a world of difference. Not knowing her hardly at all before claiming her, he'd not known how much she was holding onto in that head of hers.

And thus holding back.

Now he knew.

Fucking hell, but he knew.

She was like an all new Sonia, and if he thought the old Sonia was perfect, he'd been wrong.

This Sonia, sitting in her robe with her hair pulled back in her kitchen with her new friends, having a laugh, getting him coffee, muttering jokes in her dry humor, and leaning into him was fucking *perfect*.

And this all worked exceptionally well for Callum. In fact, he couldn't have been fucking happier.

His mate was *meant* to be there for him to talk to, to work out his frustrations with, and he'd found, since he'd never done it with another female, human or she-wolf, it was an extraordinary release.

Telling Sonia about Desdemona, about the letters he had to write, the order he had to give, all the while feeling her soft body against his as they lay in their bed, it was like being liberated from a mental prison. He could and did talk to Ryon and his brothers, but nothing was like Sonia's face gentling and her body melting into his as he let that shit go. Nothing. He'd never experienced anything like it. It was beautiful.

But, with Sonia, it was more.

Nearly three weeks ago, Ryon had asked how lucky he could get and Callum had thought he was lucky then with the mate destiny had chosen for him.

Now he couldn't fathom the depths of his fortune.

It started the day after their fight, after she'd had her breakfast and he'd given her the injection. He took her back to his study and sat her on his lap as he bent to the task of writing more letters.

She sat quietly for a short while then she started to arrange things on his desk. Then more things. Then she slid off his lap and started tidying in earnest.

He allowed this. Mainly because his mind was on other matters, but also because he'd noticed she was very organized and if she wanted to organize his desk, he'd let her.

Callum, he found out too late, should have paid attention. Though, in the end, he was glad he didn't.

"What's this?" she asked and he looked up to see her head tilted to the side and she'd flipped a piece of paper to face him.

Callum's gaze dropped to the paper.

It was the report that Caleb had sent him with the list of the names of the fallen warriors, their next of kin, and the kin's address. About a third of the way down the list had tick marks, letters he'd already written.

"Those are the fallen, honey," he explained softly.

Her brows drew together in confusion and she started, "The fall—?"

Realization dawned, her face paled, and her hand pressed the list to her chest. He stood as she flipped the list around and he saw her eyes scanning it. She stepped back when he stepped forward, not raising her head to look at him when she did.

Callum stopped.

"I know him," she whispered and flipped the list back to Callum. Peering over it, she pointed to a name then her head snapped back and her eyes caught his. "I met him at the mansion. We talked a couple of times. He was very sweet to me."

There was more than one name of one wolf she talked to a couple of times at the mansion on that list. Which meant, from the troubled expression clear to read on her face, Callum had to get it away from her.

He held his hand out and ordered, "Baby doll, give me the list."

She defied him and took another step back, shaking her head, and she looked at the list again.

He started moving toward her but she kept moving back, her eyes scanning.

"Sonia—"

He stopped speaking and moving when she halted and gasped. Her head snapped back again, this time the movement sharper, her eyes were wide, her face ashen.

"Honey—" he began but she cut him off and when she did her voice was trembling.

"Tell me there are two of your men named Waring."

Fuck!

He moved faster but she retreated just as fast, skittering across the room, her gaze locked to his all the while begging, "Tell me, Callum. Tell me that's a common name for your people."

It was rare his people's names were common. Since wolves didn't have last names, their parents often had to get creative. At the very least, they carried a name that no one in their town or village shared.

Callum had lived over three hundred years and he'd never met another wolf named Waring.

Except the one Sonia knew.

She ran into the wall but lifted her arm, hand out, palm up, to ward him off.

"Tell me, Callum."

He ignored her arm and her palm hit his chest as he got close and framed her face with his hands.

Then, trying to be gentle with her, he whispered, "I can't, little one."

She closed her eyes tight and turned her head away.

She didn't open her eyes when she whispered back, "He saved my life."

He did.

But Waring did more than that.

"I know," Callum shared. "He saved mine too."

Her eyes jerked back to his and Callum saw stark terror mixed with her grief.

"What?" she breathed.

He swiftly debated the merits of telling her the story but her hands came up to his at her face and her fingers curled tightly around them, fisting the paper in her hand as she did so.

Then she demanded loudly, "*What?*"

Callum sighed then quickly he explained, "I'd been targeted. I was defending myself against six attackers, maybe more. Waring drew several of them away, dispatched two, but was killed by the third before I could aid him."

"Oh my God," she breathed in horror as her fingers tensed.

"Honey, it's war," he explained gently.

His gentle explanation had no effect for she repeated, "Oh my God."

Before he could move to comfort her, she tore violently away from his hands and stepped to the side.

"Who's this?" she demanded to know, turning the paper and pointing at the name beside Waring's.

Cautiously, Callum answered, "That's his mother."

"Right," Sonia snapped and walked stiffly to his desk, sat herself in his chair, and rolled herself forward.

Callum watched as she grabbed a piece of paper embossed with his crest at the top and started writing.

Silently, he walked to stand beside her and looked down to watch as she wrote:

> Dear Michaela,
>
> By now, you've likely heard of me. I'm Sonia, queen to Callum, and I knew your son.
>
> In the few weeks I'd known him, he did several kindnesses for me, two very important. One of those saved the life of my mate.
>
> He also made me laugh.
>
> There is nothing I can write in this letter which will help you during this time of sorrow. But I hope it gives

you some small measure of comfort to know that there are two beings very grateful for the fact that they shared this glorious planet with your son, even if it was for a short time.

Please know you and your family are in my and Callum's thoughts.

Forever indebted to your handsome, brave, fun-loving son, Waring,

—Sonia

Once she'd finished writing her extraordinary letter, writing it without hesitation or difficulty, she folded it, dug through his desk until she found an envelope, inserted the letter, sealed it, and handwrote the address.

Then her head tipped back to look up at him. Callum saw the trail of wetness on her cheeks and the tears still shining in her eyes.

All right, it was abundantly clear she didn't write it without difficulty.

"Okay, Callum," she said in a trembling voice, picking up the report filled with names of dead soldiers and shaking it at him. "Who's next?"

At first, Callum didn't move.

There weren't many times in his long life that Callum, king of the wolves, was uncertain what to do, but in the face of his queen's profound but poised compassion, that was one of them.

So he did what his instincts told him to do. He leaned down to his mate, curled his fingers around her neck, and marked her hair with his temple. Then he kissed her softly on her lips.

He pulled her out of his chair, sat in it, tugged her gently into his lap, and together they wrote letters to the kin of the fallen. Callum writing the letters, Sonia sitting in his lap, addressing them, ticking off the names, and writing personal notes to the next of kin of the few wolves she knew, however briefly.

Her assistance made it a less difficult task, if not a less wretched one.

And, in that day and age of phones and e-mail, news of her notes, especially those received quickly by the kin of his Royal Guard who lived in the village (including Waring's mother), spread widely and it spread rapidly.

Just like he expected but much more swiftly, in fact, before most of his people even met their queen, they fell in love with her.

———

The new Sonia continued to emerge when, three nights later in their bedroom, the firelight dancing on her skin, her face tucked into his neck, her body straddling his, their physical connection still held but their breath having recovered from their orgasms, she lifted up with her fore-arms on his chest.

Her eyes moved over his face before they caught his and she asked, somewhat timidly and even with a hint of embarrassment, "What's your last name?"

He was surprised at her question but he shouldn't have been. Most immortals, including vampires (although Gregor and Yuri had adopted one and they did it for her) didn't have surnames. But humans, of course, did.

"My people don't carry surnames," he informed her.

She looked surprised for a moment as she whispered, "Oh," and her gaze drifted away as she went on, "This is a problem."

His arms about her gave her a squeeze, bringing her attention back to him before he queried, "Why?"

"Well, in my world, we *do* have surnames," she told him. "People will expect you to have one and they'll expect *me* to take it or explain that I didn't." She sighed and finished, "Which I guess is what I'll have to do."

There was one thing he liked about the human's mating ritual, the female accepting the male's name. Callum liked this not because it denoted possession, but because it signified the birth of a single unit, a family.

He found at that moment to his further surprise he wished he had a name to give her.

It was with delight when he heard that Sonia had an even better idea.

"Mara told me your father's full name was McDonagh," she remarked.

"It was," Callum confirmed.

"Well," she started, her gaze drifting away and her manner again became tentative before she looked back to him. "That's a last name for my people."

"I know," he replied.

"Well," she went on after giving a brief nod, "I thought..." she hesitated then forged ahead, "if you don't mind, and, um, if Regan doesn't, maybe, when we're in my world, I can tell people my new name is Sonia Arlington-McDonagh."

At her quiet faltering words, he had the same exact reaction he had when she gave him his ring. Something shifted inside him, so big it was as if the bed moved. His gut and chest tightened and all he could think of was her being known by the name of Sonia Arlington-McDonagh.

She stared at him and her face grew worried before she whispered, "I don't have to—"

But he cut her off by rolling her to her back so he was pinning her to the bed, his hips snug between her legs, his cock still inside her and hardening again as his mouth took hers in a hungry kiss.

When he lifted his head, both their breath was coming faster.

His eyes locked on hers and he decreed, "You'll be known by that amongst my people as well."

Then he started moving slowly inside her, and automatically, her hips moved with his.

One of her hands glided up his back as her other one came to rest at the side of his face before she said softly, "I take it you like that idea."

He stopped moving, slowly pulled out and surged back in, burying himself to the hilt before he growled against her mouth, "Yes, I fucking like it."

At his surge, her arm had clasped around him, her knees had come up to press against his sides and the fingers of her other hand had slid into his hair.

But she grinned against his lips.

At her reaction, his hips started to move faster.

Her lips went to his ear, and beginning to pant, she breathed, "Mara also told me you're known as 'The Wolf.'"

His body stilled and at his reaction her head fell back to the pillows so she could gaze at him curiously.

"Sorry?" he asked, a different feeling seizing him.

He'd planned carefully with Regan and Ryon as advisors as to when to share the information with Sonia that his people were werewolves. Her reaction could be anything and Callum wanted to control it.

Werewolves were fantasy creatures to humans and not good ones. Vicious, murdering, and abhorrent, something to be frightened of, the villain in a horror story.

Back in the day when wolves were less careful about who witnessed the transformation, humans had sometimes seen it. And, being humans, instead of trying to understand it, they feared it.

And hunted it.

Which was one of the reasons the rebellion they'd been fighting for millennia had remained so staunch in their beliefs that humans should be enslaved.

Sonia might fear what his people could do, and unless he took the time to allow her to experience the fact that wolves were friendly, good-humored, and kind, there was little doubt she would.

He also wanted their bond to strengthen. He felt confidence in their connection but this would be a shock. Callum wanted her life thoroughly entwined with his in a way she couldn't imagine it without him, no matter what secrets and how great they were that he may hold.

Regan and Ryon had agreed with his plan and it was even Ryon's suggestion to keep this knowledge from Sonia until she was securely inserted into their fold.

However, after their blowout, Callum had concerns about this plan.

Sonia seemed to prefer to understand what was happening to and around her. The longer he waited, the less it felt he was protecting her, the more it felt like a lie.

So much so, he'd begun to feel something he'd never experienced before. A twinge of something unpleasant. Almost as if he *feared* she'd discover his secret and consider his keeping it from her a betrayal.

Werewolves were half man. They weren't immune to fucking up, say, taking to too much gaming or drink. Though wolves never strayed. Infidelity to your mate was unheard of. Before you found your mate, finding play partners (and numerous of them) for both males and females was the norm. After you found your mate, never. Callum had known many a wolf to succumb to the weaknesses of drink and gambling, and in so doing, betray their mate through deceits. And, with a she-wolf, it was never pretty and it was often the female would never get over it.

Living an eternity paying for a betrayal was a daunting prospect.

Living an eternity expecting another one, he reckoned, would be far worse.

Callum didn't want anything to mar the perfection of what he had with Sonia.

And he didn't want her to think he'd betrayed her, not for an instant, but especially not for the short time that represented her eternity.

He didn't want this so much he actually thought that unpleasant feeling was that he *feared* it and fear was not something that he'd experienced before.

Further, he didn't fucking like how it felt.

"Mara told me you're known as 'The Wolf,'" she repeated quietly, watching him closely.

"Honey—" he started.

She interrupted with, "Why didn't you tell me?"

"I—" he began again but she lifted her mouth and pressed it to his at the same time she tilted her hips and he slid in deeper. Both felt so good, his word ended in a growl.

"I like wolves," she whispered against his mouth and her hand put pressure in his hair. Her head tilted slightly to invite his kiss and her eyes turned hungry before she finished, "I like them *a lot.*"

Her enticement was nearly too much.

But the time had come. He had to tell her.

So, he said, "Baby doll—"

But she cut him off again, cut him off with the words that always shattered his control at the same time her sex clenched around his shaft, making her invitation a demand he couldn't ignore.

"Fuck me, wolf."

With another growl, Callum did as she asked, in three different positions, as hard and rough as both of them liked it.

It was so hard and rough and exhausting, by the time he forced her off her knees to her belly and settled between her widespread legs, his forearms tucked into her sides and his lips at her ear to whisper his secret, Sonia was fast asleep.

Two days later, Callum had still not found the appropriate time to explain things to Sonia.

The first day it was Sonia again who took his mind off his determination to share his secret.

After breakfast, as usual she wandered into his study. However this time she did it with a funny look on her face that Callum couldn't quite read.

After their extensive play the night before, he'd left her arms that morning without waking her and started his day.

This was unusual. Since coming to the castle and giving her time to acclimatize, he'd usually wait for her to wake and he'd either take care of her or the both of them before he started his day.

However, he remembered her complaints of aching when he'd taken her "vigorously" when he brought her home, and as the night before had been nearly as vigorous, he'd decided she needed her rest.

It was also unusual when she walked to him and he turned his seat toward her to offer his lap that she didn't immediately sit.

Instead she stopped, tilted her head to the side, and stared at him, seemingly mesmerized.

"What is it?" he asked but her body gave a soft jerk at his words as if he'd woken her from a daydream.

She bit her lip, looking indecisive, then she sank to her knees before him.

It was Callum's turn to stare.

She put her hands to his knees and then she put pressure there to pull them apart.

Then, Callum watched, his cock responding instantly, as her pretty head dropped and she nuzzled his crotch with her face.

"Fucking hell," he breathed and she lifted up, pressed her front to his groin, and placed her hands on his chest.

"You didn't play with me this morning," she accused quietly, her expression no longer unreadable but greedy.

Always in heat, his Sonia.

Clearly, the night before hadn't been *that* vigorous.

Callum marked that knowledge in his mind and his fingers slid into her hair at the side to cup her head.

"No," was all he had the capacity to say.

Her hand dropped to his crotch to palm it softly and she whispered, "Can I play with you?"

"Fuck yes," he gritted through his teeth and she smiled.

Then she dropped her head and he watched as she pulled his sweater up, exposing his stomach, and put her mouth there, then it slid down while she undid his pants and freed him.

Without leading in to it, she gripped his rock-hard shaft with her hand and took him in her mouth, stroking and sucking simultaneously. Often, she'd lick while she stroked, her eyes would rise to catch his as she did so, and each time hers were hungrier, like she couldn't get enough of him.

For his part, Callum didn't take his eyes away from her for a second.

And what he saw was fucking beautiful.

It wasn't much later when he'd had enough and roughly maneuvered her body so it was bent over his desk, pulled her jeans and underwear down her thighs, that he found she was so aroused by sucking him off that the minute he buried himself in her abundantly wet silkiness, she slammed back to receive him and cried out her instant release.

Callum didn't long follow.

Allowing them both time to recover, Callum eventually righted their clothes. But it was Sonia that curled herself fully in his lap, pulling her legs up and bent to rest them against his front, her forehead tucked in his neck, her arm around him.

"Is that what you wanted me to do to you in your chair?" she asked softly.

It was.

But it was also far better because she did it of her own accord rather than because he told her to.

"Yes."

"Mm," she replied and snuggled closer.

Callum held his queen for a while then he resumed work.

Sonia didn't move, just stayed cuddled close in his lap.

As he worked with his wife held close, Callum decided that day wasn't the day to tell her his secret.

The next day, Callum didn't have time to tell her because Caleb returned.

Regan had taken Sonia away for a more in-depth perusal of town, something which it was obvious Sonia wanted to do by the look of excitement on her face when Regan suggested it. So Callum allowed it.

While she was gone, he was holed up in his study with Caleb and Ryon discussing the aftermath of the rebellion, the cleanup of the Western Territories, the sweep across the various regions to locate and neutralize all remaining rebels that Calder was leading, and he'd lost track of time.

Regan had called explaining that she and Sonia were having dinner with Maraleena and Drogan in town and by the time Callum and his brethren emerged from his study it was late. It wasn't only late, it was time for bed and Sonia hadn't had her injection.

He went in search of her and found her alone in the knitting room. The fire obviously Regan had laid and started was burning, for Sonia had no clue how to start a fire. This was something Callum learned days earlier when he walked into their bedroom in the middle of her adorably frustrated attempts and she made him promise he'd teach her to do it. He had lied (not exactly a betrayal in his mind) and promised he would when he had no intention of doing it because if she didn't ever learn, she'd have to find him to do it for her and he liked that idea.

She was standing at the window but she wasn't looking out.

Her head was bent and she was watching the fingers of one hand at the other twisting the wedding bands he'd given her around and around.

Something struck him then and he stopped in the door, leaning a shoulder against the jamb, crossing his arms on his chest, and he studied her.

During their fight she had said that when she gave him his ring, she didn't know if it meant anything to her.

He'd not called her on that. He was satisfied with the outcome of their altercation. There was no reason to dredge it up, process every word she'd said in anger when, from her behavior since then, she'd given every indication that she wasn't only settling into her life with him splendidly but enjoying it thoroughly.

But now, watching her, her face thoughtful and far away, twisting those bands, which had meant nothing to him when he'd given them to her, but an hour later when he'd heard her call him "husband," they meant everything, he felt a definite and acute unease. An unease akin to that unpleasant feeling he thought might be fear.

Without looking up, she said softly, "I know you're there."

"I know you know," he replied.

She finally looked at him and her fingers stilled in their turning but they didn't release the rings. "So why are you standing all the way over there?"

"I'm wondering what's on your mind," he told her truthfully.

She dropped her hand but wrapped her arms around her belly and explained, "What's on my mind is, I'm wondering why my husband stopped in the doorway when he *never* stops in a doorway when I'm in a room. He *always* comes to me. So, what's on my mind is, I'm wondering what's on *your* mind."

She was probably telling the truth.

Just not all of it.

He walked to her and when he arrived she slid her arms around his middle and leaned her body into his, tilting her head far back to look up at him.

It struck him then that she did this a great deal recently. Effortlessly putting her arms around him, leaning her weight into him. Before, her hugs and moments of affection were rare, and when they came seemed, compared to the recent ones, uncomfortable.

Now they were relaxed and natural and Callum preferred them greatly.

He returned the favor, wrapping her in his arms, pulling her deep in his body, and dipping his chin to look down at her.

"All right, Sonia, now what's *really* on your mind?" he asked.

"I told you," she fibbed.

"You weren't standing at the window twisting my rings for the fuck of it," he informed her, his voice meticulously even and calm, that unease he felt still acute.

She scanned his face. Then she sighed. It wasn't the fluttering sigh that he loved. It was a frustrated sigh.

He knew this by the sound but he also knew it by the irate flash in her green eyes.

"You're too perceptive," she muttered, her voice just as irate, then she informed him of the obvious, "It's annoying."

He preferred his topic of conversation so he gave her a gentle squeeze and said warningly, "Sonia..."

"Oh all right," she breathed out, her frustration still clear. Suddenly her eyes left his and she looked at his shoulder a moment before they came back. "Okay, Callum, what I was thinking was..." She hesitated a moment before stating, "And you can say no because, well, I'm sensing you're not big on human stuff and, well, this is *definitely* human. Obviously I wouldn't dream of asking you to go whole hog or anything, because considering, even for my Christmas party, you wore cords and a nice sweater..." She paused and went off tangent, "Though, the boots you wore were really nice that night. I liked them. You should wear—"

He couldn't help it. He started chuckling and gave her another squeeze, cutting her off by saying, "Honey, your point?"

Her eyes got big a moment, she pulled in breath and whispered, "Right." Then she went on swiftly, "What I was saying was, you don't have to do the big thing for me, you know, even though, outside your sixteenth birthday, it's the most important day in a girl's life. But I wouldn't ask you to wear the tuxedo and get a photographer and all that formal stuff, but can I...?" She looked at him, her eyes filled with discomfited yearning. "Would you mind if...?" She hesitated yet again and then forced out the words, "I know it isn't the done thing, but at our Mating, can I at least wear a pretty white dress?"

He stared at her a second, thrown, because he had no fucking clue what she was on about. At Matings wolves would dress up but dressing up for wolves was just wearing nicer but still casual clothes.

Then, unusually slowly, it hit him. Her twisting her wedding rings, talking of tuxedos and formalities and the most important day of a girl's life.

Fuck, she was talking about a human wedding.

Which, being his mate, she'd never get.

But, being his human wife, she would want.

And she *wanted* it and her wanting it meant she wanted *him*.

That unease sifted away leaving Callum feeling only the soft warmth of her body pressed to his and her arms around him.

"Baby doll—" he started.

"You can say no," she blurted. "It's probably a stupid idea. Your people will think..." Her eyes got big again and she said, "Oh no, would they be offended?"

One of his hands traveled up her back and tangled in her hair as his face got closer to hers. "No, they wouldn't be offended. Wear whatever you want."

He saw excitement light in her eyes for a second before it extinguished. "Will I look stupid?"

Callum grinned, pulling her tighter to him. "Impossible."

"I don't want them to think I'm holding on...I mean, I don't want them to think I don't take my responsibility—"

He cut her off. "They'll think you're proud of who you are and proud of who you're bound to, *both* of which my people will find honorable."

The excitement came back in a flash.

"Really?" she whispered.

"Yes," he answered.

"Seriously?" she pressed both verbally and by pushing closer to his frame.

Callum bit back laughter at her adorable earnest look but he didn't manage it entirely and still said through chuckling, "Yes, little one."

She gazed at him as if looking for evidence of dishonesty.

Then her weight sagged into him, she put her cheek to his chest and she gave him a squeeze. "Good."

He kissed the top of her head, enjoying the far different feeling he had now rather than the one he had when he first stood in the door to this room.

It was more than her embrace. It was more than the knowledge that she yearned to be tied to him through his rings, bearing his father's name, adhering to the traditions of her people.

It was enjoying giving her something she very much desired.

Which meant what he had to do next hurt like a bitch.

"It's past time for your injection."

He felt her body tighten in his arms before she forced it to relax and he was glad he couldn't see her eyes.

"I know," she replied.

"Let's go, baby doll."

She nodded, her cheek sliding against his chest. She pulled away. He took her hand and guided her to their bathroom.

Callum shifted in his seat behind his desk and lifted his hand to his forehead pressing away the tension that formed there after the reminder of the injection.

Last week, he'd taken her to Aberdeen to visit the specialist who simply decreed that what Dr. Mortenson said about tolerance for the drug and life changes were to blame for her "turn." He explained (three times) that there were no other treatments. He took more blood, which, again, came back normal. And he suggested they titrate off the morning dose, injecting half for a few days then stopping altogether.

"Let's hope that works," he said on a distracted doctorly smile while simultaneously writing notes.

Callum had wanted to break his jaw for it *not* working meant unendurable pain for his mate, which was what, through gritted teeth, he'd informed the doctor after he'd tersely called the man's attention back to his patient and her husband.

"You know what to do now. Just give her another dose if she becomes symptomatic and go back to twice daily injections," the doctor had replied calmly in the face of Callum's controlled fury.

It was then Sonia had squeezed his hand and Callum made the decision not to throw the doctor out the window, which was the decision he'd made the instant before she'd squeezed his hand.

Luckily, the titrating had worked and Sonia hadn't become symptomatic.

Then again, if it was stress and life changes that had affected the efficacy of the drug, she was settling in and hopefully they wouldn't have another "turn."

Callum heard Ryon approaching and his mind moved directly to what filled it any time it wasn't filled with Sonia's smile, her affection, her laughter, her kindness, her humor, her sweet little body and how it responded to him, her deepening connection to him and his family, and her fucking injection.

Where his mind moved also wasn't to his duty as king.

It went to the fact that every day he didn't tell her his secret, their life was becoming a lie.

Ryon came in on a smile and closed the door.

Since discovering Sonia had had her abilities her entire life, long enough for her father to explain she should hide them, they no longer held suspicions against the vampires.

However, they were also all aware that Sonia's abilities rivaled theirs and clearly Ryon closing the heavy door meant there was something he wanted muted should Sonia be in hearing distance.

He approached Callum's desk and sat opposite, declaring, "All is in place for tomorrow."

Callum's mouth got tight.

Ryon still felt Sonia needed time with the wolves and was against Callum telling her. They'd had words about it. Callum disagreed and decided he'd bloody well tell her when the right time arose.

Unfortunately that hadn't happened and tomorrow hundreds of wolves would be celebrating in the streets.

Shit happened. Especially with wolves.

Therefore, like Drogan, Maraleena, and Callista, his Royal Guard had been warned by Ryon that Sonia was to be protected from witnessing any transformation or talk of werewolves and tomorrow everywhere she went she would be with him, his family, or under escort of his guard.

"I don't like this," Callum told his cousin. "I'll find time to tell her tonight."

"You should wait until after tomorrow," Ryon differed. "She'll enjoy tomorrow. She'll see the true wolf nature. You need to give her more time."

Callum watched his cousin, again questioning his motives when it came to Callum's mate.

"What makes you think she needs more time?" Callum asked.

Ryon grinned. "Call it instinct."

Callum didn't find anything amusing.

"Have you not noticed the change in her?" he queried.

Ryon's expression turned serious and he shared, "Yes, Cal, I have and I don't fucking trust it."

Callum felt his blood run cold. "And why the fuck not?"

Ryon shook his head and his eyes went vague as did his tone when he said, "I can't put my finger on it but I feel she's holding back."

It was then Callum's hands clenched into fists.

First, if Sonia was holding anything back then the true Sonia would be beyond perfection, which was impossible.

Second, because his cousin was still clearly keeping a close eye on his mate and he didn't like it.

And last, because it felt like Ryon was trying to make Callum doubt his *wife*.

"I think," Callum said calmly and evenly, a tone that Ryon knew and it caught his immediate attention therefore his distracted gaze cleared and focused on Callum, "that perhaps you should stop worrying about my mate so fucking much."

"Cal—"

Callum leaned forward and said deceptively softly, "She's *my* mate, Ry. *Mine.*"

"Cal—"

"Leave it," Callum warned and Ryon leaned forward as well.

"Have you been talking to her as I told you to?"

"Leave it."

"Cal, have you?"

"Yes, I fucking have. Now, *fucking leave it!*" Callum bit out.

Ryon scowled at him then sat back. Callum watched the muscle work in his cousin's jaw for long moments before Ryon spoke again.

"You should know. I've given a vial of her medicine to a friend of mine who knows someone who can analyze it."

Callum sat back too. "I thought we'd covered this. She's had her abilities since birth."

"I know. It doesn't hurt to check though," Ryon returned.

Callum stared at him before asking, "What are you thinking?"

"Well," Ryon replied, still aggravated but, Callum sensed, not because of their earlier exchange of words. "I've had my fair share of experience with humans. I've never run across anything like her abilities."

"Yes, we've had this conversation before."

"It's unusual."

"Yes."

"I don't like it."

"Ry—"

"You don't protect a life-threatening condition behind nearly unhackable passwords, Cal. Something's wrong here. I don't like it and I haven't had time to give it my full attention."

Callum sighed. "You do if she's destined queen to a secret society and that knowledge in the wrong hands would make her vulnerable. She's had her gifts since birth, her father knew about them for fuck's sake. She and I have talked about it. Her father likely made some explanation to her doctor. Gregor nearly came out of his skin when he heard she'd had a turn and he's not a male prone to showing his reactions. My instincts tell me his reaction was not because of some nefarious plot, but because the thought of her in pain hurt *him*. Lassiter probably told him about her gifts as well, but even if he didn't, he's a vampire who's lived with Sonia for years. He'd notice it. It took me a bloody week. If Lassiter didn't tell Gregor, it probably took him about as long as it took me. What she can do is unusual for a human but she's amongst those who'll accept her now. It's fine. *She's* fine. Let it go."

At that, Ryon uncharacteristically lost patience and clipped, "Just let me do my fucking job, all right?"

Callum studied his cousin. He'd known him a long time and Ryon's instincts were as sharp as Callum's.

And what would it hurt?

Therefore, he gave in. "All right, Ry, if you feel so strongly about it, do your job."

It was then, both their heads cocked as they sensed Sonia's approach.

Ryon's eyes locked on Callum and he whispered in a voice so low Sonia wouldn't hear but also that strangely sounded like a warning, "She's in love with you, you know. She has been for years."

Callum simply smiled because he knew and that was exactly why Sonia Arlington-McDonagh was absolutely fucking perfect.

Therefore, he replied with contented kingly arrogance, "I know."

Ryon regarded him closely, communicating something Callum didn't understand.

He also didn't care.

His mind, again, turned to his mate.

There was a short soft knock on the door before she stuck her head in.

"Am I interrupting anything?"

"Come in, baby doll," Callum called and she came through the door still wearing nothing but her robe and socks, her hair back in that pretty pink band.

He wondered as he watched her walk gracefully toward him, what she had on under the robe.

He hoped it was just his chain.

He turned his chair to her, she sat in his lap, and as he twisted to the desk, she looked to Ryon.

"Hey, cuz," she greeted on a smile.

"Hey, cuz," Ryon smiled back, either over it or hiding his earlier intensity.

She turned to Callum and announced with mock irritation, "I've just been treated to a thirty-minute interrogation about my claiming in the kitchen. Mara and Callie are screamingly nosy. My excuse of 'being human' isn't working anymore."

Callum grinned at her and advised, "So tell them."

Her eyes grew wide and she cried, "No way! That's between you and me." She gasped on some sudden thought, her head twisted sharply toward Ryon, and then back to Callum where her eyes narrowed. "You haven't—"

"No," he cut her off and her body relaxed against his. "At least not yet," he went on and her body got rock solid. He was chuckling when he finished on a tease, "I just haven't had the time."

"You...!" she cried shortly, clearly too incensed to go on.

At the same time, Ryon noted roguishly, "I'll look forward to *that*."

She twisted her head to look at Ryon before twisting it again to Callum. He lifted his hand to cup and therefore control the movements of her neck so she didn't give herself whiplash.

"Don't you dare!" she snapped at him and he smiled yet again but this was a different smile.

"Will it piss you off if I do?"

"Yes," she returned instantly.

Callum replied just as swiftly, "I like you pissed off, baby doll. Haven't had that in a while." He nuzzled her stiff neck and flicked her ear with his nose before saying there, "I miss it."

She growled in her throat.

Callum chuckled in his.

They both went still and all three of the inhabitants of the room looked to the window. A car, or by the sounds of it, a truck or SUV was approaching.

"You expecting company?" Ryon asked deceptively casually.

No, he wasn't.

Then again, there were hundreds of wolves in his hills, some of them with mates, others with family members, most with both. The town and its vicinity, as Mara noted, were heaving.

However, his wolves wouldn't approach. Not without an invitation or a reason. This was not only the standard, but also because he'd newly claimed his mate. They'd need a good excuse to interrupt him during this time even if a celebration was commencing tomorrow.

Which meant this could be bad tidings.

He got out of his chair, lifting Sonia to her feet as he did so, mumbling, "I need to see who's at the door."

His mind finally off his mate and on whatever was coming, Callum didn't notice at first that Sonia fell in step beside him.

When he did, he stopped, looked down at her, and ordered, "You stay here."

She gazed up at him. "But...someone's at the door."

"Yes," he agreed. "And I'm going to see who it is."

Her expression changed. For some Sonia reason it became stubborn and she retorted, "And I'm going with you."

Callum sought patience and replied, "Baby doll, you're in a robe."

"So?" she returned instantly. "It covers me doesn't it?"

It did.

However, considering her sweet little body and her pretty face, it didn't leave much to the imagination even if you didn't have much of an imagination. And most wolves had excellent imaginations.

"You're staying here or getting dressed," Callum commanded.

"I'm going to the door," she rejoined.

"Sonia—"

Her head tilted. "Is this my house?"

"Sonia—"

"Is it *my* door?"

Still seeking patience, Callum looked to Ryon, who was grinning at them and obviously not about to assist, then he muttered, "Bloody hell."

"I'm going to the door," Sonia finished and commenced striding out of the room.

He sighed his defeat. Ryon chuckled. Callum glared at him and he moved out of his study, leaving Ryon behind. He caught her up, took her hand, and together they went to the door.

He smelled vampire as he hit the large stone entryway.

A vampire with a female human.

More precisely, Lucien, likely with his mate.

Relief hit him at the same time as curiosity and Callum maneuvered Sonia partially behind him but still beside him as he opened the door.

A shiny black Porsche Cayenne was glinting in the sun at the foot of the steps.

Lucien, tall, black-haired, and powerfully built, wearing jeans, boots, and a black turtleneck which could be seen under his black, wool, hip-length, double-breasted coat was climbing them. Climbing beside him, her hand linked in his, was a beautiful blonde with dark blue eyes. She had a fantastic figure covered in charcoal gray cords, a stylish, fitted, black leather jacket with an eggplant-colored pashmina wrapped around her neck, and she was wearing high-heeled black boots.

Pure fucking class. Both of them.

Gazing at the female, her eyes as alive as her expression, like she couldn't hide her love of life nor did she want to, not to mention smelling her exquisite scent, Callum realized immediately Lucien's fate had also led him to the perfect match.

Pleased for the vampire, his eyes moved to Lucien's as Callum tucked his own perfect match into his side and he smiled.

"This is a surprise," he greeted as Lucien led his mate across the landing to the door.

"A pleasant one, I trust," Lucien replied, also on a smile, but the vampire's black eyes were, as usual, carefully blank. Lucien never gave anything away, at least not to Callum's recollection.

"That depends on its purpose," Callum returned, shifting himself and Sonia to the side to allow Lucien and his mate entry, and then he closed off the cold behind them by shutting the door.

Lucien stopped himself and his mate just inside, and pulling her protectively close, he said, "I'd heard you'd finally claimed your mate. I was curious."

Lucien wasn't curious. Lucien had a reason to be there.

Callum also hid his reaction and turned to Sonia. "Honey, this is a friend of mine, Lucien." He looked to Lucien. "Lucien, this is my queen, Sonia."

She was gazing at Lucien, openly unsure of what to make of him, and she held out a tentative hand, which, after a glance at Callum, Lucien took.

Bending low, Lucien brushed his lips against her knuckles and all in the entryway (except, perhaps, Lucien's mate) heard Sonia's soft intake of breath.

A soft intake of breath Callum didn't like.

Nor did he like it when Lucien kept hold of her hand and pulled her closer.

Callum tensed and only partially relaxed when Lucien turned Sonia to his mate.

"Sonia, this is Leah, my bride," he said softly but Leah was smiling openly at Sonia.

"Hello," Leah said in an attractive alto voice, her smile never wavering.

However, it was plain to see in the face of her stylish company, Sonia was having belated second thoughts about appearing at the door in her socks and robe, cashmere or not.

"Hi," Sonia replied on a shy smile and then she politely pulled her hand from Lucien's and scuttled back. She nearly ran into Callum before he caught her and folded her again into his side where she wrapped her arm around him.

It was at that, Callum fully relaxed.

"Leah, meet Callum," Lucien invited and it was Callum's turn to take Lucien's mate's hand but he didn't brush his lips against her knuckles. He just squeezed and released it.

"Coffee!" Sonia suddenly cried and looked up at Callum. "I'll order coffee and something to eat and um...get dressed." She looked to Lucien and Leah. "Are you hungry?"

"Starved, but I'd kill for a cup of coffee," Leah replied, still smiling.

"Brilliant. We have coffee," Sonia announced. "Good coffee. Mara only gets the best." She turned again to Callum. "You, um...take them somewhere warm. I'll be right back."

Then, with a self-conscious grin at their guests, she broke from Callum's hold and ran down the hall.

Callum watched her go.

He realized that Lucien did too when he heard the vampire mutter, "Fetching."

"I *am* still standing here, you know," Leah remarked, her severe tone belied by her unwavering smile.

Lucien's eyes turned to his mate before he murmured, "Mm, I know, my pet."

Callum watched, concealing his surprise as Lucien looked down at his bride with blatant warmth.

Christ, he loves her, Callum thought, examining the couple.

This shouldn't have taken him aback. She was his lifemate and to have her Lucien had put both their lives at risk and turned the vampire world upside down. Further, Callum had spent his entire existence feeling the intensity of that kind of connection between his own people.

But not from a vampire. Never from a vampire. Not that transparent adoration. Not in hundreds of years.

And, for some asinine reason, Lucien's display and Leah's artless acceptance of it rattled Callum.

He was pulled from his thoughts when Mara bustled in calling, "Well, hello there! I'm Mara, housekeeper at Canis. Let me get your coats and we'll get you somewhere warm. Callista is preparing coffee and a bite to eat."

Mara took their outer gear and Callum led the way to the sitting room on the first floor. It was a circular room at the bottom of a turret with heavy comfortable furniture and a spherical fireplace in the middle, already blazing, making the space warm.

"Please sit," Callum invited Leah and she again smiled at him.

"You have a lovely castle," she noted, looking around while sitting on a couch and crossing her legs before she tipped her face up to Lucien and asked mock petulantly, "Why don't *we* have a castle, darling?"

"You want a castle, sweetling, I'll get you a castle," Lucien answered casually.

Leah had been joking.

Lucien was not.

Callum watched as Leah's stunning face absorbed this fact. It softened to a look of such extreme devotion, Callum felt himself melting from the room. They were the only two there. Callum had ceased to exist.

That was when he knew what rattled him. He knew what Ryon couldn't put his finger on. He knew his cousin was correct.

Something wasn't right with Sonia.

He knew this because, since Christmas, unless he was fucking her, except for during their fight, she never called him "wolf."

Not mock petulantly.

Not at all.

He had her warmth. He had her affection. She enjoyed his attention and she was a brilliant queen in every aspect.

And she loved him.

He knew that.

But something was missing.

Christ, he had all that, and it was magnificent, but she was *still* holding something back.

"Callum?" Lucien called and Callum's unfocused eyes concentrated on the vampire.

"Sit," Callum grunted, uneasy with his newfound knowledge but more at what might be behind it, and Lucien took a seat beside his bride as Callum did the same opposite them.

Leah instantly curled into Lucien's side as his arm slid around her shoulders, pulling her closer.

Seeing this made Callum grit his teeth.

Then Lucien announced, "We need to talk before Sonia returns."

Callum's attention sharpened and his instincts made him brace.

"Then do it quickly," Callum invited. He wanted this to be over, needed to have a word with his *wife*. His gaze shifting briefly to Leah, deciding she likely had full knowledge of Lucien's abilities, he went on, "But if you sense Sonia anywhere near, stop speaking."

Lucien's brows went up. He'd smell her before Callum did while he was in human form. If he were a wolf, his senses would have been slightly more acute than the vampire's, but at that moment he was not a wolf.

"Would you like to explain that?" Lucien suggested.

"Not right now," Callum replied, giving Lucien the correct implication that he might not later either. It depended on how this conversation progressed.

Lucien nodded, let it go, and continued without preamble, "I've spoken to Gregor."

Callum didn't respond.

"He's explained things," Lucien went on.

"And what did he explain?" Callum asked.

Lucien's arm tightened protectively around Leah before he said, "He's shared The Prophesies."

Leah's body tensed and her happy face grew serious as she gazed at Callum.

She knew as well and her fear was palpable.

As it would be.

Lucien was watching him closely and he queried, "You know of them?"

"Some of them, yes," Callum answered.

"I was told you didn't know," Lucien murmured and Callum didn't respond. Therefore Lucien continued, "They're vague as prophesies tend to be but they appear to be coming true. You and Sonia were obvious. Leah and myself..." He hesitated. "Not so much."

"There is another," Callum informed him.

Lucien's chin went up before he noted, "Yes, but they'll be found soon."

"They don't have to be."

Lucien gazed at him a moment before saying quietly, "Yes, Callum, they do."

Callum knew what he meant and he felt the muscle jump in his jaw.

The third lifemates needed to be found, the female claimed and bound, before The Prophesies could come true.

Leah, being mate to a vampire, would have eternal life.

Sonia, being mate to a werewolf, would always be mortal.

The third lifemate would need to be found before Sonia died, which meant soon, in the life of an immortal.

Callum decided to change the subject. "Do you have any idea if it will be wolf or vampire who claims the third mate?"

Lucien held his eyes and replied, "A hybrid." Callum felt his brows go up and Lucien nodded. "Werewolf, vampire hybrid. The first of his kind."

This was news.

Lucien kept speaking. "It's important we form an alliance, and when they're discovered, we ally with them."

Callum thought no truer words were spoken.

"Absolutely," he agreed.

"Therefore, you should know about Leah." Callum's eyes moved to Lucien's bride but Lucien kept speaking, explaining simply, "She dreams."

Callum's gaze sliced back to the vampire as his body grew taut.

"Dreams?" he used that word to persuade the vampire to go on.

"I dream," Leah put in. "They're better now but, well..." she trailed off and looked up at her mate.

"She dreams the future," Lucien continued for her. "Vividly. So vividly the dream can take hold in real life to the point that what's happening in her subconscious can happen to her physically."

"Curious," Callum muttered and watched Lucien's mouth tighten in irritation.

"She dreamed of The Sentence," he declared and at that it was Callum's mouth that grew tight.

The Sentence was what, centuries ago, vampires carried out against their own who had human mates who they refused to denounce. A ruthless verdict which included the vampire tied to a stake and set alight in front of the human so she could see her mate's imminent death. Then the human was hung in front of the vampire so he could watch his mate swing before his own life was extinguished.

At the thought of Lucien's stunning mate dreaming that into reality, Callum bit out, "*Christ.*"

At that, Lucien shared, "She nearly strangled by hanging while doing nothing but lying in bed."

Callum looked to Leah and murmured with feeling, "I'm truly sorry."

"It's okay," she whispered.

But it wasn't.

He could see the memory of her fear hadn't faded and Lucien was no longer blanking his reactions. This had shaken him and he showed it visibly.

Another surprise for Callum and an indication of trust from Lucien.

It was Lucien's turn to change the subject. "She has other abilities."

Callum almost couldn't control his reaction to another trait Lucien's mate shared with his, but he did it.

"And those are?"

"The most important one, considering The Prophesies," Lucien answered. "She can sense danger."

Interesting, Callum thought.

But he asked, "Heightened senses? Hearing, smell, sight?"

"Not quite," Lucien answered, watching him closely. Correctly, Callum knew, assuming from Callum's earlier warning that Sonia had these gifts. "She simply can sense a threat in enough time to prepare should a situation be uncertain."

"That's fortunate," Callum remarked.

"It's more than fortunate," Lucien returned. "And it would help matters greatly if all the prophesied lifemates shared these abilities."

Callum decided to ease both their minds and disclosed, "Sonia dreams. She's done it all her life. She dreamed of me repeatedly years before she met me." He glanced at Leah and then to Lucien. "Leah knows of my people?"

Lucien nodded. "She knows."

This was surprising as well.

Werewolves, unlike most of the other immortals, shared their secrets with humans. However only with those they trusted implicitly, for instance, if their mate was human or they'd formed a friendship bond with someone they could trust. They were far more careful of sharing about other immortal cultures. In fact it was rare if they did because all of them guarded their own secrets, as well as the knowledge of other immortal beings, obsessively.

Vampires also interacted with humans, for obvious reasons, but did so under tight strictures, until recently. As with other immortals, however, if a vampire shared the knowledge of other immortal races, the vampire *and* the human would be hunted and put to death.

Simple as that.

Cold-blooded.

And, to Callum's thinking, totally fucking insane.

Callum jerked his chin at Leah before he continued, "Sonia met me as wolf when she was a child. She dreams of me as wolf too."

"Has she dreamed of danger?" Leah asked softly and Callum could thankfully shake his head.

"No," he replied.

Leah leaned slightly toward him. "I think, and Lucien agrees, as he mentioned before that these dreams tell the future. They don't tell what it *is*. They tell what it *could be*. For me, it was a warning which thankfully we were able to avoid. Now," her smile grew partly fond but mostly intimate, "I dream of something else. For Sonia," her smile changed, the intimacy left it and it became friendly, "well, obviously, she was dreaming of her future but," Leah's smile faded, "now that has occurred, they might become something else."

Callum's teeth clenched as Lucien took up the conversation. "You should know, shortly after Leah and I connected, I started to have her dreams."

"Fucking hell," Callum muttered, but it wasn't with displeasure.

He'd fucking *love* to know what Sonia was dreaming when she dreamed of him.

Lucien carried on, "It was vivid. It told a version of the future but it wasn't connected to me in a physical way where it could harm me, like Leah. It was just a further warning."

"This is good," Callum declared.

"It is," Lucien concurred on a small smile. "But, we'll need to monitor and share these dreams, obviously."

"Obviously," Callum agreed.

Leah turned to look at her mate and observed, "Sonia seems pretty settled here and it's safe for her. Perhaps she's had no need to exhibit abilities to sense danger."

"She has abilities," Callum announced and both Leah and Lucien turned to him. "Not like yours," he told Leah but carried on, "She has the sensory capabilities of wolf as human."

Callum heard Lucien pull in a breath.

Leah just stared at him blankly, so Callum explained, "Heightened hearing, sight and smell. She can also sense danger and unfortunately has had the opportunity to do so. But for Sonia, it's more. As it's nearly wolf, she has instincts. She can sense menace but she can also sense anything even if a presence is close but not a threat."

"Fucking excellent," Lucien murmured, for tactically it would be should The Prophesies unfold.

"I'm not done." The thread of pride veined his voice when Callum continued by telling them what he'd learned on the several hikes he'd taken with his queen. "Sonia has an affinity with wildlife. She thinks it's just animals but its more. She's at her most comfortable in natural surroundings. The animals sense her but find her no threat. Some even move to get closer to her. I reckon, if she developed this, she could call them to her, maybe even communicate with them."

"How cool," Leah breathed.

"Again, lupine," Lucien remarked thoughtfully.

"Not exactly," Callum replied. "We call to canis, wolves, jackals, dogs. Any other creature would sense us as predator. Sonia is not sensed as predator. She's sensed as one with any species be they wolf or bird or bear."

"How *cool!*" Leah exclaimed and Lucien smiled, likely to Leah's exuberance, but also to this fortunate news. Leah turned to her mate and said excitedly, "I hope I get something like that."

"You have it, sweetheart," Lucien replied and in doing so revealed.

"That would be?" Callum cut into their short conversation and Lucien's eyes came to him.

Forthright, he informed Callum, "She can mark me, communicate with me nonverbally and fight mesmerization for brief periods of time."

Callum didn't bother to hide his surprise. He whistled low.

If vampires had kings, Lucien would be theirs. He was more than an epic warrior, stronger than the lot. He had added abilities, some of which other vampires had, none of which they had with the strength and control Lucien did. He could read and control minds. He could also mark humans or immortals, which meant he could manipulate their heart rates and anticipate their actions.

If Leah even had a hint of these abilities, including fighting mesmerization, if developed, they could be powerful.

This was all fucking *excellent* news.

"It seems the fates have provided weapons for the vulnerable,"

Callum noted softly, realizing finally and with a sense of relief why his Sonia was gifted.

"Indeed," Lucien replied just as softly.

"We girlie girls might be able to help you big strong boys kick ass," Leah declared proudly and both Lucien and Callum grinned at her.

And after Lucien grinned at her, he turned her face to his for a brief kiss, which left Leah with that fond intimate look when he was done.

Then he looked back to Callum. "I wanted to speak of this without Sonia because Gregor suggested you hadn't told her about immortals and you didn't know about The Prophesies."

"This first is true," Callum disclosed.

"She thinks you're human?" Leah breathed in horror and Callum looked at her.

"No."

Leah let out a sigh of relief and said, "She knows you're a werewolf."

"No," Callum repeated, this time curtly.

Leah's brows drew together and she looked toward the door before she turned back to Callum and asked, "How long have you been together?"

"Six weeks."

Leah's eyes got wide and she mumbled, "Uh-oh."

Bloody hell.

There it was, just as he suspected. A female human's reaction indicating his protection would be considered a deceit.

"She's not like you, Leah. She's not grown up knowing her place in his culture," Lucien told his bride. "If I was in his position and I understood what was at stake with my mate, I would do the exact same thing."

Callum felt slightly better.

"Then you'd be in serious trouble too," Leah stated firmly.

Callum stifled a growl.

Lucien looked at Callum and said with the experience of an immortal male who lived with a female human, "It'll be fine, Callum."

Leah looked at Callum and said with the experience that simply *was* female human, "It will be, but only after she makes you put your tail between your legs, erm...no offense intended."

"Perhaps we can stop talking about this," Callum suggested in a way that stated clearly the wording was a courtesy, the words were a command.

Leah bit her lip.

Lucien's mouth twitched.

Callum stifled another growl.

"Your housekeeper's coming," Lucien finally noted and Callum would have kissed Mara for her timing if he didn't know Drogan would challenge him for doing so.

"Coffee!" Leah declared delightedly. Lucien chuckled and Callum smelled that Callista had, as usual, made him a gracious host because there was far more than coffee heading their way.

Mara arrived with a tray of coffee, platters of homemade cakes and biscuits, and admonishments of, "Callista is preparing a huge spread for lunch, don't fill up."

Sonia arrived while Leah was pouring her second cup and it was clear to see why her appearance was delayed.

She'd showered, put on light makeup, and her hair shown, falling in sleek waves over her shoulders and down her back, but the front was pulled back at her crown with a tortoiseshell oval threaded with a matching stick. She was wearing dusky-pink cords and she put on a belted, cream-colored cardigan that fell to her hips and had a shawl collar. The soft fall of material was heavy enough to open the front wide, exposing a skintight army green camisole underneath.

As she had when she met their guests in her robe at the door, but probably didn't realize, Sonia looked, from top to toe, the queen of a werewolf's castle.

They all stood when she arrived. Sonia moved toward Callum with a smile at their guests and he saw her claiming chain was hidden behind the material of her cardigan but her wedding rings shown more brightly than usual as if she'd cleaned them.

Callum's gaze turned to Leah's finger to see she too was wearing Lucien's symbols. Hers were black diamonds set in platinum, the engagement diamond was cut in an emerald shape rather than Sonia's solitaire. Although the diamond was smaller, the engagement ring was layered between two bands. One embedded with smaller baguette diamonds at the bottom, the other embedded with lustrous black onyx at the top.

At the sight, Callum instantly decided to send his mother out to get an accompanying band for Sonia. Something set with tiger's eye.

Sonia's fingers found his and threaded through when Leah noted, "You were right, Sonia, your coffee is *good*."

Sonia's smile deepened and he noticed she'd lost her earlier discomfiture now that she was groomed for company and her innate sociability was clearly in evidence. "It isn't mine. Mine's average. Callista is an artiste. Wait until you taste her cooking. You'll think you've died and gone to heaven."

At her innocent words, Callum's eyes caught Lucien's and he knew they both had gone tense.

For The Prophesies were known but they were far from clear. Therefore their mates' fates were unknown, and as humans, both could easily perish, and as immortals, both Lucien and Callum faced a desolate eternity if they did.

Unfortunately, Callum faced it anyway, sooner or later.

"Have you asked them to stay?" Sonia inquired of Callum, taking his mind from his dismal thoughts.

"No." Callum forced his smile. "But you just did."

"We couldn't," Leah cut in.

"You are," Sonia replied, firm but friendly. She let go of Callum's hand and moved to Leah. "Let me take you on a tour. You can pick a bedroom. There are twelve in total but *eight* of them are at the top of a *turret*. Five are taken, but trust me, the other three are *fantastic*."

Sonia guided Leah out of the room, tossing a seemingly carefree smile over her shoulder at Callum.

Leah walked with Sonia out of the room, tossing a genuinely carefree smile over her shoulder at Lucien.

The difference was miniscule but it bloody well existed.

"Callum," Lucien called softly as Callum glared at the door and he turned his head to the vampire.

Lucien didn't speak for several long moments, waiting until the women were well away, and when he finally did, it was low.

"I hesitate telling you but I feel you should know so you can prepare."

Callum remained silent when Lucien paused.

Then Lucien shared, "Gregor is hiding something from you."

Callum's gaze narrowed on the vampire. "Sorry?"

"He's hiding something about Sonia." Callum tensed and Lucien went on, "When he was explaining things, I sensed it. I didn't like it. After I read The Prophesies, I asked him about it and he told me neither you nor Sonia knew anything about The Prophesies. Later, I pressed him about it and he shared with me."

Callum didn't respond.

He knew about The Prophesies. He'd been told by Mac, though for reasons he didn't entirely understand and he didn't fucking like, he'd never been allowed actually to *see* them.

Before he could react to the knowledge Lucien had, Lucien got closer and his voice dipped lower.

Then he said with unconcealed emotion, "I'm sorry, my friend."

Callum felt that feeling; the one he reckoned was fear but this time it was piercing.

"Sorry for what?"

Lucien lifted a hand to grip Callum's biceps as if in an effort at containment. "Sorry to tell you that The Prophesies state your mortal's life will be a short one."

Callum's body jolted before it locked as this statement seared straight through his system.

Lucien went on quickly and quietly, his fingers holding fast. "The Prophesies are vague, simply stating her human life will be fleeting. I haven't told Leah and I suggest you do the same with Sonia."

"You lie," Callum whispered.

"I don't and why would I?" Lucien replied gently.

He wouldn't. There was no reason. They were in this together.

He yanked his arm from Lucien's grip and took a step back, recognizing that feeling *was* fear.

Definitely fear.

And alongside it ran a new, agonizing thread of pain.

"We'll fight it," Lucien vowed. It was a vow, no mistaking it from the vein of steel in the words. "I'd offer my services but Leah would hate it so I suggest you find a vampire to feed from her—"

"You've got to be joking," Callum growled at the very idea of a vampire feeding from his queen.

First, she was his fucking *queen*.

Second, she was *his* and no male would touch her for *any* reason.

Third, she was Sonia, not a meal.

And last, humans reportedly found the feeding of vampires a sensual experience. A *highly* sensual experience. A sensual experience his sexually responsive mate was not going to have.

Ever.

"We can ask a female vampire," Lucien proposed, reading Callum's thoughts, or perhaps understanding them for they'd be his own.

"It takes years of constant feeding for vampire saliva to work its magic," Callum noted dismissively. "And you suggested we don't *fucking have that.*"

"She'll survive until the war begins, Callum," Lucien returned. "We have time."

"Not enough," Callum bit out.

Not enough.

There had never been enough, but now, evidently, there was even fucking *less.*

His senses sought her in his castle. Opening up and reaching out, he found her somewhere on the second floor. Her discourse indistinct but there was laughter in her tone and it cut through him like a blade.

"Callum," Lucien murmured.

"You'll excuse me," Callum returned and didn't wait for a response. He was already exiting the room.

"This is troubling news but we'll fight it, Callum," Lucien called after him and made his vow official. "I vow it."

This didn't make Callum feel better.

"Tell Sonia I had something to attend to," he ordered. "I'll be gone awhile and I don't want her worried."

Again, he didn't wait for a response.

His skin was prickling and his blood was heating and he was finding it difficult to fight the urge to howl.

He walked out of the room into the entryway, down the hall to the back door. Tucking his wedding band into his pocket, at the back door he leapt to wolf and ran through the snow and into the wood, the only way he could soothe his ravaged thoughts.

Then he ran as wolf for hours in a failed effort to assuage the fear that had settled like a weight in his gut and the ache that tore at his heart.

When that didn't work and night had fallen, he sat in the snow at the rise at the side of his castle, his eyes on the light that came from the windows of the room he shared with his mate and he howled his inconsolable fury at the moon.

CHAPTER EIGHTEEN

DREAMS

CALLUM WALKED as wolf into the room he shared with Sonia.

The fire was ebbing but it still danced light throughout the room.

Her eyes fluttered then opened, she spied him and whispered, "Hello, puppy."

He sat by the bed watching her.

She grinned at him.

He continued watching her.

"Is my handsome wolf coming tonight?" she asked.

Callum growled, knowing he would be coming and she would be coming too, as hard as he could force her to do so.

Sonia blinked, slowly, dreamily, knowing herself that his thoughts would come true.

Her eyes drifted closed but her hand fell out as if reaching toward him.

He moved forward, slid his muzzle along her fingers, and in her sleep she smoothed her hand against him lovingly.

Tired of this type of affection and wanting a different kind, Callum turned from her and leapt to man.

As he approached the bed, her eyes fluttered open and focused on him.

Without a word, he slid the covers from her beautiful, naked body, and without hesitation, he covered that body with his own.

He pulled the hides back over them.

"Hi," she breathed.

Callum stared at her.

God, he loved her.

And he loved the fact that she loved him too.

And he loved the fact that she could express the enormity of that love in one two-letter word.

Therefore, he smiled.

Her arm wrapped around him as her other hand went up to touch his face. Her fingertips in his hair, her thumb glided along his brow, then down over this cheekbone, then down again along his bottom lip.

She watched her thumb and she did this as if fascinated.

Callum waited as she did this, also loving the feel of her memorizing his features like she did every time he came to her after he roamed.

However, he thought, as she did it, he should be memorizing hers for she would be gone from this earth long before he would.

She lifted her head from the pillow and placed her mouth against his, taking him from his thoughts. "Where have you been, my handsome wolf?"

Instead of answering, he glided his tongue along her lower lip.

Sonia shivered and opened her legs so his hips could fall through.

An invitation.

As ever, his greedy little queen wanted his cock.

Then she wrapped him lovingly, protectively, in her limbs. As ever, her movements were an eloquent indication of her adoration of more than his cock, of all that was him.

At the reminder of this, Callum growled against her mouth.

She shivered again underneath him.

His deep voice rough with approval, he said, "Always in heat, my little one."

"Only for you," she whispered, her breath catching, her heart racing, her skin warming, all without anything but his presence.

"What do you want?" he asked low, his hips pressing into hers, knowing, when he buried himself inside her, she'd be wet, slick, ready for him.

"You, inside me," she answered.

"Just like that?" he teased.

"You've been gone a while," she told him and arched her back. "I missed you."

He felt his face gentle.

He knew she missed it when he was gone, even if it was a minute, but especially when it was hours while he roamed.

He knew it because he missed her just the same.

He knew he shouldn't do it. He had so little time with her and he'd wish this time back when she was gone.

But he was wolf, he needed to roam.

Understanding her yearning for him in a way he was glad she'd never know just as he detested the fact that he carried that same yearning every moment and would hold on to it for eternity, he murmured softly, "Baby doll."

She was done talking. He knew this too as she pressed her lips against his, tightened her limbs around his body, lifted her hips into his, dug her nails into the muscles of his back, and begged, "Please, my handsome wolf, fuck—"

He didn't let her finish. He was done talking too.

His hips reared back, he heard her breath catch and he prepared to invade.

———

Sonia lay with her head on his shoulder, her fingers sifting lazily through the hair on his chest.

He loved it when she did that.

"You okay, little one?" His voice was still gruff from his orgasm and from other things besides.

He asked because he'd taken her hard, as usual, and she'd loved it, as usual.

But he didn't want her to ache.

"Mm," she murmured, her fingers tensing to drag her nails along his chest and her legs shifted against his, tangling with them, her body pressing closer, entwining with his.

Callum smiled.

She was okay.

She did this now, entwining her body with his, getting closer.

She did it often, now that she understood.

Now that she understood everything.

He thought he'd miss her before when she was gone.

Now, these times were exquisite torture.

"Cal," she called, her voice sounding like she sensed the turn of his thoughts.

"Yes, baby doll?"

Her hand flattened against his chest as if his skin could absorb it.

Or she could absorb something integral from his skin. Something she needed. Something she couldn't exist without.

Then she whispered, "You know I love you, right?"

He closed his eyes before his arm about her tightened and his other hand came across his chest to slide into the soft golden hair at the side of her head.

How could he ever not have fancied blondes?

Because, he knew, they were never *her*.

"I know, honey."

"You'll never forget?" she was still whispering.

His neck arched slightly but he forced his body to relax.

"I'll never forget."

She cuddled close and her hand slid across his chest to wrap around him tight. "I want you to promise to be happy but I don't want you ever to forget."

"I won't forget."

"Promise to be happy?"

Impossible.

"I promise."

"Thank you," she whispered.

"I love you, baby doll."

"I know," she said on a fluttering sigh and his chest got so tight, Callum found it hard to breathe.

They were running, roaming, as wolves, he and his mate.

Not Sonia.

A wolf.

She was fast and kept up with him, close to his right flank, where she always ran.

Callum took them deeper into the trees. They'd been running for hours. He could hear her pants. He knew he was pushing her. He knew what she wanted.

He kept pushing her, knowing the anticipation would be worth it.

How could he ever have imagined he'd feel content with a human queen?

Then again, he had no idea he was missing *this*.

Finally, he turned, headed for home, and he sensed her instant excitement.

He felt it too.

She was beneath him, on her belly, her long, thick, mahogany hair spread across her back, obscuring her face, tangled with pine needles. Her sweet, musky wolf scent assaulted him, coming from her hair, her skin, between her legs.

But there was something familiar about it. Something beautiful. Something nostalgic. Something he fucking *adored*.

He was up on his hands, giving his hips leverage to thrust into her wetness with savage brutality.

Her moans weren't filled with pain but each one a temptation to take her harder.

So he did.

"Spread your legs wider," he ordered.

She did as she was told.

"Tilt your ass, take all of me," he commanded.

Again, she did as she was told and he drove inside her then ground his hips between her spread-eagled legs and her moan was so deep, he could feel it vibrating against the tip of his cock.

That felt so fucking good, Callum ground into her deeper and he knew he couldn't take much more.

"Let go," he demanded, but she defied him, clenching her sex around his shaft in an effort to hold off her climax. He shifted his weight to one arm and twisted her dark hair around his fist, yanking it back, arching her neck, and driving her further down on his cock. "Let go, wolf."

He got off on calling her "wolf" as Sonia had done to him. He fucking *loved* it.

Her legs spread even wider. Her ass tilted further. He dropped his head and saw its perfection. Not an ass marred with pinpricks, a constant hideous reminder of his old mate's vulnerability and he felt a feeling of triumph so complete, the sight set him thrusting into her again.

Which was what she wanted.

"Harder, Cal," she breathed her demand, her voice barely a whisper, even he could hardly make out the words. "Fuck me harder."

He was losing control, his orgasm was coming and he knew it would be staggering.

With her, it always was.

The best he'd ever had.

"Goddamn it, *let go!*" he roared the instant her sex convulsed around his cock.

She lifted up on her own arms, propelling herself onto his shaft so intensely he feared he'd split her in two.

But she threw back her dark head, her hair flying over his hand still fisted in it, over his forearm, down her back, and she howled her release.

He pulled out and surged back in, burying himself to the root one last time, and then howled his own.

Callum woke with a start, still wolf, lying on his side in the snow under a pine tree.

The dream was still vivid. His skin under his fur heated not from his coat but from fucking the faceless, dark-headed she-wolf.

Fucking hell, he thought, coming to his paws, his mind troubled.

The parts of his dream were not syncing. So contradictory to each other, to his feelings for Sonia now, the deeper ones he had in his dream, the heartbreakingly deeper ones he felt from her. His instinct as wolf to be faithful to his mate abrading against the episode with the she-wolf, an episode so lucid, so fucking *real* it was like it happened.

Like he'd actually been disloyal to Sonia.

The thought was so vile he felt his gut roil and he started to run.

But he ran toward home.

Toward Sonia.

He leapt to man outside the back door, which was always open in case he or his family needed to roam, which was often.

He opened the door and mindlessly pulled on the clothes he left there when he'd transformed earlier.

He slid on his wedding band and was shrugging on a shirt while moving into the house when he noticed his mother there.

She was wearing a robe, her hair disheveled, her face as troubled as his thoughts.

Atypically, Callum had no time for his mother's troubled thoughts.

"Not now, Regan."

"Cal—"

Impatient to get to Sonia, he stopped and leaned in to her. "Not... *now.*"

Without another word or processing the look of distress on his mother's face, Callum took the stairs three at a time to get to his *wife.*

She was lying on her side, the fire ebbing but still dancing in the room. So like his dream it sliced through him.

But, unlike the dream, she was facing away from the door.

And she wasn't asleep.

He went immediately to the bed.

He sat next to her and put a hand to her hip over the hides.

"Baby doll," he whispered, cursing himself mentally for giving in selfishly to his instinct to roam. "Your injection—"

"I took it," she replied in a voice strangely flat. "Don't worry, Callum. I made sure Regan was in the room when I did."

He'd just run for hours, for miles, slept rough and run for miles again, and still his gut was tight. His thoughts a torment. Feelings of guilt and fear and grief all snaking insidiously through his brain.

He needed her.

"Sonia—"

She cut him off and her voice was still flat, so flat it sounded almost dead.

"Listen, Callum, I'm really tired, okay?"

"Baby doll—"

He stopped speaking when her body visibly tensed at his words and then he watched in grim fascination as she forced it to relax.

She rolled to look at him and Callum caught himself before he flinched.

Her eyes were as flat and dead as her voice.

What the fuck?

"I've been trying to get to sleep for a while and I can't do it. I nearly drifted off before you came in so, would you mind...?"

Worry was added to those snaking thoughts tormenting him.

He cupped her jaw with his hand. Her jaw tensed under his touch but her eyes never left his.

"What's the matter?" he asked.

"Nothing," she answered immediately. "Like I said, I'm just really tired."

She was lying.

He pulled her from under the hides into his arms and sat in the bed, back to the headboard, Sonia in his lap.

This felt better, tremendously better. Sonia in his lap, her body against his, her scent all around.

"Right," he said when his mind had finally settled. "Now, the truth this time. Tell me what's the matter."

She was looking at him but her eyes stayed flat, emotionless. Not blank, like they were when he told her she had to take her injection, but lifeless.

"Sonia—" he started, that fear edging back in but she interrupted him.

"Do you really want to know?" she asked as if she doubted that he really would.

"Of course I fucking want to know," he replied, beginning to lose patience.

"All right, Callum, I'll tell you," she stated. "I miss them all the time, but sometimes, I miss them more, and tonight, I miss them *loads*. That's what's the matter. That's why I can't sleep."

She was talking about her parents and he wasn't surprised her manner was listless. It was a defense mechanism, like her eyes going blank before getting the injection.

Missing her parents had to be worse, even than that fucking injection.

He slid a hand in her hair and pressed her cheek to his chest saying, "Honey."

"You should know, this happens a lot," she told his chest matter-of-factly.

"That's okay."

"If I have trouble sleeping, I'll find another room so I won't disturb you."

His fingers gripped her head and he said, "That's *not* okay."

"I like this room but really I don't mind."

He pulled her head away from his chest and maneuvered it so they were face to face before he growled, "I *do* mind."

He didn't know what he minded more, the thought that she would move somewhere else to sleep or the thought that she didn't mind not sleeping with him.

Something was fucking wrong and it was more than just thoughts of her dead parents. She liked to talk and she couldn't sleep and he'd never fucking get to sleep after what Lucien told him and that goddamned dream.

So they were going to talk.

"I need you to explain something to me," he announced and her eyes slightly narrowed in confusion.

"Callum, it's the middle of the night."

"You're awake. I'm awake. We're talking," he told her and she sighed.

Not a fluttering sweet sigh. An annoyed, I'm-putting-up-with-Callum sigh.

"All right, Callum, what do you want *me* to explain?" she asked, a sarcastic emphasis on "me," which made his already tight gut tighten sharply.

He ignored it.

"When we had our discussion after Regan returned my wedding band..." he began and felt her body get stiff against his but he ignored that too and carried on, "You said, when you gave me my ring, you didn't know if it meant something to you. Then you said it did. I'd like you to explain that."

"Would you *like* me to explain that, in, say, I have a *choice* as to whether I do or not? Or are you *telling* me to explain that, in, say, I have *no* choice as to whether I do or not?"

Her questions were a quagmire in which he knew, if he gave the wrong answer, he'd find it very difficult to extricate himself.

Therefore, he answered carefully, "I'm asking you to explain it, Sonia."

She stared at him.

He waited.

She pulled in breath and said in a voice that was no longer flat but defiant, "All right, I will. You can be very kingly," she told him absurdly for he was bloody well a king. "I've realized now, with time, that this is *you*, but back then it worried me because when you get kingly, you forget I exist. This bothered me and I suspected you didn't care anything for me but only your duty to me as your queen."

Callum's jaw tightened before he clipped, "Tell me you're fucking joking."

"I'm not," she replied instantly. "I'd never been around a king so of course I didn't get it. But even after you claimed me, which in my people's world is a pretty significant thing, and as I've been told time and again by *your* people is an even *more* significant thing, you forced me into a shower. Then into a car. And then you didn't speak to me for hours. I melted from your world." She stared at him calmly and finished,

"I think it was five, ten minutes after you'd made me yours when you forgot I existed except as your duty to put me in the truck and take me down the mountain." She continued to stare at him a moment before aiming dead on target and hitting a bulls-eye. "That, Callum, didn't feel very good."

He could imagine it didn't and he *did* do that to her.

Exactly as she said.

Except for the fact that she ceased to exist.

"Sonia—"

"No," she interrupted him, still calm. "I get it now. You don't have to worry. I get it. You had a lot on your mind, more than I knew or understood. Now I understand. I was being selfish."

No longer angry, he explained gently, "You weren't being selfish. You didn't understand what was going on."

"Well, yes, true, but now I do so it's not a big deal, okay?"

He slid his fingers through her hair while he said softly, "Baby doll."

Her body tensed and she asked, without a flat voice, without calm, sounding impatient and annoyed. *Not* adorably impatient and annoyed but something different. Edgier, angrier but almost desperate, "Now that I've explained that, can I try to get some sleep?"

Something was still wrong. Something she wasn't giving him. Something she was holding back.

Knowing that, suddenly he asked, "Do you love me?"

She instantly sucked in breath and tried to pull away.

His arms got tight.

She started struggling.

He registered his surprise at her actions and his gut registered worry when she just as suddenly stopped.

She'd been pushing against his chest with both hands but she bent her elbows, bowed her back, and dropped her forehead to rest on them.

"Yes," she whispered to his chest, uttering that one word in a way that sounded like it was torn from her. But the chest she muttered into felt like iron bands, bands that had been clamped tightly around it for centuries, were finally released so Callum could, for the first time in his life, actually breathe. "Yes," she repeated in a whisper to his chest as he looked down at her hair shining in the firelight. "I fell in love with you during my first dream when I was seventeen. And I fell in love with you all over again Christmas Eve when you wiped the tears from my face during the general's scene in *White Christmas*."

Without willing them to do so, his arms crushed her to him, forcing her body flat against his, her arms caught between them, her face coming up to rest against his neck.

All of his torment was lost in his current sense of triumph.

And he could tell her now he was wolf.

"Sonia, baby doll—"

She pressed her face against his neck and her body against his, "Please, Callum, *please*. Can I *please* just go to sleep? *Please*."

He lifted a hand and trailed his fingers along her hairline, curling them in at her jaw to pull her hair away from her neck.

"Has it been bad tonight, missing your parents?" he asked quietly.

She pressed deeper into him and her fingers, like in his dream, tensed in his chest hair, her nails dragging through it. This caught at his memory, pulling up his guilt at fucking the she-wolf, glorying in her faultless ass, calling her by Sonia's pet name for *him* as he ground into *her*, betraying his own mate even if it was only in his unconscious mind.

"Yes," she whispered, "it's been bad."

It had been bad.

And he'd been gone, leaving her to face her sorrow alone while he selfishly, no, as she put it, *kingly* focused on his own thoughts instead of protecting his mate.

"I'm sorry, little one. Of course you can go to sleep."

She pressed even closer and said with feeling, "Thank you."

He exited the bed, taking her with him and placing her under the hides. Then he took off his clothes and joined her there. He pulled her into his arms and she acted as if she'd resist at first before she relaxed and melted into him.

Then, surprisingly, considering she said she'd had so much trouble getting to sleep, she drifted off quickly.

And, with Sonia close, Callum could set his thoughts in order.

No, with Sonia close, his queen, his mate, who *loved* him, had loved him for decades but who *he'd* made fall in love with him on Christmas

Eve (which would, forever, be *his* favorite fucking holiday), Callum could finally set his thoughts in order.

He had a victory celebration tomorrow.

Then he'd tell his *wife* he was wolf.

Then he'd give her a Mating *and* a fucking wedding because she was human and she deserved it, but also because she loved him and he'd tie himself in knots to give her everything she desired for as long as she was breathing on this earth.

Then he'd talk with Lucien and Gregor in an effort to create a strategy on how to beat The Prophesy that said her life would be shortened.

In the meantime, he'd make every fucking moment count.

And the dream...

At first he thought it was Sonia's dream, as Lucien said he had Leah's and he could see how she fell in love with him if that was how she dreamed of them together. For, if he'd had that dream without knowing her, he'd have fallen in love with her too.

It was better than what they had an hour ago even if you told him that he wouldn't have believed it.

It was what, he determined, they would have starting from now.

It was *everything*.

But it couldn't be her dream, obviously.

So, it was just a dream.

Not foreshadowing of the future.

Sonia turned in his arms.

He followed her, tucking the back of her body into the front of his and wrapping his arms around her.

Unconsciously in her sleep, like she did after her injection, her hands slid along his forearms but this time the fingers of both laced with his.

His fingers tightened in hers and he smiled into her hair.

So deep in thought, he didn't notice her left hand was bare.

He also hadn't noticed her wedding rings sitting on her nightstand.

It took some time but finally Callum, with his queen wrapped safe in his arms, followed her to sleep.

"Wake up, honey, we have company and we've got a celebration to attend," Callum whispered in her ear.

Sonia's eyes fluttered. They focused hazily on him and he saw the hunger flow into them before she blinked, her body jerked, and she got up on an arm, pulling the hides to her chest.

"Good goodness," she breathed. "Leah and Lucien, I should..."

She trailed off and looked around the room as Callum stared at her, stunned by her behavior.

She always wanted play in the morning, even if she was sleepy.

"Sonia," he called and she blinked again and looked at him sitting on the edge of the bed, "Are you okay?"

"Yes, fine, um...yes," she stammered and then twisted so her back was to him, threw the hides aside, and swung her legs off the bed.

She was heading to the bathroom when his eyes narrowed and his temper frayed.

"Sonia," he repeated and she stopped and turned to him, clearly distracted.

"Yes?"

"Come here," he ordered.

She stilled then asked, "What? Now?"

Callum's temper frayed a little more.

This wasn't, exactly, what he thought their lives would be like after she'd admitted she loved him.

And this wasn't, at all, what he'd determined they'd be like, which was what they were like in his dream.

"Yes," he said evenly. "Now."

She pulled breath into her nostrils and walked to him.

The minute she was within arm's reach, he hooked an arm around her hips and pulled her into his lap.

When she settled, he looked down at her and clipped, "Before you start your day, would you at least like to give your king a fucking good morning kiss?"

She stared at him in shock, like she'd never kissed a man before and the very idea was repugnant to her and she'd fucking kneeled between his legs and took his cock into her mouth not a week ago.

His temper disintegrated and he hissed, "What in *the* fuck?"

She looked into his eyes, her face paled, and she declared loudly, "Callum, I'm freaking out!"

It was his turn to blink and he did it slowly.

"Sorry?"

"Today, I'm going to...there are going to be lots of your..." She swallowed then, her voice filled with panic, she cried, "*What if I do something wrong?*"

He stared at her a moment before he burst out laughing, pulling her close in his arms as he did so.

"This isn't funny!" she wailed through his laughter. "I'm representing you and Regan and Caleb and Calder and *you* and Ryon and even *your dad*!"

His fingers slid into her hair and he pulled her head back and brushed her mouth with his.

It was like he'd not moved when she stated, "I need a shower."

"Honey, calm down."

"Calm..." She shook her head as if clearing it. "No, really, Callum, I need a shower. I need to be alone, get my thoughts straight, sort my head out. I'll be fine. I just need a long hot shower."

Callum grinned and informed her, "You can have your shower, little one, you just have to earn it."

She went stiff in his arms and her face again paled. "Earn it?"

His grin deepened. "Yes. Earn it."

"How do I...?" She paused and tested his arms by pushing against them. They tightened so she gave up and he tried not to laugh as she finished, "Earn it?"

"You can choose two of three things," he stated.

"Two of three—"

"First," he cut her off and dipped his head to mark her hair with his temple before he said at her ear, "You can tell me you love me again."

She stilled in his arms.

He ignored it and went on, lifting his head to look at her. "Second, you can describe one of your dreams about me."

She stared at him in horror.

He grinned and ignored that too.

"Third, you can kiss me." He rested his forehead to hers and concluded, "Now, pick two."

"Can I do one now and one—?"

He lifted his head then shook it. "Two."

She glared at him.

Then she snapped, "Dream."

When she said no more, he gave her a squeeze, bit back his smile, and encouraged, "Go on."

"Well, the last one I had," she hesitated and revised, "the last *real* one went like this." She sat up straighter in his lap and turned fully to him. "I was sleeping and my puppy, um...that would be my wolf. You know, the one I told you I met when I was a child?"

She waited for him to nod. He did, his amusement diminishing and his mouth tightening about the fact that he *still* hadn't told her he was her "puppy" as she went on.

"Anyway, he always comes to me in the dreams first. So he came to me. I was sleeping. I woke up and he was beside the bed. I said hi to him and he sat down. I asked where you were and then closed my eyes. Then I opened them and my puppy was gone but you were there. I felt the covers slide down me and..."

Callum's body tightened as she continued, explaining, to every last detail, the dream he'd had last night.

"Then you start to...you know and I woke up," she finished.

Callum stared at her.

She stared back.

Her brow furrowed and she whispered, "What?"

"That's your dream?"

She bit her lip, released it, and continued quietly, "I told you they weren't actually sexual, as such. It probably doesn't seem like very much to you but...you have to *feel* it."

Oh, he'd felt it.

He'd fucking felt it.

"What about after we have sex?" he demanded to know.

Her brows drew together in confusion and she repeated, "What?"

"You never dream of us having sex. But what about when you dream about us *after* we've had sex?"

"I've never dreamed of that."

He stared at her, trying to assess if she was lying.

She still looked confused but serious.

"Never?" he pushed.

"Never. Why do you—?"

"You never dream of us lying together, telling me you love me and never to forget it?"

Her face paled again and she whispered, "No, Callum, I've never dreamed of that."

At once distracted and needing to find Lucien, completely forgetting Sonia's explanation of how it made her feel when he lost sight of taking care of his mate, Callum ordered, "Kiss me."

"Wh-what?"

His eyes focused irately on her. "Sonia, kiss me."

"But—"

"Fucking do it."

She jerked in his arms.

Then she did it. Her hands curling around his neck, she pressed her lips against his quickly and then just as quickly, she pulled away.

"Now tell me you love me," he demanded.

"But you said only two—"

"Sonia," he warned, impatient to talk to Lucien.

She stared at him and he was so preoccupied he didn't notice the life ebbing from her always lively eyes nor did he notice her flat voice when she said, as if by rote, "I love you, Callum."

He touched his lips to her forehead, stood, putting her on her feet, and he strode from the room.

Therefore he wasn't there when Sonia stared at the door, her lips trembling, silent tears sliding down her cheeks.

And he wasn't there when she snatched her rings from the nightstand and she dug until she found her stuffed wolf and tore it from under the covers.

And he wasn't there when she walked by the fire Callum had stoked that morning and blindly threw the rings and the wolf into the fire.

But Sonia was so blinded by emotion that, luckily, her stuffed wolf bounced off the side and onto the floor to come to rest, unharmed, under the couch.

And her rings bounced too, but fell into the fire, landing safely to glint in the firelight at its edge.

"Callum, I really need a moment to speak to you," Regan pleaded, following her infuriated son down the stairs.

In response, not missing an enraged step, Callum asked, "Where's Sonia?"

"Callum, hold still a second and—"

Callum did as his mother told him, stilling then swinging around to face her. "I asked you, where *the fuck* is my *fucking queen?*"

Regan took one look at him and stepped up and away from him.

Then she straightened her shoulders and stated, "Callum, something's wrong. I know. I can see it. I felt it yesterday but I need to explain something to you. Something important. Something you must know *right now.*"

Callum's hand clenched around the rings he'd found in the fire while he searched for his mate and his mind thrashed with the memories of his *wife* laughing, talking, joking with his people, all day. Cheering, drinking, eating, clapping, dancing, making them fall in love with her.

But she'd done all of this far away from him.

Far, *far* away.

She'd ridden silently in the truck beside him as he took her into town but almost the instant they arrived she melted into the crowd.

And they'd accepted her gladly. The day having the feel of *two* celebrations. One of victory, one at their luck that Callum's queen was so fucking perfect.

He'd heard it time and again, his people telling him of the widespread talk of her notes to the kin of the fallen. The stories that had gone far and wide of her taking their women into her home and, together, waiting out the battle as she demonstrated strength of will, instilling hope in their females' hearts. How brilliant they thought it was that she, a human, proudly displayed his chain around her hips as she did that day and *every* day. The chain flaunted boldly outside her cords, his people not knowing it was *Callum's* fucking idea in the first fucking place.

And Sonia's high spirits were evident every moment during the celebration. Clearly up for anything, his Sonia, drinking copious amounts of cider. Tasting every bit of food sold by the vendors. Laughing with abandon. Grabbing handfuls of huge, yellow and gold wolf-head-shaped confetti. Throwing it in the air and giggling as it drifted all around her and those close to her, in her hair, their hair, floating to the pavement, only for her to grab more and do it again as his wolves watched her worshipfully or joined in. Kneeling low to wrap her arms around pups and hold their wrists safely away as they twirled sparklers, all the while gleaming up at the pups' parents as they stared down at her dotingly. Linking her arm with Leah's, their blonde heads, the only blondes in the crowd, bent together as they talked low and giggled with each other. Not as if they'd known each other a day, but as if they'd known each other a lifetime while the she-wolves smiled at their camaraderie but the wolves watched them with hungry eyes.

But the minute Callum would start to get near to share the day with his enthusiastic fun-loving queen was the minute she'd move away. He kept getting caught in the revelry making it easy for her to escape.

And she was escaping. There was no doubt about it.

So much, when night had fallen, she'd eventually disappeared from town, and when he searched for her, he couldn't find her. No one had seen her, of the numerous people he asked, until one of his guard told him another had taken her, for some unknown reason, to the castle.

But when he arrived at the castle, concerned at her disappearance, but more, the meaning behind it, he found she was not there.

And thorough was his search. So he found the rings he'd given her had been tossed into the fire.

Now, his mother *was* there and he could hear more trucks arriving. He could sense a large number of wolves, probably smashed and looking for fun because the main celebrations were over as the fireworks had gone off as planned. But they'd gone off without their king being there to witness them, or their queen, for no one knew where the fuck *she* was.

Twisted with this were the thoughts of what Lucien told him about how Leah's dreams would be events in which she participated, nearly real, but Lucien dreamed more, more events, more detail of their plight. He participated too, in his dreams. He participated in things Leah *never fucking dreamed.*

Like Callum dreamed last night of betraying his queen with a wolf, the first of his kind to ever fuck around on his mate.

"No," he answered his mother. "*Right now* I need to find my fucking *wife.*"

As he stalked to the entryway, he heard more trucks were arriving and there were voices on the steps. He could hear Caleb, Ryon, both sounding irate, and Lucien's voice, cooler, controlled, but cautiously so. And another, a voice he knew, it was familiar, but Callum didn't take a moment to process it.

Because none of the voices were Sonia.

However he smelled her there and he was going to have a word, or likely several of them, with his queen.

He threw open the door, his mother on his heels, and he stopped and stared at the scene.

Ryon, Caleb, and Lucien were standing shoulder to shoulder at the top of the steps and there were eight of Callum's guard, four flanking each of the sides.

At a quick glance from Callum, there were in the drive seventy wolves, not his wolves, not his guard, lined at the bottom facing off, clearly on the offensive, in attack formation against them.

Automatically, Callum assessed the six to one ratio and the fact that this, for his wolves, was not a problem.

Titium, Desdemona's father, was standing three steps up wearing a face like thunder.

The distant sounds of town still locked in drunken carousing could be heard through the utter silence.

Fucking hell.

Callum noticed Sonia and Leah, both standing close together to the side of the top landing, eyes riveted to the men, and Regan moved toward them.

"Nice you could join us," Ryon remarked dryly.

Callum ignored his cousin and speared Sonia with a glance. Her already pale face grew paler when she caught it and he slid his hand into the pocket of his cords, depositing his mate's wedding rings there.

Rings he never expected her to take off because first, she fucking *shouldn't* and *knew* she shouldn't, and second, because of how she behaved when *he* did.

Rings he never expected her to throw in the fire and he couldn't bloody well imagine why she did.

It was like she'd taken off her claiming chain and thrown it in the fire.

An act which was unforgivable.

He walked between Ryon and Lucien and down three steps toward Titium.

At his bold advance, the entire assemblage tensed and several wolves started to crouch.

He heard Sonia's intake of breath.

It was only that which made him stop.

"What's the meaning of this?" he asked Titium.

"I'm challenging you," Titium replied idiotically and Callum fought back a frustrated sigh.

"Fuck me," Caleb muttered in annoyance and Titium's infuriated eyes flashed to Callum's brother.

"*Look at me!*" Callum's voice whipped out like a lash and the tense group tensed further and at once he sensed fear from some of Titium's wolves.

The smart ones.

However belatedly so as Callum would punish them all for their insurrection.

Titium's eyes sliced back to him.

"You sequestered my daughter," Titium accused.

"I did," Callum agreed.

"It's unthinkable," Titium snarled.

Was he mad? He had to know what the crazy bitch had done.

Further, what she hadn't.

"What's unthinkable is what her inattention caused, Titium. *That's* unthinkable," Callum stated. "Desdemona should have had worse and you know it, now she's getting the attention she needs."

"My daughter is not mad," Titium declared, visibly working himself up. Still spoiling his daughter and she wasn't even fucking *there*.

"She refused to seek her mate," Callum returned.

"She was a little busy doing her duty for her king!" Titium shot back.

"Not very well," Callum replied. Titium started to crouch, and Callum warned, "You don't want to do that. She'll need you when she's out."

Titium's eyes narrowed angrily and he snorted derisively, "You think you can best anyone."

"That's because I can," Callum stated calmly.

Titium's legs bent deeper. "You—"

"She's unwell," Sonia stated from behind them and Callum sensed, rather than saw, Sonia move their way.

That was when he sighed and only just stopped himself from rolling his eyes to the heavens.

After he found out what was in her head *this time* he was going to smack that sweet ass of hers until it was red for her latest inappropriate behavior.

For now she knew. Mara and Callista had been instructing her on royal protocol, not to mention *he* had told her on several occasions how she should behave. This might not be official but she knew to keep her mouth *shut*.

"Sonia, be quiet and stay where you are," Callum ordered.

She defied him. He heard her boots coming closer as he smelled her scent getting sharper.

Surprisingly, Titium's eyes moved to Sonia and his face gentled before he said, "My argument is not with you, little queen."

"I know," Sonia said softly, stopping wisely just out of arm's reach of her mate. "But, I saw her, sir. She is not well."

"She's crazy as a fucking loon," Caleb muttered and Sonia twisted.

"Quiet, Caleb, that isn't helping," she whispered.

"She is," Caleb returned.

Sonia sucked in breath and turned back to Titium before resuming. "Callum didn't want to do it, but you have to know, the results of her... um, lack of concentration were disastrous."

"There are things you likely don't know, little queen," Titium told her.

"I know them." She was still speaking softly but now her words were pained. "Please, come into the castle. We'll sit down and talk. This doesn't need to get heated."

"It should have gotten heated centuries ago," Titium replied, Sonia tensed as did Callum.

"Centuries—?" she whispered but Titium kept talking.

"He misused her," Titium announced, his face hardening and his eyes moving back to Callum, and Callum, in preparation, removed his own wedding band and slid it in his pocket with Sonia's. "As he did many a she-wolf. Misused her knowing how she felt about him and he set her aside and didn't look back. Not like she was daughter to a warrior, but like she was nothing but a paid tart."

"Enough," Callum ordered as he felt Sonia's tension intensify.

"Mac was a decent king, loyal to his mate, like the wolf," Titium's voice declared proudly before it turned snide. "You, with your sweet human, won't last for more than—"

"*Enough!*" Callum thundered.

Titium started crouching and declared, "It'll never be enough. Not until you're brought low."

"Don't do this!" Sonia shouted, sensing the escalation, her panic palpable.

"I should have done it ages ago!" Titium shouted, definitely as mad as his daughter and just as adept at hiding it.

"Ry, get Sonia out of here!" Callum demanded as he watched Titium's skin darken, the change was coming.

And then it happened.

Titium crouched, Callum following, and Sonia screamed, "*Don't!*"

Both wolves leapt as Sonia moved, faster than any human he'd seen, within a blink of an eye she was between them. Like she was when he was wolf and she was a child, throwing herself in front of him to protect him, but this time stopping what would have been face to face.

But by the time she arrived, he was no longer there. He'd changed, and to avoid her, at the last second, he leaped over her head.

Titium's reflexes weren't as swift and he'd reached out a set of claws through the transformation in an effort at catching Callum unaware.

So by the time Callum landed on a skid at the foot of the steps and turned, Sonia was down, her body facing him. Titium was standing over her as wolf, panting and pawing the step beside her as if trying to help her.

Her head was up, her neck twisted, and she was staring at Titium, mouth open in shock.

Then her head turned and Callum saw blood trickling from her temple where it had cracked against the steps and at the sight he growled.

But he didn't move because her eyes were wide as she gaped at him as wolf, face to face with her "puppy."

Her expression changed. She winced in pain but Callum knew it was the pain of betrayal.

She took in a breath that sounded both surprised and ragged before she lost consciousness. In so doing, she fell forward and rolled down a step as Callum tensed to leap but he stopped when Sonia came to rest on a wide step with her back facing him, Titium's claw marks oozing blood through her jacket.

Titium's men behind him all shuffled back at the sight of their fallen bleeding queen.

But Callum didn't notice.

He howled his fury and his muscles bunched to attack.

However Titium howled as well but Titium's howl wasn't fury.

It was the fucking tone of surrender, which meant Callum couldn't bloody well attack when his mouth salivated to tear into the wolf's throat.

In the seconds that transpired, Ryon, Caleb, and the guard had leaped into wolves. Ryon and Caleb were prowling, snarling, and circling Sonia's prone body. Callum's guard was at the foot of the steps, snapping at Titium's men to warn them back.

Lucien, with lightning vampire speed, ran to Sonia, carefully lifted her in his arms, and again like a flash, he was up the steps, disappearing into the castle.

Callum, as wolf, bounded after him.

There were *way too many* fucking people in the room.

Sonia lay on their bed on her belly, her head to the side, her weight pressed into her forearms, cords still on, but back bared as Orphenon saw to her.

Younger brother to one of his guard, Orphenon was also simply a young wolf, being only a century and a half old. But his calling made him a human doctor currently practicing in Glasgow. He'd come to be with his brother for the celebrations, his brother was one of the eight who'd witnessed the scene, and after had called Orphenon in for human medical attention.

Luckily, Orphenon had learned that anything could happen anywhere and he brought his doctor's kit with him to town.

He'd cleansed the wounds at Sonia's back and head and had injected her to numb the pain as he stitched the claw marks together when she regained consciousness while he was still stitching.

She'd panicked, fear filling her face, and started to resist, causing tearing at her stitches when she did so. It took some effort before they could calm her enough for Orphenon to administer to her.

However, it was only Leah who could calm her and only Leah who she'd allow to touch her.

Only the human.

His cunning little queen, she could smell the difference in them now.

The rest of them, *all* of them—including Callum and every last one of his family were in the fucking room—she stared at with wary silent fear that didn't even begin to mask the pain she felt at their treachery.

As Orphenon stitched and Leah sat on the side of the bed holding her hand, Callum saw his mate's mouth get tight. Then he saw Leah start to wince repeatedly as Sonia's hand squeezed hers with each insertion of the needle.

But she still remained silent.

"She's feeling it," Callum growled to the wolf.

Orphenon stopped and leaned closer to Sonia's ear. "Sonia, do you feel what I'm doing?"

She didn't speak, simply closed her eyes tight.

Orphenon noted this, his eyes slid to Callum, and he muttered, "I'll administer another dose."

Callum watched the doctor inject another dose of the anesthetic and Sonia flinch when he did but he spoke to his mother as it was happening.

"Get everyone out of here."

"Callum, sweetheart, we're worried and Sonia needs her family close," Regan demurred and she was right.

In times of trouble for wolf, family would always be there.

"She's not wolf. She's uncomfortable with this. Get them out," Callum ordered.

"Cal—"

Finally, he turned to his mother and barked, "*Out!*"

Sonia jumped at his tone, the fear in her eyes escalating, and Callum gritted his teeth.

"The vampire should remain," Orphenon noted. "He could be useful. He can monitor her heartbeat."

At that, Sonia's eyes widened and she moved, skittering on her forearms up the bed, fleeing and protecting her nudity at the same time she cringed and her eyes flew about the room in a panic, trying to source the vampire.

"I can report her heartbeat is erratic, now she knows I'm vampire," Lucien drawled with irritated dryness.

"Whoops," Orphenon mumbled. "Didn't know."

"Calm, Sonny," Leah cooed, scooting urgently up the bed with her. "It's okay. Lucien's okay. He's good people. They're *all* good people and they're worried about you. Just calm down and let the doctor see to you."

Sonia's eyes moved to Leah. She took in a breath and held it before she let it out and nodded, settling again.

"Regan—" Callum warned.

"All *right,*" his mother snapped, approached the bed.

Sonia's terrified eyes watched her as she did so, and his mate's body tensed, preparing to flee.

Regan saw it, felt it, and her face gentled even as tears filled her eyes. She leaned toward the bed and stopped moving closer.

"Sonny, sweetie, I'm just downstairs if you need anything," his mother told his mate.

Sonia didn't reply.

Regan made a sound that was half whimper, half sob. Her wet eyes moved to Callum and then she left.

Callum's glance sliced to his brethren, his order nonverbal but understood all the same.

Caleb approached the bed next only for Sonia to have the exact same reaction, so he stopped.

"Hey, sis," he called in a tender tone and Callum was surprised for he had no idea Caleb even had a tender tone.

However, his words and tone had opposite to the desired effect on Sonia as her expression filled with a different kind of pain and she shut her eyes.

Not deterred, Caleb went on, "It's doesn't look bad, darlin', probably feels it though. You'll be sparring with Callum again in no time."

Sonia made no response and kept her eyes closed.

Caleb, too, looked at Callum, jaw clenched, and exited the room.

Ryon didn't approach as Sonia kept her eyes closed.

But he spoke to Callum, "I couldn't have had any idea she'd learn like that."

Callum turned cool eyes to his cousin. "Shit *always* happens, Ryon." When Ryon's face grew hard, Callum went on, "But it wasn't you who didn't tell her. It was me. You bear no responsibility and you know I'll sort it. You go down and see how Magnum is handling Titium and his wolves."

Ryon nodded and with one last glance at Sonia he too left.

When Callum looked back at her, Sonia's eyes were open and her expression clearly stated she'd heard him and it was doubtful his job of sorting his mistake would be quick and easy.

Callum sighed.

Lucien moved to leave, Orphenon's head came up, and his mouth opened to speak.

Lucien got there before him. "She's frightened. I'm doing more harm than good being here."

Orphenon nodded and went back to work. Lucien cut a reassuring look to Callum, a gentle one to his bride, then he left as well.

Callum stood at the side of the bed, arms crossed, legs planted wide, and watched, impatient, as Sonia's wounds were closed.

Finally, Orphenon clipped the last thread, smoothed some medicine on the wounds and bandaged her back loosely. Throughout this, he spoke in low comforting doctor's tones to Sonia even as he cleaned his mess and packed his bag.

The whole time Sonia stared blankly at the pillow or her eyes sought Leah's for support.

Packed up and ready to go, Orphenon got close to Callum.

"The wounds on her back are deep but still superficial. As you can see, he didn't even score her with his fourth claw which means the swipe was light." Callum, who listened to this without looking from Sonia, nodded once. "I'm more concerned about that bump she had to her noggin," Orphenon announced, clearly a different kind of doctor than Sonia's specialist, for his wording was meant to be humorous and reassuring. "She was out for a while. You'll need to wake her frequently in the night. She'll have a headache which is expected. The pain shouldn't be extreme and if she experiences dizziness, lethargy, double-vision, I'll want to know immediately. Yes?"

Sonia watched the doctor the entire time he spoke, her face registering nothing.

"Yes," Callum agreed tersely.

The doctor went on, "I'll leave some pain pills with Regan. Once the anesthetic wears off, she'll experience some discomfort." Callum felt a muscle jerk in his jaw before Orphenon finished encouragingly, "In a few weeks she'll be good as new and your queen will dance at your Mating."

Sonia's eyes closed again, this time tightly.

"Thank you," Callum bit out but the words were unintentionally ungracious.

"My pleasure to be of service to my king and my queen," Orphenon mumbled, took one last look at Sonia, and exited the room.

Leah glanced at him and tilted her head, giving him a small smile before she turned and leaned in to Sonia.

"I'm going now, Sonny," she said and Sonia's eyes flew open.

Sonia looked at Leah, then Callum, then Leah, and she shook her head frantically, clutching tight to Leah's hand.

Leah brought their hands to her chest and leaned farther toward his mate.

"It's okay. You're okay. You just need to rest, get some sleep if you can, be with your mate," Leah told her but Sonia kept shaking her head and Leah's voice dropped when she continued, "Tomorrow, after you've had some rest, we'll talk. I'll explain a few things." Leah grinned at her. "I'll tell you my story. It's a good one," she confided as if sharing an exciting morsel of gossip before she concluded, "But you'll understand a whole lot more once you've heard it."

Sonia gazed at her new friend then her eyes went blank, she nodded and released Leah's hand.

Leah bit her lip as she tucked Sonia's hair behind her ear. Then she sighed, stood, and walked to Callum. She touched his hand briefly while giving him another small smile then she walked through the room and closed the door behind her.

Once he heard the click of the door in the latch, Callum moved to the bed.

Sonia lay motionless, all but her eyes, which watched him.

He put a knee to the bed and settled carefully on his side, up on a forearm, close to her immobile body, and cautiously he reached out and laid a hand flat against the small of her back above her cords.

She turned her face away.

"Baby doll, look at me," he ordered gently.

Sonia didn't move.

Callum decided not to push it even though he disliked her resting her head on its injured side.

He slid down the bed so his head was in his hand, his elbow in the pillow, his body nearly brushing hers as he leaned forward, and way too late whispered his secret in her ear.

"I'm a werewolf. My people are werewolves. As you know, I'm their king, as my father was before me, his father before him."

Her body tensed tighter and tighter with each word he spoke, but other than that she didn't move.

His hand slid along her skin to curl his fingers around the side of her waist and he continued, "I'm immortal. I'm three hundred and eighty-three years old. I was there that night thirty-one years ago when your parents died. I was there on instinct, to protect you because you were alone. I'd got shot because I'd gotten cocky and *you* ended up protecting *me*."

No movement, no sound.

Callum pulled in breath.

Then he kept going, "Werewolves are not what you think we are, not what you've seen in movies. We don't change only during a full moon, we can change whenever we want and change back just the same. You can shoot us with silver bullets and our flesh will just eject it and heal. We live our lives in wolf settlements, like the town, or amongst humans. Like humans, we try to do no harm and we mean no ill-will to anyone. As you've seen, my people are kind and friendly, different than yours in many ways, but none of them bad."

No response.

Callum kept going, belatedly sharing with his queen information he should have told her weeks before. "We're born wolves. We have no capacity to make humans into wolves with a bite. No one understands truly how we came about, though there's a great deal of research that's been done. We do know we've evolved from wolves, unlike vampires, which you've learned also exist, who evolved from humans. There's no magic, nothing supernatural, nothing sinister, we're of nature, just like you. A she-wolf gives birth and a pup grows, slower than a human child, five years for wolf to every one for a human. Then we lock in our development somewhere in our late thirties and we never show any signs of further aging."

Still, no reaction.

"Honey, please look at me."

Her head turned on the pillow again and when her eyes caught his, hers were blazing with hatred.

His gut wrenched and his face dipped to hers.

"This, what you're feeling, how you're looking at me, is *exactly* what I wanted to avoid by not telling you," he explained, his voice thick with emotion.

Finally, she spoke.

Her voice trembling with loathing, she whispered, "Obviously, you failed."

"Little one—"

"Go away, Callum."

"No," he replied and she closed her eyes.

When she opened them, she asked, "Why would I ever think you'd give a gosh darn about what *I* wanted?"

Then without hesitation she again turned her face away.

Briefly Callum weighed the virtues of giving her what she wanted and asking Leah to stay the night with her. Then he decided she'd not benefit from his absence because she could think she could get used to it.

Which she could not.

Carefully, he moved from the bed. He felt his jaw harden when she didn't fight nor did she move at all when he pulled off her boots, lifted her ass gently at the hips to unbutton and unzip her pants, and he pulled them down her legs, leaving her panties. Then he disrobed, turned out the lights, and joined her in bed, sliding again along her side, pulling up the hides, and slowly and cautiously, forcing her body to her side, facing him.

She had to turn her head again when he did this and she glared at his throat.

"Does it hurt to lie on your side?" he asked softly.

She gritted her teeth then bit out, "I don't feel anything."

"Good," he murmured. "I don't want you lying on that wound at your temple."

She made no response, simply continued to glare at his throat.

He pulled in a deep breath and let it out just as deeply.

Finally, he admitted on a whisper, "I fucked up, baby doll. I wanted to tell you time and again but I just couldn't find the right moment." She remained silent so he continued, "I didn't expect that to happen. I didn't expect that to be how you'd find out. I wanted to control it, protect you, manage your reaction. I knew it would be a shock and I wanted to cushion the blow." She didn't speak so Callum lost patience and demanded, "Baby doll, fuck, give me *something*."

Her eyes lifted to his and she asked with acid curiosity, "How can I give you something, Callum, when you've already *taken* everything I have to give?"

Callum froze at her words.

With a hand in the wall of his frozen chest, she pushed away and resumed her place on her belly with her head turned from him.

Callum came unstuck, his temper flared and his arm snaked out, hooking her at the waist, and with a carefully controlled movement, he slid her toward his body so that her side was tucked in his front.

Then he leaned down to her ear. "I understand you being pissed, little one, you've a right. Especially considering you were injured in the fray, but I'll point out only this once because we're *never* fucking speaking of it again, that was your own damned fault." Her body got tight in his arm but he ignored it and carried on, "I'll give you time. But you've never experienced anything from a single one of my people to continue having this reaction to them after the shock wears off. As for me, I'm willing to pay my penance, but I've explained I was coming at this from a good place with your best interests at heart. If you don't come to terms with that, and soon, I'll not be pleased." She didn't speak so his fingers gripped her waist, still gentle but in a way she couldn't miss. "Now tell me I'm understood."

Instantly, still facing away, she replied bitterly, "Oh, you're understood, your grace."

Callum growled low.

Sonia didn't make another noise.

Callum scowled at her hair.

Then his hand moved and his thumb encountered bandage. His anger evaporated, his eyes closed, and visions of her little, prone, bleeding body lying on the steps to their home filled his brain. To dispel the images, his eyes shot open.

That night was not the night for her to die.

But, for one unbearable second, when his eyes took in her wounds, he felt that sinister sliver of fear score through him.

Callum leaned into her cautiously and shoved his face in her hair.

"No one can piss me off like you do, honey," he whispered there. "But I'm sure as fuck relieved you're all right."

Her body tensed at his first words and stayed tight for long moments after he finished speaking.

Then, slowly, it relaxed.

And, with it, so did Callum's.

Callum woke several times in the night to check his mate and stoke the fire.

It wasn't until a muted, gray dawn started slowly to sweep the sky that he woke her one last time.

Sonia mumbled sleepily that she was all right as she'd been doing all night.

But this time, she turned into him. Still on her belly, she pressed her soft body into the side of his hard one, rested her cheek on his pectoral, and her arm stole across his stomach.

Her weight settled heavily into his and he knew she was asleep.

Callum also knew it would be all right.

For actions, especially when they were instinctive, for both humans and wolves, said a great deal more than words.

He gathered her hair in one fist, twisted it until it was a long rope, and then he coiled it around his palm, and he too, finally fell asleep.

For all of ten minutes because, soon, he'd learn, they were coming.

"Regan, the plan was agreed."

Regan stared out the window at the dawn's very early light, in fact, there was almost none, and snapped into her mobile, "Well, *I* didn't agree."

"Yes," Gregor returned calmly. "But Mac, Lassiter, and I did." He saved his winning point for last. "And so did Cherise."

Regan knew that.

She knew it.

She shut her eyes tight.

"Gregor, they're suffering," she whispered. "Especially Sonny."

She heard Gregor's pained sigh before he replied softly, "They're meant to, Regan. You know this has to be the way."

"Why does it have to be them?" Regan cried.

"I don't know, it just *does*," Gregor answered in a way that stated eloquently he liked it about as much as Regan did then he finished, "Regan, you know, this isn't just the way it has to be, it's the *only* way."

Regan was silent.

This silence, they both knew, was her agreement.

"Describe her wounds again," Gregor demanded and Regan did as she was asked even though it was the third time she did, then Gregor went on. "Tell me what Callum's done to Titium."

"Ordered Ryon and Caleb to incarcerate him and his men. They'll all stand trial."

"He has too much of Mac in him," Gregor grunted, and despite her escalating sense of despair, Regan smiled.

Only Gregor, a vampire, would think Callum had too much Mac in him. By the wolf's standard, Regan's son was ruthless.

Though, not as ruthless as a vampire.

"As I told you," Regan reminded Gregor, "Titium howled surrender before Callum could attack."

"Too much Mac," Gregor repeated.

Regan changed the subject. "You'll need to come to her."

"Yes," Gregor agreed. "Earlier than expected."

Regan held her breath a moment before saying, "You're going to—"

Gregor interrupted her, "There's no reason to delay."

Regan sagged against the windowsill in relief.

Soon it would be over, for her son and for Sonia.

Thank God.

Then she blinked into the slowly rising dawn.

Not because it was bright.

But because the cars had started coming.

She stared.

"Regan?"

"I've got to go," Regan said distractedly.

"What is it?" Gregor asked as Regan saw the shadows forming on the hills, coming from tents, moving slowly, making their way to the castle.

She felt a thrill slide up her spine as tears filled her eyes.

And softly, but with immense pride, she whispered, "My people are attending their queen."

CHAPTER NINETEEN
WEREWOLVES

SONIA FELT like she'd just fallen asleep when Callum moved, sliding gently away from her but holding her body still. Only when he'd disengaged did he settle her carefully on the mattress, a pillow under her cheek where his chest had been.

She felt his heat leave the bed but the hides came up to her neck and then they were tucked softly around her.

She drifted, but on the edge of her consciousness she heard a door open and close.

Then she drifted again until she heard hazily from somewhere far away Callum muttering, "Bloody hell."

She smiled into the pillow and then let out a soft fluttering sigh. She loved it when he got annoyed, she thought it was cute.

Though she'd never tell *him* that.

On that fuzzy thought, she fell asleep.

For about thirty seconds.

"Baby doll," his big hand was curled around the side of her head, "you need to wake up."

Her eyes fluttered open and she tilted her head to look up at him.

A nagging ache struck her temple and a dull pain which hinted at something more piercing dragged her back and she remembered.

She closed her eyes and twisted her neck on a half wince. She heard him curse and her eyes opened again.

His mouth was hard when she looked at him.

"Does it hurt?"

Did it hurt?

Her head and back, sure. She'd banged her head on a stone step and had a freaking *werewolf* claw through her jacket.

But she hurt other places worse and for reasons that she knew down to the depths of her mortal soul, *those* wounds would *never* heal.

She decided to answer his question. "Just a little bit."

His handsome face softened and she wanted to scratch it with her nails. She wanted to lean into it and scream. And she wanted to tilt her head and kiss him. She couldn't do any of those things and she hated *him* for it.

"I'm sorry but I need you to come with me, honey, just for a little bit. Then we'll get you back into bed and you can sleep," he told her, and before she could blink, he was gone.

She stared at the place where he'd been, suddenly uncertain that he'd even been there.

Then he was back, the hides were pulled away, and he put his large hands under her arms and tenderly lifted her from the bed.

When she was on her feet, she tipped her head back to look up at him and started, "Callum—"

"Lift your arms for me, little one," he murmured, his hands up, holding a stretchy, pink cotton nightgown.

Since she was naked (mostly) and a nightgown would be good, she did as she was told.

She winced when, at her movement, the dull pain became piercing.

"Fuck," he hissed low at her wince, making fast work of pulling the nightgown over her head, and then he commanded, "Arms down."

Gratefully she lowered her arms as he carefully pulled the night-gown down her body, rounding to her side to yank it out before he tugged it down her back and it fell over her hips to her knees. She registered this vaguely as a novel experience, considering Callum was putting a nightgown *on* her rather than taking it *off* as he'd stated repeatedly he preferred her naked in their bed and usually did something about it.

He sat her down on the edge of the bed and she stared, this time in out and out shock, as he knelt in front of her and put thick, woolen gray socks on her feet.

King Callum kneeling at her feet.

He'd only knelt for her once but that was to put his mouth between her legs.

Now he was putting socks on her feet to ward away a chill.

Before she could cope with this, he took her hand and cautiously tugged her up from the bed and then leaned into her, reaching to the side as she reared back (trying not to look as if she did) and he brought up her cashmere robe.

"Now this," he stated. "Turn around."

She did as she was told, mainly so she wouldn't glare at the robe, which, if she had been thinking, should also have gone in the fire with her rings and her wolf. She was doubly glad she threw the wolf in the fire *now* that she knew *he* was her puppy and *he* hadn't told her that, not for weeks. Not, apparently, for *years* (though, she wasn't actually doubly glad, she'd miss her stuffed wolf like crazy).

He pulled her robe up her arms, and, hands at her shoulders, turned her around and gently tied it closed.

When he was done, his hands came to her neck, and with thumbs at the undersides of her jaw, he tilted her head back to look at him.

"You can walk okay?" he asked quietly.

"I'm fine," she lied. "Where are we going?"

"You'll see," he replied, his eyes soft. He took her hand in his and guided her out the door.

They were down two flights when she tugged on his hand. "Callum, really, where are we going?"

She didn't want to see anyone. She didn't want to talk to anyone. She didn't want to eat, drink or, possibly, breathe.

Since not breathing would be bad, she decided she'd breathe but she wanted to do it somewhere alone so she could get her thoughts in order and sort out her crazy unbelievable life. A life which was already pretty unbelievable, say, because it included kings of secret sects of society and enchanted castles in tiny, unknown, independent countries in the depths of Scotland. But now she was forced to come to terms with the fact that she had to share that life with an arrogant, self-absorbed, philandering *werewolf*.

"It'll only take a minute, baby doll, and then back to bed," he told her, not pausing in leading her down the steps.

If whatever it was would only take a minute, which seeing someone, talking to them, or eating and drinking the way Callum's people did would take longer than that, she followed without protest.

At the front door, he stopped her and turned her to him.

"One last thing," he muttered and his hand went into the pocket of his jeans.

She watched, her breath catching, as he pulled out her wedding rings.

How?

What?

Again, how?

What, did he have backups or something?

He lifted her limp hand and slid them on her finger.

Then he lifted her hand farther and bent his head to it where his lips touched her rings and brushed her finger.

Her stomach clenched, her heart leaped, and her sinuses tingled with unshed tears.

That was how you put wedding rings on a woman's finger.

Just his eyes came to her, his lips remained at her hand, and he said quietly, but very, *very* firmly, "Never take these off again, little one. Hear me?"

She was so stunned she could do nothing but silently nod.

He lifted his head, squeezed her hand, and then pulled her a bit back from the door. He opened it, and hand still in hers, he guided her numb body outside.

She almost stumbled at what she saw.

Across the clearing at the foot of the steps, around the fountain, even up the hill, not to mention tall warriors flanking the sides of the steps, stood Callum's people.

Even Regan, Ryon, Caleb, Lucien, and Leah were standing along the top of the landing.

All of them silent, some of them carrying candles, others holding bunches of flowers or tins.

All of them looking at the castle, looking at *her*.

In her *robe*!

Callum led her to the edge of the top landing where he stopped and pulled her into his side with his arm carefully wound around her shoulders.

Nearly the minute they stopped and nearly at once, every last wolf dropped to their knee, hand to the snow or stone, head bowed (though Lucien and Leah didn't, of course, not being wolves and all).

Sonia quit breathing and learned that, even not breathing, you could still cry.

When she started breathing again, she whispered, "Oh my God."

"They need to see you're all right," Callum murmured.

"Make them rise." Sonia was still whispering.

Callum ignored her and carried on, "They heard you moved to protect me."

"Callum," she whispered, not able to tear her eyes from the bent multitudes, "let them rise."

"Though," he continued to ignore her, "they would have come all the same."

"Please," she breathed.

His arm came across his chest to her chin where his fingers grasped her and he tipped her face back to his.

Then he kissed her lightly, a brush on the lips.

His head lifting nary an inch, his sky-blue eyes looked into hers, and he said quietly, "These are *my* people. These are *your* people. These men and women bowing to you are *werewolves*."

With that, he released her chin, turned to his people, and in a clear, carrying, deep voice, he commanded, "Rise!"

His people stood.

They also moved.

As the warriors at the steps stood sentry, flowers, tins, and lit candles were placed on the steps as wolves came forward giving Callum a nod and Sonia a smile before giving their gifts.

This all happened silently before they turned to their cars or to make their way back up the hill to their tents.

It took longer than a minute and she was chilled through to the bone by the time the last wolf dipped his head to Sonia's mate and sent a smile Sonia's way.

But Sonia barely felt the cold or the biting pain that had begun to torment her back.

As any queen would, she stood for her people, injuries and all.

When it was done, without a word, Callum guided her back to their room, slid the robe from her shoulders, and carefully pushed her into bed.

He kissed her injured temple at the bottom of the torn skin.

Then he slid his temple along her hair and in her ear, he whispered, "Sleep now, baby doll."

He pulled the hides higher and he was gone.

Sonia didn't think she could sleep. Not after *that*.

But it didn't take long before she did.

CHAPTER TWENTY

RECKONING

Today was the day of reckoning.

Sonia knew it.

She could feel it.

Callum was *angry*.

He'd been patient.

For a while.

That wore off and he'd been patiently *impatient*.

For another while.

Now he was mad.

And she didn't care (or, that's what she told herself).

It had been three weeks since the incident where she'd learned his true nature (*all* of it) and those three weeks were the longest of her life.

Sonia had forgiven Regan, Ryon, and Caleb for their duplicity the very next day.

She'd done this because she knew they'd lied to her because King Callum ordered it, or, if she was being fair, just kept things from her.

Things that would seriously freak her out but that was *almost* like lying even if those things were things that would seriously freak her out.

But she'd also done it because she cared about them.

Regan had come up with a late breakfast tray and the moment she looked at Sonia, Regan's obvious hesitancy instantly tore at Sonia's heart.

Sonia, who'd been awake for a while and had been lying in bed, feeling sorry for herself, and lamenting her fate at the same time contradictorily feeling both honored by the remarkable and touching display the wolves made for her that morning, sat up carefully when she saw Regan's shaky smile.

Then she reached her hand out to her mother-in-law.

Regan all but dropped the tray on the nightstand, sat on the bed, and, taking care with Sonia's wounds, gave her a gentle hug.

"It was a shock but I still was awful," Sonia whispered in her ear, able to hug Regan back far more tightly.

"We shouldn't have waited. Callum wanted—" Regan started but Sonia gave her a squeeze.

She didn't want to hear about anything that Callum wanted.

"It doesn't matter now," she assured Regan.

Regan pulled back and framed Sonia's face in her hands. "I'm so sorry. I'm so, so sorry about all of this."

"That's the last time you apologize for being who you are," Sonia said firmly curling her fingers around Regan's, pulling them down, and holding their hands between them. "It was a shock. It's over. It's all good now," she finished on a lie and her own shaky smile.

Regan's eyes searched Sonia's and hers remained troubled. "So, you're not angry with Callum?"

No, she wasn't angry with him.

Not anymore.

She'd never be *anything* with him anymore.

Not because he was a gosh darn *werewolf* and didn't tell her (or not *only* because of that).

Not because *all* of his people were werewolves and he didn't tell her (or, also, not *only* because of that).

Not to mention the existence of *vampires* which, she realized, feeling immensely stupid (and she blamed Callum for that too), Gregor and Yuri were too by their smell, which was like Lucien's which, like wolves, *wasn't* like humans (but, in her defense, how could Sonia know werewolves and vampires existed!).

And not because he was not only her handsome wolf but also her beloved puppy and he'd torn *both* of them away from her (or, again, not *only* because of those).

But because he'd disappeared for a day and most of a night, doing God knew what with God knew who and then returned to *their* bed, proving her fevered suspicions true by smelling how he smelled after they had sex and pretended to be caring and kind and thoughtful but doing it in an arrogant bastard type of way.

Naturally, she knew he'd find someone else eventually.

She just didn't know how much it'd hurt, and when she'd thoroughly processed it, lying and crying in *their* bed, how dead she'd feel and how surprised she was that feeling dead hurt *worse*.

She also didn't know the depths of that pain and her torture were not even close to being plumbed until he made her admit she loved him.

God, it was too humiliating to even contemplate.

She admitted she loved him!

Which, because evidently she was weak, weak, *weak*, was all she could contemplate while lying in bed that morning.

"I'm sure Callum and I will be fine," she lied again to Regan, who gave her a look like she knew Sonia was lying but she let it go.

She stayed while Sonia ate and then gave Sonia pain pills because the stitches at her back were, by then, killing her and the pills made Sonia drowsy.

Therefore, Sonia slept.

She woke in Callum's arms.

Or, more precisely, with her head and hand resting on his stomach, his shoulders were against the headboard, his long legs stretched out straight in front of him and his arm was around her shoulders with his fingers drawing lazy circles on her skin.

"You awake, honey?" he asked.

She clenched her jaw at the empty endearment.

"Yes," she answered.

"How are you feeling?"

Like garbage, through and through, she thought but did not say out loud.

"It hurts." And that wasn't a lie. It was just an understatement.

"Poor baby," he murmured and he was lucky she was wounded or she'd have attacked, even though he could rip her to shreds with his claws and his teeth.

"Regan said you had a nice visit," he told her.

"We did," Sonia affirmed.

His hand squeezed her shoulder with approval.

She again fought the urge to tear her stitches out of her back by attacking him.

"Do you feel like moving around?" he asked. "I'll help you in the bath."

She did not *think* so.

"Are you telling me I stink?" she snapped irately.

He chuckled before he said (false) fondly, "You never stink, my little one."

She'd had enough and therefore started to pull away from him saying, "I should move around. I don't want to get stiff."

She didn't get very far before his hands went under her arms and he pulled her gently up to rest on his chest with their faces close.

She put her hands on his chest and pushed back but his arm slid around her lower waist and he held her still.

When she stopped moving, his other hand went behind her head, grasping her hair in one big fist, pulling it over her shoulder and twisting it again and again until it formed a long twine. Then he wrapped it around his palm at the side of her neck.

He watched his hand doing this as if enthralled.

"Callum," she called and reminded him, "I was going to move around."

His eyes came to hers and he announced, "You're still pissed."

Oh, he was right about that.

Apparently she *could* be something with Callum but "pissed" was all she was *ever* going to be.

"Can I have a *day* to get used to the fact my mate is a *werewolf?*" she asked caustically and then went on, "Or is that asking too much?"

He grinned at her (the arrogant bastard!).

Then he used her hair to pull her face to his and he touched his lips to hers.

Looking into her eyes, still grinning, he granted, "You can have a day."

Now, *that* was when she would have attacked if she could have attacked.

But he simply marked her hair at her good temple (that particular business finally explained by him being half-wolf), let her go, moved away, and left the room.

She washed as best she could, dressed, and decided to hang out in their room because she couldn't face anyone.

Leah came up with a tray of food in the late afternoon.

At that moment Sonia was grateful for Leah. It was good to be around her kind, for one, even if that made her a bad person for thinking it. For another, she liked Leah. Leah was funny and sweet and a little bit crazy and Sonia could be herself around her because, obviously, Leah was used to a life filled with vampires and such.

While Sonia ate, Leah talked, telling her wild stories of vampire concubines and captivating stories of places called Feasts and terrifying stories of something called The Sentence. All of this sharing how she'd fallen in love with Lucien.

The story had taken over an hour to tell and Sonia, long since having cleaned her plate, stared at her new friend when she was done talking.

"As you can see," Leah concluded, "I'm safe, healthy, and happy and Lucien is..." she smiled a sweet eloquent smile before finishing, "happy too."

"And I'm happy for you," Sonia replied softly, meaning every word.

Leah grinned at her. "If you embrace it, Sonny, you'll be happy too and, I promise, it'll be beyond your wildest dreams."

That was doubtful.

Sonia had had her "wildest dreams." She knew how good it could be and it was *not* that.

"I don't have much choice but to embrace it," Sonia told her. "It's destiny."

"I know. Mine was too and destiny is *my best friend*," Leah declared on a giggle.

Sonia laughed softly, not agreeing in the slightest but also not wanting to break Leah's happy mood.

Ryon came up shortly after and she let him off the hook by smiling at him the minute he walked through the door.

Caleb came up not long after and she visited with them while Leah returned her tray but she came back with Lucien.

Lucien regarded her carefully as he walked in, but even though he freaked her out more than werewolves, she'd lived with vampires all her life (apparently) so she knew better than to fear him (hysterically rather than generally because Lucien, the individual, was still kind of scary).

Regan arrived a few minutes later with a board game and they all started playing. Even Lucien who didn't strike Sonia as a board game type of...*being*. Then again, she was getting the sense cold aloof Lucien would do just about anything to make his bride happy, including playing a board game.

Therefore, hours later, Sonia was lying on her belly on the curvy couch by the fire. Regan and Lucien were in chairs pulled around to the side of the fireplace by the couch. Leah was sitting cross-legged on the floor at Lucien's feet. And both Ryon and Caleb's long bodies were spread across the floor as they lay on their sides with pillows under their elbows, heads in their hands when Callum walked in.

He stood at the couch by Sonia's feet and stared down at them from his colossal werewolf height.

"We're almost done with this game. You can sit in the next one," Caleb announced.

"There won't be a next one," Callum declared meaningfully (and, incidentally, kingfully), walking down the couch and pulling Sonia up cautiously before sitting down, stretching his long legs out in front of him, crossing them at the ankles, and setting her down with her upper torso on his thigh.

She wanted to pull away but she couldn't mainly because her back had begun to really hurt and she hadn't wanted to mention it and worry anyone, but also because they were all watching her with Callum.

So she just settled in like she didn't care (when she *did*).

They finished the game, folded it up, and said their goodnights and Sonia decided now was the time for pain pills because she didn't mind Callum worrying.

She started to push up from the couch (he'd followed everyone to the door and closed it behind them), but quick as a flash, he was crouched at her side with a big palm in the small of her back.

"Just stay there, I'll bring your injection out here," he told her and then moved to the bathroom.

Holy cow.

She'd forgotten about her injection. How could she forget about *that*? And how could she take it with her back already on fire?

"Callum," she called. "I need my pain pills."

"After the injection," he replied, walking in with the syringe already loaded.

She stared at it like it was a living thing which existed only to do her harm.

Callum saw her look, crouched at the head of the couch and his hand cupped the side of her face. "Two minutes, baby doll," he said gently. "Then it'll be over and that whole time I'll be right here."

Boy, she hated the fact that she loved him, that there were so many things to love, and that all of them were lies.

He moved to her side and murmured, "Can you get your jeans down for me?"

It hurt but she did.

He injected her.

The burn was ten times worse and seared through her back like wildfire.

She was panting when it was done but felt Callum's warm hand cupped at the back of her neck, which she told herself didn't feel good (when it did).

Then, when she fully recovered, Callum did something strange.

He usually righted her clothes before she recovered but her jeans were still low on her hips and his palms went to her bottom, fingers spanning her hips, and his thumbs slid over the pinpricks exposed by her jeans. He was sitting by her thighs and he started talking as if to himself.

"I hate these," he said softly. "Fucking hate them."

She got tense (or, she should say, *more* tense) but he wasn't done.

"But I should love them because they're a part of you."

Sonia pressed her lips together and closed her eyes tight.

She gave it a moment before she asked, "Can I get up and get my pain pills? My back is beginning to hurt."

His fingers curled into the waistband of her jeans and he pulled them up before he offered, "I'll get them, baby doll."

He gave her the pills, helped her dress for bed (another nightgown, a miracle!), and he held her close when they were under the hides, acting like the devoted king to his injured queen.

They were in the same position as she woke up early that afternoon when he asked, "Would you like me to tell you more about my kind?"

She'd get Regan, Mara, Callista, Ryon, and Caleb to do that.

She wanted nothing from him.

"The pills make me drowsy and they work pretty fast." That wasn't a lie. "I don't want to miss anything." That *was* a lie.

"All right, honey," he murmured and went on to comment warmly, "You know, you're taking this a lot better than I expected."

She could have laughed.

She didn't.

"You don't know me very well," she told him the truth for once.

His fingers slid into her hair and cupped the back of her head. "True, but everything I learn, I like."

Liar, liar, liar, she thought but she just let out a fluttery, stupid sigh.

His fingers tensed against her scalp.

She prayed the pills would work their magic and, luckily, shortly after, they did.

The next week, Callum was patient mainly because Sonia was still feeling goodly amounts of pain which he took great care in assessing by often asking the soft, sweet, "How're you doing, baby doll?"

He also demanded that he be the only one to clean, put ointment on, and re-bandage her wounds. And, surprisingly, other than that, he gave her space to rest and heal.

Also, Callum gave her space because Gregor turned up since Regan told him Sonia had been injured.

Gregor gave her the whole, "Callum's a big boy and doesn't need you to protect him so you've no business throwing yourself in front of an angry werewolf even if you didn't have any idea he *was* an angry were-wolf," lecture (although it didn't go quite like that).

Then Sonia gave him her, "So, you and your son are vampires?" interrogation (and that was exactly how she started it).

Then it was done and Gregor settled in like he was going to stay a while. This was evidenced by him having a lot of luggage, not Sonia being overly perceptive. This also made Callum's patience slip a little bit, but for some reason, made Regan seem really happy.

Lucien and Leah left several days after the My Mate, The Werewolf Incident, which Sonia found distressing as she'd grown fond of Leah very quickly and she liked being around them. There was something beautiful about the two of them. The way they looked at each other, acted toward each other. The quiet but obvious way they were just *in love*.

Normally, considering Sonia's circumstances, this would be added torture but Sonia cared about Leah and she also started to like Lucien. He seemed the sort of man who deserved to be happy and he acted like the kind of man who'd waited a very long time to be so and appreciated it deeply now that he had it. Considering Leah told her that Lucien was older than Callum by *four entire centuries*, a long time for him was liter-ally, a *long time*.

Regan, Mara and Callista shared with both Sonia and Leah a good deal about werewolf nature, history, lore, and just about anything else they could share because Mara, as ever, liked to talk. It was a fascinating culture with a rich history and they were proud of it (as they should be).

There was only one hiccup in the first week and that was close to the end of it.

Sonia was in bed reading and hadn't switched out the light and settled in long before Callum came up. This was what she'd made a habit of doing, saying she was going to bed early because of pain and needing to rest, and, considering Callum didn't know an awful lot about humans, he didn't know any better. But Gregor gave her knowing looks and Regan gave her increasingly penetrating ones.

By the time she sensed him walking up, she couldn't feign sleep as he'd know since the door was open and he'd see the light go out, not to mention, he probably would hear her moving.

Luckily, he smiled at her when he walked in but went directly to the bathroom. She had time to turn out her light, turn on his, put her book aside, and get in a sleeping position before he walked out, naked and heading to bed.

She told herself he didn't hear her sucking in her breath at the beauty of his naked body (but she didn't believe herself) and this was proved false anyway when he grinned at her knowingly.

Once in bed, he immediately, and adeptly (totally ignoring her painstakingly crafted sleeping position), slid her closer to him, rolled her to her belly then to her side, avoiding her back, and pulled her to him, face to face.

Then his hands started roaming.

She tucked her face in his throat and bit her lip because his hands on her felt way too nice and she missed them.

Way too much.

"Sonia, baby doll, do you want to play?" he asked softly.

She shook her head.

"I'll be gentle, little one."

She loved it when he was gentle almost as much as she loved it when he was rough.

"I'm in a little pain. The pills aren't working as well as they used to," she lied for she felt okay. The pain was mostly a twinge by then and the wounds had started itching, indicating they were healing.

"All right, honey," he murmured but his hands still roamed, though they'd slowed and the caresses felt soothing rather than exciting.

Then he asked, "Do you want to talk?"

"About what?" she asked back and her voice sounded higher than normal.

His hand slid up her arm, his fingers curled in at her neck then her jaw and they tipped up her chin so she was forced to look at him.

"About anything," he replied.

"Not really," she told him.

His brows drew together and he commented, "A good deal has happened to you. With me, my family, my people, moving, finding out about Gregor and Yuri, meeting Lucien and Leah. Are you okay with all of that?"

God, he'd be sweet if he wasn't such a jerk.

"I'm coping," she told him, and when he looked like he didn't believe her, she went on, "I mean, it's so much, you get used to your world rocking under your feet every few days. If Frankenstein walked through that door right now and asked if we wanted to go to a barbeque at his house tomorrow, I probably wouldn't even blink."

He burst out laughing and wrapped his arms around her, low at her waist to avoid her injury, falling to his back and taking her with him so she was on top.

She planted her forearms in his massive chest and lifted up to watch him laugh.

She told herself it was clinically (when it was not) that she noted he was unbelievably handsome when he laughed, and therefore, since she was like a scientist observing nature, she could watch him do it.

When he got control of himself, he informed her, "There is no such thing as Frankenstein."

"I trust you." And that wasn't a total lie.

She didn't *trust* him, trust him, but she trusted, with his statement, he was telling the truth and he, of all people, would know.

"Would you go?" he asked.

"What?" she asked back.

He grinned. "To a barbeque at Frankenstein's house."

"I don't know," she answered. "What do Frankensteins serve at barbeques?"

He roared with laughter again, and with a hand cupping the back of her head, he forced her down so her arms had to slide out and around him and he pressed her face into his neck.

Then he took her hair in his big fist and wrapped it into a rope again, coiling it around his palm.

"I fucking love your hair," he murmured and she forced her body to stay relaxed.

Because that was a lie. He hated blondes.

That was, supposedly, until recently.

"I was thinking of cutting it," she lied yet again just to be mean.

His fist tightened in her hair and he decreed, "I'll not allow that."

She bit back a, "Yes, your grace," and stayed silent.

He used her own hair to rub against her jaw when he whispered, "Are you happy, little one?"

It was an odd, endearing, and unbelievably poignant question, and furthermore, he sounded like he cared about her answer.

She felt the sting of tears in her sinuses again, but with effort, she controlled them.

Then she sighed and stated, "Well, I guess a girl could do better than a fairytale castle in a beautiful wood with a handsome wolf as her husband who happens to be king, making her queen of a kind and loving people who think good things about her...but I don't know how."

Except, of course, having that king love his queen beyond anything in the whole world, like Lucien loved Leah and like Regan loved Mac and like Mara loved Drogan.

Or like Sonia's father loved her mother.

Or even a *little* of what they had.

Not knowing her thoughts, at her words, he released her hair and his arms wound around her. For the first time since she was injured, they did this powerfully, crushing her to him and making that twinge of pain in her back magnify.

"I'm glad," he said and his voice sounded strangely hoarse.

"Callum, my back," she whispered.

His hold loosened and he slid her off his side but kept her close with an arm about her waist. He reached and turned out the light, settled her with her cheek on his shoulder and he pulled her arm around his stomach.

"Sleep," he murmured.

"Okay," she murmured back.

He gave her a squeeze.

Her sinuses started stinging again because it hurt so much, more than she thought she could endure, wanting him to be real and knowing he was not.

But, somehow, she fell asleep.

Much later, she woke sensing him gone. She laid awake until he returned and he slid into bed at her side, his skin cold when he tucked her into him, but he again smelled of sex.

And her broken heart broke just that little bit more.

The next two weeks Callum's patience waned considerably, more and more each day.

First, he wasn't Gregor's biggest fan and Gregor had made it a habit to monopolize any time not taken by Regan, Ryon, Caleb, Mara, Callista, and wolves from town who had, at Regan, Mara and Callista's invitations, begun to drop by to meet and get to know Sonia.

Therefore, Sonia didn't spend hardly any time in Callum's lap in his study or with Callum anywhere. Practically the minute she sat there, Gregor was at the door asking if she wanted to go into town, if she wanted to go for a walk, telling her Yuri was on the phone and wanted to speak to her, and the like.

Second, Callum wasn't buying the "I'm in pain" excuse anymore considering she was going into town and taking walks but also he was seeing firsthand that her wounds were healing well. Even if he hadn't seen it, Orphenon popping by to have a look deep into week three and announcing they were healing surprisingly rapidly gave it away.

Sonia had always been a quick healer and she had the freakish capacity never to scar and she wondered if this was part of her gifts but she never mentioned it to anyone and didn't, for obvious reasons, then either. In fact, Orphenon had clipped away the stitches which kind of hurt and left her feeling a bit raw, which Callum, upon examining her face closely, believed because she was for once telling the truth.

Third, because Callum was beginning to get frustrated that Sonia was finding the willpower to fight back the urge.

Deep into the second week he made it obvious he wanted "to play." But *why* he wanted to play when two or three times a week he disappeared from their bed in the middle of the night and came back obviously having been outside and smelling of that intense and beautiful musk he always smelled like after they'd finished, she would never know.

Sonia had put him off both morning and night and some afternoons besides with a variety of excuses which were wearing thin.

He started to get suspicious then he started to get dubious and this melted straight into extremely annoyed.

Luckily Calder turned up the third week and Callum lost interest in her as he holed himself up with the boys in his study. But this still left the nights for Sonia to find ways to fend off his hands, his mouth, and his quiet, gentle, sweet bedtime interrogations (but getting less gentle and less quiet and definitely less sweet).

Just last night, quiet, gentle, and sweet went out the window.

Sonia was in bed reading (again) when Callum hit the room.

He didn't smile at her when he walked in.

Considering it was 8:30, he stopped two feet in, crossed his arms on his chest, frowned ominously and stared at her in bed.

"It's 8:30," he informed her.

Sonia tensed and decided not to look at him anymore because he was freaking her out. Therefore, she looked back at her book.

"This is a really good book," she told him (though it wasn't). "I've been waiting all day for an excuse to get back to it." (Though she hadn't.)

Suddenly her book was pulled from her hands and her eyes automatically and irritably shot back to him.

"There's the small matter of your injection," he clipped and she closed her eyes and looked away.

She hated those injections always but told herself they were a necessary evil.

Now, they were pure torture with Callum giving them to her and Sonia emerging from the burn always wrapped lovingly (but insincerely) in his arms.

She opened her eyes when she felt the bed depress with his weight, his fingers sliding into the side of her hair, and she saw him sitting beside her on the bed.

His anger was gone, the gentle look was back, and he murmured, "Two minutes, baby doll, then it's done."

"I hate those injections," she whispered and his fingers flexed in her hair.

"I do too," he agreed.

He gave her the injection, led her back to bed, and threw the hides back. She started climbing in but he stopped her, turned her to face him, and then his hands bunched the material of her nightgown at her hips and, *whoosh*, it was gone.

"Hey!" she cried, shocked at his actions.

"Now your pants," he ordered.

Sonia was covering her breasts with her arms and she looked in confusion, as she was not keeping up, down at her underwear.

Then she looked up at him. "You mean my undies?"

"Off," he demanded, leaning in and hooking his thumbs in the waistband.

"*Callum!*" she shrieked but her panties were already at her ankles and he was lifting her up so she repeated, "*Callum!*"

Like she didn't utter a word (or, in this case, *shriek* his name *twice*) he placed her in bed and pulled the hides over her.

Sonia got up on an elbow and Callum sat on the edge, leaning into the hand that he'd planted in the bed behind her.

"I thought I told you I wanted you naked when you don't have to wear clothes," he declared calmly.

She glared at him. "I'm not comfortable sleeping naked."

His brows drew together. "It didn't seem to bother you before you found out I was wolf."

This was true but only because, by the time he let her sleep, she was already naked, exhausted, and slept the sleep of abandoned contentment.

Now they weren't having sex, were *never* going to have sex again, so she wanted to wear a nightgown.

As she didn't feel like getting into that particular subject at that time, she just glared at him.

He absorbed her glare for a while then reached out, grabbed her book, and handed it to her.

"I'll be back soon," he muttered, leaned down, kissed her temple, and then walked from the room.

Without him to glare at, Sonia glared at the door instead.

Then she got up, put her undies and nightgown back on, and got back into bed.

Callum could do a lot of things, considering he was king.

But he could *not* tell her what to wear to bed.

She was dead asleep when she felt her body move and she didn't tell it to do so.

Then she felt her nightgown sliding up, up, and, *whoosh*, it was gone.

Her eyes opened and she stared groggily at Callum who was in the process of pulling her panties down her legs. Then, *whoosh*, they were gone too.

"What...?" she whispered but wasn't awake enough to get her brain functioning.

He lay on his back, pulling the hides over them and yanking her roughly in his arms.

"Did you...did you just do that?" she asked his chest, her mind still fuzzy with sleep.

"I did," he answered calmly.

"I...I can't believe you just did that," she whispered.

"Believe it," he replied.

"*Why* did you just do that?" she queried.

"Tomorrow," was his strange response.

"Tomorrow?"

He rolled into her so they were face to face.

"I'm too fucking pissed right now to have this conversation, Sonia," he informed her, sounding pissed. Sounding downright *mad*. "But tomorrow morning, after breakfast, we're fucking talking," he finished.

In the face of his anger, Sonia thought it was prudent not to say anything further.

So she didn't.

He rolled to his back again, taking her with him so her head was on his shoulder. Then he hauled her arm around him so it was resting across his stomach and his arm, curled at her waist, tightened so she was pressed into him close.

When he settled, it occurred to her that *he* had nothing to be pissed about.

She wasn't sneaking off at night for liaisons with whoever (or multiple whoevers).

She wasn't pretending to be his devoted queen when *she* wasn't attracted to *him*.

She was just doing the best she could in a really bad situation.

However, she didn't feel like getting into these subjects at that particular juncture either.

Or, ever, really.

So she forced her body to relax and she listened to his deep breathing, smelled his heady scent and wished she could go back to a time when she could, at least, pretend this was real.

But she could not.

It was the morning after and Sonia was curled in the little oval alcove trying to concentrate on her book but she couldn't because she knew that day was the day of reckoning.

She'd woken alone, showered, dressed, had a quick breakfast, and ran back upstairs before anyone could catch her.

She had no idea why she woke up alone because Callum always woke her if he was leaving her even if just to give her a kiss and tell her he was going.

She didn't take that as a good sign.

When she heard him approaching, she didn't take hearing that he alighted the stairs at least two at a time as a good sign either.

When he hit the room and slammed the door so hard that the sound it made seemed to undulate through the room like a shockwave, she didn't take *that* as a good sign either.

The instant she saw the look on his face she realized that today was not the day of reckoning.

Today was the day of the apocalypse.

Without hesitating, he walked right up to her, jerked the book out of her frozen-with-fear hands, and tossed it across the room with such force, the sound it made when it hit the doors of the wardrobe all the way across the room was like a gunshot.

She stared at her book on the floor for a second, lips parted in shock, then she looked back at him. What she saw terrified her to such an extreme, the only thing she could think to do was flee.

So she tried.

She shot out of the alcove and ran past him as fast as her feet would carry her, her heart beating a mile a minute and her mind totally blank.

She wasn't fast enough.

He hooked an arm across her waist and lifted her up, her back to his chest, her legs kicking out, and her hands pushing at his arm.

"*Let me go!*" she squealed but he just turned, took three long strides, and tossed her on the bed.

She instantly rolled and kept rolling until she rolled over the other side, got to her feet, and glared at him standing opposite the bed to her. His chest was heaving and he was visibly having difficulty controlling his anger.

Sonia was panting with fear but that fear was replaced by fury on the spot.

"*What's the matter with you?*" she shrieked.

"You didn't come to the study after breakfast," he replied, his deep voice even but far from calm.

He was enraged. His voice said it. His face said it. Every line of his big tall body said it.

But Sonia didn't care.

"You just slammed the door, accosted my book, and tossed me *across the room* because I didn't come to the study?" she shouted.

"I didn't toss you across the room but I *did* tell you we were talking this morning and you didn't come to my goddamned *study!*" he shouted back.

"Don't you yell at me, King Callum," she yelled.

He put his hands to his hips and leaned forward, yelling back, "I'll yell until I find out what in *the* fuck is wrong with you, Queen Sonia!"

"*There's nothing wrong!*" she screamed her lie, leaning toward him too.

"There isn't?" He leaned back. "Then my *wife* is denying me her affections because...?"

He let the last hang but Sonia didn't.

She lied again, "I'm not denying you my affections!"

"Really?" he asked mockingly. "Have you been fucking me in the night and I haven't felt it?"

Her hands clenched into fists, so angry she couldn't have stopped herself even if she'd tried.

Which she didn't, she'd been holding on to this long enough.

So she just let loose.

"Well, I figured, since you're out fucking whoever at night, you wouldn't need *me*!"

His body jerked but he scowled at her through the movement, muttering angrily, "What the fuck?"

"You're cheating on me, Callum. I know it. Remember? I have gifts! I can *smell* it! You go off in the middle of the night, come home, and you *reek* of it!" she screamed.

He stared at her looking both stunned and furious and shouted, "Fucking hell, are you *mad*?"

"No!" she shouted back. "I'm not mad!" She shook her head and threw out an arm, looking away and talking mostly to herself but still doing it heatedly. "I shouldn't care. I keep telling myself I shouldn't care. Why do I care?"

"You shouldn't care?" Callum muttered, low and dangerous, his tone making Sonia's eyes go back to him, and if she thought he was angry before, she was wrong.

Now he was incensed.

But she was too far gone.

"No, I shouldn't care," she hurled at him.

"You shouldn't care that you think I'm fucking around on you?" he asked, still in that low tone.

"No!" she shouted.

"Why?" he shot back. "Because you want me to get it elsewhere now that you know I'm wolf and you don't want that sweet little body of yours defiled by an animal?"

Sonia gasped in outrage at his words and screeched, "*How dare you! I love wolves!*"

"Yes, honey," he said cuttingly. "And three weeks ago you told me you loved *me*. The next day I find my *fucking* rings in the fire and you *fucking* avoid me all day and then you find out I'm wolf and do everything you can to avoid me for the next three *fucking weeks*! Is that what love is to you?"

"No, *Callum*. I did all that because you *made* me tell you I loved you while *making* me sit in your lap after you'd come home from *fucking* someone else and still *reeking* of it!"

"*I'm not fucking anyone else!*" he roared, losing what little hold he had on his temper.

But something broke inside Sonia. It had broken before, time and again, and it still hurt so much it was a miracle she didn't fall to her knees.

Instead, her anger and heartbreak kept her breathing, standing, and fighting.

She turned and rounded the bed, her eyes locked on her mate, her hand lifted with finger jabbing the air at him all the while screaming back, "You are so *full of it*! You don't want me. You *never* wanted me! I'm just your *duty*. Another in a long line of *duties*."

She was still screaming as she made it to him and she used both hands to shove his chest, rocking him back on a foot as he stared down at her looking shocked.

"*You* said in the beginning we were a *farce*! *Your brother* said you wanted to get the claiming over with, that you felt *forced* to be at the cabin with me *and* that I'd have to understand your need to fuck around with *your own kind*."

She shoved him again and kept screaming.

"Your *other* brother called being up at the cabin with me '*dicking around*.' That crazy Desdemona woman said you *hated* blondes and *I'm blonde*! And everyone, but *everyone*, Calder, Yuri, even *Titium*, talks about your legendary prowess with women."

He caught her wrists and hauled her up to his chest, muttering, "Sonia—"

"*No!*" she screeched in his face. "I've got good news. This is over for you, Callum! Over. You don't have to pretend anymore. You don't have to playact. I promise, I'll do my duty as queen and you can just go off and do...whatever it is you have to do and somehow I'll deal with it. I'll cope. I'll find a way to be happy even though I'm with you but I'm still, like I've always been, *alone.*"

She tore her hands from his wrists and started to run but he caught her around the waist and tugged her straight back, front to front.

"Baby doll—" he started.

The tears hit her eyes at those two words and she shrieked, "*Stop calling me that!*" She pushed at his chest with her hands and struggled in his arms. "Stop calling me that when I'm not that to you. I've *never* been that to you. I'm only that in my stupid, *stupid* dreams!"

He barely controlled her struggles while whispering, "Honey, settle down and listen to me."

Working hard to hold back the tears, Sonia stammered, "N-no!" and kept right on fighting.

But Callum kept right on controlling her thrashing so she had to do it harder.

She had to get away, *far* away. Far enough to get her head together and piece her heart together and find some way to get on with her hideous destiny.

She managed to break away but he caught her again and pushed her on the bed.

She rolled and almost got to her knees but his fingers wrapped around her ankles, twisted her back, yanking her down the bed, and his big body landed on hers.

In a panic because this was *not* where she wanted to be (even though it was), she bucked and pushed at his shoulders, shouting, "Just let me get away. I need to get away!"

"Baby doll, you need to calm down," he murmured softly.

Something in his tone struck her.

Her body stilled and her mind cleared but her hands still pushed at his shoulders as she looked away from him and stared at the side of the bed.

She took in a ragged breath.

She took in another one.

Then she realized what she'd said and what she'd done and how much it betrayed about how very much she felt about him.

Deflated and crushingly humiliated, she made an attempt to salvage a very bad situation, whispering, "You're right."

His hand rounded her jaw and he said softly, "Look at me, honey."

She closed her eyes tight and resisted, but finally, taking in a breath, she looked at him.

God, he was beautiful, watching her with tenderness etched in every feature.

Seeing him looking at her that way, she realized she was so caught up in the hurt, she forgot that he was dealing with a hideous destiny too.

"I'm sorry," she was still whispering. "You don't need this. You have a kingdom to worry about. I should have...I should...I should have just learned to deal on my own."

He stared at her a moment then his eyes went over her head and she could almost hear him counting to ten in his.

His gaze came back to hers and he stated, "I'm not fucking around on you, Sonia."

A hated sob welled up in her chest and she swallowed it down on the word, "Don't."

"Baby doll, I'm running at night."

She blinked at him, sudden confusion swept through her at his words and she asked, "Running?"

"Transforming to wolf and running. I did it at the cabin too. I have to do it, compelled to by the wolf in me," he told her and she stared because no one had told her *that*. "I couldn't do it when we were in the city but I do it here all the time. You always slept through it, me leaving and returning." He paused and then finished, "Until lately."

She kept staring, trying to wrap her mind around this strangely logical fact.

"Do you...do you," she shouldn't ask, she really shouldn't ask, but on a barely-there whisper, she asked, "run with someone else?"

His lips twitched and he said, "No, little one, I'm a lone wolf."

"But you smell like—" she started.

He cut her off. "I smell like wolf."

"But, I'd never smelled it before except when—"

"The scent wears off quickly, definitely by morning."

"But it smells like after we—"

He grinned. "Yes, honey, that's *exactly* what it smells like."

She thought that was kind of neat, and definitely sexy, and she felt her body getting soft under his. "So you're not meeting someone?"

His face grew serious when he replied, "I'd never fuck around on you, Sonia." His face dipped closer when he finished on a growl, "*Never*."

Relief started sliding through her but she couldn't let go. "But...why? You don't want me. You said...and Caleb and Yuri—"

"Forget what Caleb and Yuri said."

She was back to staring at him and getting annoyed so she snapped, "Forget?"

"I've lived for nearly four hundred years and you know I like to play," he calmly explained.

Yes, she was definitely getting annoyed. "Right, so—"

"No, baby doll," he cut her off firmly. "You said what you had to say. It's my turn to talk."

She clamped her mouth shut and glared at him.

He watched her as if waiting for her to defy him and then he went on, "I've had a lot of lovers but I've never had a mate."

She opened her mouth and shot back, "A mate you don't want."

Now Callum looked like *he* was getting annoyed when he informed her, "Sonia, you're talking."

"Yes, I am," she retorted. "There's no reason to do this. I get it. I understand my place. You know I understand it, so it's over."

"But you *don't* understand your place," he bit out.

And yes, he was definitely getting annoyed too.

"I—"

"Sonia, shut *up*," he clipped.

Sonia glared.

Callum scowled.

This lasted a while.

Sonia finally lost patience. "You wanted to talk...*talk.*"

"Christ, you're a pain in the ass," he told her.

"Thanks," she snapped.

His eyes narrowed and he lost control of his temper. "All right, baby doll," he gritted out through his teeth, "I never thought this was the way I'd tell you but here it is. You're perfect."

Sonia stopped glaring and her mouth dropped open.

Callum kept talking, "You have to know, I didn't think I would feel that way at first but every fucking second I was with you I realized it more and more. Every day, I would wake up and think you were perfect and every night I'd go to sleep thinking, somehow, during the day, you got even *more* perfect. If I could have wished what I thought was my perfect mate on the wind and had her come back to me in a storm, I could never have come up with anything as exquisite as you."

Sonia gazed wordlessly up at her king.

She had never, in her whole life, heard anything so beautiful.

Not said about her (even if it was said with clipped irritation).

Not ever.

She felt the tears welling in her eyes as she whispered, "Callum—"

But he talked over her. "I don't know what you heard when you were listening and no one knew you were eavesdropping or what was said to you flat out, but whatever it was, they didn't know what the fuck they were talking about. The minute you woke up in my bed in the cabin, I wanted you. I questioned it, that first day wasn't great, but I questioned it for about an hour before you started to get interesting. Then more interesting. And when we lay on the couch that first night I thought our lives together would be sweet..." His hand slid in her hair as she stared at him in loving shock. "And I knew by the night of your claiming when I fell asleep connected to you that our lives would be beautiful and I've never thought anything since except, every day, it seemed to grow impossibly more beautiful."

"Callum—"

Then he concluded, "Until the last three weeks."

She closed her eyes and everything that was him danced across her eyelids.

Callum holding her in his lap and telling her she had family.

Callum holding her close in his arms while the Christmas lights twinkled, telling her she was home.

Callum fiddling with her charm on her chain, wanting her to wear it outside her clothes so he could see it, his people's symbol, like her wedding bands, telling everyone that she was his.

Callum taking her sledding, playing board games and watching Christmas movies, then later, taking away the pain when her blood started to boil.

Callum bending over backward to give her the best Christmas she'd had in thirty-one years.

Callum coming direct to her after a bloody eight day battle and sleeping his exhaustion away with her held close and later trusting her to bury the hideous memories by taking her, again and again.

Callum's gentleness when she discovered Waring had died.

Callum letting her be who she was, the first person since her momma and papa died.

Just who she was, without hiding anything.

He'd been right those weeks and weeks ago.

And she'd been there for weeks and weeks.

She was there at that very moment.

She was *home*.

"I love you, baby doll," he said, his voice no longer annoyed. It was filled with tenderness and her eyes flew open to see his face was filled with the same thing. "I loved you before you took your first breath on this earth because that was my fate but *you* made me love you because you're just...fucking...*you*."

Her heart fluttered, her belly melted, and of its own accord, her hand lifted to the side of his face. Her fingers slid in his hair and she watched as her thumb smoothed his eyebrow then along the beautiful angle of his cheekbone and across the fullness of his bottom lip.

When her eyes went to his, they were closed and he looked, for some reason, as if he was experiencing a weirdly painful ecstasy.

"Cal?" she called. His eyes opened instantly, they were golden, she loved that so much she felt her heart swell, and she whispered, "You love me?"

He answered without hesitation. "With everything I am, baby doll, and everything I'm meant to be."

She felt the sob move up her chest. She lifted her head to shove her face in his neck and her breath hitched from the effort of holding it back.

Callum heard it, rolled to his back, pulling her on top of him, and he held her close, one arm at her waist, the other cocked along her spine with his fingers in her hair while she pressed her face into his skin, battling the tears.

A thought occurred to her. It was so huge, her body jerked with it and her head snapped up.

"You're real!" she cried with joy as if she'd made some fabulous discovery that was going to light the world on fire.

He grinned at her and said, "I'm right here, baby doll."

She stared at him, her dream man, her handsome wolf. She was in his arms in their bed in their room in their *castle*.

"You're real," she whispered.

His arms got tighter and he whispered back, "I'm real."

"And...and," she gulped as the enormity hit her, blocking her throat, "you're my puppy too."

His grin turned to a smile as he moved a hand around to caress her cheek tenderly with his thumb. "I'm thinking me being your 'puppy' should stay between you and me, little one. Not likely to strike fear in the hearts of my enemies, being known as *The Puppy*."

She giggled, shoving her face back into his neck. His arms wrapped tight around her and she felt him there. Right there. Not a dream. None of it a dream.

All of it real.

"Cal?" she called into his neck.

"Yes, honey?"

"You remember you asked me if I was happy?"

"Yes."

"I lied."

His arms tensed.

She lifted her head and looked at his wary eyes a moment before she put her mouth to his and whispered, "Now...I'm happy."

His hand slid back into her hair as his head slanted, crushing her mouth to his at the same time he rolled and he kissed her.

And his kiss was hot, sweet, wet, deep, long, and best of all, *perfect*.

Sonia woke in the middle of the night held close in Callum's arms.

They'd spent the entire day in bed making up for lost time with Callum leaving her only to go down and order food to be brought up.

All day, she'd been what she told him she was.

Happy.

Ecstatically so (as well as hot and bothered, but that was ecstatic too, as only Callum could do).

But things happened to your mind when you woke in the middle of the night and they happened to Sonia.

Taking in a quiet breath, she slid carefully out of his arms, out of the bed, and walked to her robe. Pulling it on and tying it tight, she went to the window and stared out at the night, the cloudless sky allowing the moon to shine bright on the snow making the forested hills a winter wonderland.

For a moment, she wished with everything that she was out in it, like Callum could do, turning to wolf and running through the snow in the night.

Or, at least, like she'd do with her papa, walking, seeing, listening, hearing, smelling, *experiencing*.

But then these pleasant thoughts melted away and Sonia realized that the cosmos wasn't quite done with its joke.

"Honey?" Callum called and she turned to him.

He was up on an elbow, his beautiful eyes on her.

"What are you doing up?" he asked.

"Thinking," she replied.

"Well, think over here," he ordered.

She felt her mouth quirk into a smile because he was really so gosh darned bossy.

She didn't, however, hesitate and she walked to the foot of the bed and then crawled up it on all fours, his body between her moving limbs.

When she got face to face with him, his arms came around her and pulled her down on his powerful frame.

His hand slid into the side of her hair and tucked her face in his neck when he asked, "What were you thinking?"

Again, without hesitating, she answered, "I was wondering how old you were when you locked in your development."

"Around one hundred and ninety-five."

Her head came up and she stared at him.

"You don't *look* one hundred and ninety-five," she told him and he grinned.

His hand came around to the back of her neck and he gathered her hair in his palm and twisted it into a rope, explaining, "In human years, around thirty-nine."

He was coiling her hair around his fist when she noted, "So, you're still older than me."

His face softened with understanding when he replied, "I'll *always* be older than you, Sonia."

She dropped her head down to tuck her face in his neck again, knowing this wasn't true.

It was the cosmos's last, big, huge, ugly joke.

He rubbed her hair at her jaw and called, "Baby doll?"

"Mm?" she answered, not wanting to talk anymore that night or *any* night if it was on this subject.

"You can think about it tonight, worry about it, be sad about it, but then get it out of your head," he offered on a command.

She felt the tears collecting behind her eyes when she whispered, "You'll always be beautiful."

He released her hair and rolled into her so she was on her back, he was mostly on her, and he lifted up on an elbow to loom over her.

Then he announced, "Wolves mate for life."

"What?" she asked.

"We mate for life. We never cheat. We're never unfaithful. We never leave. We mate for life. Our instinct, everything that makes us, everything that *is* us centers around our mate, our pack, our family. It's the only thing that matters. Not beauty, not youth."

"Easy for you to say," she mumbled, her eyes sliding away. "You'll be forever young."

Her eyes came back to him when he stated, "Right now I *feel* about as old as I am."

Surprised at this, she queried, "Why?"

He looked at her a moment, shook his head, and said, "It doesn't matter."

Then he bent his neck to touch his mouth to hers before he rolled again to his back, taking her with him.

But it was her turn to get up on an elbow and look down on him.

"Why do you feel that?"

"Sonia, let's just—"

"Is it because you know you'll have to watch me get old?"

"Baby doll—"

She cut him off. "No, really, Cal. Tell me."

"I shouldn't have mentioned it."

"But you *did*," she pushed.

"Yes, I did and it was a mistake." His arm came around his chest and he tried to pull her into his embrace, but she resisted and he unusually relented.

She planted a hand in his chest, beginning to feel funny. The happiness was sliding away and the despair was returning at the thought that he'd watch her get wrinkled and gray and weak and stooped while he stayed forever beautiful, tall and strong and, therefore, she demanded, "Cal, talk to me."

"It isn't because I have to watch you get old."

"Then what is it?" she pressed.

His brows drew together as his patience started to ebb. "Just let it go."

She put pressure on his chest and insisted hotly, "No, tell me what it is!"

"It's because I have to watch you *die*."

She sucked in breath and stared at him. That heinous thought hadn't occurred to her and she didn't know what to say.

"All these weeks we've been together, you've been thinking that I didn't want you. Do you know what I've been thinking, little one?" he asked softly and she didn't want to know, she really didn't, but she nodded anyway and he went on even softer, "I've been wondering how I'm going to carry on for centuries without you after you're gone."

Sonia felt her breath hitch painfully, and unable to hold herself up any longer, she dropped down, rested her forehead against his collarbone, and slid her arm around his chest.

Then she murmured into his chest, "You can't love me. I'm so self-absorbed. All this time, all I've been thinking about was me. How on earth could you love me?"

His hand slid into her hair and pressed her cheek to his chest as he said quietly, "Unfortunately, baby doll, we don't have enough time for me to explain all the ways I love you. That, in itself, would take centuries."

She laughed but it was without humor, pushing closer to his body, holding him tighter and tangling her legs with his. His fingers slid through her hair then again and again, until some time later when his hard warmth and his soothing fingers quieted her rampaging thoughts, she took a fluttering breath.

"So now you know," he said gently. "Our time is precious. So we won't waste it talking of this again. Agreed?"

She lifted a hand and sifted her fingers lazily through the hair on his chest.

God, she loved his chest.

On that thought, her fingers curled and she dragged her nails through the hair there as she whispered, "Agreed."

She went back to toying with his chest hair and decided at that moment he needed to know something very, *very* important.

"Cal?"

"Yes, baby doll."

God, she loved it when he called her "baby doll."

She took in a breath and asked, "You remember when you asked me if I loved you?"

His body grew still under hers and he answered, "Yes."

Quietly, she said, "That time, I didn't lie." She felt his still body grow tight and she finished, "Not about any of it." Both of his arms came around her but she pushed up, pressing her body to his and she whispered her story in his ear, "The first time I met you, my first dream, I felt you slide in bed behind me. You held me in your arms and I told you I was glad you were home. You kissed my neck and I lay in your arms thinking, 'This is the man I love.' It was short, just that before I woke up, but I felt strangely happy." She lifted her head, stared in his now tawny eyes and concluded, "In that first dream, I never even saw your face."

Both his hands came to her head, sliding into her hair, pushing it back.

Then he stated throatily, "You love me."

Sonia rested her lips against his but with her eyes open, and staring in his, she whispered, "With everything I am, wolf, and everything I'm meant to be."

Callum's fingers tightened in her hair and he rolled Sonia yet again.

He was kissing her by the time her back hit the bed.

It took a while before they fell back to sleep.

And when they did, they were connected.

In more ways than one.

CHAPTER TWENTY-ONE
UNDERSTANDING

CALLUM WAS SITTING in his study, going through a report on some of his investments when he sensed Sonia's approach.

She was wearing another pair of her thick socks so her footfalls were soft.

But that morning before he left her, he'd made love to her and she hadn't showered. He could smell the essence of them getting stronger as she got closer.

And he fucking *loved* that smell.

It had been a month since she'd finally unburdened her mind.

It was also only days before their official Mating.

And Callum couldn't fucking wait.

The hills were again filling with tents and the town was again bursting. Everyone wanted to be there, not because the king was formally binding his queen to him but because Callum was formally binding Sonia.

He'd been to many a Mating and he'd enjoyed them.

But he knew he'd like this one best for their last month together was better than the months before that.

Infinitely better.

It was beyond perfect.

It was a dream.

However, with Regan's assistance and Leah's long distance advice, he was planning a surprise to happen during their Mating. A surprise for his *wife*.

He was looking toward the door when Sonia rounded it and came into the room smiling.

The vision of her pretty, smiling, happy face settled pleasantly somewhere in his gut, he dropped his report, sat back in his chair, and returned her smile.

She made short work of the distance, her cashmere robe parting and exposing her shapely legs as she walked. He noticed, yet again, that she'd put on weight in the last month. As he suspected it would, it had hit all the right places and he was pleased with the result. But he was more pleased that she'd given up her obsession with calories and was simply, as she should, enjoying her food.

"I told Mara and Callista my claiming story," she announced when she came around the desk and he turned his chair to face her.

His brows went up when she seated herself in his lap and then curled up, her knees bent, feet close to her ass, torso twisted to face him.

"You did?" he asked, his arms wrapping about her small body, surprised at this news.

She shrugged as if it was all the same to her and she hadn't been guarding this secret for months.

Then her mouth quirked in a smile (something she did a great deal the past month) and explained, "They were relentless." Her body started shaking before she went on while laughing, "I think they didn't believe me though. Apparently, wolves are pretty excited during a claiming and they don't have the wherewithal to do it in multiple positions the first time." Her hand cupped his jaw and she brushed her thumb along his lower lip before finishing softly, "I think I've made you a legend, wolf."

He'd been smiling at her as she told her story, but at her endearment, he growled before he bent his head and took her mouth in a hard rough kiss that she returned instantly.

When he lifted his head, she emitted a fluttering sigh, tucked her face in the crook of his shoulder, placed her hand in the center of his chest and rested it there, something else she'd done a great deal in the past month.

His queen, he'd learned through a variety of delightful ways, was fond of his chest.

"I like how you kiss," she whispered.

"I know," he whispered back.

She shook her head in his neck and muttered, "So arrogant."

He gave her a squeeze.

She snuggled closer.

He loved these times when she'd come to him after breakfast.

Fuck, he loved every time he was with Sonia.

"Cal?" she called, her fingers toying with his sweater.

"Yes, baby doll?"

"I feel funny this morning." His arms tightened reflexively at this news and her head came up to look at him. "Not like that," she said quickly. "No, it's something else. I felt funny yesterday morning too and the morning before that." Her eyes went dazed and drifted over his shoulder. "I don't know how to describe it." Then she looked back at him. "It's almost like jetlag, though kind of nauseous but I don't get sick. It just like, I'm not one with my body somehow."

Callum's arms tightened again and he bit back a triumphant howl.

"We'll get you to a doctor," he told her.

She shook her head, still looking dazed, her mind preoccupied. "That's not necessary. I don't think it's that bad."

She'd be right, since she was pregnant with his pup.

She hadn't had her period since she'd been at the castle. He wasn't that familiar with humans but he did know they had their cycle monthly, rather than every five months like a she-wolf. And since she'd been there over two months, he reckoned she was at least that far gone.

If not more.

And he fucking *loved* that idea.

"Humor me," he ordered, her dazed eyes cleared and she looked at him.

"Bossy," she muttered but her lips quirked again.

His hands moved on her and her eyes widened in understanding before they got soft.

"Cal, the door is open," she whispered.

He didn't fucking care.

"Don't worry about it."

"Cal—"

He pulled the robe open, exposing her breast.

She sucked in breath.

Bloody brilliant, she was naked under the robe.

His head dropped and he took her nipple into his mouth, and not leading into it, sucked deep.

Her mind clearly no longer on the door, her head fell back and her fingers slid into his hair to hold him to her.

There were a myriad of ways he loved Sonia but one of them was how much he fucking *loved* how responsive she was.

He lifted his head, yanked the robe away from her other breast and did the same.

She shifted her soft ass against his hard cock, a low moan escaping her arched throat.

His hand went to her knee, pulled aside her robe and slid down the skin of her inner thigh, between her legs to find she was wet, already ready for him.

Always ready for him, his Sonia.

She was perfect.

He touched her, her hips jerked immediately, and she whimpered softly.

He smiled against her nipple then sucked deeper.

With his hand between her legs, Sonia arched over his other arm, and his mouth alternating between her breasts, he took her there. He listened as she came quietly (for once). She pulled in a soft breath and held it as he felt her sex clutch the two fingers he had embedded inside her and he rolled his tongue around her nipple as his thumb pressing against her sweet spot prolonged her release.

When she relaxed against him and her hands holding his head became fingers stroking his hair, he lifted his head and stared at his pretty little queen, her beautiful heated body exposed to him, her face soft, eyes hooded, gazing at him contentedly, and for once he could forget his future and feel at peace with his cruel fate.

His hand gently slid away from between her legs, he gathered her closer, and murmured, "You know I love you, baby doll?"

She nodded as her hands slid down through his hair so she was holding his neck. "You know I love you, wolf?"

He didn't answer, he kissed her lightly.

"You're still hard," she whispered against his mouth.

"Your sweet ass is in my lap," he explained, grinning against hers.

She grinned back before asking, "Do you want me to—?"

He cut her off. "Later."

He had things to do. When she put her mouth on him, he wanted her to take her time, which was how she preferred it too.

"Okay," she breathed, catching his meaning, and her eyes, even after just coming, were again hungry.

Fucking...

Perfect.

He heard Ryon's approach as did she and she straightened while he pulled her robe closed.

Then her eyes flew to his and she hissed softly, "God, Callum! I smell like sex."

Callum's grin changed and he said smugly, "Yes, you do."

She only had the chance to glare at him before Ryon hit the door.

When Callum looked at his cousin all thoughts, pleasant and smug, left his head.

"Hmm," Sonia mumbled, also looking at Ryon. "This appears to be my cue to go get a shower."

She turned Callum's face to her with a gentle hand at his jaw, taking his mind from his duties and bringing it back to her. Something she also made a habit of doing lately and something that he also liked.

She gave him a quick kiss and an understanding smile before scrambling out of his lap. Pulling her robe tight around her she tossed another smile at the frowning Ryon as she walked across the room, and with one last look at Callum, she closed the door behind her.

Ryon stood at the front of the desk and remained silent, his ear turned partially to the door waiting for Sonia to be out of earshot.

This, Callum didn't take as a good sign and he felt his jaw go hard.

After several long moments, Ryon tossed the two file folders he was holding on Callum's clean desk. Sonia had taken to keeping it ordered, which was a blessing and a curse. A curse because he never knew where anything was. A blessing because he had to find Sonia to ask when he needed something.

The files skidded and came to rest on the cleared blotter.

"Both of those came in this morning," Ryon announced in a low voice but Callum didn't touch the files. He just watched his cousin silently and Ryon continued, "The results of the analysis of Sonia's medication came in some time ago. But, in the end, I had to find one of our own to do it. I didn't understand it but what I *did* understand made me dig deeper. I gave it to Orphenon."

A muscle flexed in Callum's jaw but he still didn't speak.

"Orphenon called me the minute he, personally, finished a second analysis. He couldn't believe Sonia was being injected with that cocktail and I asked him to research it. I gave him her medical records and he looked into it. Then he did it more, talking to colleagues and even professors he'd studied under."

Finally Callum spoke. "I'm not thrilled that you shared Sonia's illness with others without asking me, Ry."

Ryon leaned forward and put his hands on Callum's desk. "And I knew you wouldn't be, that's why I didn't tell you." When Callum opened his mouth to speak, Ryon got there before him. "Her illness doesn't exist, Cal."

Callum closed his mouth and his chest tightened.

"Sorry?" he asked quietly.

Ryon leaned further into his hands and hissed, "It doesn't *exist*."

Callum also leaned forward in his chair. "I saw it happen to her. I felt her body. She was burning up. She was fucking *roasting*."

"I can't explain that," Ryon replied.

"It's rare," Callum reminded him.

"It's not rare, Cal. It...doesn't...*exist*. It isn't in *any* medical literature. No one's bloody heard of it."

"That's impossible," Callum returned.

"It's true," Ryon shot back, and pointing at the folders on Callum's desk, demanded, "Look at the report, top folder."

Callum did as he was asked, opening the folder and seeing on top a lab report identifying the various components in Sonia's medicine. The entire page was filled with the list and most of it made little sense, but at the top, the three items which made up the largest parts of the substance were easily identifiable.

"What the fuck?" he muttered.

"Human estrogen, werewolf estrogen, and human testosterone," Ryon clipped.

"Why the bloody hell would they inject her with werewolf estrogen and human testosterone?" Callum asked tersely.

"Who fucking knows?" Ryon replied. "Orphenon can't believe her system would even take a wolf hormone. He says some of the other things on that list are toxic to humans. Long-term use would be deadly."

It took all of Callum's self-control not to come out of his chair.

Instead, his hands simply balled into fists and he fought back the instant prickling of his skin.

"That's not it," Ryon continued, watching Callum closely.

"What?" Callum barked.

Ryon didn't delay. "Calder's boys finally discovered the source of who leaked the information to the rebels that Sonia is your queen."

Callum felt a chill slide up his spine before he prompted, "And that would be?"

"Yuri."

Callum stood so fast, his chair flew back toward the grate of the fire. His fury was palpable, his blood boiling, his mind focused on two things: halting the change and making someone pay.

"Bring Gregor to me," he ordered in a dangerous voice and then a sudden thought occurred to him and he went on, "And my mother."

Ryon nodded and he left at once to carry out Callum's order.

Callum took the time Ryon was gone to scan the contents of both folders. He wasn't in a better mood when Ryon guided Gregor and Regan into the room.

"Callum, what—?" Regan started but took one look at her son's face and her mouth clamped shut.

Callum didn't even look at Gregor. He turned to Ryon who was standing at the door. "I want Sonia occupied far away from this study. Talk to Mara."

Ryon nodded.

Callum continued, "Yuri's arriving this afternoon?"

Ryon nodded again.

"You'll meet his plane," Callum commanded. Ryon smiled in grim satisfaction and exited the room.

Callum took in his mother and the vampire.

"Sit," he snarled.

They did as they were told, Regan visibly agitated, Gregor, the cold-hearted prick, completely composed.

Callum didn't sit, couldn't, he was hanging on to his control by a thin thread.

He stared down at them and announced, "Sonia's disease doesn't exist. The medicine she's being given is a deadly toxin and Yuri is responsible for exposing her to the rebels as my queen."

"Oh dear," Regan muttered and Callum's eyes narrowed on his mother.

"Callum, there's an explanation," Gregor replied coolly.

Callum's gaze sliced to the vampire and he demanded, "Then you better give it to me quickly or I'll rip your bloody head off but you'll die knowing I'm going to play with your son until he fucking *begs* me to kill him."

"Sonia's dying," Gregor stated.

Those two words ripped through Callum's fury and all he could do was stare.

Gregor took in a breath and continued softly, "She became symptomatic as an infant. Naturally, as you experienced her symptoms first hand, you'll understand that Lassiter and Cherise were frantic to find some solution. Her illness, whatever it is, and even though they took her to dozens of doctors, they never discovered what it was, is unique. Like her abilities, which, I presume, since she's not hiding them anymore, you also understand."

Gregor let this sink in, and when Callum didn't respond, he carried on.

"When no answers were to be found, Lassiter and Cherise were forced to go on a voyage of discovery. They tried everything, and knowing of immortals, they widened their search. Wolf blood, vampire blood, vampire saliva, a cocktail of this, that, the other, *anything*. Some worked but only for a time and she'd display symptoms again. It took years but they finally found the solution, her current injection. But they knew, as did Mac and I, that it would only be a matter of time. We knew, because of The Prophesies, that the injection would only work for so long. We knew we weren't saving her life, we were simply prolonging it."

"It's my understanding that she inherited this illness from her father," Callum noted.

"That was a lie," Gregor replied.

Callum pulled in breath looking down and to the side. His chest had tightened again, powerfully, and the breath he'd taken did nothing to alleviate the pain.

Gregor continued, "We never told her. We wanted her to live her life free of the burden of this knowledge." Then he finished, "I'm sure you'll agree that was the right decision and keep to the pact that we three made."

Callum looked back to Gregor then to his mother and asked, "Perhaps one of you would like to tell me why *I* lived my life free of the burden of this knowledge?"

Regan stood and placed her hand beseechingly on the desk. "What would it have gained? You already knew she was human and struggled with that. To know her human existence on this earth was shorter still..."

Regan trailed off as her eyes slid away and she caught her lip between her teeth.

Callum stared at his mother, unwilling to process the emotions that were smoldering inside him.

Then he looked to Gregor. "And Yuri?"

"Let's just say that Mac and I disagreed as to when you should meet your mate," Gregor responded vaguely.

"Why don't you fully explain *that*?" Callum shot back.

Gregor exchanged a glance with Regan as she sat back down.

He looked back at Callum. "Mac knew you. He knew you'd want to have control of the meeting, the courtship, the claiming. He knew you'd go after her when *you* were ready."

When he stopped speaking, Callum prompted curtly, "And?"

"You were taking too long," Gregor immediately replied.

"I wouldn't have taken so fucking long if I knew she was *dying*," Callum bit out and it took him everything he had not to roar the words. "Which brings us back to the fact that you," his eyes included his mother in his words, "knew this fact and you didn't share it."

"It's forbidden for you to see The Prophesies," Regan stated quietly.

"Lucien has seen them," Callum returned.

"He did, indeed." Gregor put in steadily. "But he wasn't able to see all of them, however, only the parts we allowed him to see."

"Maybe someone can explain to me again *why* the major players in these Prophesies can't fucking read them?" Callum commanded through suggestion then finished with eyes narrowed on Gregor, "Or *all* of them."

"You've asked that question before, Callum—" Regan began.

"And I never liked the goddamned answer," Callum cut her off.

"Do you think *we* like this?" Regan retorted hotly. "Do you think it's been easy for *me* to keep this from *my son*?"

Before Callum could reply, Gregor spoke.

"I understand what you're feeling, Callum," Gregor said quietly. "And trust me, it doesn't stop the pain even knowing for all these years."

Regan shot Gregor a look but Callum missed it because he sat and swiped his eyes with his thumb and forefinger.

Then he looked at Gregor and changed the subject. "So you and Yuri decided to speed things up by putting Sonia in danger?"

"She was never in any danger. Why do you think we arranged for the information to be leaked to Saint that the rebels were amassing?" Gregor replied smoothly.

Callum leaned forward and clipped, "They broke into her house in the middle of the night, put their hands on her and terrified her."

"Yes, but she was unhurt," Gregor remained calm.

"She was thrown *across the room*," Callum hissed. "Hit her head and went unconscious. That is *not* unhurt."

Gregor held Callum's furious stare and rejoined, "We did what we had to do." When Callum opened his mouth to speak, Gregor went on quickly, "And, even as angry as you are right now, you can't have any issues with the results."

Callum sat back.

The cold-blooded bastard was right.

Callum had planned to meet Sonia at her Christmas party, weeks after he actually met her, and give her a human courtship, which would have lasted months.

Now, she was in his bed and his home. She was wearing his claiming chain and wedding rings. She was striding into his study every morning after breakfast with a smile aimed at him and curling in his lap, telling him stories while laughing.

And he was in her heart.

With nothing to be angry at, Callum was left only with that constriction in his chest that was making it difficult to breathe.

Gregor read Callum's altered mood. "I'd appreciate it if you'd continue to keep this knowledge from her. Protect her from it. Show her a good human life for as long as she has it and," he paused when Callum's eyes focused on his, "call Ryon and tell him not to harm my son."

Callum stared at the vampire for a second before he nodded.

Then he took in a deep breath which didn't seem to make it to his lungs before he ordered, "Leave me."

Gregor immediately prepared to leave but Regan again stood, leaned toward him, and put her hand on his desk.

"Callum—" she started but when her son's gaze met hers, she stopped speaking and her pale face grew pained.

He knew what she saw and he knew it was bleak.

"Please, Regan, leave," he asked quietly.

His mother's face softened, she nodded, and silently she and Gregor left, closing the door behind them.

Callum turned his chair and aimed his unseeing gaze out the windows.

He needed to run, *needed* it.

But he'd do it later when she was sleeping. He wasn't missing another fucking second of her life.

He stood and rounded his desk, his thoughts not on the variety of things he had to do that day. They were on finding his queen.

But he stopped suddenly and stared at a heavy glass paperweight

Sonia had purchased in town and brought in his study to use to hold papers down on his desk.

He picked it up and studied it, never really having seen it before.

The glass was clear with tawny swirls in its depths, the feel of it was cool and heavy in his hand.

It was actually quite extraordinary.

In a flash, he turned and hurled it across the room, and with the force of his wolf's throw, it turned to dust the minute it struck the stone wall.

He stared at the debris thinking that didn't make his chest any less tight either.

Then he went in search of his *wife*.

That night it was Sonia's idea to go out with him while he ran.

And, to be with her, Callum agreed.

As a human, she couldn't run, but even though it was night, as she always did when they were in the wood, she seemed at peace with her surroundings and the creatures in it were at peace with her there.

She wandered contentedly while he ran, coming back to circle her. To catch her eyes on him in tender awe. To move by her side for long minutes while she walked through the snow, her hand often coming to the fur on his head or his body and sliding through it lovingly.

Then he'd roam again and come back to her. And while roaming, he decided they'd do this every time he needed to run.

Eventually, he guided her home, and once she opened the back door and stepped inside, he crouched low and leaped, changed to man by the time his feet hit the floor.

When he straightened and turned to her, she was gazing up at him with shining eyes. She'd seen him change to wolf now three times. The first being when she was injured, the second before they'd gone out, and the last just now.

Still gazing up at him, she breathed in wonder, "That is *so cool*."

Callum smiled at the same time he pulled her in his arms.

Then he kissed her.

Then he lifted her and walked naked through the house, carrying her to their room, where he placed her in bed and he took her.

He wanted to go slow, take some of the little time he had with her to memorize her skin, her smell, her touch, the taste of her, the sounds she made. But Sonia was in the mood to play rough. The more Callum tried to be tender, the more demanding and hungry Sonia became.

So he gave her what she wanted.

After, Sonia lay with her head on his shoulder, her fingers sifting lazily through the hair on his chest.

He loved it when she did that.

"You okay, little one?" he asked.

He'd taken her hard and he wanted to make certain he hadn't hurt her. His voice was still gruff from his orgasm but also the memory of their time outside and the agonizing memories of his morning that were somehow, with Sonia close, less agonizing.

"Mm," she murmured contentedly, her fingers tensing to drag her nails along his chest and her legs shifted against his, tangling with them, her body pressing closer, entwining with his.

Callum smiled.

She was okay.

She did this now, entwining her body with his, getting closer. She did it all the time and Callum loved it when she did, even though it was exquisite torture, for underlying it he always knew he'd not share nearly enough of these moments with her.

"Cal," she called, her voice sounding like she sensed the turn of his thoughts.

"Yes, baby doll?"

Her hand flattened against his chest as if his skin could absorb it.

Or she could absorb something integral from his skin, something she needed, something she couldn't exist without.

And something hit him about this gesture, something he couldn't quite put his finger on, but Sonia spoke before he could call it to mind.

Then she whispered, "You know I love you, right?"

He closed his eyes at her words, remembering the dream.

They were living part of his dream.

He and Sonia said that now, "You know I love you?" It had become their way.

He hadn't recognized it as being from the dream before.

Now he did.

His arm about her tightened and his other hand came across his chest to slide into the soft, golden hair at the side of her head. It was thick and gleamed in the firelight, and studying it, he knew his next thoughts but he had them anyway.

How could he ever not have fancied blondes?

Because, he knew, they were never *her*.

"I know, honey."

"You'll never forget?" she was still whispering.

His lungs burned and his neck arched slightly as the living grief tore through him but he forced his body to relax.

"I'll never forget."

She cuddled close and her hand slid across his chest to wrap around him tight. "I want you to promise to be happy but I don't want you ever to forget."

"I won't forget."

"Promise to be happy?"

To live the perfect dream with the perfect woman what amounts to a blink in your long life only to have it swept pitilessly away and then find a way to be happy for eternity?

Impossible, Callum thought.

"I promise," Callum said.

"Thank you," she whispered.

"I love you, baby doll."

"I know," she said on a fluttering sigh and his chest got so tight, Callum found it hard to breathe.

She lifted up, pressed deeper into him, and he watched as she reached out to his nightstand and grabbed the wedding band he'd taken off earlier in preparation for transforming. She settled back beside him, her fingers curled around his wrist, and she unwound his arm from her body, lifting his hand toward her face.

Then she slid his ring on his finger and lifted his hand to her mouth. Her eyes soft with adoration never leaving his, she kissed the band.

She linked her fingers with his and whispered, "If you don't want to, you don't have to wear this forever."

He clenched his teeth and gripped her hand tightly.

When he could speak, he said low, "I'll always wear it."

"You don't—" Sonia started.

Callum cut her off. "Always."

She closed her eyes and Callum watched a single tear trail down her cheek.

At the sight, it took everything he had not to howl with grief and fury.

She opened her eyes and repeated, again on a whisper, "Thank you."

He was pleased he'd not dreamed this part.

That was, fortunately, the only thought he had time to have. Sonia slid up and onto his body, her fingers gliding into his hair at the side of his head and she leaned in to kiss him.

He rolled her and kissed her first.

That time he had her, he went slow.

He took his time and he committed to memory his mate's skin, her smell, her touch, the taste of her, and the beautiful sexy sounds she made.

CHAPTER TWENTY-TWO
CHANGES

"We could *try*," Sonia, sitting beside Callum in the SUV, snapped.

"Baby doll, we're not talking about this," Callum replied, trying to keep hold of his temper and stay calm.

They were on their way to Titium and his men's trial, which had been the source of their first disagreement that morning.

They'd had three.

Callum forbid Sonia to go.

Sonia didn't feel like being forbidden.

They had words. The words turned into a tussle. The tussle turned into play, and before Callum knew what he was doing, he was agreeing to let her attend the trial with him.

"All right, you can go," he'd gritted while fending off her hands, legs, and mouth, which were pushing, kicking, and biting intermittently with caressing, clutching, and licking. He'd had enough. He could smell her excitement, hear her panting, and at that point he wanted nothing but to bury himself inside her and he'd say just about anything to get what he wanted.

She'd grinned, stopped her struggles instantly, and lifted her head, running her tongue along his neck.

He'd taken a moment to memorize that sweet sensation before he flipped her, grasped her hips, and pulled her up to her knees, positioned himself between them and took her. Hard. Her reward for winning which was his reward too.

Christ, but she was the most sexually voracious human he'd ever met. He'd had her twice only six hours before.

And once already that morning.

Though, he wasn't complaining.

Now, he didn't even know what she was on about. Their second argument, God help him, about which boots he was going to fucking wear (another argument he lost, this time purposefully because it was so bloody ridiculous) had segued into a third and he wasn't paying attention.

He had a number of things on his mind, chiefly the unpleasant business of the trial, and further, what Sonia's reaction would be to it. Not to mention their Mating, which was scheduled for the next day, his secret plans, and what Sonia's reaction would be to that, something he hoped would be far more pleasant for the both of them.

"Why is it that you think you can say we're not talking about something and then we're not going to talk about it?" she asked crossly and he glanced from the road to her to see her glaring out the windscreen.

"Because we can talk about it later," he replied, not even knowing what "this" was and looking back to the road. "Now, it's important I explain what's going to happen at the trial so you'll be prepared."

Callum felt the air in the cab get tense and he reached out a hand to grasp hers in a warm grip, pulling it to his thigh and stroking her fingers with his thumb.

"That bad?" she queried softly, her fingers curling strong around his.

"To you, likely," Callum told her honestly then explained. "Our way of justice is not your way, little one. Wolves have very few rules, very few laws. We live and let live. Therefore, breaking one is treated harshly so others will be deterred from doing the same."

Sonia gave herself a moment to process this before she asked, "Are there attorneys? Solicitors? Will he have a chance to have his say?"

"He'll be allowed to speak," Callum answered. "They all will."

Sonia was silent another moment, he glanced at her again before looking back to the road and saw that she was no longer angry but looked reflective.

Then she asked, "What does harsh mean?"

This was the part Callum wasn't looking forward to, making his judgment, casting his sentence, and having Sonia hear it. He knew she wouldn't like it. He also knew, no matter how cunning and playful she could get, she would not be attending the executions. They were gruesome, even by a wolf's standards. A human, especially a human like Sonia, wouldn't be able to endure them.

"He committed treason, baby doll," Callum reminded her quietly and he felt the air in the cab grow tenser and her eyes turn to him.

"It's my experience that there are wolves who can be hot-headed, Cal, and he's a father. It's clear he was blinded to his daughter's illness by fatherly love, and although wrong, it's understandable. Perhaps, since it happened, he's had time to reflect."

"He challenged me, and in doing so injured my queen," Callum pointed out then concluded, "Who is, incidentally, also *his* queen."

"But what if he's—?" she began but he squeezed her hand and glanced at her again before turning his eyes back to the road.

"I am rarely challenged except during a rebellion or skirmish, little one," he told her gently. "One reason for that is I cannot be bested. This is not a boast. This is the truth. The other reason is, if it's done, the punishment is harsh. I do not have time for this. You've worked beside me now for weeks. You know my duties are onerous. We're having our Mating tomorrow. My attention being on this and away from other, more important matters has a ripple effect throughout the kingdom. If a statement wasn't made, anyone who was angry at a decision I'd handed down or simply drunk and acting stupid could think they could try their hand at besting the king. I could be spending all my time on the steps of Canis, engaged in challenges. This is one of the reasons why any ruler, any government, must deal with situations such as these harshly."

"Okay," she replied slowly. "So what does harsh mean?"

"What is the usual punishment for treason, baby doll?" he returned quietly and heard her pull in a swift sharp breath.

She knew what it was.

Then she noted, "I thought wolves were immortal."

Cautiously, he explained, "If you sever our heads from our bodies, that is something we cannot survive."

To this he received another swift intake of breath.

Then she began, "Callum—"

He cut her off to tell her something she had to know. "I do not relish this any more than you do, Sonia."

"I know that!" she cried, her voice suddenly rising. "But this isn't a drunken wolf, trying his hand at besting you like it was a Wild West gun-slinging faceoff, may the fastest draw win, and the winner gets nothing but the opportunity to brag. Family is all-important to wolves, you've said that to me yourself *dozens of times*. He was defending his daughter. Yes, it was misguided, but that doesn't negate the fact that was what he was doing, and I think somewhere deep you understand why he did it. And loyalty has to be almost as important, which was what Titium's wolves showed to him and yet they, too, will receive this punishment? The end of their lives for doing nothing but standing there and being loyal?"

Callum felt his temper again start to rise. "I told you we would not speak of this again but it seems you've forgotten he hurt you. The fact he did it at all is unforgiveable, but he did it *in front of me*. You were in harm's way, he knew it, and he still acted, and that, my queen, is indefensible." He gave her hand another squeeze. "I cannot let it stand."

"Then don't let it stand, Cal," she returned swiftly. "You're right. He did wrong and caused harm in the process. But I will point out, you were in a mood when you met him on the steps of Canis and that mood was not the mood to sit down like men with honor I, at least, know *you* are, and talk things out. I know I'm your mate and protecting me is serious business for you wolves, but I don't want you to be upset when I say that it really is *me* who gets to forgive or not forgive that he hurt me and I forgive him, Cal." She paused a moment before she told him quietly, "It was an accident. He surrendered immediately after he saw he harmed me. He knew he did wrong and felt badly about it, so perhaps you can think of another punishment that's less..." she paused and finished, "*final*."

Callum felt his temper rise further. "Are you suggesting, little one, that *I* was partly at fault for what happened?"

"I'm not suggesting anything," she retorted. "I'm saying that maybe then and now there's another way to go about things, and perhaps, before you do something that cannot be undone, you may want to reflect on both."

Callum drew in a long breath to calm his anger before he replied firmly and with finality, "This is the wolves' custom, Sonia."

She fell silent and Callum drove, still angry and part of this had to do with the fact that Sonia riled him up prior to one of the few loathsome duties he had as king of the werewolves. By now, she should know better, but apparently she did not.

Every moment of every day he was aware that his time with her was short and just as aware that she didn't know it. He very much wanted to explain yet again that in times like these, he needed her support, not a confrontation. However, it was highly likely (he hoped) that in her short life, she wouldn't need to endure another time like this, so he decided to let it, and the inevitable argument it would cause, go.

He drove up the winding, ill-kept road, through the wood and turned right, driving through the thick trees. He heard another swift intake of breath when the trees suddenly cleared and there it was.

The Lodge, a huge, circular building with a large, paved car park around it, and beyond it on either side, two four-story parking structures. It was made of reddish, gold-brown Canis stone, and had ten of his royal pennants flying from its crenelated roof. It looked like a human's sporting arena, albeit small, but with the stone and crenellations, more imposing. The inside held stands, also like a human's stadium, in a circle facing down to the pitch. Although small by human standards, it could hold ten thousand wolves.

That day, considering the vehicles parked around, he reckoned it would be half full, something else that grated on Callum's frayed nerves.

This was expected, considering the hills were full to celebrate The Royal Mating and therefore he'd planned for it, his guard being there to keep order as well as several detachments of soldiers.

It wasn't that Callum expected anyone to disagree with his judgment. It was that wolves could be vengeful and, thus, bloodthirsty. They loved Sonia. They expected the verdict he was about to give, he had little doubt they would rejoice in it, and with wolves, that could easily get out of hand. Further, Sonia might find this at best, distasteful, at worst, repugnant.

Callum, on the other hand, did not rejoice in giving the order to bring about the end of lives. It was a weight on his soul that only Sonia had the ability to alleviate, but again, he held the bitter knowledge that his mate would not always be there to provide this succor to him.

With this heavy on his mind, he drove around the curving entrance that led to the doors closest to where the royal dais would be set inside as Sonia noted, "This place is amazing."

"The Lodge, little one," he muttered distractedly, putting the SUV in park, and switching off the ignition, still muttering. "Games are played here. Official business is conducted here. As you know, our Mating will be here tomorrow. And, last, trials are held here."

"Cal," she called.

"Mm?" he murmured, his hand on the door handle, his mind on what was imminent.

"My handsome wolf, please look at me," she requested softly.

Her endearment slid through him like silk and he twisted his body and moved his eyes to hers.

Then his gut clenched at the gentle expression on her face, an expression filled with love and understanding.

She leaned forward and placed her hand against the side of his head, running her thumb along his eyebrow, down his cheekbone, and over his lower lip as her pretty green eyes watched.

All right, so maybe she did support him, just, as ever, in her way.

Her gaze moved to his.

"I have not been a good queen this morning," she admitted quietly.

"Baby doll—" Callum started, leaning toward her but she leaned further into him and pressed her thumb against his lips.

"Can I finish?" she asked and he held her eyes but nodded.

She pulled in a soft breath then whispered, "Tradition is a beautiful thing."

Callum felt his jaw tighten but he said nothing.

She continued, "But, my wolf, compassion is often mistaken for weakness when the fact is, there is very little that is more powerful than the courage it takes to give it. The one thing I know that's even more powerful is the courage it takes to forge your own path, make your own mark and in doing so, make change. Leaders who follow are never remembered because they aren't actually leaders. Leaders who are trailblazers, who lead their people to better horizons, who do that with strength, wisdom, *and* compassion are revered. You must do what you must do in there, as king to your people and as mate to me. But the reason you find it so difficult to show mercy is because it's difficult to be merciful."

She leaned closer and her voice dropped softer, lower, sweeter as her eyes held his.

"And the last thing I know, *my* handsome wolf is the strongest werewolf there is and this is not only because he is a great warrior. I saw him write letter after letter to the families of those who had fallen so I know it's also because he's compassionate. He can do anything and he can do it not just with his claws and his teeth."

After that, she leaned in, swept her thumb away so she could touch her lips to his then she sat back in her seat, her eyes on him, her smile small and gentle, and waited for him to exit the truck and open her door for her.

Callum drew in another breath as her words settled in his mind, his gut, and around his heart.

Then he turned to his door, his lips twitching because his little queen had demonstrated yet again one of the myriad of ways she was absolutely fucking *perfect*.

She proved this further when he helped her out of the cab and she walked silently at his side, shoulders straight, head held high, tipping her chin up and giving a small smile to Ryon, Calder, and Caleb, who were standing outside the door waiting for them. She held his hand fast as he tucked it to the side of his chest, keeping her close as they walked through the doors Calder and Caleb opened and into The Lodge.

Half his guard was lined up inside. They fell into step in front of Callum and Sonia, Ry, Calder, and Caleb moving in behind and Callum led his mate to the dais.

Looking around, he saw he had been correct. The Lodge was half full and there was a low din of conversation. As his guard moved and it became clear the king and queen were in attendance, the din quieted and Callum pulled his mate closer to offer her reassurance as he felt thousands of eyes move to them.

She clutched his hand and walked at his side, their bodies brushing as he moved her up the steps. As per custom, those in their seats kept them because there wasn't enough room to take a knee in the stands, but the accused and the soldiers standing at the foot of the dais all dropped into the heads bent ceremonial bow.

Callum seated himself on the throne. Sonia moved of her own accord into his lap, her face, carefully blank, was turned to the men in front of them.

Callum waited until Ryon, Calder, and Caleb situated themselves to the left and right of his throne and his guard lined the steps of the dais before he called his order in a loud deep voice, "All but the accused, rise."

The soldiers moved to their feet. Titium and his men kept their heads bowed.

"Titium, you and your men keep your knee but face me," Callum commanded, his voice ringing out in the silent huge space helped by microphones situated at the foot of the dais.

He watched as Titium and his men lifted up from their hand in the pitch and faced him on their knee.

"For official purposes," Callum continued, dipping his head to a small table off to the side where a she-wolf sat, her fingers moving on the keyboard of a laptop to record the proceedings, "even though what you've done has spread far, I must proclaim the charges against you."

Titium nodded and Callum moved his gaze from the warrior to look amongst the wolves in attendance, sitting in the stands and watching avidly.

Then he called, "I will remind my brothers and sisters that my mate is human and today's proceedings are not a celebration. The men standing accused are warriors who have all, over the years, and I will remind you, very recently, put their lives in danger to stand gallantly against those who rebelled. I will be displeased if you show them less than the respect they deserve. In other words, throughout the proceedings and until your queen and I leave, I expect silence."

A short-lived murmur swept the crowd before Callum got what he commanded.

His eyes moved back to Titium and he began.

"You are charged with treason, warrior. As your men stood with you when you challenged me, they face the same charge. You carried through this challenge, and in so doing, you injured your queen. I will remind you this was witnessed by a prince, a duke, the dowager queen, and many of my personal guard. I will now listen to how you plea as well as the pleas of your wolves."

"I speak for myself and my wolves, your grace," Titium replied, his voice ringing loud and strong and Callum again was reminded of how loathsome this duty was. Titium was a bad father but he was an excellent warrior, loyal to Mac, loyal to all wolves, strong, brave, confident, and until recently, noble.

"And how do you plea?" Callum prompted, feeling Sonia tense against him even as he tensed himself.

"We plead guilty, your grace," Titium called, chin up, bearing proud in the face of the dire consequences that he knew would happen not only to him but to his men after giving this plea.

Another murmur swept through the crowd before Callum's eyes sliced through it and it silenced.

He looked again to Titium and opened his mouth, his gut twisting, his chest burning.

Then he shut his mouth.

His eyes moved through the wolves on their knee behind Titium. He recognized only one. He was a wolf who had fought at his side, though Callum couldn't recall his name. He was young. He needed training with his teeth but he made up for it being excellent with his claws. Callum didn't remember his name but he remembered he had not found his mate, not back then, sixty years ago. He had not, thus, started a family, and if he had since, his children would still be mostly pups, his life with his mate barely beginning.

After the verdict, he would have no chance to be father to his children, if he had them, and his mate was right then in the stadium, facing Callum's future.

His gut twisted sharper, the burn in his chest searing through him, he drew in breath, looked back at Titium, and Sonia's words rung in his head.

What it was, was your way because you are king.

Yes, and I believe that it was also once the way of my people to treat diseases by using leeches, but they found another way that works a whole lot better so now they're doing that.

Leaders who are trailblazers, who lead their people to better horizons, who do that with strength, wisdom, and compassion are revered.

Callum stared at the wolves in front of him.

What it was, was your way because you are king.

You are king.

He was king.

"Rise, Titium," Callum commanded, watched Titium's body jerk in surprise, and ignored the stunned murmur that swept through the crowd.

Titium took his feet but did so not taking his eyes off Callum.

"Your love for your daughter is honorable, your loyalty to her is as well, and your wolves' loyalty to you is the same," Callum announced, ignoring Calder muttering, "Fucking hell," at his side.

"That said," Callum continued, "all of it was misguided, you acted on it, and the result could have been disastrous."

Titium's eyes shifted to Sonia, remorse filled his features, and he lowered his head.

A proud warrior stood in front of his king and queen, filled with remorse, swiftly taking responsibility for his actions, admitting his guilt, speaking for his wolves, bowing his head in defeat, awaiting judgment.

You are king.

Callum kept speaking and Titium looked back at him.

"However, my queen has grave concerns for you, your wolves, and even your daughter, regardless of your actions and what pain they caused her." He watched Titium's lips part in shock as he felt Sonia turn rock solid in his lap but he went on, "She has had my ear on this subject and she wishes for me to show mercy. I find this difficult. Your claws drew my mate's blood. But if she can forgive you for the damage you inflicted on her, then I can show mercy for your actions, which were, indeed, treasonous, but I believe, if we had time for cooler heads to prevail, it would have had a different outcome."

Titium blinked up at him as his wolves behind him swung their heads back and forth, glancing at each other, and the murmur of the crowd swelled before it silenced when Callum kept speaking.

"Therefore, I strip you of your Governorship of Europe and your command of the European Armies. I sentence you to attend your sequestered daughter until she has been brought to her right mind. If that should occur, which is doubtful, you will stay at her side when she is released from sequester and while she quests for her mate. Only after her Mating will you be free to resume your life, but you will not ever, while I rule, hold office or command men. Your wolves will not be eligible to hold office or assume a command for one hundred years. They will, prior to returning home, denounce fealty to you and announce it to me. You, Titium, will personally pay a fine of one million dollars to Canis, which will be submitted to our war chest. Your wolves will each pay a fine of fifty thousand dollars for the same purpose."

As a louder ripple went through the crowd and Callum watched the shoulders of the wolves in front of him slump with relief, one even bowed his head and covered his face with his hand as she-wolves sitting to the sides, mates and mothers of the men before him, burst into tears, Callum kept speaking.

"If any one of you again moves against Canis, there will be no trial. You will be executed immediately and burned on a pyre without family allowed to attend. Your ashes will be scattered without ceremony, a dishonor even traitors do not receive."

Callum watched Titium swallow, his face reddening with emotion, his eyes darting back and forth between Callum and Sonia even as he heard Sonia's breathing escalate, her chest rising and falling rapidly, her ass squirming minutely in his lap.

"Do you have something you wish to say?" Callum asked Titium.

"I..." Titium cleared his throat then asked in disbelief, "You show mercy?"

"Were you not listening?" Callum asked impatiently in return.

"But—" Titium started.

Callum felt his brows rise. "You prefer execution?" he inquired and a titter of humor went through the crowd as the men in front of him tensed.

"No!" Titium said loudly and swiftly, shaking his head. "No, no. I..." His eyes moved to Sonia. "My queen—"

Callum suddenly leaned forward, taking Sonia with him, and he growled, "My wife has my ear, warrior, and she has spoken for you, but *you* address *me*."

Titium looked quickly back at Callum, squared his shoulders, sucked in a visible breath, and announced, "I only wanted to thank her for her mercy and offer her my apologies for the pain I inflicted, your grace. You are correct. My behavior was loyal but misguided and I have, these past weeks, thought long and anguished on the hurt I caused our little queen, who was doing nothing but trying to save me from myself and causing that hurt by acting rashly and in anger. I will never, not ever, your grace, forget her lying on the steps of Canis, brought low by my claws and my pride. A human female who tried to persuade me to see reason and who moved in defense of her mate."

He shook his head as if he still didn't believe he'd witnessed this or caused it before he continued.

"For myself, my mate, and my wolves, I...there are not words to say how...how much our queen's forgiveness and your mercy means. My mate would..." He swallowed then pressed on, "My daughter, my sons, the families of my wolves," he looked to Sonia then hastily back to Callum, "you and she have saved them centuries, *millennium* of grief. She...you both have saved our loved ones that and..." He shook his head, swallowed yet again, and finished, his voice rough, "I'm sorry, I don't have words."

"If you don't have words, Titium, then I suggest you accept the mercy shown and my judgment so my queen and I can go home. We've important things to do tomorrow," Callum suggested and another titter moved through the crowd.

"I accept your mercy and judgment, your grace, for myself and my wolves, and I thank you on behalf of my family, my wolves, their families, and myself," Titium proclaimed loudly.

"Good, then we're fucking done," Callum muttered, ignored the relieved giggle Sonia barely suppressed, the chuckles Ryon and Caleb didn't try to suppress, and stood, taking Sonia with him and putting her on her feet. He turned to the she-wolf at her laptop. "This concludes today's business." He looked to Ryon. "See to the arrangement of the sentences and fines." Ryon, grinning like an idiot, jerked up his chin. Callum looked to the crowd and called out, "Tomorrow, we'll see you here under better circumstances."

There was a moment of silence before a cheer rang out, loud and deafening, hitting Callum and his queen with a wave of sound and Callum had to hide his surprise, for they weren't simply cheering tomorrow's joyous festivities.

They were cheering his decision.

It wasn't entirely shocking they would accept his verdict. He was king, they had no choice.

It was just a surprise that they did it so readily and apparently so soundly.

Then again, many of them had found their mates therefore many of them had their mates whispering in their ear. It was likely they were not fazed by the changes Callum had demonstrated that day knowing a human like Sonia whispered in his. Or, not so much whispered, but she found her way to get her point across and he, finally, learned how to listen.

He tucked Sonia's hand against his side, drawing her close, and he got them the fuck out of there.

They were in the SUV, going down the winding road surrounded by wood and Sonia was surprisingly silent.

Then she wasn't.

"Callum?" she called.

He braced, wondering if what she'd say would piss him off or make him want to kiss her.

"What, baby doll?" he asked on a sigh, knowing, either way, it was better to get it over with.

"You know I love you, right?"

It made him want to kiss her.

"You know I love you?" he replied then he heard her shift before he felt her lips against his neck and her fingers curl around his thigh.

"Yes," she whispered, her voice throaty. She shifted again, straining against her seatbelt to slide her nose the length of his neck before she buried her face there. Her voice was low and hoarse with feeling when she went on, "Yes, Cal, I know you love me. Today, I also know just how much."

He did indeed love her.

A great fucking deal.

Absolutely.

"Good," he murmured, his own voice thick.

"Yes." She was still whispering. "It is good. *Very* good." She gave a fluttering sigh that he not only heard, but felt against his skin before she finished, "Perfect."

She was right.

Very right.

In a number of ways.

He had his pretty little mate pressed up against him, her back to his front on the hide covered couch when the film ended and Sonia shifted to reach out to the remote. She hit off, threw it on the table, and the minute it clattered, he pulled her under him and rolled over her.

She looked up at him, smiling a small smile, her eyes dropped to his mouth and they went hungry, something, as ever, he felt in his groin.

But he, unfortunately, had to ignore that in order to say, "Time for me to find my bed and you, ours."

She blinked and her eyes moved to his. "What?"

"I believe, and correct me if I'm wrong, which I'll point out, I hope to fuck I am, it's tradition amongst humans for the bride not to see the groom before the wedding," he told her and her mouth dropped open.

She closed it to repeat a now breathy, "What?"

"Am I wrong?" he queried hopefully and she blinked again.

"Uh...no, you aren't," she whispered. "But—"

He interrupted her by dropping his head to touch his lips to hers before lifting it and concluding, "So I'll find my bed and I'll see you at the wedding."

"Are you serious?" she asked softly.

"Unfortunately, yes, and after tomorrow, I'll ask you to explain why humans do something that's that bloody stupid," he replied and her mouth twitched.

"It's supposed to be bad luck," she explained.

"Stupid," Callum returned then amended, "Bloody stupid."

Her lips curved into a grin and her arms curved around him. "You're going to let me sleep alone to give in to a human tradition?"

"Yes," he replied but he didn't even attempt to squeeze the reluctance out of his word.

"You're going to let me sleep alone for the first time, notwithstanding the nights you were away at war, of course, since I met you so you can give me one of my people's traditions."

It was a statement and a repetitive one, but Callum treated it like a question and repeated, "Yes."

Her hand slid up his back, around his neck, and framed the side of his head as her thumb came out to sweep his cheekbone but her eyes never left his and he thought that if she didn't stop holding him and touching him, he was taking his offer back.

Before he got the chance to warn her of this eventuality, she spoke.

"If you find your own bed, Callum, I'm moving to that one. I was your mate before I was born. I've been your wife for months. It means the world to me you'd do something like that for me and I love you for being willing to do it. Just as I love you for doing what you did today, not only for Titium, his wolves, their families, but also proving you listen to me and care about what I say. Just as I love you for taking Calder's bad mood and sharp words and Caleb and Ryon's ribbing for doing exactly that. Just as I love you for a million and one other things we don't have time for me to enumerate because I'm tired, I want you to make love to me and sleep beside me in order that I can wake up tomorrow refreshed so I don't look a mess when I stand beside you in front of thousands of wolves during our Mating. But we were destined to lie by each other's sides since before we were cells in a womb. Therefore, I'm not going to sleep without my wolf. In other words, if you find another bed, you're also going to find me in it."

Callum stared down at his *wife* for half a second before he growled then he growled down her throat because he was kissing her.

He pulled away, got to his feet, lifted his *wife* in his arms, and carried her to their bed thinking, *fuck it.*

If it was true, this human nonsense of bad luck, so be it.

They already had bad luck. The worst there was.

And he wasn't going to lose a moment of Sonia that he didn't have to lose.

She wanted him.

She had him.

As always.

As it would always be.

Until that dreaded day she no longer was.

CHAPTER TWENTY-THREE

THE MATING

"Um...don't you think it's a bit much, Mara?" Sonia asked hesitantly as Maraleena moved around the back of her, aiming a mirror at Sonia's hair while Sonia held a mirror in front of her face, taking in the complicated, but artful and lovely, twists and curls that Mara had pinned in a thick wide bunch at the nape of her neck.

"No, Sonny! Absolutely not! Today's a big day and there will be pictures of you and Cal in every wolf newspaper in the world. It has to be perfect!"

The butterflies in Sonia's stomach, already out of control, went into overdrive.

She'd found a pretty, but simple, ivory dress online and had it delivered. It was definitely more than what Mara and Callie had described a she-wolf would wear at her Mating but far less than any self-respecting human bride (unless she was a hippie or just not that into dressing up) would wear. Sonia thought it was a happy medium, although she had to admit, if only to herself, that she would have preferred the pomp and circumstance. A dress encrusted with lace and pearls, her hair just as it was, fabulous shoes, and all the trimmings of a wedding.

Actually, a Royal Wedding.

She was queen, it had been a bumpy ride, it would have been nice if she'd had something amazing to remind her how glorious it was and would always be.

Until she was no longer.

She pulled in breath through her nose, hiding the fact she was doing it and deciding it was good she wouldn't have pomp and circumstance.

It would always be a happy memory for her.

For Callum, once she was gone, it would be a tortuous one.

So this was good. Simple. Fast. Then a big party.

"You look lovely," Regan whispered from close and Sonia's eyes slid to the side to see her mother-in-law standing there, tears shimmering in her eyes, which made wet hit Sonia's. "Or, *more* lovely than you usually do," she corrected.

"Thank you, Regan," Sonia whispered back.

"Lassiter and Cherise," she pulled in breath, Sonia did the same, and Regan continued, her voice husky, "they would be very proud."

"Thank you," Sonia said softly, lowering the mirror to her lap.

Regan reached out and pulled it from her hand then she set it aside, pushed her hand into the pocket of her smart trousers and pulled out something that glinted but Sonia couldn't see it. Regan's hand curled around Sonia's and she pulled it to her. Pressing out Sonia's pinkie finger, she slid a thin, gold, antique-looking band with a small yellow diamond in it on her pinkie.

Sonia stared at the ring and her startled eyes went to Regan when she stated, "Your mother's mother gave that to her when she was a girl. Your mother gave it to me for safekeeping to give to you today."

Sonia drew in a shocked, painful, joyous breath as her fingers curled tight around Regan's and tears flooded her eyes.

"Oh Sonny!" Mara cried. "Your makeup!"

"Let her cry," Sonia heard Callie say quietly. "We'll fix it."

"I—" Sonia began.

"Say nothing," Regan cut her off then finished on a whisper. "I know. What you need to know is that Cherise knew, Lassiter knew, they knew you loved them just as much as they loved you."

Her lips quivering, she could hold them back no more and Sonia whimpered as Regan pulled her into her arms and held her close.

"I'll get the makeup again," Mara muttered from behind them as Sonia held on tight.

And she kept doing it for a long time.

Regan returned the favor.

Sonia stared at herself in the full-length mirror that had been brought up to her and Callum's room.

Her hair was not right and her makeup, again fixed after crying in Regan's arms, was also too much for her dress.

Way too much.

Way, way, *way* too much.

Her eyes flew to the clock on Callum's nightstand. They had thirty minutes until she had to be in the SUV with Gregor and Regan, who were taking her to meet Callum at The Lodge.

"Um...maybe we should—" she began but stopped because she heard and smelled him.

She also heard something else and smelled it too, the scent familiar and her heart started beating hard as she turned and trained her eyes on the door.

Seconds later, Callum, so handsome he hurt her eyes wearing a well-cut, beautifully tailored tux, strolled through carrying an enormous white garment bag over his forearm.

Sonia stopped breathing even as her mouth dropped open.

Callum looked at her from head to toe then caught her eyes, grinned his sexy grin, and declared, "Baby doll, that's pretty but it just won't do."

He then turned to the bed, threw the garment bag on it, and strolled out of the room, Kerry and Mabel streaming by him on their way in as he made his way out.

Sonia started breathing but only to hyperventilate.

"Oh my God! Can you believe this place?" Kerry shrieked, racing to Sonia and throwing her arms around her.

As usual, not to be outdone, Mabel screeched, *"Scotland is awesome and Callum McDonagh is even awesomer!"* and Sonia felt Mabel's body hit her and Kerry's embrace and they moved to fit each other in their clinch.

"I can't cry, I can't cry. We already did my makeup twice," Sonia told them, holding on tight.

Kerry pulled back, held on with one arm, and lifted her other hand to fan Sonia's face, and, as Mabel followed suit, Kerry ordered, "Don't cry. We don't have time. We have to get you dressed and then we have to get dressed too."

"Yes, sweetheart, we have to get you dressed," Regan proclaimed from beyond them.

Sonia looked to her and she lost her breath again for Regan was holding up a beautiful wedding gown encrusted with lace and pearls, and standing beside her was Callie, holding up a fabulous pair of elegant, sophisticated, stylish, stiletto-heeled, ivory slingback pumps with pearl-encrusted, pointed toes.

Cinderella shoes. Absolutely.

"Oh good goodness," Sonia whispered.

"Callum thought you might want something special so he sent me shopping," Regan informed her.

"Oh good goodness," Sonia repeated on a whisper and how she managed it with her throat closed was a miracle.

"She asked our opinions and we all agreed," Mabel announced.

"As did I," Sonia heard said from the direction of the door, her eyes shifted from the beautiful wedding gown and fabulous shoes to the door and she saw Leah standing there.

Leah had told Sonia that she and Lucien were tied up, they couldn't come to The Mating, but they'd come for a visit as soon as they could.

She'd lied.

"Oh good goodness," Sonia moaned promptly before she burst into tears.

Kerry and Mabel folded her in their arms and only stepped aside when Leah took over.

"I'll get the makeup again," Mara muttered on a sigh.

Sonia burst out laughing but she did it through tears.

Happy ones.

Sonia sat between Regan and Gregor in the Rolls Royce, the fabulous car another surprise, on their way to The Lodge.

Leah, Kerry, Mabel, Mara, and Callie had all changed into their lovely, but secret, deep jade bridesmaid dresses after they'd helped Sonia dress. Regan had donned her stylish, pale yellow mother-of-the-groom dress. Before Gregor helped her fold into the Rolls, Regan had handed her a huge stunning spray of calla lilies intermingled with fluffy tufts of lilies of the valley that not only looked regal as well as just plain stunning, but smelled divine.

Her gown, shockingly, fit like a glove, but then again, Regan had long ago measured her for a, "Sweater I'm going to knit for you, sweetheart." Sonia, at the time, hadn't thought why Regan smoothed the measuring tape from hip-to-sole and everywhere besides. She'd had too much on her mind and didn't knit, so what did she know?

Now, she knew.

Her gown, as everything Callum, his mother, and Leah (she found) put together, was *perfect*.

Elegant and opulent, yet somehow simple, the gown skidded over her figure perfectly, the entirety of the ivory silk covered in delicate ivory lace, including the five foot train that trailed behind her. Pearls and opalescent beads decorated the lace, but not in abundance, simply catching the eye and giving the gown even more personality. The neckline was princess, the gown sleeveless, the line graceful, skimming her body to her knees then flaring out slightly in an elegant fall to a lace, scallop-edged hem and train.

She couldn't have picked better.

Teardrop pearls suspended from diamonds, a gift from Regan, dangled from her ears.

Something new.

The ring of her mother's Regan gave her on her pinkie.

Something old.

A single strand of pearls with a diamond and gold clasp sat on her wrist, loaned to her by Leah.

Something borrowed.

A garter made of blue satin and edged in intricate lace circled her thigh, given to her by Kerry and Mabel.

Something blue.

Her claiming chain hung from her hips, given to her by Callum.

Something wolf.

She was ready for her wedding and she looked *exactly* like a woman about to marry a king.

But she was feeling funny, as she had been now for weeks. Strange, like jetlag, not herself, but lately it was accompanied by what felt like hot flashes, the skin on her entire body getting warm for sometimes seconds, sometimes whole minutes before it would cool.

She lifted the bouquet to her face, took in a breath, and then let it out, but it didn't help.

Nothing, she'd found, did.

"Are you quite all right, Sonny?" Gregor murmured and Sonia looked to her vampire.

"Yes, I'm wonderful, Gregor," she told him and his lips tipped up but his eyes moved over her face.

"You're a bit flushed, my dear," he noted and she lifted a hand to fan her face.

"Just...feeling strange. Probably stress. It's been going on for a while. I suspect, after this is over, it'll be over," she told him and was too focused on what was to come, she missed his eyes moving swiftly to Regan before coming back to her.

"Sonny, sweetheart, are you and Callum, um..." Regan trailed off and Sonia turned her head to her mother-in-law.

"Are we...?" she prompted.

"Uh, planning on pups sometime soon?" Regan finished and Sonia grinned.

"No, I'm on birth—" she stopped abruptly on a gasp, leaned into Regan, and asked in a panic. "Do human birth control pills work with werewolves?"

Regan smiled a gentle smile, reached out, and gave Sonia's hand a squeeze before she replied, "Yes, Sonny. Usually a doctor will prescribe a certain brand as, obviously, werewolves have, uh...a different hormonal make up, but it's unusual for a she-wolf or human to become pregnant if a woman is taking any kind of oral birth control."

Sonia sat back in her seat on a relieved sigh.

"Does Callum know you're on birth control?" Regan asked and Sonia looked to her again.

"I, well, I think so. I mean, we've been together awhile. I don't recall if I've ever taken it in front of him but he's never brought it up so I assumed he knew I had it covered. I mean, we would discuss having, well," she grinned, "*pups* and decide together when the time would be to start trying for a family."

Something which, on their honeymoon (Callum told her they were going to have a honeymoon thus it was not a surprise) she'd be bringing up.

For her, the sooner the better. Mara, Callie, and Regan had explained werewolf DNA always won out over human and any offspring created in a wolf/human interaction was wolf and therefore immortal.

Callum would have centuries with their children. Sonia, decades.

She wanted to start right away.

"I think, sweetie, you may want to discuss this with him at your earliest convenience," Regan advised quietly and Sonia again grinned at her.

"Oh, I will," she whispered, Regan's eyes lit and they shifted to Gregor.

Sonia's followed and she saw Gregor slightly shaking his head and frowning.

"Vampire grandpa, of sorts," she muttered her tease, sliding into him and burrowing so he had to lift an arm and wrap it around her shoulders.

He looked down at her and muttered with distaste, "Vampire grandpa to werewolves."

Sonia grinned.

Gregor kept frowning.

Sonia pressed closer and kept grinning.

Gregor's eyes moved over her face, his frown faded, and his gaze grew warm. "Vampire grandpa to my Sonia's children."

Sonia took in a quick breath and warned, "Don't make me cry, Gregor."

"Fine, Sonny. So deep breathe or do whatever you humans have to do to withstand enduring something like this," he warned then he gave it to her. "You're beautiful today. You're beautiful always, but today, you glow. I love you, my dear, I have from the moment you came to me even if that moment was a sad one. And I'm immensely proud of you."

She deep breathed, taking those breaths in through her nose and letting them out of her mouth as she stared at him.

Then she whispered, "I love you too. I have for ages and I'll do it forever."

He nodded, a muscle in his cheek twitched and he turned his head to look out the window but his arm around her curled tighter.

Regan grabbed her hand and held just as tight.

Twenty minutes later, on Gregor's arm, Sonia received all the pomp and circumstance a woman walking toward her husband the king should have.

Following Calder and Caleb escorting their mother then her string of bridesmaids, who wandered the length of The Lodge to the dais where Callum, Ryon, Drogan, Magnum, joined by Calder and Caleb, stood, all looking breathtakingly handsome in tuxes, Sonia noted the entirety of the space not taken up by wolves was festooned in ivory silk rosettes, bunting, and so many calla lilies, lily of the valley, and white roses, Callum had to have bought every bloom, not only in Scotland, but all of Europe.

The building so big, the procession took so long, the women walked the space to Beethoven's "Ode to Joy," a full symphony and chorus behind the dais filling the beautiful acoustics of the space with some of the most extraordinary notes ever put together.

And on that day, as Sonia looked around in wonder and beamed up at her mate who gave her all of this, the song was aptly named.

For she was joyous.

Surrounded by friends and family.

People who accepted her for who she was, exactly who she was.

People who loved her.

And in love with a man, well, a wolf, who she loved with everything she was, everything she was meant to be.

Therefore, Sonia Arlington-McDonagh beamed as the horns and strings played a masterpiece accompanied by a hundred voices, the air was filled with the scent of lilies and roses, thousands of wolves stood, their eyes watching her progress, their faces wreathed in smiles, and she, a queen, walked to the mate the benevolent hand of fate had given her, a man she'd dreamed of most of her life, her handsome wolf, a king.

And she did so having no idea that in thirty short minutes, she was going to die.

CHAPTER TWENTY-FOUR
DEATH

CALLUM STARED in Sonia's shining green eyes as he listened to her sweet, throaty words, up close and broadcast through the space via microphones, as she said, "I do."

He smiled.

Tears filled her eyes.

"Right, uh...now, wolf," the wolf official at their sides muttered and Callum tore his gaze from his queen and looked at the male. "Callum," he prompted with a nod of his head Callum's way.

Callum nodded back and looked back down at his *bride.*

"Are you mine?" he asked, his voice gruff.

"Yes," she whispered immediately, her voice still husky and her eyes got brighter.

A deafening cheer tore through the crowd.

The official leaned toward Sonia. Callum, holding her hands in his, felt her start and her head turned slightly as the male whispered something in her ear. Callum's smile grew wider as she blinked in shock, her head jerked to look back at him, her lips parted, her eyes warmed, and she spoke.

"Are you mine?" she asked, this new nuance of The Mating something he came up with just that morning.

He was king.

He could do anything he wanted.

And he wanted to give to her what she gave to him.

"Yes," he replied in a strong carrying voice and another deafening cheer filled the space.

Sonia smiled, her hands tightening in his. Her smile was shaky, but even so, it was beautiful.

Callum let her hands go but only to push his into his trouser pocket and pull out what rested there.

A gold charm for her claiming chain, this one another wolf but with tiger's eye for eyes to match the band he'd added to the ones he'd already given to her. He opened the link with his thumbnail and closed it on her claiming chain.

When his eyes captured his *bride's* and his hands again caught hers, he could see, even though her head was tipped down to stare at her new charm, she was biting her lip.

She lifted her gaze to his and it was still beaming, but brighter, luminescent.

Happy.

He grinned.

"It's my pleasure to pronounce you, King Callum, and you, Queen Sonia, husband and wife and, er, wolf and lifemate!" the official declared and both Callum and Sonia looked his way to see him smiling broadly. "I've always wanted to say this," he went on then finished, "You may kiss the bride!"

Finally, Callum thought, *the good part of this human ceremony.*

He turned back to his *bride* and grinned what he didn't know was a wolfish grin, her wet eyes dropped to his mouth and he heard her fluttering sigh.

Then he bent his head, tightening his grip on hers, and he kissed his *bride*.

Another roar tore through the space.

Even as he heard it, tasted Sonia on his tongue, smelled her scent in his nostrils, he felt her hand rip from his and move to clutch his lapel.

He broke the kiss to look down at her and saw she was suddenly flushed, her eyes vague.

"Baby doll?" he muttered low so the microphones wouldn't catch it.

"I'm fine," she whispered. "Just fine," she stated quietly but she tore her other hand from his and pressed it to her forehead even as her fingers at his lapel gripped tighter and she leaned her body to his.

"Sonia," Callum called when her eyes drifted to his chest.

He lifted a hand to her jaw and his gut twisted when he felt how hot her skin was. He gently pressed up, forcing her eyes to his and they were beyond vague.

They were pained.

"Little one," he murmured, dipping his head close.

"Okay," she said softly. "I think maybe I'm not fine."

The instant she finished her statement, her legs went out from under her, and this was such a surprise, she nearly dropped to the dais before Callum caught her in his arms.

The roaring crowd stopped roaring as a hush filled the space.

Callum didn't notice it because, even through the lace and silk of her gown he could feel his wife's body was afire.

As he lifted her to cradled in his arms, his eyes sliced to his pale-faced mother sitting in the front row, and he shouted, *"Regan!"* right before, with long strides, he moved to the side of the dais, down the steps and around the back, under the stands and into a short hall where there were training rooms, dressing rooms, and locker rooms.

He took her to a dressing room, laid her on a couch, sat at its edge, and took her hand.

Her eyes fluttered open.

"Cal, get the gown off me," she begged in a pained voice.

"Hang on, baby doll. Regan has an injection," he cooed, holding her hand tight as she started shifting on the couch.

"I need this gown off me," she repeated, clutching his hand and beginning to move with agitation.

"One second, honey," he told her and smelled Regan before he saw her rush in, Gregor on her heels, Yuri not far behind, and after him, Caleb, Ryon, Calder, Sonia's bridesmaids, and Lucien.

"A guard on the door, Ry," he ordered, his eyes then moving to his mother, "Injection."

She was already digging in her purse as she rushed toward them.

"Cal." Sonia's hand gripped his in a death hold. "Please, honey, *please*, get this gown off me. I'm burning up."

"The injection's coming," Callum assured her.

"Sonny, my dear, did you forget your injection last night?" Gregor asked.

Having moved close, he squatted down beside the couch.

"No," she shook her head, her eyes heated and dazed, "Cal gave it to me as usual."

Gregor looked to Callum. "Stress?" he murmured.

"Maybe," Callum murmured back as Regan handed him the loaded syringe.

"Get a cool cloth, hurry." He heard Yuri order someone as Callum looked down at his mate.

"Roll to your side, little one, I'm injecting through your dress," Callum told her and she stopped shifting with agitation and rolled to her side as ordered.

Callum made swift work of injecting the medicine.

He then carefully pulled her up and into his arms. "Two minutes," he whispered in her ear. "Two minutes, baby doll, hold on."

She writhed in his arms, fighting him as he counted it down in her ear.

At one minute five seconds, her back arched so violently she nearly tore herself out of his arms, her head flew back and she screamed a scream filled with agony.

Callum's blood ran cold.

"Fucking hell, what the fuck?" Yuri growled from close.

"Here's a cold cloth," Leah said, handing it to Gregor, who immediately moved in to press it to Sonia's forehead.

He had it there for not a second before she bucked again, letting out a primal scream that tore through the space and straight through Callum's heart.

Sonia shot double, her hands forming claws, tearing at the bodice of her gown as she cried, "It's not working. It's not working. I need this gown off. *I need this gown off!*"

Callum's head shot around and his eyes pinned Calder. "Find the wolf who's been trained to see to this. Get me another injection," Callum ordered.

Calder, also pale, nodded and sprinted from the room.

Sonia's hands moved from her gown to claw at Callum. "Cal! *Get this gown off!*"

"We're getting another injection," Callum told her, trying to sound soothing, but even he could hear the worry in his voice.

"I'm calling her doctor," Gregor snapped, straightening to standing, reaching into his jacket to pull out his phone.

"Do something, for fuck's sake. More cool cloths. Ice. *Fucking something!*" Yuri shouted.

Callum tried to control Sonia's thrashing. "Hang on, Sonia. Hang on, baby doll. It's been too much for you. We should have planned. The trial, The Mating. We should have planned."

She stopped thrashing, her hazy eyes finding his. "This isn't right," she whispered, her voice panicked, anguished, terrified.

Callum felt a presence, he knew who it was before he looked up, and saw Lucien standing close.

"Let me feed," he requested gently as Leah moved in with the cool cloth to press it to Sonia's forehead.

Distractedly, Callum noted Leah's head jerk before it snapped up to look at her mate, her face shocked as well as pained.

"Vampire saliva has healing properties, Callum, powerful ones. You know this. Perhaps, until her medicine arrives, it will give her some relief," Lucien suggested.

"Do it, anything," Sonia begged. "Anything."

Callum looked to Leah to see her face had blanked and she was pressing the cloth to Sonia's forehead.

He knew in that instant, if Lucien fed from Sonia, it would be a betrayal to his mate and it might not be worth that large of a sacrifice because it might not work.

"You can't," he muttered, looking back to Lucien, and he finished, "Your mate."

"I can," Gregor stated, stepping forward.

"She's your daughter," Yuri hissed, his voice repulsed.

"Yes, and I want her to *survive*," Gregor fired back.

"Then I'll do it," Yuri announced moving toward them.

"Fuck, *fuck*," Callum clipped, looked down at his agonized bride, took in her torment, and made a decision. "Yuri is going to feed from you, honey. Try to stay calm. It won't hurt."

She nodded, clearly in agony, clearly willing to try anything.

Callum moved away and Yuri moved in, gently pulling Sonia up, twisting her in his lap as he sat in the couch, and Callum felt his entire body turn to stone.

"Please, darling, try to stay still so I don't do you more harm," Yuri murmured in a soft voice, his arms tenderly gathering Callum's mate to him, one hand cupping the back of her head, moving it to the side, exposing her neck, and Callum tasted bile in his throat.

Her eyes came to him and he forced his lips to curl up. "It's going to be all right, baby doll," he assured.

She nodded.

Yuri ran his tongue along her neck and it took everything Callum had to fight back the instinct roiling in him to tear his mate from the vampire's arms and rip him apart.

Powerless and hating fucking *everything* about that feeling, Callum watched as Yuri tore his bride's flesh open and he fed.

This lasted too long, way too long as Yuri gathered her closer, closer, fucking *closer* and took more.

Again, suddenly, Sonia's body arched violently, ripping her throat from the vampire's teeth, blood poured down her chest and she screamed that hideous scream.

Yuri moved in quickly to lash her neck with his tongue, the healing began slowly, but Callum was there, tearing his wife from the vampire and pulling her into his arms.

She again thrashed, struggled, clawed at him, now keening animal noises that seemed physical, shredding him.

He could take no more.

"*Where's that goddamn injection!*" he roared, moving to sit on the couch that Yuri vacated, holding his mate as close as he could get her, feeling her flesh burn to the touch.

"This isn't good, Cal. This isn't good, my wolf," Sonia said, her voice weak, the fear in it palpable, her body's struggles unceasing.

The door swung open and Orphenon followed by Calder ran into the room and straight to Sonia.

"The injection?" Callum bit out and Calder handed it to him as Orphenon got close, grabbed Sonia's flailing wrist, and then dropped it immediately.

"Jesus," Orphenon whispered, glancing quickly at Callum before he went for Sonia's wrist again and demanded to the room at large, "A tub, ice, immediately! Get someone to my car to get my bag!"

Callum turned his mate and moved to inject her.

"How many is that?" Orphenon asked, his tone dire and urgent and Callum stopped.

"Dose two," Callum told him.

"Your grace, I don't think—" Orphenon started.

"It's the only thing that works," Callum clipped.

"It's poison, your grace," Orphenon whispered, Sonia gasped then bucked then arched and shrieked so loud, so long, and so horrifying, it was a wonder everyone's ears didn't immediately start bleeding.

Callum held her close but leaned into Orphenon. "It's worked for decades."

"I'm not sure it's wise," Orphenon replied but Sonia jerked mightily and shrieked yet again.

"If you don't think it's wise then what do we fucking *do?*" Callum snarled, setting the injection aside and again fighting her struggles in order to pull his mate close.

"We need to get her temperature down immediately," Orphenon answered.

"Do you think?" Callum's tone was snide.

"I can see you're upset and I understand that, I do, but I know what's in that injection, Callum, and two doses is absolutely not advisable."

"She's burning alive."

"That's why we need to get her temperature down."

"Then how about we cease discussing it and *do that?*" Callum gritted.

"Cal, Cal, Cal, my wolf," Sonia called suddenly, her voice strange, hideously weak at the same time desperate, and Callum jerked his gaze to his wife, his blood now ice in his veins at the sound. "Cal, Cal, Cal," she chanted feebly.

"Baby doll, I'm right here."

"Cal, it's happening," she whispered, her hand moving to clutch his lapel again.

"We're going to get your temperature down, honey," he assured her.

"It's happening," she repeated, her hand in his lapel tightening, drawing him to her, pulling him close, but she didn't have to. He bent into her as frantic activity bustled in the room.

"We're getting a tub of ice. It's going to be all right," he promised.

"You know I love you?" she whispered and Callum felt his heart squeeze because her tone was frail, but it was also final.

"Yes, I do and I love you too, baby doll. Now, hang on."

"With everything I am," she stated, so softly, her voice fading with each word and Callum felt her body burn into his as her fingers started to loosen on his lapel.

No, this was not happening.

He pulled her closer, tighter. "Stay with me, Sonia. Stay with me, little one."

Her eyes filled with tears and held his as she whispered, "With everything I was meant to be."

This was not happening. It wasn't happening. It *couldn't* happen. She had to survive, at least until it began.

This was *not* fucking happening.

Then it happened.

His mate, his bride, his wife, his *queen* went limp in his arms. Her green eyes open and still on him, there was nothing behind them. No focus. No light.

They were vacant.

Dead.

Dead.

Just.

Like.

That.

He stared into her pretty face and whispered, "This is not happening."

Sonia didn't move, her hand had fallen away from his jacket, he felt no breath from her lips touch his face, the room around him was still, a dread feeling creeping through the space, slithering, cold, ugly, heinous.

"This is not fucking happening," he whispered, cradling Sonia close, smelling her smell, feeling the burn of her body cooling.

He didn't twitch as Orphenon moved in, placing his fingers to Sonia's neck as Callum stared into her face.

Vacant.

Dead.

"Please, God," he begged, "make this not be happening."

Orphenon's fingers moved away and he said quietly, his voice grave, "Your grace, I'm so sorry."

It was happening.

Rage tearing through him, Callum surged up, holding his mate's lifeless body tight to his massive chest, he threw his head back and thundered useless words, *"This is not fucking happening!"*

He felt a hand light on his arm and his mother's soothing voice, "She's gone, Callum, sweetheart. We knew this day would come. Please—"

Callum twisted, leaned in, and barked in his mother's face. *"This can't happen!"*

She didn't flinch.

She lifted a hand to the side of his face, hers was tortured, understanding of his pain etched in her features, and she whispered, "I'm so sorry, my beloved boy."

It was then, he felt it. His skin prickling. The change was coming and he knew he couldn't stop it. He couldn't.

He didn't even fucking want to.

He turned, bent, and placed his bride's body on the couch like she was a piece of priceless crystal, which she goddamned was, and he stared into her eyes one last time.

Then he lifted a hand and closed them, his throat tightening, his skin beginning to burn. He bent deeper, taking in her scent, his eyes moving over her still flushed skin, registering she looked peaceful and hating it. Wanting her to sit up and argue with him. Tease him. Smile at him.

Fuck, he'd take her writhing and shrieks if it meant she was still breathing.

But she wasn't breathing.

He closed his eyes, pulled in her scent one last time, then bent close and touched his mouth to hers.

"My bride," he whispered against her motionless lips. He opened his eyes and they met hers that were closed and would be for eternity. "With everything I am, everything I'm meant to be, baby doll. Always."

He heard quiet, muffled female whimpers but he ignored them. He took off his wedding ring, lifted her hand and placed the band in her palm. Closing her inert fingers around it, he pressed it to her belly.

His pup.

He closed his eyes.

He lost his wife and his pup.

On his fucking wedding day.

Yes, he could take no more.

He turned, crouched and gave in. Leaping to wolf in mid-air, he landed on his paws and bolted through the bodies. Out of the room, past the guards, through the onlookers held back at the mouth of the hall who stared and gasped as they saw their king race through them, stepping back to give him room. One opened the door to the building and he shot through.

And he ran.

He ran for miles, for hours through the wood, his heart pumping, his paws moving, the needles on the trees brushing his fur.

He felt nothing.

Nothing.

In a way he knew he'd never feel anything again.

Except the pain.

Callum sat as wolf, howling his agony through the trees to the full moon.

It didn't help.

It couldn't help.

Nothing would help.

This was his eternity.

An eternity of agony.

He thought he was prepared for it.

He fucking wasn't.

Suddenly, he smelled it. He stopped howling, his head jerked down and around as he came up off his haunches.

There was a she-wolf out there.

He stared through the dark trees, his body tensed as the scent came closer. It was familiar but it was not his mother, who he would imagine would come looking for him. It was also not any she-wolf he knew.

But, fuck, it was familiar.

Then she appeared, stumbling through the trees, clumsy, as if she'd transformed while inebriated, but as he watched he noted she moved not drunken but disoriented.

She crashed toward him, seeming, strangely, not at one with her wolf. In fact, her movements actually appeared frightened. Then her body suddenly jerked sideways and she stopped.

Her muzzle turned his way and the she-wolf went completely still.

Christ, even through his grief he registered she was a beautiful wolf. He'd never seen a she-wolf as beautiful.

Just as suddenly as she stopped, she charged straight at him, so fast, he barely had time to shift to the side to miss her. As she drove past, he bared his teeth and nipped her warningly but gently on a flank.

She whirled, moving toward him, whining.

He barked at her.

She came closer as he shifted away but she kept coming, trying to butt him with her head, her movements awkward, unpracticed, her wolf whine constant.

Fuck, she was a young wolf. So young, maybe it was one of her first transformations outside of pup. Young pups transformed constantly and with no control. Parents worked with them when they grew older to teach them how to manage the transformations to do it at will. It was likely she'd gotten away from her parents, but what was clear was that she was terrified.

He barked at her again and reached out with his teeth to nip her flank. She pulled her hind end away after she received his careful bite, so awkward, she fell to her haunch in the needles.

Callum barked again but she seemed unable to understand the wolf communication. She righted herself and kept trying to nuzzle him with her snout, constantly whining.

The noise, seemingly desperate and trying to communicate something she hadn't yet learned to convey as wolf, tore at his shredded heart.

He wanted peace to attempt what he knew would be futile, soothing his ravaged mind.

As a wolf, and king of the wolves, he had to get this terrified she-pup to safety.

He rounded her and began herding her, something she clearly didn't understand and fought, keeping on her course of attempting to butt him with her nose, her head, as if she was trying to mark him with her temple.

Definitely a pup. Instinctively, pups marked sires, mothers, siblings, and, sometimes, elders. She-wolves, as wolves and in human form, marked their mates and offspring. He sensed this pup attempting to mark him was an attempt to mark an elder.

He moved around her, continuing to steer her toward Canis, and it took some time but she finally seemed to understand what he was trying to do and began to run with him, falling to his flank and staying there as he led her to Canis.

Once they arrived, he'd turn her over to Regan to find her parents then he would lock himself in his study with a bottle of whisky (or five).

Or he'd transform again and spend the next year in the woods as wolf.

He was coming to the decision of doing the latter when he led them to the back door of the castle. Instead of transforming to man and in doing so maybe making himself incapable of controlling her, he pushed in through the tall, wide lower door set into it that was there to allow entry as wolf.

She followed.

He then crouched to make the transformation in order to latch the lower door so she couldn't escape, but her deep brown eyes held his and suddenly she jerked around and started running through the castle.

Fuck, Callum thought before he darted after her.

Like she knew exactly where she was going, she raced to the steps and up them.

Fuck, Callum thought again as he raced after her.

Up she went, up, up, and she dashed straight into his and Sonia's goddamned room.

He skidded to a halt outside the door.

He didn't want to be there. He could smell her scent from outside and that scent, her scent, all that was left of his Sonia, he couldn't bear it.

He didn't want to be there. He never wanted to enter that room again.

He heard the she-wolf howl.

Fuck, he thought yet again as he snarled and shot into the room then he skidded to another halt and stared.

She was jumping around, leaping, her body twisting this way and that. She abruptly stopped, whined, got down on her forepaws then leaped again, twisting her body in mid-air.

She was trying to transform.

Callum used his haunch to slam the door closed in order to contain her, crouched, and leaped to man.

Quickly, he prowled to a wardrobe, yanked it open, and pulled out a pair of jeans.

Tugging them on, he ordered, "Calm, wolf, focus and crouch. Do nothing more. Hold there and then listen to me."

She didn't listen. She got down to her forepaws again, jerking her mahogany-furred head this way and that, then her wolf body stilled. Unexpectedly, she started digging under the couch, whining desperately, so frantic, she pushed the couch back with her body, her entire head shoved under the couch.

Then she backed out, lifted up, and twirled to him, Sonia's stuffed wolf in her jaw.

Callum's heart lurched and it was pure unadulterated agony.

That stuffed wolf, the symbol of him her parents gave her that she held close before she met him and continued to hold close even after she had him had disappeared around the time he found her rings in the fire.

He had not questioned Sonia about it. Knowing she'd acted in anger with his rings, he suspected she'd done the same with her wolf.

Apparently, like the rings, her wolf had survived.

Now, with her scent that lingered in the room and his wedding band held in her lifeless hand, it was the only thing he had of her that held any importance.

"Drop that!" he snarled but she didn't.

She rushed him, racing around him, circling, butting his thighs with her head, all the while whining.

"Drop the goddamned wolf!" he barked, leaning into her only for her to jump up to her hind paws and claw his chest with her front ones.

He pushed her off, made for Sonia's wolf, but she jerked her head away and pranced out of reach.

"Goddamn you, drop my wife's fucking wolf!" he roared.

She dropped the wolf, backed up until her tail hit the wall, then she burst forward. Suddenly stopping on a skid and crouching through it, she leaped, transformed in mid-air and dropped to the floor on her belly as human, her body naked and flushed, a mass of shining, extraordinary mahogany hair falling down her back and over her shoulders.

She was facing the floor, her hands to her sides, palms flat to the rug, and she was panting.

But Callum was frozen.

Completely.

He knew her scent because he knew her.

He'd dreamed her.

She was the she-wolf in his dreams.

"This isn't happening," he whispered.

"It seems," she spoke and it was so quiet, even with heightened hearing he could barely hear her, "that I *am* like your people." She lifted her head, arching her neck way back and Callum stared in shock, his body still frozen, as beloved, familiar green eyes caught his and she finished, "Wolf."

Callum blinked as something inside him shifted, fluttered, lightened.

Hope.

But, even staring at her, he couldn't believe it.

She pushed up to her knees, sat back on her calves, wrapped her arm around her breasts, the other around her belly, her eyes never leaving his, her glossy, magnificent dark hair framing her cherished face, and she noted, "Uh...the naked thing, not so fun. And, for a while there, I thought I'd be wolf forever. It was pretty cool until it was terrifying."

"Sonia?" Callum called, his voice low, quiet, disbelieving.

She stared up at him.

Then she smiled.

Then she whispered, "Get this, wolf. I'm a wolf."

She was wolf.

She was alive and *she was wolf.*

Callum came unfrozen and he was on her in less than a second. Hands under her arms, he hauled her up then tossed her across the room. She landed on her ass in the bed and he moved, landing on her.

Covering her body with his, his hands framed her face, his eyes caught hers, he watched the warm dark brown filter out the green and there she was.

His wife, his mate, his bride, his queen.

His wolf.

He dropped his head and kissed her.

Sonia curved her arms tight around him, spread her legs and then wound them around him, protectively, lovingly, and kissed him back.

It was just the same. Absolutely the same. Her taste, her kiss, his Sonia.

Just wolf.

Her human life will be fleeting.

But her wolf life could last an eternity

On that thought, Callum kissed her harder, and Sonia, as ever, returned the gesture. Her hands moving to the waistband of his jeans, she rounded it to the inside and he lifted his hips so she could get to his fly.

She made short work of it, pressing into him to pull his jeans down his hips.

She broke her mouth from his. "Now," she ordered.

Callum didn't make her ask twice. He buried his cock inside her heated wetness, straight to the hilt.

Her neck arched, her moan filled the room, her legs around him convulsed as her sex around his cock tightened.

"Yes," she whispered.

"No," he growled.

Her neck righted and she looked at him, perplexed, her brown eyes hungry.

"No?"

"Assume the position," he ordered, felt his lips curve even as they muttered, "Wolf."

Her eyes went hooded and he knew she understood. He pulled out, moved minutely to give her the ability to shift and she crawled out from under him. She got to her hands and knees in front of him then looked down the length of her body at him as he turned to a hip, yanked off his jeans then lifted up to position between her spread, quivering thighs.

He guided his cock to her opening, sinking just the tip inside.

"Cal," she breathed, pushing back, but he withheld as he reached forward and wrapped a fist in her thick, lush, dark hair even as he kept his eyes to hers.

"Are you mine?" he asked and he watched her face go soft even as it grew hungrier.

"Yes," she answered quietly. "Are you mine?"

"Fuck yes," he growled and drove into her, yanking her head back by her hair, but she'd already arched it, crying out her pleasure.

She reared into him as he drove into her, hard, deep, fast, rough, hot, fucking, *fucking* beautiful until he felt her sex spasming around him, her pants turned desperate, and her rearing turned to bucking.

"Cal," she breathed.

Callum pounded hard and deep, the momentum growing, his consuming orgasm nearly over him. "Give it to me, baby doll."

She gave it to him, arching her neck again, the sounds of her climax piercing the air, drowned only by his roars.

As it left him and Sonia's left her, he gentled his strokes, his hands at her hips drifting over her skin, the pinpricks of her injection, he noted with some surprise, were completely gone.

Then again, wolves healed swiftly. Gaping wounds might take hours but needle pricks would take only moments.

It occurred to him then that there were a variety of people who had some explaining to do.

But he'd demand that later.

Now it would be about him and his *bride.*

He shoved his hips into hers, she knew what he wanted and came off her knees, spreading her legs wide and clutching his cock with her sex to keep their connection. He settled his body on hers, but even if she was wolf, she was still tiny and therefore he did what he always did, resting some of his weight into his forearms on either side of her.

With his chin, he nuzzled the hair at her neck.

"Good news for you. Apparently, I'm not a blonde," Sonia muttered, he lifted his head and saw her eyes slide to the side to look at him.

They were still brown.

They were also smiling.

She was sated.

Happy.

Happy to be wolf. Happy to be his.

Callum moved his eyes to her hair and muttered back, "I'm going to miss it."

"Liar," she whispered and he looked back at her.

"No," he stated firmly, lifting one hand to pull the thick softness away from her neck, running his fingers through it as he rested it against her other shoulder. "It's true, baby doll. It was you."

"I could dye it," she suggested, her lips twitching.

He stared at her, feeling her under him, her sex surrounding him, wet and silky, her scent, part Sonia, part wolf, filling his nostrils, her eyes, now green with spikes of brown in them, warm and tender, and it hit him.

"We have eternity for you to try whatever color you want."

Her mouth went soft as tears filled her eyes. Callum pulled out, rolled to his back, and pulled her on top of him. She shoved her face in his neck and his arms closed tight around her.

He held her as she struggled to hold back the tears and this lasted a good while before he felt her calm.

He took one arm from around her so he could pull her hair from her face as he asked, "Do you know what happened?"

She shook her head against his neck but answered, "One second, I was sleeping really deeply, the next, I was on fire again and suddenly up and..." She paused, lifted her head, looked down at him in wonder and cried, "*Boom!* I was a wolf. It was crazy. I didn't know what to do, but my wolf body did and it took off. I know I caught your scent, even if it was only lingering. I followed it and I ran and ran and then I heard you howling and I ran right to you."

He stared up at her trying to glory in the fact that first, and most importantly, his mate was not dead, and second, and nearly as important, she was not ever going to die, instead of giving in to the searing anger he felt permeating his joy.

"I think I destroyed my gown," she muttered before biting her lip.

The searing anger dissipated because he burst out laughing. His arms closing around her, he rolled her to her back with him on top.

He lifted up and looked down at her face.

Her dark hair spread on their pillow framed it and he wondered if he'd get used to it. He had an eternity to do it so it was probable, but he was surprised that he liked the idea of her dying it. Just for a while. Just until he got used to this new Sonia.

He still needed the old.

He'd always need the old.

Then again, he had a feeling, as it all came clear, she was always this Sonia. She'd exhibited wolf traits and tendencies since the very beginning.

He should have caught it.

He didn't.

Then again, this was unprecedented, human to wolf, so he'd never consider it. He also, in those precious moments, wasn't going to allow himself to think of the indisputable conspiracy behind it.

He didn't share any of that.

He muttered, "You'll learn to leap out of your clothes."

"Well, unfortunately, I wasn't wearing an old pair of jeans but a fabulous wedding dress when it first happened," she replied.

"If it's torn, we'll have it repaired," he told her.

"That would be good," she murmured, he grinned, dipped his head, and touched his mouth to hers.

His grin faded and he whispered, "You died in my arms."

Her head jerked and her eyes grew wide. "I did?"

She didn't remember.

"You don't remember?" he asked to confirm.

"I remember collapsing in your arms." Her nose scrunched in a way that said she found it distasteful which Callum found an enormous relief. "I remember Yuri feeding. I remember you arguing with Orphenon, but then it all gets hazy and then...nothing."

He nodded but stated, "You did, my little one. You died in my arms."

She stared up at him, stunned. "How can that be?"

"I don't know," he answered.

Her head tilted to the side as her brows knitted adorably. "So you don't know what's going on."

"I have an idea," Callum replied. "What I do know," he stated ominously, "is that someone is going to fucking explain it to the both of us."

"This also would be good," she whispered, her hands moving on his skin soothingly then her arms wrapped around him, her gaze on him grew assessing, and she pulled him close. "I died in your arms?"

"You did, honey," he affirmed quietly, his voice suddenly ragged at the memory.

Her hand shifted to the side of his head, her thumb coming out to smooth his brow, his cheekbone, and then sweeping his lips.

He closed his eyes, memorizing that yet again even though he no longer needed to.

Her words were ragged as well when she whispered, "I don't know what's happening but I'm so sorry, my handsome wolf."

He opened his eyes. "Don't be. You're here. You're wolf which means you'll *always* be here." He pressed his chest to hers on the "always." "We'll soon understand why it happened and I'll make certain that nothing this fundamental is kept from us again."

She studied him even as she nodded.

Then she smiled a tremulous smile. "Cal, I'm wolf."

Callum smiled back and his was not tremulous. "You are, baby doll."

"I'm wolf," she breathed.

"As I always knew, perfect for me," Callum told her and her eyes focused on him.

"Perfect for you," she repeated, her smile strengthening.

"As I'm perfect for you," he declared.

"Yes," she whispered, her hand at his head became an arm wrapped around him again and both her arms went tight. "Can I ask one thing?"

"You can ask anything."

Love and gratitude gleamed in her eyes before she lifted her head from the pillows to touch her mouth to his.

When she set it back, she requested, "When you unleash all holy hell on whoever did all this, uh...*stuff*, can you do it fast so we can still go on our honeymoon?"

Callum stared at his *bride*.

Then he burst out laughing again and he did this while rolling her and then he did it while knifing to sitting and kissing her.

With his mate straddling his lap, his hands in her mahogany hair pulling it away from her beautiful face, he answered, "Absolutely."

Then King Callum brought his queen's lips back to his and he kissed her again before he did other things to her.

And all of it was *perfect*.

EPILOGUE
ETERNITY

"Sonia! Call your wolf off me!" Gregor ordered Sonia.

He was on his back on the floor with Callum pinning him there, his wolf nose close to Gregor's face, his teeth bared, a snarl sounding low from his throat.

She glared at her vampire then looked at her mate. "Cal, honey, maybe you should let Gregor up."

He swung his handsome wolf head her way and growled. Then he looked back down at Gregor and snapped viciously at his face with his sharp wolf teeth, purposefully missing. But he was so close, Gregor's body jerked and then he scowled.

She looked back at Gregor. "As you can see, he's a little angry." She leaned in, planting her hands on her hips. "As he *should be*."

And he should. They'd begun to tell Sonia and Callum all that had gone on, and obviously but understandably, Callum didn't like it very much.

"Callum, Sonny, please," Regan beseeched. "If you'll give us a moment to finish explaining, without bloodshed, I promise you'll understand."

Callum swung his head his mother's way and snarled.

Regan went pale.

Sonia sighed, moved toward her husband, and ran her hand soothingly down his fur, leaning in. "My wolf, let's give them a chance to finish explaining...without bloodshed."

He turned his head to her, turned it back down to Gregor, bared his teeth on another low snarl, then slowly backed off Gregor's body. As Gregor pushed to his feet, again, Callum's eyes went to Sonia and he barked sharply. She nodded and went directly to the clothes he'd leaped out of. Gathering them up, she followed her mate as he prowled out of the room.

He leaped to man in the hall and Sonia handed him his clothes, but even when he had them, he didn't don them. Instead, he stood there naked and lifted his big hand, palm up. She instantly put his wedding band into it that he'd given her moments before transforming to wolf and he just as instantly slid it on his finger.

Only then did he tug his clothes on but he did it muttering furiously, "I cannot believe this fucking shit."

Sonia couldn't either. Prophesies. Plots. Oracles. Potions to suppress the wolf traits Sonia's father gave her (her father was a werewolf!) and bring out the human ones of her mother (sadly, her father's mate was a human, weirdly, this made their demise happening together, rather than her father enduring an eternity without his mate, something bittersweet).

Sonia had to admit (not then, of course, with Callum being so infuriated), it was a relief to understand things about herself that she hadn't since she could remember. Her abilities and why she had them. Why she healed so quickly and didn't scar. Why her periods came every five months instead of every month, like a human's. This last she never imparted on anyone since it was none of their business, except her doctor, who told her a lot of women had irregular cycles. This might have been true, but what was truer was that he was lying through his teeth. About a lot of things.

"I also can't believe you're on fucking birth control," Callum went on.

Sonia's body started and her eyes snapped to his.

"What?" she asked.

"Baby doll, don't you think that's something you should have told me?"

"I assumed you assumed I was taking care of it," she replied.

"What I assumed was, when you weren't feeling yourself because my *mother* and *your* guardian were conspiring to titrate you off that fucking poison so your wolf could come out, you were pregnant with my pup. So when you died, I thought our pup died with you."

Sonia felt her face get soft as she moved to her husband and put her hand on his chest. "Cal, I'm so sorry. I thought you knew."

"Ryon mentioned it in passing months ago but that doesn't negate the fact *you* didn't. I didn't know you were wolf. You weren't having regular human cycles. What the fuck was I supposed to think?"

Suddenly, Sonia felt her brows draw together. "How did this swing around to me?"

Callum scowled at her brows then into her eyes. "Baby doll, *you died in my arms.* This is not something I'll forget *ever* and you can't know this and won't for fifty, one hundred, two hundred years, but our forever is a long...fucking...time. With you, I'll add, I thought I lost *our child.*"

"It wasn't *me* conspiring to hide *my* wolf self," she returned. "I didn't even *know* I had one! And anyway, a husband and wife discuss when they're going to start a family. If you wanted to start having pups, maybe you should have *talked to me* about it. I'll admit, I made assumptions, wolf, but you did too."

His scowl getting scarier, Callum leaned in to her. "Don't call me wolf when you're pissed, wolf."

"Don't *you* call *me* wolf when you're pissed, either." She got up on her toes to get closer to his face and finished, "*Wolf.*"

"Do you two want to quit arguing so we can get this done and maybe kill Gregor and possibly Yuri so you two can get on the plane and go on your honeymoon?" Ryon called from the door they'd exited and Sonia whirled to him.

"No one's killing Gregor *or* Yuri," she snapped.

"We'll see about that," Callum bit out as he stalked by her, grabbing her hand as he went and dragging her with him as he prowled back into his study where everyone, Regan, Gregor, Yuri, Lucien, Leah, Calder, and Caleb were all waiting.

Sonia followed him but announced upon entry to the room, "By the way, wolf, I want to start having pups immediately."

"Oh, Sonny, how exciting!" Regan cried but Callum let her hand go, whirled on her, and glowered at her.

"No fucking way. I've got you for eternity. I'm enjoying you for at least a hundred years before we introduce *more* mayhem into our lives."

"Children aren't mayhem," Sonia retorted.

"Yes they are. You like your shoes, baby doll, and werewolf pups like *chewing*."

Oh good goodness. She hadn't thought of that.

She bit her lip. Callum's eyes dropped to her mouth and his scowl got even *scarier*.

"Stop being adorable," he ordered.

Sonia quit biting her lip and exclaimed, "I'm not being adorable!"

"Jesus, are you two serious?" Calder asked, sounding exasperated, and Callum's eyes sliced to him.

"Stay out of it, Calder," he commanded.

"Brother, you forget, me and *everyone in this room* watched your mate die in your arms and *he*," Calder swung a pointed finger at Gregor, "masterminded not only that scenario but Sonia enduring a fake disease and a tortuous treatment *her entire life*."

"Yes," Callum whispered sinisterly, his gaze moving to Gregor, his mind clearly back to the matter at hand. "Let's get back to that."

Gregor, again cool as a cucumber, surveyed Callum. "If you take a breath and think on it a moment, Callum, you'll understand, considering The Prophesies, the necessity for all of this."

"How about you save us time and explain it," Callum suggested in a way everyone in the room knew it wasn't a suggestion.

Gregor drew in a breath not hiding the fact he was seeking patience.

Then he started, "Callum," his eyes moved to Sonia, "Sonny, my dear, of The Three destined in The Prophesies, two of the mates are human. One, you," he dipped his head to Sonia, "are not." He looked back to Callum. "In order to communicate solidarity with humans through supernatural beings being mated with them, Sonia had to live the triangle."

"More," Callum growled when Gregor stopped speaking and Gregor sighed before his gaze went back to Sonia.

"Born of werewolf and human, lived a human life, and, I'm sorry, my dear, suffered for it, and raised by vampires in order to deliver you safely to a werewolf mate. The triangle."

To Sonia, this made sense. Considering the prophesied three sets of lifemates would save humanity from slavery (or, she hoped not, expire in their efforts), humans, who mostly didn't know of werewolves or vampires, would need a strong statement to make them trust immortals.

Not to mention, werewolves and vampires would need to trust humans as well, and thus, as Gregor had explained earlier, all of the life-mates had to endure tribulations in order to prove their commitment to each other and, eventually, the cause.

"She is wolf, Callum, but your people accepted and loved her as human. They showed that when she was injured and they showed it in the short time they thought she passed yesterday by instantly shifting into widespread mourning," Gregor explained to Callum and looked back at Sonia. His voice dipped low and there was deep, unmistakable emotion threading though it when he told her, "This was not easy. It wasn't easy for Regan. For Mac. For your parents. For me and Yuri. We did not suffer as you did, Sonny, but we suffered. We hated it, every moment, and, my dear, in comparison with our lives, yours has been short, but trust me, making you endure what you endured all of your short life felt like an eternity."

Sonia felt her face get soft as she felt some of the anger sift out of the room but Callum wasn't finished being livid.

"Now that you've explained that, can you explain why you didn't tell me, at least, so perhaps, even if I couldn't have talked to my mate about it, I would maybe have been able to do something, *fucking anything,* to make it easier on my *wife?*"

"It's obvious," Gregor returned.

"What's obvious is, she's my mate. I would accept her however she came to me. It's the wolf way," Callum fired back.

"Humans, as you know, are not wolves," Gregor retorted.

"Please, do not try my patience further by telling me things I already know," Callum warned, his tone deadly.

"You had to accept her as human, too, Callum," Gregor told him. "Her frailties. The understanding of her life being short. Your love for her as human and demonstrated with such ferocity was essential. You went so far as to go against all your instincts as a werewolf and allow a vampire to feed from your mate in an effort to ease her pain. If you knew, this trial you had to best would not have been bested. Wolves, vampires, all immortals would understand you would love her however she came to you, but humans needed that statement to be made and I'm sure we'll all agree it was a compelling one."

Sonia heard Callum draw a sharp, annoyed breath in through his nose.

He understood.

He didn't like it but he understood.

"All of it," Regan put in and everyone looked to her, but she was looking at Sonia, "was carefully planned from well before your parents died." Her eyes moved to Lucien and Leah. "Once your situation...well, *commenced*, we put into action our plan." She looked at her son. "As The Prophesies foretold, Lucien and Leah had to be mated then you and Sonia had to find each other." Again, her eyes went to Sonia. "Wolf children, as you know, sweetheart, age far slower than humans do and part of giving you that injection was to force your aging process to accelerate to a human one so that you and Callum could find each other at the right time. If not, right now, by wolf age, you'd be just over seven human years old. Instead, you're an adult female and thus could be mated to your king."

"Now that I'm not taking the injection, is my aging going to slow again?" Sonia asked and Regan shook her head.

"No, you're locked here, Sonny. Your development has stopped as it would naturally around this age as wolf. Unfortunately, however, you now must learn how to be wolf, but," she smiled, "not woman."

This was true. Yesterday, her wedding day of all days had started out wonderful but it ended not all that fun. She didn't remember "dying" (fortunately) but she did remember waking and transforming almost immediately to wolf. It scared her silly and more, her wolf instincts to find her mate taking over and making her new body not at her mind's command, scared her more. It got worse when she found Callum and couldn't communicate with him nor did she know how to turn back to human. It was pure luck and a huge amount of desire that made her able to do it.

Callum had told her that morning before they had their confrontation with the family that he'd work with her, teach her, they'd transform together, and he'd take her out running.

She was looking forward to that.

She was also looking forward to being her age for eternity. That was far from a bad thing, never growing old, never getting wrinkled and gray, but best of all, her husband not having to watch her do it.

"Why did she die?" Lucien asked and Sonia focused her attention on the vampire because she thought his was a very good question.

"She didn't. Her human did," Yuri stated.

"Explain that," Lucien ordered and Yuri's jaw got tight at the command.

Then he looked to Sonia. "You know, of course, that wolf DNA is dominant."

She nodded.

Yuri went on, "That does not mean you don't have your mother's DNA as well. It's latent, and when the wolf DNA was suppressed, as explained, it came to the fore. Regan and Father have been titrating you off the medication now for weeks, the actual dose smaller and smaller, even if the injection was the same amount, the rest was taken with vitamins and hormones that would not alter or harm you. You didn't actually die since you cannot die as an immortal. However, your body did shut down to finalize the change." He looked to Callum. "We also knew this would happen. It was explained by the physicians who created the injection, it was closely monitored, and the ill-effects, which could have been worse, were calculated, controlled, and monitored so they weren't. Last, it was necessary, if difficult to witness and experience."

"Difficult is not the word I'd use," Callum gritted out and Sonia moved to him.

The instant she got close, he curled an arm around her shoulders and pulled her front deep into his side. She rested her hand on his stomach, wrapped her other arm around his back, and pressed closer

"It was hideous, Callum, for all of us, not just you. Do you think it was easy keeping this from you? From Sonny?" Yuri asked.

"I would suspect it was easier keeping it from us than it was for us, living your lies," Callum shot back and a muscle ticked in Yuri's jaw, nonverbally acceding the point.

"It's my understanding, Lassiter and Cherise Arlington were assassinated by the wolf rebellion," Lucien stated at this point and a different feel came to the room, a feel Sonia decided was not good considering how tight Callum's body became beside her. "Is that true?" he asked Gregor.

Again Gregor drew in breath before he admitted, "No. They were assassinated by vampires."

"What?" Sonia breathed but no one answered her.

"My father," Lucien clipped and Sonia felt her body jerk in surprise as her eyes shot to him.

She saw Leah's face was knowing and angry and her eyes were also on her husband.

"Yes," Gregor confirmed. "Etienne with a retinue of vampires and werewolves who disagreed with Lassiter's efforts within the American government to lay the groundwork for immortals and mortals to live peacefully with the knowledge of each other hunted Lassiter and Cherise and murdered them."

Sonia's heart squeezed.

"I do not believe this," Lucien hissed and Sonia pressed closer to Callum because the vampire was angry, quietly but terrifyingly so.

"You know you mustn't precipitate The Prophesies," Gregor warned, to Sonia, confusingly. Then again, this entire turn of the conversation was confusing.

"Have the last lifemates been located?" Lucien returned.

"Not yet," Gregor answered.

"I suggest you find them, Gregor. Talk to The Dominion," his eyes cut to Callum, "you request an audience with the Oracles."

"Done," Callum grunted.

"This must play out as it's intended to play out," Regan hurriedly put in.

"Etienne," Lucien stated then looked to Sonia and explained curtly, "my father," he looked back to Regan, "harmed my mate, touched her, terrified her, sent her running from me and into what could have been danger or even death from her own *fucking dreams*. He murdered Sonia's parents. And yet he runs free." Finally, he looked to Gregor. "I have been patient, Gregor, as I promised I would be, but I will warn you, my patience is running out."

"Mine evaporated five minutes ago," Callum declared and Sonia pressed even closer to her mate.

"The Prophesies state that, once the second lifemates meet, the third will be fast on their heels," Gregor explained.

"Let's hope that's true," Callum replied.

"So far, they all have been true," Gregor retorted.

The room fell silent on this not altogether (though some of it was) happy news.

Regan broke it by asking, "Now that this unpleasant business is over, can we have a lovely meal, celebrate the bride and groom, and then get them on a plane so they can enjoy their honeymoon?"

"Yes," Callum agreed but continued, "And about that." He looked to Ryon. "The two weeks we planned just turned into two months." His eyes swept Calder and Caleb as Sonia's heart stopped squeezing so it could swell with happiness. A two month honeymoon was very good news. "Adjust your plans. Sonia and I won't return until then."

"And hopefully I'll be pregnant when we return," Sonia announced and Callum dipped his chin to look down at her.

"You won't be pregnant," he declared.

She looked up at him. "We'll see."

"We won't see. You won't be pregnant," he repeated his declaration and Sonia's swelling heart turned into swelling anger.

"Callum, you don't get to be King Callum when we're discussing starting a family and thus what you say just goes," she snapped.

"Sonia, you don't get to be Queen Sonia when we're discussing starting a family and thus you being pretty, beloved, and recently, for all intents and purposes, *dead*, does not mean what you say goes either."

"Perhaps we can discuss this later, wolf," she snapped.

"Oh, we'll discuss it later," he leaned down so he was nose to nose with her, "*wolf*."

Her heart fluttered at her mate calling her wolf even if it did this while she was angry.

"Great, now can we eat?" Calder asked. "Or do we all have to stand around and watch you two bicker for the next half an hour?"

"Let's eat. I'm starved. Sonia dying then suddenly coming back to life and morphing into wolf, freaking me out because I didn't fucking know she *was* wolf, put me off my food last night," Caleb stated as he started sauntering to the door. "Time to party, and by that I mean, stuff ourselves and drink until we're sick."

Sonia forgot to be irritated mostly because she thought Caleb was hilarious.

"The town is feasting now and the fireworks are rescheduled to go off tonight. I know you're keen to be away, Cal, but it might be nice if you and Sonia took some time to make an appearance before you board the plane," Ryon suggested, getting close.

"Set that up," Callum ordered, shifting and beginning to move Sonia toward the door.

Ryon nodded and moved away.

Sonia got close to her husband and requested, "Later, can you tell me what that last part was about, the part with Lucien and his father and Leah's dreams killing her?"

"I will, little one, once I find out from Lucien what the parts I don't know about were about," Callum muttered irritably and Sonia suppressed a grin.

Regan got closer, and even with Sonia curled in Callum's arm, she shoved hers through Sonia's.

"Are you angry at me, sweetheart?" she asked Sonia softly.

"Of course not, Regan," Sonia answered softly and felt Callum's arm tense around her as Regan pressed closer. "All of that wasn't easy, on *any* of us. But now it's over."

They moved toward the door, Regan smiled at Sonia then leaned partly across her, her eyes lifting up to her son. "Are *you* angry at me, sweetheart?"

"Yes," Callum replied, Regan and Sonia tensed, but Callum went on, "But I'll get over it after fireworks and when I'm on a plane taking my bride on our honeymoon."

Regan looked at Sonia and grinned.

Sonia grinned back.

Regan let Sonia go so she and Callum could walk through the door but Sonia turned back so she could aim her smile at Gregor.

She saw his eyes move to Callum's back before they came again to her and he sighed.

Her smile got bigger.

Then she went with her groom to the dining room to feast with her family in celebration.

In other words, with abandon.

Like a wolf.

Callum stood at the front door waiting for his *bride* to join him so he could take her into town, let their people see them healthy, happy, and, for Sonia, alive, and watch fireworks before he finally took her away to somewhere it would only be them for a good long time.

He figured he had a wait since he could hear Sonia giggling with Leah, Kerry, Mabel, Mara, Callie, Regan, and fucking Caleb, and they were all doing it drunkenly.

Listening to their happiness and hilarity, he looked to his boots and grinned.

His wife was wolf and the sounds of her drunken cheerfulness, embracing all that she was, were far from unwelcome.

His head came up when he smelled vampire.

He watched as Gregor approached him and he braced. He knew what was coming.

"We must talk," Gregor said low when he got close.

"You're correct," Callum agreed. "Not now. When we return."

"This will happen fast," Gregor told him.

"My mate died yesterday regardless of the fact she didn't. She's wolf. We have not had but scant time alone. We're taking it and we're celebrating. When we return, we'll talk. And when I return, you'll show me The Prophesies," Callum replied.

"Callum, we cannot—"

Callum leaned in to the vampire. "You'll show me The Prophesies," he growled.

Gregor pulled in a deep breath before he nodded.

Then he stated, "She's wolf and that explains her senses amongst other things, but you know she has additional abilities."

"Her affinity with wildlife, her dreams," Callum confirmed.

"We must understand that," Gregor stated.

"First, she and I will," Callum told him.

"Callum, we're preparing for *war*," Gregor reminded him.

"I'm aware of that, far more than you since it's myself and my mate who will be in the thick of it, Gregor. And any warrior knows, prior to war and after it, you savor the beauty of life so you always have close exactly what you're fighting for."

Gregor held his eyes then he inclined his head.

He turned and started to move away before he stopped and turned back.

"Thank you," he said softly.

"For what?" Callum asked.

Gregor stared into Callum's eyes.

"Making her happy."

Then, in a blink, the vampire was gone.

"Jesus," Callum muttered to the space where Gregor disappeared.

He heard Sonia's giggle.

His mood shifted and he grinned.

Then he bellowed, "*Sonia! Wolf! Get your ass out here!*"

"*Patience, wolf!*" He heard his *bride* bellow back and his grin turned into a wide white smile.

***

The fire in the cabin's grate roaring, Callum, flat on his back on the couch, heard the door to the bathroom open, and his *wife's* feet padding on the floors.

His eyes caught her as she rounded the end of the couch and walked to him, hair in a towel, body encased in a short robe.

He moved only his hands to settle on her hips as she moved over him to settle astride him.

She leaned down, her face irritated, and she rested her forearms in his chest.

"Guess what," she ordered.

"What?" he asked, fighting a grin, knowing from her disgruntled tone and the times they'd been through this before exactly what.

She lifted one hand away, jerked at the towel, and her dark wet hair tumbled around her face and shoulders. "Project So Much Bleach Marilyn Monroe Would Balk was a failure. Wolf hair is immune to peroxide," she announced.

His hands slid up her sides, drawing her closer as they did, and his lips twitched. "Baby doll, this has now been proved five times."

"You want me blonde," she pointed out.

He did. He missed her golden hair. The mahogany was beautiful but he fell in love with a blonde.

"With time, I'll get used to it," he muttered.

"How much time, a century? Three?" she asked, still disgruntled.

"Maybe four," he answered while fighting his grin.

She glared at him then her glare melted as her body melted into his as she whispered like she still couldn't wrap her mind around it but it made her blissfully happy all the same, "Maybe four. I have four centuries with you and more."

His arms circled her. "Yes, my little one, four centuries and more," his arms gave her a squeeze, "and about the time we hit four, we'll be ready to start a family."

Her eyes flashed, the brown spiking out to obliterate the green.

Perfect. She was getting angry.

That meant a tussle.

Which meant that tussle would end phenomenally.

His arms got tighter.

Suddenly, the brown receded and her hand slid up to curl around the side of his neck.

"You brought me home for our honeymoon," she said quietly and Callum felt his brows draw together.

"Sorry, baby doll?"

She vaguely threw out a hand. "This has always been home to me," she explained. "My parent's cabin, *our* cabin. Where I brought you when I first met you even though I didn't know it was you. The only home, until you gave me the castle, that I ever knew. And you brought me here for our honeymoon." She bent even closer, brushed her mouth to his, and whispered against his lips. "Perfect."

It was.

She was.

Everything was.

Apparently, they weren't going to tussle, they were going to do something else, and Callum found he was fine with that.

He was again wrong.

"Can we run?" she asked, her thumb sweeping the thick stubble on his jaw.

He stared into her eyes. She was a fast learner, becoming quite adept at controlling her transformations. She loved the wood, nature, she loved running with him, and they did it every night and some days besides, three weeks of it at their cabin.

An idea struck him.

No, a memory.

No, *a dream.*

And this made his look turn wolfish as his lips whispered, "Absolutely, little one. We can absolutely run."

He was lone wolf no more.

They were running, roaming, as wolves, he and Sonia.

She was fast and kept up with him, close to his right flank, where she always ran.

Callum took them deeper into the trees. They'd been running for hours. He could hear her pants. He knew he was pushing her. He knew what she wanted.

He kept pushing her, knowing the anticipation would be worth it.

Finally, he turned, headed for home, and he sensed her instant excitement.

He felt it too.

Sonia was beneath him, on her belly, her long, thick, mahogany hair spread across her back, obscuring her face, tangled with pine needles. Her sweet, musky wolf scent assaulted him, coming from her hair, her skin, between her legs.

There was something familiar about it. Something beautiful. Something nostalgic. Something he fucking *adored*.

His human Sonia.

He was up on his hands, giving his hips leverage to thrust into her wetness with savage brutality.

Her moans weren't filled with pain but each one a temptation to take her harder.

So he did.

"Spread your legs wider," he ordered.

She did as she was told.

"Tilt your ass, take all of me," he commanded.

Again, she did as she was told and he drove inside her then ground his hips between her spread-eagled legs and her moan was so deep, he could feel it vibrating against the tip of his cock.

That felt so fucking good, Callum ground into her deeper and he knew he couldn't take much more.

"Let go," he demanded but she defied him, clenching her sex around his shaft in an effort to hold off her climax. He shifted his weight to one arm and twisted her dark hair around his fist, yanking it back, arching her neck, and driving her further down on his cock. "Let go, wolf."

He got off on calling her "wolf" as Sonia did with him, especially when he was fucking her.

He fucking *loved* it.

She did too.

Her legs spread even wider. Her ass tilted further. He dropped his head and saw its perfection, not an ass marred with pinpricks, and he felt a feeling of triumph so complete, the sight set him thrusting into her again.

Which was what she wanted.

"Harder, Cal," she breathed her demand, her voice barely a whisper, even he could hardly make out the words. "Fuck me harder."

He was losing control, his orgasm was coming and he knew it would be staggering.

With her, it always was.

The best he'd ever had.

"Goddamn it, *let go!*" he roared the instant her sex convulsed around his cock.

She lifted up on her own arms, propelling herself onto his shaft so intensely he feared he'd split her in two.

But she threw back her dark head, her hair flying over his hand still fisted in it, over his forearm, down her back, and she howled her release.

He pulled out and surged back in, burying himself to the root one last time, and then howled his own.

Naked on their bed of pine needles, Callum on his back, Sonia on top of him, his mate moved. Shifting up, she pressed her temple to his and slid it through his hair, marking him.

He growled into her ear, rolled her to her back, him on top, and did the same.

When done, he lifted his head and looked down at her in the moonlight.

"You know, you gave me another wedding band, another charm, and a fabulous honeymoon for my wedding gifts and I've given you nothing but, well...me," she said softly.

"All I need is you," he replied just as softly and felt her already relaxed body melt under his as her arms grew tight around him.

"Okay then, how about, for your wedding present, I give you more of me and agree to wait fifty years before we start a family?" she suggested.

"Seventy-five," he countered, her head jerked slightly before he saw her eyes light and her mouth twitch.

"Deal, wolf," she whispered. "Seventy-five."

He grinned and dropped his head to touch his mouth to hers again.

He lifted his head and she shifted a hand and framed the side, her thumb moving to smooth his brow, his cheekbone, his jaw, her eyes watching.

Finally, they came to his. "You know I love you?" she asked.

"You know I love you?" he asked back by way of answer.

"With everything you are," she whispered.

He dipped his face to hers and murmured with feeling, "With everything I am, baby doll."

"And I you, my handsome wolf. With everything I am, with everything I'm meant to be, and with eternity to be it in, that's a lot."

Callum grinned at his *wife*.

Then he shifted his head and again marked her temple.

His.

And, as he did it, she did the same.

Hers.

As it was.

As it always would be.

For eternity.

At that exact moment...elsewhere...

Oh my God, they were hunting me.

Hunting me!

I ran, my breath ragged, a stitch cutting agony through my side, as I heard them getting closer. Closer.

Fast.

Too fast.

I was a girl and maybe not Jackie Joyner-Kersee but I wasn't out of shape. They'd gain but not that fast.

No way.

That didn't mean they weren't gaining that fast.

They were.

And I was terrified.

I turned into an alley, hoping in the darkness to lose them, and ran with everything I had left.

Straight to a dead end.

"Shit," I breathed, panting, turning, feeling them closing in on me.

Then there they were, on me as in *on me.* In the blink of an eye I was on my back, one of them pinning my body down with his on mine, one holding my arms down over my head, one my legs at my ankles while, I stared to the side in disbelief, two humongous, terrifying *dogs* circled, snarling and snapping their sharp, alarming teeth in my direction.

"Rip her throat out and have done with it," a voice coming from over my head bit out and my attention went back to the enormous man who was lying full on top of me, pressing the breath out of me, and staring down at me in a way I did...not...*like.*

I tried to struggle but the hands at my wrists and ankles held so strong, it was preternatural how strong they were. I wasn't pinned. I was completely immobilized.

"In a minute," he grunted, his eyes not leaving mine. "Christ, smell her. Divine. Fuck me, absolutely fucking divine." His face changed to a look I liked even less and he finished, "First I'm going to feed."

He was going to feed?

Oh man. What did *that* mean?

I didn't know. What I knew was, it was not good.

"Are you insane?" a voice coming from my feet asked like he thought the dude holding me was, indeed, insane. In fact, *very* insane. At the same time, ugly scary growls came from both of the dogs.

It seemed to me these were warnings, but the guy on top of me was, apparently, insane because he ignored the warnings of the huge, vicious, snarling dogs. His head dipped toward me, slanted, then his mouth was at my neck.

Oh shit. Oh *shit!*

This was *definitely* not good.

I belatedly opened my mouth to scream.

Not that first sound came out because suddenly I wasn't immobilized. Nothing was on me, nothing holding me down.

I still didn't move.

This was because something I couldn't see, and not only because it was dark but because it was happening so...damned...*fast*, was whirling around me.

I would know what that was when sickening, warm gushes of blood spurted across my chest and neck about a half a second before I saw a canine head (with no body, mind) roll across the asphalt in front of me. More blood splashed the pavement beside me in a hideous surge and I heard the heinous noises of body after lifeless body thudding to the ground.

Then I was up, my own body swinging like it was flying through the air, but I felt hands on me. A breeze was blowing through my hair, I was moving so fast, and then my back slammed against the brick wall of the building at the side of the alley.

I blinked, feeling the wall at my back but the intense hard-muscled warmth of a body pressed to my front and before my eyes, a man.

A shock of black hair.

An intriguingly tilted set of eyes, the hue I couldn't make out in the dark, but shockingly, I could see one was a color that was light, the other a color that was definitely dark.

Strong jutting jaw, sharp cheekbones, heavy brow.

The slash of an angry scar that went across his forehead, through his left eyebrow, disconnected then rejoined on his cheekbone to slide all the way down his face, curling around his jaw and disappearing.

I panted in his blood-stained face.

He stared, intense and frightening, into mine, his gaze, honest to *God,* like a touch.

I stopped panting because I stopped breathing.

His face came closer and my stomach clenched, my muscles tensed near to snapping, my chest burned, but his head veered and he touched his temple to mine, slid it back, rubbing it through my hair.

I sucked in breath only to hold it again when his hands left my armpits. One to travel down my side and then curve to become an arm around my back holding me so strong, I was plastered to his front. One going up, over my shoulder and in to curl tight and freakishly warm around the side of my neck.

His chin dipped and I felt his lips at my ear.

"*Mine*," he growled in a deep, guttural, forceful way that even I, who

had no clue what was happening, I just knew I didn't like it one...single...
bit, agreed.

When he said "mine," he meant *me*.

Uh-oh.

Lucien stood in the alleyway with Gregor who had summoned him.

They both stared at the smoldering remains of three vampires and
the blood and gore of the beheaded corpses of two violently mutilated
wolves still in wolf form.

He felt Gregor's eyes on him and he cut his to the vampire.

"Five against one," Gregor noted.

Two immortals could do that.

Lucien and Callum, King of the Werewolves.

Now, the third.

"I'm thinking the third set of lifemates have been found," Gregor
went on to mutter drolly.

Lucien cursed and pulled out his phone. He hit one button and put
it to his ear.

Four rings later, he heard a wolf growl, "This better be good to interrupt my honeymoon."

"The third lifemates have met."

"Fuck," Callum grunted.

"My thought exactly," Lucien concurred.

There was silence from Callum then he remarked, "My wife and I
have had a good night. I'd like her to enjoy the rest of it as I intend to
enjoy the rest of it with her. We'll be on a plane tomorrow."

"I'm sorry, Callum," Lucien murmured.

"It's begun, therefore it's closer to done," Callum replied.

"Indeed," Lucien muttered.

"We'll taste victory," Callum told him.

"We fucking will," Lucien agreed.

"Tomorrow," Callum stated.

"Tomorrow, Callum."

He heard Callum disconnect and he slid his phone back in the inside pocket of his leather jacket.

His dark eyes again surveyed the carnage.

Then, without another look at Gregor or any of the other members of The Vampire Council on the scene, he turned away and strode to his Porsche so he could leave the slaughter behind for now and get home to his bride.

It had begun.

They had very little time

So he and Leah were going to fucking enjoy what little they had.

The End

The Three Series continues with the story of the final two.
Wild and Free

WILL LOVE CONQUER ALL?

Abel Jin and Delilah Johnson have lived their lives with a hole in their soul, yearning for something they don't understand.

Until one night, Delilah is in mortal danger and a man who's otherworldly strong and supernaturally fast saves her. Delilah is then cast into a world where fiction comes to life in the form of Abel, her destined mate, a vampire/werewolf hybrid who claims her at first breath as his.

But Abel knows the danger isn't done. He's dreamed for centuries that his mate will perish, and he will stop at nothing to keep her safe.

For Delilah, she's not only coping with fantasy come to life, but a mingling of very different families. Not to mention, she has on her hands a man who doesn't understand his true nature and has lived his long life thinking he's a monster.

Abel and Delilah together fills the hole that has been clawing at them for decades. But finally finding each other, it also tips their destinies as the last of The Three. They must unite with the other destined lovers who, with Abel and Delilah, are fated to save the world.

Or die trying.

WILD AND FREE
PROLOGUE

Mine
Delilah

Oh my God, they were hunting me.

Hunting me!

I ran, my breath ragged, a stitch cutting agony through my side as I heard them getting closer. Closer.

Fast.

Too fast.

I was a girl and maybe not Jackie Joyner-Kersee, but I wasn't out of shape. They'd gain but not that fast.

No way.

That didn't mean they weren't gaining that fast.

They were.

And I was terrified.

I turned into an alley, hoping in the darkness to lose them, and ran with everything I had left.

Straight to a dead end.

"Shit," I breathed, panting, turning, feeling them closing in on me.

Then there they were, on me as in *on me*. In the blink of an eye I was on my back, one of them pinning my body down with his on mine, one holding my arms down over my head, one holding my legs at my ankles while, I stared to the side in disbelief, two humongous, terrifying *dogs* circled, snarling and snapping their sharp, alarming teeth in my direction.

"Rip her throat out and have done with it," a voice coming from over my head bit out, and my attention went back to the enormous man who was lying full on top of me, pressing the breath out of me, and staring down at me in a way I did...not...*like*.

I tried to struggle, but the hands at my wrists and ankles held so strong, it was preternatural how strong they were. I wasn't pinned. I was completely immobilized.

"In a minute," he grunted, his eyes not leaving mine. "Christ, smell her. Divine. Fuck me, absolutely fucking divine." His face changed to a look I liked even less and he finished, "First I'm going to feed."

He was going to feed?

Oh man. What did *that* mean?

I didn't know. What I knew was, it was not good.

"Are you insane?" a voice coming from my feet asked like he thought the dude holding me was, indeed, insane. In fact, *very* insane. At the same time, ugly-scary growls came from both of the dogs.

It seemed to me these were warnings, but the guy on top of me was apparently insane because he ignored the warnings of the huge, vicious, snarling dogs. His head dipped toward me, slanted, then his mouth was at my neck.

Oh shit. Oh *shit*!

This was *definitely* not good.

I belatedly opened my mouth to scream.

Not that first sound came out because suddenly I wasn't immobilized. Nothing was on me, nothing holding me down.

I still didn't move.

This was because something I couldn't see, and not only because it was dark, but because it was happening so...damned...*fast*, was whirling around me.

I would know what that was when sickening, warm gushes of blood spurted across my chest and neck about a half a second before I saw a canine head (with no body, mind) roll across the asphalt in front of me. More blood splashed the pavement beside me in a hideous surge and I heard the heinous noises of body after lifeless body thudding to the ground.

Then I was up, my own body swinging like it was flying through the air, but I felt hands on me. A breeze was blowing through my hair, I was moving so fast, and then my back slammed against the brick wall of the building at the side of the alley.

I blinked, not feeling the wall at my back but the intense hard-muscled warmth of a body pressed to my front and before my eyes. A man.

A shock of black hair.

An intriguingly tilted set of eyes, the hue I couldn't make out in the dark, but shockingly, I could see one was a color that was light, the other a color that was definitely dark.

Strong jutting jaw, sharp cheekbones, heavy brow.

The slash of an angry scar that went across his forehead, through his left eyebrow, disconnected then rejoined on his cheekbone to slide all the way down his face, curling around his jaw and disappearing.

I panted in his blood-stained face.

He stared, intense and frightening, into mine, his gaze, honest to *God*, like a touch.

I stopped panting because I stopped breathing.

His face came closer and my stomach clenched, my muscles tensed near to snapping, my chest burned, but his head veered and he touched his temple to mine, slid it back, rubbing it through my hair.

I sucked in breath only to hold it again when his hands left my armpits. One traveled down my side and then curved to become an arm around my back, holding me so strong, I was plastered to his front. The other went up, over my shoulder and in to curl tight and freakishly warm around the side of my neck.

His chin dipped and I felt his lips at my ear.

"*Mine*," he growled in a deep, guttural, forceful way that even I, who

had no clue what was happening, I just knew I didn't like it one...single...
bit, agreed.

When he said "mine," he meant *me*.

Uh-oh.

Wild and Free
is available for purchase in all formats

NEWSLETTER

Would you like advanced notification about Upcoming Releases? Access to exclusive content? Access to exclusive giveaways? The first to see a new cover reveal? Sign up for my newsletter to keep up-to-date with the latest from Kristen Ashley!

Sign up at kristenashley.net

ABOUT THE AUTHOR

Kristen Ashley is the *New York Times* bestselling author of over one hundred romance novels. She's a hybrid author, publishing titles independently and traditionally, with books translated into fourteen languages and millions of copies sold.

Kristen's novel, *Law Man*, won the *RT Book Reviews* Reviewer's Choice Award for best Romantic Suspense, her independently published title, *Hold On*, was nominated for *RT Book Reviews* best Independent Contemporary Romance, and her traditionally published title, *Breathe*, was nominated for best Contemporary Romance. Her titles *Motorcycle Man*, *The Will*, *The Hookup* and *Ride Steady* (which won the Reader's Choice award from *Romance Reviews*) all made the final rounds for Goodreads Choice Awards in the Romance category.

Although Kristen is super proud of all those accolades, she's just happy that—after years of writing with no publisher or agent interested in what she did—she now has a loyal readership who, on social media, she can share recipes with and regale with stories of her bent toward being a klutz.

Kristen was born in Gary and raised in Brownsburg, Indiana, but since leaving her home state (Hoosier by birth, Boilermaker by the grace of God!), she's lived in Denver and the West Country of England. All of these places were home, and she's put them in her books with all the love she still has for them.

Now, after years of cold, misty days in the UK (that she still misses, along with cream teas, custard and battered sausages), Kristen resides in almost constant sun. She writes at her desk in Phoenix or among the deer and javelina in her little cabin up in the Arizona mountains, regretting often that she forgets to put the sunshade over her windshield, thus her car often doubles as a human oven. Even so, she loves calling all the sun, saguaro and beautiful mountains home.

You can read more about Kristen and her books at KristenAshley.net.

facebook.com/kristenashleybooks

instagram.com/kristenashleybooks

pinterest.com/KristenAshleyBooks

goodreads.com/kristenashleybooks

bookbub.com/authors/kristen-ashley

tiktok.com/@kristenashleybooks

ALSO BY KRISTEN ASHLEY

Rock Chick Series:

Rock Chick

Rock Chick Rescue

Rock Chick Redemption

Rock Chick Renegade

Rock Chick Revenge

Rock Chick Reckoning

Rock Chick Regret

Rock Chick Revolution

Rock Chick Reawakening

Rock Chick Reborn

Rock Chick Rematch

Rock Chick Bonus Tracks

Avenging Angels Series:

Avenging Angel

Avenging Angels: Back in the Saddle

Avenging Angels: Tenderfoot

Avenging Angel: Bad Medicine

The 'Burg Series:

For You

At Peace

Golden Trail

Games of the Heart

The Promise

Hold On

The Chaos Series:

Own the Wind

Fire Inside

Ride Steady

Walk Through Fire

A Christmas to Remember

Rough Ride

Wild Like the Wind

Free

Wild Fire

Wild Wind

The Colorado Mountain Series:

The Gamble

Sweet Dreams

Lady Luck

Breathe

Jagged

Kaleidoscope

Bounty

Dream Man Series:

Mystery Man

Wild Man

Law Man

Motorcycle Man

Quiet Man

Dream Team Series:

Dream Maker

Dream Chaser

Dream Bites Cookbook

Dream Spinner

Dream Keeper

The Fantasyland Series:

Wildest Dreams

The Golden Dynasty

Fantastical

Broken Dove

Midnight Soul

Gossamer in the Darkness

Four Realms Series:

Night's Fall

Ghosts and Reincarnation Series:

Sommersgate House

Lacybourne Manor

Penmort Castle

Fairytale Come Alive

Lucky Stars

The Honey Series:

The Deep End

The Farthest Edge

The Greatest Risk

The Magdalene Series:

The Will

Soaring

The Time in Between

Sharing the Miracle

Embracing the Change

Finding the One

The Three Series:

Until the Sun Falls from the Sky

With Everything I Am

Wild and Free

The Unfinished Hero Series:

Knight

Creed

Raid

Deacon

Sebring

Wild West MC Series:

Still Standing

Smoke and Steel

Smooth Sailing

Other Titles by Kristen Ashley:

Heaven and Hell

Play It Safe

Three Wishes

Complicated

Loose Ends

Fast Lane

Perfect Together